THE SOULS OF FIRE

A Portal Fantasy (The Chosen, Books 5-7)

AMY PROEBSTEL

BETHANY HALL

Cavaliers Publishing

ISBN-13: 978-1-946292-65-0

ISBN-10: 1-946292-65-6

Printed in the United States of America

Cover art by Wynter Designs

First Printing, 2019

Second Printing, 2022

Website: https://geni.us/LOA-Home

BookBub: https://geni.us/BBFollow

Goodreads: www.goodreads.com/aproebstel

Facebook: https://geni.us/FB-LOA

Twitter: https://geni.us/Amy-T

Instagram: www.instagram.com/amyproebstel

BOOKS IN THIS SERIES

Chosen Origins Trilogy
Book One: The Keeper of Secrets
Book Two: The Secrets of Magic
Book Three: The Magic of Time

The Chosen Series
Book One: The Time of Shadows
Book Two: The Shadows of Destiny
Book Three: The Destiny of Hunters
Book Four: The Hunters of Souls
Book Five: The Souls of Children
Book Six: The Children of Fire
Book Seven: The Fire of War
Book Eight: The War of Realms
Book Nine: The Realms of Rising
Book Ten: The Rising of Dragons

There are certain people who come into my life who are just shining stars. My mother-in-law, Ann, has been one of those people. Her Pollyanna attitude is so endearing, inspiring, and contagious. She always pushes me to write my next book as she eagerly waits to discover where the story will go next. I'm so thankful for her expert grammar lessons and her eagle eyes, as she finds the most obscure errors in my manuscripts.

To the readers of this series, I greatly appreciate all of your kind words, suggestions, and support along the way. A special note goes to Gail and Jutta who are the best super-fans across two continents any writer could hope for. None of these books would be possible without your enthusiasm for the world of Tuala.

THE SOULS OF CHILDREN
BOOK FIVE OF THE CHOSEN

CHAPTER 1

Amanda Stel watched Neal closely as he sauntered out of the Ascension Gate room in Manzanit with Vinia close to his side. He certainly did not look like a man who had been drugged senseless only a few minutes before. Now came the interesting part where they had to decide what to do with Neal. He appeared to have his memory back where Tuala was concerned, but his memories of Earth were now gone.

Originally, Amanda had wanted to get Neal out of Tuala because he was being drugged and held captive by Elder Vargen for his knowledge of Earth's engineering. Now she had helped him escape from a similar scenario from a deranged doctor on Earth for his knowledge of Tuala. She was pulled from her thoughts by Rasa touching her arm in sympathy.

"Come on, Amanda, we'll get this sorted out," Rasa said as she pulled on her arm to lead her out of the room and into a more comfortable place to discuss their options.

Barla came to Amanda's other side and asked, "What happened Amanda? Why was Dr. Gascon at the Gate on the Earth side?" She continued to stare at Amanda even though it was clear she was not going to get an answer. Barla could practically see the wheels turning in Amanda's head as she reviewed her recent escapade.

Amanda's gaze returned to the Ascension Gate where she had seen Dr. Gascon's face mirrored in the center of the energy source. She shivered violently and allowed herself to be led out of the room between Rasa and Barla. There were other matters which needed her attention more, namely what to do with Neal.

Rasa followed Vinia and Neal as they slowly navigated the long hallway leading to the main areas of the Residence. She called ahead to them when they came near the room she wanted to use, "Go into the next doorway on your right, Vinia. We need to get some things worked out."

Vinia did as she had been instructed and turned Neal to their right and settled herself and Nealan in one of the overstuffed, foxl-hide loveseats by a lit fireplace. The room was large, and yet it retained a quaint feeling with the tall bookshelves lining all of the walls except where the fireplace took precedence on another whole wall. There were no windows and yet the room was well-lit by sconces of elemy spheres.

As they all took their places around the room, Amanda wished Chelesa had stayed with them. She understood her desire to connect with her samara once again. However, she could really use her sound advice as a wise-woman at this time with Neal. She sighed in resignation and sat down. For several moments nobody said anything as they all tried to take in the recent events.

"Is anyone going to tell me what's going on?" Neal asked petulantly.

Amanda sighed and began, "It would be too long of a story to tell, Neal, and I don't expect you to believe all of it right now. Really, it's pointless to go into all of the details since we're going to be taking you back home and you won't remember this conversation anyway."

Neal scowled at Amanda's answer and decided to turn to Vinia for an explanation, "Maybe you'll be more helpful, Vinia. We've been together for a long time now, and I expect more from you than I would from a stranger." He tipped his head to indicate Amanda was the stranger.

Vinia looked guiltily at Amanda and answered softly, "Suffice it to say, we are in a world called Tuala, but you are really from Earth. Amanda's going to have to take you back home for a while, so you can get some things straightened out with your parents. After that, we can decide whether you want to live here in Tuala or back on Earth."

Neal's scowl deepened since Vinia seemed to be spouting off the same drivel as the other woman named Amanda.

Rasa turned to Amanda and asked, "Is that what you want to do as well, Amanda? Do you want to take Neal home to his parents? You know there will be a lot of questions which will be really hard to answer. Neal won't have any memories, even the things he regained from this last week will be gone as well."

"I know it'll be complicated, but I owe it to his parents. They've already lost their son once; they can help me bring him back this next time. I'll probably have to tell them the truth, although I'm not sure how it'll be received. With the luck I've had lately, they'd probably push to have me committed." Amanda sighed deeply at the difficult position into which she had put herself.

Barla could see her niece was in turmoil and finally came to the conclusion she had thought she never would when she offered, "I'll come with you to help with Neal."

Amanda stared at her aunt in amazement. She knew how much Barla feared going back to Earth after all these anons. She had rightly been afraid of losing her memories of her husband and children in Tuala when she passed through the veil. Because Barla now had her own birth crystal, she no longer had to fear the loss, yet she had not come to terms with it until just this moment. "Are you sure? I don't want you to feel pressured about this," Amanda asked in disbelief.

"Yes, I'm sure. You need the help, and I've been selfish enough. Besides, I'd really like to see my sister again!" Barla kept talking to convince herself it was the right thing to do.

"Okay, well I guess we should probably get going then," Amanda said as she stood up. She looked over at where Neal and Vinia sat on the loveseat, and she realized there were still two more problems. "Neal needs a different outfit. He's kind of conspicuous in his hospital gown."

"I can arrange for something for him to wear," Rasa said. She got up from her seat and pulled on a cord by the door. She resumed her seat to wait for a staff member to come at her call.

"Also, Vinia, do you want to come, too?" Amanda asked softly.

"What about Danika? She's here too, remember?"

"We can bring her with us."

"I don't know. Don't you have enough to worry about without dealing with my daughter and me?"

"It'll be fine. Besides, it might help Neal regain his memory faster if you and Danika are there as well. What do you say?"

Neal had been moving his head back and forth as he listened to the two women talk about him as though he were not in the room. "Don't I get a say in all of this?"

"Not today, Neal, I'm sorry to say," Amanda answered matter-of-factly. "Once we get you back home and you've had time to recover, then you can do as you like. Until then you're just going to have to understand we know what we're doing and it's for the best for you and your family."

"You keep talking about my family, what family?"

"Your mother and father, Neal."

"Why do you keep calling me Neal when my name is Nealan?"

"Actually your real name is Nealand Taivas, but we all call you Neal for short."

Neal sat back in the sofa and contemplated what Amanda just told him. Something about the way she said his name brought a memory forward and he wanted to try to figure out what it really meant.

A knock sounded on the door just before it opened. A staff member waited expectantly to be asked to perform a service for which the bell had been rung. Rasa stayed seated and asked, "Can you please find some suitable clothes for this gentleman? We're going to need them in the next couple of minutes. Thank you."

"As you wish," the woman replied with a small curtsy. She turned sharply and left as quietly as she had come.

Amanda appreciated the efficiency of the staff here in Manzanit. She was getting antsy to get going. Now that they had a plan of action, Amanda wanted to be on her way. She really did not want Barla to have enough time to change her mind about coming with her.

CHAPTER 2

It was early in the morning in Richmond Heights, Florida, when Shemalla knocked on the door, smiling over at Willian beside her. The red door opened and Shemalla turned her gaze back to the middle-aged man. "Marcus, it's so good to see you. Thank you for agreeing to meet with Willian and me on such short notice."

"Shemalla, dear; come on in. We can take care of introductions once everyone's together. It's been way too long. Melissa has been cleaning all day in anticipation of you coming over," Marcus said. He stood to the side to allow Shemalla and her guest to enter the house.

The house was pretty small with only two bedrooms. The couple had given up on ever having kids and eventually had downsized their house to make it easier for them to travel. Willian took note of everything as they entered the narrow foyer, moving sideways to get his rolling suitcase across the threshold.

"Just leave your bag there for now," Marcus instructed.

Willian turned and saw the living room. They sat down on the worn couch as Marcus went to get Melissa.

Soon enough Marcus returned, promptly followed by Melissa. She rushed forward and gave Shemalla a hug and warm welcome. "It's so good to see you! And who do we have here?"

"This is Willian Potts. Willian this is Melissa and Marcus Parker."

"It's nice to meet you, Willian," Marcus replied with his hand outstretched to shake his in welcome. "We're excited to have you with us. Do you know how long you want to stay?"

"Thank you for having me. I'm not exactly sure how long I'll be, I hope that's going to be okay," Willian said as he looked swiftly from Marcus to Melissa and finally to Shemalla.

"No problem. Shemalla has told us what your plans are and we know relationships can take time to heal. Don't worry about a thing and we'll do our best to make your stay here as easy as possible. I'm sure there are many things about Earth with which you are unfamiliar, so feel free to ask us any questions you may have."

Willian nodded and remained silent. He was thankful for Shemalla already explaining his mission. Just then there was a strange noise which caught Willian's attention, and he looked beyond his new hosts to see a fluffy animal racing toward him. He was unsure what he should do as he tried to recall what the creature was from the studies he had made of Earth animals.

Melissa leaned down and picked up the incredibly furry animal and pet it soothingly as it kept barking at the two new people in the house. "Hush now, Pesi. These are our new guests, and you're going to be nice to them," she spoke to the black Pomeranian as though the dog would understand what she was saying.

Shemalla took a moment to lean over to Willian and say, "This is their pet dog. The breed is called Pomeranian."

Willian nodded only slightly as he kept his eyes on the little animal who had ceased barking and was leaning toward him and trying to lick his arm. He did think it was pretty cute and wondered what it would feel like to pet. He stretched out his hand cautiously and waited for it to sniff his fingers before she began to lick him. He smiled up at Melissa and said, "I think she likes me!"

"Of course she does, she'll lick you to death if you let her. Let's sit down and get to know one another shall we?" Marcus offered even as he reached out to pet the furry little dog.

Willian looked over to Melissa and watched as she sat down in the chair next to Shemalla. He noticed her silver tree-of-life pendant necklace and remembered hearing about the 'friends of Tuala' each having one to wear. Having this physical proof somehow made him feel better.

"We can take you over to the school today and get you registered, unless you want to wait until tomorrow," Melissa suggested. She set Pesi down on the floor now that she had calmed down and watched as she went over to Shemalla and began sniffing and licking her shoes and pant legs.

"No, today would be great. I really want to get started as soon as possible."

Marcus smiled down at Melissa and commented, "Isn't it strange to have a young person so eager to get to school?" He reached down and touched Pesi's head and said, "Leave Shemalla alone, Pesi. Do you want to go outside?"

Melissa looked up at him with a matching grin. She patted his hand as it rested on her shoulder. This was what they had always wanted for themselves. They would enjoy the time they had with Willian and make his stay as fun as possible.

"Let me show you your room on my way to putting Pesi outside," Marcus said as the silence dragged on in the room. "Bring your bag so you can start unpacking."

Willian jumped up and took the four steps to the foyer where he had left his bag. He grabbed the handle and rolled the bag in the direction Marcus had taken down the short hallway. His room was the first door on the left. There was not much to see as he noticed a twin-sized bed, a dresser, and a small desk filling the small room.

Marcus went to the far wall and folded back the door to the closet he could use for his clothes. "This whole room is yours, feel free to spread out. If you want privacy, simply shut your bedroom door, and we'll respect your need to be alone. The bathroom is right next door to here."

Willian rolled his bag over near the closet and left it to deal with later. He wanted to explore the house and see what else was different from what he knew in Tuala. The tour was really quick since there was only the kitchen, dining room, and the master suite to see. The biggest change Willian would realize would be that he'd have to make food by hand instead of using his powers.

Marcus continued to carry Pesi as he went out the back door. Willian could hear him talking to the dog as if she were a little child. He imagined they probably treated the dog as if she were their child since they had none of their own.

SOFIA STILL COULD NOT BELIEVE her suspicions had been validated when Jon had called her to talk about the story of his mother. She knew there had been something strange about the 'experimental aircraft' in the Stel garage. It made even more sense for it to be the vehicle the Stel family used to get to and from Tuala.

Just the name 'Tuala' gave her a small thrill of excitement. To know the actual name of another world and her friends were from there. Actually, if Jon's story panned out, it would mean all five of her best friends were aliens visiting from another world.

She started thinking about the injuries she was sure she had received after being hit by the car at school. Juila and Jena had been the first people to be on the scene, and they had been touching her. Now she was certain they had used healing powers to fix her broken and bloodied body. Ever since that fateful afternoon, she had seemed to feel differently inside.

When she was around Juila, it almost seemed as though she could read thoughts or images from her friend's mind. She had no way of proving it without talking to Juila, but so far it was what she had determined on her own.

It had been a week since her accident. So much had happened during the last seven days, almost as if the accident had set everything in motion. She wished she had more energy to keep up with it all. *Heck,* she thought to herself, *I'm just glad to be alive to think at all. I have Juila and Jena to thank for that.*

She got into her car to go to school. This was the first day her mother had agreed she was well enough to drive herself. It had been so embarrassing to have her mother take her to school and pick her up in the afternoons. Life seemed to be getting back to normal.

After driving around the parking lot several times, she finally located a parking space pretty far back in the lot. She got out, grabbed her book bag, and trudged up to the entrance of the school. She got to the front door just as a woman and young man were reaching for it.

"Hi," she said to the boy who seemed to be her own age. "Are you new here?"

"Yes, I'm getting registered right now," he replied. He liked the way the young girl looked at him.

"Cool, I can show you around later if you want," she offered.

"That would be great, although I don't think I'll be starting here until tomorrow."

"I'll look forward to it then. See you around," she said. "The office is right there, good luck." She pointed them in the right direction and then she kept walking to get to her locker. They were already in the office when Sofia realized she should have introduced herself. *Oh well,* she shrugged, *I can find out tomorrow.*

She navigated the crowded hall until she got to her locker and dumped off her bag of books. The first bell rang, and she picked up her writing books and set off to be in the same class as Juila and Jena. She would be watching them more closely now that she knew their secret. This was going to be very fascinating.

CHAPTER 3

Amanda parked the telepod in her garage once again. This time she had a full complement of people with her. She hit the button on the console to open the side door as she unbuckled her seat belt. She had timed her return to directly after she had originally left that morning. Her best alibi for her whereabouts would be to create a scenario where she would indisputably be in her home town all morning long.

"Are you okay, Barla?" Amanda asked as her aunt remained motionless in the co-pilot's seat.

"I think so," she said haltingly. "I was just trying to figure out if I've forgotten anything about my life." She looked over at Amanda with a sheepish smile.

"And?" Amanda prompted.

"It's all still there," she grinned foolishly and began unbuckling her seatbelt. "Let's get Neal situated, shall we?"

Amanda led the way to the rear of the telepod. She stopped in front of Neal and waited to see what he would have to say about his new location. His response did not surprise her.

"Where are we? What's going on, Amanda?" Neal's head turned as he took in the view all around him.

To keep from confusing him with unnecessary details, Amanda simply replied, "We're at my house in Florida, Neal. Let's get you inside, and we can call your parents. Your mom has been very worried about you." She bent forward and released his seatbelt. She offered her hand to help him out of his seat, but he refused it.

He put his hands on the armrests and levered himself to a standing position.

Barla came around to his other side, and they flanked him down the ramp to the garage floor with Vinia, carrying Danika on her hip, following close behind them. To avoid any further questions Amanda tapped the cloaking button on her remote, and the telepod disappeared as though it had never been there.

Neal had missed the whole thing. When he turned his head to look around, he only saw an empty garage which made him frown in confusion. "What happened to the car?" he asked even as he was being pulled toward the house.

"Don't worry about it right now, Neal. Come inside so we can sit down," Amanda urged.

They trooped through the house until they reached the living room. Amanda made sure everyone was seated before she kept walking to get to her office. She closed the door behind her and dug her cell phone out of her pants pocket.

She scrolled through the numbers until she got to the Taivas house. She dialed the number and waited for the phone to be picked up. When Jessica's voice answered, Amanda said, "Jessica, this is Amanda. I have Neal. Can you please come over here to get him?"

"What? How is that even possible? Never mind, you can tell me when I get there. I'll be right over."

Amanda was unsurprised when the phone disconnected. She

could understand how distraught Neal's mother would have been thinking her son was still in danger at the psychiatric center in Queens, New York. To know he was only a short drive away, she definitely did not want to waste time talking on the phone when she could satisfy her curiosity in person.

The next call Amanda made was to Dr. Medin. She knew she could trust her with their lives, so she had no reservations as she dialed her number from the speed dial. Even though it was early, Dr. Medin answered on the third ring. "Hi Dr. Medin, this is Amanda."

"Oh, Amanda. I'm so sorry I haven't figured out a way to help you get Neal released from Dr. Gascon's facility. I swear I've been trying."

"I didn't call for that. I already got Neal out of there this morning."

"Seriously? How?"

"I don't have time to discuss it right now, I'll tell you later. Can you do me a favor?"

"Sure. What do you need?"

"I'm wondering if you will agree to treat Neal with hypnosis."

"Are you sure it'd be wise? Do you want him to remember?"

"I do. There's someone else involved, and I think it's only fair for Neal to have his memories intact so he can decide where he wants to live. The hard part will be convincing Neal's parents of the truth."

"Yes, I can see what you're saying. His story would seem rather nutty to the uneducated."

"I think the uneducated would accept it quicker than Neal's parents. They're pretty old-school about everything."

"When would you like me to see Neal?"

"Today, if you have the time."

"I can make time. I'll leave you a message when I'm available. Talk to you later."

"Thanks, Dr. Medin. See you later."

There was still one more phone call to make. Amanda dialed her own parents' home phone. Diane answered.

"Hi, Mom. I know it's early, but can you come over right now?"

"Is everything okay?"

"Mostly. I have a surprise for you. Can you come?"

"I'm already on my way," she replied cheerfully.

Amanda shut her cell phone and breathed a sigh of relief. She went over to the computer and pulled up the security program for the front gate. She set the gate sensor to open for the next two cars to arrive. With all of the details handled, Amanda turned off the computer and returned to the living room to wait for her guests to arrive.

Everyone turned their heads to watch Amanda walk into the room and seat herself. They had been watching Danika play on the floor. Nobody seemed to have anything to say.

She made sure she had a view of the door so she would be forewarned when Jessica pulled her car up front. "I've made a few phone calls. Jessica should be here in a couple of minutes."

"Who's Jessica?" Vinia asked.

"Neal's mother."

Vinia's mouth made the shape of an 'O,' and she hastily shifted her gaze back down to her own daughter on the floor. Danika had become fascinated with the television remote. She repeatedly shoved it in her mouth and then slapped it on the rug-covered floor. It seemed only Danika seemed unaffected by the strange moods of the people in the room with her.

Amanda wished she could be as oblivious. Her mind was racing through all of the different scenarios of how Jessica could react to her son's return. For the most part, she thought Jessica would be angry because Neal's memory was even worse than it had been a couple of days before he had gone to be treated by Dr. Gascon.

Soon enough a flash of light shot through the room as the sun reflected off of Jessica's car as she pulled up to the house. Amanda rose from the couch and went to the door before Jessica had even made it out of her car.

"Thanks for coming over so fast."

"Where is he? Is he okay?"

"He's inside on the couch. You'll see for yourself how he is." Amanda trailed behind Jessica as she rushed through the house to get to her son.

"Neal! Neal, are you okay honey?" Jessica cried as she kneeled in front of her son and put her hands on both of his cheeks while she looked into his eyes.

"Do I know you?"

Jessica's head pivoted to look at Amanda with an expression of horror. "What did that doctor do to him?"

"Give him some time. Dr. Gascon drugged him almost into a coma. I have called a friend of mine, and she has agreed to take over his mental care. I promise she can be trusted."

Jessica looked up at her like she had spoken blasphemy and sneered, "You expect me to trust him to a doctor after this? I don't think so. Neal is going to stay at home where I can keep him safe."

Vinia sobbed at Jessica's statement.

Jessica looked over at the other woman and did a double-take. She recalled Neal telling her about someone who he thought he remembered who looked like Amanda. This had to be the woman; only she could not recall her name at the moment. She turned her head back to Amanda and asked, "Who is this woman?"

"Her name's Vinia. I told you about her yesterday. She and Neal are dating, or they were, up until he lost his memory."

With another appraising look, Jessica stared at Vinia's expression and at her relative closeness to her son on the couch. Her inspection was interrupted when Danika decided to crawl over and pat Jessica on her hip as she kneeled on the floor. "What? Who's this?"

Vinia spoke for the first time, "She's my daughter, Danika. Danika, leave the woman alone right now." She bent down and picked up the squirming child and settled her down in her lap. The remote was still firmly held in her hand, and Danika brought it to her mouth and happily began chewing on it again.

Jessica looked from Danika to her son to see if there were any similarities.

Vinia caught the look and instantly spoke up, "Danika is not Neal's child, although, he's been a wonderful father to her."

"Oh," Jessica said even as she had a hard time concealing her disappointment. It would have been wonderful to have a grandchild, to know her son's legacy continued on.

Neal had been silent during the exchange although he had kept turning his gaze to each person as they spoke around him. He reached up and gently removed Jessica's hands from his face. He continued to hold her hands as he moved them down to his knees. "I can see you know me, but I'm sorry to say I don't remember you right now. I'd like to take Amanda up on her offer of seeing her doctor friend."

Jessica's expression changed to fear at her son's admission of not knowing his own mother. She could not understand what could have gone so desperately wrong under Dr. Gascon's care, but she was certainly not going to let him get away with it. She was going to sue him and make sure his medical license was taken away. Dr. Gascon had messed with the wrong family!

Amanda looked at her watch. Her mother should be arriving soon. She really wanted the reinforcements of another person before she told Jessica what had actually happened to her son. This was going to be hard enough for Jessica to believe.

Jessica pulled her hands away and picked herself up from the floor. She sat down on the other side of her son and noticed Barla for the first time. Her focus had been so completely on her son that she had missed seeing everyone else in the room. Now she felt slightly foolish and wanted to find out what had happened. "Tell me how you got Neal here so fast. We just spoke yesterday afternoon, and you didn't sound like you knew what you were going to do."

Amanda was spared from having to answer as the flashing light of another car pulling into the driveway sparkled through the living room. "Hold that thought. I have to answer the door." She rushed back to the front entrance and raced outside to speak to her mom privately for a moment before she came inside to the tense setting.

"Thank goodness you got here so fast, Mom. Just listen to me for a second really fast. I got some help from people in Tuala to rescue Neal from the hospital where Dr. Gascon was treating him. I'm afraid I might have been too late because Neal was heavily drugged when we got him out of there this morning. Anyway, we traveled through Tuala, and now Neal has lost his memory again. Jessica's inside, and she's wanting answers to how I accomplished the feat. I'm afraid I'll have to tell her the truth, and I need you to back me up. Can you do that for me?"

Diane was floored by everything her daughter had just shared with her. It seemed as though a lot had happened since she had last spoken with her daughter. All she could do was nod her head as she hugged her daughter before they walked inside. Diane had gotten as far as the entrance to the living room when her gaze fell on the sister she had believed dead for over twenty years. She stopped dead in her tracks and stared dumbfounded as she said, "Barbara? Is that you Barb?"

Barla stood up with a huge grin on her face as she moved across the living room to hug her sister. She shifted her gaze to Amanda and said, "You never told me you asked my sister to come over!" She folded her arms around Diane and rubbed her back as she felt her sister begin to cry. "Hey, Diane, it's okay. I'm right here now."

Diane was overwhelmed with emotions. She never thought her sister would be able to come back to Earth; she never imagined being able to hold her, touch her, or talk to her ever again. Her happiness at seeing her long-lost sister overcame her powers of speech or anything else for several minutes. Finally, she was able to get a grip on herself, and she pulled away from Barla and held her at arm's length as she said, "I just can't believe it, Barbara. It's really you!"

"I go by Barla now, but yes, it's really me. Come on let's sit down. We have a lot to discuss and not just me, but Neal needs our help right now." She took Diane's hand and led her over to the loveseat, and sat down right next to her.

Jessica could not understand what she had just witnessed. She had not known Diane had a sister who was missing, and she was intrigued but did not want to be distracted from finding out what was going on with her son. She asked again, "Tell me what happened with Neal."

"I asked my mom to come over, not only to reunite with her sister but because I knew I would need her here to convince you of what has been happening with Neal. It's a very complicated story, and I'm sure you'll have a hard time believing what I'm going to tell you."

"Get on with it Amanda. I've waited a long time to hear the truth from you, and I'm ready!"

"We'll see about that," Amanda muttered as she looked down on her folded hands as she tried to decide the best way to tell the story.

Jessica scowled darkly at Amanda's doubt and wished she'd get on with her explanation. She decided, at that moment, to believe whatever Amanda told her. Any explanation would be better than imagining all of the possible heinous scenarios.

Amanda took a deep breath and looked around the room to all of her guests. Some of them knew almost everything, so this would not be a complete revelation. She decided to start at the beginning as she looked only at Jessica, "You remember when Neal and I went sailing just after we were engaged?"

Jessica nodded.

"Well, everything was wonderful until a sudden electrical storm hit us. I was knocked unconscious when a rogue wave knocked me over, and I hit my head on the bed stand. When I woke up, I had no idea where I was or who I was with. I didn't know what had happened to Neal or to our yacht.

"The simplest explanation is that we were found by a man named Petre MacVeen and he sold Neal, me, and the yacht to a man who's known as Elder Vargen. The boat was disassembled to find out how it was engineered. Neal was kept hostage and forced to work for Elder Vargen in his Old Soul Engineering Facility. Neal's knowledge of engineering is what Elder Vargen exploited, and he kept him docile by addicting him to a drug called *resh*.

"I was held captive in another area and had no idea what had happened to Neal. Elder Vargen had me impregnated because he wanted to have a child from me. He never counted on the fact that the wise-woman called in to attend me would take pity on me and help me escape. Unfortunately, she wasn't fast enough, and I ended up having my twins before she was able to send me home. She sent me home alone, and so I missed out on Juila and Jena growing up.

"You know how I was when I was found off the coast of Cancun. The trauma kept me in a coma for seven years, and I was unable to do or say anything to help you locate Neal. After I woke up, I had a hard time remembering just what really happened. I was even more confused and scared than Neal is right now. I wrote down all of what I remembered in a journal, at the insistence of Dr. Medin.

"The dreams I'd had while I was in a coma were very confusing and seemed quite contradictory. One person who was prominent in my dreams was Riccan. You can imagine when I met him for the first time while I was awake, it got me very excited. He and I discussed my memories, and he became convinced something quite extraordinary had happened to me. He took me to his parents to talk about what I knew, and they agreed."

Jessica shook her head and interrupted, "That's really great, Amanda, but what does this have to do with Neal?"

"I'm getting to that, just bear with me a few more minutes. When I told them about what Elder Vargen did to me and how I suspected he still had Neal, they helped me locate him. A few other people were involved, including Barla," she nodded her head toward her aunt, "and we contacted Vinia to ask her to help us get him home." Amanda and Jessica both looked over to Vinia to see her look down to avoid seeing their stares.

"So a group of us got together when we knew Elder Vargen would be out of town, and we flew in and rescued Neal. Riccan and I brought him home to you and hoped that would be the end of it. Unfortunately for you, the therapist you had Neal seeing must have spoken about Neal's case with Dr. Gascon.

"You see, Dr. Gascon approached me before I was released from the hospital and wanted me to answer his questions. I knew he could not be trusted because I had lived through very traumatic events in my dreams about Dr. Gascon's 'treatment' plans for his patients. He loves to use drugs and electric shock therapy to force people to tell him what he wants to hear about his latest research ideas.

"So when you told me Neal was being treated by Dr. Gascon, I knew he had to be rescued. I gathered another group of people, and we were able to get him out of the hospital and back home as fast as possible." Amanda knew she had left out some key points and hoped her strange explanation would satisfy Jessica's curiosity. She looked around the room to gauge how her story sounded to the listeners.

Jessica remained silent as she absorbed everything Amanda had said. It seemed as though some major points had been glossed over, but she fixated on one point in particular. "So you don't actually have any proof of Dr. Gascon being unethical except for your dreams?"

"Oh, no, there's plenty of proof. I told you about the patient records at Cannon Memorial. I researched Dr. Gascon after I regained my memories of the past. Although I was never actually his patient, there were plenty of people who were tortured by him through his so-called 'treatment protocol'. My friend, Dr. Medin, has first-hand proof as she has worked for Dr. Gascon in the past and she can verify everything I've told you. Neal was almost comatose when we took him out of his hospital room; he was definitely in danger."

"How can we find this Elder Vargen? He obviously can't be left unpunished after everything he did to the two of you. I want to have him arrested."

"I'm afraid he's out of your reach, Jessica. Please try to forget about him."

"Forget about him? Are you serious?"

"I'm very serious. Please focus your attention on people within your grasp. There's Neal's recovery, and then there's Dr. Gascon. I'm sure you'll be hearing from him shortly." She looked down at her watch and realized it was still another forty-five minutes until they actually broke into Neal's room to rescue him.

She was going to have to hurry if she were going to have a solid alibi. She did not believe visiting with Jessica would be a good enough alibi to a police investigation as Neal's mother could be believed to be complicit in the plan.

"Here's the thing, Jessica, unless I tell you things you absolutely won't believe, then we're at a stand-still. The truth of the matter is I broke Neal out of his room at Creedmoor forty-five minutes from now. I have been to Queens and back in a matter of seconds because I have a special way to travel. Do you think the police will believe it? No. I can see on your face that even you don't believe it.

"So here's what you're going to do. You are going to take Neal home now. When the police come to you, you are going to tell them that Neal came home first thing this morning of his own accord. Tell them you arranged a private jet for him to come home. Tell them whatever you like. There is no explanation I can give to the police which will be believed; therefore I cannot be part of his return.

"I am going to go out in public and make sure there are plenty of records saying I've been here in town all morning. I'm going to take Vinia with me so she can be seen around here as well so nobody can then say it was her either since we look so much alike."

"Speaking of that," Jessica broke in, "Neal told me about you before he went to be treated by Dr. Gascon. I know you two were seeing one another. Would you, and little Danika there, like to come and spend some time with him? It might speed up his recovery."

Vinia enthusiastically nodded as tears started to roll down her cheeks. She had never wanted anything more than having a family want her around. Since her own family was dead, it would be very special to get to know Neal's parents.

She looked at her watch again and stood up. "I think you need to take Neal somewhere public right now. Take him out for breakfast, go through a drive-thru, anything where he can be seen with you right now."

Neal looked up at her dumbfounded. "You mean you want me to leave with this woman?"

"Yes, Neal, I do. She's not some random stranger; she's your mother. In time you'll remember, but right now we don't have time for you to argue with me. You need to go and be seen in public. I'll call you, Jessica, and let you know what time Dr. Medin will be able to meet with Neal. When Dr. Gascon or the police call, let them know everything is fine and you've already made alternate arrangements for Neal's mental health."

Jessica seemed rather daunted by the task set to her. While she had been so thrilled to come and get Neal before she had arrived, now she had second thoughts about taking him home when he was so obviously confused. She looked over at Neal and asked, "Do you think you can trust me until you can get your memories back? I promise to make sure you get to see this doctor friend of Amanda's if it would make you feel better."

Neal looked back and forth between the two women. It seemed he was not going to get any say in the matter since both women seemed to be of the same accord. He nodded and saw Amanda's face transform into one of relief. He was glad he had made the right decision. Eventually, he would remember everything, and he hoped it would be soon. He stood up and said, "I guess we should get going then."

Jessica still seemed hesitant as she remained sitting on the couch.

Amanda went to Jessica and kneeled beside her as she spoke rapidly, but quietly, "I assure you he'll be better, maybe even by the end of the day. He's traveled quite a bit today, and he's still suffering from the effects of the drugs he was given. Go get him something to eat; it might make a great improvement."

Jessica slowly nodded much as her son had just done. She decided to trust Amanda to know what was best in this strange situation. After all, what could it hurt? She rose from the couch and said, "Okay, Neal, let's get something to eat. Where do you want to go?" She walked slowly with her son across the foyer.

"Can we go to Denny's?" Neal asked quietly.

"Sure," Jessica replied as she opened the front door and waited for Neal to exit the house first. She looked back one last time before shutting the door. The look on her face clearly said Amanda had better be right about all of this.

CHAPTER 5

"Two down, one to go," Amanda said almost to herself. "Vinia, why don't you come upstairs with me and I'll find you a nice change of clothes. These hospital outfits clearly won't work for what I have in mind." She looked Vinia up and down and nodded, "I think we wear the same size even."

Vinia hastily stood up and said to Barla and Diane, "Barla, would you mind watching Danika?" At Barla's nod, Vinia put Danika back on the floor and followed Amanda upstairs to get ready for another adventure.

Diane, now left pretty much alone with her sister, cleared her throat and said, "I hear you have two children of your own. Amanda said your daughter, Rasa, right? She said she's really amazing."

"Yes, she has just been accepted and the successor of an Elder."

Diane nodded without really understanding the significance of the position.

"Women have never been Elders before now; Rasa will be the first when Elder Wilken steps down or dies."

"Oh," Diane said. She felt slightly stupid for not having anything more interesting to add to the conversation. Finally, she just asked what was really on her mind, "What happened, Barb…I mean, Barla? Why didn't you come back like Amanda did? Why did you change your name even?"

"Well the simple story is similar to Amanda's, and Neal's, for that matter. I had lost my memory when I was transported to Tuala; even my name was a mystery. When Captain Ahn found me in the ocean, he gave me the name Barla until I could remember my own. It took a long time for my memory to return and by then everyone already knew me as Barla, so I kept it. It was also amazing since Diane had nicknamed me Barla when I was little, so it was perfect.

"I'm sure Amanda told you that Captain Ahn and I fell in love. How could you expect me to leave my soul-mate to return back to Earth? Eventually, we had our son, Gravin, and then it was just impossible. I knew that I would lose everything if I ever returned to Earth, even for a visit, and it wasn't worth it. I'm sorry, it sounds callous, but it's the truth."

"But you're here now, how is it any different than before?" Diane asked with a confused expression.

"You have your daughter to thank for this blessing. She figured out the key to retaining memories through the veil. You see, only people from Earth lose their history. The people from Tuala can travel back and forth without any problems. Amanda asked Jehoban to give me my own birth crystal which, in essence, made me a citizen of Tuala with all of their natural-born abilities.

"Even though it's been a few mesans, or I guess you'd say months, since I got my birth crystal," her hand came up to caress the bright blue crystals woven in to the shape of a tree-of-life pendant suspended from an ornate chain around her neck, "I've been too afraid to make the trip for fear Amanda had been mistaken."

"What made you willing to try it now?"

"Amanda needed my help with Neal. After everything she's done for my family and me, I had to do what I could to help out. I had to let go of my fears and trust in Jehoban's protection built into the birth crystal he personally picked out for me."

"Can I see it?" Diane said as she leaned forward to inspect the beautiful jewelry. The pendant was only about an inch across, and the metal was all gold. "It's beautiful. When you said you now have all of the natural-born abilities, what exactly does that entail?"

Barla smiled and held out her hands in front of her. She concentrated for only an instant before a sphere of elemental energy pulsed between her cupped hands. She had it float above them both and then return to her palms where it dissipated into nothingness again.

Diane's eyes widened with the display of what appeared to be magic. "What would you use that for?"

"Light mostly, much like you'd use a flashlight, except mine is always with me. There's so much more to accessing the elemy which makes life a lot easier. I can create meals by thinking them into existence; likewise, I can clean up the mess with only a thought. There's really no limit to what a person could do with the elemy."

"I can see this gift has made you a very happy woman and I'm glad for you. I'm also thankful that you can now come and visit! Wait until you meet my husband and my other two daughters! Do you think Ahn would ever like to come for a visit?"

"I'm sure he will at some point, because we really hate to be apart. He's never been to Earth, as far as I know. It'd definitely be an adventure for him!"

Diane laughed and the tension between them dissolved completely. They settled into talking about their children and what kept them busy during the day. Diane was not surprised to hear her sister had started an orphanage and was kept busy with as many children as she could surround herself with. Barb had always wanted to have lots of children as far back as she could recall.

The conversation was interrupted as Amanda and Vinia returned from upstairs. Amanda leaned on the back of the couch and asked, "Barla, would you be okay to keep watching Danika while Vinia and I go out to create an alibi for my morning? Vinia didn't want to ask you to do more for her, but I tried to assure her you wouldn't mind."

"Oh, Vinia, really it's no bother at all. Danika is a wonderful little girl. We may even take her out to the pool to splash around a bit since it's getting pretty warm. We'll have loads of fun," Barla leaned over and rubbed Danika's cheek and said, "Won't we, Danika?"

The little girl giggled and nodded her head enthusiastically.

Vinia laughed as well and said, "Okay, okay, I give up. Hopefully, we won't be gone too long." She turned her gaze back to Amanda as though asking her to keep the outing short.

"Barla, spare bathing suits are upstairs in my chifforobe, top left-hand drawer. Feel free to help yourself!" She turned to Vinia and said, "I was thinking about doing a little bit of clothes shopping, and then we could stop for some breakfast of our own. This has been a long morning, and the fruit and steena tea I had for breakfast really aren't enough!"

"Why don't we eat first then since I was too nervous to eat anything at all," Vinia suggested. She was curious to see if the restaurants were any different on Earth than they were at home. She would be lying to herself if she said she was not worried about this outing. After their adventure in New York, this was surely going to be an easier task, she hoped.

"Okay, then, let's go!" Amanda replied enthusiastically. She was going to have to be in a cheerful mood, completely unconcerned about life in general if she was going to look innocent of having kidnapped someone earlier in the day. This plan had to work, or she was going to be in loads of trouble with the authorities.

She walked out to the other garage and opened the door to the 4-Runner for Vinia. She showed her the seatbelt and how it worked, and then she went around to the driver's side and started the engine. As the garage door was opening, she said, "Remember to act as if everything around you is normal. I can't have you staring at everything or asking too many questions. I'll answer everything for you once we return home so just keep a catalog of questions for then, okay?"

Vinia swallowed her nerves and said, "I'm ready." She had decided she was going to need this education sooner or later if she were going to be a part of her children's lives. After all, they had been living and experiencing life on Earth for the past eight anons; years she corrected herself.

This led her to another thought; she was going to have to remember two sets of vocabulary which could not be confused when she changed dimensions. She would have to pay more attention to how Amanda and Riccan handled the language differences and try to emulate them as much as possible.

They pulled out of the driveway, onto the main road, and into the life of Richmond Heights, Florida. Just as Amanda had planned, they ate breakfast at one of her favorite restaurants where the servers all knew her name. They spent a leisurely time eating, including having dessert for Vinia's benefit.

They went to the bank where Amanda asked about setting up accounts for her two girls, even though she had no intention of actually going through with it. She knew the banks had security camera systems which would be irrefutable evidence of her being in town during the time of day where Neal had been taken from the hospital.

As their last stop, Amanda pulled into the shopping mall along the way home. She really hated shopping, but she thought it might be fun for Vinia to see the fashions of the people of Earth. To make the trip out worthwhile, she decided she would buy Vinia a few outfits to keep at her house for when she came to visit her children.

CHAPTER 6

Amanda glanced at her watch as she was turning into her driveway. They had spent almost two hours out on the town, and she suspected there would be some action happening pretty soon. She pulled the truck into the garage and shut the garage door. Vinia helped her gather all of their bags of clothes and take them into the house where they put it all down on the living room floor.

Vinia had been anxious about taking so long since Barla was watching Danika for her. She spotted her daughter out in the pool with Barla. Diane sat on the edge of the pool with her pants rolled up and her feet splashing in the water playfully. Clearly, Danika had not missed her mother's presence.

As if on cue, the gate intercom buzzed. Amanda took a calming breath and went to answer it. "Hello," she said into the box on the wall.

"Kendall District Police, we'd like to ask you a few questions," the man's voice replied.

"Sure, come on up," Amanda said as she pressed the button to open the gate. She turned to Vinia and said, "The questions will begin. Do you want to stay in here with me or go out by the pool to say hello to Danika?"

"I'm sorry, Amanda, would you be too upset if I went outside?" Vinia felt as though she were abandoning a friend in her time of need.

"Oh, Vinia, I love you. Don't feel bad. I've got this handled. Go outside and enjoy yourself. Hopefully, I can get this squared away."

Vinia smiled sheepishly and practically ran out the back door.

Amanda watched as Danika's smile lit up her face, and she started to babble nonsensical things to her mother. She wished she could join them as she went to answer the knock on the front door. She did have everything covered. She just had to remain calm and unconcerned; it was all going to depend on her acting skills.

Two officers stood facing her, both looking uncomfortable with their assignment. "Amanda Stel?"

"That's me."

"We're sorry to disturb you, Mrs. Stel. Would you mind letting us come in and ask you a few questions?"

"Not at all, come on in. Can I get you anything? Water? Coffee? Tea?"

"No, ma'am, we're fine," the one officer replied for them both as they stepped into the foyer and looked around in amazement at the sheer size of the house.

Amanda led the way into the living room and, pushing aside a few of the bags of clothes, said, "Please sit down, we may as well be comfortable. What can I help you with, officers?" She hoped they would not see her hands trembling as she folded them in her lap as she sat down across from them.

"We've been informed of a patient escaping from Creedmoor Psychiatric Center in Queens, New York. The patient's name is…," he looked down at his notepad and continued, "Nealand Taivas, Jr."

"Oh my goodness, is Neal okay?" Amanda said in a surprised tone.

"We haven't found him yet. Do you have any knowledge of his whereabouts?"

"If he's not at the center, then I'd assume he'd be with his parents. Have you contacted them yet?"

"No, ma'am, we were given to believe you participated in Mr. Taivas' escape from the center. Given what time it is and the fact that he went missing only about an hour ago, then it would be impossible for you to have been personally involved since it would take at least three hours to fly here."

"Wait, let me give Jessica a call, and we can see if she knows where her son is," Amanda said as she stood up to get her phone from the kitchen island. She flipped open the cell and punched in Jessica's phone number. She heard several rings before she heard Jessica's voice. Amanda turned to face the police as she spoke, "Hey, Jessica, it's me, Amanda. Hi. Yes, the police are here at my house, and they're looking for Neal. Have you seen him? Oh, he's with you right now? Oh, that's wonderful. Just a sec."

Amanda loosely held her hand over the receiver and asked the two officers, "Would either of you like to speak with Neal's mother? She says Neal's with her right now."

One of the officers nodded his head and went over to stand beside Amanda. He held out his hand for the phone and put it up to his ear, "Hello, is this Jessica Taivas?"

"Yes, what's going on? Is there a problem?"

"We had a report that your son escaped from Creedmoor in New York."

"I think there's been a grave mistake, Officer. I'm sorry someone has wasted your time and caused such a fuss. Neal contacted me last night and said he was leaving Creedmoor because he didn't feel he was being treated properly. I made arrangements for him to fly home last night. He and I are out eating breakfast right now."

"Mrs. Taivas, we're going to have to speak to both you and Neal. Can we come over to your house in twenty minutes?"

"Yes, we were just finishing right now. I believe we can be home by then."

"Okay, thank you for your cooperation. We'll be over shortly." He flipped the phone shut and spoke to Amanda, "Thank you for your assistance, Mrs. Stel. I'm sorry to have bothered you."

"Don't worry about it. I'm just glad I could help you out. Let me walk you to the door," she smiled up at the officer.

When the two uniformed men finally got back into their car and drove away, Amanda shut the front door and leaned her back against the door to hold herself up. Her knees were shaking along with the rest of her body. Never in her life had she been so scared. Her only hope now was that Jessica and Neal could both remain calm and able to keep up the story they had fabricated.

Diane found her daughter slumped down on the floor by the front door. Instantly she screamed, "Amanda? Amanda, are you okay?" She ran across the living room and into the foyer. She slowed her run as Amanda lifted her head from her knees and looked up at her.

"I'm fine, Mom. I only had a slight panic attack after the police left. Help me up," she said as she held up her hand for her mom to support her while she stood back up.

"I'm sorry you're going through all of this, Amanda. I only wanted you to have a happy life once you woke up from your coma." Diane pulled her daughter to her and wrapped her arms around her to give her as much love as she could show. She rubbed her daughter's back until she no longer felt the quiver's of fear pulsing through Amanda's body. She pulled away and asked, "Are you better now?"

"Yes, much better. Thank you for being here today, Mom. I'm so glad you were able to get to see and talk to your sister again. At least one thing has gone right today."

"What do you mean 'one thing'? Did something go wrong?"

"Not yet. The police are on their way to the Taivas house to question Jessica and Neal. As long as neither of them cave, then we are all going to be fine. If either one of them says the wrong thing, then we are all going to have a lot of explaining to do."

Diane listened carefully to her daughter and then smiled.

"What could you possibly have to smile about, Mom?"

"You!" Diane laughed out loud at her daughter's expression. "Don't you see, Amanda? How can they come back to say it was you when you were clearly here in town shopping? It would be impossible for you or even Vinia to have been in New York and here at the same time."

"All true, Mom, except for the fact I was there. They probably have security footage of Rasa and me. I don't know why I didn't think about that when I was walking through the halls of Creedmoor. How could I have been so careless?" Amanda slapped her thigh as she left the foyer and her mother behind.

"At least you won't have to worry about them ever finding Rasa. She's from Tuala, and she won't be visiting Earth anytime soon." Diane sped up to stand beside her daughter. She touched her arm and spoke softly, "Don't ever berate yourself for being a good friend and doing the right thing. I've always loved you for your loyalty. Everything will be just fine. Besides, if it came right down to it, you could always move to Tuala until the statute of limitation ran out."

Amanda simply stared at her mother. Suddenly she burst out laughing at the absurdity of her last statement. Her giggles resumed as soon as she said, "Until the statute of limitations runs out!" She collapsed on the couch and brushed the tears away from her eyes as her chuckles finally stopped. "Thanks, Mom. I needed to hear a voice of reason."

Barla held the door open for Vinia who was carrying Danika. They stopped at the door when they saw Amanda and Diane seemingly in deep discussion and asked, "Is now a bad time?"

"No, no, you're fine. Mom was just making me laugh. Come inside and cool off. I'll get everyone something to drink." Amanda went to the kitchen and stood staring at the contents of the refrigerator. She really hoped it would not come to them having to leave town for several years.

CHAPTER 7

Jon finally cornered Sofia at school the day after his phone call complaining about his siblings' trick on him regarding their mother. "What did you mean on the phone last night? It almost sounded as though you believed Behn and Val's story about us being aliens!"

Sofia's eyes got huge as she rapidly looked around them. She grabbed his arm hard and whispered, "Hey, keep your voice down! Do you want everyone to know?"

"Know what, that my brother and sister have gone off the deep end? You're right; I probably should try to keep that in the family!" he whispered back to her even though he felt like yelling.

"And just so you know, I do believe them. I want you to think about everything you and I have talked about since I got hit by the car. Really think about it with what Behn and Val told you as well. I know you will come to the same conclusion." She kept her hand on his arm and began moving him out of the flow of students so they could speak more privately in the alcove next to the girls' bathroom.

"I can't believe they got to you, too. I'm really starting to think I'm the one going crazy!" He shook his head and closed his eyes in frustration.

"Listen to me, Jon! You are not going crazy, but you are in a very unique situation. We all are, for that matter. The easiest way to resolve this whole thing is for you to go along with what you've been told. Tell them you have reconsidered and you're willing to meet with your mother. Have them take you home. Have them show you the, what did you call it…oh yeah, the telepod in the garage. If they can do all of that, then will you believe?"

Jon stared at Sofia in horror at her suggestion to go along with the plot. Suddenly he realized what he could do. "I like it. I can go along with it until I can prove that they've all been duped. Good idea, Sofia. Have you seen Behn or Val? I want to tell them right now. Let's get this thing over with once and for all!" He pulled away from Sofia and began scanning the faces in the crowds trying to find his brother or sister.

"Jon, we've got to head to class right now. Sit through this next class, and then you can tell them at lunch. You know where they'll be then."

Jon nodded even as he was thinking about his new plan. "Good idea. Okay, I'll see you at lunch!" He continued to nod even as he stalked off in the opposite direction.

Sofia watched him go and wondered what his reaction was going to be when he found out everything he had been told was actually true. She shook her head and walked slowly to her typing class. She was going to have to pay more attention to her lessons after her last conversation with her teacher, Mrs. Shoreham.

Soon enough the bell rang to end class and Sofia shot out of her seat and rushed out the door to get to her locker. She definitely did not want to be late for lunch and the conversation which was bound to be interesting. Sofia tossed her book and binders carelessly into the locker and slammed the door shut as she turned and entered the flow of students into the cafeteria.

Sofia spotted Jon first and shoved her way through the crowd to get beside him. She tugged on his sleeve, and he looked down from his active search to smile at her.

"Good," he said absentmindedly, "You can help me find everyone."

"Jon, seriously, there's no need to be so obvious. Grab a tray and get your lunch. We always sit at the same table together. Good grief, you can be so…so focused!" She tugged on his arm to get him to follow her directions. She stumbled slightly as he actually came along easily. Sofia looked up at him to see if he were planning something else, yet all she saw was him acting nearly normal again.

"I'm sorry, Sofia. You're right about this, too. Besides I'm really hungry anyway since I was too upset last night to eat dinner with Behn and Val sitting across the table glaring at me to believe their crazy story. Of course, Mom and Dad asked what was going on, but nobody gave them a real answer." Jon picked up a tray and began filling it with several different dishes of food.

Sofia followed along behind him and only grabbed a salad and a bowl of fruit. Her mind was working through what could possibly go wrong at the table once they were all seated. She hoped they would at least keep their voices lowered so it would not draw too much attention.

They sat down and waited for everyone else to join them. Juila and Jena were the first to arrive. Both of the girls were smiling and on their best behavior as though the night before had not even happened.

Juila sat down next to Sofia and asked, "How are you feeling today? Did I see your car out in the parking lot?"

"I'm feeling much better than I was! Yes, my mom finally agreed I was well enough to drive myself to school again. Of course, the only parking spot I could find was out in the back forty! I'm not sure I ever really thanked you for helping me right after the accident."

"What do you mean?"

"You know, you..." Sofia looked up as there was a shifting of positions at the table.

"Hey, Jena, scoot over so I can sit down beside Juila," Behn said as he tried to fit in between Juila and Jena.

Sofia saw the look on Jon's face and decided to let the conversation with Juila drop. There were certainly more important matters which would be discussed. They only had one more person to wait for, and she was nowhere to be seen. She leaned around Juila and asked, "Where's Val?"

"She'll be here shortly. She said she wanted to go to the bathroom first," Behn replied. He picked up his fork and began eating as though nothing were wrong.

Sofia poked Jon in the ribs with her elbow and whispered, "Eat while you can." She looked down at his full tray meaningfully.

Jon scowled at her even as he picked up his fork and stabbed the meatloaf harder than was absolutely necessary.

Sofia valiantly contained her grin as she turned to concentrate on her own salad. She had her mouth full when Valentina and Luke came over to sit down. Instead of taking her customary seat next to Jon she set her tray next to Luke's when he sat down beside Jena and hopped over the bench. It appeared as though the teams were formed, the four of them were sticking together, and she and Jon were on the opposing team. Sofia almost felt bad for Luke since he was actually clueless while secretly she was rooting for team Tuala to win this upcoming battle.

Jon set down his fork and leaned forward as he spoke quietly, yet distinctly, "I want you to make arrangements for me to meet our mom."

All eyes shifted from Jon to Sofia. She took in their gazes and tried to act innocent as she picked through her salad for another bite to stab.

Behn broke the silence and asked, "So you believe us now?"

"I don't know what to believe just yet, but I want to meet our mother. I'll decide what to think after I talk to her. Will you do it?"

"Sure," Behn said and then turned to Juila and asked, "Do you think your mom can arrange it?"

"I don't see why not since she's the one who did it before. I'll ask her after school."

Jon rudely interrupted and demanded, "Call her now on your cell phone. Tell her I'd like to see her today."

Juila frowned slightly and then shrugged her shoulders as she dug her phone out of her coat pocket. "Okay, okay, don't get so testy, Jon. I'll see if my mom has time today."

"Fine," Jon said sullenly, and he stopped leaning across the table. He thought about trying to finish eating, but he was too anxious to even make the attempt until after he heard what Mrs. Stel had to say.

"Hey, Mom, it's me, Juila. Hi, yeah, no there's nothing wrong. I was wondering if you could arrange for Vinia to come over so Jon could meet her. What? Cool! I'll let them know. Thanks, Mom. I love you." She flipped her phone shut and smiled, "Done! You can meet her after school today at our house."

"Just like that?" Jon asked in disbelief.

"Yep! Oh, this is so exciting, don't you think, Behn?" Juila asked her boyfriend as she started to eat her lunch with enthusiasm.

Jon started to feel as though he'd been set up. Everything worked out a little too easily for his mind. He picked up his fork and finished eating everything he had picked out even though he tasted none of it.

Luke looked around the table and noticed, for the first time, how everyone was acting strangely. He elbowed Jena in the arm and asked, "What's going on?"

"Nothing," Jena mumbled and busily occupied herself with eating her lunch.

Luke frowned and tried to make eye contact with anyone. He realized he was being left out of something, but now was definitely not the right time to find out. He felt certain he could get the truth from Jena the next time they were alone together. It had been a while since they had gone on a date, maybe he would find out after school if she were busy.

Sofia watched Jon and fervently wished she could be present when he got to meet his mother for the first time. She was certain how the meeting would go, and she wanted to witness Jon's acceptance of who he really was. More than anything, she wished the whole group would allow her to be in on their huge secret.

CHAPTER 8

Captain Ahn arrived back to an empty home. He hated it when Barla's work took her away from the house so often even though he knew it made her so happy and fulfilled. He guarded his time with her jealously because she was his other half, or as Barla liked to put it, his soul-mate.

He had expected her to be home long before now, and he was beginning to worry. He went into the kitchen to check the patil to see if she had left him a message. Sure enough, Barla had been kind enough to let him know she was visiting with her sister. *Wait. What?* he thought, *Her sister lives on Earth. What is she doing there? Was it possible? Had Amanda finally convinced her to overcome her fear and go to Earth with her? Or was this some kind of code from Barla to him letting him know she was somehow in trouble?*

Ahn shut down the patil and worried through the possible scenarios. Nothing he came up with made him feel at all happy. Finally, he decided the only way to resolve this would be for him to go to Earth himself to see. He grabbed the remote for his own personal telepod which seldom ever saw flight and then he realized he had no way of getting to Earth without the help of an Elder. His shoulders slumped in defeat as he realized this new plan of action was not going to work since his telepod did not have a portable Gate built into it like Amanda or Riccan's telepods.

He dropped the remote back onto the table and went back to the patil. Maybe Barla was with Alena. Since Vinia had come to stay with them, Barla had been talking with Alena about their past together. It was a long-shot. However, Ahn was willing to try.

He turned on the patil and decided to activate a video call. He touched the screen, entered Alena's call sign, and waited for her to answer. Chances were she would not be near the patil in order to hear his call. His hand was almost touching the screen to end the call when Alena's face filled the display.

"Hello, Ahn. I was expecting to see Barla. How are you doing?"

"Well, I was hoping you might know where Barla is. She's not home yet, and I expected her to be here before I got here."

"I'm sorry, she hasn't talked with me today. If I hear from her, I'll let you know."

"Thanks, I'd appreciate that," Ahn replied in a defeated tone. "Have a nice evening."

"You too," she replied as she reached up and disconnected the call.

"Where are you, Barla?" Ahn asked the empty house. "Did you really go to Earth?"

ALENA DISCONNECTED the call and wondered what was going on with Barla. Usually, her friend was predictable and stable. Ahn had to be really worried to start calling around to find her. She wished she had been able to assist him, yet she had other worries of her own.

Her children swarmed around her and wanted to know when dinner was going to be ready. They had plans with their friends, but they needed to eat before they could go. Alena wondered where the time had gone for her children to be so grown up to have plans of their own. Justan and his betrothed, Andera, had just turned eleven, whereas Kyelon was close behind them at age ten.

Her own time was taken up more and more with her wise-woman practice. The community had embraced her, and they trusted in her skills and abilities. It felt nice to be needed, and yet sometimes she wished she could have her quiet life back.

She could not concentrate and gave up trying as she went to the kitchen and looked into the icebox to figure out what to make for dinner. Since the children seemed to be in a hurry, she wanted to make them something portable and quick to eat. She decided on foxl sandwiches with a dipping sauce and also a side of fruit. With a few seconds of concentration, she had their meals prepared and ready for them on the dining room table.

The kids did not need to be told to get ready as they were already heading to the bathroom to wash up. Alena was certain the task would be only half-done as they reappeared almost instantly and seated themselves around the table. Just this once Alena did not have the desire to make them do it over.

She really wanted to look into the mystery of where Barla had gone. As she used the few moments of peace while the children ate, Alena went into the living room and sat down. She rested her head in her hands as she reviewed the last few conversations she had had with Barla.

Eventually, the only thing she could come up with was that Barla had seen a lot of Amanda as of late. Maybe they were off on an errand together. She contemplated getting back on the patil and telling Ahn about her theory when she was interrupted by a knock on the door.

With a sigh of resignation at the disturbance, she got up and opened the door. There was a woman who was hugely pregnant standing with one hand on the doorframe and the other under her belly. "I need help," the woman said.

"Obviously, come inside quick," Alena reached forward to steady the woman as she took her through the house and into the room designated for patients. All thoughts of Barla and her situation were gone from her mind as she began channeling her energy into this woman's life-line to alleviate her pain and assist in the imminent birth.

After Petre had finished his conversation with Rualin, he resumed his post watching Captain Ahn and Barla's house. Since he knew where Jinya was now staying, he did not have to hang around the market place. Now his only concern was keeping out of sight of the neighbors so they would not call the authorities on him.

He knew Captain Ahn's opinion of him, yet he did not care. Jinya was staying in his house, and he wanted her back. The next time she left the house alone, he would convince her to come away with him again so they could really get married this time. He would do right by her.

The waiting was the hardest part since he had not seen anyone come or go from the house up until Captain Ahn got home. He had barely gotten into the shadow of the neighbor's tree before Captain Ahn had walked past him. Luckily, the old man seemed preoccupied with something or else he probably would have seen him.

Petre sat down on the grass and thought about how he had discovered Jinya's whereabouts. He had grown curious about the increased amount of telepod traffic going to and from the landing field. Usually, people steered clear of the port town, because of the unpredictable winds coming from the water, unless there was a serious matter to handle.

Always one to keep his eyes open for an opportunity to discover secrets and exploit them to his advantage, Petre stayed near the landing field for a few days. His patience was rewarded when he watched a woman, who he originally believed to be Jinya, land the telepod and go to Barla's house. He had followed at a discreet distance, of course.

He had been ecstatic when the woman left the house with Jinya beside her. Thinking it could be a one-time occurrence, Petre remained on watch until they returned. After that day, he had moved closer to the Harbor Master's house to better assess the situation.

He had learned there were a lot of kids still living in the home. He had also seen one young girl, who appeared to be lost, had come over from the landing field and left with another girl and boy who looked around her own age. The light had been fading or else he would have gotten a better look at all three of them. In any event, the telepod was always the same one; he would know it if he ever saw it in the future.

CHAPTER 9

School let out, and all of the kids met in the parking lot. Luke pulled Jena off to the side and asked, "Do you want to do something tonight?"

"Sure, what were you thinking?"

"How about a movie? I could come pick you up around seven."

"Sure, I can't wait." She looked over and saw everyone starting to get into Behn's car and said, "I gotta run. I'll see you tonight!" She leaned up and gave him a quick kiss on the cheek before she turned around and ran to get into the back of the car.

Sofia was there as well, and she wished she were bold enough to invite herself to come over, but she held back and watched as they all piled into Behn's car and left. She drove herself home and imagined what would be happening at the Stel house.

Jon was missing Sofia's confidence on the drive. He had missed his opportunity to invite her along, and now he regretted it. He had to keep wiping his palms on his jeans since they were wet from nerves as he thought about meeting a woman who could possibly be his mother. There were a lot of things going through his mind over how he would react, questions he would ask, and memories he would like to regain.

They pulled up to the front door and parked. Jon was the last to get out of the car as if delaying would make any of this meeting any different. As a group, they walked inside the house and through the foyer.

Jon looked up and was surprised to see a group of women in the living room. Somehow he had imagined it would only be his mother at this meeting, so he was at a loss of what to do or say now that the dynamics had changed. He glanced over at Behn and raised his eyebrows in question.

Behn moved forward and greeted Barla with a nod and then bent over and hugged Vinia. When he stepped away, she immediately stood up and turned to meet her other son. The look on her face was wary, both expecting a reaction, and noticing the changes in his appearance. She smiled tentatively and said, "It's great to finally see you, Jon. I hope you will let me know what your life has been since you've been here. I'd love to hear all about it."

Her voice was exactly as he remembered it. He blinked as the memories came flooding through his mind. Without any hesitation, Jon moved forward with tears in his eyes and gave his mother a long-overdue hug. "Mama!" he cried out as he tucked his face into her hair and took a deep breath.

Vinia had not expected to be accepted so swiftly, so it took her a moment to register what was happening. Her arms wrapped around her son's torso and she felt tears of her own slipping down her cheeks. Her family was back together again; they would be fine now.

Valentina stood back and watched the scene unfold. She was relieved that Jon had come around so easily because she had made it hard enough on their mom. Now they would be able to move forward and find out everything they had missed over the past year of their mother's life. She felt bad that their mother had missed out on eight years of their lives, but they would not have experienced what they had if they had grown up in Tuala.

A giggle broke into the silence, and Valentina noticed for the first time that Danika was playing on the floor on the other side of the coffee table. She rushed over and kneeled on the ground as she put her arms out for her little sister to come to her. "Hi, cutie! I didn't know you were here too. How lucky! You'll get to meet another of your big brothers."

Danika threw herself into Valentina's arms, and she stood up with her. Valentina turned around and walked back to where her mother and brother still held one another. "Jon, you need to meet our little sister, Danika."

Jon turned his head and raised his eyebrows at the sight of the adorable little toddler. "How old is she?" he asked his mother.

"She's almost one. I was so blessed to have her with me after the three of you went away; she's been the brightest spot in my life during your absence." She reached out and touched Danika's cheek as she spoke.

"Can I hold her?" Jon asked. He had never really cared too much for babies or small children, yet he felt drawn to this little girl. He held out his arms and waited anxiously for Danika to decide if she wanted to be transferred over to him. When her pudgy arms reached across toward him, he was elated and immediately nestled her against his hip as he smiled down at her. "You were pregnant with her when you sent us away, weren't you?" He suddenly remembered seeing her belly getting bigger and wondering if she were sick as well. Now he knew it was because she had been pregnant.

"Yes. It's hard to believe the time difference, isn't it?" she asked.

"It's remarkable," Jon said as he shifted his gaze back to his little sister who was smiling at him and reaching up to touch his birth crystal which was resting against his tee shirt. He sat down on the couch and moved Danika onto his knees where he gently bounced her up and down while she cooed her contentment with the new arrangement.

Vinia sat down next to her son and looked up with an amazed expression at Behn and Valentina. She gestured for them to sit down as well so they could enjoy family time together. This was going to be a moment forever imprinted in her memory as the happiest she had ever been.

Amanda, Barla, Diane, Juila, and Jena all moved into the kitchen to give them some privacy. Amanda could hardly believe all that had been accomplished in just this one day. It felt like a lifetime had passed, and she was already exhausted. She still had to take everyone home to Tuala before it was over and it seemed like a daunting task.

"Is anyone hungry?" Jena asked. "I could make something if you wanted."

"I think you're amazing, Jena. That would be wonderful," Amanda said as she made herself comfortable on one of the bar stools at the kitchen island. She was sure she would feel better after she got something into her system.

"Does anyone have any suggestions?" Jena asked.

"How about sandwiches," Barla suggested.

"Perfect," Diane agreed and got up to get the supplies from the refrigerator to help out.

Amanda grinned at what she knew was going to happen. Before her mother even made it to the refrigerator, plates of prepared sandwiches appeared on the island. Her mother about jumped out of her skin when she saw them materialize out of thin air.

"Oh, that's handy," she exclaimed as she suddenly looked over to Jena. "Did you do that?"

Jena grinned mischievously and reached for one of the plates. She held it out to her grandmother and asked, "Do you want to try one?"

"Don't mind if I do," she said cheerfully as she picked one up.

"What was Luke talking to you about before we got into the car?" Juila asked.

"He wants to take me to the movies tonight at seven."

"That sounds like fun. Are you two getting serious?" Amanda asked.

Barla frowned as she heard their conversation. She knew Jena was betrothed to Willian and wondered what was going on here. While Amanda may not be from Tuala and would not know better, surely Riccan would know this was a bad idea. She was going to have to talk to him about it before this went too far.

Jena blushed and shrugged. She picked up a sandwich and said, "I think I'm going to eat outside in the sunshine. Do you want to come with me Juila?" She had read Barla's thought and wanted to talk about it with her sister in private.

Juila grabbed a sandwich of her own and walked beside her sister. Instead of going to the pool to dip their feet, they chose to walk along the garden paths in the shaded part of the yard. She waited for her sister to talk while she nibbled on her sandwich.

"Do you think Barla's right? Am I doing the wrong thing by going out with Luke?"

"You know exactly how I feel about Willian. I'm glad you're meeting new people and discovering what a real man is like, if, for no other reason, you'll have a good comparison."

Jena nodded and kept her head down as she continued to walk slowly. "I like Luke a lot better than I like Willian," she admitted.

"I know," Juila said simply.

"He's so much nicer to me. He always smiles when I'm around, and I don't feel as though I have to act stupid to get him to be nice to me."

"That doesn't put Willian in a very good light if you asked me."

"Nobody asked you. Besides, I've known exactly how you've felt about Willian from day one. Is it me or just him? Do I flaunt my skills when he's around to make him feel inferior?"

"No, he's just insecure about his own abilities. He tries to make you feel like you should hold back so he can be better at what comes naturally to you."

"I suppose. I just wish I could make him happy like I make Luke happy. This would be so much easier if Willian would just let me."

"After what Willian pulled, I doubt you'll have to worry about pleasing him anymore. From what Dad said, I think they're going to push to have the betrothal annulled. Clearly, Willian isn't the right man for you."

"But the shame of the whole thing, Juila! I don't know if I could bear to show my face in Tuala if the betrothal is called off."

"Trust me, Jena, nobody would blame you in this matter. Everyone who has eyes could see it was Willian's fault it didn't work out."

"I hope you're right. Although Willian would probably blame me for that as well," she said with a sigh of resignation.

CHAPTER 10

"It's getting pretty late, Barla. I should probably think about taking the three of you back home," Amanda suggested.

Barla glanced over to the family still reuniting in the living room and hated to have to break into their time. She nodded her head and said, "Ahn is probably getting worried about me as well. I was gone a lot longer than I had originally planned. I'm glad I was able to witness the family reunion, though."

She hopped off the stool and went to rest her hand on Vinia's shoulder.

Vinia looked up and behind her and smiled at her friend.

"We should head home now. You can make arrangements with Amanda to see your kids again; I'm sure."

"I know. I was thinking the same thing. Danika will be ready for dinner and bed by the time we get home. I just didn't want this visit to end." She squeezed her son's hand warmly for emphasis.

"Why doesn't Jon come with us? I'm sure he'd like to see Tuala," Amanda suggested.

"They could all come," Vinia agreed enthusiastically.

"I'm afraid not, Vinia. I only have enough seats for us and one other person, and Danika will have to ride in your lap as it is."

"Oh," Vinia said in disappointment.

"That's okay, Mom. Val and I have already been there. Jon can go this time, and we'll arrange another time for all of us to come over."

Vinia shifted her gaze from Behn to Valentina and saw they both agreed with the new plan. She nodded and smiled over to Jon and asked, "What do you say? Are you up for a ride in the telepod to come to Tuala and see where I'm living right now?"

"Are you kidding? It sounds amazing!" Jon replied enthusiastically. He stood up with Danika still in his arms and then offered a hand to help his mother up from the couch. He was more than ready to take a ride in a space ship since that was how he still thought about it.

Without any further delay, they trooped out to the garage. At first, Jon thought they were playing a dirty trick on them because the garage appeared to be completely empty. He was just about to make a snide comment when suddenly the aircraft appeared in front of them. His eyes grew wide as he took in the cylindrical shape and the dull grey exterior. It definitely looked like a space ship and did nothing to dissuade his mind of the name.

Amanda touched a panel on the side of the craft, and a door dropped down onto the ground making a ramp for them to walk up. Jon expected to see strange shapes and mechanicals inside and was disappointed at how much it just looked like the interior of any private airplane. He walked up the ramp and took a seat in the ordinary looking chair.

Vinia sat down next to him and fastened her seat belt. She took Danika from him and settled her on her own lap and said, "You'll want to fasten your seat belt even if the ride only lasts a few seconds."

"A few seconds?" he asked in confusion. "I don't understand."

Amanda heard his comment on her way through the cabin and stopped to answer, "We will be teleporting directly from the garage to the Port of Cresdon landing field in Tuala. The transfer will only take about six to eight seconds, but it will feel much longer because there are absolutely no sensations during the transfer."

"What do you mean by no sensations?" he asked nervously.

"Everything will go black, and you won't be able to feel, see, or hear anything until we've reached Tuala."

"Oh," he stupidly said even as he felt his hands begin to sweat against the armrests. This was going to be much different than he had imagined.

Amanda and Barla both sat up front. Amanda palmed the side door shut and waited to see the green light indicating the cabin was secure. She began the start-up procedure and was pleased when the telepod rose several inches and maintained its balance effortlessly. She entered in their destination and shifted her hand over to the manual control lever. "We are all ready to go. Remember to count in your head to eight seconds and keep breathing! Here we go." She pressed the activation button, and they disappeared from the garage.

Right on cue, they hovered above the landing field where the wind caught them slightly. Amanda was ready for it and countered neatly. She set the telepod down as rapidly as possible and powered down the systems. As soon as everything was off, she turned her head and asked, "Are you still doing okay, Jon?"

"Yes! That was absolutely amazing. Are we really in Tuala now?" he asked as he continued to stare out the windows at their new surroundings.

"Yep, let's get out and walk to Barla's house," Amanda suggested as she hit the button on the control panel to open the side door.

"It even smells different," Jon commented as he stood outside.

"That's the ocean you smell," Barla teased as she pointed across the way to where they could see the water on the horizon. "This is a port town."

Jon felt stupid for having commented on the smell, but he soon forgot it as he turned his head to take in all of the sights. "Which house is yours?"

"Down the road a bit. Are you ready?" Barla asked.

Jon's impressions of the streets and the house almost identically mirrored that of his brother. They went inside the house, and Vinia got a meal ready for Danika. Everyone else snacked on tocolas and some fruit salad.

Corva came in the back door and stopped dead in her tracks. She had not been expecting to come home to a crowd. She spotted Barla and brightly smiled as she said, "Dad has been worried about you. I'll let him know you're home." The young girl turned around and flew out the back door.

They could hear her yelling for Ahn, and Barla grinned at her daughter's enthusiasm. She did feel bad about worrying her husband, but she had done so much good that day it was hard to feel too guilty. A moment later, Ahn came charging through the door, saw the crowd of people in his kitchen, and marched across the room to take his wife into his arms and lift her off her feet with his enthusiastic greeting. He planted his mouth on her and kissed her soundly before setting her back onto the floor.

Everyone smiled at his unabashed greeting; they all knew that was his way with Barla. Their love for one another was hard to miss. "I'm glad you're home safe. Who is this young man?" Ahn turned to look over at Jon.

Vinia proudly announced, "This is my youngest son, Jon. He wanted to see me and Danika home safe."

"Good man," Ahn said as he held out his hand for Jon to shake. "It's nice to meet you, Jon. My name's Ahn. Barla is my wife."

"It's nice to meet you Ahn. Thank you for letting my mom live with you; it's really good to know she's safe," Jon replied as he pumped Ahn's hand enthusiastically.

"We love having her and her little one. Can we expect to see you around more?"

"I hope so. I guess it's up to Mrs. Stel," he answered as he looked over at Amanda hopefully.

"I'm sure we can arrange a schedule to get all of you kids over here," Amanda replied. "We should probably head back now. I've had an exhausting day."

"Oh, I'm sorry, Mrs. Stel. I didn't even think about that," Jon began.

Amanda chuckled and said, "Don't worry about it." She looked over to Ahn and said, "Barla can fill you in on everything we got done today. We were successful, and that's all that really matters."

Vinia looked troubled. She had been hopeful when Nealan had remembered who she was when they had initially transferred to Tuala before bringing him back to Earth. Now she was back in the same situation where he had no idea who she was. She was thankful he was safe again, so there was some consolation to the outcome of the day's adventures.

Amanda and Jon retraced their way back to the landing field. They had declined an escort knowing everyone there had things to do and to say to one another. Amanda knew the way, and she wanted some time alone with Jon to find out how he was coping with all of the changes.

"How are you doing, Jon? A lot has happened this afternoon, and I'm sure you have a lot of questions."

Jon scuffed his feet along the grassy path as he tried to form a good answer. "I'm really happy to have my mom back. I just don't know what it's going to mean for the Wilsons. They've been wonderful parents, and I don't want to hurt them after everything they've done and sacrificed for us. It seems kind of ungrateful of us to say we have our mom back now, so thank you very much, we're going to go home now. Do you know what I mean?"

"Yes. You don't have to make any decisions right away. Vinia knew the situation was complicated. Her main concern was reconnecting with all of you. She doesn't have any means of taking you back right now anyway since she's living with Ahn and Barla."

"Why doesn't she have a place of her own?" Jon asked suddenly.

"It's a long story, and I'm partly to blame for it. I'll let your mother tell you about it when she's ready. Okay?"

Jon could hardly hide his disappointment, but he could understand why Mrs. Stel would decline to answer. He hoped his mother would feel comfortable telling him the story. There was a lot about his mother he wanted to find out, but he would have to be patient. Maybe Behn and Valentina would know more when they got home. He would ask.

WILLIAN SAT ALONE in his new bedroom and thought about everything he had seen and done in the past two days. It was slightly overwhelming to experience all of the new things on Earth. Reading about everything was vastly different than actually experiencing them, but he was relieved to finally be close to reuniting with Jena again.

His first look at the school was intriguing, and the young girl who he had met sure had been friendly. The stack of paperwork they had been given was slightly daunting until Melissa and Marcus had said they would handle it for him with Shemalla's help. While they were working on getting that taken care of, he was free to do whatever he liked around the house.

He had already put all of his things away in his room. He had investigated the house both inside and out. For a while, he had sat on the front porch and watched the strange vehicles pass in front of the house. He wondered how many different types and colors of vehicles the people of Earth had, it seemed slightly ridiculous for there to be so many options when on Tuala they only needed a few. When he got tired of being out in the heat, he went back and rested on his bed for a while.

Pesi had come into his room and began jumping up at the side of the bed. Willian grinned as he realized the dog could not jump high enough, so he reached over and brought her up. She bounded eagerly across the whole mattress until she flopped herself down right next to him and threw her back legs out behind her. Willian laughed at the silly animal and stroked her soft fur from the top of her head down to the base of her tail where it flopped back up over her back. The tail seemed to have a mind of its own as it wiggled back and forth with Pesi's anticipation of receiving another pet.

Melissa enjoyed the scene in front of her for a moment before she tapped on his open door and asked, "Are you hungry for dinner?"

"Sure!" he answered and hopped off of the bed and met her in the hallway. Pesi also jumped down from the bed and raced alongside his feet. Willian looked down at her and realized having a pet in the house could be quite enjoyable as well as entertaining.

The four of them enjoyed a meal which Willian was told was typical for Earth. He wished he could have had some foxl, but they did not seem to have anything like it here. He was going to have to get used to new foods for the duration of his stay.

"Are you excited to go to school tomorrow?" Melissa asked. "What did you think of it today when we visited?"

"Yes, I'm curious to find out how they do it here. The school was huge, and there were so many other kids. Our schools are much smaller at home." Willian answered and then returned to eating his dinner.

CHAPTER 11

Alena could not stop thinking about Barla and Ahn, so she decided to take a day off of her healing to head over to the Port of Cresdon. It had been ages since she had last visited so she thought it would be perfect timing. Just as Bryon was heading off to work, she asked, "Would you mind if I dropped you off at work so I could use the telepod today?"

Bryon got a quizzical expression on his face since his wife seldom flew on her own and asked, "Where are you going?"

"I thought I'd stop in and see how Barla is doing. Ahn called yesterday wondering if I knew where she was, and it got me thinking. Ever since we met with Jehoban and told we were supposed to work together to help Amanda, we've been even further apart than ever. I thought it would be good to find out what she's been up to and to catch up on any progress."

"Sounds like fun. I wish I could go with you, but I have a meeting today with Kenen in Beewa. Be sure to tell everyone hello for me," Bryon said.

"Are you ready to head out? I'd like to get back home before the kids are out of school."

"Sure, just let me get my files out of the office and then I'll meet you outside."

Alena picked up her purse from the hall table on her way out the door. She was excited about this change of pace, although she was slightly nervous about flying into the port town. Any air traffic near the ocean breezes could be tricky unless you were a confident pilot which she felt herself to be even if she flew infrequently.

Preparations took longer than the actual flight and Alena set the telepod down in the designated area of the Kirma Shipping and Receiving facility where Bryon worked. Bryon kissed her on the cheek before he exited the vehicle. Alena lifted the aircraft in order to leave and saw Bryon meet up with his assistant, Frasnia, and head toward the office together.

She smiled to see him so happy with his work before she turned her attention back to flying. She kept the destination coordinates firmly in her mind and activated the transfer. As expected she arrived to gusting winds as she hovered over the landing field in Cresdon. She rushed her landing and touched down harder than she would have liked with a cringe for her carelessness.

After she exited the craft, she circled around it to check for any damage. She would hate to have to tell Bryon she had caused any harm to the transport when she got home and was relieved to see everything looked just as it should. With a relieved sigh, she left the landing field and walked down the pathway to get to Barla's neighborhood.

The day was quite pleasant with the sun shining and the warm breeze blowing in her face. She missed being able to smell the ocean air every day. Ever since she and Bryon had moved inland for his work, she dreamed of the day they would be able to return to a location closer to the water. She imagined it would be quite a few anons before that dream could come true.

Turning up the graveled path into Barla's yard, she admired the beauty and symmetry of the grand house with its four columns and grand staircase. It was by far the biggest and highest house in the entire town, befitting the status of Harbor Master Ahn. She admired and respected both Ahn and Barla for their commitment and constant contributions to their society.

Alena knocked on the door and waited. For several moments she could not hear anything from inside and wondered if it would have been better to schedule a time to visit. When the door swung open, and Barla's expression showed immense pleasure, Alena was grateful she had surprised her instead.

Barla flew out the door and hugged her friend whom she had not seen since they had met with Jehoban so long ago. They had been close until marriage, jobs, and children had demanded more of their time. "Come in, Alena! What a wonderful surprise! Come in." She tugged on Alena's arm to propel her into the house faster. She looked around outside before turning herself and following her guest inside.

"I hope I haven't come at a bad time. Captain Ahn called me yesterday asking if I knew where you were and it got me thinking it's been way too long since we've talked."

"Your timing is perfect. We were just sitting down to some steena tea in the living room. You just missed Ahn; he went down to the dock to get some work done before the quarterly audit."

"Hmmph," Alena chuckled as she knew how Ahn hated dealing with the hassle of the paperwork. "How did you get out of it this time?"

Barla smiled knowingly and answered, "I didn't have to since one of the apprentices has been assigned to the task of entering the invoices into the patil every day. Now all Ahn has to worry about is making sure all of the numbers align properly to show a profit for the town."

"How convenient for him," Alena commented as she turned into the living room and saw Vinia and Danika playing together on the floor. "Well hello! I'd heard you'd come to live here for a while. It's been forever since I've seen you, Vinia. And who is this young little beauty?" Alena dropped onto the floor and touched the beautiful little girl's rosy cheek in greeting.

"This is my youngest daughter, Danika," Vinia replied proudly. She knew her daughter was special and she was even more pleased to see Alena thought so too.

Alena entertained Danika for over an hour even though she had come to see Barla. Being able to play with a toddler was a rare treat for her anymore, and it made her wish she and Bryon would try to have a few more children before they were too old to handle the responsibility. Her own children were of an age where they were more interested in being around kids their own age rather than spending time with their mother. She missed having the special time with her little ones, and Danika only reinforced her idea of having more.

When Danika began to fuss, Vinia picked her up and took her into the kitchen to feed her before her nap. Alena watched her go and felt a tug at her heartstrings for the loss. She picked herself up from the floor and sat down in the chair across from Barla. Not knowing quite what she wanted to discuss she remained silent and contemplated different ways to begin.

"I'm assuming you didn't come over here to play with children. What's going on, Alena?" Barla cut right to the chase. She poured a cup of steena tea for Alena and passed it to her.

Alena chuckled at Barla's directness. She accepted the tea and answered, "I'm not sure. I just had this overwhelming feeling I should come out here to talk to you. I've learned, over time, to heed my instincts and act on them promptly. What do you think it means?"

"Well, let's see," Barla answered as she mused on the possibilities. "The last time we saw one another was when Jehoban brought us all together…"

"I was just thinking the very same thing as I was walking up to your house. I think it might have something to do with it."

"Maybe, let's focus on that train of thought and see where it takes us." Barla leaned forward and asked, "Has Amanda come to you asking for any help?"

"Not to me, no. As you know, she asked Bryon to help her out with Vinia. I'm still amazed to discover Vinia is actually Jinya! All this time, I never knew that wasn't her real name up until Bryon told me about it when he came home from helping Amanda. Now everything seems to be back full-circle with Vinia living with you. The only difference is that Petre isn't after her this time, thank goodness."

Barla shook her head sadly and said, "If only that were true."

"What do you mean?"

"Petre spotted Vinia in the marketplace, and he's been hanging around town trying to find her. Knowing him, he's probably discovered she's living here and is watching our house. I just can't shake the feeling of being watched, but I keep telling myself I'm being overly paranoid."

At Barla's revelation, Alena's hand came up to cover her mouth in dismay while her other hand began to shake enough for her to worry about spilling her tea. The first time around with Petre had been bad enough when the triplets were babies, but to have it happen again with another baby in the house was even more upsetting.

They were quiet for a moment while Vinia passed by the doorway on her way to putting Danika down for her nap upstairs.

After she heard the footsteps on the stairs, Alena asked, "What are you doing about it?"

"Ahn has alerted everyone down at the docks to keep tabs on Petre's movements. Hopefully, he'll get tired of being blocked at every turn and decide to pursue other interests elsewhere."

"I can't see that happening after the last go-around with him."

"I don't know; he hasn't been the same since your husband cold-cocked him and took him into the authorities. I don't know if it were he being threatened with mind swiping or if Bryon knocked some sense into him, but he is definitely less devious."

Alena did not comment, but one of her eyebrows rose in doubt of Barla's assessment. "Not to change the subject or anything, but I have an idea."

"What's that?"

"What if we were to get everyone back together again and invite Amanda and Riccan to attend? It's possible we could work together to figure out the prophecy or at least help move it along faster."

"That's true…" Barla began as her mind began to go through various possibilities. The logistics of bringing all of them together without Jehoban's request were astronomical.

"I was thinking we're far too busy in our ordinary lives to make proper time to address this project. Jehoban believed it was important enough to assemble us, so shouldn't we do our best to honor his wishes to help Amanda?"

"You know what? You're right. Let me send a message to Amanda and find out if she wants to do something like this. She has a lot going on right now, so maybe it would take some pressure away from her if she had all of us working as a team rather than waiting for her to come to us." Barla rose from her chair and left the room.

Alena sipped her tea and stared into the unlit fireplace. The suggestion to gather everyone together felt right in her soul. This had to be the reason she felt drawn to Barla's house. They were supposed to be doing more in assisting Amanda with the prophecy; otherwise, what was the point of Jehoban assembling them in the first place?

Vinia entered the room and picked up her cold cup of tea. She picked up the teapot and topped off her cup with the hot tea to make it slightly warmer. "Where's Barla?" she asked as she took the seat she had vacated earlier. She kept her eyes on Alena while she lifted the teacup to her mouth and took a large sip of the minty beverage.

"She went into the kitchen to send a message to Amanda."

"Oh, is she going to ask when my kids are going to come visit again?"

Alena looked at Vinia quizzically and asked, "What would Amanda have to do with that?"

"It's a very long story, but the short version is that my kids live on Earth and they are friends with Amanda's kids. Amanda reunited us and said she would work on a schedule where I could get to know them again."

"Get to know them again? How long have they been on Earth?"

"Eight anons for them, only one for me."

Alena shut her eyes and shook her head in confusion. "What are you saying? Why is the time different for each of you?"

"I had to send the kids away to Earth, but I didn't know what would happen, so I accidentally sent them back in time eight anons."

"What? They're only eight anons old right now, are you saying that's not right?"

"Exactly, they're sixteen anons now. I've missed out on almost all of their childhoods by sending them away. I don't want to miss another day, but I have to rely on Amanda's generosity in being able to see them."

"Wow, that's so sad. Why don't they just come home?" Alena asked in wonder.

"They have wonderful parents on Earth, great friends, and they want to finish going to school. They don't remember much from here, and they're adjusting to finding out how different they really are other than the adopted orphans they previously believed themselves to be."

"Oh, that's rough. I'm sorry, Vinia. You have been through so much. When will it get better for you?" Alena gushed.

"I wish I knew. I'm more than ready for my life to get easier. I thought it was getting happier with Nealan, but now he's on Earth as well, and he doesn't even remember me. I feel as though my life has been in a circular mode, repeating the same terrible things over and over." Vinia held the cup of tea between both hands and stared down into the liquid as though it might contain an answer for her tragic life.

Alena didn't know what to say in reply, so she kept silent. She felt so blessed in her own life, happy to have a husband, family, and career, none of which Vinia could claim for herself. She wondered why some people's lives seemed destined to have so much sorrow while others hardly had to work at keeping their happiness.

Not wanting to take up too much of Barla's day, Alena stood up when Barla entered the living room again. "I should probably get going, Barla. I'm really glad I got to visit with you and Vinia today. It has eased my mind to know we are still on the same page. Hopefully, we'll be able to get together again real soon."

Barla stepped forward and hugged Alena. "I'll walk you to the door," she said as she kept her arm around her back. When they reached the door, Barla whispered, "I'll let you know what I hear from Amanda about the meeting."

CHAPTER 12

"I've paid you good money to deliver pictures to me every day," Dr. Gascon screamed over the phone. "I expect today's pictures to be in my hands within the hour. I don't need your excuses; I need results. If you can't deliver, then I'll hire someone more capable." He slammed down the receiver with his pent up frustrations.

After he had told the police who had been responsible for abducting Neal from his facility, he had expected Amanda to be hauled into jail when they apprehended her at the airport. He could not understand how she could have gotten away from him in Central Park and then again how she had somehow gotten out of New York entirely still baffled him.

He needed the pictures from his private investigator to find out who had come and gone from the Stel residence the day before. When he had been told that the police had questioned Amanda at her home only an hour after she had abducted Neal from the hospital, he knew there had to be some kind of scheme going on to confound him. He needed to see for himself who had been posing as Amanda for the police so he could present the evidence to the police to get her brought in for him to question.

His phone rang again, and he picked it up with irritation as he spoke curtly, "Dr. Gascon."

"Hello, Dr. Gascon. This is the Kendall District Police Department. We have an update on your missing patient, Nealand Taivas, Jr."

"Yes, where is he? He needs to be brought back directly for evaluation."

"I'm sorry, doctor, but that won't be possible."

"What? I'm his doctor, and he has left without being discharged. He is legally within my medical care, and I demand he be brought back to me at once."

"Mr. Taivas has declined to return and has obtained medical treatment here in Kendall. Since we are in Florida, you have no legal right to have him brought across state lines to be returned to your care."

"No legal right? Are you kidding me? When did you talk to him? Who's his new doctor?"

"I'm sorry, Dr. Gascon," he replied while looking through his notes to find the answers to Dr. Gascon's questions. "We talked with him yesterday at 10:33 am. I am not at liberty to tell you his new doctor's name as that falls under the doctor/patient confidentiality clause. Your only recourse now is to discuss this matter with the Taivas family. Have a good day, doctor." The line went dead as the police department hung up.

Once again, Dr. Gascon slammed the receiver down even harder than before. This was certainly not adding up. There was no way they could have spoken with Neal at 10:33 am in Florida when he had been taken from his room at 9:45 am in New York. It was logistically impossible, and he felt as though somebody was lying to him. He would get to the bottom of this mystery if it were the last thing he ever did; nobody ever got away with trying to make him look stupid.

BEFORE THEY HAD TAKEN Neal up to be treated by Dr. Gascon in New York, Jessica had felt confident in her son's full recovery. Now they seemed to have taken many steps backward in only a few short days. She watched her son sleep on the living room couch and wondered if he would ever be the same cheerful boy he used to be. The lines and wrinkles on his face troubled her more than anything since he seemed to be ten years older than he should be.

It was obvious that although Neal slept, he did not get any rest. He had lost weight again, and she was constantly worried about him. Now that he was home, she certainly did not want to let him out of her sight again. The world was too hard on him, and he needed to be protected at all costs.

The phone rang, and Jessica rushed over to answer it before the ringing woke Neal up. "Hello?" she answered.

"Is this Jessica Taivas?" a female voice asked.

"Yes."

"Hi, my name is Dr. Jasmine Medin. I've received your phone number from Amanda Stel because she and I both believe I can help your son, Nealand. Is now a good time to speak?"

Jessica sank into the chair next to the phone and closed her eyes in fear. "Sure," she replied softly.

"I understand you've had quite the experience with Dr. Gascon and I want to tell you how sorry I am that you and Neal had to go through that pain. I've worked for Dr. Gascon in the past, and I know his treatments can be rather...how would we say it...harsh."

Jessica snorted at the understatement.

"I can see you agree with my assessment. Anyway, it's really important that I can meet with Neal today. It would have been better had I been able to see him yesterday when he got home."

"Yes, I'm sorry about that. After the police left, Neal was exhausted, and I didn't have the heart to wake him up to talk to him about it. I got your messages, but I...I was scared," she admitted reluctantly.

"As well you should have been considering what your son has been through this last week. I'd really like to help him get through the trauma and start him back on the road to recovery. Could you come to my office in an hour?"

Jessica felt panic rising in her at the idea of taking Neal outside of the house again. Yesterday's breakfast had been a nightmare as Neal stared at her as though she had been a stranger. She did not want to have to take another chance with him in public.

"Time is of the essence in cases such as Neal's, Mrs. Taivas. Please tell me you'll bring him in to see me today," Dr. Medin prompted when the silence continued.

"Where is your office?" Jessica asked with a resigned tone.

Jasmine almost fainted with relief as she hurriedly gave her address and directions to Jessica. For a moment there, she believed Jessica would refuse her offer to help her son. She had no idea how she was going to tell Amanda that she had failed.

"We'll be there," Jessica said and then she hurriedly hung up the phone without saying goodbye. She stared down at the paper with the address. She wanted desperately to rip the page to shreds and pretend the call had never happened. Then she could go back to her vigil of watching Neal sleep in the safety of their home and pretend nothing was wrong.

She returned to the living room and was startled to see Neal sitting up on the couch.

He turned his head at the sound of her footsteps and asked, "Who was on the phone?"

"Dr. Medin. She's a friend of Amanda's, and she's going to begin seeing you in an hour," Jessica replied with a flat tone.

"Good," Neal replied brightly. "I want to get answers. The sooner, the better if you asked me!" He pushed himself up from the couch and began to leave the room as he said, "I'm going to take a quick shower, and then I'll be ready to go."

Jessica's head was about to spin at the complete change in her son's behavior. She had felt certain he would want to stay home. She dropped to the couch and tried to think about what could have caused this drastic change in Neal's attitude. She took a huge breath and slowly exhaled as she realized this was one hurdle which seemed to have crumbled without any effort on her part. Maybe there was hope after all.

NEAL SHOWERED SPEEDILY and got a change of clothes from the ones he had been sleeping in since the day before. His fingers noted the difference in the fabric of the unfamiliar outfit, and he wondered where it had come from. Maybe he would ask Amanda about it the next time he saw her. With one last check of himself in the mirror, he left his room and went back downstairs to get his mother.

He almost missed a step as he realized he remembered that she was his mother. Already he was making progress, and he had not even seen the doctor yet. He hoped this would have a much better outcome than their decision to see Dr. Gascon. Just the idea that this doctor was a friend of Amanda's already gave her the proper endorsement where he was concerned.

"Hey, Mom, I'm ready whenever you are," he said with a huge grin as he saw his mother's expression change as she registered the meaning of his statement.

"Do you remember me now, Neal? Do you really? Is your memory coming back?" She rushed over to him and grabbed his arms in excitement.

"I remember that you're my mom. That's a start, isn't it?" he grinned foolishly.

Jessica pulled him into a hug and about crushed his ribs in her enthusiasm.

"Hey, Mom, don't smother me!" he chided gently.

"I'm sorry, Neal. I'm just so happy to have you back, even if it's just a start!" She reached up and cupped his cheek lovingly with her hand. "I love you, Neal."

"I love you, too, Mom. We should probably get going; don't you think?"

With a lighter heart, she nodded and turned away before he could see the tears beginning to form in her eyes. Her hope returned for her son's recovery. Yesterday had been wonderful and terrifying all at once, and today was definitely a new day with hope on the horizon. She grabbed her purse and led the way out the door to the garage.

They drove in silence and parked right in front of the doctor's office. Jessica was first to get out of the car, and she shut her car door before she realized Neal had made no move to get out. She walked around to his side of the car, opened the door, and asked, "Are you having second thoughts?"

"No, I'm just worried, I'll be fine. I need to do this," he said with resolve as he swung his legs out of the car and stood up beside his mother.

She put her arm around the small of his back and gave him a little squeeze for comfort. "You'll do fine; I have a good feeling about this doctor. I think you'll like her. She sounded very kind and competent on the phone."

"Are you trying to tell me she didn't sound pompous and rude like Dr. Gascon?" he teased as he smiled over at her.

She laughed nervously and said, "Yes, that's exactly what I was implying."

"Good, then I think we'll get along famously. Let's get this started! Is it this door?" he asked as he lengthened his stride and went to the door in front of them and opened it for his mother after she nodded in affirmation.

The receptionist had them go back through the main door directly upon arrival. They had been expecting to have to fill out another round of papers and were relieved to be able to forego the task. They saw a woman standing outside of an office and figured she probably was who they were meant to be meeting.

Jasmine stepped forward and asked, "Are you Neal?"

"Yes and this is my mother Jessica Taivas," he replied. He liked the look of this doctor very much. She was a young and very attractive woman whom he did not think he would have any problem interacting with for an ongoing treatment plan.

"Come into my office, and we can discuss the strategy Amanda suggested," she said as she stepped back and gestured for them to go into her office. She closed the door behind herself as she followed them in. "Please be seated over here on the couch so we can be a bit more informal at the moment."

Neal sat down on the long couch with his mother right beside him. He watched as Dr. Medin seated herself directly in front of him. He noticed she wore an interesting tree pendant on a leather cord around her neck. Thinking it was a strange item for her to wear he wondered if there were a story behind it, possibly a gift from a loved one or maybe a boyfriend.

"First of all, I wanted to thank you for coming in today. I know it has to be scary to put yourself into the hands of another doctor after what you've already experienced. I want to say I'm sorry for what Dr. Gascon did to you under his care and I promise you will not have that type of experience here."

"That's a relief," Neal replied, and he felt his shoulder muscles loosen as the tension began to flow out of his body.

"I will not be giving you any drugs either so you can experience your recovery on your own terms and not under chemical coercion," Jasmine continued. She knew Dr. Gascon's beliefs on keeping his patients practically comatose to make them more receptive to his own agenda.

"Good because I would have refused anything anyway. I've had quite enough of being incoherent. What is Amanda's plan for my treatment?" Neal asked.

"She and I both agree that hypnosis will be the best course of action for your memories to be reactivated."

"How does Amanda know you exactly?"

"She was my patient when she was in her coma. I've watched over her for eight years now, and I'm very pleased with her recovery. We're both hoping you can experience the same type of results for yourself, that is if you'll allow me," she finished almost as a question.

"I agree Amanda seems to be doing great. I want the same thing for myself. I would love to have you treat me, Dr. Medin," Neal agreed wholeheartedly.

Jessica stared at her son and was encouraged by his decisiveness. She turned her head back to Dr. Medin and smiled weakly.

"Are you okay with this as well, Mrs. Taivas?"

"What? Oh, yes. I want Neal to be comfortable with his choice, and I believe he is," she agreed readily.

"Okay, well now that we've settled this then I guess we can begin right now. Mrs. Taivas, I'd like to have my sessions with Neal to be in private, if you don't mind."

Jessica's fear returned, and she began to object.

"Mom, it's okay. I think Dr. Medin is right. I'll be able to relax better knowing I'm alone."

"As long as you're sure, Neal," she said even as she wished he had objected and wanted her to stay. She got up from the couch, touching his shoulder, as he nodded for her to leave. At the door, she turned and looked at her son one last time, hoping he would change his mind before she opened the door and left the room.

Neal shifted his gaze from the closed door over to Dr. Medin. He was unsure what to expect, but he was willing to try. To bridge the awkward silence, he commented, "I like your necklace. It reminds me of something, but I can't remember what right now."

Dr. Medin's hand went up to touch the tree-of-life pendant, and a small grin appeared on her face. Neal had provided her with the opening for which she was searching. "This was a gift from a very dear friend. She's from a place far away called Tuala. Have you ever heard of it?"

Neal thought about it for a second. It seemed as though the name of the place should mean something to him, but the though proved elusive. Finally, he shook his head and answered, "No, I don't think I have."

"That's okay; we'll work on your memories. Have you been hypnotized before?"

"Yes, the counselor I met with before Dr. Gascon hypnotized me once."

"Good, so you are familiar with how it works. It'll be easier to go deeper into relaxation each time we do it. I want you to be able to recall everything from the past seven years. However, I'm going to ask you to write down your memories rather than discuss them with your family. I know your family means well, but they can keep you from realizing the whole truth based on their limited understanding of what you've been through. Can you agree to not talk to your parents about what you recall?"

"You mean ever? I don't know." Neal thought her request seemed slightly strange.

"No, I don't mean you can never talk to them about what we discuss. I just want our sessions to be complete, and all your memories returned before you start to share with them. At the point we're done, you will be free to say whatever you want to whomever you want. Can you agree to that?" Dr. Medin felt as though she were explaining this badly and wished she could clarify it better to keep Neal feeling comfortable with her.

He nodded slowly since Dr. Medin's offer seemed to be his only option for help at this point. After all, he could always decide to talk to his parents on his own.

Jasmine could see he was thinking over his options and added, "I'm serious about this, Neal. I only want you to write down your thoughts and feelings and bring them back here to discuss. Do not include your parents in this until we are through. I can't express how vitally important it will be for you to follow my instructions."

Feeling guilty that she had somehow read his mind, he looked down at his hands and said, "Okay, I can agree."

"If it'd make you feel better, then I'll allow you to talk to Amanda about anything. She can be your confidant in this, if you feel you need one."

Neal raised his eyebrows at this new concession. It did make him feel more comfortable with the doctor's arrangement. This time he nodded more certainly and said, "Okay, I can agree with that."

"Good. Let's begin right now then. Why don't you go ahead and stretch out on the couch and get comfortable? I'll grab a notepad to take notes and be right back." She reached over and grabbed her paper and pen and adjusted herself to be at ease for the long session ahead. She would do her best to help Neal for Amanda's sake.

CHAPTER 13

Willian entered the school building prepared for his first day. The paperwork was already turned in, and the receptionist was getting his schedule put together. He sat down in the office chair and tugged at his new clothing. He felt ridiculous in the outfit Shemalla ensured him was in style. As he waited, he looked out the window to see the other kids his age and had to agree his clothing did not look any different than theirs.

"Willian?" the receptionist called out.

He stood up and walked over to her with a smile.

"Here is your locker number and the combination," she said as she handed him several slips of paper, "and here is your schedule. I'll call a student to escort you around so you can find your way. Wait here one moment."

He looked down on the paper and wondered what he would learn in these strange classes. His most pressing concern was to locate Jena and smooth things over with her. The fact that his father had insisted on the condition of him enrolling in school had seemed a bit much until he realized there was a lot to learn about what Jena had been experiencing.

He did not want her to have knowledge of this other world that he did not possess since it made him feel inferior to her knowledge. In almost every other facet of their lives, Jena was better at everything. He was tired of trying to demonstrate his superiority only to be showed up by her. Instantly he realized he had slipped into his old way of thinking and he chided himself for it. If he wanted to win Jena back, he needed to show her he had changed.

The girl he had met before walked into the office, and his attention was straightaway taken by her appearance. She went up to the receptionist, and they spoke for a few seconds before she turned and walked toward him. "Hi, I'm Sofia. I'm sorry we didn't introduce ourselves yesterday. I'm going to give you a quick tour before classes begin and get you settled in."

Willian stood up as she began talking. Instantly, he noticed she had a different way of saying things than he was used to. He had never heard an accent before, and the rhythm and cadence of her words intrigued him. "Hi, I'm Willian. It's nice to see you again. Thanks for helping me out."

"We can talk while we walk or you're going to be late for your first class. Let me see your locker number and schedule," she said as she held out her hand.

Willian thrust the papers toward her as they walked out of the office. He tried to pay attention to where they were headed, but he soon lost track of the direction since he kept staring at Sofia instead of their surroundings. When they stopped walking, Willian wondered why since they were in the middle of the hall and not at any class.

"This is your locker," she said as she pointed out the same number which was on his paper. He had no idea what the locker was for and simply smiled at her.

"Do you have anything you want to put in there?" she asked patiently.

"I don't think so," he replied. He even sounded dumb to himself and started to wish he had been able to figure this out on his own.

"Go ahead and try out the locker combination to make sure it works. Do you want me to show you how it works?" she asked as Willian seemed to hesitate. She was beginning to get a strange feeling about this boy. She leaned over and read the paper in his hand and then made an exaggerated effort at demonstrating how the dial worked as she said it all out loud for his benefit. She pulled up on the handle, and the locker opened.

Willian leaned over to see what was inside. He was even more confused when he saw a bunch of stuff in the metal box already. "What is this?" he asked.

"You share this locker with another student. This is their stuff in here. When you get books from your classes, you'll want to keep them in here until right before your class. Otherwise, you'll be lugging a lot of books around unnecessarily. Okay," she said as she leaned over to see his class schedule, "let's head over to the gym so you can get to the locker room to change."

"What am I changing for?" he asked.

"You have PE first period so you would normally change into shorts and a tee shirt in the locker room. You'll leave your school clothes in the locker in there until the class is over. I'll show you the next couple of classes you're going to be in since they are on the way to the gym anyway."

She shut the locker and twisted the dial before she began leading Willian down the now-crowded hallway. They had only passed a couple of classroom doors before she pointed to the left and said, "This is your third-period Anatomy class."

Willian peered through the door as they kept walking and saw rows of tall desks with two chairs at each one.

"This's the room you'll come back to for your fourth-period Psychology class. Right around this corner is where you'll go to get to your Algebra class for second-period. You can see the class numbers outside the doorways in the hall. Just follow them until you find the right one for each class.

"I'm sorry I won't be able to take you to each of your classes throughout the day, but your classes are nowhere near mine. Oh, wait! You and I have the same class for seventh-period English III. Your lunch is after your Pottery class in fifth-period." She stopped walking and pointed down another long hallway and said, "Do you see that big open space down there at the end?"

"Yes." Willian was starting to feel overwhelmed.

"That's the cafeteria, we all call it 'The Commons.' You'll go there to pick up a lunch to eat. Did you bring a lunch or are you going to buy one?"

Willian pulled out a wad of money which he still did not know how to differentiate and said, "I'll be buying lunch, I guess."

"Good. Go down there to The Commons after your pottery class gets out. Lunch lasts fifty minutes so don't take too long about getting your food and finding a place to sit down to eat. After lunch is over, you only have two more classes."

"Will I see you at lunch then?" Willian asked hopefully. He thought it would be nice to see at least one familiar face in the crowd.

"I'm sorry, I have first lunch which gets over just when yours begins. I will see you in English class." She resumed walking until they reached the boy's locker room. She pointed to it and said, "I'm not allowed to go in there with you since this is the boys' side. This is the place where you will normally change into gym clothes before you go out the door on the other side which leads into the gymnasium. Your teacher will let you know what you'll need to bring on Monday so you'll be able to participate."

"Thank you for showing me around. I really appreciate it," Willian said as he watched several boys enter the locker room. "I guess I'll be seeing you around."

"Good luck," Sofia called over her shoulder as she jogged away to get to her writing class before the second bell rang. She could not believe the bad luck of being called to assist a new student today of all days.

She had planned on finding Jon and asking him how his meeting had gone with his mother the afternoon before. Thinking he would have called her yesterday to let her know all about it, she had been disappointed when she went to bed without hearing anything. His meeting could have gone very well, or very badly and she was desperate to know which. Now she was going to have to wait until lunch before she learned anything and that was possibly the most agonizing wait of all.

CHAPTER 14

Jena and Luke walked down the school hallway hand-in-hand. Their movie date had brought them closer together ever since Jena had decided she needed to discover how a relationship should be. Her thoughts of Willian's treatment of her in the past were becoming something she refused to bring forward into her present.

Luke imitated one of the lines from the movie which made Jena laugh at how silly he could be. She realized Willian had never done or said anything purposely which had made her laugh. Willian was always so serious about his position in society, so much so that he refused to participate in anything which might be construed as inappropriate or beneath his dignity.

She looked up at Luke and realized he was everything which Willian was not. He made her feel special and cared about. He wanted to spend time with her, getting to know her, wanting to hear her talk about anything including nonsense. It was a refreshing break from the reality of her betrothal, and she was beginning to think the betrothal had been doomed from the beginning. She and Willian were an ill-fitting combination.

"What are you thinking about, Jena? You're frowning so I can only assume it's something unpleasant." Luke asked.

"I was remembering someone from my past."

"Do you want to talk about it?"

"Not really, he's a million miles away anyway."

"You know you can talk to me about anything, right?"

"I know. Thank you for being such a good friend and listener. I really feel free when I'm with you, and it's so nice. I had a really good time last night, even though the movie sucked!" She chuckled as she recalled how ridiculous the movie plot had been. They were expecting a romantic comedy, yet it had turned out to be so poorly acted and predictable that they had made fun of the actors rather than actually watching it.

"I agree. I think we need to go to another movie to make up for how bad that one was," he said with a grin. "How about tomorrow night?"

"Sure," she agreed. They had reached her American Government classroom, and she felt a pang of regret for having to go their separate ways again. She felt a thrill of delight when Luke leaned down and kissed her cheek before he turned and walked away. Her fingers touched the spot on her cheek where his lips had made contact with hers, and she imagined she could feel electricity tingling.

Luke had a spring in his step at daring to kiss Jena in public. He had wondered how she would react to him being so forward, but the time had felt right. She had seemed so sad while she was thinking about her past and he wanted to remind her that he would be a part of her future. In his ruminations, he was not paying attention to where he was going, and he ran into another student.

"Excuse me," he said to a boy he had never seen before. "I'm sorry."

"It was probably my fault," Willian replied as he looked back down onto his class schedule in confusion. "Hey, do you know where room 36 is?"

"Sure, it's back this way. I have to go by it to get to my next class; you can walk with me." He waited until the other student turned around and they walked together. "Are you new here?"

"Yes, today's my first day. Is it always this crowded?" Willian asked peevishly.

"Yep, but usually it's a little calmer. I think everyone's getting antsy for Christmas break, so they're a little more wound up than usual. I'm Luke Thompson; what's your name?"

He looked at him strangely for a second before he answered, "Willian Potts." Hearing a boy's name without an honorable 'n' at the end threw him momentarily until he recalled that rule did not apply here on Earth.

"Here's your class. I'll probably see you around," Luke said with a jaunty wave as he kept walking to reach his own class before the second bell rang.

"Yeah, see you around," he replied as he watched the boy leave and wished he could have spent more time talking with him. So far he had been the nicest person he had met with the exception of his morning guide, Sofia. Everyone in the school seemed to be too preoccupied with their own friends even to bother talking with Willian. He felt rather lonely and out of place and he did not much like it.

All of his classes had been very confusing. He found himself reading the minds of everyone around him, including the teacher, just so he would not be caught out not knowing the answers. He really wished this school piece had not been one of his father's conditions for coming to Earth. It would have been much easier to confront Jena at her home and left this mess out of the equation.

He looked up at the wall clock and realized he still had almost two hours to go until lunchtime. He was starving, and it was not helping his mood at all. The teacher continued to drone on and on about health services issues which seemed pretty basic to Willian.

In bored frustration, Willian pulled out his schedule to see what torturous class he had next. Almost laughing out loud he saw it was a pottery class. *What could possibly be learned in a pottery class?* he thought to himself. *At least I won't be plagued with all of these boring details while I'm slinging mud around.*

AT THE END of her typing class, Sofia was desperate to find Jon. It seemed rather peculiar to her that she had not seen him anywhere in the hallways between classes. She raced out of the classroom and down the hall toward his locker. For certain, he would be dropping off his books before heading to The Commons for lunch.

Even before she reached the locker, she spotted him up ahead. With an elated squeal of excitement, she ran full-tilt to catch up to him. She grabbed his arm and whispered, "What happened yesterday? Why didn't you call me?"

Jon foolishly grinned down at her and said, "It was so amazing, Sofia! It really was our mom, and we had the best time visiting and catching up. I even got to meet my new little sister, Danika."

"Why didn't you call me?" she asked again.

"I went with Mrs. Stel to take Mom, Danika, and Barla home. By the time we got back, it was really late, and I didn't think your parents would appreciate a call at that hour. Besides, I'd rather tell you about it in person so I could see your reaction."

She leaned in closer and asked, "So it's true? You are really from Tuala like Behn and Val told you?"

"Yeah, isn't that crazy? I don't feel like an alien!" he laughed at his own joke and then sobered up when he started to worry about what Sofia would think about him now. She did not seem upset, yet she did seem slightly troubled.

"So what's going to happen now? Does this mean you'll be going home with your mother? Are you going to leave here?"

"No! We'd never do that to our parents. We owe them more courtesy than that. Besides, we still need to spend time getting to know our mother and our past before we'll decide to do anything drastic. I'd never leave without telling you anyway."

"That's good," she replied. Her grip on his arm tightened, and she said, "I'm so happy for you, Jon. It's so cool that you've met your mom and you have a baby sister, too. When are you going to see them again?"

"I don't know yet. Mrs. Stel said she'd make some visitation arrangements and she'd let us know."

Sofia nodded as they moved together through the crowd on their way to the lunch room. Her mind was reeling with the implications of Jon's revelation. If they were all from Tuala, and they all had special powers, then it was a definite that Juila and Jena had healed her. Maybe it was no coincidence that she was starting to be able to read their minds since the accident. There was so much to consider now that the pieces of the puzzle were starting to come together.

By the end of the school day, Willian was even more exasperated than he had been in his health services class. Sofia had been warm and welcoming when she had walked into their shared English class, but it had done little to assuage his frustration at not even seeing Jena at school all day. He wished there was a way to track her down so he could begin working out his differences with her.

Sofia came up to him after class and asked, "How was your first day? Pretty rough?"

"To say the least," Willian confessed with a big sigh. "I must have gotten turned around after every class."

"I'll walk you to your locker," she offered with a smile of understanding.

"That would be great," Willian said in relief. He picked up the stack of books he had been amassing from each class and followed after her.

She noticed his books and said, "Why didn't you put those in your locker?"

"I couldn't find it in time to not be late for my next class!"

"Not even at lunchtime?" she asked.

"Trust me, it was bad," Willian admitted with a chuckle.

She had to laugh at his expression. "I'm sorry, I should have found you after your class and made sure you were getting around better. Normally, the office has someone escort a new student for the whole day; I'm not sure why it wasn't done for you today."

"That would've been nice," Willian admitted.

"Are you riding the bus home?" Sofia asked.

"No, my guardian is picking me up."

Sofia frowned slightly at his phrasing. She wondered what his story could be that he would have a guardian instead of a parent. Wishing she were bold enough to ask about it, she instead asked, "Do you want me to walk you out front? It's the least I could do since you didn't get the proper guidance during the day."

Willian smiled at her friendly offer and said, "I'd really appreciate it. Thanks for being so nice to me."

"I know what it's like to be the new kid," she answered with a slight shrug. "Did you get much homework assigned? It's kind of a rough time to start in a new school with Christmas break right around the corner."

"I've been getting the same impression. I really wanted to get going right away. There didn't seem to be much point in delaying the inevitable." He shoved all of his books into the locker and shut the door. "I'm ready."

"No homework?" she asked in amazement.

"I did it in class already."

"Wow, that must be nice!" she teased as she thought about how much homework she still had to get done. The accident had caused her to get behind, and she was still playing catch-up. Now she had other distractions with Jon's mother coming into the picture.

They had reached the school's front entrance, and Willian watched Sofia walk away yet again. He exited the school and searched for Melissa's car as he worked his way around the other students. Finally seeing her standing outside the driver's door, he waved and walked faster.

"How was your first day?" she asked as they both sat down inside the car.

"Tiring and really confusing," he admitted with a sigh of relief.

"Well, you'll have a couple of days off for the weekend to get your bearings back." She started the car and pulled out of the parking lot. "Did you make any friends?"

"Hmmph," he grunted with dismay, "I don't know if they'll be friends, but I met two people who seemed nice. Sofia was my guide this morning, and then I literally ran into another guy named Luke who helped me find one of my classes."

"Well, that's a start at least. Did you eat lunch?"

"I ate something," he admitted. "I got into the wrong line first and then by the time I finally got an apple, the first warning bell rang for us to get back to class. I ate it while I wandered around looking for my classroom."

"I'm sorry. Why don't we stop for something on the way home then? There's a Burger King up the street, we can get you a hamburger, and you can let me know what you think of one of America's favorite meals."

"Sure, sounds like fun," he answered even as he wished for a foxl sandwich from home.

By late afternoon, Amanda finally had time to sit down at the patil and see if she had any new messages. She was delighted when she discovered one left by Barla. As soon as she finished reading it, she sat back in the office chair and wondered why she had not thought about doing the same thing. A gathering of everyone involved seemed the easiest way to figure out the answer to the prophecy she had discovered. Now her only problem was finding the time in everyone's busy schedules to get them together to talk it over.

Looking at her watch, she realized Riccan was due to come home from work at any minute. She would bring this up with him and see if he had any ideas of his own. She turned off the patil and stored it back away. She left the office and went out to the living room to wait for her husband to arrive.

The house was strangely empty as the kids had decided to go over to the Wilson's house after school rather than coming home to study. She wished she could have talked with Jon to see how he was faring with all of the new information he had absorbed the day before.

Thinking about absorbing information made her think about Neal and what he must be going through. Deciding to do the right things, she went over to the phone and dialed his number. On the second ring, the call was picked up.

"Hi, is this Mrs. Taivas?" Amanda asked.

"Yes."

"Hi, this is Amanda. I was just calling to find out how Neal is doing."

A moment of silence went by as Jessica absorbed the shock of Amanda actually calling. "He met with Dr. Medin today. Neal seemed eager to work with her which is encouraging. Do you think you'd want to come over and talk to him about everything?" Jessica could have bit her tongue for even asking.

"Maybe after he's met with Dr. Medin a few more times. When is his next appointment?" Amanda just imagined what types of questions Neal would have after his memory began to return.

"Monday afternoon," she answered.

"Good. I'm glad he's getting in so fast. I know how confusing it is to remember only bits and pieces. Pretty soon Neal will be back to normal."

"Do you really think so?" Jessica could only dream of such a recovery for her son.

"I do. It happened for me, and I don't see any reason why it won't happen for Neal as well."

"Can't you tell us what his story is? Don't you think it would speed things along?"

"It's not my place to talk about it, Mrs. Taivas. I'm really sorry. I'm not trying to impede his recovery; I just think it'll be healthier for him to regain his memories as he's ready to know them."

"I still don't understand," Jessica complained.

"Oh, I'm sorry, Mrs. Taivas, I have to get going. My husband just got home. I'll keep in touch. Bye," she hurriedly said as she hung up the phone and turned to greet Riccan.

"Who was that?" he asked as he stopped in front of her to lean down and kiss her cheek.

"Mrs. Taivas," she answered as she put her arms around his neck to greet him properly with a kiss on the lips.

As soon as their lips parted, he asked, "Any progress with Neal?"

"He saw Dr. Medin today and is scheduled to go back to her Monday. Hopefully, he'll get his memory back soon and then we can all move on."

"Do you think it'll be that simple? What about Vinia? She's going to want to be with him, and maybe he'll want to go back to Tuala."

"Maybe," she conceded and then changed the subject, "but we have concerns of our own." She told him about Barla's idea for the meeting, and she could see Riccan approved.

"That plan makes sense. We could let each person in the group try to work out their part of the prophecy. We could also talk about what samaras have been found and the possible connection between the aura and the birth crystal color."

"Possible connection? You aren't convinced of it yet?" Amanda asked in dismay.

"I'm convinced, it's just the others in the group who don't have a samara yet will need to be persuaded."

"Okay. I think we should bring some of the samaras with us so we can start to distribute the power source. After we had that break-in, I'm certain that was just a warning for us to do something different. I'd hate to see what happened in the event we had all thirteen samaras here in the same location," Amanda finished with a shudder of fear.

"Maybe we can have the two Elders involved keep them at their guarded and warded Residences. The power influx would hardly even be noticed."

"There's a third Elder's Residence now, you know since Rasa's been confirmed. She was also at the meeting which would make her eligible to receive her own samara."

"True," Riccan said as he nodded agreement. He put his arm around Amanda and began leading her through the house so he could change out of his work clothes. If the journey happened to lead to something else, then he was not about to complain. "Where are the kids?"

"They are studying over at the Wilson's house."

Even better, Riccan thought as they began to climb the stairs.

Amanda could sense a change in his mood. She looked up into his face and saw the gleam of excitement in his eyes. Her worry, for the time being, could be put on hold for them to have a proper home-coming. They could always think about their options much later.

THE PATIL BUZZED for the third time, and Riccan began to wonder if his parents were unavailable. He looked at his watch and thought his mother, at least, should be around. Raising his hand to disconnect the video call he almost hit the button when his mother's face appeared on the screen.

"Well hello, Riccan! I'm glad you rang me up," she cheerfully said.

"I'd like to ask a favor of you," he replied.

"Sure, what is it?"

"Can you arrange a time and place where everyone who was at Jehoban's meeting can get together again? We'd like to have me,

Amanda, and the twins present as well, so maybe we can find some answers faster."

"Oh, what a wonderful idea. You should have Amanda bring copies of her journal so each person can read his or her own account of Amanda's memories of them and see if they can identify the discrepancies. Maybe we can find a pattern or something."

"You're brilliant, Mom!"

She beamed with pride at her son's compliment.

"Will you be able to set up the meeting?" Riccan asked again.

"Sure. It'll have to be sometime in the afternoon since the girls will be there. It'll also be easier for myself and you to get together. When were you wanting it to happen?"

"As soon as possible. Also, Amanda wants to begin redistributing the samaras to keep the power signal dispersed a bit more. I'm hoping to use the separate Residences since they are already warded against intrusion or attack."

Nena frowned slightly. She was still leery of the other samaras even if she knew hers to be harmless ever since she had bonded with her own. "I'll talk to your father about it and let you know what he thinks," she answered noncommittally.

Riccan knew his father would agree with his own assessment and took it as an affirmative and replied, "Thanks, Mom. I'll let you go for now."

"Thanks for calling. I can't wait for the girls to come over and spend time with us."

"Yes, that's right around the corner, isn't it?"

"Yep and I've made so many plans for us!"

"You know you don't have to entertain them, right?" Riccan cautioned.

"Oh, I know. I'm just having fun," she childishly grinned.

"I love you."

"I love you, too," Nena replied and then she tapped the screen to disconnect the video call.

Riccan turned to Amanda and said, "There, now Mom will get it all together and you won't have to worry about a thing until she tells us when to show up."

"I'm glad. I think everyone will be more receptive to Nena's request."

"You give yourself far too little credit, Amanda. Nobody you've ever spoken with has refused anything you've asked of them, you know."

"That's true," Amanda replied as she reviewed all of her previous contact with the Tualan people. They had always been more than willing to do whatever she had proposed. "I like your mom's idea about sharing my journal. I'll have to start making each person's packet so they will only have to read the parts which pertain to themselves."

"We'd be there forever if everyone read the whole thing, wouldn't we?" Riccan teased.

"I think I hear the girls in the other room. Let's go tell them what we're planning," Amanda said as she stood up and left the office.

The twins were inordinately pleased to be included in such an auspicious meeting. "I hope Grandma can arrange it before the winter break," Juila said.

"Do you have plans for the break?" Riccan asked.

"No, I just don't want to wait that long!"

Everyone laughed at Juila's reply and then Amanda asked, "Do you have any plans for this weekend?"

Jena answered, "Behn, Val, and Jon are coming over tomorrow afternoon to practice their crystal skills."

Juila dug her elbow into Jena's ribs to tease her as she added,

"And then Jena is going to the movies with Luke again in the evening!"

Jena blushed at her sister's implications. It was true she had developed feelings for Luke, but she still was unsure what to do with them.

As if reading his daughter's mind, Riccan said, "We're going to be discussing a dissolution of your betrothal with Willian. It's pretty clear it's not working out for the two of you."

Jena's posture loosened in her relief. She had not wanted to bring it up, yet she wanted to get it over with.

Juila suddenly whooped in delight at their father's announcement. "It's about time! Jena, isn't that amazing? You'll finally be free of his controlling demands."

Jena sat down on the couch and worried about what the Tualan people would say or do. This was not a matter to be taken lightly. She did not want to hurt Willian or his status.

CHAPTER 16

It was mid-afternoon before the Wilson triplets were able to come over to the house. They were in high spirits because all three of them would be learning to use their birth crystals. They had also discussed at length what they wanted to do about visiting with their mother in Tuala.

"Do you think your mom could arrange for us to spend time with our mom both here at your house as well as in Tuala?" Behn asked Juila.

"I'm sure she'd love to. She knows how hard it is for a mother to be without her children."

"That's right," Behn beamed. "You two are so close with your mother that I keep forgetting you've spent your entire lives apart. Was it hard to get into a rhythm?"

"No, we had a unique situation when we were living on Acaim. Jehoban allowed us to have dreams at night where we interacted with our mom. She had the same dreams, so we have shared memories."

"But none of it was real," Behn said with a confused expression.

"It didn't have to be real for us to love her. Reality is what you make it, Behn."

Behn tilted his head and raised his eyebrows as he considered her statement. "I guess that's true."

Juila was about to make another comment about their upbringing when she was interrupted by Jon entering the living room. She could tell he was excited about something and wondered what had happened during his initial training with Jena in the library. "What's going on, Jon?"

"I'd like to see where we used to live in the Roanoke Colony," Jon said to Juila. "Val said you had taken her and Behn there where they regained a lot of memories. I'd like to see if it brings anything back for me as well. Val said she recalled all of the initial crystal training sessions with our mother and it'd be a heck of a lot easier just to know it again."

"I think we can probably arrange something for you," Juila answered as she looked over to her father to see if he would offer to take them.

"You should see if Valentina or Behn want to go with you," Riccan suggested without committing himself to the journey.

"Do you mind if I take them, Dad?" Juila asked hardly breathing until she got an answer.

Riccan smiled at her thinly veiled excitement at the prospect of getting to fly on her own. He had few reservations about her piloting skills since they had flown together on many occasions and she had always performed flawlessly. In any event, his own telepod was much more advanced technologically than anything she had ever trained on so it practically flew itself. "Go ahead and take my 'pod, Juila. It still has the coordinates in its history from the first time we went there as a group."

"Really? You mean it, you'll let me take them alone? Cool!" she flew across the living room and practically smothered him with her gratitude as she hugged him tight around the neck. "I love you, Dad! You are the best!"

"I would have offered a long time ago if I knew this was the reaction I'd get!" He laughed and hugged her back, liking the feel of her cuddling with him.

Juila rushed into the library where Jena was giving Behn and Valentina more birth crystal lessons. She had their immediate attention as she came to a breathless halt in front of them. "Dad said I could take you guys back to the Roanoke Colony if you want to go. He even said I could take his 'pod since the coordinates are already in it. Who wants to go?"

Jena and Behn both looked at one another conspiratorially and then turned back to Juila. Jena shook her head as Behn answered, "I think I'll skip it this time. Jena has agreed to teach me some new things with healing. What about you, Val?"

"I've been wanting to get back there, but I didn't know how to ask you; I figured your parents would have to take us and they're always so busy. When do you want to go?"

"Right now!" Juila practically shouted.

Valentina jumped up from the wing chair and straightened her clothing as she looked down at her brother and asked, "If we stay out late, can you run blocker with our parents?"

"Sure thing, Val. Have fun," Behn answered as he grinned up at his sister. He was grateful his brother would finally get to see the home they had been born in and grew up in for the first seven years of their lives. He hoped it would spur as many memories for Jon as it had for himself and Valentina.

Valentina's excitement was evident as she grinned over at Juila as they left the library side-by-side to get Jon from the living room and then be on their way. As soon as she saw her brother Valentina announced, "I'm coming with you. Let's go!"

Jon joined them on their way through the kitchen and out to

the garage. He still marveled at the sight of the bright red telepod. It still seemed amazing that the aircraft actually existed even though he had only been speaking in anger when he suggested the mode of transportation between the two dimensions. This would be his first flight in Riccan's telepod since he'd gone to Tuala with Mrs. Stel in her older telepod.

The first thing he noticed was how classy and sharp the interior was with two glass panels for the controls and polished surfaces everywhere. Even the covering of the seats was a tanned foxl hide left natural in an ivory tone which was silky soft to the touch. This telepod would definitely be categorized as first-class accommodations.

He chose one of the back seats where he would be able to see out of all of the windows. Valentina took the right co-pilot seat whereas Juila sat in the left front seat. He watched as Juila activated the telepod and he could see out the still-open door that they had risen a couple of inches off of the cement floor. His view outside was diminished as the side door rose up until it sealed completely.

Juila maneuvered through the screens until she came to the travel history so she could scroll through previous trips until she came to the Roanoke coordinates. She did not have to look very far into the list as her father seldom went anywhere other than work or home. Juila raised her eyebrows when she saw the Port of Cresdon come up, and she briefly wondered what her father had been doing there. She would ask him when they got back home.

Focusing her attention to the task at hand, she selected the Roanoke trip and waited until the proper map showed on the screen to display their intended destination. She took a few seconds to memorize the surrounding area, as she had been taught with lesser telepods, so she would have an emergency plan of action should anything go amiss.

Before doing anything further, Juila turned and asked, "Jon, is your seatbelt fastened?"

"Buckled and ready," he announced with a broad grin of excitement.

"Val, are you secure?"

"Yep," she answered as she tugged on the shoulder harnesses to demonstrate its proper tension.

Juila nodded approval and double-checked her own before she tapped on the activation button. Her hand was resting comfortably on the manual control when the transfer took them into the darkness between the two locations. Several seconds more than she was used to traveling, they arrived over the beach in the bright sunshine.

Immediately, Juila knew they were in trouble. The wind was blowing over the water in fits as the waves came crashing to the shore with more force than normal. She held tighter to the manual control and tried to keep the craft level and steady as she moved over the place on the shore she wanted to set the telepod down. They were within two feet of the ground when another rogue gust of wind blast from the front of the telepod and instantly dropped them to the sand in a jolting strike.

All of the occupants felt the whiplash of the sudden landing. Juila powered down the telepod and noticed her hands were shaking with fear. She asked in a quavering voice, "Is everyone okay?"

Jon laughed nervously from the back as he replied, "I'm glad it was only sand under us and not concrete. I'm fine."

"I'm fine, too, Juila. We were really lucky just then, weren't we?" Valentina asked as she waited to do anything with her seat harness until she saw Juila do something with hers.

"That was the worst landing I've ever had; the wind just came out of nowhere. Jon's right, we were lucky it was sand underneath us. Come on; let's get out of here and thank Jehoban for keeping us safe!" Juila flipped the buckle to release it. She pressed the button on the control panel to open the side door and moved through the cabin to go outside.

Expecting to be blasted by the wind, Juila simply stood on the edge of the ramp and stared in wonder at how completely still the air had become. She squinted her eyes and looked along the shoreline to see if there had been any clouds to indicate a squall had passed. Nothing. The sky was clear blue as far as she could see. "That was really weird," she muttered as she stepped into the sand and waited for her two passengers to join her.

Juila remembered her father's caution about maintaining the safety of the telepod, so she made sure the door was securely shut and that she used the cloaking feature to prevent anyone from finding their aircraft. She looked around the location to make sure she would know where to come back, and then she set off over the sand dune to get to the brushy trail leading to the village.

CHAPTER 17

Valentina stayed right by Juila's side as she recalled the way as well. This second trip seemed so much more familiar, and she began remembering different landmarks from when she was a small child. It had only been about fourteen months Tualan time since she had last been here, but in Earth time she had been away for eight years. She still wondered why the community had abandoned the village they had inhabited for two hundred years. On this trip, she hoped to find some answers to her questions.

Jon followed behind the two girls and frequently stopped to look around him. He had absolutely no memory of this place, and he hoped when they got to the house itself that maybe something would come back to him. He jogged to catch back up with the girls as they had started down another smaller trail where they had to go single file.

The walk from the beach to the middle of the town took about ten minutes at the pace Juila had set. Jon felt a small tingle of familiarity at the look of the buildings, yet he had no idea where their home had been located in relation to the others. He now walked beside his sister as they were out in the open space of the town center.

Valentina pointed out their old home and said, "That's where we used to live. Go ahead and check it out, I'm going to look around a bit. I'd like to see if anyone left anything behind which might say why they all left." She took off in the opposite direction and turned down a side street out of Jon's view.

Jon shrugged his shoulders at his sister's curiosity and moved forward to go inside the home Valentina had said was theirs. He pushed open the wooden door and waited outside while the door swung on creaky hinges. The house appeared to be empty, and he moved closer to see inside without actually stepping over the threshold.

The first thing he noticed was the amount of dust covering everything. He could see a crude wooden table in the middle of the room with benches on either side of it. His eyes roamed to the far side, and he saw the kitchen. Further over, he saw a cot which no longer had any coverings other than a mat of moldy straw. About four feet away he saw two other cots in similar condition to the first.

He had no recollection of ever stepping into the house, yet the next thing he knew, he was kneeling down next to the furthest cot from the door. This had been where he had spent so many winters drowning in his own sweat and phlegm from the pneumonia which almost killed him. As he looked around now, he could see the fire softly lighting the room with its wavering flickers and his mother sitting at the table with Behn and Val teaching them to use their birth crystals.

His hand came up to touch his own pendant in reverence of the memory. He had learned the same lessons, although he seldom had the strength to practice using them. Tears of forgotten pain began to fall down his cheeks as he realized how much his mother had given up to keep them safe. He felt terrible for ever believing she had been selfish in sending them away. She had done her best for them out of love.

Jon could feel his lungs tightening up, and he started to gasp for air. He had to get out of this house and breathe the fresh air outside. He stumbled out of the small house and held onto the doorframe as he heaved oxygen into his painful lungs. Knowing it had to be a psychosomatic reaction to the memories he had to shake his head at himself as he tried to relax and breathe normally again.

Without any concept of how much time had passed, Jon began walking through the village to find either Juila or Valentina. Even as he walked along, memories were coming back to him about places they had played or where other children had lived. He also remembered they seldom were allowed to play with the other kids since their parents told them to stay away from the strange triplets who did not belong in their colony.

Jon could not recall why they had been outcasts in the community. He would have to ask his sister about it when he found her. Looking away from a dilapidated cabin, Jon spotted Juila moving from one house to another. He quickened his pace to catch up to her before she decided to move again.

"Hey, Juila," he called from the doorway. His eyes could not see into the dim interior as the sunlight outside had blinded him. His nose told him there was something rather unpleasant inside.

"I'm right here," she called from several feet away. "Wait there; I'm coming back out."

Jon stepped back as she suddenly appeared in front of him. "What was in there?"

"Nothing but a lot of trash and a dead animal of some sort," she replied as she snorted a couple of times while trying to dislodge the terrible smell from her nose. "Val is across the way; let's see if she's found anything."

They found her inside the largest building in the entire community. Kneeling down on the floor, Valentina was rummaging through a wooden crate. Dust was flying up around her, and they had to laugh as she pulled her torso out of the mess and turned around to face them. All of her hair was covered in cobwebs and dust, and she had dark smears of dirt on both of her cheeks as she had used her filthy hands to brush her hair out of her eyes.

"Did you find anything useful?" Jon asked as he tried to contain his laughter.

"Not much," she answered with disgust. "I did find this one piece of paper which might be interesting to look into further. It looks like a page out of a diary or something. The writing's pretty faded, so I'm going to take it home to investigate it further in front of a lightbulb or something." She handed the paper over to her brother as she needed both hands on the edge of the crate to assist her up from her cramped position on the ground.

Jon looked at the almost blank sheet of paper dubiously. If his sister could resurrect anything intelligible from this page, she had more skill than the average person. He brought it closer to his face as he angled himself into the light, he could just barely make out scrawling script on the page.

Valentina walked over to the kitchen sink and turned on the faucet hoping the water still worked. She almost cheered as the gurgle of clean water began to fall into the basin of the sink. She rubbed her hands together and watched as layers of dirt began to flow in muddy puddles into the sink before swirling into the drain. Without soap, she managed to clean herself reasonably well, including her face.

She rubbed her hands on her pant legs to dry them off. She

flipped her head down and vigorously shook her hair to try to dislodge as much filth as possible before using her hands to pull cobwebs and brambles from the ends. One more quick rinse in the sink and Valentina declared, "I've seen enough here. What about you, Jon? Did seeing everything help your memory?"

"It did. I'm glad we came. I don't think I'd want to come back, though. This place's really depressing."

"I agree. Let's go home where everything is clean and has pleasant memories," Valentina agreed as she slung her arm around her brother's waist. She tipped her head against his shoulder as he put his arm around her shoulders. She was glad Jon was being friendly with her again. It had been a rough couple of months when they had had to keep him in the dark about their mother. Now everything seemed back to normal, or as normal as their lives would ever get considering from where they actually came.

The three of them trooped back to the shoreline and decided to play in the ocean water for a bit before they headed back. It felt good to giggle and play after the tenseness they had experienced while they were in the town. The sun was starting to get low on the horizon when the three teenagers, wet, sandy, and tired, decided they should head home.

Juila pressed the cloaking button on the remote as they walked in the general direction of where they had landed. The telepod appeared, and they boarded the aircraft. They sat in their same locations as before, and Juila closed the side door before activating the aircraft. She had a strange feeling of being watched and wanted the security of being enclosed as soon as possible.

She activated the telepod and issued all of the commands of the start-up procedure. She scrolled through the destination history and tapped down one to get to the home coordinates. "Everyone ready?" she asked and waited for the replies before she pressed the selection which would send them back home to Earth.

Several seconds ticked by, then several more. The lights of the garage did not appear as they should have. Instead, she saw pinpricks of light all around them. The telepod's system turned on several red lights on the glass panel as the emergency systems kicked on. Juila began resolving the issued one by one until all of the warning lights were gone. They had stable pressure in the cabin as they appeared to be floating in space rather than several inches above the concrete in the garage at home.

Juila tapped the mapping section of the glass panel and groaned as she realized what had gone wrong.

"What's going on, Juila?" Valentina asked as she stared out the windows with sheer terror evident even in her tone of voice.

"Juila, I don't think this is home," Jon stated the obvious as he turned and saw the round ball of Earth circling slowly beneath them.

"We are exactly above home, actually," Juila said as she continued to study the coordinates of their intended destination. "It seems as though the Z coordinate did not compute when the transfer occurred. We are approximately 50,000 miles above our intended target."

"What? How did that happen?" Valentina could feel herself starting to come unhinged at the idea of floating helplessly out into space to die.

"I'm not sure yet, give me a few minutes to check some things out," Juila answered even as her mind was going over every possible scenario.

"Do you think our hard landing did something to the navigation system?" Jon asked. He could not help but stare at the beautiful planet far beneath them. The swirling of the clouds was mesmerizing as the land appeared and disappeared beneath them.

"I think you may have the answer, Jon. Unfortunately, the crystal compartment is not part of the pressurized cabin, so I won't be able to check on it to see if it requires repairs. I'm going to try the radio to see if we can get anyone to assist us." Juila dialed as many frequencies as she knew and none of them produced any results other than static.

"This isn't looking good, is it, Juila?" Valentina asked as her breathing came faster as she imagined the air was getting thinner the further they floated away from Earth.

"No, it's not good, Val." Juila ran her hands through her hair, and she tugged fistfuls to help her focus her mind on solving the problem. It was possible there was a manual override to the crystal drive allowing her to use mental coordinates. She began tapping on different selections on the glass panel as she searched for the manual selection. "Ah, I found it!" she announced triumphantly.

"What? What did you find?" Valentina asked urgently.

"The manual override section. I can use this to have the crystal drive take the coordinates from my mind rather than from the computer system. Give me some quiet for a few minutes while I mentally guide us back home."

Juila closed her eyes in concentration and recalled all of her lessons on the older telepods which required only mental navigation. This should be a simple matter of thinking their destination into a reality. She took a deep, calming breath, and then she pressed the activation button on her mental destination.

Everything went black inside and out of the telepod as it shifted through space. Only three seconds passed before they appeared back in space. Juila stared in disbelief as she realized they were further off course than they originally had been.

Jon said it best when he declared, "I can't see Earth anymore out of any window. I think we have a problem."

"You think, Captain Obvious?" Valentina shouted at him.

"Stop it, you two, I need to think!" Juila studied their new coordinates and groaned. They had doubled their distance away from

Earth instead of moving closer. The crystal drive had to have a loose connection in order for it to behave in such a manner.

She could almost kick herself for being so hasty and confident when they were leaving Tuala. Any good pilot knew to check all of the equipment and fuselage before departure. She had been feeling so anxious to get away that she had neglected to heed the most basic lesson on safety. Now they were stuck in space without any form of communication and no way to fix the crystal drive without losing the vacuum inside the cabin. The situation was hopeless to say the least.

CHAPTER 18

Jena instantly knew that there was a problem. The part of her brain which was always in contact with Juila was suddenly gone. "No, no, NO!" she yelled as she stood up and ran out of the library.

Behn stared after her and wondered what could have happened to make her act so strangely. He began to get a terrible feeling inside that something bad had occurred and it would most likely involve Juila. He jumped up and raced after her.

"I can't feel her anymore, Dad! Juila is gone!" Jena kept calling out.

Riccan stood up from the couch and held out his arms to Jena even as he tried to make sense of what she was saying. He spotted Behn as he came to a halt in the hallway and he yelled at him, "Go get Amanda, quick! I think she's upstairs in our room!"

Behn nodded and changed direction to go through the foyer. He took the stairs three at a time and pounded on the bedroom door twice before flinging the door open to a startled Mrs. Stel.

"Something bad has happened, and Mr. Stel needs you downstairs straightaway."

"What is it?" she asked as she brushed past Behn and flew down the stairs without any conscious memory of touching any of them. She took in the scene ahead of her as she bolted into the living room and took Jena's face into her hands. "What happened? Tell me what you know!"

"I can't feel Juila with me anymore; she's gone! She's gone, Mom!" Jena's eyes were huge with fear.

"Come, sit down, Jena. Let's go over this very slowly. I remember this happening before when the two of you were separated."

"Mom that was in a dream, it wasn't real! This is real, Mom, Juila is gone!"

"My dreams have all meant something before. Maybe this was to prepare us to look at this situation differently and not to panic. Tell me everything you felt up until you could no longer sense Juila."

"Behn and I were in the library studying, and everything was normal. Juila was getting ready to come back home. She was feeling anxious, almost as if someone were watching her. She wanted to come home as fast as possible. I don't know anything after that because the link just vanished."

Amanda looked up in horror at her daughter's revelation. It sounded as if there had been a problem with the telepod transfer home. If the aircraft had malfunctioned, then it would mean their daughter no longer existed in any dimension, she would be lost forever from either side. She looked over to Behn as she realized it also meant that both of his siblings were also lost.

Riccan sat back in stunned silence. He had thought there was something wrong with the telepod when he had landed at his parents' house, but he had dismissed it as being the tracking device attached at transfer. How could he have missed something so basic? Had his negligence just cost him one of his daughters and two other teenage lives?

An idea struck him, and he abruptly stood up and left the room. He went into the office and pulled out the patil from its secret cubby. He tapped in a few commands and sat back in his chair as he realized the transmitting beacon was still operational, if not faint. They were still alive, but the question of where remained a mystery.

He pondered the implication as he returned to the living room where everyone stared at his abrupt exit. "I was able to confirm the aircraft is still functional. The beacon is still functioning, but the tone is very distant. I don't know where they are, but they definitely still exist."

"Then why can't I feel Juila anymore?" Jena cried.

"I have an idea," Amanda offered.

"What is it?" Riccan asked.

"This scenario happened in my dream, remember? Rasa was able to help Juila re-link with Jena when she had been taken to Earth. Maybe we should go see Rasa and see if she can do it again for Jena."

Riccan looked at his distraught daughter and said, "Unless anyone can come up with a better plan, then I think Rasa is our only option. Let's go!" He helped pull Jena up from the couch. Her limbs seemed limp and uncooperative as she began to shiver and cry as if in pain. He picked her up and carried her out to the garage. He gently placed her in the back seat of Amanda's telepod and buckled her in. He waited for Behn and Amanda to board the aircraft before he closed the door and activated the flight to Manzanit.

SEVERAL TENSE HOURS passed and still they were no closer to finding a way to return home to Earth. Juila had reviewed every screen on the glass panel and yet there was nothing to be done for their free-floating in space. She was afraid to attempt another transfer for fear of taking them further out into space.

Juila was thoroughly sick of hearing Valentina's comments about how they were going to die, and they were going to run out of oxygen. While Valentina did have a point about the finite amount of air available, they were by no means in any imminent danger of suffocating. Juila attempted to put Valentina to sleep using her skills with her birth crystal only to find out there was no elemy accessible.

She had a moment of panic herself as she searched in vain for any traces of elemy only to come up empty-handed. She took deep breaths to focus her mind and tried again, with the same negative results. Juila finally had to admit the idea of being so far away from the Earth's energy source was impeding her abilities. It was not an idea which sat easily with her since she had always relied on being able to use her gifts whenever she felt the need. Now she felt absolutely ordinary; she almost chuckled as she realized this was how people from Earth felt all of the time: helpless.

For once Valentina had something constructive to say. "I think we're moving," she said as she pointed to the display screen.

Juila confirmed Valentina's suspicion as she watched the X and Y coordinates begin to move in a synchronous line rather than the random fluctuations they had been performing as they drifted in space. "I think you're right, Val." Juila swiveled her head in every direction trying to see what could be causing them to change course so suddenly.

Jon cried from the back, "I think I see something off of the port side. Juila, do you see anything out there?"

Juila stared intently and finally made out a small smudge in the distance which seemed different than the surrounding stars. "I do see something. I have no idea what it could be, but if it has the ability to draw us in, then it must be sentient."

"What?" cried Valentina in increasing panic. "What do you mean sentient? Are you suggesting we're being drawn in by aliens? Could this get any worse?"

"I'd say this was a lucky break because they probably have communications for us to contact Earth and arrange for help. If nothing else, they would have a place with gravity and compression where I could fix the crystal drive so we could use our own telepod to get back home ourselves." Juila nodded her head at her own ideas; this was going to work out just fine. She felt confident they were on the way to being rescued from a potentially deadly situation.

Several minutes passed by, and they were able to make out the shape of a large spaceship in the distance. Juila had never heard of anyone actively pursuing space travel in Tuala, but she could not rule out the idea of some of the Elders probably entertaining the idea. It was possible Elder Vargen's Old Soul Engineering Facility had created something space-worthy in all of the time they had been amassing ideas from Earth's people.

The closer they came to the foreign ship, the more anxious Juila became. Not only was the vessel a good fifty times larger than their own telepod, but she also did not recognize any part of its design. The structure was oblong with very few windows, a dull silver finish, and a very large opening on the side they were approaching.

"It looks as though all of our questions will soon be answered," Jon stated as their telepod began to pass through the entrance of a large internal cavern.

Valentina glared back at her brother's obvious comment yet refrained from further comment. Her knuckles were white where she gripped the arms of her chair. She failed to find anything comforting about this new turn of events.

Several things happened all at once, the forward motion of their telepod stopped, the opening behind their ship began to close, and the darkness around them began to change as a circle of lights began to turn on around the perimeter of the cargo bay in which they were floating.

Juila imagined the gravity would be restored as soon as the external door shut, so she put her hand on the manual control to ease the telepod down onto the cargo room floor. The last thing she needed was to crash the 'pod again. As if on cue, Juila could feel the telepod regaining spatial control as gravity returned. She set the telepod down with ease and powered down the systems.

"What are you doing?" Valentina asked of Juila as she watched her friend unfasten her seat harness and jump out of her chair.

"I'm going to go check on the crystal drive to see if I can fix the problem. If it can be repaired, then we can get out of here." She had not stopped her movement through the telepod, but she did come up short from her task as the external door was opened and she came face to face with a strange, terrifying-looking man holding a gun up and aimed at her.

CHAPTER 19

"Hold it right where you are, missy. Now be a good girl, and walk on down this ramp. We're going to check out what business you have out here so close to us. You there," he pointed to Jon and then to Valentina, "come on out and join your friend. If you cooperate, then nobody will get hurt."

Soon enough they were all three standing on the cargo bay floor beside the telepod and watching as a swarm of unwashed men entered their vessel and pawed through everything. Another man had taken over the duty of guarding them, and he kept leering at Juila and Valentina. Jon put his arm protectively around Valentina and pulled her closer to him to offer whatever protection he could give her.

"The ship is clear," a man said as he stepped out of the telepod. He turned to the three kids and asked, "Who sent you and why?"

Juila cleared her throat before she answered, "Nobody sent us, sir. We had a system malfunction, and we were unable to navigate back to Earth."

"Earth, you say?" the man raised his eyebrows and tilted his head with interest. "Come with me." He turned and began walking toward a door they had not seen before.

The three of them held hands as they walked behind this fierce-looking man. He led them through various dimly lit hallways and up a short ramp. He pointed to a room and said, "Leave the other two in here. Bring the girl who spoke to my room." With the tone of voice, he used it was clear he was used to being obeyed at once.

Jon realized what had been said and he spoke up, "She stays with us. If you want to talk, then we'll all be going together."

The man turned on his heel and stepped right up to Jon until their noses were nearly touching, "You do not call the shots around here, boy; I do. If you value your life at all, then I suggest you do exactly what I say and keep your mouth shut. When I want your opinion, I'll ask for it." He looked him up and down and sneered, "I doubt you'll be talking much from the looks of you." He chuckled, turned, and walked away. "Bring the girl now!" he spoke loudly without even turning his head to make sure his orders were being followed.

Valentina grabbed Juila's arm and said urgently, "Don't go with them, Juila. I'm afraid."

"I don't see where we have a choice in the matter at present. I'm going to get to the bottom of this and be back as soon as I can. Stay with Jon; keep believing we'll be fine."

Juila's words were barely finished before another man grabbed her by the upper arm and began pulling her in the same direction the leader had taken. She jerked forward and released her arm from his grasp as she continued to walk forward. "Don't touch me," she spoke with as much authority as she could muster and straightened her shoulders to give herself as much confidence as she could gather.

To her surprise, the man did back off and followed her two steps behind. She had seen the other man turn at a doorway up ahead, so she knew where to go. Once she stepped into the room, the man behind her shut the door, and she thought she heard a snigger of amusement from him as the door clicked shut.

Without any preliminaries, the leader said, "My name's Viceroy Blair. You can either call me by my full title or Viceroy, but you will not call me Blair. Do you understand?"

Juila nodded.

"Good! Now state your name, rank, and where you're from."

"Juila Stel, I am a student of Jehoban. I'm from Acaim, Tuala." Juila wondered if she should claim Tuala or Earth as where she had come from. She opted to go with the most influential place and hoped it would be enough to gain some respect, and possibly help, from this Viceroy Blair. *Where better than the home of the creator of the universe?* she thought to herself.

"Yet you claimed to be trying to return to Earth. Which story is it, girl?"

"Both, Viceroy. I was taking my two passengers home to Earth."

"I see. How did you come to be acquainted with your passengers?"

"I met them in school on Earth."

"I thought you said you were from Tuala?"

"I am."

"I see," Viceroy said even though he failed to understand the situation. Regardless of their reasons for being out in space, he had a problem, and he believed they possessed the solution. "You do realize you're now indebted to me for rescuing your ship, right?"

"I am, Viceroy. We'd be glad to repay your kindness once we're safely returned to Earth."

"I think you will be paying long before then, Juila," Viceroy quietly said as he turned and fiddled with some of the paperwork on his desktop. "Will you be able to repair your ship to fly again?"

"I'm not sure what the exact problem is with it, Viceroy Blair. If you'd allow me to go back to the telepod, then I can give you more details."

Viceroy pretended to consider her request even though his mind was already made up in the matter. "I think not at this time," he replied as he turned back around to face her. "I have more pressing matters at present. Do you have any experience with aquaponics?"

"Yes, I do. Is your system down as well?" Juila began reviewing all of the lessons she had ever learned on the subject. She hoped to be able to offer her assistance so the Viceroy would be more accommodating to their situation.

"Unfortunately, yes. Everything began to malfunction after we picked up our last shipment in Tuala, actually."

"If you can take me to your grow-room, I can see what I can do to help," Juila said reasonably.

"Perhaps, perhaps. Sit down for a bit." He gestured to a chair and remained standing. He hastily reviewed what he knew of Tuala and wondered why the place she said she came from worried him. "Tell me about Acaim."

Juila clearly had not expected the request and remained silent for a few seconds. "It's the home of Jehoban. The people who live on Acaim are all there by Jehoban's invitation and are His special students."

"And who *is* this Jehoban?"

Juila's eyebrows rose, and her eyes widened as she replied in astonishment, "He's the creator of the universe."

"Hah!" Viceroy tipped his head back and laughed out loud for several seconds before he looked back down at Juila and asked, "Who is he really?"

"Viceroy Blair, I would not joke about such a matter. Jehoban is the creator of everything around us. All of the worlds were made by Him, all of the dimensions, the creatures, the very air we breathe was His thought made manifest."

The tone of her voice triggered a memory in his head, and he recalled the truth behind her words. He could not show his ignorance of the matter and be seen at a disadvantage, so he laughed and said, "It's good you know the truth. I had to make sure you truly believed or else I wouldn't be able to work with you."

"That's good to know," Juila replied even as she wondered about his sincerity. He did not seem to be a particularly religious man. "What do you need me to do?"

Since he had no other option and she was just a kid anyway he decided to be straight with her. "The ship's crystal drive shattered and the replacement crystal we just installed from Tuala has cracked in half. For all intents and purposes, we're also stuck here in space on very minimal power and even lower food supplies with the aquaponics plants not performing up to their expectations. If we don't get everything back online soon, we're all going to die out here in space."

Juila's eyes widened as he explained their situation. Her original plan of using the ship's communications to get help was no longer an option with their crystal drive inoperative. To get right to the heart of the problem she asked, "How many people are on board?"

"I have ten crew and nineteen new recruits."

"How long has this situation been going on?"

"The first crystal shattered as we were landing on Tuala to resupply the ship about two months ago. We were able to get the new crystal and install it almost immediately. While the new crystal was nothing like the old one, it worked even better than the previous one up until seventeen days ago when it broke in half."

Juila nodded as she processed his information and asked one

final question, "How many reserve supplies do you still have available?"

"If it were just my crew, we'd be good for about one week. As it stands, there's only enough for about one to two days, and that's on rations."

The situation was worse than Juila had imagined it would be. She wracked her brain for a solution for everyone and kept coming up blank. Deciding to take it step-by-step, she asked, "Show me the grow room and I'll see if we can get something going before it comes to starvation." She stood up and made to move for the door.

"Not so fast, Juila. We need to set up some ground rules before you leave this room. Sit down."

Juila took the one step back and resumed her seat. She looked up at him and wondered what he could possibly mean by being so bossy.

"First, you are not to be talking to my crew. Second, you will not poke around in areas where you are not supposed to be. Third, you will come right back here to this room when you are finished. Do you understand these rules and agree to follow them?"

"Yes, Viceroy Blair, I agree." She could not possibly understand why these rules were so important to him, yet they seemed easy enough to follow.

"Do not cross me," he warned as he moved over to the door, opened it, and told the man outside, "Take our guest to the grow room. Make sure she stays in the room and escort her back here when she is finished."

"Yes, Viceroy!" The man saluted him and stood ready for Juila to come out into the hallway.

Juila took this as her cue to go ahead and leave the room. As soon as they were out of earshot of the Viceroy, Juila turned and asked the man, "I'm Juila. What's your name? I'd prefer to be able to use your name instead of hey you."

The young man looked confused as he answered, "The name's Ozias, ma'am."

"It's nice to make your acquaintance, Ozias. Where're you from?"

"I shouldn't be talking to you about this, Juila."

"Really, Ozias? What could it hurt?" she teased him, hoping to keep him talking. She slowed down her paces wanting to keep him talking longer. Unconsciously, he slowed down where he was leading her.

"All of the original crew is from a planet called Heliok. We're really far away from home right now, and we should have been back almost a month ago."

"So might your people have sent a ship out to find you?"

"I don't think so." He looked away and cleared his throat.

"Why not? Don't you think they're missing you?" Juila really was starting to wonder at his strange response to such a reasonable question.

"Our planet's dying, and we have the last operation space ship on the planet. At least we did until it stopped running. Do you think you'll be able to fix it so we can go home and try to save what's left of our planet?"

Juila touched his arm in sympathy and replied, "I don't know, Ozias, but I promise to do my best. Okay?"

His throat choked up with emotion, so he merely nodded his agreement and then began walking faster to get to the grow room. He believed this young woman would be able to help them. He was going to do everything he could to help her succeed.

CHAPTER 20

Dr. Gascon waited for his next appointment to arrive in his office. This was not going to be a typical appointment as this man was not seeking treatment, rather he was seeking payment. The door opened, and the young, thin man entered the room.

It was pretty obvious from his medical experience that this person was used to taking drugs, probably methamphetamines based on the lesions on his skin. If he could have avoided this meeting, he would have; however, the Creedmoor Psychiatric Center was used to seeing all types so he would be less recognizable here than anywhere else. Mr. Smith sat down in the chair across from him and promptly began to fidget.

"I want to know if you were successful in getting into the estate. Also, tell me what you found out," Dr. Gascon asked without preamble. There was no point in making small-talk with this man as he was not going to need any further association with him. He had been told his name was Mr. Smith which he knew to be false and yet satisfied him.

Mr. Smith crossed his ankle over his knee and began to shake his foot uncontrollably. He looked around the office and saw all of the awards hanging on the wall and the fancy desk. Thinking about how much money this doctor was worth made him wish he had taken more time in the other guy's house.

"I don't have all day, Mr. Smith," Dr. Gascon spoke curtly.

"Yeah, I got in. It was easy walking into the gated driveway once the gardeners left. I walked around the perimeter of the property to make sure nobody was home. The house wasn't even locked, and I came in through the back patio doors. That guy must be really rich to have a pad like that one."

"Of course he's rich! I want to find out how he's making all of his money! What did you find out? Get to the details already!"

"I tore the whole house apart. I couldn't find any records of any cult dealings as you suggested I might find. They didn't even have any loose change or jewelry sitting around. I even checked both of the garages for any safes or hidden caches. One garage was completely empty, and the other one was full of vehicles. I'm telling you, I was thorough, and they do not have any records within the house."

"So you're telling me you have nothing to report," Dr. Gascon said in disgust.

"I'm telling you there is nothing in that house to show they are doing anything illegal. There weren't even any people living there except the parents and the two children. There's nothing more to tell you," he said with a firm nod. "I've done your job now where's my payment?"

"I paid you to get me answers," he complained even as he opened his desk drawer and pulled out a thick, white envelope. He negligently tossed it onto the desk in front of Mr. Smith. "There's your money! I don't ever want to see you again. Do you understand what I'm saying to you? Never again will you try to make contact with me."

Mr. Smith uncrossed his leg and stood up. He picked up the envelope and weighed it in his hand to make sure it felt heavy enough to be the agreed price for the job.

"It was a pleasure doing business with you," Mr. Smith grinned as he pushed the envelope into the back pocket of his blue jeans. He swaggered out of the office wishing he could have figured out a way to get a second job from the wealthy doctor.

As soon as the door shut, Dr. Gascon pounded the top of his desk with his fist. That ploy had been a colossal waste of time and money. He still had one more ace up his sleeve. He called his secretary and informed her he was ready for his next appointment.

The private investigator entered the room and sat down in the same chair Mr. Smith had vacated. He put a briefcase down on the chair next to him and flipped the side locks open to open it up. He withdrew a thick manila envelope and put it on the desk for Dr. Gascon. He knew better than even to try to have a conversation with the doctor, so he remained silent while he waited for his client to review the reports and pictures.

Dr. Gascon pulled the envelope into his lap and pulled the thick stack of papers out. He skimmed the report and frowned at several of the entries. Next, he flipped through each of the pictures showing him who had come and gone from the Stel house. The more he looked, the angrier he became because it was obvious someone had messed up.

"How come you don't have any record of Neal coming to the house and yet, here," he flipped through the pictures until he found the one he wanted and poked his finger down on it hard, "clearly show him leaving the house with his mother?"

"He had to have been hiding in a vehicle because there is no error in the report. This is not the first time there have been people coming or going who were not reported. There has been someone on active duty outside their property ever since you have hired my firm. They are the best investigators, and they don't miss details. There is definitely something strange going on in that house, but I can't tell you what it is."

"Is there another entry point to the property? A back gate? Anything?" Dr. Gascon asked as he tried to make sense of the inconsistencies.

"No, there is only one point of ingress or egress."

"I want you to keep on this case. I also have another case for you, if you have enough men to spare."

"Absolutely, Dr. Gascon. What else would you like us to do for you?"

"I'd like to get copies of all of Riccan Stel's financial records. I'd also like you to put a tail on Nealand Taivas, Jr. so you can tell me the name of the doctor he's seeing for treatment."

"No problem. We can begin on both of those things right away. Would you like daily updates on Nealand as well?"

"Yes. How long for the financials?"

"I can have those for you within seven days. I could do it faster, but I want to make sure we leave no stone unturned."

"Good enough. That will be all. I'll expect to hear from you tomorrow then."

The private investigator nodded and turned to shut his briefcase. He picked it up at the same time he rose from his chair. With a nod of his head in Dr. Gascon's direction, he turned and left the room.

Dr. Gascon felt another stab of anger as he realized Amanda had thwarted him once again. He had been sure the pictures would show her bringing Neal to her house. On the contrary, it left him with yet another mystery surrounding their house. He did not like the idea of being outsmarted by a young girl, and he was going to find a way to take her and her husband down.

Sofia did not know how to explain it, but she felt the overwhelming need to drive over to Juila's house. Without second guessing her instinct, she grabbed her keys and headed out to her car. The drive only took about ten minutes, but she became increasingly agitated the closer she came to the estate.

She pulled into the driveway and was grateful for the gate recognizing her car as it swung open silently. Driving faster than normal, she parked her car next to Behn's. She wondered what he was still doing here so late even as she got out of the vehicle and went to knock on the front door.

Nobody answered, so she knocked again louder. She wondered if everybody had gone around to the backyard by the pool, so she tried the doorknob and found it to be unlocked. She poked her head into the house and saw everyone sitting silently on the couches in the living room across from the front door.

"Hey," she called out as she closed the door behind her. "Is something wrong?" She walked through the foyer and became aware of the stranger in the room.

"Oh, Sofia, now isn't a good time," Amanda began to say.

"Is there something wrong with Juila? I had the strangest feeling she needed my help, so I came over. Is there something I can do? Is she in trouble? Where is she?"

Rasa looked over from where she sat on the couch with her hands on Jena's head. "If she felt something then she may be the key we need. Have her come in and sit down."

Amanda leaned over to Rasa and said, "Sofia doesn't know about our family, she can't stay!"

"If you have any other ideas about finding Juila, by all means, send away the messenger."

Amanda's eyes widened at Rasa's attitude. When Rasa had insisted they all return to Earth to help Jena re-link she had agreed immediately, now she was not so sure. She turned and addressed Sofia, "Yes, Sofia. Please come in and tell us what you know."

Sofia wondered if the family was finally going to come clean about their origins and she was both excited and terrified to find out the truth. In any event, Juila needed her help, and she was going to do everything in her power to assist. She sat down next to Jena and grabbed her hand to offer comfort.

Deciding to tell them what she already suspected, she said, "I know you are from Tuala and I know Juila and Jena healed me after I got hit by the car. I also know about Behn, Val, and Jon being from Tuala as well. Please don't keep me out of the loop because I might be able to help."

Stunned silence met Sofia's proclamations. Riccan was the first to recover as he asked, "How did you know there was a problem tonight?"

"I've been noticing something strange ever since Juila healed me. I've been able to see her thoughts even before she says them out loud." She looked over at Jena and said, "I've been able to do it a little with Jena; it's just not as strong as it is with Juila."

Jena perked up and said, "Juila did take the lead on healing Sofia. It is possible there was some transference in our rush to keep her alive."

Rasa nodded confirmation even as she was amazed to hear someone from Earth talk about everything so calmly. "So what did you see in your mind tonight?"

"This may sound crazy, but it seems like she's in a giant space ship," Sofia finished in a rush. Now that she had said it out loud it sounded even lamer than it had in her head.

Amanda frowned even as Riccan's expression lightened with realization. "She might be on to something, guys! It would make sense if she were somehow in space, then she would not have access to elemy to be able to make contact so easily."

"That's great, but how did they end up in space when they were going to and from Tuala in the telepod?" Amanda asked what she believed to be the most obvious question.

Sofia's eyes became huge as she heard their strange discussion. This situation was much worse than she had originally believed. She sat forward and listened avidly to what was going on with Juila.

"I don't know that part, but it would also explain why I could still get a faint signal of the transponder on the telepod. It's not designed to work in space. Luckily the telepod is pressurized and has its own oxygen supply."

"Which won't last forever. How much time do they have?" Amanda asked with growing anxiety.

"With three of them on board, I'd say it would probably last several days. We have time to locate them now that we know where to begin," Riccan jumped up from the couch to go back to his patil to do some research.

"I'm glad he sees hope in this situation," Amanda muttered.

Rasa turned to Amanda and said, "There is hope, Amanda. Trust in Jehoban, and He'll never let you down. Everything happens for a reason; we just have to figure out what the reason is in this situation."

Jena turned her attention back to Rasa and asked, "Do you think you could link Sofia and me together to try to touch Juila's mind? Both of us have an established link, maybe combined we can reach her even if she's so far away."

"I don't know, but I'm willing to try it if Sofia is," Rasa answered as she moved her gaze over to the eyes of a scared girl.

Sofia could feel her heart begin to race even as she nodded her head in agreement. "It's the least I could do after what Juila has already done for me. I'm glad to be able to return the favor. Do whatever you need; I just hope it won't hurt."

Rasa chuckled and said, "No, it won't hurt at all; although, you might feel a strange tingling sensation in your scalp." She put one hand on top of Sofia's head and the other on Jena's. She closed her eyes and began to pull a cord of elemy from the earth to join together with the life-lines of both girls. She mentally braided the powers together and began to search for a common strand between the two girls.

Just as she was about to give up, she found what she was looking for and pushed forward to connect with the spark of light which was Juila. All three of them gasped as they could see and hear everything happening around Juila. They watched as she stopped dead in her tracks and widened her eyes at the renewed contact.

CHAPTER 21

"Are you okay, Juila?" Ozias asked as he saw Juila stumble beside him and stop walking.

Juila shook her head and inwardly smiled in recognition of her sister's touch. What troubled her was she also felt the presence of two other people. She did not have the time to investigate at the moment as she had to pretend nothing had happened.

She could not believe she had not even noticed her connection with her sister had been missing. Since it had returned so forcefully, she realized her sister had been terrorized with the sudden departure. *I'm sorry,* she thought to Jena. *We're in big trouble, sis. The telepod malfunctioned terribly, and we ended up in outer space. When I attempted to make a correction and use the manual controls, it only made it worse. We couldn't see Earth anymore and then we were brought into a large spaceship where we're being held captive by a man named Viceroy Blair who's from a planet named Heliok. I'll tell you more later. I love you!*

They had reached the grow room, and Ozias opened the door

for her and remained outside. As soon as she stepped in, she could smell the musty odor of stale water. She knew the first order of business was to get the aeration going through the water. Nothing would grow in scummy water.

She checked the controls and the small power supply and realized one of the brackets had come loose on the small crystal powering the system. Juila was able to hand-tighten the bracket until she felt the small vibration of tuning flow through the crystal. The system began to move the water in the troughs again.

Next, Juila checked on the fish in the tank. There were several dead ones floating on the surface. Even though they felt repulsive in her hand, she knew they could not remain in the tank, or they would kill the other fish as they rotted. She pulled them out and dumped them in a compost bucket she found under one of the troughs.

The aeration was running in the large fish tank as well, and she looked around for fish food. She wondered if anyone had thought to feed them as she finally located the pellets in a cupboard to the left of the tank. By the way the fish sluggishly rose to the surface, she imagined they had all been near death. Juila threw in another handful before setting the container down on the counter.

She looked through every drawer and cabinet trying to track down the seed supply. They still had a rather large selection, yet most of them would require more than three days to mature. She set about seeding as many containers as she could find with lettuce, kale, green beans, tomatoes, beets, and corn. Much of it would take too long to mature, but they had to start somewhere. The lettuce would be large enough to harvest in only a week since she had found the booster fertilizer in with everything else.

When she had the last tray floating in the water, she straightened up her back and groaned with the cramped muscles protesting the new position. She rubbed the sore area and looked around the room to see the amazing progress she had achieved in such a short amount of time. Checking one last time in the fish tank, she removed another two dead fish which had floated to the surface.

With a sigh of relief at a job well done, she leaned against the cabinet to ease the tension in her body. Using the time alone, she again could feel her sister's link. Instead of it being effortless like when they were at home, this connection required concentration and focus to keep it open.

Why does the link feel different, Jena?

Because we're also linked with Rasa and Sofia.

Sofia? What's going on there?

She knows about all of us. She can tell you all about it when you get home. Do you know the coordinates of where you are?

Not exactly. The first malfunction had us exactly over our house in Florida except the Z coordinate took us out fifty thousand miles into space. I think my second attempt doubled the distance away from Earth. That's the best I can do since I'm not able to get back to the telepod until Viceroy Blair gives me permission.

Are you in immediate danger?

I don't think so. They are almost out of food, so I think the situation might change drastically in the next couple of days. I'm hoping we won't still be around to witness it.

What happened with the telepod?

Again, I'll have to try to figure it out when I regain access to the telepod. We had a hard landing in Roanoke so something might have come loose with the bracketry of the crystal drive.

Please try to be careful, Juila. I don't know what I'd do if I lost you. Losing the connection was heart-wrenching enough.

Believe me; I'm going to be extra careful around this crew. I think my knowledge of aquaponics will keep them from doing me any harm. I just hope Val and Jon will have the same safety. They've separated us, so I don't know how they're faring in this. Val was pretty shaken up with the misadventure.

Okay, we're going to let you go since I can feel your power's being taxed just by having this conversation. We'll keep checking in, but we won't try to talk unless you need something. I love you!

I love you, too. I'm glad you're here with me, it's really a comfort.

Juila pushed herself away from the cabinet and walked through the grow room to get to the exit. She opened the door expecting to see Ozias waiting for her and rocked back on her heels when a different man leered back at her. "What happened to the other guy?" she asked stupidly.

"He's on break. Follow me," the older man said gruffly.

Juila would have taken longer if she had known she would be faced with another guard. Her palms began to sweat with nerves as he began taking her down a different hallway than the one she had been in before. "Where are we going?"

The guard did not even move his eyes in her direction as he continued to ignore her as he kept his pace brisk. He stopped abruptly and turned to the left, where he opened a door, waited for Juila to enter, and then shut it immediately behind her.

"You were gone for several hours. I hope you were successful in the grow room?" Viceroy Blair asked even though he never turned around to see her.

Juila could see he was typing on a keyboard to a blue backlit screen. She imagined it was a sort of computer even though she had never seen one quite like it. "Yes, I believe you'll have quite a bit of food in the next week or so. I used the booster, but even I can't make it grow faster than a week. I'm sorry."

Viceroy turned abruptly in his chair and stared at her. "You're sorry? For what? Getting us back online for food? You've done more than any of my team could do and you've asked nothing in return."

"That's not true, I've asked for assistance in getting us back to Earth. Are you still going to honor our deal?"

"As much as I can. I have other concerns more pressing at this time. Feel free to lie down in the bed over there; you'll be spending the night in here with myself."

"I'd like to go back to be with my friends," Juila said promptly, trying to keep her voice calm in the face of this new, and possibly dangerous, situation.

"No," he answered as he turned his back on her again as he went back to typing.

Juila could not understand the need to keep them separated. She really wished she could check up on them to make sure they were okay. She did not have a good feeling about this at all. "Can I at least go and check on the mechanics of my telepod?"

"No. Please be quiet and let me work on this problem."

"Is it something I might be able to help with?"

"NO!" he shouted and then in a calmer voice he continued, "Please go lie down and try to be quiet."

Juila moved slowly to the bed and sank down onto the edge. She definitely did not want to fall asleep, so she remained sitting with her mind working furiously on how to get out of this situation.

A MAN GRABBED her arm and forcibly hauled her away from her brother. She was moved into another room, and the door slammed shut even before she could regain her footing. There were voices arguing in the hallway and Valentina moved across the room to get as far away from them as possible.

The door opened again, and a man stepped in and leaned on the door as he closed it behind him. He moved forward slowly as if he were stalking his prey. His eyes roamed over Valentina's body with his intentions clear in his eyes.

"Who're you? Where's my brother? Where's Juila?" Valentina kept asking questions as she tried to think of any way to distract him from his obvious intentions.

"My name's Grobin. And what's your name, sweet thing?" he purred as he stopped right in front of her.

Valentina's eyes widened as she recognized the name and then looked closer to see it was the same man she remembered as the leader of the Roanoke Colony. "What're you doing here?"

"You haven't answered my question, sweet girl. What's your name?"

"Valentina," she answered. She would have picked another name except she did not know if her brother had already told them. The last thing she wanted was for her brother or friend to be hurt because she lied about her name.

"Valentina, hmm," he practically purred as he stroked her cheek with the back of his index finger. "I almost married a girl named Valentina. She was a bit young for me, but you, you're just the right age for me. Why don't you give me a little sugar, sweet thing?" He moved closer until his mouth almost brushed against her lips.

She worked up her nerve and spit into his face as she buckled her knees to not be face-to-face with him.

Grobin jerked backward as though she had slapped him and his rage was instantaneous. He dropped down on his knees and grabbed both of her shoulders, slamming her back up against the wall. "You want to play it that way, huh? You like it rough?" He used the back of his hand to wipe away her spittle from his face.

"Touch me, and I'll scream!" Valentina spoke through clenched jaws.

"I don't mind screaming, feel free; nobody'll come to your rescue." He let go of her entirely and began unbuttoning his pants.

Grobin's prediction proved correct. Valentina had screamed the entire time he ripped off her pants, pinned her to the floor, and took her body violently. The only good thing about the entire encounter was that it was mercifully short. Grobin finished swiftly and then left the room without a backward glance.

Valentina could hear his laughter and then his whistling as he moved down the hall. Frozen with fear, she could not even move enough to pull on her pants to cover herself. Her body started shaking as shock began to take over. Hearing a loud moaning cry, she suddenly realized it was her own voice. Her hands flew to her mouth to stifle the horrible sound as her mind began to register what had just happened to her.

She rolled onto her side, curling up into the fetal position as tears of rage and fear burned in her eyes. She kept both of her hands covering her mouth as her sobs ran into one another. Fear of hyperventilating overcame her as she struggled to breathe.

As if she were waking from a horrible nightmare, Valentina opened her eyes and slowly sat up. She pulled her pants over to her, fumbling in her attempt to put her feet into the legs holes. Her hands were shaking so badly she had to stop for a few seconds before she could continue. She managed to put her feet all the way through, and she bunched the fabric up by her knees.

With a hand on the wall for support, she managed to lever herself up from the floor and then pull her pants up the rest of the way. There was no way she could tell her brother what had happened if she planned on both of them leaving the ship alive. She had to protect her brother from ever finding out.

Jena repeated the details she had learned from Juila to everyone in the room. She saw varying expressions between concern and hope. Their mother was anxious, whereas their father became excited to have a clue with which to work. Behn feared for both of his siblings since he had no idea what had been done to them because Juila had been separated from them. Rasa and Sofia had both shared in the experience with Juila so they had already processed the conversation and felt more confident because of Juila's certainty that she could turn their situation around to their good.

Riccan returned to his office to look up information on his patil based on the new names and places Juila had reported. He also wanted to try and triangulate their last known location with the newest coordinates. If he could get close enough, he could use Amanda's telepod to rescue them.

Amanda looked at the clock on the microwave and asked Behn, "Should you go home and tell your parents that Jon and Val are staying over tonight?"

"Probably, but I don't want to miss out on any updates," he replied with a shrug. He had promised his sister he would go home if they stayed out late and cover for them. It almost seemed as though she had known they would encounter a problem. He had to let go of that line of thinking since he was clearly reading more into an innocent comment than it deserved.

"We can call and let you know if we find out anything," Amanda offered. She understood his fear since she felt the same thing because Juila was also involved. If she were in his shoes, she would probably want to stay the night as well.

"While we're waiting, can anyone share with me why you all are here?" Sofia asked.

Rasa sat back on the couch with a grin on her face. She did not envy anyone in the room the answer to that question. She looked at Amanda to see what she might reply.

"It's a very long story, Sofia. Seeing as we have some time on our hands while we're waiting for an update, I guess we can tell you. My husband's maternal line is completely from Tuala. His grandfather is originally from Roswell, New Mexico. Like his own father, he has spent half his lifetime in both places. It's a similar situation for our daughters since I'm from here in Florida."

Sofia tipped her head as she thought of something to ask and wondered if it would be impertinent for her to voice it. "Can I ask you something...kind of personal?"

"Sure," Amanda answered, thinking she already knew what it was going to be.

"How is it you're so young with the girls being sixteen. You don't seem much older yourself than they are." She glanced swiftly at Amanda before returning her gaze down to her hands in her lap.

"That's a fair question, Sofia. I knew I'd have to answer it at some point. The fact of the matter is there was time-travel involved. When I was sent to Tuala by accident, I was also transported back in time several years. Likewise, my transfer back to Earth was not achieved through a sanctioned Gate, so the timing was also messed up. Needless to say, I'm technically only ten years older than my girls, which would be confusing for anybody." Amanda had to chuckle at how ridiculous it actually sounded when she said it out loud.

"It must be hard," Sofia began.

"It was at first. I was expecting them to be eight or nine when I went searching for them. When I found out they were almost sixteen, I wasn't sure what to make of it. Mostly I was sad for all of the missed time."

"We had a good life, Mom. We visited you in your dreams, that was a gift to us from Jehoban," Jena said to her mom. She did not want her to feel as though she had failed them in any way.

"I know, it's still sad though. When you have children of your own, you'll know what I'm talking about."

Sofia turned to Behn and said, "Jon told me what you said to him about your family. Is it true? Were you transported back in time as well?"

"Yes. Our mother did the best she could when she sent us away. She had no idea we'd be sent back eight years. For her, it's only been just over a year since it happened. I'm sure she's had to face the same feelings of loss at how old we've gotten without her knowing." Behn nodded his understanding as he looked over to Amanda.

"Do you all have healing powers? What else can you do?" Sofia asked. She knew she had been changed by the healing and wondered if she also had powers of her own.

"Healing's an advanced skill, and not everyone wants to learn it. We use elemental energy through the help of our birth crystal so we can do almost anything imaginable. You would consider it to be almost like magic," Jena replied.

"You mentioned something about transference when Juila healed me. Does this mean I now have some powers as well? After all, I've been able to read both yours and Juila's minds. And now I've helped you link minds with Juila even though she's thousands of miles away. Can I learn to do the things you know?"

"I'm really not sure, Sofia. What happened with you is not common practice. Usually, when we heal someone, he or she is also from Tuala, so this doesn't happen. Only time will tell what you are capable of doing now that you've learned to access that part of your brain."

"I'd like it if you could help me learn as much as I can. I think it would be cool to be able to heal people. Imagine what would happen if everyone from Earth learned how to do the things you're able to do!"

Rasa spoke up and said, "There's nothing genetically different between the Earth's people and the Tualans. We've often wondered and studied why the people here are unable to achieve the same things as we do so easily. It's always been believed the birth crystal made the difference, but maybe we were wrong. Maybe it's as simple as unlocking the right part of the brain."

"When you talk about birth crystals, do you mean the pendants all of you wear around your necks? I've seen them before, but I never realized they had any real significance. Most of the time I don't even notice them. In fact, I've never seen one on Mr. Stel or Mrs. Stel." She looked over at Amanda.

"We both have them, yet it's not required for us to wear them to be able to use them. As for the kids, they are unable to remove them until after they turn eighteen. The crystals give them protection from harm while they are young."

"That's good to know. At least we can take comfort in Juila, Valentina, and Jon each being protected then, huh?"

"I don't know," Rasa said slowly. "Since they are so far away from the Earth's energy, I doubt they have access to the power or its protection. Juila is skilled enough that she could have translated herself as well as Val and Jon back to Earth if she had been able. I think she feels just as crippled as if she had been born on Earth."

"That was the impression I had from her," Jena agreed. "I think your assumption is correct."

"That sucks," Sofia said in the silence that followed Jena's statement.

"I'd like to try something with you, Sofia. Would you mind?" Rasa asked.

"What are you thinking?" Jena asked before Sofia could reply.

"Sofia brought up a good point about learning to access the elemy. If I'm able to help her learn how it works, she might be the perfect amplifier for keeping in contact with Juila."

Before Jena could interrupt again, Sofia spoke, "I'll agree to anything which might help Juila."

CHAPTER 23

"Okay," Rasa said as she moved over on the couch, so she was sitting next to Sofia. "I'm going to put my hands on your head as I did before, but this time I want you to follow my movements inside your head. You need to know where to go in order to access the elemy."

"What's elemy?" Sofia asked uncertainly.

"It's a Tualan term shortening the actual words of elemental energy. You see all of the earth is surrounded by rivers of energy. Most of the energy is underground, and a little of it leaks into the air which causes magnetic variations above ground in places like the Bermuda Triangle and the Oregon Vortex. In any event, as children, we learn to tap into this resource and use it to do our bidding. Pay attention so you'll learn the path," she advised as she rested her hand on Sofia's head and they both closed their eyes to better focus on the task.

"I feel a tingling sensation, is that you, Rasa?"

"Yes, that's a positive sign that you can feel my energy. Focus your inner mind on following where I'm leading you. Good, you're

152

doing it very well, Sofia. Now we're going to go down your body, following your veins until we reach the ground. Then we're going to keep going down until we feel the flow of energy in the earth. Tell me what you feel."

"It's very strange, almost like I have electricity running through me. What do all of the colors mean?"

"You see colors?" Rasa asked as she opened her eyes and frowned with concern at Jena. "Have you ever heard about that anomaly, Jena?"

"No, but it might be the difference for which we've been looking." Jena wished she could be a part of this exercise so she could experience what Rasa was seeing. She felt she could be so much more helpful if she had first-hand knowledge. She had to let Rasa continue as she was her senior in all matters related to crystal skills; after all, Rasa had been her own teacher.

"Tell me about the colors," Rasa instructed.

"There is every color of the rainbow including white and black. There are even some colors which I've never seen before. What do I do with them?"

Rasa pulled a few strands of the elemy forward and asked, "What does this look like to you?"

"It's mostly white with a little bit of light blue mixed in."

"Okay," Rasa said, "Can you use your mind to hold this where I leave it?" Sofia's explanation of the colors led her another realization; the elemy's colors corresponded with the birth crystal colors. Her own birth crystal was mostly clear with two stones of the lightest blue. She wished she could see the colors for herself to verify her new theory. The next time she met with Jehoban she was going to ask Him about what Sofia had pointed out and see if it were true.

Sofia began to feel beads of sweat form in her hairline as she struggled to try to do as Rasa asked. Holding the elemy was harder than she had imagined it would be and yet she was doing it. She imagined over time, and with a lot of practice, this would get a lot easier. She hoped this would be the start of many lessons.

Rasa praised her and told her to release the strands. "Now I want you to use your mental power to pick up strands of your own. Only choose the ones which feel like they belong to you."

Sofia concentrated on the rainbow of energy swirling beneath her and felt most drawn to the yellow colors. She focused her attention on them, and they seemed to leap toward her of their own volition. This was much easier than holding the white and blue strands. "I'm doing it!" Her enthusiasm caused a break in her concentration and the elemy slipped away from her and melted back into the flow around them.

"I think that's enough for now, Sofia. You may not realize it right now, but this is a very tiring exercise even for a Tualan. I don't know how this will affect you. Follow me back to your core, so you know what that feels like as well," Rasa showed her the path to take for future lessons and then withdrew her power entirely.

She brought her hand away from Sofia's head and then opened her eyes to check on the young girl's color. Even though she had begun to sweat, her breathing and color were both good which meant it had not taken too much out of her. They would definitely have to keep training together to see how far Sofia's skills could be taken.

"Well? What happened? Did it work?" Amanda asked.

Sofia looked at her strangely since they had already talked about it working.

Rasa smiled conspiratorially at her and said, "We never spoke out loud, Sofia, everything was in your mind alone."

"Really? That's so cool. To me, it sounded just exactly like your voice, so I assumed it was said out loud." She looked over to Jena and said, "I can't believe you do this every day!"

Rasa spoke to Jena, "If you want to continue to practice with her, I'll make sure you won't get in trouble for it."

Jena nodded enthusiastically. She still had a hard time believing her cousin was the successor to an Elder. Now her hopes and dreams of becoming one herself did not seem so far-fetched. When Juila got home, she could not wait to let her know about this latest turn of events on Tuala. She sobered instantly as she realized Juila might never make it home alive. She shut her eyes and took a deep breath as she shook her head and refused to believe in such a negative outcome of this problem.

"What is it, Jena?" Rasa asked. She had been watching the girl intently and felt like she was holding something back.

"I had a dream about this a long time ago," Jena confessed.

"About what exactly?" Amanda asked for clarification.

"About Juila being gone. She made me promise not to say anything about it for fear it would prevent you and Dad from ever letting her fly alone."

"Tell me exactly what happened in your dream, Jena," Amanda spoke slowly as her fear began to rise into her throat and made her feel as though she were suffocating.

"In my dream, she flew away and never came home. I felt lost and confused because our link was broken."

"What happened next?" Rasa asked.

"I don't know because I woke up then. I was terrified, and I ran into Juila's room and crawled in bed with her. As soon as I woke up, I could feel our link, so I knew it was just a dream. I've had the same dream at least a dozen times over the years."

"It sounds more like it was a premonition. We just need to make sure the outcome is the same as when you wake up, and everything is fine again, now don't we?" Rasa asked. She put her hand on Jena's arm to comfort her.

"I like the way you think about it, Rasa. I'd hate to have to live with the alternative," Jena replied.

Amanda did not like that this was the first time she was hearing about the reoccurring dream. She believed her daughters knew they could come to her with anything. Now she realized there was still a separation between them and it made her wonder if there were more they were keeping from her.

The doorbell rang, and everyone in the room jumped. Amanda recovered first and asked, "Who do you think it is?" She did not want to interrupt Riccan in the office, yet she had no desire to answer the door herself.

Behn stood up and said, "I'll check." He strode across the foyer and then flung the door open. His eyes lit up in surprise as he said, "Hey, Luke! What are you doing here?"

"I'm taking Jena out to the movies. Is she ready?" He looked over Behn's shoulder and spotted Jena sitting on the couch. She looked terribly unhappy, and he became instantly alert. "What's wrong, Behn?"

"I'm not sure it's my place to say anything..." he began.

Amanda rescued Behn from having to speak when she walked up beside him. "Tonight might not be such a good night for the movies, Luke. I'm sorry we forgot to call you, and you wasted a trip out here."

"I'd like to see Jena if that'd be alright. She doesn't look very happy."

Amanda looked back at her daughter and could see the same thing Luke must have. She shrugged and said, "Come on in. I don't think Jena will want to visit very long."

"That's fine," he assured her. He stepped into the house and kept his eyes on Jena as he made his way to her.

Behn hurriedly shut the door and grabbed Amanda's arm, "Why did you let him come in?"

"We couldn't very well slam the door in his face. Besides, he'd already seen Jena and knew something was wrong."

Luke sat down next to Jena on the couch and asked, "What's wrong?"

"It's Juila, Luke, there's been an accident of sorts," Jena replied as she hastily tried to come up with a story which would satisfy Luke while not revealing the actual truth. "She took Val and Jon flying, and the aircraft malfunctioned. We're not sure where they are, and I'm really worried for them."

Luke drew her into his arms and hugged her. He was stunned at the news and wondered why Behn was still so calm considering both of his siblings were involved in this. He saw Sofia for the first time as well as another woman he did not recognize. Pulling her back so he could look into her face he said, "I'll keep good thoughts for them to come home safely. Do you want me to stay or go?" He really hoped she would want him to stay, but she began to shake her head.

"I'm sorry, Luke. I don't have the energy right now. I'll call you when we find out anything," Jena hated to send him away. It would be so wonderful to tell him everything and be able to lean on his shoulder for support. She realized this would always be a problem between them if she were to continue to date him and possibly get even more serious. It gave her serious pause in continuing a relationship with him when she was almost positive she would be returning to Tuala once they were done with high school.

He stood up to leave and was pleased when Jena stood as well. They held hands on their way to the door where they stopped before opening it. He turned to her and put his hands on her cheeks as he stared into her eyes. "I know everything will turn out fine. You'll see."

Jena teared up at his proclamation. She wanted to believe he had the answer because she desperately needed her sister to return safely. "Thank you, Luke. It means a lot to hear you say it. I'm sorry you wasted a trip out here. I should have called to cancel, but I completely forgot all about it once I found out about Juila."

"Hey, you don't have to apologize. I completely understand, and I don't consider it a waste any time I get to see you. I'll talk to you soon, okay?" He leaned forward and kissed her lips lightly even as they trembled with emotion.

Jena was flustered since her family and friends were watching from the other room. She pulled back and promptly opened the door. "Drive carefully," she cautioned as Luke stepped outside to leave.

"Always," he jauntily replied as he got into his car.

Jena shut the door and leaned her back against it. She saw the way Rasa was looking at her and knew she was going to have to explain the situation. This would be the first person in Tuala for her to share with, she hoped it would go well. She looked at the floor on her return to the living room.

"What's going on with him, Jena?" Rasa asked curiously.

"Luke is my boyfriend," she answered simply.

Amanda chimed in, "We're working on dissolving Jena's betrothal with Willian. There have been extenuating circumstances for us to go through with it even though it's considered taboo."

Rasa raised her eyebrows at Amanda's statement. Things must have gone terribly wrong for it to have come to this. She knew Willian was here in town somewhere trying to work things out. She could only guess he had yet to make contact or else this discussion would have been very different. "Are you sure there's no way to reconcile?"

Jena shook her head sadly. "I don't see how. We have never gotten along very well, even though I tried really hard. He's just very possessive and domineering. Juila says he's jealous of my skills, so it makes him lash out at me. I don't know. I'll just be glad when it's all over and settled."

Sofia looked over at Behn and shared baffled expressions. This was a serious conversation which made very little sense. If Jena were in another relationship in Tuala, they were worried for their friend Luke and how this might affect him in the future. There was something about the other boy's name which bothered her, yet she could not place what it was at the moment. If she stopped trying to think about it, she knew her mind would connect the dots and let her know later.

CHAPTER 24

Juila unintentionally fell asleep sitting up while leaning against the wall. When she woke up her neck was stiff, and she had no idea how much time had passed. Immediately she searched for the mental link with her sister and found the spark of it with a sigh of relief. Knowing her sister was only a thought away gave her the courage to look around the room and see what had happened with Viceroy Blair.

She turned to find him curled up on top of the bed, fully clothed. She felt some amount of relief to know he had no sexual intentions where she was concerned. It made her feel a bit more relieved even though she still desperately worried about the well-being of Jon and Valentina. There did not seem to be any good reason to keep them separated.

Viceroy was still deeply asleep since she could hear his rhythmic breathing. She edged herself off of the bed, stretched her neck until it cracked, and then crept quietly over to his desk. If she could find out what challenge the Viceroy was facing, she would have a better chance of getting them released faster.

The desk was spectacularly messy, and she had no idea how to activate the computer so that angle was out. She kept her ears attuned to the Viceroy's breathing sounds while her eyes and hand rooted through the paperwork. She discovered what she would consider a captain's log and she read through several of the pages.

She was pretty sure she had misread the entries from several weeks before so she slowed down and reread them...

Had to land in Tuala to acquire provisions. Met with a band of villagers who requested passage back to a place known as Earth. The community leader, named Grobin, promised to provide supplies as well as a sacred object in exchange for my transportation services. The stop lasted longer than usual as Grobin had to gather comestibles. In the end, Grobin as well as twelve men ranging in age from sixteen to seventy-two, and six women ranging in age from eight to thirty-six were brought on board. As we have no idea how to access Earth, we will be transporting them to Heliok where they will be taken to the labor camps until passage can be determined, if ever.

Juila turned the pages to see if any more mention of the Roanoke Colony were made and found nothing more. Her mind was working furiously to figure out what she would do with this new information. It was probably a good thing Valentina and Jon were being kept apart from the general population to keep them safe from discovery.

She was thankful Behn had opted to stay home since he had plans for seriously injuring, if not outright killing, Grobin for his role in breaking up their family. Juila wondered if Grobin were the only unstable person in the group or if the others were innocent bystanders of their leader's misguided notions. Knowing they were going to be taken to another planet to be enslaved made her want to figure out a way to rescue those who wanted a different fate.

She knew how to get them to Earth. She could easily take

several of them with her if they wanted to go. For sure, she would not give transportation to Grobin, no matter what he wanted. He had gotten their colony into this mess, and he would have to deal with the consequences of his own actions.

Viceroy Blair shifted on the bed causing Juila to move promptly away from the desk. She sat down on the chair she had used earlier and thought about a new plan of action. There were several children and teenagers who would have to be taken away from this space ship. Not knowing the layout of the vessel or the locations of the other people, made talking to them to find out their end goal much more difficult.

Her father's telepod could carry more passengers than her mother's so she was thankful it was the vehicle she had to work with. Unfortunately, only six people would be able to be harnessed. If it came right down to it, she could probably accommodate a total of fourteen passengers, not enough to take everyone, which disturbed her more than anything.

She jumped with alarm when Viceroy Blair's voice sounded immediately behind her.

"I trust you slept well. You didn't look very comfortable, but it left me lots of room on the bed so who am I to complain." He moved across the room and went to sit down at his desk. He looked up at her and said, "I'd like you to check on the grow room, and then we'll take it from there. There's a guard outside who will escort you."

"I've been thinking," Juila started.

"I thought I made myself clear that I wasn't interested in your ideas. Go to the grow room." He shifted his gaze back to the desk, picked up a pencil, and began writing in the journal she had already read.

Juila began to form a rebuttal when she realized it was not in her best interest to interrupt him from his work. She went to the door, opened it, looked back over her shoulder to see him still writing, and stepped outside. When she saw the guard was once again Ozias, she smiled and said, "Good morning, Ozias. I missed seeing you after I was done in the grow room."

"I would have stayed except I didn't expect you to take quite so long. When dinner time comes, nobody is dumb enough to miss it, even if we are only on rations."

At the talk of food, Juila realized just how hungry she was. She did not even bother to ask about eating when she knew how desperate their situation actually was. "I need to use a bathroom before I start working in the grow room. Is there one nearby?"

"Why didn't you use the one in Viceroy Blair's room?"

"I didn't know there was one. Is there another one nearby?" She could see he was not happy about deviating from his assignment and hoped he would overcome his scruples since she really did have to go pretty urgently.

"Right this way," he said as he changed direction at an intersection.

Juila avidly memorized everything they passed so she could learn the layout of the ship or find any other people. She still did not have a plan for getting back home, but she was going to have to figure it out right away or be a part of a mutiny when the crew discovered there was no more food. She would like to be well away from the ship before it came to a desperate situation. Plus, she reasoned with herself, the Viceroy would benefit from her leaving with most of the hungry mouths to feed.

Deciding to talk to Ozias about the matter she asked, "Do you think Viceroy Blair would allow me to take as many of the passengers back to Earth with me? Since you're so short on food, it would help alleviate the strain of trying to feed everyone. If I could look at my telepod, I might be able to find out what caused the navigational system to malfunction."

"I'm sorry, Juila. I have orders to take you only to the grow room. I'm already deviating enough by taking you to a bathroom. Please don't ask me to do more."

"I don't mean to bring any trouble to you; on the contrary, I'm trying to keep all of you from even more trouble when the food runs out tomorrow. You do know it's that short of a supply, right?"

It took a moment for Ozias to answer her and she knew she had told him something he had not known. "I'll see what I can do. I'm not making any promises. Here's the bathroom. I'll be waiting outside to escort you to the grow room. Please don't dally; I'd rather not have to answer any questions as to why you're in this part of the ship instead of where you're supposed to be."

"I'll hurry," Juila announced brightly. She had planted a seed of doubt and also offered a solution to the problem. If she knew Ozias' type, he would be weighing the options and find her solution to be the best. All she had to do was be patient and hope he would decide to help her.

The bathroom looked like any other she had ever used, so she was unable to glean any new information from the detour. She finished as fast as she could and went to wash her hands. She took several handfuls of water to trick her stomach into thinking it had been fed. She dried off her hands and face and then went back out to the hall for Ozias to lead her to the grow room.

"Thank you," she said as she fell into step with him as they continued on their way.

"You're welcome. I'm afraid you haven't been given much consideration as a guest of the ship. Viceroy Blair is under a lot of pressure to get us back home. It seemed as though this voyage had been doomed from the start as we've had one problem after another."

They reached the aquaponics room, and Ozias opened the door for her.

"Why don't you come in and keep me company while I check everything over?" Juila asked as she stepped into the room. She tried not to sound too desperate to keep him talking.

"I suppose it couldn't hurt," he replied and stepped into the humid room along with her. "It sure smells better in here today."

"Yes, it does. It smells fresh like it should." She moved over to examine the fish tank and asked, "Tell me some of the things which have gone wrong with this trip. How long have you been flying?"

"We left just over a year ago. Things were pretty bad on Heliok then, so I imagine it's gotten worse since we've been gone. We were supposed to be back a long time ago with new recruits as well as a new power system. It looks as though we're going to fail on all aspects at this rate."

"I don't know. Maybe we can work something out if I go back home. I might be able to help out with the main power system if you let me look at it. I'm pretty good with mechanicals, as you can see from this room."

Ozias looked around the room which had been set to rights in a matter of hours. Even the equipment was working again when they had been told it was hopelessly broken. She might be able to help them after all. If not, they were doomed to starve to death as they floated in space. Nobody would come to their rescue from their home planet. They had made plenty of enemies in their travels due to Viceroy Blair's acquisitive nature. They really were running out of options pretty rapidly.

"What else has gone wrong?" Juila asked as Ozias remained silent.

CHAPTER 25

"We've run out of supplies twice. The first time, everything spoiled. There was a plumbing leak which caused water to drip all over the stored supplies, and they grew moldy and unusable. The second time, there was an infestation of bugs which fouled everything, so even the fish refused to eat it. Then the power system on the aquaponics stopped working almost a week ago and then we knew we were in trouble."

"It looks like your starter seeds are all doing well. Look here," she pointed to one of the grow trays floating in the water trough, "there's already a curl of the first two leaves poking out of the top of the pearlite."

"Does it normally happen this fast?" he asked as he leaned forward with fascination at the start of the new plants which meant they would soon have food.

"The trick is to soak the seed in a bath of water and booster before you plant them. If the seeds are viable, then they should begin to sprout the same day." She went down all of the rows to check each pot individually. Of all of the plants, there were only four pots which were not showing some sign of life.

Juila asked, "How far away are we from Heliok?"

"If we were moving at regular speed, it's probably still about two to three weeks away."

"What's happened to your power supply?"

"More bad luck, I suppose. Our original crystal worked fine up until we resupplied the first time. Once we got back into zero gravity, the crystal shattered into a million pieces and killed our only engineer in the process."

"Oh, that's bad. Who did the clean-up?"

"There was a group of the crew who did it together. It took them several days to locate all of the pieces."

"How did you get the second crystal?"

"We got that from one of our newest passengers named Grobin. It wasn't a conventional crystal, but it seemed to work better than the first one, so we didn't mind."

"Viceroy Blair told me it cracked in half. Do you have any idea why it might have done that?"

"Your guess is as good as mine."

An idea struck her, and she asked, "When the crew cleaned up the crystal shards, did they happen to go over the whole area with a microfiber cloth to gather any remaining dust from the explosion?"

"I doubt it. Why?"

"That's probably why the new crystal cracked."

"What?"

"The dust left behind most likely created a resonating frequency which increased in volume the more you demanded energy from the new crystal. The conflicting frequencies probably caused the crystal to crack."

"That makes sense because we were under full power when it happened."

Juila nodded when she heard him explain the circumstances. She could think of two solutions and yet only one in which she would voice out loud. "I could probably redirect the power from the grow tank to the main thrusters to get you moving again."

"Seriously? You know how to do that?"

"I'd have to study the wiring diagram, but I'm sure I could patch it together. The thrusters don't typically take a lot of power to keep them going after the initial startup. I might be able to use one half of the crystal to generate the extra boost to get it started."

Ozias stared at Juila in amazement. On his planet, nobody as young as she was would ever be taught the skills in which she professed knowledge. He wished he could spend more time with her and find out what else she might know.

At that moment Ozias decided to help Juila. He would find a way to get her to her telepod to see if her navigation system could be repaired. He was also going to talk to Viceroy Blair about her idea of rewiring their ship's controls to get them running again.

Juila dropped another handful of food into the fish tank and announced, "I think I'm done here. Everything looks like it's running just as it should, and you should have fresh greens by the end of the week."

Looking at his timepiece, Ozias realized the majority of the crew would be lining up for their morning ration. He could take Juila to her telepod right now and have her back to Viceroy's room before anyone noticed. He opened the door and motioned for Juila to walk in a different direction than she had planned."

"Where're we going?" she asked, slightly alarmed at the change in plans.

"I'm going to let you see your telepod. We'll only have a few minutes, so please be as fast as you can."

Juila's eyes widened in surprise, and she merely nodded her assent. She lengthened her stride to keep up with Ozias as he practically ran to get them to the loading bay. Within minutes they reached the rear of the space ship, and he opened the small door to the massive space beyond.

"I won't be able to turn on the overhead lights, or it will draw attention. Your eyes should adjust by the time you get to your telepod. It's straight ahead about thirty paces. Go, hurry!" He shoved her to move her forward.

Juila stumbled slightly and felt awkward as she moved across the smooth floor without being able to see at all. She counted her steps and held out her hands in front of her so she would not run into anything. On her twenty-seventh pace, her fingers touched the hull of her telepod. She felt a rush of relief at finally being back with her father's aircraft.

She felt down the side of the craft until she reached the palm control on the side to open the door. She sighed with relief as an interior light came on to let her see. With more confidence, she ran to the back of the cabin and kneeled at the panel enclosing the crystal drive. It hurt her fingers to pry the wingnuts loose, but she persevered until the panel was able to be removed. She set it aside and peered into the hole where she found exactly what she expected: one of the brackets holding the main crystal had come completely undone.

Without positive contact on all of the brackets, it would never be able to function properly. She reached into the opening to realign the bracket only to have it break off in her hand. Pulling her hand out with the broken piece, she stared at it dumbly. This was not good, and she was running out of time.

Wracking her brain for a solution, Juila recalled a small pen-torch kept in the emergency bag under the back seat. She dived under the seat and felt around for the foxl-bound bag. Her fingertips found the strap, and she pulled it out as she sat back down on her rear to dig through it. When she found it, she almost cheered in relief.

She placed the bracket back into place and activated the pen torch. The metal heated up until she had to let go and blow on it to cool it down enough to finish. The last thing she needed was to warp the metal until it was useless in performing its function. The repair was definitely not pretty, but she knew it was a solid enough job to take care of the problem until they got home where her father could replace it entirely.

Juila had to fine-tune the contact until it was properly seated against the crystal. She knew her time was up and she shoved the torch back into the bag. She brought the panel back over to cover the crystal drive. After tightening the wingnuts as tight as she could make them, she tossed the bag back under the seat and almost leaped out of the cabin. She palmed the door release and waited the few seconds for the panel to completely close before she turned to head back to where Ozias stood impatiently waiting for her at the outer door.

"Did you find the problem?" he asked as he led them back through the corridors to Viceroy Blair's private chambers.

"Yes, it was a broken bracket on the main drive system," Juila answered. She purposely did not mention that her craft had a crystal on board for fear he would think it could be an alternate power supply for their own space ship. He would be right, but then she would no longer have an escape route to get back home.

"Were you able to fix it?" He could not see how she would be able to fix it if it were broken and yet he could not resist asking.

"Yes, I welded it back together. It should hold until I get home and can get it repaired properly."

Ozias shook his head in wonder at her endless capabilities. She was definitely their best opportunity for making it home alive.

"Here is our stop," he announced as he came to a stop. Wishing he could stay in her company, he opened the door and entered the room with her. "A moment of your time, Viceroy?"

"Yes, Ozias, what is it?" he asked as he looked up from his journal.

"I have seen this woman's work on the grow-room systems, and I think she might be of assistance in getting our main thrusters back online. If I may be so bold, I'd like to tell you my idea." He cast his eyes down and waited for the Viceroy to grant him the opportunity to speak.

"Go ahead," he replied as he moved his fingers into a steeple on the desk and wondered what this man could have possibly come up with. He had never shown any initiative in the past, so this was a new side of him in which he was intrigued.

"Since the crystal is functional in the grow-room, it would be possible to rewire the main thrusters to the same system. While the initial start-up takes extra power, the grow-room crystals have more than enough power to sustain the thrust needed to get us home in a reasonable amount of time."

"And just how would you suggest getting the initial power to start the main engines?" Viceroy Blair taunted him thinking this was the part of the plan which would fall short.

"I think we could use the larger half of the split crystal to provide the power needed."

"You do, do you? Why wouldn't we just move the grow-room crystal into the main power system and save ourselves a lot of time?"

"It would, Viceroy, except for two major problems."

CHAPTER 26

"Yes, please tell me what those problems would be."

"First, the room was not properly cleaned with microfiber which allowed the remaining dust particles to cause enough dissonant resonance to crack the replacement crystal. It would be foolish to take the remaining crystal into that environment."

"And the other reason?" Viceroy could hardly believe this boy knew so much about the systems. He wondered why he had not come forward earlier.

"If we move the crystal now, the crops would be unable to mature, and we would starve to death before we reached home."

"Very good thinking. What made you come to this conclusion so suddenly?"

"I believed the initial report of the grow-room system being permanently inoperable and did not make any investigations of my own. When I went into the room today, I realized the possibilities and have brought it to your attention to see if you would approve of the plan."

"All on your own, huh?" Viceroy shifted his gaze over to Juila who refused to look him in the face. He narrowed his eyes in suspicion yet allowed the deceit to continue. "What would you need to get the system back online?"

"I would need the wiring diagram, Viceroy, and the assistance of Juila who has already proved she is a capable engineer."

"Very capable, I see," he mused in a low tone only for himself. He really had nothing to lose and everything to gain if this were to work. Without saying another word to either of them, he turned in his chair and typed several commands on his computer. After a few minutes, he pressed another couple of keys, and the printer began spitting out several pieces of paper. He picked them up, tapped them square on his desk, and then held them out for Ozias to take. "Take Juila and get started immediately. We don't have any time to waste."

"Yes, Viceroy! Thank you for giving me this opportunity to prove myself," he saluted his captain and turned smartly on his heel. He tucked the papers under his arm and strode across the office to the door. He waited for Juila to leave before him and he quietly closed the door leaving them alone in the hallway. "I'm sorry for taking all of the credit, Juila."

"I don't care. You know the Viceroy better than I do, and even I know he wouldn't give my suggestion any consideration. In fact, I tried talking to him earlier about it, and he sent me out of his room. You did the right thing, Ozias. Now let's get this big tub moving, shall we?"

Juila used the walk to take the opportunity to update her sister on what was happening. *Jena, I was able to get back to the telepod and fix a broken bracket on the crystal drive. Right now, I'm working with one of the crew members to make a patch on their main thrusters to get them moving again.*

I'm hoping to be able to bring ten refugees home with me, so please make some arrangements for them. Many of them will be women and children. I'll let you know when I'm able to get on the move again. I love you!

Once they arrived in the grow-room, Juila took the papers and spread them out on the planting counter. She spent the next hour going over the diagrams and following the lines throughout the structure of the ship. More importantly, she was able to see the rooms and corridors of the ship and memorize them for future use.

They got to work on pulling various panels and accessing the wiring system. Occasionally they left the room to pull panels from the hallways to reroute specific wires to come back to the grow-room. Ozias left her alone for a while when he had to retrieve the late engineer's toolbox. As soon as they had all of the proper tools to reconnect the wires, they ended up in the grow-room, where they made quick work of the job.

"This step's complete, Ozias. Now we need to go get the broken crystal shard to get this thing going. Let's go!" She followed along as Ozias led the way.

She had been amazed at how easy it had been to shift the wires to where they would be most effective. Of course, there were plenty of conveniences which would no longer function until they were back on their home planet. The alternative was to die in space, so she shrugged off any pangs of guilt for butchering their normal systems for the greater good.

They entered the small crystal room, and Juila immediately felt something unexpected. She stared ahead and could not believe what her eyes were showing her. The new crystal drive had been one of the missing samaras. It was clearly broken in half which just about broke Juila's heart.

Ozias went to pick up the shards when Juila yelled out, "Don't touch that, Ozias!"

He jerked his hands away and looked up in alarm. "What's wrong?"

"This's a powerful crystal, and it could have wild residual energy flowing through it. Let me get it, okay?" She pulled her sleeves down to cover the flesh on her hands.

Even through the thin fabric, Juila could feel the power pulsing through the two pieces of crystal. She wondered if it could somehow be repaired. In any event, this samara could not be left behind; she would have to figure out some way to spirit it aboard her telepod when she escaped.

Before they left the small room, Juila urgently asked, "Will you help me get my friends back to the telepod? You know when we get this running, Viceroy may decide he needs me to stay on board until you reach Heliok. If I were to leave and take eleven of the women and children with me, then you would be assured you'd all have enough food to stay alive all the way back home."

"I don't know how I can get that all accomplished in such a short amount of time," he temporized. He realized what she was saying was probably true. It was not fair for her to remain with them after all she had done to save their lives. He would have to repay her somehow. "I'll try," he replied.

"Why don't you begin gathering the women and children into my telepod while I get this crystal set up?" she suggested. She tried to make it seem like an offhanded comment, but it was the only way to make this work.

"Okay. How many extra people can you take with you?"

"Eleven, possibly twelve if a couple of them are small. Use your best judgment and make sure you tell them not to touch anything inside the telepod or else we'll never be able to leave. Tell them it's important to remain quiet and that they are not to bring anything with them or we won't have enough room."

"It sounds like you've put a lot of thought into this," he accused.

"No, it's just common sense," she fired back and then smiled to take the sting out of her words. This man was her only hope of getting off of the ship so she would have to stay on his good side.

He nodded agreement and left her at the door to the grow room. "How much time do you think it'll take you to get that running?"

"Not long, maybe thirty minutes at the most. Will you be able to get everyone, including Jon and Valentina, on board in that time?"

"I guess I'll have to, won't I?" he chuckled at the impossible task to which he had just agreed.

Juila watched him march down the hall on his errand. She turned and let the door shut behind her as she needed to finish her task. Setting the crystal shards on the counter, she pulled out an extra length of wire from the toolbox and spliced it into the existing wire which was hooked up to the aquaponics system.

Her original plan was to have Viceroy Blair use his computer to start the main thrusters. Since she had discovered their power source was the samara, she knew she would be able to perform the duty herself with mind power. By eliminating the step involving the leader of the ship, she would gain precious moments alone to be able to get to her telepod. She hated the idea that her plan was only going to work if Ozias actually got everyone on board.

She used electrical tape to secure the wire to the larger piece of the samara so her flesh would not be in contact with the bare wires. For once, she cursed her efficiency as she noticed only ten minutes had passed. She would have to wait anxiously for another twenty minutes before she could start the engine.

Jena, she thought, *I'm almost ready to put my escape plan into action. Please keep really close with me so I can be sure to end up in the right place this time.*

She was startled out of her thoughts as the door to the grow-room opened and closed swiftly. Without looking behind her, she assumed the person walking across the floor to be Ozias. Her body froze when she heard an unfamiliar voice.

"I'd heard there was another new woman on board. I'm glad to find you alone. I have the same plans for you as I had for your friend," he drawled as he reached out a hand to grab her shoulder to turn her around to face him.

"Touch me at your own risk," she warned.

"Another spitfire, I like that in my women," he said as he grabbed her anyway.

Juila used the power of the samara to charge her own body with electricity. She smiled wickedly as she heard the man scream in pain and remove his hand immediately. She turned to face him and asked, "What's your name? It wouldn't by chance be Grobin, would it?"

"How'd you know?" he stammered.

"I didn't think there'd be too many mentally deranged bastards on this ship," she spoke through clenched teeth. "Just what were you saying about my friend, Valentina?"

He recovered some of his swagger as he recalled the good time he had experienced the evening before. "She's not likely to forget me anytime soon. Ask her how she liked it," he bragged.

Completely unbidden, Juila could feel a rage of energy course through her body. If she had wanted, she could have killed the man where he stood. She smiled instead as she thought of the future in store for him on Heliok and she restrained her desire.

She knew her time was up. This unbalanced man had changed her plan, so it had to be now or never. Keeping her eyes on Grobin, she used the energy drawn by her anger to surge through the wires into the thruster engine. Under her feet, she felt the rumble of the motor coming to life and pulled the wire away from the samara. She taped off the end to prevent an arc shorting out the system.

With both pieces of samara in her bare hands, she made a daring decision. She gathered elemy from the samara itself and translated herself from the grow-room directly into the open space beside the telepod in the cargo bay. The exercise should have been terribly taxing on her strength, but her fear and anger had pumped her full of adrenaline.

Several people had seen her appear from out of nowhere and they fell backward to keep their distance from her. She had neither the time nor the energy to deal with their ignorant beliefs. She turned and walked up the open ramp into her father's telepod. Jon was in the same seat he had used on their previous trip.

After sitting down in the pilot's seat and settling the samara in her lap, she looked over and saw Valentina was also present. She gave her a weak smile as she began the startup procedures. Never before had she sped through the process as she had just then. She selected the home coordinates and saw them displayed correctly on the glass panel.

"We are leaving in six seconds. If you are not on board already, then you will be left behind!" she announced. She heard shuffling of feet and a small sob before she hit the button to close the side door. As soon as she received the green light letting her know the cabin was secure, she punched the activation button to begin the transfer.

CHAPTER 27

"She's on her way home!" Jena shouted in excitement. Even though they were all tired from waiting for news through the night, Jena felt her energy surge as she jumped up from the couch and ran out to the garage to see the telepod appear. While the transfer took place, she was unable to touch her sister's mind, but it did not keep her from knowing her sister was soon to arrive.

Several more seconds ticked by and Jena began to worry something else had gone wrong with the repair Juila had done to the telepod. She had to keep herself from panicking as she waited still longer. Her father came up behind her and put his hand on her shoulder as he waited with her.

"The telepod signal was getting stronger when I left the office. She should be here any second," he stated in an authoritative tone.

Everyone crowded around the doorway when the telepod popped into the garage exactly where it was supposed to park. The aircraft settled to the floor and powered down. They began crossing the empty bay of the garage when the side door opened to expose the mob of people crowded within the cabin.

Rasa immediately began to identify which occupants might require mental assistance with the change of scenery and possibly the first telepod ride they had ever taken. She noted the expressions on two people in particular who looked about ready to faint with the shock. She stepped up onto the ramp and put her hand out to the first person who needed her help.

As soon as the first woman moved to walk down the ramp, the others began to follow. They were a silent group who looked around them with wide, terror-filled eyes. They huddled together, not knowing where to go or what to do now that they were off of the transport ship.

"Everyone, please step inside so we can eat and find out what your plans are now that you're on Earth," Riccan spoke loud enough for his voice to carry over the entire crowd. "Right this way." He ushered the first woman through the doorway and into the house. He could see the announcement of being on Earth seemed to enliven some of them.

Jena barely noticed the strangers getting out of the telepod since she was only focused on seeing her sister again. Their mental link was strong again, so she knew Juila was still inside the aircraft. *Are you okay?*

I am, but Valentina isn't. I'm afraid something terrible has happened to her.

What happened?

I think she was raped.

Jena could not form a response to her sister's proclamation. She immediately felt sick for their friend and wanted to be able to help her in any way Valentina would let her. *How do you know?*

I had a run-in with Grobin just before we left. He made sure to tell

*me all about what he had done last night with Val. I wanted to kill him,
Jena. I came so close.*

What did you do?

*I translated myself out of the room and into the telepod. We left
immediately after that. I don't know what we should say or do for Val.*

I'll ask Rasa for advice.

Is Rasa here?

*She came to help me relink with you, and she wanted to stay until you
returned.*

Juila unbuckled her seat harness and folded the samara into her
shirt. She then helped Valentina out of her seatbelt as well. She
pulled her friend's arm to get her to stand up and turned her
around to allow her to exit the cabin out the back door. We're
coming out now.

Jena looked around the garage and saw Rasa was just stepping
up to go into the house. She called out, "Rasa! Wait just a moment."
She rushed forward and grabbed her arm as she leaned closer to
her and whispered, "We think Val was raped. Can you please talk
to her before she has to go inside?"

Rasa nodded without speaking as she turned away from the
house and went back across the garage. She rapidly thought about
all of the ways in which she could help Valentina up to and including
mind swiping. She really did not like the most drastic option considering it took the entire memory away and left a blank space which
could cause more damage than the event being removed.

Jon had been relieved to see his sister as they were ushered so
rapidly into the telepod when they were on the spaceship. He
hated how they were separated for the night, and he really wanted
to talk to her. She seemed so closed off to him, and he thought she
was probably anxious to get home. When she came back through
the cabin, he reached out to touch her arm. She pulled away from

him as if in fear, and he frowned with concern as he looked at her face. "What's wrong, Val?"

"Nothing! Go inside, and I'll talk to you in a little bit. Tell Behn I'm going to spend the night here," Valentina said in clipped tones.

"Okay," he answered slowly and glanced over Valentina's shoulder to Juila to see if she had any answers for his sister's strange behavior. He dropped his hand which was still outstretched toward his sister, and he left the cabin. With a final look behind him, he walked across the garage and went into the house.

Jena fell into step beside him and asked, "Are you okay, Jon?"

"Yes, I'm just really tired and hungry," he answered.

"We'll get you fed right away," she laughed in relief. While she felt terrible for what Valentina had experienced, she was overjoyed to have them all return home. "I'm going to call Luke and let him know you are all back. We told him that you guys were in an airplane accident. He's been worried sick."

Jon looked down at her and began to laugh. "If only he really knew."

"No kidding," Jena agreed and left him in the kitchen while she went upstairs to call Luke from her room. The sooner she got the call done, the faster she could return downstairs to help with all of the new people. The last thing they needed was for Luke to show up unannounced at their house with all of these strangers.

CHAPTER 28

"We're alone now, Val. Can you tell me what happened to you yesterday? Did Grobin do something to you? Did he rape you, Val?" Juila kept asking questions hoping to get some reaction from her other than the blank stare she had acquired. At her last question, Valentina flinched and crossed her arms over her body as if to protect herself from another attack.

Rasa moved forward, refraining from touching her since she had seen the girl's reaction to her brother's touch. "Let's sit down for a moment," she suggested and pointed behind them to the rear seats of the telepod.

Valentina moved woodenly and sat where she was told. She refused to make eye contact with anyone. Her mind kept going over the events of the day before, trying to find a way in which she could have prevented the attack. Surely she could have fought harder, screamed louder, or done something to keep Grobin from violating her body. This was all her fault. She had brought this on herself.

"Val, you're safe now. Grobin is not going to ever hurt you again. He's going to become a slave on Heliok where he can pay penance for what he's done to you. Will you please tell us what happened? I promise it will help." Juila really wished her friend would talk to them. She was on the verge of reading Valentina's mind when she finally spoke.

"I should have stopped him. It was my fault; I should have stopped him." She looked up, but her eyes were not seeing anything in the garage. All she could see was Grobin lying on top of her, his foul breath in her face, his body invading hers. She was frozen with fear, anger, and pain.

"She's suffering from shock," Rasa announced. "We need to get her upstairs and put some blankets on her to warm her up. She's as cold as ice."

"I could translate us to my room. Would you like me to do that?" Juila asked.

Rasa nodded. "I'll make excuses for us, and then I'll meet you there. Which room is it?"

"It's upstairs, first door on the right."

"Okay, give me a few minutes."

Using the extra power from the samara in her shirt, Juila put her hand on Valentina's hand and focused her mind on translating them to her bedroom. Immediately, the power rose to her call, and they shifted instantaneously, so they were seated on her bed. She could not have asked for a better transfer.

She stood up and went to her nightstand where she opened the top drawer and placed the samara inside. She shut the drawer and planned on revisiting the damaged artifact when she was not so urgently needed. Juila immediately turned back to her friend and did what she had promised she would not do: she read Valentina's mind.

The pictures and feelings she received were so vivid that Juila felt as though everything had been done to herself. She could not believe what her friend had endured, nor could she agree with the overlying monologue in Valentina's mind.

"No, Val, it was not your fault! Look at me! Look at me, Val! Listen to what I'm telling you; this was not your fault. That man took advantage of you, and he was easily twice your size. You could never have stopped him once he'd made up his mind to hurt you."

"I could have done something, anything, other than just let him do that to me! Don't you see? I should have hit him over the head, or choked him, or scratched his eyes out. I didn't do any of those things and he…he…" she could not continue as she began sobbing.

Rasa entered the room at that moment and was relieved to see the girl had begun talking. She knew it was important to have her share what happened, even if it were painful. Otherwise, the story she replayed in her mind would paralyze her forever. She nodded for Juila to keep her talking.

"What did he do, Val? Talk me through everything. Start from the beginning."

"One of the guards came and took me to a different room. I thought they wanted to question us separately. I sat down in the only chair in the room and waited. The door opened, and a different man walked in." She looked up at Juila and said, "I thought I recognized him."

"Was it the leader of the Roanoke Colony? Was it Grobin?" Juila asked.

"Yes! That's why he looked familiar. How did you know?"

"I met up with him right before we left. Please keep telling me what happened."

"He said I reminded him of someone he once knew, someone he was going to marry. He was talking about me, Juila. He asked me my name and laughed and said it was the same as the girl he was going to be with. After everything Mom tried to keep us safe from, it wasn't enough. Grobin still took what he wanted anyway. It was all for nothing! All of those years without our mother and he still got what he wanted!"

"Tell me what happened, Val," Juila prompted again. She had already seen everything from her mind, but she needed Valentina to say it out loud.

"He grabbed my shoulders, and I screamed. He told me he liked a feisty woman. I spit in his face and dropped to the floor to get away from him. He pinned me to the ground with his body as he ripped my pants off. I kept screaming even as he unbuttoned his pants. He put his hand around my throat, and I thought I was going to pass out, I wish I would have. I saw black spots in my vision, and still, I screamed.

"He pried my legs apart and pushed himself into me. It seemed like it went on forever as he kept breathing his foul breath into my face. Finally, he laughed and then he got up. As he buttoned his pants, he kept looking at me as if he were trying to fix the scene in his mind and then he left. I'll never forget his chuckling and whistling as he walked down the hall.

"I don't know how long I stayed on the floor. I couldn't stop crying, and then I was gasping for air. After a while, I was able to put my pants back on, but the crying still wouldn't stop. I should have fought more! I should have killed him!"

Rasa spoke up for the first time, "I'd like to link with your mind and body to check you out. Will you let me?"

Valentina left her head down and nodded.

Rasa gathered elemy, touched Valentina's life-line, and followed it up through her body. She healed the small tears caused by the rape as well as the bruises she encountered. What she really wanted to know is if she had contracted any sexually transmitted diseases or, worse, if she were pregnant. She mentally sighed with relief when she found nothing on either account and took the extra precaution to seal her womb to prevent any embryo from attaching in the next few days.

She continued her scan up Valentina's body and healed all of the bruises around her arms and neck. Rasa sent the elemy into her brain to cause soothing energy to calm her mind and help ease the shock from her. The last thing she did was to relax her body and allow her to fall asleep. She pulled her powers away and helped Juila ease Valentina down onto the bed.

"I think she didn't sleep much last night. Rest will be the best medicine right now. Leave the light on so she won't find herself in a strange place in the dark. Then we can go downstairs and check in on all of the people you brought home. I must say, they are an interesting bunch. What made you decide to bring them along?"

"They were refugees wanting to go to Earth. I think their ancestors were from Earth, but I can't be sure of that just yet. I read through the captain's journal and found out he planned on making them all into slaves on his world, and he had very little incentive to find Earth for them. I couldn't take everyone, but I was able to ask for all of the women and children. I wish I could have done more."

"You did the best you could. Come on, let's talk to them and find out what they want to do now that they're here," she whispered as she led the way out of the bedroom.

They walked down the stairs expecting to hear the voices of the guests; however, the room was silent. Juila led the way through the foyer and saw everyone sitting around in the living room and kitchen with plates of food in various stages of being eaten. Juila imagined her father had created the dishes since her mother's skill in the art was unequal to the large task.

Just as she turned toward the kitchen, she gasped and said, "Ozias! What are you doing here?"

"I hope you don't mind. I wanted to see where you were from and how you could have learned so much at such a young age. We don't get opportunities like that on Heliok."

"But what about the refugees? I only had so much room, and you took someone's place? How could you be so selfish?" Juila could feel her anger rising.

"Everyone who wanted to come was already on board. I didn't leave anyone behind, Juila. Don't you see? I would never do something so terrible. Besides, Viceroy Blair would have punished me for lying to him about the plan to restart the thrusters."

"You didn't lie; the thrusters were going when we left."

"They were? I never dreamt it would actually work. Well, that's a relief, at least they will all be able to make it home."

"What about you? What are you going to do about getting home?"

"I want to stay here...with you."

Behn walked over since he could see Juila becoming agitated. He put his arm around her and asked, "Is there a problem here?"

Ozias looked from Behn to Juila and noticed the proprietary way in which he held Juila. He had been mistaken in his ideas regarding Juila. She was obviously involved with this other person. Now he had no idea what his plan would be.

"No, it's fine," Juila said and turned away from Ozias to prevent any kind of scene.

"Where's Valentina?" Behn asked.

"She's asleep in my bed. She was up all night last night, and she was exhausted. Don't you think you and Jon should be heading home now? Your parents must be getting worried about you."

"I called them last night and said Jon and I were spending the night at Luke's house and Val was staying here. It almost sounds like you're trying to get rid of me. What's going on, Juila?"

She chuckled nervously and answered, "Nothing, Behn. We

have a little bit of chaos going on around here unless you hadn't noticed. We need to talk to these people and get everything sorted out. Jon's exhausted, just look at him," she said as she pointed over to where Jon was almost asleep over his plate of food.

"Okay, you have a point!" He laughed and gave her a big hug. "I'm glad everything worked out so well, and you all came home safely. Don't ever do anything like that again!"

"Trust me; I don't plan to!" She returned his hug while pressing a kiss to his neck. She pulled away, playfully pushing him toward his brother. "Take him home now."

Juila breathed a sigh of relief when she finally saw Behn and Jon go out the front door. Her mind reeled from everything which had happened over the last two days. She did not want to have Behn see his sister until she had her emotions under control. Luckily, they had not missed any school which would have been interesting to explain to the Wilsons. Hopefully, they would never find out about any of this adventure.

She turned around and surveyed the people in the house. They were a ragged looking group of women, children and a couple of men. She counted and found there were only nine of them. Her eyes were drawn to one teenaged girl who sat curled in on herself in the corner of the couch. She went over to her and sat down next to her. "My name's Juila. What's your name?"

The girl raised her head enough for her to see Juila and whispered, "Gevena."

"That's a pretty name. How old are you?"

"Sixteen anons."

"So am I," Juila replied excitedly.

Gevena's eyes lit up a bit. She drew her arms around her thin body a little tighter.

"Are you cold? I could get you a blanket."

"I'm fine," she whispered.

"Did you get something to eat?"

"Yes, thank you."

"I'd like to help you and your family. Please let me try."

"I don't have any family here."

Juila frowned a little at this new revelation. She wondered what this girl's story could be if she had no relations among the other refugees. "Do you want to talk in another room where it's more private?"

She nodded and slowly stood up. She followed Juila down the hall and into the library. They sat down in the wing chairs facing one another. She lowered her arms until the book she had was resting in her lap.

Juila wanted to ask her about the book but decided to wait until the girl felt more comfortable. "Were you part of the Roanoke Colony?"

"No. I..." she could not think about how to explain her strange situation. This girl could not possibly understand what she had been through. She glanced around her and saw all of the books and opulence. No, this girl would definitely not understand.

"Where are you from?"

"I lived in Desio with my father."

"Is your father still in Desio? Can we contact him so you can go home?"

"NO!" She looked up in alarm and then realized her outburst was uncalled for and continued on in a more subdued voice, "I don't want to go back to him. He's a drunk."

"I see. Is there anyone else we can contact for you? Any family who you could stay with?"

"No, I don't have anybody other than my father. I won't ever go back to him."

"How did you end up on the space ship?"

Gevena clasped her hands tightly over the book in her lap. She did not want to talk about it, but it seemed this girl would keep asking questions until she knew her whole story. She sighed and began talking, "My father drank a lot, and he liked gambling. He met a man named Politun who was from the Roanoke Colony. The colony had recently started camping outside our village, causing all kinds of problems as they stole food and clothing from our people.

"We don't know why they came, but my father was only interested in his gambling and drinking. Nobody in town would play with him anymore because he couldn't pay what he gambled. Politun was an outsider, and he was willing to play cards with him. For a while, my father was winning. He bought more liquor and got sloppy.

"After losing several nights in a row, my father came home and told me to gather my things. I had no idea what he had done, and I did as he asked. He took me away from our home and gave me to Politun. He took my arm and began dragging me away from the village. I kept crying and asking my father to help me. He turned around and walked back to our house.

"Politun told me to shut up. He said he had won me fair and square in their last card game. I could not believe what he said was true. I called him a liar and told him to let me go home. When we got to his tent in the woods, he shoved me on the ground and told me I was home. He ordered me to make him dinner, so I did it. I figured I'd be able to sneak away when he was sleeping and go home.

"He must have anticipated my plan because he tied my leg to his tent stake that night. After we were done eating he told me to take my clothes off. I refused, and he ripped them off of me. I screamed and screamed knowing someone would come and help me. Nobody seemed to notice. Politun hit my face until my eye swelled shut and my nose was bleeding.

"He told me I was his property and he could do to me whatever he wanted. I had no idea how far he would take this idea until he removed his clothes and pinned me to the ground. I couldn't get away with my leg tied to the tent. I didn't have anywhere to go since my father had betrayed me. I was alone." Her last words came out in a whisper.

For the second time that night, Juila was confronted with a young girl being raped. She wondered what was going on that would make these things happen. An idea came to her that it might be a good idea for Valentina and Gevena to talk to one another. They would be able to understand the pain they had each endured; and they might be able to help each other through this terrible time in their lives.

"I'm sorry all of that happened to you, Gevena. You don't have to go back to Tuala if you don't want to. We can find a family for you here on Earth, and you can start your life over. What do you want to do?" She tried to think of how she could get her and Valentina to talk to one another without betraying either of their confidences; this was a sticky situation.

"I don't want to go back. I have nothing there; nothing and nobody."

"Okay. I'll see what I can do."

Gevena smiled for the first time. Her life just might be okay with this girl's help.

"What is that book you have?" Juila asked.

"I took this from Grobin's things when we were leaving the space ship. I thought it might be important. Maybe it could help you," she said as she picked it up and handed it over to Juila. She was glad to give it to someone else.

"Thank you for trusting me," she replied as she took the book and stood up. "I'm going to give this to my mother and then I'll be right back, okay?"

"Don't let anyone see it, they might get upset," Gevena cautioned.

"I'll be careful," she said as she left the room. She almost ran down the hall and slowed down only when she got near the living room. She looked all around for her mother and could not locate her. Scanning the room, she made eye contact with her father and tipped her head to get him to come over to her.

His curiosity was piqued as he wove his way around the furniture in the living room. "What's going on, Juila? What is that?" he asked as he gestured to the book in her hands.

"The girl, Gevena, who I took into the library, said she took it from Grobin's things before she got onto the telepod. She thinks it might help us figure out what's going on. I was going to give it to Mom, but I can't seem to find her. Do you want it?"

"Sure!"

"Gevena said it shouldn't be seen by any of the people from the Roanoke Colony. Maybe you should take it to your office," she suggested since it was closer to them than any other private place.

"Good idea," he said as he turned her around so they could head in that direction down the hall. In a quieter voice, he said, "I'll put it in one of the secret cubbies until we can have some time to investigate it. What do you think we should do about all of these people?"

"We have enough room here at the house if they share beds. They could stay the night at least and then we can find out more in the morning."

"You're full of good ideas. I think I might place protection wards around our rooms just to be on the safe side. We don't know what these people might do now that they're in a strange place. I'm sure they're worried and scared; that combination drives people to do extreme things."

Juila wished her father were not right with his assumption, but she could see the wisdom in being cautious. She tried unsuccessfully to cover her yawn of exhaustion. She just realized how tired she actually was.

"Your mom, Rasa, and I can take over from here. Why don't you head on up to bed?"

"I'm going to say goodnight to Gevena first. Dad, she's had a bad time recently. She's…I don't know how to put it…delicate?"

"They all seem to be. We'll tread carefully. I'm so grateful you made it home safely!" As they stood in the office, he pulled her into a hug and rubbed the back of her hair to comfort himself that she was actually okay. He had nearly lost her because of his negligence in maintaining his telepod. "I'll check the mechanics on the telepod before work tomorrow."

"Yeah, I had to make a repair weld on the crystal's contact bracket. It's going to have to be replaced. I'm sorry I damaged your telepod, Dad."

He sputtered and said, "You have nothing to be sorry for, I'm the one who should have made sure it was safe to fly. I'm sorry I put you in danger."

"I was the one who crashed it down onto the sand at the Roanoke Colony. I'm pretty sure the impact is what caused the damage to the bracket."

"Maybe we're both to blame then, in any event, I'll check it out later."

CHAPTER 29

School seemed rather mundane after the excitement over the weekend. Sofia cornered Juila and Jena in their first period writing class before the final bell rang. With her back to the classroom, Sofia whispered, "I'm so glad everything worked out so well with you Juila."

"Me, too," Juila agreed wholeheartedly. "It could have gone a lot differently if Ozias hadn't agreed to help us."

"I still can't believe you two didn't tell me the truth!" Sofia accused.

"We're not really at liberty to talk about it, Sofia. Besides, how do we explain the reality of our situation? It's not really very believable; you have to agree," Jena reasoned.

"True, but after you healed me, you could have told me. I already suspected something because of that day anyway."

Juila hugged Sofia and said, "We can't change the past, but I'm glad you know now. I hated having to lie to you and keep secrets. It will be so much easier now that you know everything."

Sofia squealed a little with happiness at being included in their inner circle. The second bell rang, and the students began to take their seats. Since the teacher had yet to arrive, the girls continued to talk.

Jena asked Sofia, "Have you seen Behn, Jon, or Valentina yet?"

"We saw their car in the parking lot, but I have yet to lay eyes on any of them yet. If nothing else we'll be able to get together at lunchtime."

"True," Jena agreed and then had to end their conversation because the teacher had arrived.

After class, they parted company with Sofia. They kept their eyes roaming the faces of the students around them as they made their way to the biology classroom. Again, they were unable to find any of the triplets.

By the time lunch rolled around, Juila was concerned. Usually, Behn walked her to each of her classes, and yet she had not seen him at all. Juila and Jena met up with one another at their locker and they shoved everything inside haphazardly and hurried their way to The Commons.

They spotted Behn first as he was entering the room from another hallway. Rushing against the flow of students, Juila grabbed Behn's arm and said, "Where have you been all morning?"

"I'm sorry; I should have found you earlier."

"What's going on? What's wrong?" Juila demanded.

"There's something wrong with Val, and she won't talk to us about it. She claimed she had a migraine and needed to stay home from school."

"So she's home alone?" Jena asked.

"Yeah, I don't like it much myself."

They got to the lunch line and began filling their trays with food. Jon cut into the line and joined them with a grin at Jena's look of mock sternness. They paid the cashier and made their way over to their regular table where Luke and Sofia were already seated. Jena sat down beside Luke.

"Hi," she said shyly. "I'm sorry about the movies on Saturday night."

"Don't worry about it. You had something more important going on," Luke shrugged.

"Do you think we could reschedule?"

"Of course. I'm not available tonight since my parents invited some friends over and asked me to be there. What about tomorrow night?"

Jena nodded enthusiastically. Feeling as though she had mended the awkwardness between them made her feel much better. She had dreaded thinking about what kinds of questions Luke would have. She was relieved he respected her privacy and did not push for any explanations. Luke was certainly easier to work with than Willian ever had been. This was just one more point in Luke's favor.

Juila nodded in agreement as she read Jena's thoughts on comparing the two boys. She was lost in her own thoughts and missed what Behn had asked her. "What was that?" she asked as she turned her head and looked directly into his eyes.

He leaned closer and whispered, "Do you still have all of the refugees at your house?"

"Yes, I have no idea what's going to happen with them. Our house is big, but there are so many of them that they seem to be everywhere."

Behn chuckled under his breath. "Do you want me to come over after school?"

"You'd better not. I hope you don't mind," Juila answered.

"No, I should probably see how Val is doing anyway. If she'll let me into her room, that is," he spoke with resignation.

"She was really scared, Behn. The moment she discovered we

were in space she freaked out and immediately said we were going to die. I think she really has a bad case of astrophobia. Give her some time to adjust to being safely back on terra firma."

"If you say so," Behn agreed. It was still hard for him to imagine the adventure his two siblings had been on. If he did not know better, he would say it sounded like a bad movie plot, and yet it was their new reality.

THE STEL HOUSE was very chaotic as the refugees began to relax and spread out throughout the rooms and the yard outside. Rasa had agreed to stay and help Amanda work with the people. Riccan used Amanda's telepod to go and get Barla to come over and offer her guidance as well.

Riccan returned to work in order to craft and manufacture a new bracketry system for his own telepod. He realized there was a design flaw which could fail in similar circumstances and he knew there was a way to create a safer option. This was an element of his job which excited him, and he was soon lost in the creation of the new part. Once the new part was tested, he would be able to use the newest version to roll out to other telepods to make them safer as well.

By the time Riccan returned home at the end of the workday, he was surprised to see there were fewer people left at their home. He cornered his wife and asked, "Where did the people go?"

"My mom came over to visit with Barla. They decided to go shopping, and then several of the women wanted to go out and explore Earth with them. I never would've expected that cowed bunch of refugees to have any desire to learn or try new things. The women have amazing resilience. I'm still not so sure about the men and a couple of boys, however, as they're harder to read. How was your day? You look pleased with yourself."

Riccan smiled at her assessment of his mood and nodded. He held up the new part he had created and said, "I've solved the problem with the crystal drive. Never again will we have to worry about what happened to Juila. This new part will revolutionize the crystal drive system as it will be nearly foolproof."

"That's awesome, honey. When are you going to install it?" She hoped it would be soon since she had gotten used to the freedom of having her own transportation to Tuala, and she missed it.

"I was hoping Juila would want to help me out with it. Is she home?"

"Yes, she's upstairs in her room with Gevena. Do you want me to get her?"

"That's okay; I'll do it. I have to go upstairs to change anyway." He leaned down and kissed her cheek and then rushed past her to head to his bedroom. He put the bracket down on the kitchen island and winked at her before he continued on.

Amanda studied the new bracket and wondered how it differed from the old one. She thought it looked almost the same, yet she really had no notion of the intricacies as Riccan did since it was his job and his passion.

"What is that?" Ozias asked Amanda.

She jumped slightly since she had not seen him walk over to her. She looked up and smiled as she said, "This is the replacement for the part which broke in the telepod. Riccan just made it today, and he's going to install it when he comes back downstairs." Amanda could not place why this man tended to make her uncomfortable. He never did or said anything out of line. She wished Riccan would return and rescue her from this man's company.

"Do you think he'd let me watch as he made the repair?"

"I don't see why not," Amanda said with a smile. "Excuse me;

I'm going to go check on a couple of people." She moved away as speedily as she could while still keeping tabs on Ozias to make sure he kept his hands off of the replacement part. She probably should not have left him alone with it, but it was too late now to return.

Riccan hurried to change his clothes and then walked across the hall to knock on Juila's bedroom door. He heard her say to enter, so he went into the room. "Hi everyone. I was wondering if you wanted to help me replace the bracket in the telepod, Juila."

"Sure!" she said excitedly as she jumped off of her bed and met her father at the door. She didn't even bother asking Jena if she wanted to go since she knew her sister could care less about mechanics. "Do you want to come, Gevena?"

"No thanks," she replied shyly. Riccan made her nervous even though he was the nicest man she had ever met.

"Okay, let's go," Juila prompted her dad.

As they walked together, Riccan asked, "How was Val at school today?"

"She didn't go to school. Behn said she had a headache and begged to stay home. I hope she'll decide to go tomorrow. It'll do her good to get back into a normal routine."

"I agree. What were you talking to Gevena about?"

"Rasa asked her to come and live in Manzanit with her. She was wanting to know what we thought about the idea."

"I think it's a perfect solution. She probably wouldn't be happy here on Earth, and her father doesn't deserve to get her back."

"I agree. I'm pretty sure she'll agree; she's just nervous."

"Understandable after everything she's been through," he said as they crossed the foyer. He saw Ozias inspecting his part as they approached and he asked him, "Do you want to come watch as we put that into the telepod?"

"I was hoping you'd let me," Ozias said with a big grin on his face.

Riccan picked up the part and handed it to Juila. He wanted her to familiarize herself with the design so she could envision how it would be installed. It pleased him to have a child who had the same interests in engineering as himself.

Juila's amazement at the simplicity of the design was apparent. She turned the light metal object over in her hands and looked at it from every conceivable angle. "This is really cool, Dad. Why hasn't anyone done it this way before? This is so much better."

"I agree. I guess it's true that necessity breeds invention."

They entered his telepod, and the two of them crouched down at the back panel while Ozias sat in the rear seat and watched from a distance. It did not take much time for them to have the crystal removed from the old bracket. Juila held onto it carefully while she watched her father position the new part into place.

The whole repair took less than ten minutes, and they grinned foolishly at one another once the crystal was put back in line. "I guess we should take it for a spin and make sure it works properly. Do you think we should tell your mom first?"

Juila shook her head emphatically as she giggled, "Are you

kidding? She'd be a wreck. I think I'll pass on the test run myself, though. Sorry."

"Are you doubting my brilliant work?" he asked in mock sternness.

"Not exactly," she answered seriously. "I just don't think Jena would forgive me if I took off again so soon after what happened." She stood up and turned around to exit the vehicle. Her gaze spotted Ozias, and she felt guilty because she had forgotten all about him being with them.

"I'd like to go with you, if you'd let me," Ozias offered.

"Sure," Riccan agreed, eager for an audience to his brilliance. "Go sit in the right-hand seat up front and get buckled in." He finished fastening the cover panel on the crystal drive system. "I'll make this a quick trip," he said to Juila as he moved to the pilot's seat and sat down. He waved over to her as he hit the button to close the side door.

"Have you had much flying experience?" Riccan asked Ozias as he readied the vehicle for its first test flight.

"None other than my trip here to your house," he admitted.

"What about in the spaceship?"

"Viceroy Blair took care of everything. The ship was so large you never even noticed when we traveled between places."

Riccan nodded understanding and entered their destination coordinates before he asked, "Are you ready?" He saw Ozias swallow nervously and tip his head forward in agreement. "Here we go then," he said as he pressed the activation button to send them on their way.

The trip was quick and perfect, which pleased Riccan immensely. He had missed flying his telepod to work that morning and would be glad to have it back for the next day. He grinned over at Ozias and received the same expression back from his passenger. "Did you like it?"

"That was amazing. I'd love to learn to fly my own someday."

"What are your plans? Do you know yet?" Riccan asked. He stayed sitting in the telepod as it was quiet and he hoped to get some answers from Juila's stowaway passenger. It had seemed strange that the man would abandon his ship and crew in favor of seeing Earth.

"I don't know yet. I'm torn between staying on Earth or going to Tuala. Juila's knowledge is what intrigued me in the first place, so maybe I should go to Tuala and see what it has to offer. What do you think?"

"I'm not sure. I think in either place you will find it hard to adjust. Tuala doesn't take well to people who aren't native-born, and Earth is very suspicious of people they consider aliens. To the people here on Earth, aliens should be small, grey people with big heads and large black eyes who will steal their children onto their spaceships."

"Ugh, that sounds like Viceroy Blair, except for the physical description of course," Ozias had to admit.

"What about going back to Heliok? Isn't that an option?" Riccan asked.

"I don't see how without Viceroy Blair's help. I'm pretty sure he won't want me back on his ship after I left the way I did."

"What if there were a way to get there without Viceroy Blair? Would you go home?"

"Probably. Eventually. I really want to learn some things to improve our situation before returning. My world is dying, Riccan. We will need a miracle to keep everything going."

Riccan drew in a long breath through his nose as he considered this new information. He wondered what could be going wrong with their world. This changed things slightly. "I'll ask my dad what he knows, and then I'll get back to you on it, okay?"

"Okay," Ozias agreed even as he wondered how Riccan's dad

would be of any assistance. "Who is your dad and how could he be of any help?"

"My dad is an Elder on Tuala. He is one of Jehoban's chosen students, and he has access to an Ascension Gate and many other resources. There may be a gate to your world; we'll just have to locate it."

Ozias raised his eyebrows as Riccan kept talking about his father's station on Tuala. He had no idea Riccan's connections to Tuala were so important. His chance meeting with Juila had been more advantageous than he had even dreamed.

"How was your weekend, Neal?" Dr. Medin asked.

Neal moved his shoulders to get more comfortable on the couch as he considered her question. "I haven't been sleeping well. I keep having these strange dreams, and then I wake up disoriented. Is that normal?"

"Considering what you've been through, yes, very normal."

Neal nodded and felt better about having told her about it after all. He had planned on keeping it to himself until he realized he would probably get better faster if he had full disclosure with her. The sooner he remembered everything, the sooner his mother would quit looking at him as though he were a bomb about to explode.

Dr. Medin began the session to put him into a hypnotic state. She was grateful he was so easy to put under because it would make his mind relax faster. "Tell me about the first memory you have after you and Amanda encountered the storm on the yacht."

"There was a flash of lightning where a strange blue light rolled across the deck and railings. I stood and watched in fascination as it came closer to me."

"What happened next?"

"I'm tied up in a dark place. I can't talk because there's something wrapped around my head and over my mouth. I'm really hot."

"Move ahead until you are free of the room. What do you see now?"

"I'm in a different room where there's light from a window far above my head. An old man in a white outfit is standing in front of me."

"Is he saying anything?"

"No, he has his hands on my head, and I feel strange. I look up at his face, and he is smiling. He hands me a glass and tells me to drink. It tastes like cold, minty water and then it's really bitter. My head is pounding with a strange ache in the front. The pain passes, and then I look around as if I can see everything with exquisite detail. It's amazing."

"What happens when you leave the room?"

"The old man takes me to a cubicle and has someone show me how to use a strange computer. I'm fascinated with the engineering project he shows me. I can see flaws in the design, and I point them out to the new man. He is happy and smiles at me."

"What is the old man's name?"

Neal frowned slightly with his eyes still closed. Suddenly his expression cleared as he found the name he was after and he announced proudly, "Elder Vargen."

Jasmine looked down at her watch and notes they have been in session for over an hour. Hating to stop the session just as Neal was making a breakthrough, she sighed and said, "I'm going to count backward from ten. With each number I want you to take a deep, cleansing breath and feel more alive and awake. When I reach number one, you will open your eyes and remember everything we talked about today. Ten, feeling refreshed and alert. Nine, coming back to alert awareness. Eight…seven…six…five, another deep breath…four, that's right Neal, breathe a cleansing breath… three…two…and one, open your eyes." She snapped her fingers and smiled as Neal's eyes opened and he shifted his gaze to look at her with amazement.

"That was awesome. I saw so many new things. Was any of it true?"

"Yes, Neal. Remember to write down any new thoughts in your journal. Write everything down even if you don't think it could be true. Okay?"

Neal nodded as he swung his legs around, so he was sitting on the edge of the couch. He felt amazing as if he had slept for hours. He was alert and refreshed just as she had told him he would be. "When can I see you again?"

"Will the same time tomorrow work for you?"

"Absolutely!" he replied enthusiastically. It did not matter if his parents had other plans; he would take a cab to get to the appointment if it came to that.

"Since we made such great progress today, plan on bringing your journal with you tomorrow. We'll discuss what you write down so we can go deeper into the matter during your hypnosis."

"That sounds great. Thank you so much, Dr. Medin. I really feel like I'm going to be okay now that I'm seeing you."

"I'm glad, Neal," she said with a warm smile. "Okay, I'll see you tomorrow then." She held out her hand to shake Neal's. She watched him walk with more confidence as he left her office. As soon as the door clicked shut, she sighed and wearily sat back down.

Amanda had been right about Neal needing her help. She could just imagine any other doctor treating Neal for what he had been through. The other doctors would have him in a mental institution in a heartbeat. She wondered how many people who had experienced time in Tuala had ended up in mental institutions on Earth. It made her sad to think about it.

She pulled herself up and walked over to her desk and to begin writing her paper notes of Neal's case. She did not dare put anything down in her computer about him. In fact, he did not even have a patient file with her office, just to be safe.

CHAPTER 31

Amanda pulled urgently at Rasa's sleeve to get her attention while they were still in the hallway. "These women and children won't be able to live on Earth," she whispered quietly. "They don't have the knowledge or the means to make a living here. My mom and Barla told me how they reacted to all of the technology around them." Amanda was glad the two of them had gone back out to enjoy themselves after dropping off the Tualan women at the house. They certainly needed the time to bond with one another after so many years of being separated.

"I've seen that myself. They will be much better off back in Tuala where they already know what to expect. Let me talk with them and see what they want to do now that they've been outside of the estate to see for themselves."

Rasa returned to the living room where the refugees had congregated after their outing. All of their discussions ended as they looked up at her expectantly. "How many of you wish to remain here on Earth now that you've experienced what their world is like? Raise your hand."

The people looked at one another and began shaking their heads. Nobody raised their hand.

"I have an idea for all of you," Rasa began and noticed interest sparking in most of their eyes. "I suggest we return you to the Roanoke Colony where you already have homes. You can elect a new leader for your community, and I can speak with the Elder in charge of your district to let him know you have a new leadership structure. Would you be willing to allow the Elder to be in charge of your well-being?"

Some of the older women muttered in discord while the younger ones seemed excited about the idea. Nobody was willing to commit an answer at the moment. They had never thought about leading themselves, and it was an intoxicating idea.

"We'll give you some privacy to talk it over among yourselves," Rasa proposed as she tilted her head at Amanda to indicate they should go outside to give them time to discuss the matter.

They walked through the garden paths, and Amanda asked, "What do you think they'll do?"

"I think they'll opt to go home. It's easier to go where you already know, and they might find it easier without Grobin leading them."

"Which Elder is in charge of the Roanoke Colony?"

Rasa smiled over at Amanda as she declared, "Elder Daven. I thought you already knew that!"

"I didn't, but that's great. He already knows about them, and he'll do everything he can to help them thrive."

"Only if they'll trust him. Grobin has instilled a great fear of outsiders to the group so they'll have to learn to trust them before any changes will take place."

Amanda nodded her head and kept walking as she pondered the problem. Suddenly an idea struck her which she thought would be the perfect solution, "What if we asked Vinia to go back to lead them? She's familiar with both worlds, she has her own birth crystal—which I noticed most of them do not—and she has already lived among them before."

Rasa raised her eyebrows in consideration and said, "You might be onto something. It would certainly help Vinia with a sense of self-worth. Do you want to talk to her about it, or do you want me to do it?"

"I think we should propose the idea to the people in the house first. If they are adamantly opposed to the idea, then I don't even want to get Vinia's hopes up."

"True, good thinking. Let's go back inside and see what the group has decided." Rasa turned around and began working her way through the pathways. She opened the patio door, and the buzz of conversation abruptly ended. Amanda followed her across the room until they were both standing in front of the fireplace with the group seated in front of them.

"Have you decided?" Rasa asked.

One of the middle-aged women nodded and said, "We have agreed we do not belong here. We also would like to go back to our homes."

"And what have you decided about a leader?" Rasa pushed.

"We could not agree on who it should be."

"Could I offer you a suggestion then?" Rasa asked. So far the conversation had gone exactly where she had hoped.

The older woman looked around her and received nods from nearly everyone. She turned back to Rasa and said, "We'd like to hear what you have in mind."

"I know of a woman who used to live in your community. She

has lived outside the Colony for a while and has learned a great deal about what happens in other Elder's districts. She has also been here to Earth, so she knows what you have experienced. Her name is Vinia."

There was a commotion among the group as they heard her name. They had always been told by Grobin that she was an outsider and not to be trusted. It soon became obvious they did not know what to believe or how to answer.

"Let me ask you something," Amanda spoke up for the first time. "Did Grobin always have your best interest in mind when he led your community? Was he the one responsible for you being held captive on Viceroy Blair's spaceship? Did you know the captain planned to make all of you slaves on his home world? He never had any intention of bringing you to Earth. As we speak, Grobin is en route to Heliok where he will be enslaved for his misguided notions of leading you. I think it's safe to say Grobin was misguided himself and you should consider Rasa's proposal for Vinia to be the spokesperson for your community."

"We don't even know where she is," another woman complained.

"If that is your only objection, then we can ask her if she will come back to her old house. If she accepts the position, then we will arrange for her to meet with Elder Daven to discuss the needs of your group. We will also contact wise-woman Copa to come into your village to help with any health problems you may be experiencing." Rasa took a deep breath and added, "Will you accept Vinia as your leader in return for us taking you back home?"

After a short discussion, the refugees agreed, some reluctantly Rasa noted, to the terms of her proposal. There was an air of anticipation within the group which had been of desperation only a short while before. She was pleased to have found a solution to the group's problem and hoped they would learn something from this experience.

Amanda was already making plans for visiting with Vinia. She hoped Vinia would agree to the new arrangement. Maybe she would have a greater sense of self-worth if the community wanted and needed her. "Do you want to come with me to talk to Vinia? We can discuss the matter with her when we take your mom home."

Rasa nodded and wondered when they would be able to go. Her mother could take a while visiting with her sister here on earth. She did not want to leave these people alone here on Earth. There was no telling what they could manage to get into if they were left to their own devices.

The front door opened and Diane and Barla came inside the house laughing at some joke between the two of them. They only had a couple of bags from their shopping trip since they had spent more time catching up on their histories rather than actual shopping. As soon as they entered the living room, they noticed the tense silence and wondered what had happened.

Thinking they were going to have to leave the people alone with Diane, Rasa sighed in relief as Riccan and Ozias entered the house discussing their recent flight. Rasa tapped Amanda on the arm and said, "I think Riccan and your mom can handle being here while we go and make arrangements for Vinia's new life. What do you think?"

Amanda smiled in agreement and said, "I'll go let him know." She went up to him and asked, "Can I talk to you privately for a minute?"

"Sure, honey," he replied and turned to Ozias and said, "Excuse us." He waited for Amanda to lead him in the direction she wanted to go.

She led him back to the garage and waited for him to shut the door before she began. Still, she could not get past the feeling of unease around Ozias. "Are you going to need to use my telepod this evening?"

"No. I just took mine for a spin, and it works great. What's going on? Are you going somewhere?"

"Rasa and I are going to see if Vinia wants to be the leader of the Roanoke Colony. They have agreed to let her do it if she agrees."

"Seriously? That's amazing, Amanda. I was wondering if they were all planning on staying here on Earth and then we were going to have to find places for them to live and figure out how they could earn a living. This is the best possible option!" He hugged her in his enthusiasm, truly thankful for the situation to have a great resolution. "What made them decide to go back?"

"I think it was the shopping trip. They realized nothing is the same here on Earth as it is on Tuala. They decided it was better to go with what they know rather than the dream of living here where they no longer fit in."

"That makes sense," Riccan agreed. "When were you going to leave?"

"We'd like to go now, but we didn't want to leave the people alone here at the house."

"Wise decision. So you need me to babysit everyone, is that what you're saying?"

"Pretty much," Amanda smiled up at him brightly. "Hopefully Mom will want to keep you company."

"Okay, well hurry back home, will you?"

"As fast as we can," she agreed and gave her husband a hug in relief. "I love you, Riccan."

"I love you too. Don't you dare try to time your return either, just in case you were starting to get the idea."

"You know me too well," she grinned.

They returned to the living room where Amanda nodded her head at Rasa and Barla to indicate their plans were set. Instead of going out to the garage, they opted to go into the back yard to pretend to go for a walk. They turned to the right and followed the path closest to the house until they were parallel to the garage. They cut across the yard and entered the garage through the man door on the back side.

CHAPTER 32

Amanda made quick work of getting them landed at the Port of Cresdon landing field. She noted the time and the winds as she powered down the telepod. They left the telepod and walked the short distance to Rasa's childhood home.

Rasa was feeling unaccountably nervous as they turned into the yard of the house. The gravel crunched loudly under their feet until they reached the steps leading to the front door. "I hope Vinia's home," Rasa said.

"She should be," Barla said as she looked around them still feeling as though she were being watched. "After all, Petre is still hanging around town trying to locate her. She doesn't venture out much anymore."

Barla opened the door, and they entered the foyer, hearing Danika giggling from the other side of the house. "That's a good sign," she said in an aside to Amanda and Rasa. They followed the joyful noise until they reached the living room and discovered everyone sitting and enjoying tea and each other's company.

Vinia looked up when she saw movement in the doorway and jumped up from her chair with a squeal of delight. She raced across the room and about knocked Amanda over with her exuberant embrace. "Why didn't you say you were coming over? I would have planned a dinner or something. How long can you stay?"

"Hi, Vinia. We actually came to discuss something rather important with you," she answered hastily before she could make any other plans for their time.

"Oh," Vinia replied and looked down at Danika playing on the floor. "Is it about Nealan?" she asked excitedly. "Does he remember me?"

Amanda answered, "No, I'm sorry this visit has nothing to do with Neal."

"Oh," Vinia said sadly.

Rasa sat down on the floor next to Danika and asked Vinia, "Have you considered returning to your home in the Roanoke Colony?"

"No, there's nobody there anyway. I don't want to live so far out all alone. Why?"

"We have found the residents, and they wish to return to living there. They have all agreed they'd like you to be the spokesperson for the community. Would you consider doing it?"

"I'll never go back as long as Grobin and his sidekick, Mosan, are there." She looked down on her daughter and continued, "Danika needs to grow up in a safe environment. As long as those men are there, they would undermine anything I said."

"That's the thing, Vinia. There are only women, children, and a couple of teenagers who will be returning to the community," Rasa explained.

"I don't understand, where is everybody else?" She shifted her gaze from Rasa beside her to Amanda above her. "What happened?"

"The community tried to arrange transportation back to Earth where they believe they once originated from. Unfortunately, they made a bargain with a crooked captain, and they were going to be taken as slaves onto a different world.

"Juila took Jon and Valentina to their old home and as they were returning their telepod malfunctioned, and they ended up drifting in space."

"Oh, no!" Vinia gasped. "Please tell me they made it home safely."

"Yes, they were only gone overnight. They were taken captive by the same captain as the Colony. Their space ship was in dire straits with their ship inoperative, and Juila managed to repair enough functionality to get them home, at a much slower pace, however.

"To make a very long story short, one of the crew members agreed to assist Juila in getting Jon, Valentina, and any of the colony members back to the telepod in thanks for her help. Only nine people decided to return, and now they want you to lead them. Will you agree to try it out?"

"I don't know," Vinia began as she looked over at Barla to see what she thought of the offer.

Rasa saw the look and added, "We told the people you would have assistance from Elder Daven and from wise-woman Copa. The community would no longer function as a closed society, and you would be the bridge between until they could feel comfortable."

"Would they really want to help?" Vinia asked as she could start to see how their plan could actually work.

"Absolutely," Rasa guaranteed. "They have often worried about what to do for your people even when they refused any help."

"We didn't have a choice! Grobin refused to let any outsiders come into the village. He taught everyone to be afraid of outsiders. He said they would taint our people and try to lure them away to do the evil bidding of Jehoban."

"You know better, right?" Rasa asked gently. "You have your own birth crystal which is a gift from Jehoban, and you use the elemy to make your life easier. Do you think you could teach the other women and children the benefits of it?"

"I could certainly try," she agreed with a sense of purpose. In a matter of minutes, her life had changed from complete dependence on Barla's hospitality to the idea of leading the community she had grown up in. She could hardly believe what had led her to be chosen, yet she was thankful all the same. "I will do it!"

"Do you want to take more time to think about it? We really need you to be certain," Rasa asked promptly.

"There's nothing to think about really. For once in my life, my community needs me! I'm going to step up and be the best leader they've ever known!" Vinia's voice rose with each sentence until she was almost shouting which caused Danika to begin to whimper with concern. Vinia hurriedly picked up her daughter and lifted her into the air and laughed, "We are going home, Danika! Our people need us, and we're going home!" She brought her down and hugged her tightly until Danika's squirming caused her to put her back down onto the floor to play.

Barla frowned slightly and asked, "How soon will this happen? Certainly, it'll take time to arrange for Vinia to meet with Elder Daven and Copa, right?"

"Well, right now all of the people are staying at my house, and I think they'd be much happier back in their own homes. I think it would be best if we got everyone back home tonight. The meetings can be arranged sometime this week," Amanda answered.

"I think we should plan on having a patil installed in Vinia's home. She needs to have access to other people easier than walking for several hours to get to Desio," Rasa added.

"Good idea," Barla agreed. "If she needs anything, I'm only a message away."

"The same would go for Elder Daven, Copa, or myself for that matter," Amanda put in.

"Why don't you gather your things and we can take you home before we bring everyone else back?" Rasa suggested.

Vinia nodded happily and asked, "Barla would you mind watching Danika one last time while I run upstairs?"

"You don't even have to ask. I'm going to have to soak up as much of your daughter as I can get since I'm not sure how long it'll be before I get to play with her again."

Vinia grimaced a little even though she was terribly excited for her new adventure. Barla had been so wonderful to help her out, it almost seemed rude to be so eager to leave. It was even worse that they had no advance warning in which to plan for a better departure. She left the room hurriedly even as she regretted the necessity of leaving the house at all.

"Do you think this will work?" Barla asked quietly.

"You just don't want to see her take the baby away," Ahn teased as he reached for his wife's hand to comfort her.

"Of course I don't want either of them to leave," Barla replied with mock severity. She knew her husband was teasing, yet there was a note of truth in his statement. She looked back to her daughter for an answer to her question.

"I think it'll give Vinia a sense of purpose in Tuala. She has been rather forlorn since she had to send her kids away and then Neal was taken as well. This will help restore some of what she lost because of Grobin's warped ways. Also, she'll have a home for her kids to come back to if they choose to return to Tuala in a couple of anons."

"Barla knows she'll thrive in this new role, she's just going to miss the company," Ahn said as he continued to pat his wife's hand. "We can go visit her if you want, Barla."

Barla glanced gratefully over at her husband and smiled at his explanation. She knew they were too busy to make many house calls, yet they would probably make time to go just because he had suggested it. The solution helped ease her mind at the two of them leaving so abruptly.

A short while later, they could hear Vinia coming down the stairs. Barla scooped up Danika and rushed out of the room to see if she could offer assistance. Rasa, Amanda, and Ahn followed a little slower as they wanted to give Barla a moment alone with Vinia.

As soon as it could be arranged, Amanda and Rasa were both carrying sacks containing most of Vinia's belongings while Vinia held Danika and another small bag. Barla and Vinia had a tearful farewell in the foyer before Ahn pulled his wife away and put his arm around her to offer comfort.

"We'll walk down to the landing field with you," Ahn declared.

"Oh, can I carry Danika then?" Barla asked. She had assumed they would stay at home while they left and was glad to get one last opportunity to hold the child.

Vinia eagerly passed the heavy child over to Barla's eager embrace. She would have more than enough time to hold her daughter once they were back in the community. She felt a thrill of fear pass through her in anticipation of her new role. Never had she expected to receive such an honor from the town where they had always made her feel like an outcast. This almost felt as if she were being reborn into the village; everything would be different now.

The group strolled along the sidewalk back to the landing field. Barla spent quite a bit of time securing Danika into the back seat before she tearfully returned to Ahn's side. She held onto her husband for support as she wiped the moisture from her eyes.

Vinia gave both Ahn and Barla big hugs and said, "Thank you so much for everything you've done for me and my family again. I can't begin to tell you what it's meant to me. You two feel like family!"

"I agree," Barla answered as she held onto Vinia a second longer. She let her go and watched as she entered the telepod and sat down in the seat next to her daughter. Barla waved and felt her heart break just a little more as they left to go onto their new adventure. She hoped it would work out well for the two of them; they deserved to be happy for once.

Amanda set the coordinates for the Roanoke Colony and activated the flight. They appeared just above and beside the rolling waves of the ocean. Amanda carefully navigated the breezy landing and then powered down the telepod.

The group gathered all of Vinia's belongings and trooped back through the trails which led to the village. When they got to Vinia's house, they all realized just how long it had been abandoned. Wind, weather, and dirt had taken its toll on the interior, and they were going to have to get the place cleaned up before anyone would be spending any time inside.

Luckily Rasa and Vinia were both proficient in their ability to use the elemy to scour away the dirt and dust. Amanda watched in amazement as one thing after another became spotless. She had never had to practice this particular aspect of their skills since they had maids at her own home. She could definitely see the value in having the power to make such changes so easily.

Amanda began to unpack the bags onto the cleaned kitchen table so Vinia could decide where everything would go. She watched Rasa and Vinia go outside. Her curiosity got the better of her, and she abandoned her task to follow after them.

"What are you two doing?" Amanda asked.

"I'm setting up protection wards around Vinia's house," Rasa explained.

Amanda frowned and tilted her head as she tried to understand why Rasa would even need to do such a thing. "Why?" she finally asked.

"I asked her to do something to make sure Grobin would not be able to harm us should he discover a way to come back to Tuala," Vinia answered.

"Oh," Amanda said with raised eyebrows and a questioning look over at Rasa.

"Okay, your home is protected," Rasa announced. "We should get going so we can bring the other villagers home tonight. They're going to want daylight to clean up their homes since none of them know how to use elemy to get it done efficiently."

Suddenly nervous, Vinia asked, "Is there something I should do or say when they get here?"

"Maybe greet them as they go into their homes. Let them know you're here and available to hear their needs," Amanda suggested.

"We'll talk with them before we bring them," Rasa assured her.

Vinia nodded as she held Danika closer to her chest as she tried to decide if she were more nervous or excited for her new role. "I'll see you in a little while then."

"Do you want to walk back to the beach with us?" Amanda asked.

"No, I think I'll stay here and put my things away. I want to be ready and settled when everyone else arrives."

"Okay," Amanda said as she stepped forward and gave Vinia a quick hug. "We'll be back soon."

Vinia nodded before turning back to go into her house.

Amanda exchanged a significant look with Rasa. They were definitely going to have to set up some rules with the refugees before bringing them back. The sooner the people recognized the importance of Vinia's role, the better their lives would become.

PETRE WATCHED as the three women entered the Harbor Master's house. Since he had been watching the place, he had noticed there was a lot of people who visited. He sat back against the tree and waited to see what would happen next.

It was rather boring just sitting around, it had never been his strong suit since he liked taking action. He closed his eyes in anticipation of a long wait. He was uncertain how long a time had passed, yet a noise had caught his attention. Opening one eye, he realized something different was happening.

He did not like what he was witnessing. It appeared as though Vinia were leaving the captain's house and he could not let that happen. He jumped up from his hiding spot and began to trail after the group of people. Once he figured out they were heading to the landing field, he cut behind one of the neighbor's houses and began to run.

He had to hurry if he were going to reach their destination first. If they got into the telepod, he would never know where they were heading. He had to be in position so he could overhear their conversation. Vinia was not going to get away from him again.

After only passing two houses, Petre had to stop, bend over, and hold onto his knees while his breath came raggedly into his lungs. Living on the sea had not conditioned him for this kind of exertion. With his chest still heaving, he began to walk slowly, desperately needing to find out where the love of his life was going.

CHAPTER 33

Willian actively despised the role his father had forced him to take on Earth. He had spent another day slogging through the sea of humanity at the school, and he still had not seen Jena at all. The only way he could resolve their situation was if he could sit down with her and work it all out. Knowing how to create a stupid bowl in pottery was never going to benefit him in life, and he resented having to waste his time on such trivial matters.

Melissa had driven him home from his second day of school. She had taken one look at his dark expression and decided not to ask him how his day had gone. Willian had been grateful for her observation so he would not have to pretend to be in a better mood for her sake.

He sat alone in his bedroom and kept punching the soft mattress to vent some of his frustration. To add insult to injury, he had discovered Shemalla had left to return home while he was out so he could not even ask her opinion on the matter. He felt alone, abandoned really, and it did not sit well with his foul mood.

Pesi came trotting into his room and begged to be brought up onto his bed. Without thinking, Willian reached down and hoisted her up. He did find some solace and comfort in petting the animal, but his mood was still pretty foul. The fluffy dog lay down right next to his thigh, and he wished he could be touching Jena instead of this animal.

Unable to remain inside, Willian put on his shoes and marched out of his room to go outside. Maybe he could get some inspiration if he could take a walk in the fresh air. Just as he reached the front door, he heard Melissa calling him. He rolled his eyes in frustration before he stepped back to see her sitting in the living room.

"Are you going somewhere?" she asked kindly.

"I thought I'd go for a walk. I need some time to think about things," he added lamely.

"Don't go too far, okay?" she advised.

"I won't."

"Have fun."

"Sure," he said glumly, and he opened the door and stepped out into the sunshine. *Have fun?* he asked himself. *How am I supposed to do that when I don't know anyone around here, and I can't find Jena to talk to her? Earth is not a place I would come back to willingly.* Pesi tried to follow him, and he had to put his foot up to stop her. He swiftly closed the door and walked away from the house.

He kept walking at a brisk pace as he played different scenarios in his mind. There was always the option of returning to Tuala and waiting for Jena to come back to him. He shook his head in dismissal as he realized his letters had been too damaging to risk leaving her alone for so long.

Turning down another street, Willian became aware of another presence near him. He looked down and noticed a large black dog had decided to trot alongside him. It pleased him to realize he remembered this type of dog was called a Labrador retriever. He looked around to see if its owner were nearby yet nobody was out walking except himself.

His attention was drawn to a couple of people who were playing some sort of game. He crossed the street and stood at the fence to watch. Both players were holding some sort of a racket in their hand, and they were hitting a yellow ball back and forth between them. Willian lost track of time as he became fascinated with the number of times the players volleyed the ball.

The player furthest away from him had to almost leap to hit a fast-coming return. The angle was wrong, and the ball glanced off the edge of the racket and flew high up, over the fence, and out into the road. The Labrador decided it would give chase and ran after it.

Too late, Willian realized there was a car coming down the road at the same time. The vehicle was unable to avoid hitting the big dog, and Willian watched in horror as the animal was thrown up and to the side of the vehicle. It twirled several times before it skidded along the pavement and came to a stop when it hit the curb.

Possibly the worst part about the whole thing was the animal's cries of pain as the car never even slowed down. Willian rushed over to the injured animal, and he put his hands on its roughened fur. The dog's leg was bent in a peculiar angle, and it had several gashes where the bumper had struck it.

Willian could not stand to hear the animal whimper and whine as it writhed in pain. He immediately called on the elemy to come up and begin repairing the damage. His concentration was so complete he never noticed the two tennis players leave their game to come over to offer assistance. Luckily, most of the exterior damage had been repaired before they arrived, so they did not witness much.

After several minutes, Willian leaned back away from the

healed animal and watched as it picked itself up from the pavement. As if to thank him for helping, the dog began to lick his hands. He realized there was blood in between his fingers and then he looked up to see the two people.

"Is the dog okay?" the first man asked.

"Yeah, I think he was just stunned," Willian lied.

"That was incredibly lucky. I can't believe the car didn't even stop. What a jerk!" the other man stated. He bent down and picked up the tennis ball which had started the whole scene and put it into his pocket. Next, he stepped over to the black lab and pet the top of his head as he said, "Now don't you go running into the street anymore. You might not be so lucky next time."

The first man spoke up and said, "I think I'm done for the day. What about you?"

"Yeah, let's call it a day," he agreed.

The two men left, and Willian watched them go. He felt a rush of guilt for almost giving himself away so easily. Obviously, the men had not seen him actually healing the dog, yet he could not forget how close it had been. He was going to have to be more careful in the future. The dog sat down and leaned against him. Willian put his arm around the big dog's neck and said, "I'm glad you're okay, boy. You were really lucky I was here to take care of you. Let's go find your home."

He pushed himself up from the sidewalk and began walking back the way they had come. They walked several blocks before Willian began to hear someone calling out. Soon they came upon a man who eagerly raced out to intercept them.

The man kneeled in front of the dog and put his hands on either side of his head and said, "You're a bad boy for jumping the back fence again. It's a good thing this young man was bringing you home." The man looked up and asked, "Where did you find him?"

"Down by the park," Willian replied.

"Thank you for bringing him home," the man said as he stood back up and kept his fingers under the dog's collar to make sure he stayed with him.

"No problem," Willian answered as he continued to walk back to his foster home. At least the dog was going to have a happy ending. He hoped his would be just as fortunate.

His outlook was much better now that he'd been able to help another living creature. Touching the elemy helped to ground him, and he realized he actually missed using it daily. He felt a calmness spread throughout his body and knew he would have better luck with Jena because of it.

"I THINK we should stop off at Elder Daven's Residence before we go get the people," Amanda suggested.

"Good idea. Maybe he'll want to be at the village already when the people return."

Amanda entered the coordinates into the telepod and activated the trip. They arrived over the landing field and made a smooth touchdown. Even before they had left the aircraft, Amanda noticed Nena standing on the balcony waving over to them.

She grinned over at Rasa for her mother-in-law's predictable ways as they walked away from the telepod and toward the Residence. They went up the stairway where Nena greeted them warmly with hugs. Amanda asked, "Is Daven home?"

"Yes, yes, come inside out of the heat," Nena answered as she gestured for them to go into the house. "He's just in his office. He'll be thrilled to see you."

Amanda led the way as she knew where his office was located.

When she reached the open door, she knocked before entering to make sure he was not working on anything confidential.

Daven hurriedly rose from his chair and crossed the room with a huge smile, "Hello, Amanda!" He gave her a hug and then noticed Rasa and greeted her the same. "Come in and sit down."

"We came to ask a favor of you," Amanda said as she moved over to sit down across from him at his desk.

"What can I do for you?" Daven asked curiously.

Amanda explained what had happened with the Roanoke Colony and ended with, "Would you be willing to go out there tonight and welcome everyone back home? Vinia is really nervous about her position, and how to greet them, maybe with you by her side, the residents will understand what changes will need to take place to make their village prosperous again."

Daven was in awe of everything they had managed to achieve in such a short time. He had plenty of work to keep him busy, but he knew this was an opportunity not to be missed. He turned off his patil and announced, "I'll head over there right now."

"Maybe you should see if wise-woman Copa could come with you. Some of the people have never had any medical care. After everything they've gone through it might be nice to see if any of them need help. We might as well begin as we mean to end, right?" Amanda asked.

Daven nodded his agreement and asked, "Is there anything else I'll need to know?"

"Not that I can think of," Rasa answered and looked over to Amanda to see if she could think of anything.

"Vinia will need a patil to be able to get in touch with you. Do you have any extras around?" Amanda asked. She realized then that she did not understand how the patils were disbursed and if all households had one. She also did not know what type of infrastructure was needed to be able to work one. For all she knew, the Roanoke Colony would be unable to use a patil until electricity was brought out to them. They still lived as if it were the fourteen hundreds on Earth with all of their old-fashioned tools and ideas.

Daven laughed at Amanda's expression. "We have a lot of extras we use for the children. I'll bring one along and spend some time teaching Vinia how to use it. Do you think she's ever had the opportunity to use one before?"

"It's probably been a long time, but she did enter bills of lading on the patil for Captain Ahn many anons ago," Amanda replied.

"Let me go grab one, and then I'll walk out with you," he announced as he stood up and left the room. They only had to wait a few minutes before he stood in the doorway with a satchel slung over his shoulder. "I'm ready," he announced and then waited for the women to come out of his office to lead the way.

Nena came up beside Rasa and said, "I've been asked to assemble everyone from Jehoban's meeting. Are you available this Kamis? I think everyone has been available for getting together on that day.

"I'll make the time because it's really important we keep in touch and move forward with figuring it out. Just let me know when and where and I'll be there," she answered.

"Together, we will get it figured out," she agreed and put her arm around Rasa's lower back as they descended the stairs down to the landing field.

CHAPTER 34

Shemalla arrived back home and found Lillia was still there. "What do you have planned?" she asked.

"I don't know. I'm just keeping out of Lucinden's way for a while. I'm going to have to report back soon, but I'm not sure what I should tell him. What do you think?"

"You could try for the truth and say you didn't discover anything unusual. After all, there isn't anything going on here in Roswell." She laughed at her own joke since Roswell seemed to be the most laid back place she had ever lived.

"I have to agree with you there! How do you manage to keep from dying of boredom in this town? Not to mention working in the museum and hearing all of the visitors theorizing about what really happened!"

"I've had to bite my tongue so many times," she laughed. "Knowing Elder Vargen's son was actually responsible for the original crash makes it pretty funny, though."

"I bet," Lillia wiped the laughter tears from her eyes and then sobered. "I probably should think about returning to Tuala."

"You could travel across America and find people who are friends of Tuala. I'm sure they'd love to get an update on what's going on in our world. They really have been the nicest people I've ever met."

Lillia tipped her head and raised an eyebrow at the suggestion. She had never really spent too much time with the Tualan supporters, and she thought it might be an education. They might even lead her to find out something to share with Lucinden after all. "I think I might just do that! Do you have any suggestions on the route to take?"

"I'll print you up a map," she answered happily.

"How was your trip? Were you able to complete your assignment?" Lillia asked innocently.

Shemalla did not dare discuss what she had been doing with Lillia. While she trusted the woman implicitly, her association with Lucinden made some information ill-advised to share. She knew Lucinden could read her mind if he ever chose to do so, and the less information Lillia knew about the Elders of Tuala, the safer they would all remain. "It went alright," she answered noncommittally.

THEY ENDED up taking both telepods to deliver the people back to the Roanoke colony. Riccan had insisted on making sure the people would be secured in seats rather than standing. Amanda had piloted her own telepod and Riccan, the other. Rasa had stayed behind with Gevena to talk to her about their plans for bringing her back to Manzanit with her.

Ozias again sat in the co-pilot's seat and watched in wonder as they easily maneuvered to land on the sandy beach in Tuala. The other passengers also stared out the windows as they landed.

Never had they imagined they would see their home land again and they were eager to return to their familiar lives.

After he watched Amanda land her telepod ahead of him, Riccan opened the side door and announced, "It's safe for everyone to unbuckle their belts and leave the telepod." He saw the passengers leaving the other aircraft. He would have expected them to rush back to their homes, and was surprised to see they seemed hesitant to go until all of them had reassembled from both telepods.

As they had been coming in for their landings, Riccan had seen his father's telepod in the clearing. He hoped he had been able to get wise-woman Copa to come with him. Knowing his father, he would have made sure of it, even if he had been forced to time their arrival to get there ahead of them.

Nobody needed to lead the residents back to their village as they were all intimately familiar with the area. Amanda and Riccan lagged behind so the homecoming could happen as naturally as possible. When they rounded the last corner, they could see everyone had gathered in the middle of the town.

Vinia, with Danika on her hip, stood in the center of the people along with Daven and Copa. She spoke louder than usual to address the group, "I'd like to thank you all for giving me the opportunity to lead this colony. I will do everything I can to make sure we all prosper and remain safe from harm with the best care possible." She gestured to Elder Daven and wise-woman Copa as she spoke of their safety and well-being.

"I know we've always been told to shun outsiders and to keep to ourselves and that way of thinking has not served us well. Elder Daven has agreed to make sure we will have access to everything we need including education for every one of us, young and old alike. It's never too late to learn how to read and write.

"Wise-woman Copa has also agreed to look after all of our

health concerns. She has been brought into our community in the past with the old leader's blessing, so we should continue to seek her guidance whenever we have any troubles. We will no longer need to remain apart from other people; we've seen what can happen when we do." Vinia took a step back and tilted her head down modestly to let the people know she was not going to be a tyrant like Grobin had been.

Elder Daven cleared his throat and spoke, "I've often been concerned with your community since you've never sought any assistance even when you were entitled to it. I want to make sure you all know what your rights and privileges are as citizens of Tuala. I will personally speak to Jehoban on your behalf to find out what He wants to do for your community since you have been burdened with a selfish and uneducated leader for so long. We want to correct this error and return to you all of your natural blessings."

"Jehoban is evil," someone muttered from the crowd. "We don't need anything from Him!"

"We'll have a long way to go, I see," Elder Daven spoke softly and sadly. "We will go at a pace where you will learn to appreciate the beauty and bounty of Tuala."

"You said we were entitled to money. Why? Who would want to give us money?" another woman asked.

"I am the one responsible for paying you. It is the way our leadership is set up. Each citizen is entitled to a retirement fund until they are eligible to work according to the lottery. This is usually assigned after the completion of school. Since none of you has ever had an opportunity to attend school, special dispensations will have to be made until we can rectify the situation."

"Are you implying we are a situation?" a woman called out.

"I'm saying the circumstances in which you were brought up is a situation which is not the same as how other Tualan citizens have been raised. I look forward to getting to know each and every one of you to find out what interests you and how you want to shape your futures. I will do everything in my power to make sure you are given every opportunity to thrive and be happy."

"You have all had an eventful time these past few days, maybe even weeks. Please go to your homes and get yourself settled back in. Copa and I will visit with each one of you to find out what your immediate needs are so you can begin getting your life back in order. Consider what food, utensils, clothing, linen, and any other necessities you'll need, and we will make sure you have them."

"We don't take charity," the same woman sneered.

Several women began to nod while others seemed to like the idea of finally having the things they needed. Many were tired of always having to go without while Grobin had everything. It would be a nice change to be comfortable.

As the crowd disbursed, Amanda and Riccan moved forward to speak with Vinia. Amanda reached her first and held out her hands to hold Danika. Vinia gave her over with a sigh of relief.

Riccan spoke first, "You said just the right things. I'm sure the people will come to you as long as you remember they agreed to this. This isn't going to be like before where they shunned you. Even now, everyone listened when you spoke; nobody said anything against what you promised for them."

"They sure did with Elder Daven. I hope he doesn't change his mind," she replied with a shake of her head.

"Let's go back to your place," Amanda offered.

Riccan walked beside Vinia and spoke quietly, "My Dad has wanted to help your people for as long as I can remember. He's a very patient man, and he will continue to do everything to make sure your village prospers."

"Do you really think so?" Vinia looked up at him with wonder in her eyes. She would be so proud to lead her community to prosperity. If only her parents were still alive to witness the changes taking place, they would have been so proud.

They entered Vinia's house and sat on the benches around the wooden table. Amanda settled Danika on her knee and jiggled her up and down to make her laugh. She had missed all of this with her own daughters. Thinking of the lost time made her think about Vinia's other children.

"Now that you have your home back, what do you want to do about arranging visits with your other kids?" Amanda asked.

"I don't really know; I'm too afraid to think that far ahead. Everything has happened so fast I feel like my head is spinning. What would you suggest? I don't have my own telepod or any way to get to Earth on my own, so I guess it'll come down to your schedule."

Amanda nodded agreement and wished there were another way to make it easier. Of course, if her children decided to return to Tuala, then they could be reunited permanently. She understood why they would want to remain on Earth with their adoptive family, yet it still seemed like a bad situation for Vinia.

"We don't have to decide right now," Amanda said. "Let's give you a few days to get settled into a new routine, and we'll check in with you. I'll tell your kids what's going on and I'm sure they'll understand."

"Thank you, Amanda," Vinia said. "I think it's almost time for someone's nap." She held out her hands to Danika, and the little girl eagerly raised her arms to be picked up by her mother.

Vinia hugged her to her chest as she walked over to a bed she never thought she would be able to use again. She sat down on the edge and placed Danika in the center of the straw-filled mattress. She rubbed the little girl's back soothingly until Danika's eyes began to droop. Vinia bent over and kissed her sleep-dampened forehead before standing up and returning to her company.

"We're going to head home now. If you need anything, my father will let you know how to get in touch with him," Riccan assured her.

"I sure don't see how," Vinia replied skeptically.

"He's going to set up a patil here in your house before he leaves today. He'll make sure you understand how to use the communication programs," Amanda assured her.

"Thank you for thinking of everything." Vinia gave both of them a hug and walked with them to the door. She was saying her farewells when Daven came around the corner and began angling his way over to her house. She could see the satchel he carried and knew it contained the device which would forever change their village. They would no longer be forgotten.

Riccan patted his father's shoulder as they passed him. "Good luck, Dad. We're heading home."

"Safe travels, my boy. It was good seeing you again, Amanda," he said as he continued to walk over to Vinia's house. He began to pull the bag around to the front of him as he neared the dwelling.

Amanda grinned over to Vinia and waved encouragingly before she turned and ran to catch up with Riccan. She grabbed his elbow and pulled herself close to him in her excitement. "This worked out so well, didn't it?"

"Yes, my love. You did good! I'm glad you thought of the patil; otherwise I think everything would have returned to the old ways if nothing different had been brought in to change the status quo."

"I'm hoping the people will start to appreciate the speed of communication when they have a problem which needs immediate attention."

"True. That one woman was rather pregnant, so she'll probably feel better knowing wise-woman Copa can be contacted in a matter of minutes rather than hours."

Amanda nodded knowingly. Amanda suddenly looked around them and in a panicked tone asked, "Where's Ozias?"

"He's looking around the beach. My dad is going to take him home with him."

"Seriously? When did that come about?"

"I talked with him about it through messaging today while I was at work. Ozias had seemed receptive to the idea, for which I was grateful because I'd already made the arrangements before I talked to him about it. I think my dad will be able to help him get home to his own world using the Ascension Gate."

"Really? That'd be pretty amazing." She wondered if that meant the people from Heliok would be able to return to Tuala through the Gate. If that were the case, then would Grobin be able to somehow get back to the Roanoke Colony to create more havoc? She voiced her concerns to Riccan and was thankful he actually took her worry seriously.

"I'll talk to Dad about it," he assured her. "I don't think it's possible without my father's permission, but he can also take extra precautions when he gets ready to send Ozias home just to make doubly sure nobody can reverse the crossing path."

"That's good. Let's hurry up and get out of here. I don't know what it is about this place, but I don't' like it."

They reached the telepods, and Riccan held Amanda's hand as she climbed up into hers. He palmed the control to close the door before he turned to go back to his own aircraft. His wife wasted no time starting up her telepod, rising, and blinking out of existence. He chuckled at her wariness of this location even if he did not share her unease.

He looked around the clearing expecting to see Ozias nearby. Frowning slightly, Riccan boarded his telepod and closed the door. He ran through the startup procedure and then switched to manual control. Instead of immediately activating a flight plan,

Riccan flew up and down the coast line to see if he could spot Ozias.

Without finding him, Riccan had to assume he had decided to wait for Daven in his father's telepod. Satisfied he had done everything he could, he tapped on the glass panel the destination he wanted and then hit the activation button. His view of the majestic coastline disappeared in an instant as he began his journey home to Earth.

CHAPTER 35

His third school day was almost over, and Willian was becoming desperate to find Jena. He had decided this was going to be the day he let her know he was around. There were only two more classes until everyone would be leaving to go home. He left The Commons and kept searching the crowd for any sign of Jena.

Inspiration struck as he saw the boy he had met on his first day. Luke's head was above everyone else's since he was so tall. He wove his way through the crowd until he came to where he'd last seen him and was disappointed when he found he had moved. Again he scanned the crowd and saw him walking away.

He pushed rudely past several groups of teenagers and caught up to him. He watched as Luke turned to face him as he bent forward and kissed the lips of the girl he had been walking with. It embarrassed Willian to interrupt, so he waited. Finally, the kiss ended, and Luke spotted him and smiled in greeting.

"Hi Luke, I was wondering if you could help me find a girl named Jena," he asked and watched in horror as the girl who had been kissed turned around. Jena's eyes were huge as she spotted him standing right in front of her.

Instantly Willian felt a rage of anger and jealousy boil up inside him, and he immediately sought out the elemy to help him kill the boy who dared to touch his betrothed. He felt the elemy all around him and yet it seemed to slip around his grasp. Unable to use his preferred means of revenge, Willian opted for the more primal energy as he threw himself at Luke with his fist connecting with his face.

Almost in slow motion, he felt the impact through his knuckles, wrist, arm, and shoulder. Luke fell back in surprise and immediately took a fighter's stance to counter any further attack. The element of surprise was gone, and Willian could see he was no match for Luke. He yelled, "Don't you ever touch my betrothed again or I'll kill you!"

Luke's expression changed from anger to confusion as he glanced quickly over at Jena to see what she was making of this strange claim. The look on her face told him there was some truth in it and he put his hands down. "It sounds as though you have some unfinished business to attend to," Luke spoke softly before turning and parting the crowd which had gathered around them and walking away.

Jena finally found her voice as she leaned closer to Willian and whispered, "You have no right, Willian, not after what you wrote to me! You and I will never be together! Never!" She turned and ran away before Willian could even react.

He watched her go with a stunned expression on his face. Jena had never spoken to him in anger before; she had always been so eager to please him. He hastily looked around at the faces of the kids still staring at him. "The show's over!" he yelled and then pushed rudely past them to get to his next class.

Willian realized he had finally found Jena. Unfortunately, the meeting could not have gone worse, and he was unsure what he was going to do to fix the situation. He could hardly blame her for looking to someone else for comfort after what he had done. The only problem was the Jena he knew never would have done it.

He continued to stalk through the hall until he reached his classroom. The last thing on his mind was US History as he sat down in his assigned seat and tried to ignore the whispers of the kids around him. They had seen his embarrassing display of emotions. If only he could have used the elemy.

His rage immediately disappeared as he realized the elemy had not worked for him and it scared him to the core. There had to be an explanation he reasoned with himself. Surely he had not lost the ability since he had healed the dog only a couple of days before. He could not be his father's successor if he lost his ability to access the elemy to help the people. His mind swirled with different reasons for the unthinkable, yet he never came close to realizing his father had restricted the use of his powers while he was angry.

WHAT HAPPENED JENA? Juila asked as her sister sat down next to her in English class. She had seen her sister rush into the classroom, immediately sit in her chair, and put her head down in her folded arms on top of the desk. She could hear the soft sobbing noises coming from her and could not make sense of the scenes she could see in her mind.

Finally, Jena lifted her head and sniffled softly as she wiped the tears from her eyes. She looked over to her sister and distinctly thought, *Willian is here at school and he saw Luke kissing me. Willian told everyone that I was his betrothed and he threatened to kill Luke if he ever touched me again. Of course, this was after Willian punched Luke in the face without any warning at all. Do you think this could get any worse?*

Juila's eyes grew round as she saw the scene play out in Jena's mind. She immediately wondered how Willian had come to be at the school in the first place. Something was definitely going on, and she was going to get to the bottom of it. She was not going to sit by and watch her sister be hurt by Willian yet again, especially now that she had found happiness in her relationship with Luke.

Juila worried over Jena for the rest of school and wondered if they would see Willian again before they rode home. Now that they knew he was there, they no longer felt the ease of laughter and friendship as they continued to search all of the faces in the crowd, anticipating a new confrontation.

Just as they left the building to get a ride home from Behn, Sofia ran up to them and stopped in front of them. "Is it true?" she demanded of Jena.

"Is what true?" Jena decided to play dumb just in case Sofia knew something else.

"Did your boyfriend from Tuala really punch Luke in the hall?"

Jena groaned as she realized the story must have traveled through the entire student body for Sofia to have heard about it. She closed her eyes in dismay and nodded.

"Why is he here? Where is he now?" Sofia asked as she began looking around them as if she knew what he looked like.

"I don't know where he is, and I'm hoping it stays that way. It was mortifying enough to have Willian attack Luke, the last thing I need is for another brawl out here in the parking lot."

"Did you say his name was Willian? Is he about this tall," she put her hand up over her head to indicate his height, "with dark hair and brown eyes?"

"Yes. Don't tell me you've seen him!" Juila accused.

"I met him last Thursday when he was enrolling and then again on Friday when I showed him around the school. I wish I would have put the pieces together faster so I could have forewarned you he was here. I'm sorry Jena, I didn't know."

"Hey, it's not your fault, you have nothing to apologize for," Jena said as she reached out and touched Sofia's arm to console her.

"We should get going, Behn's probably waiting for us, Jena," Juila spoke up. She hugged Sofia and watched her friend go across the parking lot to go to her own car.

Juila was eager to get home and see if there were any updates on the Roanoke community since they had been taken home the day before. Even as they walked across the parking lot, they kept up a vigilant search around them for Willian.

Fortunately, they met at Behn's car without incident. Behn looked at them strangely which led Juila to believe Luke must have said something to him. It was not until they were on the main road to their home that Behn said, "Is anyone going to tell me what happened today?"

Jena shook her head and softly spoke, "Willian is here."

Behn's eyes grew wide as he looked back at Jena in the rearview mirror. "Your boyfriend from Tuala is here on Earth?"

"Unfortunately," Juila affirmed.

"What does he want?" Behn asked.

"Me," Jena answered flatly.

"What do you want?" Behn asked.

The numbness of surprise finally wore away, and Jena yelled, "I came to Earth to find myself! Willian had no right to follow me here and cause a scene like that. I'll never forgive him for displaying such abhorrent behavior and acting like he owned me."

Juila was relieved to finally hear her sister stand up for herself and see Willian for the selfish boy he was. "We could only wish he got the idea and decided to go back home."

"Wishful thinking, Juila. You didn't see his face as she looked at me. This is far from over."

"What are you two going to do? This doesn't sound like it's something which should be played out at school."

"No kidding!" Jena agreed wholeheartedly.

"We should try to find out where he's staying and confront him there," Juila suggested.

"How? We have no idea where to start," Jena replied dejectedly.

"We could use the elemy to search for him," Juila began.

"No, I want to talk this over with Mom and Dad before we do anything. They said they were working on breaking the betrothal. I want to have confirmation of it before I speak with Willian again. I want to see the look in his eyes when I tell him we are finished, and now he can go back home in humiliation."

Behn thought about how he would pose his next question. Finally, he decided the direct approach would be best when he asked, "When Juila's telepod got misdirected, you mentioned something about being betrothed. Are you saying you and Willian are engaged to be married?"

"Yes," she sighed. "It was arranged when we were six anons old. It was an odd situation because we were already so old, but Elder Debbon insisted this was what his vision had been about. Jehoban approved of it, so here we are. Both of us are miserable, and now Willian is going to extreme lengths to hold onto something which was doomed from the moment he decided to be jealous of me and my gifts."

Behn frowned and looked over to Juila for clarification.

"Willian was always trying to compete with Jena when they were learning to use their birth crystals. He has developed a terrible habit of speaking down to her trying to make her feel guilty for learning faster and better than he could. He thinks he should naturally be better at everything because of who his father is."

"Oh," Behn whispered quietly as he focused his attention on where he was driving. The situation was much more complicated than he had originally believed. If Willian were simply a boyfriend, then breaking up should have been easy. To know they had entered into an agreement, sanctioned by Jehoban, well that made the situation rather difficult.

Juila agreed with Behn's simple statement. She was going to have her work cut out for her to get Jena's situation straightened out. She was not about to let Willian continue to ruin everything good in her sister's life.

Behn parked in front of the house and followed the girls inside. Even though he had planned on going home to check on his sister, he never even considered leaving when he could tell the girls were so upset. What did surprise him, however, was how quiet the house was when he shut the door behind him.

Juila and Jena were thankful for the peace and quiet. They walked slowly through the foyer. "Is there any news, Rasa?" Juila asked as she looked down the hall expecting to see her mom show up because they had come home. Her parents had come home after they had gone to bed, so they still did not have any updates. She returned her gaze to where Rasa was seated on the couch with Gevena.

"Everything went smoothly. Elder Daven set up a patil for Vinia to use in her house. Your dad's at work and Amanda went to her mom's house for a little while," Rasa replied with a sigh of relief.

"Wait, what's this about Vinia?" Juila asked.

Behn also perked up and leaned forward to hear the news about his mother.

"The people agreed to allow Vinia to lead them now that Grobin is gone. Vinia and Danika moved back to her old home and is going to be the go-between with Elder Daven, wise-woman Copa, and Roanoke's people."

"That's great!" Juila exclaimed. She was really glad to hear the situation had worked out well for Behn's mother.

He could hardly comprehend what had just happened. Suddenly his mother had her own home again as well as access to a patil. It was possible for them to remain in contact with her even without the ability to travel to Tuala. This was fantastic news which he could share with his siblings. He was certain it would cheer up Valentina. Maybe she would want to go back to their old home to visit.

"What about Ozias?" Juila suddenly asked as she looked around as if expecting him to suddenly appear. He had made it clear that he was interested in herself; she hoped he would discover a new focus.

Rasa chuckled as she correctly read Juila's concern. "He went with your Dad. Riccan mentioned he had a plan for him, so I expect you probably won't be seeing him anytime soon."

"That's one less thing to worry about," Juila sighed as she wilted against the back of the couch next to Gevena.

"What else is there?" Rasa asked in concern as she watched Behn seat himself across from them with a troubled expression.

Jena plunked herself down on the couch next to Rasa and announced, "Willian made a scene at my school today."

"He finally found you, I see," Rasa confirmed.

"You knew he was here?" Jena and Juila asked in unison.

"Yes, I helped him come. His father asked Elder Wilken to allow Willian to use his Ascension Gate. I originally thought it was a bad idea, but Willian had changed so much in the week he helped Elder Wilkin, I believed he could work out your issues."

"I certainly didn't see any difference in him," Jena stated hotly.

"That's unfortunate," Rasa replied as she wondered what had gone so wrong. Willian had been so confident in his personal changes. Apparently, he had been overly optimistic.

"So do you know where he is?" Juila asked. "We'd like to talk to him outside of school, obviously."

"I don't know myself, but I can probably find out." Rasa was already thinking about contacting Shemalla and finding out the names of Willian's foster family. Surely they lived nearby if Willian were able to go the same school as the girls. If they could meet him privately, maybe they would have a chance of working out their relationship before discussions of breaking the betrothal went any further.

"We'd sure appreciate it," Juila told Rasa. "Do you know when our mom is planning on returning?"

Jena was wondering the same thing. She needed to clarify her own situation with Willian before she could make any plans to confront him. She glanced over to Behn, who had taken a seat across from her, and wondered what he thought of this whole situation.

Rasa raised her shoulders slightly and said, "Amanda left a few hours ago. I can't imagine she'll be too much longer."

Behn shifted his gaze to Rasa and asked, "You saw Val when she first got home on Sunday. Do you think anything happened to her in the transfer which would cause her to have a migraine headache? She's missed two days of school now. Could there be something wrong with her?"

Rasa glanced nervously over at Juila before she shook her head and said, "I'm sure the two things are unrelated. Give her a little time to readjust and then she should be back to normal."

"That's just what I told him, too," Juila confirmed. She hated keeping the truth from Behn, but she also knew what Behn's reaction would have been had he been told. *Besides*, she said to herself; *it was up to Valentina what to tell her brother.*

"Can I use your patil?" Rasa asked suddenly.

Juila looked at her strangely and nodded. "Sure, come with me."

Rasa waited until they were in the office before she said, "Make sure you keep an eye on Valentina. We don't want her to start cutting herself off from life over this incident."

"I was thinking the same thing," Juila agreed. "Do you really want to use the patil, or did you just want to talk to me alone?"

"I may as well send a message to my contact while we're here. She might even be around her house and be able to give us the address of where Willian is living. I really hope Jena will hear him out. You know I've never been a fan of his, but after the time he spent working in Manzanit I saw significant changes in his attitude."

Juila scoffed rudely. She walked away from Rasa and pushed on the latch to open the secret compartment where the patil was located. "I'll leave you alone to send your message," she said as she left the room in a huff.

In her mind, Willian had already used up more than his share of chances where her sister was concerned. Jena needed to have her final say about the relationship, and then Willian could go back home and leave them alone. He should have respected her privacy and allowed her to come to him if she wanted to fix their relationship. Just the fact that he practically ambushed her and created a scene spoke volumes for where his mind was at in reconciling.

Very soon after Juila returned to the living room, so did Rasa. She held out a piece of paper to Jena and said, "This is Willian's address and phone number. I'll let you decide what you want to do with it." She turned her attention to Gevena and asked, "Gevena, do you want to walk in the gardens with me?"

The girl understood their need to give Jena some privacy with her decision. From the short time she had known the two girls, she admired and respected them greatly. Her own situation with her father and Politun gave her more insight to the tough conversation Jena was going to have with her verbally abusive boyfriend. She stood up and nodded. She fell into step beside Rasa as they exited the house through the patio doors.

"What are you going to do?" Behn asked.

"I should go over there right now and confront him, but I'm too scared. I really wanted to talk everything over with Mom and Dad before I met with him." She held the note in both of her hands and kept reading the address over and over. The reality of Willian living on Earth only a couple of miles away made her slightly nauseous.

"Rasa suggested you talk things over with him before you decide to throw in the towel," Juila sneered. "I think you already know what I think of her idea."

"Well, now, just wait a minute, Juila. Maybe Willian has had time to consider what his life would be like without Jena. It is possible he wants to try to make an effort.

Juila goggled over Behn's statement, "I can't even believe you are trying to make excuses for Willian, especially after what he pulled today! Maybe you should keep your unwanted opinions to yourself."

"Juila, don't be mad at Behn. He does have a point. I'll ask Mom to drive me over there tonight." Jena sighed as she realized the inevitable had come about and now she was going to have to face it.

"I can drive you over there if you want?" Behn offered.

"Traitor," Juila hissed as she jumped up from the couch and stomped out of the room to go upstairs to fume alone.

Jena frowned at her sister's treatment of Behn as she watched her retreating back. She turned back to Behn and said, "I'm sorry for Juila's behavior. She and Willian have a long history of feuding which has made her very bitter toward him. Please don't take anything she says to you seriously."

"I heard that!" Juila yelled down from the top of the stairs.

"And you know I'm right," Jena yelled back.

Behn and Jena chuckled as Juila's response was slamming her bedroom door. Behn asked again, "Do you want me to take you over there right now?"

"I suppose," she answered as she pushed herself off of the couch and sighed deeply. "Thanks for doing this, Behn. I'll talk to Juila about apologizing to you when this is over."

"There's no need for that, Jena. She's just trying to look out for you. I'd do the same for my siblings. Now let me see that address so I can figure out where we're going."

Jena handed over the paper and opened the front door for Behn to leave first. She looked back up the staircase wishing Juila would have offered to go with her. She knew this was something she had to do on her own, but it still would have been nice. Her only consolation was that their mental link was stronger than ever and Juila would only be a thought away. Considerably heartened by this thought, she hurried after Behn and got into the front seat beside him in his car.

With her limited knowledge of the layout of the city, Jena soon became lost as Behn traversed the streets with confidence. She looked out the passenger window without really seeing anything other than the thoughts in her head. Every mile they drove brought her closer to the most important conversation she would ever have in her life. She hoped she would be able to keep her calm and remember the things about Luke which she loved and Willian did not possess.

Jena's attention was brought back to reality when Behn slowed the car down to a crawl as he tried to find the correct house on the street. She took a deep, calming breath and hoped Willian had already decided to go home after what had happened at school. She knew it was a cowardly thought, but at the moment she lacked confidence in herself.

"This is it," Behn announced as he pulled close to the curb in front of a small house. He turned to Jena and put his hand on her knee to offer comfort, "Speak from your heart. If you want to give him another chance, then that's what you need to do. As much as I care for Juila, I know she can be very vocal about her opinion. Juila doesn't have to live your life, you do. Remember that, Jena. This is your life and your future you're talking about."

"Thanks, Behn. I really needed to hear that," she said as she patted his hand. "I'm ready."

"Do you want me to wait out here or do you want to call me when you're ready to be picked up?"

"Oh, I hadn't considered that part! How far away from your house are we?"

"We're on the opposite end of the school district here. I'd say it's probably a twenty-minute drive. I don't mind waiting, or I could even come inside with you if you wanted."

"Oh, Behn, I don't know what I want. Maybe we should just go back home!" Jena could feel herself beginning to panic over the thought of confronting Willian. She was passive by nature, and this definitely put her out of her comfort zone.

"Sorry, Jena, that's not one of your options right now. I can see you are scared, but the best way to handle that is to tackle it straight on. Here's what we'll do. I'll walk you up to the door. If Willian seems to be happy to see you, then I'll come back to the car and wait until you are finished so I can drive you home. If Willian is still upset from earlier today, then we can leave. What do you think?"

"Fine," she said flatly. She was slightly heartened by the idea of having a friend by her side for the initial meeting. Maybe this would turn out better than she envisioned.

CHAPTER 37

Behn opened his door and walked around to Jena's side to open her door. She seemed to be having trouble mustering the courage to get out of the car, so he offered his hand to help her out of the seat. Jena chuckled at him as she took his hand. Behn could feel her hand trembling in his, and he gave hers a slight squeeze before letting it go.

They walked up the sidewalk to the front door together. When Jena merely stood at the door, Behn took the initiative to knock. They could hear a dog barking inside, and they both wondered whether or not anyone was home. Someone hushed the dog from inside, and then a woman opened the door with a pleasant expression on her face as she held a black Pomeranian in her arm.

"How can I help you?" she asked.

"My name is Jena Stel, and this is my friend Behn Wilson." Jena gestured over to Behn while she kept her gaze locked on the dog rather than the woman. She instantly looked up at the middle-aged woman and said, "I was told this's where Willian Potts is living right now and I was wondering if he were home."

"Oh, yes. Come on in. I'll get Willian."

"If it's okay with you, we'll wait outside until Willian sees me."

"We want to make sure Willian's in the mood to talk with Jena before I leave her alone with him," Behn put in helpfully.

"Ah!" Melissa said with raised eyebrows. Inside she was chuckling at how dramatic teenagers could be with their interactions with one another. "I'll be right back then."

Jena had done the unthinkable and had read her mind. She whispered to Behn, "She thinks we're being a tad bit overdramatic." The idea had heartened her slightly until she saw Willian walking toward her down the very short hallway to the front door. She was unable to see his expression since the corridor was dark, but she could see he still had a confident swagger to his step.

Willian's gaze immediately locked onto Jena's face and he could tell she was troubled. She was the very last person he expected to see on his doorstep. It pleased him greatly that she had sought him out rather than remain in hiding until he could find her again. His hopes for a reconciliation rose. He leaned on the doorframe and smiled down at Jena. "Who's your friend?"

"This is Juila's boyfriend, Behn. He gave me a ride over here. Do you think we could talk?"

"I came a long way so we could talk." He looked over at Behn and nodded his thanks for bringing Jena to him. "Why don't you both come inside and sit down?"

"I'll wait out in the car," Behn promptly answered as he could see Willian was willing to at least have a cordial conversation.

"Thanks, Behn," Jena spoke softly. "I don't think this'll take too long."

"Don't worry about me. Take as much time as you need." He waved half-heartedly over to Willian as he turned and jogged back to his car to wait.

"That was nice of him to give us some privacy. Will you come inside? We can talk privately in my room."

Jena was uncertain about the selected location even as she recalled Behn's advice to take the bull by the horns. She nodded and stepped into the house. She waited in the hall for Willian to shut the door and lead the way. From the short walk, she understood why Willian had picked his bedroom considering how small the house was with very little private space.

As soon as he shut the bedroom door, Jena rounded on him, "What were you thinking when you assaulted Luke at school today? I'm sure your father would be very proud of your behavior."

"Please leave my father out of this right now, Jena. That wasn't one of my finest moments. Can we sit down?" He moved over the bed and sat at the farthest edge so Jena would feel comfortable joining him.

Already Jena was off balance as Willian never would have backed down from a confrontation in the past. Maybe Rasa had been right to ask her to listen to him. Maybe he had actually changed. She nodded and stepped across the room to the bed and sat down.

"I'm not proud of my behavior today or in the past. I've treated you as if you were my property and I was wrong. I should have been rejoicing with the blessing given to me by Jehoban rather than pit myself against you all the time. I've been a complete jerk, and I'd understand if you told me you never wanted to see me again."

Jena stared in mute confusion wondering where this man had come from because he certainly was not the boy she had left in Tuala.

You aren't seriously falling for this, are you? Juila's voice spoke in her head.

I'm going to hear him out, she replied.

I think I'm going to throw up!

Then stop listening! Jena almost shouted back.

"What brought this change about?" she asked Willian.

"A lot has happened since you left, Jena. I've discovered several things about myself which I now realize were less than desirable. I'm actually shocked you wanted to come and see me after the stunt I pulled today."

"Mostly I wanted to avoid any future embarrassment," she admitted.

"I really am sorry, Jena. I don't know what came over me, well I do, really. When I saw Luke kissing you, all I could think was that should have been me you were kissing. I took out my own frustration on Luke when I should have kept it for myself. I'm going to apologize to Luke tomorrow."

"I hope you really mean that about apologizing to Luke," Jena spoke sternly.

"Absolutely, on Jehoban's honor," he promised.

Jehoban's oath was rarely given so Jena knew Willian would do as he had said. She felt so torn. On the one hand, she had a long-standing agreement with Willian, and on the other hand, she had developed feelings for Luke which would make the other agreement impossible. It was unlikely the two boys would agree to share her, so she was going to have to choose.

As if he had been reading her mind, Willian said, "I don't expect you to trust me so easily after our past together. I could see you really care for Luke and I think he's a nice guy as well. Will you promise you will at least spend some time getting to know me again? If you like the changes I've made in myself, then you can come back home to Tuala with me. If not, I won't object to a dissolution of our betrothal. Just give me some time, okay?"

Jena nodded since she could hardly refuse such an honest and heartfelt offer. She especially appreciated the fact that Willian had not discounted the relationship she had created with Luke. Willian was making it hard to remain angry at him, and she was certain that was his intention.

Willian smiled in genuine relief to Jena's agreement. "I'd like to apologize to your parents and Juila as well."

Jena's eyebrows rose nearly to her hairline in astonishment that Willian would want to put himself willingly in the line of fire with Juila.

Willian laughed out loud at Jena's expression. "I can tell you think that's a bad idea, but I really feel the need to do it. Please tell me you'll let me."

"It's your neck," Jena finally answered.

Willian breathed a sigh of relief. "Do you think I could come over sometime this week?"

"I think it'd be better to meet on neutral ground. Maybe we should get together for dinner or something."

"Whatever you want. I'm willing to do whatever will make you happier."

"Okay, I'm going to go for now, but I'll think about what you've told me. I'll call to let you know what night works for all of us. I'm assuming your schedule is pretty open?"

Willian snorted through his nose at Jena's understatement. "I have absolutely nothing going on! It'll be a relief to have somewhere to go in the evening. I look forward to hearing from you then. Can I walk you out to the car?"

"Sure," Jena replied shyly. She had never had him be so polite to her before, and she frankly did not know what to do with it. She kept waiting for something to set him over the edge and cause him to snap at her.

Give him a few more minutes, and you'll probably see it, Juila sneered.

Jena ignored her sister's comment and fell into step beside

Willian. She noticed he shorted his pace to remain beside her. This was something he had never done before. Maybe there was still hope for their relationship. Jena almost felt as though she were in a dream where everything worked out perfectly for everyone. Unfortunately, there was a third person in the mix, and she somehow doubted Luke would appreciate the competition.

"Thank you for coming over," Willian said as they neared the car. "Can I give you a hug?"

"Sure," she replied not knowing how to say anything else without giving unnecessary insult. Willian surprised her again as he put his arm across her shoulder and pulled her into a side hug. She had expected an embarrassing frontal hug where he would press against her suggestively as he had done in the past. Before it had always been a gesture to ensure she knew what to expect in the future after they were married. This embrace had been one of friendship and nothing else.

More flustered than she cared to admit, she reached for the car door at the same time as Willian. Their hands touched, and Jena withdrew hers immediately as though she had been shocked. Willian grinned as he opened the door. "I'll see you tomorrow."

"Okay," she replied lamely as she promptly sought refuge inside Behn's car. Expecting something more, Jena looked out the window to see Willian smiling as he shut the door. He waved and went back into his house.

"I take it the conversation went well," Behn stated as he started the engine. When Jena still remained silent, he asked, "Are you okay?"

"Yes. I don't know what I'm going to do, Behn. I think I'm in love with two different men."

"Hmm, that does make things rather awkward. Is Willian pressuring you to make a choice?"

"Quite the opposite, he said he wanted me to take my time."

Jena turned in her seat to face Behn as she said, "Willian is going to apologize to Luke the next time he sees him."

"Wow, that's rather good of him. I hope Luke will let him talk."

"Me, too. He seemed rather hurt that I'd kept my relationship a secret from him. Do you think I should have told him?"

"That's not for me to say. Your situation is rather unique, after all. How many other kids in our school are betrothed? You would have had a lot of explaining to do."

"My life would be easier with Willian since we are both from Tuala. If I decided to stay with Luke, then I'd have to tell him everything. What if he decided I'd lied or omitted too much in our relationship and decided I wasn't worth it?"

"I don't think that's Luke's style." Behn checked around the car and pulled out onto the residential street. "So what's next with you two?"

"He wants to meet with my parents and Juila to apologize to them."

Behn whistled his appreciation of the situation. "Brave man! Somehow I don't think Juila will let him finish." He chuckled at the scene he could easily see in his head.

Truer words have never been spoken, Juila chimed in.

Jena rolled her eyes and remained silent from both Behn and her sister. She had a lot to consider, and both of her choices were hard. At least she no longer had to fear another confrontation at the school. She felt rather pleased with herself for handling the situation as she had and knew Behn had played a significant role in the execution. "Thanks for everything, Behn. I wouldn't have gone through with this if it weren't for you pushing me. I would have spent the next few days in fear of what was going to happen next."

"I think you might still have to worry about that when you get home, and Juila gets ahold of you," Behn chuckled.

"I think I might make it work out, Pesi," Willian spoke to the dog as though she could understand him. He had returned to his room with a new outlook on the time he would be spending on Earth. As though she had felt his shift in mood, Pesi had wandered into his room and begged at the side of his bed to be brought up.

He laughed as Pesi gave him a small bark because he had paused in his petting of her. She definitely knew what she wanted, and Willian was willing to allow her to call the shots. He realized he was going to have to do the same thing with Jena.

Looking down at Pesi he thought to himself; *I wonder if pets are put into people's lives to make them less selfish.* Another bark from the dog made him laugh and focus his attention on pleasing her. The dog rolled over so he could rub the spot on her chest where she liked it the best.

"It's too bad Juila isn't as easy to please as you are, Pesi," Willian said as he kept rubbing her chest. "I'm afraid it'll be a long time before I win her over."

"It might not take as long as you think," Melissa said from his doorway. Pesi immediately rolled over and jumped off of the bed. She licked Melissa's leg a couple of times and then moved away to get some kibbles of food from the kitchen.

"Jena's sister really hates me. I can't really blame her since I've earned all of it, unfortunately," Willian admitted.

"Be patient and give her time to see how you've changed," Melissa encouraged. "Dinner is ready if you're hungry." She could tell the discussion had gone well with Jena since Willian was actually seeming upbeat now. She had been worried that he would continue to get surlier the longer he went without speaking to Jena. It had been a relief when the pretty, young girl had appeared on their doorstep.

"I'm famished," Willian announced with a huge smile. "I can't recall a time when I felt so good. Thank you for putting up with my deplorable behavior. I'll try to be better from now on."

Melissa smiled at his apology. She wished kids from Earth would be so thoughtful. She would be sad to see Willian leave to go back home.

JENA IMMEDIATELY WENT UPSTAIRS to sit in her room. Her emotions were in turmoil as she tried to reconcile her memories of Willian's past treatment of her against how he had behaved at his house. An agreement had been forged for her to spend her life with Willian and she had been willing to cast it aside in favor of being with Luke because he treated her the way she felt she deserved to be treated.

The phone on her nightstand rang, and she tried to ignore it. On the third ring, she finally rolled over on her bed and answered the call.

"Is this Jena?" Luke asked.

"Yes," she answered in a whisper. She could not believe Luke was calling her after what had happened at school earlier in the day. Maybe he wanted to talk it over with her and tell her he was willing to fight for her.

"I know we had made plans to go to the movies tonight…"

"Yes, I'm looking forward to it."

"Well, I was thinking it might not be the best timing for you. It seems as though you have some unfinished business with Willian and I don't want to get in the middle of it. I'm sorry, Jena, but I can't go tonight."

"What are you saying, Luke?"

"I don't want to interfere with you and Willian working things out."

"But what about what I want?"

"You need time to figure that out for yourself. I'm sorry, Jena. I just can't do this. Bye." He hung up the phone.

Jena pulled the receiver away from her ear and stared at it, disbelieving he had actually hung up on her. Her mind felt numb as she dropped the phone receiver back onto the charging cradle. It seemed as though Luke had made the decision for her; he did not want to be involved with her. She could not believe he was unwilling to stand by her or even hear what she had to say about the situation with Willian.

She turned on her bed and punched her pillow before she grabbed it and stuffed it against her face as she screamed her frustration into it. Why did boys have to be so complicated? Why did they have to disappoint her? Why did she care so much to allow herself to be hurt by them? Tears of anger overflowed her eyes and dampened the pillowcase.

Her inner turmoil must have alerted her sister because she was suddenly by her side. She felt Juila's arm draped across her back.

She wanted to be able to think everything through, but she was afraid of being alone.

"Luke doesn't know what he's saying right now, Jena. I think he was just embarrassed by what happened with Willian. Don't lose faith in him yet. Give him some time, okay?"

Jena was thankful for their mind link so she would not have to say out loud what Luke had just done. Even thinking about it again felt like a knife stabbing in her heart. She felt so betrayed and abandoned. She wished she had never taken Juila's advice about dating other boys; then she would not be feeling so torn up inside.

"It wasn't a mistake, Jena. You learned a great deal about what you want in a man. Luke was always respectful, caring, and kind. He was everything Willian was not, and you needed to see the difference."

Jena could tell her sister was trying to be helpful, but all her talk only convinced her she had made a mistake in letting Luke get close to her. She had allowed another person to take a piece of her heart and break it like it was worthless. She could only allow that to happen once or twice in her life before she would only feel like a shell of a person.

"Please don't think like that, Jena. I have a feeling deep within me that things are going to work out just exactly as they should. Have faith that we have been led in the right direction. When you're older, and you look back on this time, you'll laugh at how silly you're being right now."

"That's easy for you to say, you still have your boyfriend. Mine just dumped me because of Willian. Now I don't know what I'm going to do. What's going to happen at school? Will Luke stop talking to us? Will he sit at a different table at lunch? I hate this!"

"Luckily there's only a couple more days of school before the break. I think a little time and space will make Luke think twice about not fighting for you. You're worth the fight, and if he can't see that, then he's not the right man for you."

Juila spoke with such conviction that it halfway convinced Jena that she may be onto some truth. They would be leaving for Tuala as soon as the break started. She could have some time away from everyone where she could discover what it was that she wanted for herself.

BEHN DROVE AS FAST as he dared to get back home after dropping Jena back off at her house. He was glad he had been able to help out the girls with their issue even though he knew Juila was now mad at him. His focus now was finding out how his sister was faring. He could not shake the idea there was something terribly wrong with her. She had not been the same ever since she had returned from the fateful trip back to their old homestead.

Once he was at home, he knocked softly on her bedroom door and was surprised when she told him to enter. He poked his head around the door and asked, "Are you feeling any better?"

"Not really," she answered even though she never looked up from what she was reading on the desk.

"What are you looking at?" Behn asked as he moved into the room to get a closer look.

"I found this in Grobin's house in the Roanoke Colony. I was hoping to be able to read it with better lighting, but I think it's pretty hopeless. The ink is too old and faded to make out more than a few words here and there. Tell me what you think?" She moved off to the side so Behn could lean over her shoulder.

"There's probably someone who could restore the ink on the page, depending on what it's made out of. Don't throw it away. I'll do some research and get back to you on it."

Valentina sat back with a disgruntled sigh and rubbed her temples.

"I have news about our mother," Behn changed the subject.

"What?" Valentina perked up a little.

"She's been appointed the leader in Roanoke, and she and our sister have moved back to our old home. We could go back there and visit, even spend the night, now that she has her own home again. What do you think?"

Valentina was horrified to think about going back to the town where Grobin used to live. She groaned in agony as she clutched her head. "I need to lie down again. My head is killing me." She swiveled in the chair and took the two steps to flop down on the mattress.

Behn watched her curl up on the bed with her back to him. He kept feeling like he should try to keep her talking. For a moment there she had seemed like her old self, but now she was closing herself off again.

Not wanting to leave things the way they were, Behn crossed the room and sat on the edge of the bed. He reached out to touch her shoulder and was shocked when she about jumped out of her skin. "I'm sorry to have startled you, Val. Do you want to talk about what happened?"

Valentina's head whipped around, and her eyes bored into his as she asked, "What did Juila tell you?"

Behn raised his eyebrows at her sudden change of tone and then shook his head slightly as he replied, "All she said was to give you some time. A lot of people are afraid of dying, Val. Anything you said while you were up there was only your fear talking. You don't have to be ashamed of wanting to live."

Valentina shut her eyes to hide her relief. It seemed as though Juila had not betrayed her confidence and Behn was unaware of what had really happened while they were being held captive. She breathed deeply while she thought of how to reply to Behn's statement. Her heart rate began to decrease as she said, "I don't want to talk about it, Behn. Can you please let me rest?"

"Okay, but if you decide you want to, I'll listen." He wanted to stay and comfort her, but it seemed as though she wanted to be left alone. His hand hovered over her shoulder, and he thought better of touching her again. With a shake of his head at how useless he felt in this situation, he stood up and quietly left the room.

VALENTINA WAITED until she heard the door click shut before she allowed her emotions to take control. Her shoulders shook with the strength of her muffled sobs. She stuffed her pillow up against her face to keep anyone from hearing the tormented cries of fear.

Her brothers could never know what she had endured at the hands of Grobin. She was certain they would kill him, and it would ruin their lives. Secretly she wished she had been able to kill Grobin herself, but she had proved weak and paralyzed to do anything to help herself.

While the physical wounds of the attack had been healed from her body, the mental wounds were still raw and painful. Valentina's mind kept replaying the act over and over, each time creating a more violent and intense scene. She felt so violated and scared for her future. Until she knew the outcome of Grobin's physical attack, Valentina could not possibly return to a normal life. Normal, she scoffed, I will never be normal ever again. I'm tainted, used goods. Nobody will ever want me now.

Fresh tears poured from her eyes. She cried for the innocent girl who had been taken from her. She cried for how simple it had been for Grobin to take her. Mostly, however, she cried for her shattered future. After a while, the tears seemed to have run out. Valentina's wracking sobs had exhausted her entire body until all she could do was close her eyes and pray for sleep without dreams of Grobin.

CHAPTER 39

Rasa spent one more night at the Stel house before she knew she would have to return to Manzanit to continue with her studies with Elder Wilken. The extra time spent on Earth was mostly to benefit Gevena. The girl had been so traumatized by her recent past that Rasa wanted to make sure she had some peaceful time to recover before they took her to Manzanit to begin her new life.

Several correspondences had been sent and received from Elder Wilken regarding his opinion on the best plan of action for the displaced girl. He had been thrilled to hear that Gevena had wanted to return to his Residence. His own daughter was grown and had moved far away; he was going to enjoy having another young girl around. She would be like the granddaughter he would never have.

The morning arrived along with a thunderstorm. She always enjoyed the feel of the air around her and the smell of the charged particles. She sat at her open window and watched the flashes of lightning as they lit up the sky. The storm was coming closer which thrilled her.

Her bedroom door opened, causing Rasa to wonder who would need her at this early hour. She saw Gevena enter, her eyes wide with fear. Rasa swiftly left the window seat and went over to give the young girl comfort. "Hey, it's okay," she said soothingly as she rubbed the girl's bony back.

"I hate thunder," she whispered. "It reminds me of the times my father would come home drunk and tear the house apart in his rage to find more money to go out and gamble again. He always made so much noise with his yelling and stomping."

"I'm sorry, Gevena. I love the storms; they remind me of Jehoban's power. He controls everything, and I imagine each flash of lightning is a visual reminder to pay attention, and the thunder is His voice proclaiming His power." She pulled away from Gevena and said, "Let me go close my window so it won't be so loud."

"No, Rasa, you don't have to do that. I like your explanation of the storm better than mine. Maybe if I thought of it your way, then I could begin to appreciate it rather than fear it."

Rasa smiled at Gevena's attempt to please her. "Do you want to sit at the window seat with me then?"

With only a slight hesitation, Gevena nodded and followed her to the window. She sat down with her back to the edge of the window drawing her legs up in front of her with her nightgown pulled over her knees. She folded her hands across her shins and rested her chin on her knees.

"How do you feel about going to Manzanit today? I have obligations I need to get back to, and I think everything is under control here now." Rasa watched Gevena's expression carefully to make sure she was actually ready. She was pleased to see the girl did not flinch like she had previously.

Gevena rubbed her lips together and began to gnaw on them

nervously as she thought it over. Finally, she nodded her head while her chin remained resting on her knees. She already owed so much to Rasa for offering her a place to live, the least she could do would be to agree to leave when Rasa needed to go.

"You're going to love it there. We have so many private gardens where you can relax and hear yourself think. We can enroll you in school so you can catch up on the things you've fallen behind in."

Gevena groaned at the idea of school. She knew how far behind she actually was and she hated to have to admit her lack to Rasa. She decided to tell on herself right away rather than wait for Rasa to find out on her own and be disappointed. "I stopped going to school several anons ago. My father told me it was a waste of time and he wanted me to be at home to take care of him while he was drunk. I'm sorry, Rasa."

"Don't worry about it, Gevena. We'll get you caught up in no time. I will make sure I'm available to tutor you so you can catch up with the rest of the kids your age. It'll be fine, you'll see," Rasa said as she patted the girl's toes where they peeked out from the skirt of her nightgown.

Gevena wanted to believe it could be so simple. She tried to feel as confident about the situation as Rasa obviously was and she smiled tentatively. "I'll try not to disappoint you."

"Don't worry about that. As long as you do your best, I'll always be proud of you."

Feeling shy at the praise, Gevena turned her head to look out the window. She wished Rasa could have been her mother instead of the woman who had left her when she was only a toddler. All of her life she had wanted to make her father proud of her, yet he always found fault in whatever she did. Here Rasa was saying she would be proud no matter what, it was almost too good to be true.

"When are we going to leave?"

"Right after we eat breakfast. There's nothing to keep us here, and plenty awaiting us at home."

"I wish I could have said goodbye to Juila and Jena. They've been so nice to me. I've often wondered what it would be like to have a sister or even a best friend. Since I've gotten to know them, it seems like they've taken on both of those roles with me."

"They are both able to fly telepods, so I'm sure they'll come and visit you once you've gotten yourself settled in. I told them last night that we'd be going." Rasa stood up and walked across the guest bedroom where she picked up two envelopes from her nightstand. She returned to the window seat and held out the notes to Gevena. "The girls asked me to give these to you since they weren't going to see you before you had to leave."

Gevena held the paper in her hand, wondering if she should open them now or wait until she was alone. Opting for the latter, she set them down on the bench seat beside her. It made her feel even more special to have her own private notes to read. Nobody had ever written to her before, and it was exciting to imagine a little longer what the girls might have shared with her.

"It looks like the storm has blown itself out," Rasa commented. She stared out the window and wished it could have lasted longer. She sighed at the inevitable. Her time off was officially over, and she was going to have to return to her duties with Elder Wilken again. "You best get yourself ready to head out. Meet me in the kitchen when you're done."

Gevena scampered off of the bench with her letters held tightly to her chest. She looked forward to the adventures ahead of her while also worrying about learning a new place and meeting new people. Her life had definitely taken a turn for the better ever since she had been rescued by Juila. It was a debt she doubted she could ever repay, but she would do her best to find a way.

SOFIA COULD HARDLY CONTAIN her curiosity over what Jon had seen and remembered because of his visit home to Tuala. The incident with the telepod had overshadowed the purpose of their trip. Everyone had been so happy for them to return safely, that Jon's original idea of seeing his childhood home was temporarily forgotten.

She caught up to Jon as they were heading to lunch. She put her hand on his arm to be able to keep up with him in the crowded hallway. "What was your home like?" she said quietly as she leaned closer to him.

He smiled down at her and answered, "It was really cool. The house was just a small shack, but I remembered a lot more than I thought I would. Just like it was for Val, I could see us all living inside the cabin, laughing and talking. There were some things I recognized outside the house, but not nearly as much. I was a pretty sickly kid, so I spent most of my time indoors."

"Did Val have any breakthroughs from going there again?"

"I don't really know. She's been so quiet since…you know."

"Is she really okay? I mean, it's been three days now, and she still hasn't come back to school. I really doubt a migraine would last this long. Maybe there's another problem."

"Maybe, but I sure can't imagine what it would be. It's possible she just wanted Christmas break to be a week longer!" He chuckled at his own joke even though he knew it was unlike his sister to ditch school.

Sofia merely smiled to be polite. She had seen Valentina's face when they were trying to get her off of the telepod. Something was definitely wrong with her. Her suspicions were heightened when Juila had translated Valentina directly to her room rather than taking her through the house where all of the other people were congregated. It seemed there was more to Valentina's story than anyone was sharing.

"Have you had any more breakthroughs since you've been home?"

"Not really."

"What was it like up in space?" Sofia had been dying to ask him about it.

"Big!" he shivered at the memory. "It was dark, cold, and really quiet. I'm pretty sure I wouldn't make a good astronaut now that I've had some experience with it."

They got into the lunch line, so their conversation naturally came to an end. Sofia continued to fantasize about their epic adventure. She was certain there was more to what had gone on, and Jon was just downplaying the gravity of the events. Valentina seemed to still be suffering from the journey, yet it remained unclear why.

NEAL'S MEETINGS with Dr. Medin had been both amazing and disturbing at the same time. After each hypnosis session, he felt like he was more in control of his memories, even if they did make very little sense. Just as the doctor had asked, Neal faithfully wrote down all of the details he could recall of the time he had been missing.

He flipped back through several of the journal pages and reread what he had noted. It still seemed as though his mind were working in a dream-like state since many of the accounts made little sense.

One particular story had him living with a woman who looked like Amanda, who he believed was named Vinia. She had stood in their kitchen and asked him what he wanted for dinner. He had told her and then instantly the food appeared on the table. Obviously, this story was just that: a story.

He hoped the truth would eventually become apparent. He rested his temple on his left fist as he tapped his pen onto the page of the journal. He contemplated what more he could do to encourage his memories to return. So far he had followed all of the doctor's instructions of eating right, getting lots of sleep, and writing in his journal.

Thinking there was one other option, Neal picked up the phone and dialed Amanda's phone number. He hoped she would take his call. Several more rings sounded in his ear before the answering machine turned on. He listened to Amanda instructing him to leave a message after the beep.

The beep sounded, and Neal said, "Hi, Amanda. Thanks for referring me to Dr. Medin. I think it's helping a lot. I'd love to sit down with you and Riccan to talk about a few things which are still confusing. Give me a call and let me know when we can get together. Thanks. Bye."

He hung up the receiver and sighed deeply. It was too much to expect Amanda to be sitting around waiting for his phone call. Hopefully, she would call him back. With another sigh, he flipped the pages in his journal to the last page written in. After another few taps of his pen on the table top, he began writing a few more details of memory.

CHAPTER 40

Captain Ahn came home from work and walked into the eerily quiet front entrance of their house. He had grown used to the sound of Danika's giggling and nonsense chatter. He sighed as he took his coat off and hung it in the hall closet.

Barla appeared at the end of the hallway and smiled as she stepped toward him. Ahn still thought she was the most beautiful and amazing woman he had ever known. After being married to her for more than two declans, he never tired of her warm embrace when he arrived home from work. She was the reason he came home rather than work late hours down at the dock as he had once done in the past before she had appeared in his life.

He pulled back from her and gave her a passionate kiss. "I love you, Barla," he whispered with his lips still touching hers. He could feel her lips curl in a smile as he knew she would. He rested his forehead against hers and said, "The house is entirely too quiet with only Corva running around."

"I know what you mean. I spent all day going from room to

room expecting to hear Danika's babble and see Vinia carrying her around getting her tired enough for a nap. Maybe we should look at taking in another orphaned baby." She was always ready for more children, yet Ahn had been less receptive for the last several anons.

"Now it's one thing to have a baby with a mother, and it's quite another when you are expected to be the mother. Call me selfish, but I want to spend my evenings with you!" He pulled her beside him and began walking down the hall to get to the kitchen. "I'm famished. What should we make for dinner tonight?"

They reached the doorway to the kitchen and Ahn had his second surprise for the day: dinner was already made and set out at the informal table for them. "You made glawlets!" It was his favorite dish, and he promptly became distracted by the thought of eating them.

"I also made enskil dumplings with foxl crisps and butter along with baked krumpli with clotted cream. Here is a bowl of tocolas and a pot of java. I had so much time on my hands that I thought I could go all out and get this ready as a surprise for you."

"You are amazing."

"I have to admit I used my birth crystal to create some of the easier things, but it was good practice. Corva should be home any minute, and then we can sit down to eat. Why don't you go upstairs and wash up?"

"Gladly! If Corva isn't here by the time I get back, then we'll just have to be rude and start without her!" Ahn winked as he turned around to head up to his bedroom to get changed into more comfortable clothes and to freshen up.

Barla rushed to the back door to see if Corva were on her way back from the neighbor's house. She really disliked beginning dinner without everyone present. It felt incomplete when they left anyone out, even if they were late.

She could hear Ahn stomping around upstairs, and she smiled as she imagined him rushing through his routine to get back down to his favorite meal. The glawlets were a typical breakfast food, but Ahn had insisted it was proper to eat good food at any time of the day, so she made the exception for him.

Still looking outside, Barla heard Ahn coming down the stairs just as Corva jumped over the back fence and ran through their yard. Barla was pleased to see Corva was still young enough to be a tomboy. All too soon she would become a serious young adult and not want to be playful anymore unless a boy were involved. Barla opened the door and called out, "Hurry up and wash your hands. Ahn is coming downstairs right now and he's excited about the glawlets!"

Corva skidded past Barla and rushed over to the kitchen sink. She splashed the water furiously all over her hands, arms, and then face. She grabbed the towel to dry off just as Ahn entered the kitchen. "Hi, Dad!" she mumbled through the cloth of the towel as she wiped her face.

The three of them sat down and had their prayer of thanks before Ahn filled his plate with several glawlets. He would sample everything else only after he had gotten his fill of the rare delicacy.

Barla and Corva exchanged knowing grins as they chose other dishes until he became less protective of the glawlets plate. They ate silently since they were all very hungry after having been busy right up until dinnertime. When Ahn went back for second help-ings, Barla said, "I received a call from Nena today. She wants us to meet with her and a few other people tomorrow afternoon at the Pantano Residence. I told her we'd be there, so I hope you can clear your schedule."

Ahn looked at her with a puzzled expression since it was unlike Barla to make plans for them without consulting him first. When he saw her tip her head and raise her eyebrow to indicate this was not optional, he answered, "I'll make the time."

Barla nodded and resumed eating. She did not want to concern Corva with what they were getting involved in, but she wanted to make sure Ahn knew what was coming before she somehow forgot about it. She knew Ahn would want to discuss the issue further, but he had taken her hint about it being a private matter. Being married for so long had the benefit of being able to read each other very well indeed.

The evening remained quiet as the three of them sat in the living room around the fireplace. Corva sat off to the side at the small desk and worked on her homework. Ahn talked about some of the more bizarre happenings down at the dock. One piece of news stood out more than any other.

"Someone reported Petre sailing south of here, supposedly heading out of our area."

"It seems rather coincidental that he would leave at the same time Vinia left, don't you think?"

"Rather," Ahn agreed. "I wonder how he found out."

"The man who's been sleeping down the road is gone, too. Do you think maybe that was Petre?" Corva asked innocently.

"What? What man, Corva? How come you never said anything about him before?" Ahn stood up in his agitation. To think that Petre may have been spying on their house made him furious. "Did you ever get a good look at his face? Could you identify him if you saw a plasfilm of him?"

"Ahn, slow down. Can't you see you're scaring Corva?" Barla grabbed her husband's arm and pulled him back down into his seat. She turned to their daughter and asked, "Could you identify him, Corva?"

"I think so," she answered softly. She hated it when she disappointed Ahn, and clearly, she had done something bad to get him so upset with her. Unbidden, tears began to drop down her cheeks.

Barla saw it and rushed over to comfort her. "Corva, please don't cry. Dad isn't mad at you. He really doesn't like Petre, and he's upset thinking he's been hanging around our house." She pulled her daughter into her arms and rubbed her back to sooth her until she stopped crying. "That's better. Can you remember the first time you saw the man sleeping?"

"He'd been there for weeks. He tried to hide whenever we went out to play, but he wasn't very good at it. I haven't seen him since Senin morning when I went to school."

"Can you show us where he was?" Ahn asked softly, trying not to make Corva cry again.

Corva nodded, and the three of them left the house together. The walked down the road a short distance and then Corva pointed to the area. "He was right over there by the tree."

Ahn stomped across the road and investigated all around the area. He went up to the nearest house and knocked on the door. When the woman answered, he asked, "Have you seen a man hanging around that tree?"

She nodded and said, "I'm relieved he finally left. He refused to talk to me whenever I asked him what he was doing. I assumed he didn't know how to talk."

"Thanks. If you see him again, will you let me know?"

The woman nodded again and closed her door.

Ahn returned to his wife and daughter. He put his arm around Corva and said, "You did really well. Thank you for telling us. I'm going to get a plasfilm of Petre so you can tell me for certain if it's who we suspect it is." He squeezed her shoulder as they walked back to their house.

When they returned to the living room, Corva gathered up her schoolbooks and declared, "I'm heading up to bed now. Goodnight." She rushed out of their presence, eager to get to the sanctuary of her room.

Ahn frowned at how poorly he had handled the situation. She was such a sensitive child. He was going to have to find a way to make it up to Corva. Finally, he sighed and turned his attention back to his wife.

"What's going on tomorrow that you didn't want to discuss in front of Corva?"

"Amanda has requested a meeting of everyone who was present at Jehoban's meeting. I think something significant has happened, but I can't be sure."

"You've certainly spent enough time with her lately, how come you don't know for sure?"

"I've spent most of my time with Diane, actually. Amanda has been busy with the people from Roanoke, not to mention the scare of almost losing Juila in the telepod incident. That must have been absolutely terrifying for her, for all of them really." Barla shivered at the idea of it all.

"How is it being with your sister again?"

"Bittersweet, actually," Barla began and tried to find the right words to describe what she really meant. "I tell her about my life here, and I know she can never come to visit. She'll never be able to share friends with me or see the things I've seen. Do you know what I mean?"

"I get the idea," he agreed.

"I also wish I could go and see my mom and Saul. It's great to know they are alive and well, yet I could never explain to them that I've been living in another dimension. They'd never believe it, and I doubt they'd forgive me for staying away, even if it were for love. Family means everything to them so I'm sure they'd say I'd turned my back on them which hurts to even think about."

"So don't think about that part," Ahn advised simply.

"I try not to, but it seems to seep into my thoughts unbidden. Diane tells me the same thing. She seems to be very happy with her life. I doubt I'd be able to meet her other two daughters for the same reason, however. They both are married and live pretty far away so the chance would be unlikely anyhow. Do you know what's really strange?"

"What's that?"

"Neither Carrie nor Deanna has made any time to come and see Amanda since she got out of her coma. Don't you think that's strange?"

"Like you said, they're both married and have children and lives of their own. Besides, maybe they weren't that close anyway."

"Still, if my sister woke up after seven anons, I think I'd find the time to tell her I was happy for her." Barla sat back in her chair and wondered what had gone wrong among the three sisters to make them drift so far apart. Surely it could not have been as significant of a problem as Barla had experienced by being in a different dimension. There was simply no excuse for such selfish behavior.

"Leave it alone, Barla. It's not your place to interfere in their business. I can see the wheels turning in your head." He chuckled at the guilty expression on Barla's face as he called her out.

"Sometimes I think you know me too well!" she accused. "Let's head up to bed. We have a big day tomorrow, and we need to be well rested."

"I can't wait to hear what Amanda has for us next," he said as he held Barla's hand on the way up to their bedroom.

CHAPTER 41

D r. Gascon opened the latest packet of pictures and notes from the private investigator. He inspected the pictures first and frowned at the number of people coming and going from the estate at such odd hours of the day. One picture, in particular, was disturbing because it had a carload of women who could not be accounted for in the investigator's report.

Once again, Dr. Gascon was faced with a strange scenario of having people leave the house without any evidence of them arriving in the first place. He did not care for mysteries, and it angered him that he had to stoop to such levels as hiring a private investigator when Amanda could have just told him what was going on. He threw the pictures down in disgust and shifted his attention to the written report on Neal's movements.

His mood did not improve as he finally got to the end of the report and read that Dr. Jasmine Medin was now treating Neal. She had once been his employee before he had fired her for insubordination. She had been so upset with her rightful termination that she had caused a medical review board to examine his patient records to make sure he was providing legal care. It still galled him that he had had to endure the injustice of his peers questioning his methods.

"That bitch has a lot of nerve stealing my patient from me. She will regret taking him on!" He slammed the report down and began thinking furiously of how he could get even with her.

ALENA FRETTED over having the kids ready to head over to Tana's house next door so they would be able to get to the meeting on time. When she had told Bryon about it several days before, he had been concerned about getting some meetings rescheduled so he could be sure to attend. The original message they had received was the meeting was tentatively set and only found out the evening before that it had been finalized.

Finally, all three of her children were standing in front of her impatiently waiting to go. Alena gave each of them a hug, "Now you guys be on your best behavior for Tana. I know she likes spending time with all of you, but you do take advantage of her kindness sometimes."

Justan looked down at the floor in embarrassment because he knew he was the worst culprit for his mother's admonition. "We'll be good, Mom. You'll see."

Alena kissed the top of his head and wondered again how he had gotten so tall. "Off you go now, Tana is waiting. You might end up spending the night since your father and I have something important to take care of, and we're not sure how long it will take. I love you," she called after them as they raced across the yard to get to the next-door neighbor's house. She waved as she saw Tana step off of her porch to greet the exuberant children.

Bryon's telepod popped into existence in front of their garage just as she turned to shut the door. Alena sighed with relief to know they would not be late now. She waited at the door for him to power down the telepod and get out. She gave him a quick hug and kiss in greeting and then said, "Hurry up and get changed so we can go."

"I'm on it," he answered even as he kept walking past her to get to their bedroom. Not bothering to be tidy about it, Bryon tossed his work clothes onto the bed and grabbed the outfit he had already selected from the chair. He returned to the front entry while he finished tucking in his shirt. "All set. Let's go!"

Alena nodded approval of how he looked and then opened the door for him. They situated themselves in the small telepod and Alena fussed over the seatbelt until Bryon set the coordinates for the Pantano Residence. She had been afraid they were going to have to time it and that always scared her. Now they would be early for the meeting, just as she always liked to be.

"Ready?" Bryon asked suddenly.

"Yep!"

Blackness surrounded them for three seconds as they traveled between locations. Alena let out a breath of relief as the sunlight once again poured through the windows of the telepod. She looked below them to see if she could identify any other telepods to know who had arrived before them. There were only two telepods so they, indeed, were early.

Bryon expertly set the telepod down on the landing field. He powered down the craft and opened the side door for them to get out. Alena unbuckled and left the craft first with Bryon immediately behind her. He palmed the control to shut the cabin door and then took Alena's hand as they walked across the expansive lawn to get to the Residence's stairs.

THEY COULD SEE all of the other telepods already in the yard. Amanda felt terrible that they were the last ones to arrive when it was a meeting for which they had asked. She glanced over at Riccan with an 'I told you so' look.

Riccan laughed and replied, "They just got here early. I promise you we are not late!" He did, however, rush through the landing and shut-down procedures to appease his wife. Once the four of them were on their way across the grass, Riccan used his remote to cloak his telepod.

Amanda looked back in amazement and asked, "Do you really think that's necessary?"

"I don't want to take any chances after what happened before."

Amanda nodded and readjusted the bag's strap on her shoulder. The samaras were bulky to transport when they were all together. She had wrapped them each in their own hand towel so they would not rub together or damage one another.

They marched up the stairs, across the patio, and through the great room where all of them had enjoyed spending time in the past. Nobody was looking for this to be a leisurely visit, however, so they continued down the hall to the largest conference room in the Residence.

As soon as they entered the room, Amanda could see the people were milling around and getting reacquainted with one another in a friendly fashion. Nobody seemed disturbed by what she would deem a late arrival, so she calmed herself down and smiled at Nena who came over to greet them.

"You are right on time," she said as she pulled Amanda down to give her a kiss on the cheek. She then looked her deeply in the eyes and remarked, "You look wonderful. Married life is good for you."

She smiled warmly as she patted Amanda's cheek and then she left her to go greet her two granddaughters.

Amanda watched as Nena greeted each person in her family with warmth and realized she had done just the right thing to ease their tension. Obviously, Nena was used to having gatherings of varying cordiality at the Residence, and she was an expert at making everyone feel welcome. This was just another aspect of being married to an Elder which Amanda would have to learn someday when Riccan finally stepped up to fill his father's position.

Apparently, things were working out in favor of this meeting because everyone asked to come was here in the room, including Rasa who had only left their house the day before. Amanda was pleased to see Elder Debbon and Chelesa had been able to make the meeting. There had been some discussion about whether or not they would be able to get away for the time needed.

Thinking she did not want to delay the inevitable, Amanda clapped her hands to get everyone's attention. Several claps later, discussions around the room ended, and all eyes turned to Amanda. "I'd like to thank everyone for coming together today," Amanda announced to the group. "Please be seated so we can begin."

While everyone took their places around the table in front of her, Amanda removed the bag from her shoulder and placed it gently on the table. Riccan sat on her left side with their daughters next to him, while Daven sat on her right side with Nena next to him. Amanda realized her family represented over half of the attendees at this meeting whether by birth or by marriage.

A murmur of wonder sounded around the group as Amanda began to withdraw the samaras from her bag, unwrap them, and set them carefully on the table in front of her. "As you can see, I have brought several samaras with me, and they will need to be stored in the Residences of the Elders."

The first one she pulled out belonged to Barla, then Bryon's, and finally Nena's. She watched the expressions of the people around the table at the placement of each stone. The owners of the crystal skulls knew when there's had been exposed, and she still found it fascinating that they could have such a bond with them.

"For some of you, this will be the first time you have seen these crystals. They have been around for thousands of anons, so long, in fact, that they have become legends in your world instead of reality. I can assure you, as well as the owners of these crystals; these are definitely real and very powerful.

"There have been seven samaras which have been identified as belonging to people in this room. At this point, we believe it has become obvious that each person in here will eventually have their own samara. While we still don't know the significance of this, we hope to be able to figure it all out as a group." Amanda sat down and waited for the murmuring to stop. She hoped her final statement would have the people present begin to wonder how they were to get their own samaras.

Riccan watched the group carefully before he spoke. "There are several clues which have brought us to conclude what Amanda has just told you. First, the legend says there are thirteen samaras, and there are thirteen of us here at this meeting. Jehoban called the rest of you to a meeting to help Amanda after the three of us had already received our samaras, so we were not needed at His original meeting.

"Second, the Unity Song which says:

> *Crystal around the neck,*
> *Follow the next step,*
> *Changes today,*

Changes tomorrow,
We all become one.

"This seems to imply changes must be made for us all to become one. There are still some questions as to how this will happen, but hopefully, it will be revealed to us as we delve into it further.

"Third, Amanda discovered a new prophecy—from her dream, no less—in an ancient text hidden in a secret location known only to me. I know each of you has received your own copy of the prophecy, however, I will speak it again as a refresher:

When the descendants of the Watchers bring these all together, then the gates between the worlds will be open for all to pass through without a loss.

"Those of us who have linked with our samaras can tell you with absolute certainty, the true owners of the samaras are descendants of the Watchers. Only a true owner can access the histories in the crystals, so we know we are the ancient offspring of the original Watchers."

"Who were the Watchers?" Barla asked.

Riccan nodded slightly as he declared, "They are a select group of Jehoban's angels."

"Oh," Barla whispered. She stared at her samara on the table across from her with renewed wonder. Hearing how others had communed with their crystals made Barla wish she had also had the opportunity to know what her samara held within its stored memories.

Just as Riccan cleared his throat to begin speaking again, Juila touched his arm and whispered, "I'd like to address the group."

Riccan nodded and wondered what she would have to add to the conversation. He had learned to appreciate the knowledge his daughters brought to them based on their unique upbringing with Jehoban. "Go ahead."

Juila slowly stood up, and all eyes immediately turned to her. She could feel her face beginning to redden as the group waited for her to speak. "Some of you know," and she looked directly at Rasa, "I had an unfortunate incident with my father's telepod. The crystal drive system malfunctioned while I was transferring between Tuala and Earth and I ended up floating in space. As with all of the other events in our lives, this one turned out to be a good thing in many ways. This," she said as she pulled out the broken samara and placed it on the table, "is not so good."

There were gasps around the table as they saw the two pieces lying side-by-side. Her own parents were wondering why Juila had said nothing of this find when she returned. She knew she should have talked to them about it, but she felt terrible about the broken samara so she could not bring herself to tell them. When she had heard there was to be a meeting, she thought the group might be able to come up with a solution.

"Why are we just learning about this, Juila?" Amanda asked in a harsh whisper.

"I didn't want to be the one to end the prophecy," Juila whispered back with her eyes downcast.

Amanda immediately felt bad about accusing her daughter of secrecy. She should have known there would be a good reason. Her mind raced through the implications of this revelation.

Alena, in particular, leaned forward and felt a sense of loss at the sight of the fragmented crystal. "This is terrible! What happened to it?"

Relieved to have some answers, Juila replied, "It was being used to power a very large space ship. Unfortunately, the previous engine crystal had shattered which left microscopic dust everywhere. The resonance of the powdered crystal caused this one to break in half."

"And you think this belongs to someone here?" Alena asked. "How would you find out?"

"So far the aura of each samara has matched the birth crystal color of the owner."

"What color is this one's?" Alena could feel a level of excitement and fear rising within her.

"It's lavender," Juila answered.

"That's the same as mine!" Alena announced with a glance around her to see how everyone else was reacting to her statement.

"We thought the same thing," Juila answered as she gestured toward her sister and saw her nod in agreement.

"What am I supposed to do with it? It's broken, and I've never heard of any crystal being put back together." She felt so bad for the samara; she wished she could use her healing skills to repair it the same way she would one of her patients.

CHAPTER 42

Completely without conscious thought, Alena reached out and picked up the two sections. She joined them together like a jigsaw puzzle and felt the energy from the crystal begin to course through her body. It was a feeling, unlike anything she had ever experienced.

"Should we try to get it away from her?" Ahn asked with a concerned tone as Alena continued to remain silent.

"No, it won't hurt her," Amanda assured him quietly.

Several minutes passed as everyone watched in fascination while Alena held the now-glowing crystal within her cupped hands. The swirling colors surrounding the samara were mesmerizing.

Not one to waste time when there was a lot of work to get accomplished, Ahn finally asked, "So, who here has their own samara?" He looked around the table as each person raised his or her hand. When Barla put hers up, he stared at her in frank disbelief. "You have one? When did that happen? How come you never said anything to me?"

"Amanda brought it over to me almost three weeks ago. She asked me to keep it secret until she could figure out if there were an actual pattern to who would receive them. She has been keeping it at her house."

"I still can't believe you never said anything about it," he grumbled.

Amanda hoped to prevent a fight between her aunt and uncle and said, "I'm sorry, Ahn. I really did think it was best to keep it secret until we knew more. I never want you to think Barla is keeping things from you on her own."

"I don't," he said unconvincingly.

"Speaking of my keeping the crystal for Barla, I would like to change the arrangement. We need to keep the power emanating from the crystals down to a level which will not draw attention to our locations. The Elders already have the Ascension Gates creating a power vortex which will help disguise the combined power generated from the samaras. So I was thinking the rehoming would go like this: Elder Daven would keep Nena's and Bryon's samaras; Elder Debbon will keep Chelesa's and Barla's; and we will keep Jena's, Juila's, and Riccan's at our house."

"Why are you concerned with the power?" Barla asked.

"We have reason to believe Lucinden is sending out people to investigate power spikes throughout the region. We want to eliminate any reason to attract Lucinden's attention until after we have fulfilled the prophecy given to us by Jehoban," Amanda answered.

"Amanda is right," Rasa chimed in. "I have a friend who has it on good authority that Lucinden's interest has been peaked. We would do well to try to limit our exposure to risk. Amanda's idea for scattering the samaras is definitely warranted."

Debbon spoke for the first time and asked, "How are we supposed to go about finding our own samaras? I imagine there must be some way to find them. How have you found the others?"

Amanda and Riccan exchanged a knowing glance. Debbon's question fit right in with their next plan of action. Riccan stood up and drew everyone's attention, except for Alena's, and said, "We had brought the journal pages from when Amanda was in her coma. In her unconscious dream state, Amanda managed to see our lives through other people's eyes.

"Unless anyone has any other suggestions, we propose that each person who still needs to receive their samara should read through the stories to see where the account has discrepancies. Without anything else to go on, we believe it's possible the answers lie within the inconsistencies of the stories."

Juila took the stack of papers her mother handed to her and stood up. She walked around the table and passed out the sections of stories to the appropriate people and then returned to her seat next to Jena.

Her sister had yet to say anything since arriving at the meeting. Juila had noticed her glancing over at Elder Debbon and Chelesa before she returned her eyes to her lap. Juila knew this was a difficult time for Jena since she was questioning her betrothal with their son.

Before anyone could begin to read their portion of Amanda's journal, Alena gasped as her hands fell away from her samara. She looked over to Riccan with an amazed expression and said, "That was incredible! I think I know how to fix it."

"How?" Riccan asked. He had felt unaccountably disheartened when he had seen the two pieces. If there were any way to fix it, he would be the first one to volunteer to help.

"I think if each person touched their own crystal and focused healing energy toward my samara, then it would have the power to fuse itself back together again."

It was not lost on Riccan that the number of samaras needed to heal the new one was seven. It seemed as though Jehoban regularly used the number seven as a significant number. He thought Alena might have a valid option for the healing of her stone, so he nodded his approval and stood up to bring his samara closer to himself.

"Use the towels to grab your own samara," he cautioned the others. "We don't want to have to wait until you are all free again before we're able to start."

Jena, Juila, Bryon, Barla, and Nena all moved over to the head of the table to pick up their samaras to take back to their seats. Chelesa brought her own crystal out of the bag she had brought with her. When everyone was comfortably seated again, Riccan nodded his satisfaction of their arrangement.

"We will wait for your direction, Alena," Riccan announced.

"Remember to focus your thoughts only on healing this stone," she cautioned. Alena took a steadying breath and once again cupped her hands around the two halves. Just before she had them touching one another, she cried out, "Now!"

The seven others around the table immediately put their hands on the tops of their samaras. Even those without their own crystal could feel the electricity in the air as their combined energy formed a colorful cloud of light around Alena's hands. Alena focused her own mind solely on using the energy to draw the two pieces together to form a solid stone, fusing the edges together so completely that no scar was evident.

"It's done!" she cried, and she jerked her hands away to be free of the charged power still surrounding the stone.

Slowly, the other participants were able to disentangle themselves from the collective healing. Their minds felt as though they had worked very hard even though it appeared they had done very little. One by one, each person removed their hands from the samaras and looked across the table to see Alena's triumphant smile at what they had accomplished.

Alena felt tears of joy falling down her cheeks. She knew it was ridiculous to cry over the healing of a stone, yet she felt more alive than ever. It was almost as if the stone had filled a piece of her which she did not know was missing. Now she understood what her husband had been trying to tell her about his own samara. The bond was unmistakable as well as indescribable.

"I'd like to know why we would each want to have a samara. What good will they be to us? If you think it'll draw Lucinden's attention, maybe we should stop trying to find them," Ahn reasoned.

There were nods of approval from those who were still without them while the owners could not disagree more vehemently. Daven looked over to his wife's radiant expression and realized he had to speak, "We need to continue on. If Lucinden is trying to stop it, then we must carry on. We must do everything in our power to thwart Lucinden so that Jehoban's prophecy can be fulfilled. There can be no greater calling for the children of Jehoban than to serve Him."

"So we're supposed to read these papers," Ahn said dubiously, "and then we'll be able to locate our own skull." He thought there must be a better way, something more structured than simply reading someone's dreams and gathering clues by finding the errors.

"It's a starting point, at least," Barla insisted.

Amanda nodded and then changed the subject by asking, "I'd like to ask everyone to write down what you learn from your own samara. Maybe we can discover the true purpose of the crystals or see if there is some type of samara cycle which needs to be completed. I believe by documenting everything it will help us move forward faster."

Chelesa spoke up for the first time. "I've spent several days talking with my samara and learning the history from it. There has been so much lost over time, and I think Amanda is right to ask us to document everything. We are embarking on an amazing journey in which Jehoban has given us a powerful tool to ensure our success. We need to have faith that He will guide us the rest of the way, but we also need to use the brains He gave us to do so."

"I've been wondering how you've been doing, Chelesa," Amanda began. "After we rescued Neal we were so busy with the fallout from it that I wasn't able to get back in touch with you to see how you were doing with it. I'm glad you have spent time learning from it, you might be able to give the rest of us some pointers about it."

Chelesa laughed and looked guiltily over in her husband's direction. "Be sure to eat, drink, and get lots of sleep before ever touching it. Also have someone around who can force you to stop listening to it, because time flies by without you noticing. Debbon can attest to that the first time I used it at home."

"Yeah, Chelesa said she was going to her office to check out her samara as I left for work in the morning and when I got home late that night, she still hadn't moved from where I left her. It was really eerie because she looked so peaceful and content.

"After several attempts, I finally freed her hands from the stone and broke the connection. Chelesa scowled at me saying she'd only had a few minutes with it. When I showed her my timepiece, she was appalled to realize she had lost the entire day."

Chelesa nodded her agreement throughout Debbon's recounting of her first attempt to use her samara. "Since that day, I've taken extra precautions by asking staff members to help me, or make sure Debbon will be home within a decent amount of time from when I start."

"That's sound advice," Riccan praised. "What else have you noticed through your link?"

"My birth crystal is much stronger than it has ever been before.

I find it very easy to heal my patients now which is a blessing all around. There's also a feeling of rightness about it, which is more difficult to explain." Chelesa chewed on her bottom lip as she tried to find the words for what she was saying and finally shook her head. "I can't find the right words to describe it."

"I'm sure each of us who has a samara knows what you are eluding to," Riccan assured her. He looked around the table and saw each person nod in acknowledgement.

"I'd like my samara to be kept with Bryon's here at the Residence if you don't mind," Alena said as she turned her head to see Elder Daven and Nena. She was relieved when they both nodded readily in agreement. It scared her to have so much power in her home, more so than when Bryon's had been there. Now she knew what the power was like and she wanted to keep her children safe from Lucinden and his people.

"I think we should all keep in contact via messenger on the patil. I'll create a group box so we can all see what everyone is working on or thinking about. The more we share, the faster we'll succeed. Does anyone have any objections?" Riccan asked. He looked around the group and only saw heads shaking. "I guess this concludes the meeting. Go home and read through your pages. See if you can discover where your own samaras are, and we will keep working on it as well. Thank you for coming and safe travels home."

With the meeting adjourned, Nena stood up and announced, "I have refreshments and snacks available in the great room for anyone wishing to stay and visit."

Amanda rewrapped the crystals which would be going home with them and returned them to her satchel. She gestured to catch the attention of both Elder Debbon and Elder Daven. When they were both gathered around her, she lowered her voice and said, "Be sure to put these somewhere safe and build wards of protection around them. I'd suggest limiting the number of people who even know they exist just as an added precaution. I'm already uncomfortable with Chelesa letting the house staff see hers."

Debbon nodded his agreement. "I trust our staff implicitly, but I understand your concern and caution. I'll do as you ask."

"As will I," Daven agreed.

Amanda handed Barla's wrapped bundle to Debbon, and his expression changed to surprise when he still felt the tingle of power even through the cloth wrapping. "Give that to Chelesa to put in her bag until you get home."

Amanda then handed Bryon and Nena's crystals into each of Daven's hands. Likewise, his expression changed upon his first contact with the power. She watched him hurriedly leave the room to secure them somewhere in the Residence.

All of the occupants of the meeting had migrated to the great room. Most only stayed for a single glass of steena tea and a couple of sweets before they left to attend to their children at home. Only Elder Debbon and Chelesa remained with Daven and Nena on the patio overlooking the landing field.

Amanda was anxious to get home and put the remaining samaras back into their secret room. She had been unaccountably nervous about bringing all of the stones with her to this location, so it was a relief to be leaving with fewer of them. Once they were back home and Riccan had taken the satchel from her, she noticed how quiet Jena had been during the entire outing.

Between her sister's silence and Valentina's continued absence from school, Juila was about ready to scream. She was going to do something about one of them at least. She picked up the phone and dialed Behn's number. After he greeted her, she got right to the point.

"Can I come over to your house to talk with Val?"

"Sure! Do you need me to pick you up?"

"Yes, please. I don't want to ask my parents right now since they're working on something else."

"Okay, I'll be over in a few minutes. We just finished dinner, so your timing is perfect."

"Great! I'll be waiting out front then," she replied and hung up the phone.

Jena stood nearby and asked, "What are you planning?"

"I'm going to get at least one person to stop sulking. Val is going to come to school tomorrow if I have to compel her to do so!"

"I'm not sulking, Juila, so don't start with me. I have a real problem now that Willian is actually being a decent human being. Just today at school, he did as he promised and apologized to Luke. He even offered to carry my books for me."

"I'm sure Luke loved that! So now what? Is he stalking you? How did he know where to find you?"

"Juila don't act this way; it's not very pleasant. I ran into him and asked him to walk with me to our locker."

"Great, now he knows where our locker is! Now I'll probably be plagued with having to see him as well."

"I wish you'd give him another chance, Juila. Do it for me!"

Juila goggled at her sister even asking such a thing of her. She shook her head in disgust and marched out the front door. She would rather wait outside than have to hear anymore drivel about how wonderful Willian has become. "Anyone can be nice for a few minutes!" she mumbled as she sat down on the front step while she waited for Behn to arrive.

She was angry with Jena for being so cowardly and indecisive. She felt there had been a perfect opportunity for her sister to speak with Willian's parents at the meeting earlier, yet Jena had remained silent as if her silence would mend the anons of abuse she had endured. Abuse they had both endured since Willian's poor behavior usually spilled over to include Juila.

Her mood shifted slightly when she saw Behn pull around the circular driveway and stop right in front of her. He was smiling as though eager to see her. She smiled back, forgiving him only slightly for encouraging Jena to give Willian a chance. She swiftly got into the car and buckled herself in.

"What are you planning on saying to Val?" Behn asked before they even got back onto the main road.

"I don't know yet, but she has got to stop hiding at home."

"Hiding, huh? I guess it does seem a bit like that, now that you mention it!" he chuckled at the choice of words since he knew Valentina prided herself on acting brave. She had been the one to keep them all together when they first arrived on Earth and cheered them up until they had been adopted by the Wilsons. "Do you want me to stay with you when you talk to her?"

"No!" Juila answered more sharply than she intended and immediately regretted it when she saw the hurt look on Behn's face. "I just think she needs some girl talk and not her brother right now."

"If you say so," he answered. He navigated a few more streets before turning into his own driveway. He got out of the car and went around to open Juila's door for her. "She's in her room, Behn said as they walked into the house together. Behn stayed in the living room while Juila continued down the hall to Valentina's room.

Juila knocked softly on the door and entered when she heard Valentina acknowledge her. She entered the room and was appalled to see how terrible Valentina looked. It was apparent that a shower had not happened in days, and her skin had a strange color to it. "Are you alright?" she asked as she strode across the room and sat down on the bed.

Valentina rolled her eyes and answered, "How can I be alright after what happened to me?"

"So you really don't have a migraine? You just want to stay in your room, where it's safe, forever?"

"It sounds pretty reasonable to me."

"I know this is the last thing you want to hear right now, Val, but just listen," Juila said as she jumped up and planted herself in front of her friend. Valentina looked up at her with a patronizing look from where she had curled up on her bed. "You have high expectations for yourself and for other people around you. What are you willing to give up for those expectations? If Behn or Jon didn't do or say something you thought they should, would you become angry?"

"Probably," she replied uncertainly, not knowing where Juila was going with this line of questioning.

"So what you're saying is your happiness is worth less than your expectations of other people. Why are you willing to sell your happiness for so little? You deserve to be happy every day, but it's a choice. You can choose to keep your high standards for yourself, and for the people around you, and be miserable or you can choose happiness. It's your decision."

"Go on; I'm listening," Valentina prompted.

"This applies to all areas of your life. I know what happened to you with Grobin has hurt you deeply, and I'm not trying to minimize any of it, because it was terrible. There was nothing you could have done or said which would have kept Grobin from using you as he did.

"The monologue you have playing in your head keeps telling you that you should have defended yourself against him. You hate yourself for being weak, or any manner of other things for which you aren't responsible. Grobin took more than your virginity, Val, he took your self-confidence away. The problem is that you gave that to him, just as he took your body.

"Do you hear what I'm saying to you?"

"That's not what I'm doing, Juila. I'm processing everything that has happened in the only way I know how. I'm dealing with it my way!" Valentina stood up and began pacing the room with her arms crossed over her chest. Her heart began to race as she realized she was not handling the situation at all; she was only reliving it and trying to find out where she went wrong.

"How's that working for you, Val? You're not dealing with anything! You've shut all of us out of your life; you don't speak to anyone anymore. We're concerned about you. Please let us help."

"I haven't meant to; it's just I'm afraid!"

"Afraid of what?"

"I'm afraid I'm pregnant!"

Juila stared at her friend's face, searching for the right thing to say. "You aren't pregnant."

"You don't know that, and I won't know for at least another week, maybe two. I'm too young to be a mother, and I don't want to have that disgusting man's child." Tears began to pool in her eyes as she finally voiced her greatest fear.

Juila went to her friend and folded her arms around her. "I wish you would have told me this days ago; I could have saved you so much worry. Rasa checked you out the day we got back, and she confirmed you were free from any STD's and she also made sure you would be unable to conceive. It would be impossible for you to be pregnant."

"What do you mean? How could Rasa do that?"

"She sealed off your womb so it wouldn't be able to receive an egg even if one did get fertilized. You'll have your normal period in a few days, and you will see I'm right."

"Does this mean I'll never be able to have children now?"

"No, it only lasts until your next period. You'll be back to normal in a few days."

Valentina closed her eyes, the tears fell down her cheeks, and she sobbed with relief. She felt as though the weight of the world had been lifted from her shoulders. It would have been better to talk about this long before and saved herself so much grief. She unfolded her arms and put them around Juila and cried the tears of release she needed so badly.

She finally felt able to look on the next minute, hour, and day with hope instead of dread. She began to think about returning to school since her worst fear would not be realized. Her life was not going to be determined by this one terrible event. Valentina decided in that moment she would create her own destiny and not let past events shape her future.

"Thank you for coming to me today, Juila. You are the best friend I could ask for."

Juila simply smiled at her friend's transformation. She still felt a level of guilt for having put Valentina in the way of danger in the first place. She was going to have to take her own advice and let it go. The past could not be changed, and the future was still to be determined. She only had the present to live in, and she was going to do her best with it.

The moment of mental release was over for both of them. They sat down on the bed and Juila could see the color returning to Valentina's cheeks. The transformation was almost miraculous just from a single conversation. "I was wondering if you could talk with Gevena for me," Juila began.

"Who is Gevena?"

"She came back with us from Viceroy Blair's space ship. She was a girl who was taken from a town called Desio. Her father betrayed her and gave her away to a man he owed a gambling debt to," Juila answered.

"That's pretty harsh. What do you want me to talk to her about?" Valentina asked. She didn't think she had anything in common with the strange girl who had come back with them.

"I think she's had a similar experience as you've had with Grobin. Maybe you two could help one another. Would you give it a try? She needs friends right now and someone who might be able to understand what she's been through. It might help both of you," Juila suggested with a shrug of her shoulders.

Valentina raised an eyebrow in consideration and replied, "I guess I could try. I don't know what I'd say to her. Is she still at your house?"

"No, she went to live in Manzanit with Rasa at the Residence there. You don't have to pressure her to talk, just be her friend. It might be easier than you think."

"Sure, I'll do my best." She wished she had waited to agree. Finding out that Gevena was no longer on Earth would mean she'd have to travel in a telepod again and she did not much like the idea after what had happened the last time.

"Thanks, Val. I think this is important."

"Don't thank me yet; she may not even like me." She laughed, and even she noticed it sounded a bit strange. "What's this Behn was saying about our mom returning to our old home?"

"Yeah, that was a bit sudden. The refugees all agreed to let her lead them in exchange for Mom taking them back home. I have no idea how that's working out, but one good thing did come of it all."

"What's that?"

"Your mom had a patil installed in her house. You, Behn, and Jon can use the patil at our house to send her messages to keep in touch when it's not possible to travel there to see her."

"About that...," Valentina began and did not finish.

"About what?" Juila pushed.

"I don't think I'll ever be able to go back to the Roanoke Colony. That's where Grobin lived, and I'm afraid it'll make me remember what he did."

"Honestly, Valentina, you'll never forget what he did. Grobin is on his way to being a slave in Heliok, and he'll never be able to hurt you again. Don't let his actions keep you from enjoying your mother's hospitality. It was so important to her that she had a home and a position in society which would make you proud. Don't do anything to take that joy away from her. Too much has already been lost in your family to let it keep going."

"I'll have to think about it. Can we leave it at that for now?"

"As long as you promise to see it my way in the end!" Juila smiled mischievously at her friend.

Valentina laughed with a genuinely joyful sound which made Juila turn to her and hug her again. She was so glad Juila had decided to come over and talk to her. It had been a miserable four days wallowing in her room. She decided she would be going to school in the morning. It was time to begin living again.

Juila could feel the change in her friend's posture. She pulled back and looked into Valentina's face and was pleased with what she saw. "This is the girl I remember! Welcome back!" She grinned again, and they began talking about Valentina's plans for the upcoming winter break.

CHAPTER 44

Alena still felt as if she were charged with energy after her encounter with the samara. It was impossible to describe how the connection had changed everything she thought she knew about elemy and how to use it. She looked over at Bryon and wondered if he had felt the same transformation when he had linked with his.

Now that she had her own samara, she felt slightly guilty for how she had reacted to Bryon's being in the house. While she had been justified in being wary of its power, she had been wrong to think that Bryon should want to get it out of the house. If he even felt a fraction of the connection she had to her own, he would have felt the loss of the stone, and it was her fault.

"I'm sorry I reacted the way I did to your samara, Bryon. I had no idea they were so special." She recalled all of the stories she had heard as a child about the mythical objects. The tales had a common theme of danger and mystery which should be avoided at all cost. She never realized they were going to be a part of her future.

"To tell you the truth, I didn't either," he admitted.

"Can you still feel it?"

"Yes. Can you?" He raised himself up onto his elbow and looked over at his wife lying beside him in their bed. She looked positively radiant and content. He felt an overwhelming sense of love for her which was almost painful.

"Absolutely, I almost feel electric," she answered.

"I'm glad to hear you still feel it. I was afraid it might just be me."

"Did you notice any difference between the first time you linked and this last time?" Alena's analytical mind wanted to discover all of the nuances. She had noticed a vast difference between her first time when it had been broken and the second time when it had been made whole. She wanted to know if it were only because it was intact or if it became more intense with each linking.

Bryon spent a few moments trying to decide whether or not he had felt any difference. He knew how his wife's mind worked, and she would appreciate a methodical answer. It had been quite a while since the first time he had touched his samara, so he really had to work at the comparison. "I guess it was easier to focus the second time. Maybe because I knew what to expect. I'm not really sure. I'll pay more attention the next time."

Alena smiled at his answer. "When do you think will be the next time? I want to be able to really delve into how it works, and find out all of its secrets. Aren't you curious about yours as well?"

"Not as much as you are, but it's always been like that with us. You always want to know more about everything. It's what makes you a great wise-woman; you look at every detail to make sure your patients are able to get the best care."

Alena nodded and asked again, "Do you want to go over to Elder Daven's Residence to get more time with it?"

"It would probably be a good idea. Maybe it will give us some answers about the other samaras or even the reason they exist in the first place."

"I've been doing some thinking on that already."

"What did you come up with?"

"In the old language, samara means key. What do you think they would be a key for? Any ideas?"

"Hmm, I don't know, but now that you've brought it to my attention, I'll see what I can come up with. I think this might be one of those things we should share with the whole group."

"I should also ask everyone to pay attention to the quality of their connection each time they link. If it gets stronger with every use, it might make sense to set up regular times to be linked with them. It might make the difference in the end, depending on the final outcome of their purpose."

"Good point. I'll put all of this out to the group tomorrow. I'm really glad we're in this together, you know? When it was just me with the samara, I felt like you were being left out. This is a much better outcome already." Bryon leaned forward and kissed his wife. It might have been his imagination, but he could swear he felt an electrical charge pass between their lips. He decided he would have to keep testing his theory by seeing what other aspects of their intimate life could be affected.

AMANDA LISTENED to Neal's message on the answering machine. She thought his voice sounded good and hoped the sessions with Dr. Medin were working well for him. She hit delete on the machine at the end of the message and walked through the kitchen to sit down in the living room.

The meeting had gone better than she had planned, especially since she had not known about the broken stone Juila had found. Thinking about how the samara had been returned to its original state of perfection made her consider what else the crystals were capable of achieving. She imagined their power was similar to the birth crystals, limited only by the imagination of the owner.

Even though she tried to ignore Neal's repeated attempts to meet, her mind kept returning to what would be the right thing to do for him. Finally, she sighed and got up from the couch and returned to the phone. She picked up the receiver and dialed his phone number. He answered after several rings.

"Hi, Neal, this is Amanda."

"I'm so glad you called. Do you think you could come over here? I've got so many questions, and Dr. Medin said you and she were the only ones I was allowed to discuss this with."

"Sure," she answered. She had no idea Dr. Medin had restricted him so much and knew how he felt about not having anyone to talk with. "I'll be there in about ten minutes."

"Thanks, Amanda. I really need to talk. Okay, I'll see you in a couple minutes. Bye." He hung up the phone in his excitement.

Amanda smiled at his obvious exuberance and actually looked forward to discovering what he had unearthed from his inter-dimensionally cloaked memories. She rushed upstairs to let Riccan know about her plans. After a quick kiss, he slapped her playfully on the rear as she skipped out of range from his advances.

Just as she had promised, Amanda pulled into the Taivas driveway ten minutes after speaking with Neal on the phone. She did not even have to knock before Neal stood in the doorway and ushered her into the house. Amanda was pleased to see he looked well-rested and maybe even putting on some of the weight he had lost while being addicted to the *resh*.

They walked through the house and out to the back gardens. Neal led them to a private bench set off to the side of the main path. He waited for her to sit down before he joined her. Now that he had her attention, he could not decide what he wanted to say first.

Amanda began the conversation when the silence drew out to an uncomfortable length of time. "How is your mom? Where is she?"

"She's doing better ever since I've been seeing Dr. Medin. She's somewhere inside. I finally feel like she's beginning to trust that I won't wander away when she's not hovering over me."

Amanda chuckled as she envisioned Mrs. Taivas being an over-protective mother hen. "What do you think about Dr. Medin?"

"She's amazing. I'm really glad you referred me to her; I think she's really helping me."

"Good. I don't know if you knew, she was my doctor all the while I was in a coma."

"I was told about that. It's what actually made me say I'd go."

"How many sessions have you had with her?"

"Today was my fifth one. I've seen her every weekday. She asked me to write all of my memories and dreams in a journal in between sessions."

"She had me do the same thing. At first, I didn't think it was helping because everything was so confusing. Over time, it has been invaluable to look back in it and review what was important."

"I think I'm still at the confusing stage," Neal admitted. He reached behind him to pull his small journal out of his back pocket. He handed it over to Amanda and said, "I'd like you to read it and tell me what you think."

Amanda hesitantly took the book but did not open it. "Are you sure? These are your memories."

"I'm sure. I need someone to tell me I'm not going crazy. Dr. Medin speaks highly of you, and I already trusted you, so it seemed pretty obvious to me that you were the only one for this task."

"Thanks, I think," Amanda said with a grin. She set the book on her knees and opened it up to the first page. Immediately she could tell Neal had regained more than she had imagined.

He had written everything as if it were a dream, but she knew all of the details were actual memories of his time while he was being addicted to the resh. She was surprised to see he recalled having an engineering job for Elder Vargen—he had even called him by name—which told her it had been real.

She turned the page and saw the entries where Neal recounted meeting Vinia. She did not know the real story, but it was easy to imagine it had taken place much as he had written it. There was a small pang of jealousy which she immediately tamped down because it was not her place anymore.

Because he remembered Vinia, it gave her hope that their relationship could be rekindled. The problem now was where they would live. Vinia had a new start for herself in her home town so it would be unlikely that she would want to relocate to Earth. If Neal decided to go back to Tuala, he would lose his memory again and have to work hard to regain it. He might not think it was worth the risk or the trouble.

When Amanda reached the last page, she shut the book and handed it back to Neal. She could see he was anxious for her honest opinion. It was hard to know whether the truth or a lie would better serve this situation, but she opted for the truth since it felt like a better option.

"Well?" he asked when she remained silent. "Am I going crazy? Is any part of this true?"

"It's all true, Neal. Your memories are definitely coming back. Keep working with Dr. Medin, and we can set up a regular time to go over any details which you have trouble understanding."

"Are you kidding? I'm having trouble with all of the details. None of it makes any sense. Why would someone want to enslave me and force me to work on engineering projects? Doesn't that seem a bit far-fetched to you?"

"Not where Elder Vargen is concerned. Nothing he does surprises me."

"You say that as if you know the man. Do you?"

"Yes. I know of him, but I've never met him."

"So he's real?"

"Yes, as real as you and me."

"Then I want to talk to him. He needs to answer to me for what he's done!"

"Don't focus on him right now. Keep working with Dr. Medin and writing in your journal. Soon enough you will realize why your proposition to confront him is a bad idea." Amanda held up her hand to keep him from arguing. "No, I'm not going to tell you more than you already know. When you are satisfied that your memories are complete, then I'll let you read my own journal. I think that is when you will finally understand."

"I still don't understand why you won't tell me what you know."

"I won't because I want this to be all you. I don't want anyone to say I planted ideas in your head. Everything you write will be one hundred percent authentic to your own experiences."

"I guess I'll have to trust you on this," Neal capitulated. He could see he was getting nowhere and he did not want to push her away from him again. He would have to be content with what he had gotten already. One thing he had gained from this visit was the assurance that he was not experiencing strange delusions. He trusted Amanda to tell him the truth no matter what.

Amanda patted Neal's knee when she could see his expression change to acceptance. "I'm glad you asked me to come over. I've been worried about you."

"I've been worried about me, too. It's getting better every day, thanks to you and Dr. Medin."

"The best advice I ever got was 'believe everything even when it seems unbelievable'. Once you decide to go with that option, everything will fall into line really fast."

"Who told you that? It sounds slightly crazy."

Amanda grinned wickedly, "I wrote it to myself in a note which I found after I lost my memory."

"That makes even less sense." Neal shook his head at Amanda's explanation.

"It's probably more than I should have shared. That's all you're going to get out of me today. I'm going to head home now. I'll talk to you again soon."

Neal stood up and wished he could think of more to talk about to keep her longer. Finally, he gave up and asked, "Can I give you a hug?"

"Sure," Amanda said with a small chuckle. She thought it would bring back memories of a time long-past, but all it did was reaffirm they were merely old friends and nothing more. Amanda left the house feeling satisfied that she had helped her friend move forward.

CHAPTER 45

The short ride home was rather quiet for Ahn and Barla. She was thinking about how wonderful her first real experience with her samara had been. He was thinking about Barla keeping her samara a secret from him and what it would be like to have his own. He had to suspend his ruminations long enough to mentally navigate home to Cresdon and then set the telepod down in their private landing space near their home.

Ahn waited until after Corva had gone to bed before asking what was really on his mind. "Can you explain to me what it feels like to be connected to your samara?"

Barla clearly did not expect the question. She was thinking it would be more along the lines of accusing her of keeping secrets. She took a deep breath and let it out slowly as she tried to give him as accurate of an account as possible.

"You know when you go to access the elemy, and you can see all of the colors of energy flowing by. You pick the colors out which match your birth crystal because it comes easier to you than any other color, or at least that's how it works for me. Is it the same for you?" Barla's curiosity began to sidetrack her explanation.

"I've never thought of it quite that way, but I guess I could agree with you. Keep going."

"When I'm linked with the crystal, it's like the entire flow of energy is already the right color and it practically jumps through me to be used. There is absolutely no effort and no need to contain it because it's only for my use. But that's just one aspect of it."

"What else is there?"

"The samara has a memory of its own. When I'm linked with it, I could see all of the past owners and everything which they used it for, both good and bad. It all goes by so fast it's hard to make any sense of it. I'm sure if I had more time, I could investigate it and know all of its history."

"What good would that do you?"

"I'm not sure. Maybe it's there to teach us how to be responsible with it. If you knew someone was going to review your whole life, don't you think you might make some different decisions? Better decisions, maybe?"

"I suppose. What else is there?"

"Let's see, there's a sense of completeness now that I've touched it. I know I can access its power no matter how far away it is because it knows me and I know it. When I first received my birth crystal, I felt a difference in my core, and I thought that was magnificent. This experience just blew that feeling out of the water in how much more powerful it is.

"I don't think I'm explaining this right. You've grown up with your birth crystal so you can't remember a time when you didn't have it. Before I got mine, it was as if I were half of a person, unable to utilize Jehoban's gift of the elemy. Now I think maybe I was only a third of a person. The birth crystal gave me the second third, and then the samara completed me."

"How could you tell which samara was yours when Amanda put them all on the table? They all looked the same to me, and yet your eyes lit up when yours was brought out."

"Mine was the only one shimmering with a cloud of bright blue around it. I know what you mean though because all of the others looked like crystal skulls to me. They aren't linked to me, so they had no pull on my life-line. That's it! The samara is directly linked to my life-line, so it is almost the same as the way the blood pumps through my veins. It's a vital part of who I am."

Ahn was starting to get the idea of how important these samaras were to the owners. He had originally believed they were a fancy bauble, but now he could see they had an elemental tie to the proper owner. He began to think about how his life would be changed when he finally found his own.

Seeing the look on his wife's face even as she described the sensation, made him slightly jealous of its power over her mind. He had seen the same look overcome Alena's face when she fixed her samara. It had been almost embarrassing to witness the look which had passed between Bryon and Alena once they both had their samaras. He imagined the same thing would happen between himself and Barla as soon as he had his. It made him want to get his even faster.

He got up and went to the front entry. He rummaged through the pocket of his coat and grabbed the stack of papers he had folded when they had left the meeting. The sooner he discovered where his was, the better he would feel. He wanted to have the same connection with the elemy as his wife was now enjoying. There was so much he had to accomplish, and it would be easier with the help of a supercharged crystal.

"What are you doing?" Barla asked in confusion as he returned to the room and settled back into his chair.

"I'm going to read these stories from Amanda and see if I can find my own samara!" he answered with determination.

Barla smiled at his new attitude. She remained silent as she watched him read. She would read through them after he had finished to see if there were any details with which she could speed up the process. Her mind had wandered until she no longer saw the room around her. She was startled back into the present when Ahn loudly tapped the papers back into a neat stack. "Well?" she asked.

"I've read through it all. There were only the tiniest things different, and I can't see where any of it would lead to a clue, let alone to my samara." He tipped his head back and closed his eyes. He had been so hopeful for an obvious clue, and now he just hoped to find his samara sometime before he died. It seemed a rather dismal prospect without much direction from the stories.

"It's too bad you couldn't just create your crystal like we create our dinner," she joked. "Let me read those pages, and I'll see what I can discover." She held out her hand until Ahn passed them over to her. She tipped the pages to the fire so the light would make them easier to see. All too soon she lost herself in the stories of their past.

Ahn sat mutely as he pondered Barla's offhanded comment. Was there a way to think his own crystal into existence? Could he possibly visualize it well enough to make it appear? Barla had been more specific in description than she could possibly realize, or else he knew her so well that it made it easier to understand. In either event, Ahn was willing to try anything at this point.

While Barla was distracted by the journal entries, Ahn closed his eyes and focused his attention within himself. He imagined the elemy flowing beneath him in an abundance of dark, storm cloud grey colors. Feeling the call of the energy, he drew it up closer to him until it coursed through his body and tingled in his fingers. He had never attempted anything like this before, and he hoped it was not going to hurt him.

Casting aside his momentary doubt, Ahn imagined his samara resting in his hands, feeling the weight of it, seeing the colors flowing up and around it in the color of his birth crystal. Letting the vision expand, he could feel the link beginning to form and see people he had never before met. With a final rush of energy, he used the same lessons learned in creating to apply to making his samara be right here with him. Almost effortlessly it seemed, the crystal materialized in his hands.

His eyes popped open as the link formed between him and the stone in his hands. Never in his life had he felt anything as profoundly wonderful as the energy coursing through him in that moment. All of the things he had imagined were experienced tenfold more. He understood what Barla meant now about being complete. His samara was home.

Barla noticed something was different in the room and looked up from her reading. She jumped up from her chair and gasped, "What did you do, Ahn?"

"I created it, just like you suggested!" He stood up and looked into her eyes with a look of wonder. "I know what you mean now. This absolutely cannot be described with mundane words. This bond is so much more spiritual."

"Oh, Ahn! You're amazing. I can't believe you took my joke seriously, but I'm so glad you did! I wonder if the others will be able to do it for themselves now that you've done it. We need to go to Elder Debbon's estate right away. I can feel the energy emanating from it from over here."

"I wish I could have more time with it. There's so much for me to learn!"

"You won't need physical contact with it now that it's linked with you. But if you really want to hold it, then I'm sure Elder Debbon will give you a room in which you can sit and explore its histories. In fact, we might do it together since I've never spent any quality time with mine either."

"Okay, let's go then. I'm sure they'll be amazed just like I was!"

"Let me get a towel to cover it. We don't want anyone to see what you have and start asking questions."

"Good idea!" Ahn said even as he could feel the energy pulling him to listen and see what it knew. "Hurry up," he called as he felt like he was losing the battle to remain in the present.

Barla returned immediately with a kitchen towel. She draped it over the top and let Ahn tuck the cloth underneath the precious new samara. Without a word to Corva who was sleeping upstairs, they left the house again and hurried to their telepod.

THE WHOLE STUDENT body was overly exuberant because this was the last school day before Christmas break. The teachers pretty much gave up in trying to get any actual teaching done since the students were so distracted. Wandering the halls in between classes was even scary at times as people were running and yelling to one another about their plans for the break.

Willian had discovered the classes were all going to be shortened so that they would be able to only attend a half-day. He had missed three opportunities to meet with Jena between classes because of the crush of bodies. He kept looking around to see if he could spot her, but mostly he just ended up running into other students.

One student was a beautiful girl whom he had never seen before. As soon as their bodies touched, Willian felt a charge of energy course through him, unlike anything he had ever experienced before. He hastily grabbed her arm to steady her as she began toppling backward from the force of their meeting. His fingers felt as though they were on fire.

He looked at her eyes to see if she felt the same thing and he saw her own eyes widen in surprise. "Who're you?" he asked in a whisper.

"Valentina Wilson. Who're *you*? I haven't seen you around here before."

"Willian Potts."

She frowned slightly as she recalled hearing his name before. "Are you Jena's betrothed?"

"Yes, how'd you know?"

"She's one of my best friends. You can let go of my arm now; I'm fine." She stepped away from him, intending to leave as soon as she could. Instead, she felt another pulsing wave of energy as he touched her arm again to keep her from going.

"Do you feel what I feel when we touch?"

Frowning in confusion, she did not want to admit to anything until after she had spoken with Jena to find out what was going on with her betrothed. "I don't know what you're talking about. I've got to go. I'm going to be late for class."

She pulled her arm out of his reach and almost ran in her haste to get away from him. Her mind was racing through what had just happened. It scared her to think she could feel so intimately toward another man after what had taken place with Grobin. What especially disturbed her was that the other man would also be Jena's betrothed. This was a problem she was going to have to avoid.

Willian watched her run away and realized his heart raced,

unlike anything he had ever experienced before. He had heard of instant connections with people, but this had been ridiculous. The word connection did not seem to cover the extent of the feeling he had felt when he had touched her. He had just discovered his destined soul-mate and yet he was betrothed to another.

THE CHILDREN OF FIRE

BOOK SIX OF THE CHOSEN

CHAPTER 1

Amanda Stel was finally able to sit down in her living room and put her feet up on the coffee table. The house was quiet since she had just returned from dropping off her daughters, Juila and Jena, at their grandparents' Residence in Tuala. Amanda planned on spending a few days alone with her newly wedded husband. There had been so little alone time together since they had been married only five months earlier. It felt as if a lifetime had passed at least.

It was hard to believe that this time last year she had just come out of a seven-year coma. Since then, she had discovered she had lived another life in a different dimension called Tuala, and she had found and married her husband, Riccan. As if that were not enough she had then met with Jehoban, the creator of the universe, and discovered He had chosen to raise her two daughters because they had been so talented with their use of the elemental energy through their birth crystals.

If anyone had told her that at twenty-six years old, she would be married and the mother of sixteen-year-old twins, she would have told them they were crazy. Yet this was exactly as her life had turned out and she would not change a thing. The important people in her life knew what had happened, and they were very supportive of her, making her life perfect.

To any outsider, they would assume the twins were her step-daughters because she was only ten years older than them. The truth was even stranger since they were her birth-daughters. She had slipped through time and dimensions when she had been sailing with her fiancé in the Bermuda Triangle. She had been eighteen at the time, abducted, impregnated against her will, and ultimately helped back home by the same woman who rescued her daughters.

Her husband had also been raised in Tuala. He had literally been a man of her dreams since she had actually dreamed about their relationship while she had been in her coma. Riccan had never even met her when she introduced herself and told him all about his family. Their relationship had been based on trust in one another and an instant bond or recognition because they truly were soul-mates.

Riccan was due to come home any minute. They would be able to enjoy one another's company unlike they had since before they had found the twins and brought them back. Amanda had several ideas for what they could do together; it all depended on what Riccan also wanted to do with their private time.

Right on time, Riccan came through the kitchen door from the garage. He spotted Amanda sitting in the living room and length-ened his stride to get to her faster. When she turned her head and smiled a welcome, his heart almost melted with pride because she was his wife. He had waited a lifetime to meet the perfect woman, and Amanda exceeded his expectations on every angle. She was not only beautiful and smart, but she also challenged him to do better for himself and his family. He was certain his effort had not gone unnoticed since she seemed as besotted with him as he was of her.

Amanda rose from the couch and rushed forward to embrace her handsome husband. She loved how tall and muscular he was as she held him close to her. She breathed in his clean, masculine scent and it made her change her plans for their evening. They would definitely be staying in tonight.

As if reading her mind, he asked, "Are we alone? Did you take the girls to my parents' house already?"

Amanda nodded her head and asked, "What are we possibly going to do with all of our alone time?"

"I can make a guess," he answered as he swooped down and picked her up in his arms.

She squealed with delighted surprise and continued to laugh as he carried her up the stairs to their bedroom. They made short work of undressing one another, and soon they were tumbling across the bed. It was nice to have the house to themselves and not have to worry about being quiet or having someone walk in on them. Soon all considerations were forgotten as they rediscovered one another with their caressing and kissing.

The darkness overtook the room as they remained entangled together on the bed. Riccan rolled over slightly to flip on the nightstand light so he could see his bride's beautiful brown eyes while they continued to talk about their plans for the future.

Unfortunately, with the return of light, they seemed to come out of their dream state, and they began discussing strategies for finding the remaining four samaras. It was incredible to think they had located the first nine in such a short amount of time, which also led them to believe the timing was right. They both wished to have them all found so they could move on with fulfilling the prophecy.

For once in their relationship, it would be delightful for them to have nothing to do and nowhere to be except for what they planned themselves. As it was, their time was being taken in every direction until they no longer felt like they were in control. They wanted to experience the hectic life as two parents of teenage daughters instead of being in charge of Jehoban's prophecy.

"Do you think it'll be over soon?" Amanda asked with a long sigh.

"I'm not sure if I want it to," Riccan replied with a shrug. "We don't really know what's going to happen once the prophecy is fulfilled. I imagine it'll be a good thing since it is Jehoban's idea and Lucinden is opposed to it. The only thing which worries me is how it will all come together."

"I know what you mean."

"Do you ever get the idea that Juila and Jena know more than they're telling us?"

"What do you mean?" She had an idea of her own, but she wanted to see how Riccan's view differed.

"Like when we found the first samaras. The girls already knew the history of them. There's probably more stuff they learned as students of Jehoban than we'll ever know. I just hope if there's anything important, that they'll trust us enough to tell us."

"I think they will. Look how easily they've adjusted to living on Earth and with us. It had to be a great deal of transition, yet they've made it look easy."

"That's because they're amazing, just like their mother!"

"Maybe they get it from their father. You learned to live on both worlds, after all."

Riccan raised his eyebrows at her comment. He still could not believe the twins were his biological children. They were everything he could have ever hoped for, and he was so proud to say he was their dad.

They laid quietly and listened to one another breathe. Riccan inhaled and said, "I set up the messaging system for the group today. Hopefully, we can all use it to keep one another up-to-date on any news or theories. It might make it easier for us to finish the prophecy, don't you think?"

"You'll have to show me how to use it," Amanda said as she snuggled closer to Riccan's side. "I'll be grateful when all of this is over so we can have a peaceful life together."

"I know exactly what you mean." Riccan put his arm around Amanda and pulled her closer to him. He never felt as though he got enough time with Amanda and wished he could devote all of his time in being with her.

AHN HAD HAD a hard time letting go of his samara. Even though he had never been one to want power, the existence of this extension to his own power created a craving inside him, unlike anything he had ever felt before. He wondered how Barla had been able to keep hers a secret from him, especially since he had felt his own.

He was still amused at the expression Elder Debbon had on his face when he saw the samara being pulled out of the towel. To be fair, it was probably the same expression he, himself had worn when the samara had suddenly appeared in his hands. He had no idea where it had come from, but once it materialized in his hands, he felt as though his whole life had been turned inside out. There were so many unanswered questions which only spending time with the samara could answer.

Once again, Captain Ahn carefully explained how the samara had come to be in his possession. He knew the Elder was asking him with the hopes of figuring out how he could acquire his own samara. With the addition of this samara, they now had located nine of the thirteen samaras. As soon as they were all located, they assumed they would be able to complete the prophecy. They were all anxious to do their part in making it come to pass.

Elder Debbon sat back in his chair and closed his eyes. He tried to imagine the feelings Ahn had described to him. He pulled elemy around him hoping the added power would draw his samara to him. After several exhausting minutes, Debbon had to release the elemy and allow it to seep back into the earth under him. There had to be something more to the calling of the samara than Ahn was telling him.

Because he knew it was possible, based on the evidence in Ahn's hands, he would continue to try without having an audience present. He could not appear weaker in power than Captain Ahn, so he would wait until he was alone. "You have certainly given me a lot to consider, Captain Ahn. If I have any other questions, I'll let you know."

"Thanks," Ahn replied lamely. Barla was pulling on his arm to get them to go back home. He knew he was stalling, wanting to be with his crystal for only a little longer. Realizing there would never be enough time to gather all of the answers to the millions of questions he wanted to ask his stone, he hastily set it down on the table in front of him and pushed his chair back to stand, all at the same time. "It's late; I guess we should be getting back home."

"I will put your samara with Barla's in the warded room," he said as he also stood, but did not make a move to walk out with them. He did not want to leave the samara unattended for even a moment until it was safely guarded in the room with the Ascension Gate.

"We're sorry to come so late, Elder Debbon. Thank you for seeing us," Barla spoke with a shy smile on her face. She continued to hold onto her husband's arm as though she could feel his reluctance to leave the precious new object behind. "Do you think we could set up regular times to be with our samaras?"

"Certainly. I think it'd be wise for all of us to be intimately familiar with these objects. From what I hear, they contain enormous amounts of history. We might even find out what we should be doing to help with the prophecy. Come as often as you like. You know the way to the Ascension Gate, right?" He waited until he saw their nods before he continued, "You will both be able to pass through the ward in the room. I would suggest you don't leave that room, however, so you can be assured of the most privacy possible."

"Thank you, Elder Debbon. You are most considerate." Barla tugged once again on Ahn's arm and began walking toward the door to leave.

"Maybe I should take my samara to the room for you," Ahn suggested hopefully.

"That won't be necessary," Debbon replied hurriedly. "After all, I didn't have any trouble putting Chelesa's or Barla's into the room. Rest easy, Ahn, no harm will come to your new prize."

Ahn's expression altered little as he realized he was leaving without the samara. He let his wife lead him through the Residence and back to their telepod. His mind was racing with ideas of how he could shift his workload around so he could return the next day.

"Take us home, honey," Barla requested.

"I don't know why we had to come over here tonight," Ahn replied petulantly.

"Keeping the samaras safe is our first priority, Ahn. Now focus on the home coordinates and take us there. I'm exhausted and ready to go to bed."

With a shiver of fear at the idea of something happening to his newfound samara, he began tapping the startup procedures on the panel of their telepod. The process took longer than usual since he had to keep reminding himself of each step as none of the familiar routine was coming easily with his mind so torn. After he had fumbled with the controls for the second time, he glanced over toward Barla to see if she had noticed. Of course, she had which only compounded his frustration. With a new resolve, he pushed all thoughts of his samara from his mind and concentrated solely on getting them both home safely.

Barla nodded in satisfaction when she could see the shift in her husband's mindset. She had been worried about the transfer home with Ahn being distracted. The very last thing they wanted right now was to be lost in the space between during the transfer. They had heard stories of people being lost, and she loved life too much to want to squander it away on a single, inattentive moment.

CHAPTER 2

Valentina held her arms across her chest and realized she was shaken to her core. She had never expected to feel anything for another man after what Grobin had done to her. When Willian had touched her arm, she felt an electrical current course through her whole body. Nothing like that had ever happened to her before, and she doubted it ever would again.

She did not want to admit anything even to herself until after she had spoken with Jena. After all, Jena and Juila were her best friends as well as the only other people her age she knew who were from Tuala. She had a feeling she was going to be causing a huge problem when she told Jena what had happened.

Wracking her brain for a reasonable explanation, she came up with nothing. She had hoped to catch up with Jena when her last class of the day let out even though it was only noon. Since winter break was officially begun, she would have the next two weeks to figure out what had actually occurred with Willian. Surely she had overthought the event, and it would amount to nothing.

She had hurried to her locker to try to get outside before the twins left. Unfortunately, she was too late and had seen Jena and Juila leaving the parking lot inside Sofia's car. She belatedly waved to catch their attention but soon gave up when she realized none of them was looking her way. Now she would have to wait until almost the end of winter break before she would be able to talk to either girl since they were going to their grandparents' house as soon as they got home.

Now she sat in her room and wondered what she should do next. Surely she was putting too much meaning into the innocent meeting in the hall at school. When they all returned to school in a couple of weeks, everything would be back to normal, and she would not have to worry about any awkwardness. She had managed to convince herself of this just when her brother came to her bedroom door and announced she had a visitor.

She frowned over at Behn and asked, "I'm not expecting anyone. Who is it?"

Behn raised his hands as he shrugged his shoulders, "Beats me. Mom just told me to tell you as I was passing through the living room."

More curious than anything, Valentina scooted off of her bed and brushed past her brother as he remained standing in her doorway. She did not have many other friends than her brothers, the Stel twins, Sofia, Luke, and Ryan. Surely Behn would have mentioned it if it were any of those people, so she had no idea who could be coming over to see her without calling first.

She turned from the hallway to the living room and only stared in shock as she saw Willian sitting in her living room chatting with her mother. How had he found out where she lived? What was he doing here? What was she going to say to him? Her steps slowed down as she tried to figure out what she should do next.

Willian turned slightly and saw Valentina enter the room. With heightened senses, he had felt her energy before he even saw her physically. He immediately rose from the couch and turned to face her as he said, "I hope you don't mind my dropping by without calling first. I didn't have your phone number; otherwise, I would have. I'm sorry."

Valentina clasped her hands in front of her and finished walking toward the couch. "How did you know where I lived?"

"I asked a few people at school." He turned to Valentina's mother and thought she looked nothing like her daughter. "I wanted to apologize to Valentina for running into her in the hall at school today."

"That's very kind of you," she replied. "I'll leave the two of you alone." She stood up and left the room with a smile on her face. This was the first time a boy had ever come to the house for Valentina other than the school dance. She was curious to see where this would lead.

Valentina watched her mother's hasty retreat and then whispered harshly, "What makes you think you could just show up here? You should be concentrating on spending time with Jena before she goes to her grandparents' house for the break."

Willian frowned slightly at the idea of Jena leaving again but then realized it was perfect timing for him to get to know this mysterious girl before saying anything rash to Jena. "She has a life of her own. Besides, I would like to get to know you better."

"What about your betrothal contract? Don't you think you should be honoring that?" Valentina was more than willing to seem rude if it would only get Willian out of her house. Even though they had not touched, she could feel the energy coursing from him, and it made her feel things inside her which she was scared to acknowledge.

"I'm already here. Can't we talk for a while?"

With an exasperated sigh, Valentina sank onto the chair across from the couch. "Fine. Whatever."

Willian smiled and resumed his seat on the couch. It already felt as though he had won the first battle by getting Valentina to spend time with him. Unfortunately, he had not thought this through and found he had no idea what to say to her.

Valentina raised an eyebrow at his continued silence. Finally, she accused, "I thought you wanted to talk."

"I did. I mean, I do. I just don't quite know what to say. It seems as though you found out more about me than I did about you, so you have an advantage."

"Hmph." Valentina was not going to make this any easier for him. She sat back in the chair and crossed her arms. She was going to remain silent as long as he did even as she could not help but appreciate his chiseled features and admire his good looks.

Willian finally decided on what to say and leaned forward to speak quietly. "You don't seem surprised to hear that Jena and I are betrothed. It's not something which is very common here, but it is where we come from.

"I don't know how to explain our situation to you, but suffice it to say, Jena and I have a strained relationship. We always have, in fact. I hate to admit that I've been jealous of Jena's ability to do everything better than myself. I haven't always treated her right, and I came here to make amends and let her know I've changed."

"That's good of you. If that's true, then why are you here at my house?"

"I think you know why. When we ran into one another today, I felt something amazing. It wasn't what I was expecting or even looking for, but it happened all the same. I think I came here, not to fix things with Jena, but rather to find you. At the risk of sounding crazy, I believe we are meant to be together."

"You're right; you do sound crazy. Jena is one of my best friends, and I think you are out of line coming here, Willian. I think you should leave."

"Okay," Willian replied as he rubbed his sweaty palms down his thighs as he remained seated on the couch. "I'll agree to go if you can tell me you didn't feel anything when we touched. In fact, I could feel your energy even before you entered the room. Can you explain any of this to me?"

"I don't have to explain anything to you, Willian. You came here to make things right with Jena, and I think you should continue to do so. You can see yourself out." Valentina leaned forward to pick up a magazine from the coffee table. Her birth crystal came free from her shirt and swung in front of her.

Willian's eyes caught the movement, and they grew wide as he wondered if it could truly be what he thought it was. The pendant was as it should be, however, the necklace was a leather strap instead of the usual intricate swirling chain. "Valentina, where did you get your necklace?" He could not keep himself from asking. Ever since he had felt the electrical touch between them, he could not help but wonder how he could possibly be destined for someone from Earth.

Valentina's hand involuntarily rose to clasp the pendant and hastily tuck it back into her shirt. The magazine was forgotten in her lap as she tried to come up with an explanation. She opted for the truth as she answered, "It was a gift from my mother."

Willian's gaze instantly shifted to the doorway where her mother had left them. "You don't look much like your mom."

"This was from my birth mother." As soon as the words were out of her mouth, she wished she had remained silent. For as long as she could remember she had tried to believe her adopted mom was her real mom since she recalled very little of her birth mother.

Here in a moment of confusion, Valentina had told this stranger about her being adopted.

"Ah," Willian answered as he rapidly grasped the situation. "Where're you originally from, Valentina?"

"I fail to see how this is any of your business. Please leave, Willian." Valentina stood up from her chair and let the magazine fall to the ground unheeded. She stepped around the coffee table, intent on escaping Willian's questions. As if anticipating her, Willian's hand reached out and grabbed her arm gently. Liquid fire raced through her arm, and she only stared at his hand where it touched her bare skin. All of her nerves seemed to ignite, and she did not know what she should do.

It seemed pointless to deny what she felt when she shifted her gaze to his and saw the same expression on his face as she surely had. "It doesn't prove anything, Willian." Her denial sounded weak to her own ears.

"It proves everything, Valentina. Tell me where you're from; I need to know."

"Tuala," she whispered.

A huge smile spread across Willian's face as his last reservation evaporated. To know she shared the same heritage as he made everything perfect. "You know what this means, don't you?"

"It doesn't mean anything." She jerked her arm from his grasp and practically fled from the room without looking back. A sob tore from her throat at the loss of their physical touch, yet she ignored it as she somehow found her way to her room through the tears which suddenly sprang to her eyes. How could this be happening? If she had met him a week before, she would probably have different ideas, but she could not even face this situation after what Grobin had done to her. She did not want to have feelings for Willian, yet his touch had done something to her. She craved his touch, and it scared her more than she could even admit to herself.

She wished she could talk to Jena and end her emotional torment. She threw herself face down onto her bed and let the sounds of her wracking sobs be absorbed by her pillow. This whole situation was intolerable. The energy in the room changed, and Valentina knew without looking that Willian had followed her to her bedroom. She stilled her body and hoped Willian would get the hint and leave.

After a few moments of quiet, Valentina turned her face from the pillow to see Willian standing in her doorway with the most heartfelt expression of pain on his face. "Why didn't you leave?" Valentina cried out passionately. "Can't you see what this is doing to me? You need to go!"

"I can't go when I know you're in so much pain. Please tell me what's wrong. I want to be your friend if nothing else." Willian stepped into the room and stopped when he reached the edge of the bed. He wanted nothing more than to reach out and touch her again to feel the powerful connection between them. Deciding against it, he sat down on the bed careful not to have any physical contact with her prone body.

Valentina brushed the tears from her cheeks angrily and sat up. She did not like the helpless feeling she had felt when she was lying down. She needed to be on an equal level with Willian. Against all reason, Valentina wanted to prove to herself that she could not be with Willian. She knew if she had any intimate contact with him, her mind would rebel against it, seeing visions of Grobin violating her body.

To confirm her worst fears, Valentina practically lunged forward and kissed Willian on the lips. What was intended to be a quick kiss, immediately ignited passion in both of them as the electrical charge passed between them. Without knowing how it happened, Valentina found herself lying flat on her bed with Willian poised above her. Their lips never broke contact, and her mind raced with the possibilities the kiss promised.

Suddenly Willian was gone. Valentina opened her eyes in time to see Jon pulling a fist back and letting it fly into Willian's gut. She watched in horror as Willian crumpled into a heap onto the floor. "Stop it, Jon! What are you doing?" Valentina lunged across the bed to prevent Jon from landing a second punch.

CHAPTER 3

Jon looked over at his sister in surprise and asked, "What are you doing, Val? Do you even know this guy? What's he doing in here making out with you anyway?"

"I...I don't know how to explain any of this, Jon. He's from Tuala."

Jon's gaze suddenly shifted from his sister to the guy on the floor who had been wise enough to remain sitting. "Tuala? What are you talking about? What's he doing here? Why would that be an explanation for him kissing you?"

Valentina struggled to explain anything. Her gaze continued to shift between her brother and the man on the floor who made her feel things she never thought possible.

"I think I should leave," Willian murmured. "I believe I got the answer I was after anyway. Are you going to be okay, Valentina?"

"I'm all right, and yes, I think you should go. Jon, let him go!" she suddenly cried out as Jon made an aggressive move in Willian's direction. She grabbed her brother's arm and urged him with her eyes to leave it alone for now.

"Can I get your phone number?" Willian asked from the doorway.

"Are you kidding me?" Jon asked in astonishment. He turned his head to look at his sister and asked, "Is this guy for real?"

Valentina wished she could tell her brother to shut up. Realizing she desperately wanted to talk to Willian again, she pushed past her brother and went to her desk. She grabbed a pen and groped around for a piece of paper. She finally tore the corner from a page of her textbook and scribbled her number on it. Rushing across the room, she shoved the scrap of paper into Willian's hands and said, "Please go!"

Willian smiled as his fingers caressed hers. Gladly he would go now that he had her number. "I'll call you when I get home," he whispered and then turned to leave.

Valentina remained in the doorway, effectively blocking Jon from going after him. She lifted her arm to keep him in her room and realized her hand was shaking uncontrollably. Immediately she clasped her hands together and sighed with relief as she heard the front door close.

Jon stood with his feet apart, and his arms crossed tightly over his chest. "Have you lost your mind, Val?" He leaned around her and called out, "Behn! Come to Val's room so we can talk!"

"Really? What business is this of yours or Behn's? Get out of my room!"

"What's going on?" Behn asked as he came up behind his sister. He saw his sister jump in fright at his quiet arrival. He looked past her to see Jon looking angry. "I could hear you both yelling. Is someone going to tell me what happened?"

"Uhhh!!" Valentina cried out in anger as she glared at Jon.

"Come in and close the door, Behn," Jon ordered.

Behn did as he was told and wondered what had happened in the short time since he had last seen his sister. The three of them stood in the center of Valentina's room, yet nobody seemed inclined to speak. "Well?" Behn prompted.

"I was walking down the hall to go to my room, and I happened to glance in here. Do you know what I saw?" He glared at Valentina to deny what he told Behn. "I saw a guy lying on top of Val, kissing her. I'm sure it would have progressed to something more if I hadn't pulled him off of her and punched him."

Behn's gaze swiveled over to Valentina, confident she would deny Jon's accusation. He frowned in confusion as his sister merely looked down at the floor without saying anything to refute the story. Behn could hardly believe his brother's tale since his sister was usually so cautious and reserved. "Val? Is that true?"

"Yes! No! I don't know! It's none of your business!" She crossed her arms defiantly and faced her two brothers squarely as if defying them to say another word.

"None of our business? You tell me that guy is from Tuala and now it's none of my business?" Jon spat back.

"What? Wait! He's from Tuala? What made him show up here at our house, Val?" Behn asked reasonably.

"I ran into him at school today before the last period. Literally, ran into him. He apologized and asked me my name."

"That makes sense then, of course, he would come over here to practically have sex with you! Do you realize how dumb you sound, Val?"

"Not nearly as dumb as you, Jon."

"Stop it, both of you!" Behn shouted. He wanted to hear Valentina's explanation, and Jon was not helping the situation with his accusations. "Why did he come here, Val?"

"We had a strange connection when we touched at school," Valentina began lamely. "He wanted to come over and find out if there were more to it."

"I guess, based on what I walked in on, you two definitely decided there was more," Jon said sarcastically.

Behn glared at his brother to keep quiet as he tried to coax Valentina to tell the story. "Go on."

"I don't know how to explain it where it makes any sense, but he said what we were feeling was a sign that we were soul-mates." She turned around to try to figure out how to express what had happened. It was easier to think without her brothers staring intently at her face. "After what happened in space, I needed to see if..." She stopped talking as she realized what she was admitting to her brothers. They could never know what Grobin had done to her; she had to protect them from themselves.

"After what happened in space?" Jon questioned as he tried to turn her around to face them again.

Thinking hurriedly about how to cover her mistake she said the first thing which came to mind. "After thinking I was going to die in space without ever finding a man to fall in love with. I wanted to see if what Willian said was true. What if we really were soul mates and I sent him away without even looking into his claim?"

Behn frowned slightly thinking there was more to it than Valentina was sharing. He decided to let it go for now and asked, "What was he doing at school? How did Tuala come up in your conversation?"

"He saw my necklace and asked me where I got it. I told him it was a gift from my mother. He asked me where I was from, and I said Tuala. If he were from Earth, then it would mean nothing to him except the name of some obscure city. He knew what I was talking about and said he was from there too. He said it was further proof we were meant to be together."

"Gahhh, he brainwashed you, Val! Don't you see it?"

"What was he doing at our school?" Behn repeated as a suspicion began to form in his mind.

"He was looking for Jena."

"Is he Jena's betrothed? Did you say his name was Willian?"

"Yes," Valentina admitted as she sank onto her bed. She looked up at her brother to see if he had anything good to say about the situation. Behn seemed to be the only one who still seemed calm.

Jon looked from one sibling to the other as he processed this new information. "What do you think you're doing? Is this how you want to repay Jena for her kindness? I can't believe you!"

"Hold on a minute, Jon. There are a lot of problems between Jena and Willian. He's part of the reason they're living here. I met him a few days ago when I took Jena over to his house. What I don't understand is that it seemed like he was trying to make amends with Jena. Why would he suddenly start to pursue you instead?" He looked down at his sister as he tried to figure out the strange puzzle.

"Why didn't you tell me you knew him when you said there was someone here to see me?" Valentina accused.

"I didn't see him. Mom told me to get you, but he wasn't in the house yet. I never even imagined it would be him. How could I?"

"I told him to leave. I wanted to talk to Jena before I met with him again. He followed me to my room and saw me crying. He tried to comfort me. I guess I was a bit overwhelmed because I was the one who kissed him. There is something very strange which happens when we touch, almost like an electrical current passing through us."

"I don't want to hear about this," Jon said disgustedly.

"Maybe you should go then," Behn encouraged. He wanted to hear more about what had transpired between his sister and Willian, and it would certainly be easier without all of Jon's commentary interrupting.

"Talk some sense into her, if you can, Behn," Jon advised as he walked across the room, opened the door, and stormed out with the door slamming shut behind him.

"Why do you think he's so angry?" Valentina asked.

"I don't know. I want to ask you something without you getting upset with me. Do you promise to really think about your answer before replying?"

Valentina took a deep, calming breath and nodded.

"Do you think it's possible Willian brainwashed you? Or do you really think there's something real between the two of you?"

"I know it sounds crazy, and I've never felt anything so powerful. I don't think it's brainwashing because I was able to walk away from him twice now; once at school and then again here at home. Whatever it is, it is enormously powerful and intoxicating. I'm not sure what would have happened if Jon hadn't interrupted us. I know I would have let it keep going, and to be honest, it scares me more than a little bit."

"Why were you crying?"

"Because I was confused. He stirred up feelings in me which I didn't want to have because I know he's betrothed to Jena. I guess I was feeling sorry for myself."

"So what are you going to do?"

"I definitely want to talk to Jena about this whole thing. It's only fair since she has known him for so long and they are supposed to get married in a couple of years."

"You know the betrothal was arranged by Willian's father when he was only a little kid. Both Willian and Jena have not had any say in the relationship. It may not be as awkward as you imagine it to be. Granted, Jena did seem hopeful for their relationship after meeting with him, but I doubt if Juila will be heartbroken at all if the betrothal were called off." He smiled even as he thought about how Juila would react to the news of Willian being interested in someone other than her sister.

"What are you smiling about?" Valentina asked suspiciously.

"I was thinking about Juila." He waved his hand dismissively and asked, "Do you want to pursue a relationship with Willian or do you want to keep your distance from him?"

"I think I don't have a choice."

"There's always a choice."

"Not this time. Already I feel as though I'm going through withdrawals from him and it has only been a few minutes. I don't know how I'm going to stay away from him until after Jena gets back from her grandparents' house so I can talk to her about this. Besides, what would I say to her? I want your fiancé, and I hope you don't mind."

"Why don't we go over to Willian's house and see what he has in mind?" Behn asked.

"Seriously? You'd do that for me?" Valentina asked in amazement at her brother's suggestion. The idea of knowing where he lived both intrigued her and terrified her. If she could go see him whenever she wanted, she doubted she would be spending much time at home.

"Absolutely. I think you need a chaperone, though, if the attraction you feel for him is as strong as you seem to believe it is."

Valentina nodded approval of his admonition. At this point, she would probably agree to almost anything if it meant she would get to see Willian again. She could hardly even recognize herself as she made plans for what she would talk to him about. Her mind was reeling with the possibilities of her future which had seemed so bleak only the day before.

"Let's go before I change my mind," Behn's words broke into Valentina's thoughts.

She nodded and stood up from the bed. "I'm ready," she declared and led the way out to Behn's car.

Valentina had a lot of questions for her brother as they drove. "How do you know where Willian lives?"

"Jena got the address from Rasa. Rasa was the one who helped Willian get here."

Her brother had anticipated her next question, so she asked another. "Whose house is he staying at?"

"Marcus and Melissa Parker are fostering him until he's ready to go home."

"How long did Jena spend talking with Willian?" For some reason, Valentina felt a stab of jealousy because Willian had spent time alone with another girl.

"Only about twenty minutes. He walked her back to the car and opened the door for her. They seemed to be on pretty good terms, and Jena sounded hopeful for their relationship when I drove her home."

"How come this is the first I'm hearing of this?"

"You weren't exactly very social earlier this week if you'll recall. I didn't want to bother you with someone else's problems. Besides, how was I to know it would matter?"

"True." Valentina nodded her head at her brother's last comment. How would he know it would matter? Why was this happening right now? Was she overcompensating for the traumatic event she had experienced over the last weekend?

CHAPTER 4

Without even realizing it, Valentina memorized the streets and turns to get to the Parker's house. She felt a thrill of fear course through her as her brother pulled to a stop in front of the house and turned off the ignition. She asked, "Is this it?"

"Yep." He unbuckled his seatbelt and opened the driver's door.

Valentina hurriedly copied him and met him on the sidewalk leading up to the front door. "Do you think he's at home?"

"There's only one way to find out. Let's go." He walked up the walkway and stepped up onto the front porch. Without waiting for Valentina, he knocked on the door briskly. He heard a dog barking inside and waited to see if anyone answered.

Moments later, the same woman Behn had met before answered the door. She was holding a little, black Pomeranian who seemed to be struggling to get out of her owner's grasp so she could properly greet the new guests. She smiled in recognition of Behn and said, "I didn't expect to see you again so soon. Who is this?" She turned her attention to the attractive girl beside Behn.

"Hi, Mrs. Parker. This is my sister, Valentina. We were wondering if Willian were home."

"Sure, come on in." She stepped back from the door to allow the two to enter the house. She pointed down the hall and continued, "He's in his bedroom, first door on the left. Feel free to go and visit with him."

Valentina smiled and said, "It's nice to meet you, Mrs. Parker."

Behn kept in the lead as he nodded his greeting at their host and then walked down to the indicated room. He stood in the doorway and waited for Valentina to catch up with him. Just as they entered the bedroom, he watched as Willian's gaze met his sister's and he suddenly felt excluded from the meeting.

It was the weirdest feeling he had ever encountered and immediately knew what his sister was unable to adequately express with mere words. Something about the two of them together was so intense which he had not noticed when Willian had been in close proximity with Jena. Surely this had to mean something significant; he only hoped it would not cause problems between them and the only other people they knew from Tuala.

"I can't believe you came over," Willian exclaimed as he jumped up from his bed where he had been thinking about Valentina. She almost seemed like a vision made into reality as she appeared in his room so unexpectedly.

"We need some answers," Behn interrupted rudely, smoothly intercepting Willian's attempt to touch his sister.

"Certainly," Willian replied as he struggled to shift his gaze away from Valentina. "Let's sit down on the bed." He led the way across his room. "How do you know Valentina?" he asked Behn.

"She's my sister." Behn chose to sit between the two of them so he could make sure they remained as undistracted as possible given the circumstances. Almost beyond belief, Behn thought he could feel the electrical energy passing through him, and it made the hair stand up on his arms. He unconsciously rubbed his forearm with his other hand.

"So then I can assume the guy who punched me in the gut at your house was another brother of yours?" His hand went to his stomach where he could still feel the effects of the hit. He had been completely unprepared for the attack since his mind had been clearly involved in being with Valentina.

"Yes," Behn answered. "We are triplets." He saw Willian's hand move and smirked at how effectively Jon had handled the situation.

Willian's eyebrows rose at Behn's announcement of the multiple births. Triplets were very uncommon in Tuala, and it pleased Willian greatly since it was considered a blessing. He wondered briefly if Valentina's close tie with two other humans was what created the energy pull around her.

They were about to begin their discussion when there was a commotion from outside the room. They could hear a clattering sound and then the little dog came bounding into the room. The noise they had heard was her claws clicking on the hardwood floor as she tried to maintain traction on her forward motion. The ball of fur immediately sniffed and licked Valentina's feet and then Behn's before she scampered over to Willian.

She rose up onto her back legs and rested her front paws on Willian's shins. She made funny growling noises as she leaped up a pitiful inch or two, clearly indicating she wanted to be picked up. Her antics were rewarded as Willian lifted her into his lap and began to pet her chest. She seemed rather pleased with herself as she rolled her eyes toward the guests and lolled her tongue out the side of her mouth.

"This is Pesi," Willian told his visitors. "She's a bit spoiled, but she's a really good dog."

"I can see she has you well trained," Valentina teased.

Hearing her made him look down at the dog and smile as he answered, "I guess she does!" The tension in the room seemed to dissipate as they all paid attention to the playfulness of the dog. Whenever Willian's petting slowed down, Pesi would raise her paws up and down to catch his attention. Willian would immediately renew his petting efforts, and the dog remained content.

Soon enough Pesi sprawled across Willian's lap and fell asleep. Willian kept his hand on her, occasionally stroking her soft fur. He felt comforted by the little animal's trust in him.

Behn was the first to speak when he asked, "What are you planning regarding Jena?"

Willian kept his gaze down at the dog on his lap and sighed. His hand on Pesi's back stilled as he considered what his answer should be. "As I'm sure you know, I came here to try to work things out with Jena. We have had a rocky relationship from the start. I know what was expected of the two of us based on the betrothal agreement my father arranged, but it never felt right. When I was in Tuala, I felt myself being lured to Earth. Initially, I thought it was because Jena was here and I was meant to come here to set things straight. The closer I got to Florida, the stronger the pull became.

"When I started attending your school, I felt like there was something missing. I never felt comfortable, but I attributed it to the new culture and customs. When I finally saw Jena, I thought I would feel a sense of ease because I could finally begin to make amends with her. My energy was better, but by no means at ease.

"Earlier today when I ran into Valentina, and we touched, it's like everything suddenly made sense. I was certain she was the reason I was brought to Earth and Jena was just the means to get me here. I haven't been able to talk to Jena yet, but I'm positive she will be relieved to have our relationship annulled so she can move on with Luke.

"I'm sorry I hit him, he actually seems like a nice guy. She seemed genuinely attracted to him, and I became jealous. Mostly because she never looked at me the way she was looking at him. My base instincts kicked in, and my reason abandoned me."

"So your jealousy would indicate there are still feelings you harbor for Jena," Behn stated.

"I thought so at the time as well. Right before you got here, I was thinking about everything. At the time I was still under the impression I was supposed to make things work with Jena. I hadn't had an opportunity to talk with her yet, so I felt she was betraying our relationship by kissing Luke.

"Since connecting with Valentina, I realize what I feel for Jena is more brotherly than husbandly. There has always been a competitive streak between the two of us which would never make a relationship work well. She's always dreamed of becoming an Elder, even though before Rasa, no woman was ever allowed to hold the office. If she were to become my wife, she would not be able to pursue her dream because I'm destined to be my father's successor. I think she's always resented me because of the lost opportunity."

He held up his hand to forestall Behn's comment. "I've resented Jena much more than she ever did me. I was jealous of how easily she learned new skills with elemy. In my mind, it should have been easier for myself because of who my father was. At that time, we didn't know who Jena's father was, nor did we realize she had a mixed heritage which would make her abilities even stronger."

"So I think we're agreed we both need to talk to Jena before we let anything more happen between us," Valentina spoke up for the first time.

Willian nodded reluctantly. His mind was already decided against trying to make anything more happen with Jena; however, he could see it was the right thing to do. More than anything, he wanted to be able to spend more time alone with Valentina and see where the power would take them.

Valentina's thoughts were mirroring Willian's even though she did not know it. She shivered with a thrill of anticipation of the day where they could explore their mutual energy. Just the day before she had felt broken and hurt. With a single touch from Willian, it seemed as though all of her pieces had been melded together into a more perfect reflection of herself than she had ever known before.

"I'd like to try an experiment," Valentina announced into the silence of the room.

"What is it?" Behn asked.

"I want to see if you can feel what is between Willian and myself. If Willian touched one of your arms and I touched your other one, maybe you could become a human conduit."

Already feeling something, Behn was reluctant to be experimented upon. He changed his mind once he realized this was something important to his sister. He nodded and held up both arms for them to touch.

Willian was first to grasp his forearm and smile at him in anticipation of feeling even a small bit of Valentina's energy passed through her brother. His eagerness soon turned into wonder as he felt a familiar connection with Behn. Certainly, it was not as intense, nor was it as compelling, yet it was there all the same.

Behn's gaze suddenly shifted to Willian as he felt the same thing. He was just about to stand up to discontinue the experiment when Valentina reached over and took hold of his other arm. His vision immediately became dazzled by bright white lights everywhere. It was almost as if he had entered a room filled with a million LED light bulbs.

As the initial shock wore off, he could see several people walking ahead of him. He had no idea who they were, but he could see they were each holding a samara in their hands. Joining another group of people, they formed a circle with the samaras almost touching one another, and an old man wearing white robes said, "It's time."

The vision vanished in an instant, and Behn found himself kneeling on the floor of Willian's bedroom. He touched his hands to his scalp and pressed hard to try to contain a massive headache. "What was that?" he groaned as he kept his eyes shut to minimize the brightness of the sun shining through the window onto the floor in front of him.

Valentina slipped off of the bed and put her arm gently around her brother's shoulders. "Are you okay, Behn? I'm so sorry! I had no idea it would cause any harm. Please tell me you're okay!"

"I'm fine, Val. Just give me a minute to see if my head will stop pounding." Abruptly the ache disappeared as though it had never happened. Behn cautiously opened his eyes and turned his head toward Willian. "Did you do that?"

"If you're talking about your headache, then yes. Since it was my fault you were hurting to begin with, I thought it only right for me to take the pain away. Do you feel well enough to sit back up on the bed and tell us what happened?"

"Didn't you see the people, too?" He rose slowly from the floor and sank onto the bed as his mind tried to make sense of what he had just witnessed.

Valentina looked across to Willian with a concerned expression. She had no idea what her brother was talking about, and she was afraid for him. What if her experiment had caused irreparable damage to her brother? She would never forgive herself for putting him in a dangerous situation just to satisfy her curious nature.

Willian shook his head in negation as he spoke, "I didn't see anything. Did you, Valentina?"

"No, nothing." She gently placed her hand on her brother's forearm and asked, "Do you want to talk about it? Are you sure you're okay? I'm sorry I even suggested it."

"How would you know? Besides, it was pretty remarkable. I could feel the energy coursing through me like I was a human conductor. If that was anything like what you and Willian feel when you touch one another, then I wonder why you'd want to try it again!"

"It's not painful for us." She looked over to Willian to confirm her statement. When she saw him shake his head, she continued, "It's more…intense…exhilarating, you might say." Valentina finally gave up trying to come up with the right way of putting it.

"What did you see?" Willian prompted.

CHAPTER 5

Behn recounted what he had seen and kept his eyes on Willian to see if any of it made sense to him. Maybe it was part of something which occurred on Tuala with which they would be unfamiliar. Even as he finished the story, he could tell Willian was just as confused by the vision as they were.

"That sure sounds interesting. What did the samaras look like?" Willian asked.

"They are clear crystal skulls, seamlessly carved and proportional to a human skull, only smaller. It would comfortably rest in the palm of my hand."

"Oh, those!" he replied with a grin. "We all know those are just a myth anyway. I remember Jena talking about reading something from the library on Acaim. There's clearly nothing to what you saw if those things are involved."

"But…" Behn was about to tell Willian about the samara he had seen on the coffee table at the Stel house when Valentina squeezed her hand on his arm. He changed what he was going to say. "It seemed real at the time. Oh well. It was an interesting experiment. Now back to the business we came here to discuss."

"I don't think Willian and I should be left alone together until after we can all sit down with Jena."

"If then even," Behn said. "Now don't get mad at me, Val. Remember what you told me at home about Jon interrupting you."

Valentina blushed as she recalled her total lack of inhibition when Willian was on top of her and kissing her. She had enjoyed herself immensely and could see what her brother was talking about if she were to have another unchaperoned opportunity. Maybe it was wiser to take precautions until they could figure out if there were a way to harness the impulses when they were touching.

"What did you say?" Willian asked Valentina. He hoped it was something along the same lines as he had been thinking. He felt a thrill of anticipation rise like butterflies in his stomach. Nothing had ever been more important to him than being with Valentina. He could hardly wait until he could be alone with her and see where things would go.

"Never mind," Valentina hastily replied, blushing even more furiously.

Behn intercepted the awkward moment by saying, "So I can see the feelings between the two of you are entirely mutual." He turned to Willian and said, "When I brought Jena over here, you seemed content to be with her, but I can see now, that it was nothing like how you feel when you're with my sister. However, if Jena says she wants to try to work things out with you, are you going to honor the betrothal agreement you have with her?"

A pained expression crossed Willian's face as he considered a life without Valentina. He supposed it would be the right thing to do, even if his heart broke into a million pieces to be separated from his soul-mate. "I promise to honor Jena's feelings in this. You have to think about what her life would be like knowing she was married to a man who had his heart elsewhere. It would be kinder to let her go."

"Even so," Valentina interrupted, "I think we should find out what Jena wants to do before we make any declarations of intent." The statement sounded good to her mind even as her heart broke a little just imagining herself without Willian. The notion was so foreign given she had only known him for a few hours. It seemed implausible that she was willing to throw herself at a man after what she had just endured the weekend before and, yet, that was exactly what was happening to her.

"That sounds like a good idea. In the meantime, what are we going to do with the two of you?" Behn was almost teasing but mostly wanted to keep them on notice that they should refrain from physical contact.

"Maybe we could talk on the phone and get to know one another until Jena gets back," Valentina offered.

"I think that sounds like the best plan for now," Behn agreed.

Willian nodded. He could feel as though Behn were about to suggest leaving and his mind raced with ideas for keeping them longer. Finally, he asked, "How did you three find yourselves on Earth rather than Tuala? How long have you been here? Valentina did say you were from there."

Valentina had looked at Behn before she leaned forward to resume eye contact with Willian. "We had some trouble in our village, and our mom somehow sent us here. For her, it was only a year ago, but for us, it was eight years ago."

Willian's eyes widened. He realized at that moment how lucky he had been to only lose a couple of weeks when he traveled to Earth without the proper guidance. He could have been as unlucky as these teens who had lost out on so much more time with their mother. "What about your father? Where is he?"

A significant look had passed between the brother and sister before Behn answered, "We don't know who our father is." He spoke with such finality in his tone that he hoped Willian would get the idea to leave the subject alone.

Willian was about to pursue the line of questioning further when he saw how uncomfortable Valentina looked. He sighed and answered, "I see. So this problem you were having, has it been resolved?"

Valentina flinched visibly.

Willian wondered what could have caused her reaction and wished he would have read her thoughts just then. It was at that moment he realized he had not tried to read anybody's mind since arriving on Earth. Back in Tuala, it was frowned upon, yet almost everyone did it at some point during the day. It made discussions much more productive when you knew exactly where everyone stood on the matter.

Behn had missed his sister's reaction as he had been facing Willian with his back to her. He answered, "Yes. Our mother is now the leader of the community, and the problem has been taken care of."

"If it's been resolved, then why don't you go back home to her?"

"It's a long story, but suffice it to say, it was only resolved just this week," Behn said curtly.

"Besides," Valentina added with more tact, "we owe our lives to the family who we live with now. Without their love and support, I doubt Jon would still be alive. He was very sick when we first came over here. The Wilson's have been wonderful parents to us. How could we repay them by abandoning them as if their love weren't enough for us?"

"What about your mother? Don't you think she needs you, too?"

"We've only just found our mother. We're still getting to know her, and she's still adjusting to the idea that we're almost all grown up. She didn't even have a house of her own until this week, so we really didn't have much to consider up until now. She understands we want to stay here on Earth until we're done with school. It's not too much longer, and it would be expected for us to branch out on our own at that point."

Selfishly, Willian hated the idea of Valentina remaining even one more day on Earth. With the betrothal customs as they were on Tuala, she would not have continued living with her mother. He would much rather she come home and live with him and his parents as would have been the case if they were betrothed.

Another fluttery feeling appeared in his stomach at the idea of Valentina sleeping in the room across from his own. His thoughts swiftly turned the idea further, and he wondered if Valentina may have a good point in wanting to remain on Earth. He did not want to shame his family with behavior out of their control, even if the feelings were mutual. There were protocols to be followed, after all.

The siblings took Willian's silence as assent. Behn cleared his throat and said, "I think we should get going."

Willian's hand clenched on Pesi's fur making her growl with displeasure. He immediately uncurled his fingers and patted the spot to relax her again.

PETRE WAS uncertain how much time had passed; mostly he recalled the bartender's face as he handed over one bruskin after another. One day ran into another; only the drink had changed to something stronger, something which would help him forget the fact that he had lost Jinya yet again. There had been a time when he had only wanted her because she was beautiful. As time moved on, he realized he really did have genuine feelings for her. He really wanted to be able to apologize to her and see if he could make an honest go of having a relationship with her.

It seemed as though this were an impossibility since he had no way of tracking her down. Sure, he could approach Captain Ahn and see if he would tell him anything, yet the likelihood of that happening was slim to none. The Harbor Master hated him with a passion which he could hardily understand. No, he was destined to be alone and miserable. Every time he tried to find happiness for himself, he always found a way to mess things up. He picked up his glass, glared at the amber-colored liquor as if it were to blame before he silently toasted to his misery, and he downed the foul liquid with a grimace of distaste. He had changed to the cheaper stuff as he got drunker since he was in no mood to appreciate a finer vintage. This liquor almost tasted like cleaning fluid, and it burned all the way down to his gut.

He set the glass down with a loud bang and raised a finger to the bartender, asking for another round. He stared in disbelief as the man simply shook his head and refused to move. "Get me another drink," he slurred loudly.

"You've had enough." The man moved out from behind the bar, grabbed a towel, and began wiping down the tables in the restaurant. He wished Petre would take his business elsewhere. Ever since the man had taken a seat at the bar, his regular customers refused to stay for very long.

"I don't have to take this! I'm a paying customer! I want another drink!" Petre pounded his fist on the bar top with each statement.

"You won't get another drink from me, Petre. You should go back to your water craft and sober up. Whoever the woman is, she's long gone. You should look for her elsewhere."

"You know what? You're right. I'm going to go look for her. Thanks for the suggestion, man." Petre slid off of the bar stool and stumbled slightly as the floor was further down than he had guessed. He bounced off of a couple of tables as he wove his way across the room to the entrance. He held onto the doorframe as the bright sunlight suddenly blinded him. Rubbing the moisture from his eyes, he stumbled the rest of the way through the door and ran right into a man who was standing in front of him. "Sorry," he mumbled as he made to walk around the unmoving man.

"Come with me, Petre, there's someone who wants to speak with you," he said as he grabbed Petre's arm and practically hauled him along with him.

"Who are you? Who wants to see me? Why are you walking so fast? Hey, let go of me and start answering my questions!" Petre attempted to stand his ground and found himself propelled forward against his wishes.

"Shut up, you drunk fool. All of your questions will be answered in due time." He paused to open the side door of a transport, and then he shoved Petre inside. He stepped inside and over Petre's body where he had fallen on his way in. After shutting the door, he called up to the pilot, "We're ready to go back."

He brushed his hands down his thighs as he took his own seat and fastened his seatbelt. His hands felt dirty after having touched Petre. It was obvious the man had not taken a bath in who knew how long and he smelled abominable. The sooner this assignment was complete, the happier he would be.

CHAPTER 6

Jon stormed back into his room, unable to believe what had just happened in his own home with his sister. The nerve of Willian, coming to their house without an invitation and then taking advantage of Valentina. When Jena came home, he was going to let her know what kind of a boy she was betrothed to. Hopefully, by the time he was done with him, Willian would be returning to Tuala without anyone still wanting to be with him.

After slamming his door and pacing across his room several times, he picked up the phone and called the only person he knew he could count on to take his side. Besides, Sofia was the only other person on Earth who knew who they all were so he could be completely candid and not worry about revealing their truth. With the phone ringing, he continued to stomp through his room from one side and back to the other.

"Hello?" Sofia answered.

"Hey, Sofia, it's Jon. Can you talk?"

"Sure! Let me go to my bedroom, just a sec." She almost ran to her room in her haste to hear whatever had just happened. From the sound of Jon's voice, it must be something big. She shut her door and leaned back against it. "Okay. Are you okay? What's going on?"

"You're never going to believe who I just punched!"

"Who?"

"Willian!"

"What? Where?"

"In my sister's bedroom!"

"What was Willian doing in Val's room?"

"He was practically having sex with her, that's what! He was lying on top of her, and they were kissing. All I could see was red, and I grabbed him by his shirt, pulled him off of her, and punched him in the gut. He's such a wuss; he crumpled to the ground in a heap."

"Jon, you're not making any sense. What was Willian even doing at your house? Besides, I thought he was betrothed to Jena. Why would he be making out with Val?"

"That's what I said! Willian came over to talk with Val. She asked him to leave and went to her room. He followed her in and then practically attacked her. I should have done more to him, but Val screamed for me to stop. I shouldn't have listened to her."

"Where's Val now? Is she okay? Does she need me to come over?" Sofia was more than a little confused by Jon's explanation of what had happened.

"I left her in her room with Behn. For some reason, Behn isn't nearly as upset about this whole thing as I am. Can you believe the nerve of Willian? What's Jena going to say about this?"

"For sure. Wow. This is turning into quite the mess. Do you think Jena and Juila are already gone? Maybe we should try to call over to their house."

"No, I'm sure they're gone. Juila said they were leaving as soon as they got home from school."

"Oh," she replied lamely. "I'm sure there's more to this story which we don't know yet. I'm going to come over, okay?"

"Sure, go ahead. I'll see you in a couple of minutes then." Without waiting for any further conversation, Jon hung up the phone and dropped it back onto his desk. He flopped backward onto his bed and sighed deeply with exacerbation. It was a good idea for Sofia to come over, maybe she could talk some sense into Val.

Petre felt himself being roughly handled again. He felt sickness rise through him as he was picked up from his prone position into a standing one. He turned his head just in time for all of the liquid contents of his stomach to rise and come out of his mouth and nose with explosive force. He heard a gagging sound beside him as the ground quickly rose to meet his body.

Only then did he realize he had been released from being held and he had fallen back to the ground. It was a strange sensation since he could hardly feel his body. Surely the fall should have hurt, yet somehow it had not. His gaze fixated on a bit of pretzel swimming in the pool of liquid next to his face. He had no idea where he was, nor any recollection of getting to wherever he was.

"Take it easy!" Petre slurred as he felt someone grab the back of his shirt and haul him back to his feet. The sudden motion caused him to be sick again, yet, this time, he managed to remain standing while he bent over and heaved several times and spat the foul taste out of his mouth.

"If you're quite through, we need to get going. You are so disgusting, Petre! How can you stand your own stench?" The man turned his head away from Petre as he kept his fist holding his shirt to keep him as upright as possible. He could hardly wait to see what was in store for Petre at this meeting. As soon as Petre seemed okay to begin walking, he hauled him forward and kept up a brisk pace despite Petre's continual stumbling and complaining.

They marched down several long corridors before turning into a darkened chamber. Petre had been scrupulously watching his feet to keep from falling flat on his face again. He looked around curiously when they finally came to a stop. Instantly, the fog lifted from his brain as he realized who had summoned him.

"Lucinden!" Petre swallowed hard before continuing, "How may I serve you?"

"Petre," Lucinden drawled. "It's nice to know that even in your debilitated state, you recall where your loyalties should lie." He shifted his gaze to the man who still had his hand on Petre's shirt and stated, "Leave us."

The man reluctantly let go of Petre and bowed his head in submission. "As you wish, Master." He backed out of the room and shut the double doors as he moved past them. He dared not let Lucinden see how much he wished to remain in the reception room.

Lucinden waited another few seconds before he spoke again. "How the mighty have fallen. Petre, aren't you ashamed of how you've let yourself go? Look at yourself!"

Petre stupidly looked down at his own body and registered how disheveled and unclean his clothes appeared. He plucked at the front of his shirt with his thumb and index finger and replied, "I guess I have."

"Well, if you aren't going to do anything about it, then I guess that leaves me." An instant later, Petre's clothes were replaced with clean, beige robes. Lucinden smiled as Petre's shock was apparent. He still did not know why he put so much energy into this man who was obviously a lack-wit. He did have his uses, which brought his mind back to the point of this meeting. The time for fun and games were over; it was time to get down to serious business.

"You asked me how you can serve me. I've requested your presence to help me retrieve something which I have placed on Earth."

Petre gulped. "You want me to go to Earth? Why can't you just snap your fingers and bring it to you?"

"Be careful, Petre. Don't forget who you're addressing. Given the fact that you lost your samara, you should be grateful I'm even willing to allow you to remain alive, let alone giving you another assignment." He looked at him scathingly and sneered, "Maybe my trust is misplaced to believe you could accomplish this simple task. You may leave now."

"Wait!" Petre wished he would have kept his mouth shut. He hastily rethought his next sentence as he saw Lucinden scowl at being abruptly addressed. "I'm sorry, Master. I spoke out of turn. Please believe I will do whatever it is you ask of me."

"This I already know about you, Petre. Your tenacity is the reason I thought of you in the first place." He tapped his fingers rhythmically on the arm of his chair as he let the silence draw out uncomfortably in the room. He liked keeping Petre nervous and on edge.

"Please, Master, tell me the task so I can prove myself to you again." Petre would have thrown himself down on the floor and begged if he thought it might make a difference. He could see Lucinden considering his request, and he almost cried out in relief when he saw the slightest nod of his Master's head.

"Very well, Petre. I require you to go to a place called New York City. Here in Tuala, it is known as Manzanit. Obviously, you will not be able to use the Ascension Gate in Manzanit as it is held by Elder Wilken who is a devout follower or Jehoban. You will have to travel to Genip where Elder Olguin owes me a favor. You will be able to use his Gate to transfer to Earth. From there you will travel across land and water to get to your destination."

Petre nodded as he took in all of the details. He fervently wished he had been brave enough to go to Earth when he was a teenager to prove his rights of passage. This would be his first trip, and he hated to admit, even to himself, that he was terrified of the prospect. Not only would he have to go to Earth, but he would also have to stay there for an unspecified period of time. Then, if the task were not hard enough already, he would have to work out a plan for getting back to Tuala on his own.

The task sounded nearly impossible, yet he was not about to tell Lucinden he had picked the wrong man for the job. He would go to Earth and complete the task, or he would die trying. He was done being a loser; he was going to prove to himself and Lucinden that he was a man of his word; he could be trusted with the most sensitive assignment. He was going to make a name for himself.

AMANDA WANDERED around the empty house and grounds wondering what she should do to fill her time. She knew it was important for her to work on finding the next samara, yet the timing did not feel right. Somehow, it felt as though she would be spinning her wheels if she were to force it to happen, so she had to concentrate on something else.

Her mind kept wandering back to Roswell, New Mexico. For some reason, her dreams had led her to find Shemalla, yet in real life, she had never met her. The discrepancy began to become an obsession with her.

After her fifth circuit around the garden paths, Amanda gave up fighting the idea and decided to go inside and call her father. In her dream, he had been the one to get the ball rolling in the direction of traveling to the southwest. Maybe he would have some insight as to what she should do next.

With the cordless phone in her left hand, Amanda sat down at the kitchen island with a pad of paper in front of her and a pen in her right hand. Using her thumb, she dialed her parents' number and impatiently waited for someone to answer. Her impatience began to simmer when an automated voice picked up her call rather than either of her parents. *When had they gotten an answering machine?* Amanda thought angrily.

"Leave a message at the beep."

With a sigh of resignation, Amanda spoke into the machine, "Hi, Mom and Dad, this is Amanda. I had hoped to talk with Dad to run something by him…I'll call back later." Amanda was in the process of ending the call when she heard her mother's breathless voice call out.

"Amanda!? Are you still there?"

Amanda raised the phone back to her ear and asked, "Mom? Is everything okay?"

"Yes, yes. I just had to run to catch your call before you hung up. This stupid answering machine only gives me three rings."

"Why did you get it?"

"It was your father's idea. He said he thought it was important we stop missing calls."

"You know you can set it to pick up after more rings, right?"

"No, I didn't know that! I'll have to talk to Chris about changing it. Anyway, what's going on with you?"

Amanda heard the odd inflection her mother placed on the word 'you' and switched topics in her head. She asked, "Is everything okay with Carrie and Deanna?"

Unexpectedly, Diane began to sob.

"Mom? What's going on? Never mind, I'm coming over right

now. I'll see you in a couple of minutes." Amanda waited a few seconds to see if her mother would oppose her new plan.

"Okay," Diane sobbed.

Amanda hated hanging up the phone with her mother crying, but she had to in order to drive over to their house. "I'm going to hang up now, Mom. Are you going to be okay until I get over there?"

"Yes. Thank you, Amanda." Diane ended the call herself.

Amanda was even more frantic with her mother's uncharacteristic end to the call. She tossed the receiver down onto the counter, hopped off of the barstool, grabbed her purse, and ran out to the garage. She dug the truck keys out of her purse as she entered the vehicle. More than anything right now, she wished she could teleport herself over to her mother's house.

CHAPTER 7

The idea of spending twenty minutes on the roads with traffic streaming around her seemed almost unbearable. Knowing her mother was troubled enough to practically hang up on her had her so anxious, maybe teleportation would have been catastrophic anyway. Instead, she would use the drive time to calmly review the call in her mind to see if she could piece together what could possibly be going wrong.

She backed out of the garage and turned the vehicle around in the driveway. She sped down the length of the driveway and tapped her fingers impatiently on the steering wheel as she waited for the gate to open far enough for her to squeeze the truck through the opening so she could be on her way. It was not until she hit the highway that she was able to focus enough on the problem at hand.

Obviously, the problem her mother was experiencing had something to do with either or both of her sisters. Amanda had, on more than one occasion wondered about them both. Neither of them had been to see her since she had woken up from her coma over a year ago. She had often thought it was more than strange, but life had a way of keeping her busy, so she imagined it had done the same for her siblings.

Still, it seemed inconceivable she could be in a coma for seven years, and her sisters could not manage a trip out to see her or even when they found out she married or had two children. Granted, the girls were supposed to be Riccan's kids, which still broke her heart. She could not claim them as her own given that she was technically only eleven years older than her children. It would be rather hard to explain since her sisters both knew she had not had any children up until the age of eighteen when she had gone off on the ill-fated yacht trip with Nealand.

Unable to come up with any real answers, Amanda pressed the gas pedal down a little further and sped over to her parents' house. She pulled into the semi-circular driveway and cut the engine. She hopped out of the truck and slammed the door as she raced up the walkway. Without bothering to knock, she let herself in.

She found her mother in the living room, sitting in a huddle on the couch. Amanda rushed across the room, put her arm around her mother's shoulders, and sat down next to her. "I'm here, Mom. Please tell me what going on! I hate knowing there's something so upsetting to bring you to tears and I don't know anything about it."

"We should have told you a long time ago, but your father insisted you needed to be stronger before we told you."

"Okay, now you're really starting to scare me. What are you not telling me?"

"It's about your sisters," she sobbed with renewed vigor.

"I gathered as much. What's wrong with them?"

Almost as if she needed to get it out in a hurry, Diane took a deep breath and sputtered, "Carrie's addicted to meth and spiraling out of control, and Deanna's really sick, and we don't know what it is."

Amanda felt as though someone had punched her in the gut. Never in her wildest imagination had she imagined the news could be something as bad as her mother had admitted. Her mind raced through all of the past conversations with both of her siblings and realized she should have seen the signs. "So what are we going to do?"

Another round of sobs issued from her mother. Amanda tightened her hold on her mom, and she leaned into her as she said, "We can get through this together. I wish you would have told me sooner, but I know now, and we can handle it."

"We've tried everything! There's nothing more we can do but wait!"

"Why don't you start at the beginning and tell me everything? I'm stronger than Dad believes and I might be able to help if I know about everything."

Diane took a deep stuttering breath to help calm herself. "Right after you went missing, Carrie was beside herself with worry. She spent so much time with the search and rescue crew, we wondered how she was able to do it. Later we discovered she had started taking meth to give her more energy to keep going. When the search was canceled, your sister kept taking the meth so she wouldn't have to think about how she had given up on you.

"We talked to her about her mood swings, and she always had an excuse about being busy or tired, or anything, really. Of course, we didn't know anything about the drugs until recently, but we should have known."

"How could you know? We don't have any experience with drugs in our family. You'd have no way of putting it together."

Diane nodded at her daughter's reasoning. "As a mother, I should have asked more questions when she started missing work. She got fired, you know."

"I didn't know. What happened?"

"She stopped going to work. She had a lot of excuses for not going, and her boss finally got tired of it. They let her go and then things got really bad."

"Well, at least she has her husband."

"She doesn't. They got divorced several years ago when he was arrested for attempted murder."

"What? How come nobody told me?" Amanda recoiled from her mother and stared at her in hurt realization. "I'm not so fragile that I can't handle any bad news. Who did he try to murder?"

"I'm sorry, Amanda. It was your father's idea; and he was adamant we keep it to ourselves." Diane reached out and touched her daughter's leg as if begging her to understand. "Supposedly, it was a friend of his with whom he used to work. The details are sketchy and I really never bothered to find out after I knew Carrie was safe. She's better off without him. I'm really sorry."

Amanda put her hand on her mother's consolingly and said, "You don't have to apologize, Mom. But you can be sure I'm going to talk to Dad about how protective he's been with me! What other things do you have to tell me?"

"An hour before you called, I got a call from Carrie. She's in jail."

"What?!"

"She was charged with meth distribution. The police raided her house this morning, and they arrested her. Even your father doesn't know about this yet."

"Where are her kids?"

"Carrie wasn't sure. She said she walked them to the school bus stop and then she went back home. A few minutes later, the police charged into her house. Everything has been happening so fast, and I don't know what I can do to help."

"Wait, why were the kids in school, isn't it Christmas break?"

"Not until Wednesday, they start the break later there."

"Oh," Amanda said stupidly. "Do you need me to book you a flight to go get the kids then?"

"Even if I were to get on a flight right now, I wouldn't be able to be there in time to pick them up from school."

As if on cue, the phone rang. Diane jumped up and sprinted over to answer it before the machine picked up the call. Amanda had no idea who was on the other end, but it was obvious from her mother's expression that the news was not good. She waited anxiously on the couch for her mother to return and tell her what she had learned.

Diane spent several minutes on the call and rapidly scribbled down a name and phone number on the notepad by the phone. She sighed as she hung up the receiver. With a dejected step, she walked back to the living room and wilted onto the couch beside her daughter. "That was New Mexico Protective Services Division. They are going to pick up the kids from school when it lets out today."

"So you do need a flight today," Amanda said. Her head was spinning through all of the options they had available to them. Once again, she wished she could use her telepod to go and rescue the children.

"No, the lady said they would be placed in foster homes for at least the next two weeks for evaluation." Diane's composure broke again, and she folded herself forward with her hands covering her face. "They have to be so scared! They've been ripped away from everyone and everything they know!"

"There has to be something we can do!"

"The lady said if we wanted to take custody of the children, we would have to become foster parents. Can you believe it? Being their grandparents isn't enough!"

"So that's what we'll do then. We'll get started on it right away, so you'll be prepared when the children are ready to be released from their evaluation." Amanda was glad to have some positive action to take. She wished her father were home so he could help console her mother while she started putting together what they would have to do to become foster parents. This was all uncharted territory.

After the initial shock had worn off, Amanda realized an important detail she had missed before. "Why was the New Mexico Department calling you? I thought Carrie lived in Nevada."

Shaking her head in negation, Diane answered, "She moved after her husband went to jail. She said it would be better for the kids to have some separation from the situation."

"What part of New Mexico is she in?"

"Roswell."

The pieces clicked in her head; it all made sense now. Amanda declared, "We're going to Roswell, Mom. All three of us are going to leave as soon as I can arrange it!"

"What? Why? You heard me say there's nothing we can do right now."

"I can't explain it, but I feel it's important for us to go out there. When I called earlier, I wanted to ask Dad about Roswell. I didn't even know Carrie was living there. Don't you think it's a bit too coincidental? I think it's a sign we need to go out there."

"Okay," Diane said slowly. Her mind was not working properly, and she could hardly see how it would help. She was just glad Amanda was taking over; she was more than willing to do anything which might help her daughter and grandchildren.

CHAPTER 8

Sofia arrived at the Wilson's house in less than ten minutes. She walked up the walkway and noticed Behn's car was missing from where he usually parked it along the sidewalk. After knocking, and waiting for more than a minute, she nervously opened the door and poked her head inside. "Jon? Are you here?" More than a little concerned, Sofia let herself all the way in and closed the door behind her.

She knew where his bedroom was located, so she went through the living room, down the hall past both Valentina's and Behn's empty rooms, until she came to Jon's shut door. Not knowing what else to do, she tapped on his door.

Jon almost immediately pulled it open and said, "You got here fast."

"Where is everyone? I knocked outside, and nobody came. I hope you don't mind I let myself in."

"Of course, I don't mind. I've been in my room since we spoke. My guess is Behn and Val are in their rooms, but I don't really know."

"No, their rooms were empty, and Behn's car is gone."

"What?" Jon ran out of the room calling down the hall, "Val! Behn! Where are you?" The silence continued, and Jon returned to Sofia without knowing anything more than he had when he had left. "I don't know where everyone went. At this point, I'm having a hard time caring. I'm glad you came over, though. Do you want to sit down?" He walked across his room and dropped on his bed.

Sofia sat next to him and said softly, "What's going on Jon? Your earlier accounting of events was really confusing. Why don't you start from the beginning?"

Jon sighed in resignation and tried to compose his words before he spoke. "I guess Willian ran into Val at school today. For some reason, he decided to come over here to...I don't know, discuss something with her, I guess. She asked him to leave and then went to her bedroom. She told me he followed her and tried to convince her that he had an attraction to her. It's really unclear, but they ended up kissing and then somehow ended up on the bed.

"That's when I was passing by her door and saw what was going on. I knew something was wrong, so I dragged him off of her and punched him in the gut. Then something crazy happened; Val stopped me from continuing to beat him up. Val asked him to leave and then he had the gall to ask her for her phone number!"

"What a jerk! I wish Val were here so she could tell me what was going through her mind to allow things to get so out of hand."

"Well guess what Val did next?"

"What?"

"She gave him her phone number! Can you believe it?"

"Okay, now I'm really confused. It sounds as though Val wants to be with him. What is he thinking? He's betrothed to Jena, after all."

"Exactly. Why would Val want to be with her best friend's fiancé? It doesn't make any sense. If it were up to me, I'd send him home today. I don't want him anywhere near Val or Jena. He doesn't deserve either of them if he's going to be such a player."

"You got that right. I guess there's not much we can do until we can talk with Val and Jena. What else is going on with you, Jon?"

"Not much." He reached up and touched the pendant hanging from the leather thong around his neck. "I've started learning how to use my birth crystal."

"That's awesome. I bet it's pretty cool knowing you've had this power all along and not knowing how to access it. What can you do?"

"Silly stuff really. Do you want me to show you?"

"Uh, yeah! Are you kidding? Of course, I want to see!"

"Okay, I'm not an expert or anything so don't expect much," he said shyly, suddenly feeling self-conscious about his newly acquired skill. He held out his hands and closed his eyes. After a few seconds, some wisps of light swirled over his palms.

"Woah, that's cool! What is it?" Sofia leaned forward and inspected the product of Jon's thoughts.

The elemy dissipated as soon as his concentration broke. He smiled shyly and said, "That's what they call elemy, or elemental energy. It's supposed to form a ball and be a brighter light, but I'm still working on it."

"I thought it was perfect. You're too hard on yourself."

"Well if you saw how Behn and Val do it, then you'd know why I'm disappointed in mine."

"They've been doing it longer. I'm sure yours will look like theirs if you had as much practice as they've had. Is there more?"

"Yes. Okay, I have to concentrate so I won't be able to talk once I've started."

Pulling her thumb and index finger across her mouth, she said, "I promise to keep my lips zipped!"

Jon smiled at her silliness and closed his eyes again. In his still cupped hands, he gathered elemy and this time it did form a better, brighter ball. It shifted up and moved several inches away from him; then he pulled it back into the crystals of his pendant. He knew he had performed much better and he smiled triumphantly as he opened his eyes. "I did it!"

"Yes you did, and it was much stronger this time. What do they call all of that? What is it used for?"

"Those were the first three lessons which all six-year-olds learn. Our mom had taught us before she sent us to Earth, but we forgot about it over time until it all seemed like a dream. I didn't really remember any of it until I went back to the village where we were raised. It all came back to me in a rush, but now I have to practice it all over again. I'm not sure any of it actually has a use other than to teach kids how to control the elemy so it can be put to other uses in later lessons. I have a few other things to show you, but I need to get something for the last two things. I'll be right back," he said as he rushed out of the room.

Sofia watched him leave and was glad to see she had managed to distract him enough for him to be almost himself again. She wondered what he would need for his next demonstration. When he returned with two glasses of water, she was even more confounded. He handed her a cup of water, and she accepted it by saying, "Thanks."

Jon smirked and said, "Don't drink it. I'm going to need it for a demonstration in a minute."

"Okay, I'm glad you told me!" She giggled nervously.

He set the second glass down on his nightstand and then turned to face her. "This next skill is to create a breeze. Let me know when you feel it on your face."

Thinking he was probably going to blow on her and make a joke of it, she did not really take him seriously. She smirked and waited while watching his mouth closely.

Again, Jon closed his eyes and kept his mouth firmly shut. Several seconds passed without anything happening. Sofia felt a tickling as if the small hairs on her face were being moved and then she felt a definite breeze. Her eyes grew wide as she realized Jon was actually creating a breeze and he was not using his own breath to make it happen. "I felt it!" she cried out in excitement.

"I was starting to wonder if I were doing something wrong!" Jon was more relieved than he was even letting on. Creating the breeze was a harder skill than anything he had learned to date. There was something elusive about air which caused him much difficulty. "Okay, now turn your attention to the glass of water on the table. Let me know when you see something happen."

Not knowing what to expect, she shifted her gaze to the water and waited, and waited, and waited. Remembering his injunction to remain quiet, she resisted the urge to tell him nothing was happening. Then she realized there were small bubbles forming throughout the water. Even as she leaned closer, the water began to move until the bubbles rose and broke through the surface. Steam rose and then she knew he had heated it until it boiled.

"Cool," she enthused. She shifted her gaze to Jon and saw he was pleased with what he had done. "Why don't you keep your eyes open? It might make it easier if you can see your progress."

"You might be right," he conceded as he reached for the glass she still held in her hand. "I'll try your idea for this last demonstration." He put the glass down in front of the now simmering water and stared intently at the liquid which was gently moving. Without missing a beat, he used the movement to increase the activity of the water and drop the temperature at the same time. Much quicker than ever before, he had the water frozen. "You're right! That was much easier." He turned and grinned at Sofia. "I can't tell what use any of these skills are yet, but that's what I've learned so far."

"Well, as you said, it's teaching you control of the elemy. I'm sure they have a good reason for the order of the lessons. When you learn more, I know it'll make more sense. Until then, I must say, I'm very jealous you can do this and I can't!"

"Maybe you could learn it. Do you want to try? I could try to teach you."

Sofia held up her hands and said, "Once you learn more, then maybe, but until then, I think I'll just live vicariously through you."

"Are you scared?" Jon accused jokingly.

"A little," Sofia answered seriously.

Jon sobered immediately. "You're not scared of me, are you?"

"No! Never! I just don't know if it'd be dangerous for me to try to do what you just showed me without having my own birth crystal. We don't know what could happen and I don't want to risk it yet."

"I guess it makes sense. I'll talk to Jena and Juila about it when they get home. I'm sure they'd know since they've already finished all of the levels of crystal skills."

"Really? They've really learned them all? How many levels are there?" Sofia raised her eyebrows at this new revelation.

"There are twenty-seven known levels, but Jena once said they were only limited by our imagination, so I'm sure there's bound to be more."

"Wow, that's amazing. What else did they say?"

As Jon began explaining, Sofia soaked up everything she learned. She was going to have a lot of questions for the girls when they returned in two weeks. She was so glad she had been on guide duty at the school the day the girls first came to town. Sofia was certain the twins were probably the most fascinating people she would ever meet.

CHAPTER 9

The arrangements were made, and Petre found himself in yet another transport. The journey lasted only three seconds as the telepod erupted in the air over Genip proper. He leaned toward the window to see the palatial Residence sprawling beneath the rapidly descending telepod. The pilot remained silent as he efficiently landed the telepod in the designated landing field.

Petre did not even bother to address the pilot as the door opened whisper quiet beside him. He unlatched his seatbelt, stood up and walked out of the telepod. Before he even took two steps away, the telepod was already ascending. Petre scowled at the pilot's disregard for his own safety and raised a fist in anger. He could almost swear he saw a smirk on the pilot's face just before the telepod disappeared from the sky above him.

Before his new resolve, he would have planned ten ways to get revenge on the pilot for his slight to himself. Now Petre decided to keep focused on his assignment and forget all about the lowly pilot who would never see such adventures as he was about to embark upon. He marched across the landing field and stood in the short line of visitors to the Residence.

When he was finally at the front of the line, the bored attendant asked, "State your name and your reason for going into the Residence."

"Petre MacVeen, I'm here to use the Ascension Gate."

The guard did a double-take at Petre as he recognized the name. "The Gate is by appointment only. You'll have to come back later. Next!" He leaned around Petre to address the person behind him.

"Wait!" Petre moved to block his view. "I have it on good authority I will be granted permission today. Allow me through!"

"Step aside while I send a request. Next!"

Petre had no other option than to stand in the cold breeze to the side of the guard shack. His patience was wearing thin as more than a dozen other patrons were allowed entrance to the Residence before the guard called Petre back to the shack. Petre could tell the guard had enjoyed keeping him waiting in the cold. He kept his expression blank as he took several steps to be at the front of the line again.

"Permission has been granted. Proceed into the Residence." The guard barely made eye contact, and he was already busy tapping requests on his patil keyboard.

Unsure of the layout of this particular Residence, Petre asked several people along the way for the proper direction to the Ascension Gate. More than one person seemed hesitant to tell him, so he shrugged and continued on his way. As he suspected, his questions had caused someone to report him to the staff. Before he got too much further into the main hallway, an older man stopped in front of him.

"Are you Petre MacVeen?"

"Yes, Sir, I am."

"Follow me," he replied curtly as he turned on his heel and set a quick pace through the expansive hallway. Before long, they were winding their way through narrow, dark corridors.

Petre gave up trying to memorize the path they had taken. He soon realized it was a moot point anyway since he would not be returning through this Gate. Besides, the chances of him ever having to come back to Genip were remote at best.

Each step brought him closer to the unknown destination, and he could feel his palms and armpits sweating. He tried to keep his face drawn to neutrality, but he could feel the tension around his eyes as his fear made his heart beat faster and his breathing became irregular. It would be humiliating to pass out in front of his guide, so he tried to think of something other than the feared Gate at the end of this walk.

"Have you used a Gate before?" the guide asked.

Petre looked over at him sharply, wondering if he had been rude enough to read his mind. He saw only curiosity, so he curbed his reply to, "No, this will be my first. How about you?"

"Sure, it's one of the perks of working here. My family is from the Telae District, so I make certain to go out to see them several times an anon. I know how you must be feeling, with this being your first time and all. There's nothing to worry about, you know. Elder Olguin is an expert at using the Gate; besides the journey only lasts three seconds. There's hardly any time at all to get nervous." The guide kept his head facing forward to continue navigating the hallways, so he did not see Petre's look of relief.

This was the first time Petre had experienced someone genuinely trying to be nice to him. It felt pretty good to be on the receiving end. He did gather some measure of comfort from his guide's advice, and he was also thankful to know how long the journey would take. From what the guide had said, the transfer would only take as long as a telepod relocation, so it did not seem too bad. He felt the constriction in his chest begin to loosen and his breathing became easier and less labored.

"And here we are, Petre. Just go through this last door. Elder Olguin will be waiting for you. Have a safe journey." He patted Petre's arm as he moved past him and back up the hallway the way they had come.

Petre looked after him and then turned to face the final door. He felt a chill run through him as he realized this was a one-way trip through the door. How many other people had walked through this same passageway and never returned? His thoughts turned darker as he wondered how many people had been lost for all time on their journey.

Shaking his head abruptly, Petre dismissed his last macabre idea and had to believe Elder Olguin knew what he was doing. Besides, the Elder would hardly want to anger Lucinden by sending Petre somewhere other than his intended destination. With this in mind, Petre confidently took the last remaining steps, reached out and turned the knob, and stepped through the entrance.

With his hand still holding the doorknob, Petre was surprised to see how plain and dark the room actually was since it was windowless and only spheres of elemy were used to light the middle. After seeing all of the grand opulence of the Residence, it seemed odd that the most important room should be left unrefined.

"Shut the door and come forward, MacVeen. I'd like to get this transfer finished promptly so my final favor to Lucinden can be discharged."

Petre jumped at the seemingly bodiless voice since he had yet to see where Elder Olguin was located. Knowing the direction from where the voice had sounded gave him his only clue as to where to look. He promptly shut the door behind him and then boldly looked toward where he thought the Elder would be, only to be startled again when the Elder appeared right in front of him. His eyes grew wide as he tried to control his sharp intake of breath. He hated seeming weak to anybody, especially in front of powerful people.

"This way, MacVeen. Come swiftly!" He plucked at Petre's sleeve for emphasis before turning and leading the way, confident in Petre's compliance.

"Why is it so dark in here?" Petre asked as he fell into step behind the short, old man.

"I already know where everything is, and I hate to waste my energy creating more light than is necessary. Step down into the depression, just there," he said as he pointed several feet ahead of him. "I'm told you wish to go to Winnipeg, Manitoba, on Earth. Is this correct?"

"More or less."

"MacVeen, this is no time for games. I must be certain of your destination, so please say yes or no."

"Yes," Petre answered with a slight rolling of his eyes at how dramatic Elder Olguin was acting. He kept his final destination to himself, as he was beginning to feel as though all of this were a test regarding his discretion. He was not going to reveal anything unnecessarily to anybody. He stepped down into the shallow, dirt hollow. Again, he wondered why the space was left in its natural state rather than being made to look pristine.

"Good, good. Now keep your hands to your sides, you don't want to lose them in the transfer," Elder Olguin admonished as he turned to the control panel and began tapping out commands on the plascreen.

"Wait just a minute," Petre began to protest as his mind registered Elder Olguin's last words. "Is this going to be dangerous?" He started to raise his arms in protest until his fear of losing them stopped the motion.

With a final tap to his plascreen, Elder Olguin looked up with a glint in his eyes as he answered, "All transfers contain an element of danger. Goodbye, MacVeen." He smiled wickedly as he could see the fear register on Petre's face as he hit the activation button to send him on his way.

Petre wished he were anywhere other than where he currently was, yet he was terrified to move a muscle since he could feel the elemy gathering around his body. The sensation was similar to that of a telepod transfer, yet so much different because it was only him. Instantly he began counting in his head, certain he could endure three seconds of the unknown. Panic began to rise faster as he counted five then six seconds. Surely Elder Olguin would not have purposely sent him to his death; the Elder had more scruples than that.

Relief rushed through him as his mind registered full feeling throughout his body again. The transfer had worked, yet he had no knowledge of his actual destination. Supposedly, he had arrived on Earth, yet what it should look like remained a mystery. The utter darkness surrounding him surpassed what he had experienced in Elder Olguin's room.

Recalling the Elder's elemy spheres, Petre conjured one of his own in his outstretched hand. He soon discovered he was inside of a cave. He turned around in a full circle before he decided on which direction to attempt to leave. Only two tunnels were leading off of the place where he had been standing.

He had a fifty percent chance of choosing the correct path. Of course, he had chosen the wrong one as he found himself facing a dead end. With a growl of displeasure, Petre turned around and followed his own dusty footprints to lead him back to his starting point. He hated small dark spaces, and this cave was not inspiring any confidence with its seemingly endless twists and turns. He chose the second tunnel and soon found himself outside, facing a vast expanse of forested land and a steep drop off.

Laughing at his own idea of where this Gate would have brought him, he realized the error of his thinking. Civilization was nowhere near. Not only would have to navigate unknown territory, but he would also have to rely solely on his own survival skills until he could ask anyone for assistance in getting to New York City. This task just turned monumental.

Everything came together in a whirlwind of activity. Amanda found herself sitting next to her mother in the first row of the airplane with her father sitting across the aisle. Now that they had the next five hours of travel time to breathe, Amanda's thoughts returned to her earlier conversation with her mother.

"Tell me what's going on with Deanna. Earlier, you said she was sick."

"She keeps fainting at work. She's been to the doctor several times, but they can't seem to figure out what's going on with her. There doesn't seem to be any rhyme or reason for why she passes out, and, of course, it never happens at the doctor's office. They've run all kinds of tests, but there're no answers."

"Does she have any other symptoms?"

"She said she's tired all of the time," Diane answered. She sighed and tried to think of anything else her daughter might have mentioned. "She's also lost weight."

"Hmm. Anything else?"

"Well, she hasn't said anything, but there have been many times when I've talked to her that she's forgotten things she said she'd do. When I reminded her, it was like it was the first time she'd heard it. I always thought it was because she had a lot going on, but do you think it could be something more?"

"Maybe. Once we get things squared away with Carrie and the kids, I'll call her and see for myself." Amanda closed her eyes. She could hardly believe her perfect, idyllic life could be unraveling so easily. Just that morning she had only to worry about what she was going to do to occupy her time while the girls were on vacation. Now her family was in major crisis mode, and she had no idea how she was going to fix any of it.

Amanda sighed with exhaustion and turned her head to talk to her mother again. Just as she opened her mouth to speak, she realized her mother had fallen asleep leaning against the window. Relieved because her mother was getting the rest she needed, she turned and leaned across the aisle to whisper, "Mom is finally getting some sleep. Why didn't you tell me everything going on with my sisters?"

"I didn't want you to worry about them. There's nothing you could have done, and you had your own recovery to focus on."

"Still, Dad, you could have said something. I've been perfectly fine for the last six months; why not then?"

"You just got married, and then you got your children back. There was nothing you could have done."

"I don't have to do anything, Dad, but I can be there to support them. If I had known, I could have made more of an effort to go see them or talk to them on the phone more often."

"To what end, Amanda? We didn't even know what was going on with Carrie until it all started to unravel."

Amanda unbuckled her seatbelt and moved over to the empty chair next to her father. "I wanted to talk to you about Roswell. I called today to ask you about it when I found out that's where Carrie lives now. Don't you think it's too coincidental that my dream had us all going to Roswell to find a way back to Tuala, and now we're all going there because of Carrie?"

"It is rather odd," Chris mused. He liked puzzles, and this seemed like the ultimate one. Being personally invested in the outcome did make it harder to figure out, but he was willing to focus his attention on Amanda's question. "So we're clearly not needing to find a way to Tuala since you have that angle covered. What else did we learn while we were there in your dream?"

"We met with Shemalla. Do you think she's also real?"

"I can't see why she wouldn't be since everybody else in your dream was real. Maybe we should plan on going to the UFO Museum to check."

"If nothing else, we'll be able to see if the displays in the museum are anything like reality."

"That would be cool." Having seen, touched, and flown in an actual telepod did take a little of the excitement away from going to look at a display. He was, however, always willing to investigate for any discrepancies.

Amanda smiled at her father's instant enthusiasm. She usually appreciated his ability to look at the bright side of things, and right now, they needed as much optimism as possible. With the end of their journey being a visit to her sister in jail, they were all going to need to be as positive as possible.

CHAPTER 10

Vinia had her work cut out for her with all of the demands from the people of the Roanoke Colony. In the past, they had always been self-sufficient, but with the installment of the patil in Vinia's house, suddenly they all had specific needs which had to be taken care of immediately. While she had been grateful for their easy acceptance in the beginning, she was starting to feel as though they were testing her to see how much they could get away with before they were told no.

It was not until one of the women insisted she needed a specific type of food to remedy her delicate stomach that Vinia finally put her foot down. "I'm sorry, Agetha, that's just not going to happen. The patil is to be used for requesting necessities, not for personal pleasure. I'm sorry; I just will not allow this to continue."

Agetha simply stared at Vinia in disbelief. Finally finding her voice, she scoffed, "Who are you to tell me no?"

"I'm the one you all appointed as your leader. Go home to Romen and let me get back to work." Vinia began to shut the door when the woman's hand struck out and held the wooden plank open.

"You haven't heard the last of this, Vinia, I promise!" She turned on her heel and stomped along the path back to her own cottage. Her indignation was apparent by the stiff way she carried her shoulders and head.

Vinia shook her head in dismay and wondered what type of trouble Agetha could cause for her. She knew this day would happen sooner or later; she had only hoped it would be later. "I better send a message to Elder Daven and let him know what's brewing." She murmured to herself as she shut the door and leaned back against it for support.

After writing and re-writing the perfect message to the Elder, Vinia hit enter and then sat staring at the blank patil screen. Her role as the village leader was both harder and easier than she had hoped, yet she still felt unfulfilled. She wanted to have her children back, and she knew the villagers looked down on her because they failed to come home with her.

Vinia shook her head at how paranoid she was becoming. She realized the people around her did not even know where her children were, only that they had gone away. Maybe she should try to get them to come and visit with her. Then there was the problem that her kids were no longer children, they were almost adults, after only having been gone for one anon. This was getting more complicated by the minute. Her thoughts were interrupted by a knock on her door.

With a sigh of resignation, she pushed away from the table and stood up. She smoothed her tunic and prepared for another battle with Agetha. She was certain the woman was coming back to make another go at getting something special brought into the village. She shifted her expression into one of determined resignation and flung the door open.

Her expression changed immediately as the person on the other side of the opening was none other than Ozias. "What are you doing here?"

"I…" he looked away as if he were suddenly uncomfortable. He saw several women watching him surreptitiously. "Do you mind if I come inside to talk? It seems as though those people are rather interested in me."

Vinia looked over his shoulder and instantly understood. "Yes, come inside. I'm afraid the women around here are rather anxious to see a man in their midst."

"Thanks," he said as he moved across the threshold and entered the small cabin.

As she shut the door, Vinia tried to figure out why Ozias would be at her house. "I thought Elder Daven was going to find a place for you to stay. Did that not work out?"

"I never gave him the chance. I left his telepod when he brought you and the other villagers back here. I've been wandering along the coast ever since."

"That was four days ago! What have you been eating? You must be starving!" Vinia began to plan something for him to eat even before he answered.

"I don't want to be any bother," he began and cut off any further statement as a plate of food suddenly appeared on the table in front of him. He shifted his gaze in amazement from the meal back to Vinia. Never in his life had he seen anything so amazing as what she had just done. "How did you do that?"

"It's something anyone can do." She realized he probably never would have seen such a display since he was from another planet. His only experience with people had first been with Juila and her family on Earth, and then the wilderness of Tuala when he walked away from Elder Daven's telepod when he brought him back with him. She indicated the chair in front of the table and said, "Please sit and eat."

Without any hesitation, Ozias sat down and pulled the plate closer. He picked up the sandwich and took his first bite of shredded foxl. The flavors were perfect, and the meat was still warm. He had no idea how Vinia had accomplished the task, yet he was grateful to have something to eat so soon. He had been feeling lightheaded and slightly delirious, which was what had actually driven him to make contact with Vinia again. Initially, he had thought to make a life for himself on Tuala, but he soon realized he lacked any ability to survive on his own.

"What have you been doing these last few days?"

Not wanting to appear rude by not answering, he spoke around the bite in his mouth. "I've been trying to find a place to settle down and live."

"My guess is you didn't have much luck?"

"Very accurate guess," he said with a rueful shake of his head. "There's nothing around here! How did your people survive all this time?"

"There's plenty around when you know what to look for. Do you want me to contact Elder Daven? He said he had a plan in mind for you."

"I wish you wouldn't."

"So what do you plan on doing?"

"I'd like to stay here and help out your people. I feel partially responsible for the lack of men because of my association with Viceroy Blair. Do you think I might be able to stay?"

Vinia sat back in the chair she had taken across from him. She had been wondering what they were going to do without the men to do the harder chores. The women of the community resisted most usage of elemy and tended to do every task manually. Ozias' offer might be just the change they needed.

"We might be able to make some arrangements, but I'd need to discuss the matter with the villagers first. I'm sure you understand." Vinia could not help but wonder if Ozias might have some ulterior motive for coming back to the colony. She hated having to be suspicious; however, she had to keep the best interest of the people in mind rather than her own beliefs and opinions.

"Absolutely." He looked back down at his food to escape Vinia's penetrating stare. This plan was going to have to work because he did not have any other options at this point.

Vinia stood up after making her decision. "I'll go have a word with the people while you eat. Hopefully, I'll have an answer for you in a couple of minutes. It shouldn't be too hard to gather everyone since it seems they all noticed you coming here in the first place." She smiled at the recollection as she opened the front door and stepped outside.

Just as she suspected, the women rushed forward and bombarded her with questions. The overwhelming demand was to know what he was doing in her house and what he was doing back. Vinia held up her hands for silence and spoke to the restless crowd. "Ozias has asked to stay on in our community to help out. Does anyone have any objection to his request?"

As if on cue, Agetha pushed her way through the crowd and planted her feet aggressively right in front of Vinia. With hands on her hips and a hard expression, she asked, "Why would he want to stay here? Who's going to take care of him? And where do you propose he would live? With you, I suppose!"

Taken aback by Agetha's vicious attack, Vinia tried to maintain her composure of leadership as she answered calmly, "He knows about our situation and has offered to help out with chores which would be too strenuous for the women. Since it was his former leader who took away all of the men, he feels some measure of responsibility for our welfare. I would suggest he would live at

Grobin's old home unless there are any other ideas. As for who would take care of him, I think we could all share in that duty."

Agetha could not find any faults with Vinia's proposal and ungracefully stepped away from Vinia. While she did not like the idea of another man assuming he might have any say in their lives, she had to agree they were going to need help through the winter mesans. After all, they could always send him away if he became a burden. "I don't have any objections," she sneered.

Vinia held back a sigh of relief since Agetha had been her biggest worry. She would do well to keep her eye on the discontented woman to make sure she did not create any mischief. With a nod of satisfaction at Agetha's statement, she looked around the rest of the crowd to see nods of approval. Although some of the women seemed reluctant, nobody else came forward with any objections.

"I'll let Ozias know after he's finished eating his meal. Will anyone volunteer to freshen up Grobin's house?"

Dilela, Mitelda, and Edda stepped forward after looking at one another and nodding agreement. "We'll go and do that for you," Dilela spoke quietly.

"Thank you all!" Vinia turned to go back into her house. From the corner of her eye, she noticed one of the only older male teenagers, Semsen, who did not seem happy to hear about another man coming into the community. She would be certain to keep an eye on him to make sure he did not cause any trouble. She opened her door and swiftly left the crowd behind her. "It's all set, Ozias," she said as she leaned against the inside of the door with relief.

"Are the people being hard to deal with? You seem slightly out of sorts."

She pushed away from the door and slowly advanced across the room. "Not exactly hard." She searched for the right word to describe the villagers. "They aren't used to making decisions on their own. Grobin always dictated what would happen and they would blindly follow. Now that he's gone, they're cautious of every choice, fearful of doing something wrong. I can't blame them. Up until Viceroy Blair took them, their whole lives' experiences revolved around the area surrounding this village. Outsiders had always been turned away."

Ozias nodded his understanding.

"You'll be staying in Grobin's house for now."

"He was the leader here, wasn't he?" He recalled how arrogant the man had been.

"You might say that. I'd call him a tyrant, personally."

"Do you think they'll resent me for coming back?"

Vinia shrugged her shoulders and said, "Don't give them any reason to. Since you're done eating, I'll give you a tour of the village while the women get your place ready."

Ozias picked up his empty plate as he stood and wondered what he could do with it. He hated leaving a mess for Vinia to clean up.

"Don't worry about it," Vinia said. As soon as he put the plate back on the table, she used a small amount of elemy to take care of the mess. Again, seeing his expression of disbelief, she added, "Most of the people here don't use the skills they were born with. Grobin, and all of the other leaders for that matter insisted it was unnatural and evil. My family disagreed, but we never did anything within sight of the other people here. If we could keep this to ourselves..."

"You can trust me, Vinia. I'm grateful for everything you're doing for me, and I'll support your leadership in whatever way I can." Ozias raised his hands, practically pleading her to trust him. He would do anything to prove his worth to this amazing woman.

CHAPTER 11

Petre felt lucky when he discovered a strange clearing in the forest. He looked up and saw several lines suspended from giant towers following the same pathway. Since the footing was much better in the cleared area, he decided to follow the overhead lines to see where it would lead him. Certainly, the people would not decide to build such a device unless they planned on utilizing it in some way.

There were several large bodies of water where the path wove its way around them. More than once, he wished he had his water craft available so he could rest comfortably as he traveled over the calm waters. He had already spent one anxious night exposed to the intolerably cold elements. More than once, he wondered how the people on Earth could stand to live with such cold weather. Then again, he had yet to see a single person yet, and he hoped he would discover any civilization soon since he was hungrier than he could ever recall. All of his muscles protested as he kept moving one foot in front of the other.

His lifestyle on the oceans certainly had not prepared him for such a physical journey. He would have stopped to rest, except the biting wind made him too cold to stop for more than a few seconds at a time. He was going to have to find something to eat soon. If he had known the trip would be so physical, he would have packed provisions. As it was, he was forced to only stop for water breaks at the streams and lakes.

When Petre encountered a black-topped surface, he wondered at what it could mean. He stepped back suddenly as a large object sped along the way, and he realized it must be some sort of trading route. With more eagerness, he turned left and almost jogged alongside his new discovery. As another object appeared ahead of him, barreling toward him, he paid more attention to it and realized there was a person seated in the front.

Petre only had a couple of seconds to realize the speeding objects were vehicles of some sort. Initially, the noises emanating from them had kept him from registering their function. Now that he had seen several, he noticed the vehicles came in all sorts of shapes and sizes, unlike back home where there were only a few size differences and hardly any variance at all in design.

He kept jogging, not only to keep warm but also to get to wherever all of the vehicles were going. Surely, civilization had to be nearby. Just as his breath was coming out in ragged sobs, and plumes of white air obscured his vision, he felt the stiff breeze of another passing vehicle, bigger than any other. His steps slowed down as he realized the vehicle had decelerated and finally stopped ahead of him. Now was the time for him to finally meet someone from Earth on their own soil.

Excitement at the prospect of getting help soon turned into fear as he came up beside the large vehicle. He had no idea if this person were friendly or not; he was just going to have to hope for the best. Once he got to the front of the vehicle, he looked around him with more than a little confusion. He almost jumped out of his skin when he heard a voice calling out to him.

"Are you okay, mister? It's freezing out here. Get into the cab and get yourself warmed up! Here, let me get the door for you," the burly man said as he reached up behind Petre and pulled on a shiny lever. He looked back at Petre expecting immediate compliance.

Realizing belatedly that he should comply, Petre mumbled, "Thanks," as he stepped up onto the shiny metal step and used a handle on the doorframe to help him up into the high cab. Immediately, he could appreciate the heat coming out of the vents in the dash. He held up his hands in front of it even as the man shut the door behind him. Being so consumed with getting warm, Petre barely registered the man walking around the front of the vehicle and getting into his own seat behind a big circle sticking out of what Petre imagined was the control panel.

Petre was literally shaken from his heat-soaking trance as the man began to drive the semi. The shifting, contorting, and shaking of the cab appalled Petre into wondering if the vehicle were safe. He had been in some poorly maintained telepods, but this took his worry to a whole new level. The noise coming from the front of the vehicle seemed even louder than a racing telepod, which he thought was ridiculous in any event.

He glanced over at the stranger and saw his neutral expression, so he had to assume all was well with the vehicle. There was much he needed to learn about Earth, and this was his first valuable lesson in transportation. Some of the noise instantly went away as the driver turned a knob on the control panel.

The man shifted his gaze from the view of the road as he addressed Petre, "Where are you headed?"

"New York City," he mumbled.

"You know you're heading the wrong direction, right?"

"Not really. I've never been there, and I got turned around while I was walking."

"Where's your vehicle? I didn't pass anything along the way."

Having to improvise hastily, Petre gestured toward the hills and said, "I got stuck up there."

The man looked dubiously toward where Petre had indicated. He was unaware of any driving trails anywhere near. He shrugged indifferently and had to assume the man was suffering from hypothermia. "If you're set on getting to New York, then I'll drop you off as close as I can to the bus station, unless, of course, you have other transportation arranged already."

Petre shook his head. While he did not know what a bus station was, he hoped someone there would know how to get him to his desired destination. Still holding his hands up in front of the warm air vent, Petre was beginning to be able to feel his fingers again. He had no idea how anyone could possibly want to remain living in an area with temperatures so cold.

His body started to relax as the heat settled around him. His eyes closed and he slumped against the window and door frame. Before many more seconds passed, Petre was fast asleep and missed the hour-long journey to Winnipeg.

THE WOMEN STOOD in small groups, pretending occupation all the while they kept their covert attention on the house in the center of the village. They were intensely curious about Ozias now that he was staying in Grobin's former house. Not everyone felt secure with a stranger in their midst even though a vote had been taken allowing him to stay.

"It's just not right," Agetha grumbled to Fraya. "What do we really know about him, after all? He doesn't even have a proper, honorable name."

Fraya looked over at Agetha and wondered if there were something to what Agetha was saying. She personally thought Ozias was handsome, not to mention old enough to take as a husband. The shortage of eligible men in their community was even more prevalent since they had returned to Tuala.

"Maybe we should suggest he change his name," Fraya suggested quietly.

Agetha glared at the attractive, young girl for her comment. "He doesn't belong here, Fraya! We were doing just fine without him!" Thinking about how peaceful her life had become ever since her husband had remained captive with Viceroy Blair, she did not wish to have to answer to any man ever again. She felt protective of Fraya's innocence and did not want to see her get involved with this stranger who could prove to be more harmful to their community than even Grobin had been.

Their conversation was interrupted when the front door of the house opened, and the man in question stepped out into the daylight. Agetha tore her gaze away from his lean, masculine form and looked over at the girl by her side. The expression she saw on her friend's face instantly infuriated her with jealousy. In disgust, she threw down the rake she had been barely using, let out a loud sigh, and stomped off to her own home.

Fraya jumped with surprise at Agetha's poor manners. She blushed prettily and immediately bent to retrieve the abandoned tool. Without looking back over to Ozias, but painfully aware he was probably watching her, she scurried away to hide behind her own house.

Unknown to either of the women, Ozias had been able to overhear their conversation. He had originally planned on going for a walk until the women's concern changed his mind. Ozias firmly shut the door behind him and walked with purpose to Vinia's house to find out what she thought about his name. Never before had it occurred to him there might be something socially wrong with his name.

Arriving only seconds after deciding to go, Ozias knocked swiftly on the door. As soon as the door opened, Ozias hurriedly asked, "What's wrong with my name?"

Vinia's expression turned puzzled, and she stammered slightly before stepping back into her house and saying, "Come inside."

Ozias barely cleared the doorframe before he started talking. "I overheard some women saying my name wasn't honorable. What were they talking about?"

"Oh," Vinia replied lamely as she shut the door silently. She turned around and rested her back against the wood as she tried to come up with the easiest explanation. "There's nothing wrong with your name, at least not where you come from. The problem is that you're in Tuala now and here all of the men's names end with an 'n' unless they've lost honor." She pushed herself away from the support of the door and took several steps across the room to where she could sit at the table.

Vinia gestured for him to sit down with her as she thought about possible solutions to their new dilemma. She watched him carefully to see if she could read his face enough to discern what he was thinking. As he sat next to her, she suddenly felt something click inside her head. She hastily looked away as she realized she was flustered by the idea of having a man inside her house, sitting at her table.

She had told Amanda she wanted to be able to reunite with Nealan as soon as he had recovered from his ordeal. Now she felt as though she were betraying his memory with her lecherous thoughts. Surely, Ozias did not entertain the same ideas about herself, and she could not understand what had suddenly over-come her good judgment.

Returning to the original discussion, she said, "In Tuala, we're supposed to report any foreigners to the Elders. Usually, the people who come here would be from Earth, and they call them *old souls* here." She stopped talking as another realization hit her; Ozias had not lost his memory when he entered Tuala. "I think you're special, Ozias. More than you'll ever know, really." She had to look away again as she felt the same attraction pulling at her when he looked in her eyes.

"Elder Daven already knows I'm here. Doesn't that take care of your social obligation then?"

"Yes." She could not remain idle, and she pushed herself away from the table and started to pace the room. "The women did have a point, however. If we don't do something about your name, then anytime you meet someone from outside the village, they'll think you're not honorable. How would you feel about modifying your name…say something like Ozian?"

"Ozian," he said quietly and slowly, feeling the sound of it on his tongue. "I think I could live with that change."

"Alright, I'll be sure to tell everyone in the village what we've decided then." She did not want him to leave and swiftly asked, "Are you hungry? I could make us something to eat."

"I'm always hungry, but I don't want to put you to any trouble."

Gathering elemy, she created two plates of lunch which appeared instantaneously on the table. "No trouble at all." She sat in her recently vacated chair and smiled proudly at the look of surprise on his face.

"I'd forgotten about you being able to do that!"

"Would you like to say the prayer before we eat?"

Ozian looked uncomfortable as it was not something he prac-ticed for himself.

Vinia saw his expression change and hastily offered, "I can do it if you'd rather."

"Please. I'd like that."

Vinia folded her hands on the table, bowed her head with eyes closed, and spoke softly, "Jehoban, we thank you for this food which we are about to receive, and pray that thou will bless it, and us to thy service, in Emmanuen's name we pray. Amen."

Ozian smiled at her when she opened her eyes and said, "That was really beautiful. Will you teach that to me?"

"Sure, but I think we should eat first, while it's still hot." She picked up her shredded foxl sandwich and dunked it into the bowl of broth.

Ozian chuckled at her response and followed her lead with the food. One day, he hoped he would be able to learn how to create food out of thin air. Somehow, he thought it was going to be a skill which would be difficult to acquire.

Ever since arriving back in Tuala, Jena had been experiencing a strange feeling. At first, she simply believed it to be the energy rising from the land itself. Now, as she lay in a pool of sweat in her bed, she knew it was something much more. The nightmares which had plagued her for almost her whole life were more intense than ever. It was almost as if the dream were trying to prepare her for something to come.

As if on cue, Juila entered the room and sprawled out on the bed beside her. "I'm here now," she whispered as she threw her arm across her sister's stomach. "It seemed worse tonight."

"It definitely was worse," Jena whispered. "The dreams have been less intense until tonight. What do you think made the difference?"

"Probably being back in Tuala. Don't worry about it. I'll stay here for the rest of the night. You won't be alone." Juila thrust her arm up under the pillow to raise her head a little higher as she prepared herself to sleep again.

Jena knew exactly when her sister fell asleep. She counted the breaths as Juila took them, hoping the monotony of it all would bore her back to sleep. Unfortunately, the rising sun found her still awake as she tried to make sense of the disturbing dreams. Trying not to wake Juila, she wiggled out from under her arm and off the edge of the bed.

She freshened up in the bathroom by splashing cold water on her face. Staring at her wet reflection in the mirror, she could see the dark circles under her eyes. She used the smallest amount of elemy to revitalize her body and watched with pleasure as the darkness seemed to seep away. This was hardly the first time she had used this unorthodox method to make it through a day after a bad night. She wished she could say it would be her last, but she knew that to be untrue as long as she still had to live through what the dreams were showing her.

Her thoughts must have woken up Juila since she was now sitting on the edge of the bed waiting for her to return.

"Grandma Nena said we could go to Grandpa Daven's office to read through the books in his library. She said there were some really old ones in there." Juila knew how much her sister loved to read and hoped the offer would help her mind to relax. She could feel the turmoil in her own mind and knew it was even worse for her sister. She wished she could trade places with her so she would sleep better. It was hard to imagine they would have to wait for another two anons before the dreams would finally end.

Smiling at her sister's attempt to help her, she smiled and answered, "I can't wait to see what he's got. I'm pretty sure we already read everything in the library at Acaim."

"To be sure," Juila agreed as she stood up and stretched, joints cracking, and sighing deeply. "Are you ready?" She led the way to the door, planning on stopping by her own bedroom to put on a robe before heading downstairs.

Jena grabbed her own robe off of the chair next to the door as she followed her sister. She pulled it on as she walked across the hall and into Juila's room, which was identical to her own. Maybe she could find something of use inside the books downstairs which could help her figure out her dreams.

They walked around the office several times before pulling several volumes from the shelf. Jena was exhilarated to find several topics which she had read very little about. Even Juila had discovered a couple of books which she seemed interested in reading.

SHUTTING his folder with more force than necessary, Dr. Gascon ripped the glasses off of his face and pinched the bridge of his nose to try to ease the headache behind his eyes. There had to be something he was missing in these records; something which would give him the breakthrough he needed in order to submit his case study to his peers. It had been far too long since he had begun this research and told his colleagues about it, and they were pressing him for answers he was unable to provide with solid proof.

If only he had a couple more cases in which to provide supporting documentation. This line of thinking only angered him more because he had two more cases he should have been able to pursue: Nealand Taivas and Amanda Covington. Both of them had slipped through his fingers and were now firmly out of his reach. Which led him to another line of thinking entirely.

He pulled the latest envelope of pictures and reports from out of the locked top drawer of his massive desk. There had to be something going on at the Stel house. Too many people were seen coming away from the property when only very few ever actually entered. Maybe he should consider hiring another investigator to see if there truly were a second, perhaps secret, entrance to the property.

After rifling through the various photographs, he held the clearest picture of Amanda up in front of him and simply stared at her. "What are you keeping from me," he asked out loud. "One day I will have you in my care, and you will answer all of my questions."

The phone buzzed annoyingly. Dr. Gascon stuffed the investigative reports back into the envelope before he picked up the receiver. "What?!"

"Your three o'clock appointment is waiting for you, Dr. Gascon." The receptionist did not wait for an answer before she clicked off the line. She had enough experience to know when the doctor was not feeling particularly nice, and she would rather not hear any of his snide comments.

Thinking about how much trouble it would be to replace his impertinent secretary, Dr. Gascon gathered the files he would need and shoved them in his briefcase. He locked his desk up and then stomped across the large office. Once he got within earshot of his secretary, he said, "You're fired!" Without missing a beat, he continued on his way to the next patient.

CHAPTER 12

Elder Daven found the girls studying in his office and it still warmed his heart to know these brilliant young women were his flesh and blood. He had seen them on several occasions throughout the anons when he had consulted with Jehoban. He knew Jehoban was extremely proud of their accomplishments and it stroked his ego to know now who the girls were to him. For so many anons, he and his wife had lamented the lack of grandchildren from their only son. He could never have anticipated how well things would have turned out.

"It looks as though you've both found books of interest," he announced as he stepped through the doorway into his office.

As one, both girls looked up at him and smiled the exact same smile. Jena abandoned her seat and rushed over to hug her grandfather and say, "Good morning, Grandpa. You have some great books here!" With her greeting finished, she returned to her seat and asked, "What do you have planned today?"

"Unfortunately, I have a healing to attend. The parties were unable to leave their property, so I'm going to be gone for most of the morning unless the ailment cannot be contained quickly, then I'll be gone until dinner." He stopped behind Jena's chair and glanced over to see what she had picked out to read. He was more than a little surprised to see the volumes were of the most complicated subject matter he owned. With raised eyebrows, he shifted his gaze to inspect Juila's choices and found her to be reading equally challenging material. "Promise me you won't spend the entire day cooped up in here. These books aren't going anywhere so you should enjoy the grounds and get some fresh air."

Juila grinned broadly and assured him, "I'll be sure to pry Jena away. She does tend to forget to eat when she finds a book she hasn't read before."

He placed his palm on the top of Juila's head and said, "That's my girl." With more than a little reluctance he moved away from his grandchildren, gathered the supplies he would need for his day, and sighed with the idea of leaving so soon after finally getting the girls to come and visit. Daven kissed each girl on the top of her head as he passed behind them and said, "I'll do everything I can to make this short, so I can get back home. Have a great day!"

"You too, Grandpa," the girls spoke in unison.

Daven rushed down the hall and out to the landing field. He wished there were someone else he could have sent to handle this particular situation. Any other Elder would have sent their successor, but Riccan was spending some much-needed time alone with his new bride. Besides, being Sabtu, he would not have asked anyone else to handle such a delicate task.

Once he was settled in his telepod, he began the start-up procedures. The telepod rose from the ground several inches and hovered, unmoving. Instead of concentrating on his current task, Daven found his mind wandering back to the scene in his office. There had been a tension around the two girls which Daven tried to understand. He wondered if the girls were homesick, or if they had some other problem which he should try to resolve for them.

Daven shook his head in resignation as he realized trying to understand a teenage girl's mind was almost impossible and he had another task at hand. With a gusty sigh, Daven pulled up the coordinates of his destination, focused his mind to only completing the transfer, and then he touched the activation button which immediately sent him on his way.

The darkness surrounded him, and his mind maintained the necessary focus. The landing area was detailed in his thoughts, and he could feel himself moving through space, even though he knew it was most likely a figment of his imagination. Who knew? Maybe it was a special talent of his, to be able to feel space moving around him. Three seconds passed, and then the site he had noted in his head was directly ahead of him. Daven shifted the telepod into manual mode and used the yoke to navigate over to a perfect landing.

Several of the people from the small town were already waiting for him at the edges of the field. Daven could see their anxious expressions even as he worked through the steps to deactivating the telepod. The strange epidemic the town was experiencing was troublesome to his mind since they had never encountered such a widespread sickness before. He had to discover the source of the problem to prevent a second outbreak after he healed the first round of the ill.

He picked up his healer's bag as he passed through the back of the telepod on his way out the side door. He barely had time to turn around to press the button to close the hatch before the people began to advance upon him. For some strange reason, he felt uneasy about this situation, even though he had been to this town several times and personally knew most of the residence.

There seemed to be an air of evil surrounding him, and rapidly he spoke a prayer for safety before he smiled at the advancing crowd.

"It's gotten worse," a man called out across the distance between them.

"Take me to the first person to have fallen ill," Daven said as he identified the speaker and stopped in front of him.

"She's in the market square," he said cryptically.

Daven's eyebrows rose at the odd location. Something was definitely amiss with this situation. He followed the man and felt the crowd of people press around him on all sides as they tried to hurry him to their loved ones. They had walked for several minutes before they reached the middle of town. Once there, the leader stopped and stepped to the side for Daven to witness the strange actions of the people.

"We can't make them stop dancing. You can see they are exhausted, but they won't stop moving."

Daven watched for several seconds, entranced by the clumsy swaying and weaving of the men and women of the town. Their cheeks were flushed bright red, and they were all sweating profusely. Their motions were jerky, and they often bumped into one another without seeming to notice. Most of all, the blank expressions on their faces was the most bothersome.

Wishing he could make one of them stand still so he could examine them, Daven dismissed such an idea as he looked at the feet of the first woman to come down with the ailment. There were bloody footprints everywhere she stepped. She had shuffled her feet so long that she had worn through the soles of her shoes and was now scraping the layers of skin off of her feet.

Once he saw the devastation the dancers were doing to their own bodies unknowingly, Daven immediately went into action. He set his bag on the ground and held his hands out to his sides to catch the onlookers' attention and yelled to the crowd. "I'm going to begin working on these people. Please do not interrupt me or touch me. If you see any of the dancers fall, please pick them up and remove them from the market square, so they won't be trampled by any of the other people affected by this strange sickness."

"How do we know we won't catch whatever ails them if we touch them?" A male voice called out from the crowd.

"I promise it will be safe once they stop dancing." Daven could no longer wait for any more discussion, and he closed his eyes and gathered elemy from under his feet. Thinking of the number of people twirling in the market square, he pulled more elemy than ever before and searched for the woman whose feet were bloody. He tapped into her life-line and immediately felt the flow of something terribly wrong coursing throughout her body. There was a darkness surrounding the illness which puzzled him. Never before had he encountered anything as insidious as this new ailment, and he wracked his brain to find a cure.

Daven felt as though he were chasing the sickness coursing through his patient and he soon realized he would have to figure out another way of treating the problem or he would be too exhausted to work on the other victims. He stilled his thoughts and allowed the healing energy emanate from him. Without conscious direction, Daven felt his touch on the patient's life-line spread throughout her body, and all of the affected cells seemed to snap back into perfect health. Just as he had predicted, the woman dropped to the ground in exhaustion, able to rest now that her ordeal was over. He swiftly healed her feet even as the onlookers surged forward to pick her up and take her back to her home.

Having a better understanding of what he was working against, Daven shifted his attention to another dancer; an old man who seemed on the verge of collapse. Again, he tied into the man's life-line and cleared the infected cells from throughout his body. This process was repeated until all of the gyrating dancers were healed and removed from the square. Daven was both relieved and exhausted from his efforts, yet knew he was only half done with this work. Now he had to discover the cause of everyone's sickness.

He turned to the left and found the community leader standing by his side. "Lukon, can we go to your house and talk about all of this?"

"Certainly! Right this way," he spoke with alacrity. He bent and picked up the Elder's bag for him and led the man to his house. It was apparent that Elder Daven needed some refreshment, so he called out to his wife, upon entering the house, "Scarola, please get food and drink for Elder Daven."

Once the three were seated at the table with glasses of cold steena tea along with a platter of cheese and bread, Daven felt up to the task of talking. He picked up his tea and took a long drink while he composed his thoughts. "We need to find out what each of those people had in common to make them all display the same symptoms. Do you have any ideas?"

The couple looked at one another with expressions of inquiry as they both considered the Elder's question. They knew every person who had been affected, yet they could not come up with any answers.

"I'm sorry, we just don't know," Scarola finally said quietly. She felt a deep despair, as though she were letting the Elder down in some manner.

"It's okay," Elder Daven consoled as he picked up a piece of cheese and placed it on a chunk of bread. He enjoyed the sharp taste of the cheese as he chewed his bite until something strange happened; he felt a tingling in his mouth. In an instant, his body registered the same feeling as he had discovered inside the sickened cells of the other residents. He spat the bite out into his hand

and looked at it to see if he could see something amiss. "Where did you get this cheese and bread?"

Scarola stammered in confusion as she watched her guest spit out his food. "I made the cheese myself, from the milk of our foxl. I bought the bread from the vendor earlier today. I don't understand. Is something wrong?"

"I think we might have just discovered the source of the problem. How many people get bread from the same vendor?"

"Almost all of us. It's something we've become accustomed to doing ever since he came to town."

"How long has he been in town?"

"Just short of a mesan. Why?"

"Where did he come from?"

"I don't know. Do you, honey?" She turned to her husband hoping he would begin talking so she would not feel as though she were being interrogated by the Elder. Tears were beginning to form in her eyes, and she desperately wanted to hide in shame for what had just happened in her home.

"Please don't worry yourself, Scarola. Believe me when I say this was the best possible scenario, and quite possibly the quickest diagnosis I've ever encountered." Elder Daven tried to soothe his host since he did not want to create any bad feelings because of his hasty reaction to the food. Upon reflection, he should have simply used his own ability to heal, to purify the taint in the food and just swallow it.

"Are you saying there's a problem with the bread?" Lukon asked, finally comprehending the Elder's questions.

"Yes, I believe so. Can you take me to the bread vendor?" Daven pushed away from the table and stood up. His mind raced with thoughts of how widespread this epidemic could be if everyone from the town had purchased their bread from the same street vendor. He was first to the door and opened it in his urgency to find the unknown man.

The three of them almost ran through several streets before Lukon stopped in front of a shanty house and knocked on the door. The flimsy wood shook on its unstable hinges with the force of Lukon's blows. Several tense seconds passed while they waited for someone to answer the loud summons.

With no sounds coming from inside, Lukon flung open the door and marched through the opening, ready to do bodily harm to the breadmaker. He was further frustrated to find his quarry was already gone. He turned rapidly around in a circle to see if the man were in any of the corners of the small room.

"It looks as though someone left in a hurry," Daven commented as he surveyed the scattered items in the dim interior space.

"I'll gather men to begin a search for him right now," Lukon spat out as he pushed past Elder Daven.

"Don't bother." Daven put his hand on Lukon's arm to keep him from following through on his plan. "I imagine he is long-gone by now and it would be a waste of time. Our most pressing concern is how many other people are currently eating the tainted bread."

Lukon's flushed face instantly turned an unhealthy ashen color as he realized what Elder Daven was saying. Thinking about his community's welfare, he said, "I'll go to the market square and ring the meeting bell."

"We can all go together," Daven offered as the three of them made their way out of the abandoned house.

Daven approved of the speed at which the community returned to the center of town at the summons of the bell. He scanned the faces in the crowd for any evidence of sickness beginning and was pleased to see everyone appeared to be in good health. He raised his hands to help ensure silence from the crowd and bellowed, "We have determined the source of the illness has come from the bread sold from the new street vendor."

The noise from the gathering was instantly deafening as the people called out for the man to be brought to justice for what he had done to their loved ones.

Lukon finally yelled for silence, allowing Elder Daven to continue.

"The vendor has already left town, and I doubt you will have to worry about seeing him ever again. The more immediate concern is for anyone who currently has bread, or has consumed bread, from him in the past few days. If this does not apply to you, then I ask you to please return to your homes and allow me to examine and heal those who have ingested the bread."

The volume of the crowd increased momentarily as the people shifted and grumbled. Finally, after about five minutes, only the affected people remained in the square. More people stayed than Elder Daven had anticipated and he knew he would have to call on a large amount of elemy just to get himself through all of the exams he would be performing.

"Form a line, and we will begin," Daven called out to the remaining crowd even as he gathered elemy for his use.

CHAPTER 13

Valentina moped around her house on her first full day of Christmas break. Normally, she would have been excited for the time away from school where she could catch up on reading some of her favorite books. Instead of being content and lost in a good story, she was living her own real-life soap opera where all she could think about was hurting one of her best friends while she plotted to steal her boyfriend; even worse, he was her best friend's fiancé.

Try as she might, she could not help but wonder what Willian was doing and if he had been thinking about her as well. More than once she had picked up the phone to call him, only to chastise herself for being too forward.

Maybe if they spent some time apart, they would realize their mutual attraction was just…just what? An accident? No, that definitely was not right. What she felt for Willian touched the core of her being, even more than her triplet connection had ever been. No amount of time apart was going to lessen the desire she felt just at the thought of Willian.

Giving up, Valentina sat at the desk in her room and picked up the phone. She stared at the buttons for several seconds before she finally mustered the courage to dial the number. Holding her breath, she put the phone to her ear and impatiently listened to the ring tone on the other end. She silently prayed for Willian to pick it up since she had no idea what she'd say to his foster family should they answer.

"Hello?" a male voice asked.

"Willian? Is that you?" She really did not need to ask since she could already feel Willian's energy coursing through the phone line.

"Yes. Hey, Val, I'm so glad you called. I couldn't get you off my mind."

"I know what you're saying. This is too much, Willian. What are we going to say to Jena when she gets home?"

"I could probably get a message to her before then if you wanted me to."

"What would you say to her? I found someone new. Sorry...oh, and it's your best friend! Really, Willian, there's no good way to write it to her without sounding terrible."

"Well, when you put it that way, it does sound pretty bad." Willian sat on his bed, picked up Pesi so she would quit making growling noises to be lifted, and leaned back against the wall, content just to listen to Valentina speak to him. Pesi climbed onto his outstretched legs and plunked herself down, throwing her back feet out, and taking up as much room as she could. Willian looked fondly on the furry pet and began to stroke the soft hair along her back.

Valentina let out a deep breath and suggested, "Why don't you tell me about your family?"

"Well, let's see, my dad is the First Elder..."

"Why do you say it like that? Is there a second and third Elder?"

Willian chuckled before replying, "No, but I can see where you might think that. He was voted in as the First Elder; I guess you could say he is the leader of the Elders. Does that make sense?"

"Yes. Okay, I'm sorry to interrupt. Go ahead."

"It's alright. I'd rather you ask me your questions than you discover something in an embarrassing way when you get back home."

Valentina's mind immediately thought about the prospect of going back to Tuala permanently. Certainly, she had entertained the idea of visiting the place now and again to see her mother, but she had not actually decided she would move there. This notion of uprooting her life was going to require some serious consideration.

"Anyway, my father is the First Elder, and he's forty-nine anons old and the second youngest Elder."

"How old are the other Elders?"

"Senjin is the youngest at forty-three, while the other thirteen range anywhere from mid-sixties to one hundred and thirty-seven anons."

Valentina sputtered slightly and thought she probably did not hear correctly, so she asked, "Did you say one hundred and thirty-seven as in years old? Are anons somehow different than years?"

"No, they're the same. Elders and their families physically age slower than other people in Tuala. It helps to keep continuity within their Districts to have fewer changes of leaders."

"Oh," Valentina said lamely. "But what about your extended family? How would the difference in aging affect them?"

"Elders' families aren't typically large, but if they do have siblings, then they can opt to live at the Residence and age at the same rate as the Elder. No one really thinks about it much because it's always been this way. My father doesn't have any extended family, so we haven't had to do that.

"My mother's name is Chelesa, and she met my father when they were in a post-study class together. She's awesome; you'll love her, and I'm sure she'll love you, too."

Valentina kept quiet since she was having a hard time reconciling the idea of moving to Tuala permanently.

"My mom is a wise-woman as well as being the wife of an Elder, which has a lot of duties attached to it already. Her days are completely packed with patients and petitions from the community for favors and help with civil matters too small to bring to the Elder's attention. Tell me about your family?"

"My family on Earth or the one in Tuala?"

"Both, if you don't mind."

"On Earth, my father's name is Oliver Wilson, and my mom's name is Zoey. They met at the bowling alley. My dad worked there, and when my mom came in there with a group of her friends, she thought he was cute. After having him retrieve her fourth gutter ball from the lane, he decided he should ask her out. They've been together ever since.

"As for my Tualan family, my mother is Vinia who was raised at the Roanoke Colony and is now the interim leader of the community. She sent the three of us away to Earth when we were eight to keep us safe and to get medical help for Jon since he was deathly ill and the leader of the colony continually refused to allow medical attention."

"What about your real father? What's his name?"

"We don't know; our mother won't talk about him."

"That's weird. I wonder why," Willian mused. Wishing to change the subject, Willian asked, "What's with all of the strange classes you have to take in school?"

"What do you mean? They're all really normal here. How are they different than what you've done in Tuala?"

"Our main focus is on using elemy. Of course, we all learn

math, writing, and history." He tried to think about how he could explain the differences and came up without anything. It was almost as if his brain were short-circuiting while he was talking with Valentina.

"We'd probably think it was like a wizarding school if it's anything like I imagine it to be."

"Didn't you ever go to school in Tuala before you left? You did say you were eight when your mom sent you, right?"

"The Roanoke Colony keeps to themselves. They weren't much on education, and they did not allow the people to get birth crystals so there wouldn't've been much point in that training anyway."

"I don't understand. I thought you had your own birth crystal." Willian was becoming increasingly worried about the prospects of him being able to marry her if she did not even possess her own link to the elemy.

"The three of us do have them, but they have always been kept a secret from the people where we were living. Much like here, the people only see what they want to see."

Relief washed through Willian at Valentina's admission to having a pendant. Their situation just became immensely easier because of it. "So have you ever learned how to use the elemy?"

"Jena and Juila have been teaching us. We just discovered our true origins only a short time ago, and we've got a lot yet to learn to catch up with other kids our age, I'm sure."

"What's the furthest level you've mastered?"

Not sure if she had been learning the skills in the same order as Willian had, she answered, "Behn and I have both gotten through the memorization level, and Jon is a little behind, at freezing water, in fact, because he just started."

"Would you like me to give you lessons? I think it could be fun."

"I'm not sure. It's kind of hard keeping it a secret from our parents."

"We could practice it here at my house. Melissa and Marcus already know about where I'm from, and they would be sure to give us privacy to study."

"I'm not sure privacy would be wise for us, Willian," Valentina replied slowly. She instantly recalled the moment's lapse of judgment which ended with Jon punching Willian in the gut.

Wishing he did not have to say it, Willian answered, "Bring your brothers. We can all work on it together. Please say you will, it'll be fun."

"I'll ask them. If they say no, then I can't come over there alone."

Trying to keep his voice cheerful, he answered, "No problem, just let me know what they say. We can start tomorrow if you want."

"Okay. I should probably get going. I'll talk to Behn and Jon, and I'll call you back tonight to give you our answer. Thanks, Willian."

"For what?"

"Just...I don't know. Goodbye." Valentina hung up the phone swiftly and hit her thigh with her fist at how badly she had ended the conversation. Willian must surely think she was an idiot now if he had not already.

She left her room to see what her brothers thought about learning the crystal skills from Willian. Knowing Behn, he would be amenable; however, Jon was a different matter entirely. With the tense scene between Jon and Willian from the day before fresh in her mind, she opted to talk to Behn first.

Valentina leaned into Behn's bedroom and tapped lightly on the door to catch his attention. "Do you have a minute?"

"Sure. What's going on?" He set aside the magazine he was reading onto his nightstand and pulled his legs up to give his sister room to sit on his bed with him.

Valentina took the offered spot near him and jumped right in with what she was thinking. "I just got off the phone with Willian. He asked if we would be willing to have him teach us to learn more crystal skills. He said we could start tomorrow."

Behn cocked his head to the side, smiled, and said, "And it wouldn't hurt to be able to spend more time with him during the break!"

Valentina actually blushed at her brother's taunt. "I can't say I'd mind, actually." She chuckled and then became serious again as she moved on to her next point. "Do you think Jon would be willing to go?"

Raising his eyebrows, Behn considered his sister's question. It would be a tricky matter where Jon was concerned. "I'll talk with him if you want."

Rushing forward and hugging him tightly she announced, "You're the best brother ever! Does this mean you want to go?"

"Sure, why not? It'd sure beat sitting around the house for the next two weeks. Besides, you never know when our abilities will be needed."

"Hopefully never while we're here on Earth. That's another thing: Willian seems to think we'll eventually be moving back to Tuala permanently. Do you think we will?"

"There's always that possibility. I'd be willing to if that's where Juila wants to live. From what I witnessed between you and Willian, I'd also dare to guess you'd go as well."

"I don't know..." Valentina answered uncertainly. "What about our parents? We can't just disappear from their lives. That would definitely not be a good way to repay them for all of the time, effort, and love they've poured into our lives growing up."

"You're right, but there's nothing saying we wouldn't be able to come and go like Juila's parents do."

"True," Valentina agreed, starting to warm to the idea. When her brother spoke about it that way, it did seem less daunting and final. Maybe she would be able to work something out in a future which included Willian after all. "I told Willian I'd call him back tonight about our decision whether or not to train with him tomorrow. Do you think you could talk to Jon right now?"

"Sure." Behn threw his feet over the edge of the mattress and hopped off of the bed. "I'll be right back!" he said as he confidently strode out of his room.

Valentina sat anxiously on his bed anticipating a shouting match from down the hall. She breathed quietly, hoping to catch any of the conversations, but never heard anything. When Behn came back a few minutes later, she thought maybe he had not even discussed it with their brother.

"We're in," he announced triumphantly.

"What? Just like that, he said he'd go?" Valentina was trying to figure out what the catch was to this turn of events.

"Sure. I just told Jon the sooner he learned everything about using his crystal, the faster he could know how to hurt Willian if he ever attempted anything untoward to you again."

"You didn't!" Valentina's hand covered her mouth in shock at what Jon might accomplish if he had more training.

"Nah, I'm kidding. I just reminded him we are really behind in our training and we wouldn't want to have our mom blamed for the lack."

"Gah, Behn that was terrible!" She scrambled off of the bed and advanced on her brother who was still standing in the middle of his room with a goofy grin on his face. She noticed with satisfaction that he registered fear as he saw her scowl the closer she came to him. With lightning speed, her hand shot out and delivered a punch to his arm as she passed him and continued out the door, across the hall, and into her own bedroom.

She sat at her small desk and picked up the phone receiver.

Willian picked up after only the first ring.

Valentina smiled at the thought of Willian sitting near the phone anticipating her call. She almost forgot about how their last call ended until Willian spoke.

"Is everything okay, Val?"

"Yeah, I was just calling to see if the offer to teach us still stands for tomorrow."

"Absolutely. I'm available whenever you can get over here. Are both your brothers coming?"

"Surprisingly, yes, they are."

"I'll be sure to be on my best behavior for Jon. He packs a mean punch, you know!"

"I'm really sorry about that, Willian. Jon shouldn't have done that to you."

"Yes, he should have, Val. I would have done the same thing in his place. It's his job to protect you; I totally get it."

"I'm glad you understand. It must be a guy thing."

"Probably." Willian could not help but chuckle at Valentina's tone.

Without having anything further to discuss, Valentina said, "We'll call you when we're leaving the house. Will that give you enough time?"

"Sure. I can't wait to see you, all of you, I mean."

"I'm looking forward to it myself. See you tomorrow." Valentina hurriedly disconnected the call and realized it was another awkward ending to their discussion. She did not understand why every encounter she had ever had with Willian ended strangely. Surely, it would have to get more comfortable...eventually.

CHAPTER 14

Amanda had always had a hard time sitting idle when she thought there was something which needed to be done. Unfortunately, there was nothing to do until the next day when the museum opened. Of course, she could probably drive over to where Shemalla's house had been in her dream, but she thought that might not be prudent since she had never actually met the woman in real life. She could hardly be expected to go up to her front door and introduce herself as the person who dreamt about her while she was in a coma. It sounded nuts even to herself, and she had lived it.

The previous day had been filled with air travel, rental cars, and eventually checking into their hotel. Coincidentally, it was the same hotel as the one from Amanda's dream. She did not mention the detail to her father, but she got the distinct impression he already knew based on the sly looks he gave her as they had checked in.

Amanda was most worried about her mother since she seemed on the verge of tears almost all of the time. They were going to visit the jail on Monday when visitors were allowed, but until then they were going to see if Shemalla really did work at the museum. Amanda and her father both hoped the quest to find Shemalla would help to distract Diane from her preoccupation with Carrie's situation.

As a mother herself, Amanda knew it was a futile effort. She would be just as upset if one of her daughters were in jail with nobody to be able to see her. It still boggled her mind even to imagine how things could have devolved so far that her eldest sister would even end up in jail. Worse yet, they had no idea where her children had been taken, other than knowing they had been put into foster care.

A knock on her door interrupted her musings. She got off of the bed and opened the flimsy excuse for a security door.

"We're heading over to the restaurant for dinner. Do you want to join us?" Chris asked.

"Sure, let me get my jacket. It's pretty cold here, or maybe I'm just too acclimated to the Florida sun," she teased as she left the door open to retrieve her coat from the back of the chair next to the bed. Amanda joined her father and carefully shut her door behind them. They walked down the hall where Chris used his room key to open his own room.

"Ready?" he called into the room.

Diane appeared almost immediately; together, they all headed downstairs to eat. After their orders had been placed, Diane asked, "What time does the museum open tomorrow?"

"The desk clerk seemed to think it opened at noon on Sundays. I guess that means we can all sleep in," Chris answered brightly.

"That's too bad. I'd hoped they'd be open earlier so we could at least get one mystery solved quickly." Diane frowned in disappointment.

"I wouldn't exactly say anything would be solved, Mom. In

actuality, it would only be the start of a new mystery. We don't know why Shemalla was even a part of my dream. We never came here before to elicit her help, so there's a lot we still need to figure out."

"I suppose," Diane muttered.

"I think it's all exciting!" Chris announced brightly.

"You would," Diane and Amanda said in unison which caused them all to start laughing. It was the first genuine laugh Amanda had heard from her mom since they had learned about Carrie's predicament. Amanda was grateful for the release of tension her mother had been harboring.

Their conversation ceased as the waitress brought their meals. They each focused on eating. Amanda's mind raced with different scenarios which might play out at the museum the next day. She desperately hoped they would get some answers.

This trip would be very depressing if nothing came of it except a visit to the jail. There was nothing they could do for her sister except be there to show support, but it hardly seemed enough to erase the pain the family would be enduring as the drama of the trial unfolded. They had a long road ahead of them where this matter was concerned.

Because the conversation was so strained, nobody wanted to continue to sit and attempt it any longer than necessary, and they all returned to their rooms for the night. Amanda sat on the only chair in her room and opened up her cell phone. She missed Riccan terribly, but she was unsure whether or not she wanted to answer his questions about their progress. There really was nothing to report, yet she wanted to hear her husband's voice. She hit the programmed button and held the phone to her ear.

Riccan answered on the second ring. "Hello."

"Hi, honey," she sighed. "It's good to hear your voice."

"I take it you haven't gotten anywhere yet. It's okay; I know tomorrow will be different. You know, as soon as you told me about your plan to go to Roswell, I couldn't help but feel stupid for not suggesting the same thing sooner. I'm just sorry for the other reason you're actually there. Have you heard anything about your sister yet?"

"Nothing. Mom's really upset that the jail she's in doesn't allow visitors on the weekends. It seems stupid to me, too. Most people would have the weekends free, but I guess it's because she's in the county hold and not in the prison. I guess we can be glad for that, right?"

"That's for sure. Do you think it would help if I made a few phone calls? Maybe I could bargain for her release," Riccan suggested hopefully, wanting to give his wife renewed hope.

"Let's just see what happens. I don't know how things work here, and I wouldn't want our interference to cause more problems for her. Carrie has enough wrong right now.

"We're going to visit the museum tomorrow. I guess they open at noon."

"I wish I were there with you. Maybe I should fly over there and go with you. What do you think?"

"As much as I'd love that, it didn't happen that way in my dream. I think we should try to be as accurate to the original accounting as we can be."

"How's that going to work? You don't exactly have a broken arm, do you? One of the things Shemalla did in your dream was to heal you before she sent you to Tuala."

"True," Amanda mused. She wondered if she were reading more into the dream than she should. It would be nice to have Riccan with her. She shook her head and said, "I think we should leave it the way it is for now. If I need you, then I know you'll be here in a heartbeat."

"Damn straight! I'd bring the telepod if you needed me immediately. I'm pretty sure the people there in Roswell wouldn't think twice to see another spaceship in their midst. Can you imagine it? I might just come if only to see their reactions!"

Amanda burst out laughing at her husband's absurd comment. "You'd better not, mister! I like my life with you just fine, and I don't want to jeopardize anything just for your amusement."

Pleased with his ability to make Amanda laugh, he relented easily. "If you insist! I'll be a good boy."

"Good boys are often rewarded," she replied with a lowered tone in her attempt at being seductive.

"Grrr, I'll be verrry good!"

Amanda chuckled again and then asked, "Have you heard anything from the girls?"

"Not a word. I'm sure my mother has been thrilled to pieces to have them stay at their house. If there were any problem, though, they'd be certain to get ahold of me."

"Well, I guess that's all I got. How about you? What have you been up to?"

"Nothing important really. I spent the day reading through some of the ancient text in the samara room. I was hoping to find another new entry, like the one you discovered. Unfortunately, I came up empty-handed. Really, I spent most of the day moping around the house wishing I could have come with you. I love you, Amanda. I miss you."

"I miss you, too. Hopefully, we'll be able to come home by the middle of the week. Dad wasn't able to get too much time off of work, but we need to see what we can do about getting Carrie's kids moved into my parent's house."

"Good luck."

"Thanks! I feel like this is going to be an uphill battle. I'll call you tomorrow after we're done at the museum to let you know how it went."

"Cool, I'll look forward to it. Good-night."

"Good-night." Amanda shut her phone and set it on the night-stand. Without anything else to do, Amanda undressed and got into her bed. She picked up the remote and turned on the television. She flipped through the channels until she came to a program called 'History's Mysteries' and decided to watch it to hear what they had to say about the other worlds which she now knew something about personally.

DAVEN RUSHED BACK to his Residence and found the girls had abandoned their post in the library for a walk on the garden paths near the landing field. They rushed toward him as he set the telepod down on the ground and exited the vehicle. It warmed his heart to see their excitement to see him. He realized he had not received such a warm reception since the days when Riccan had been young enough to do it himself.

"How did it go, Grandpa?" Juila asked as they came close enough, even as she stepped closer to give him a warm hug of welcome. She moved to the side so Jena could also greet him.

"It was an interesting case, to be sure. Let's go inside, and I can tell you all about it with Nena there as well. From the impression I got, I think this situation involves all of us somehow."

Their grandfather's statement was sufficiently cryptic enough to pique their interest and keep them from asking questions until they were inside the privacy of Daven's study. Nena had been found in her own office and summoned on their way past.

"Please shut the door, Nena," Daven asked politely as his wife entered his office last.

More than a little puzzled by his request, she complied and immediately took a seat next to him as the girls had already occupied the chairs across the desk from him. "What's going on Daven?"

Daven spent the next few minutes sharing the story of the illness in the town and how he had come to realize the means for the spread of the sickness. "I'm afraid the man who came to town to sell bread and who happened to leave town just as I got there may have been sent by Lucinden. There was a strange darkness to the infected cells, the like of which I've never encountered before. Girls, do you know anything from your healing classes about this?"

The girls looked at one another for only an instant before Jena answered, "No, nothing. How strange."

"Strange indeed, and scary as well!" Nena agreed wholeheartedly. She did not like the implications of this new threat to the people of Tuala. She knew Lucinden was willing to go to any extreme, but she never guessed he would go so far. Nena shivered in fear of what was to come next.

"We're on to him now. I'll be sure to let the other Elders know what I've discovered. Lucinden won't be able to use this tactic again and be very successful. Forewarned is forearmed."

"That's true, but what will he do next? What will we have to discover next?" Nena asked.

"We'll have to trust Jehoban will give us insight and protect us; it's really all we can do right now." Daven leaned forward and gently patted his wife's knee, glad for the ability to have her near.

Figuring out how to get transportation to New York City proved more complicated than Petre had first imagined. Eventually, he had been able to use enough elemy to create the proper documentation he had seen the other passengers using to be granted access to the bus. Apparently, since they were crossing over into another country, he needed something called a passport.

After befriending another passenger while sitting on the bench in the terminal, Petre was able to inspect one of the infamous documents in enough detail to create one for himself. He was disgusted with how easy it was to fool the officials at the ticket booth even as he congratulated himself for succeeding.

He had been riding on the large, noisy, smelly bus for over twenty-four hours and he was weary of the tedious travel methods of Earth. If he were back home, he could have been in Manzanit in a matter of seconds instead of days. Of course, if he were back home, he would probably be drunk in a bar somewhere. Instead, he was on an important mission for Lucinden, and he did not plan on disappointing him again.

The plan seemed simple enough; he had to meet with a man named Stephen Gascon. How that was to come about was up to his own ingenuity. It seemed pretty straightforward enough to Petre's mind, and he planned on getting home before the end of the week. That part of the plan was still a little sketchy since he was uncertain how he would be getting back to Tuala unless he were to travel all the way back to Winnipeg. He shook his head in denial of that option as taking too long. He would figure out another way, something more expeditious.

One good thing about the long trip to New York, Petre did not have to try to figure out sleeping accommodations since he merely slept in his seat. When he did finally reach his destination, he was going to have to find this unknown man. Really, how hard could it be?

Surely the people of the town would be able to direct him to Stephen Gascon. Every town he had ever encountered was well able at least to be civil enough to direct him to the right house, not that they were always civil to Petre because of his reputation. At least he would not have to worry about his reputation preceding him on Earth.

His travels thus far had not disabused him of this notion. He began looking forward to completing his mission and returning triumphantly to Lucinden. He was certain there would be a great reward for him in the end. With this pleasant thought in mind, Petre rested his head against the cold window, closed his eyes, and fell fast asleep.

CHAPTER 15

Shemalla had been feeling anxious all day. She had no idea what was causing her to feel any different, but she knew something was going to happen. On more than one occasion, she had thanked her ability to perceive a situation before it occurred.

Without coming to any conclusion on the matter, she went to bed where she slept restlessly. The morning started the same as it always did with the sunlight pouring through the window. She tried to shake the unrest, and finally had to give up trying. Like any other time, she would have to wait and see what events unfolded and act accordingly.

She ate a light breakfast, took her usual walk through the neighborhood, read the paper, and then finally began getting ready for work. The museum was notoriously slow this time of year, and she sighed at the prospect of another long, boring day. With her dinner simmering in the crockpot, Shemalla left her house and slowly drove to work on the other end of town. She had traveled the route so often, she no longer paid much attention to her surroundings.

Before she knew it, she was turning into the staff lot and parking her car in the furthest spot from the employee entrance. She liked to be able to stretch her legs a little before and after every shift, it invigorated her and helped make her more cheerful. It was still another half hour before the museum opened and Shemalla went to the front to make sure all of the brochures were stocked.

"Opening time," the manager yelled to the staff as he walked cheerfully to the front door and unlocked the top and bottom lock. He threw open the door and gave a hearty welcome to the couple who had been waiting outside.

Shemalla hurried to the back stock room to get another bundle of brochures. It was a good sign to have early visitors. Maybe today was going to go by rapidly after all. She turned on the basement light and began searching for the right box among the mess of crates and shelves.

AMANDA WAS ALREADY ready to go by the time her father knocked. She shrugged into her jacket even as she walked across the room. She grabbed the room service tray from the table and opened the door. "Let me leave this outside, and then I'm as ready as I'll ever be. Where's Mom?"

"She's downstairs already. I wish she'd leave the concierge alone with her incessant questions. I'm sure we'll get everything straightened out with Carrie and the kids first thing tomorrow, but she just won't let it be." Chris shook his head in resignation as he fell into step beside his daughter on their way to the lobby.

"I'm sure she just wants to feel useful. Since we don't know anybody or anything about this town, she wants…I don't know what she wants any more than you do, except maybe to have Carrie cleared of all charges and her kids returned to her. I'm pretty sure that's not going to happen, but you never know."

"We might know someone from town if your dream about Shemalla is true. We're soon to find out that mystery, and, I must say, it is rather exciting." Chris smiled down at his daughter as he put his arm around her shoulders and hugged her close to him as they rode the elevator down to the main floor.

Ever the optimist, Amanda could not help but feel better about everything when her father spoke. She wished she could have more moments like this with her father, but life always seemed to get in the way. The elevator doors opened, and they saw Diane sitting dejectedly in one of the lobby chairs facing them.

"Are you okay, Mom?" Amanda rushed forward ready to do anything to make her mother less sad.

"Don't mind me," Diane said as she tried to paste a smile on her sad expression. "I can't wait to see what comes of this trip to the museum. Are you both ready to head out?"

"Yep. Wait here, and I'll bring the SUV around," Chris announced as he bent down to kiss his wife's cheek before hurrying out the door.

Diane stood up and walked silently beside Amanda to stand in front of the glass to see when Chris drove to the entrance as it was too cold to wait outside. As soon as they spotted him driving around the corner of the building, they exited the building and got into the 4-Runner.

Amanda, again, wondered if this were something her father had done on purpose since her dream had them using the same type of SUV. She watched out the window as they drove through the same streets she remembered even though she had never been to this city before. It was eerie having such knowledge in her mind even knowing she had no logical explanation for it.

Soon enough, they were parking in the parking lot with the giant alien mural on the side of the building across from them. Amanda's sense of déjà vu increased as they walked around the building and under the giant overhang where the entrance to the museum was placed. As if she were reliving her dream, the main lobby of the museum was exactly as she recalled, including the statue of the alien greeting them.

Once her father paid their admission, they entered the museum and wandered through the different displays. They finally came to the replica of the spaceship which had crashed in Roswell so many years before, and Chris said, "This really does look like the tele-pods from Tuala." Unlike Amanda's dream, Chris had already seen and ridden in Riccan's telepod, so he had a reference of his own to draw upon.

The difference in his comment was not lost on Amanda, and she surreptitiously looked around to see if she could locate any employees who might actually be Shemalla. The museum was unusually devoid of all workers at the moment, and Amanda wondered if this were normal. It did seem rather a stretch of the imagination for the mystery woman to show up as if on cue to her father's statement as she had done in her dream. Amanda smiled at her own foolishness in putting too much stock in the sequence of events being the same.

THE RIDE over to Willian's house was tense, excited, or curious depending on whose mind was probed. Jon sat in the back seat of the car with his arms crossed and a sulking expression on his face. Valentina could hardly believe she was going to spend the entire day with the man who made her forget everything she ever held sacred. Behn drove the car, all the while wondering what lessons Willian might try to teach them.

"I still don't see why I needed to come along," Jon protested for the third time in as many minutes.

"You didn't have to," Behn reminded him. "I just thought you'd like to continue with your crystal training while the girls are away. It'll be fun to show them how much progress we've achieved in their absence."

"I think it'll be fun," Valentina put in brightly.

"Of course, you would! I'm going to be watching carefully for any move he tries to make on you, Val. This time I won't hold back."

Valentina rolled her eyes even as she kept her head facing out the front of the car. His remark did not even warrant a response since she was going to be in full control of herself and on her best behavior. At least that was her plan, which was easy to decide when she was subjected to the tremendous power of Willian's pull on her self-control.

Looking up in the rearview mirror and catching Jon's black look, Behn spoke, "We're going over there to learn, Jon. Please at least try to be polite. I can tell you by experience, whatever is happening between Willian and Valentina is not likely to go away. The sooner you get used to the idea of Willian being a part of our lives, the happier we'll all be."

They pulled up to the curb in front of Parker's residence. Jon was the last to leave the vehicle, and he slammed his car door with more force than necessary as his final demonstration of his protest for the day's activities. Both Behn and Valentina hurried up to the door to knock and did not even give Jon another look, expecting him to follow them like a good boy.

Jon's expression changed to curiosity when he saw Mrs. Parker answer the door. She looked nothing like he expected and thought she was probably a very nice lady. He would be polite to this woman for having to put up with Willian in her house. As soon as he stepped into the house, he felt something strange on his leg and looked down. A cute, black Pomeranian was resting her front paws on him and sniffing for all she was worth. "Who's this little cutie?" Jon asked as he leaned down to let the fluffy dog sniff his hand. He was both surprised and pleased when she started to lick his fingers.

"Oh, that's Pesi. Pesi leave our guest alone! Come on; that's a good girl." Mrs. Parker leaned down and picked up the dog and cradled her in one arm as she moved into the living room to allow the guests to go down the hallway to Willian's room.

"She wasn't bothering me. I really like dogs," Jon spoke to Mrs. Parker, but never took his eyes off of the dog's big, brown eyes which seemed to be appraising him as a likely person to keep petting her. He smiled before he turned and reluctantly followed his siblings. Much to his pleasure, Mrs. Parker set Pesi on the floor, and the little dog scampered straight to him and stayed right beside him as he entered the bedroom.

Willian remained on his bed, wanting to keep as much distance as possible between him and Valentina so he could do his best to stay on track. "I'm so glad you took me up on my offer to teach you," he spoke excitedly. "Do you want to do a quick run-through of what you've learned so far so I can see how you process the techniques? It'll help me tailor your lessons to your own style."

"Sure," Behn replied easily as he plunked himself down on the bed beside Willian. He could see how their instructor was trying to keep himself as professional as possible to try to win Jon over to his side. He only hoped Jon would not feel slighted because he was further behind in his lessons and this exercise would prove him lacking to Willian.

Not one to hedge where his education was concerned, Behn did not hold back anything as he held out his hands and, pulling energy from his birth crystal, he created a sphere of light resting between his fingers. He moved the ball away from him several feet and then recalled it back into his pendant. Feeling energized by the exercise, he used more elemy than necessary to create a breeze throughout the room, ruffling the papers on Willian's desk and setting Pesi to barking.

"Sorry," he apologized as he allowed the breeze to end.

"No worries," Willian replied with a smile. He gestured over to his nightstand and said, "Feel free to use my glass of water for the next couple of skills."

"Thanks," Behn replied and shifted his attention to the offered tool. With only a slight change in his expression, Behn used the elemy to boil the water and then slowly shifted the direction of the flow until the water stilled and then began to crystallize as if frozen. Once it was a solid block, he demonstrated the next skill by picking up the glass and moving it onto the bed in front of Willian.

"Nicely done," Willian praised as he picked up the glass and instantly returned the water to a liquid state even as he moved it back to the table. He opened the drawer below and pulled out a small tea light. He handed it to Behn and asked, "Will this do, or do you need something larger?"

Letting the small candle rest in his palm, he answered, "This will do fine." Without waiting for another beat, Behn called a flame to the wick. He allowed it to flicker for only a couple of seconds before he extinguished the light with only a thought. He smiled at his success and also a bit in wonder at what they were now able to accomplish. Never in his life had he imagined the necklaces he and his siblings wore were so important and vital to their future.

Willian handed him a piece of paper which had several paragraphs written on it. Behn glanced at it for a good ten seconds before he handed it back to a surprised Willian. Verbatim, he recited back everything he had seen. He smiled smugly as he saw the shocked look on his new teacher's face at the speed at which he had accomplished the task.

CHAPTER 16

"I'll go next," Valentina offered as she could see her brother was now just basking in the pleased expression on Willian's face. She was eager to have him look at her in the same manner.

"Okay, go ahead," Willian prompted. He was most curious to feel Valentina's touch of power. He hoped it would not cause any problems because of their obvious attraction for one another. Just her presence in the room was causing his heart to beat faster and his palms to sweat. He was thankful she had opted to sit in the desk chair across the room from him, almost as if she felt the same tension between them and wanted to keep her distance.

Valentina performed the same tasks as her brother had demonstrated. Hers were achieved even more efficiently and easily as she felt how swiftly the elemy came to her call. She reveled in the feel of each lesson which seemed to caress her soul with the perfection of the process. All too soon, she was at the end of what she knew and sighed as she let the elemy sink back to the earth as she no longer called it to her need.

"Very elegant, Val. I can see there is quite a difference in how you and Behn process the steps. What about you, Jon? Do you want to go next, or do you just want to watch today?"

Wishing he would have gone before his sister, he felt trapped into performing for Willian. He did not like it, but he was glad he was offered an out. Like Behn had said the day before, maybe he could learn something useful from this smug bastard. "I'll go," Jon finally answered.

"Great! Begin whenever you're ready." Willian tried not to have any expression which would anger Jon. He kept his gaze fastened on Pesi just in case Jon felt as though his gaze were aggressive.

Jon put Pesi down on the floor so he could focus all of his attention on proving to Willian the skills he had learned. With less speed, but the same accuracy, Jon performed the first six tasks. Since he had not advanced any further with Jena or Juila, he was forced to end his performance. "That's as far as I've learned so far."

"You've learned quite a bit with the short amount of time you've been training. I noticed you used the same techniques as Valentina. You both manipulate the elemy in a unique way so as to conserve your strength. Very interesting!" He paused to consider the implications of what he had witnessed. Taking a closer look at the two siblings, Jon and Valentina looked much more alike than Behn. Maybe the similarity in looks could help account for their specific way they demonstrated their skills. "Jon, pretty soon, I believe you'll surpass your siblings in skill. You're more powerful than you know."

Blushing slightly at the praise, Jon was also suspicious of Willian's motives for saying such a thing. It could be possible that Willian was catering to his ego in the hopes of getting him to like him better. He hoped it could be true, and only time would tell him for certain – time and practice he amended. Feeling flustered, he handed the frozen glass of water over to Willian.

As soon as Willian's fingers touched the cold surface, the ice returned to its liquid state.

"How do you do that so fast?" Jon blurted before he could stop himself.

"With enough practice, you'll start to get a feel for the structure of the things you manipulate with the elemy. It's easy enough to move the molecules back to their preferred state with only a thought. It's a lot like creating when you combine ingredients to make a meal. After you practice hundreds of times, you'll be able to think something into being rather than have to go through each step individually.

"It's a lot like reading; actually, you no longer have to notice each letter of a word to know what it says as a whole. Some people even learn to read a sentence or a whole paragraph at a time. I've even heard of people being able to read an entire page at a time, but I haven't tried to master that yet."

"Interesting," Jon mused thoughtfully as he returned to his seat across the room, next to his sister. *Maybe these lessons were going to be okay,* he thought to himself. Already, he imagined new possibilities with just one suggestion from Willian.

"So, I think we should start with healing lessons. Jon, I know this is isn't the next phase for you, but I'm certain you'll pick it up, so go ahead and listen while your brother and sister learn. Once I get them practicing, then we'll move on to extinguishing a flame for you. Does that sound good for everyone?" He looked at each person and saw their excited nods of assent.

"All of the lessons you have learned up until now are designed to show you all of the pieces needed to heal. You will be using bits and pieces of each skill in various configurations in order to move the pieces of the person, animal, or plant you are trying to heal. Does this make sense?"

"I think so," Valentina spoke slowly as she started to see what

Willian was telling her. Of course, it seemed too simple to be true when he explained it. "How do we practice this? I don't have any injuries to heal, and I don't really relish the idea of hurting myself in hopes of being able to fix it."

Willian smiled at her summation of the situation. He reached over and pulled a plant off of his nightstand and held the pot between his hands. "I think we'd all rather practice on this," he said as he held it up for all to see. He set the plant down on the bed and then pushed his thumbnail through one of the leaves. "Who wants to try first?"

"That's it? We don't get any more instruction than that?" Behn asked in disbelief.

"In Tuala, the teachers let us try it first. If we were unable to figure out the proper sequence, then more instruction would follow."

With a sigh at her brother's statement, Valentina came forward and kneeled on the floor in front of where the plant was resting on the bed. "I'll go first," she said with a look of disgust at her brother for not trying. She took the plant from the bed and placed it on the floor in front of her.

Knowing Willian had given her a clue about the other skills learned to be the key, she tried to piece together what she thought should happen. She gathered elemy into herself, knowing instinctively that a visual display was not needed, and imagined the cells of the plant's leaf much like she thought of the water molecules to get them to move. She poured the elemy into the cells and focused on them moving to join together again like she would with creating ice.

Without any idea of the amount of time which had passed, she felt the cells respond to her request. As soon as she saw the damage close in on itself, she returned the elemy to the earth and sat back on her heels in relief. She took a deep breath and then smiled triumphantly up at Willian. "I did it!"

"Yes, you did." He looked at his timepiece and then said, "And it only took you fifteen minutes. Very good, Valentina! Do you want to give it a try, Behn?"

Slightly disgusted with the amount of time it had taken her, she vowed it would go faster on her next attempt. Before her brother could answer, she asked, "Did I do it right? Was there something I could have done better?"

"I'm going to refrain from answering your questions until after Behn has made an attempt. How about it, Behn?"

"Why not!" Behn said as he reached for the plant from his sister still on the floor. He watched as she damaged one of the leaves before she handed it to him. "Thanks," he said as he settled it on the bed directly in front of him.

Like his sister, he gathered elemy and surrounded the plant with the idea of well-being. As if the plant understood his desire, it began to heal itself faster than Valentina's method. In a fraction of the time, the plant was repaired to the point where not even a scar remained. "That was actually pretty easy!"

"Wait! What? Are you finished already? Let me see," Valentina leaned over and inspected several of the leaves since she was unable to tell which one was the one she had damaged. "What did I do wrong?"

Willian shook his head at the same time Behn laughed out loud at his sister's indignant tone. Willian answered, "You both accomplished the goal, but you took very different paths to get there. Do either of you think you could replicate what you just did?" He looked from one to the other and saw them both nod. Finally, he looked over at Jon and asked, "Did you figure out what each of them did?"

"I think so," Jon said slowly as he replayed the scene in his head.

In both cases, he had felt the elemy being pulled into the room, but Willian had been right when he had said the goal was accomplished in different manners. He thought he preferred his sister's overall method, but knew the efficacy of Behn's way was much more efficient.

"Do you want to try it then?" Willian asked gently, not wanting to push him too fast.

"I don't know...," he began even as he recognized the deep desire to accomplish the task.

"Here," Valentina said as she picked up the plant, punctured a leaf, and handed it over to her brother. "I think you'll find it pretty interesting." She purposely used a challenging tone to activate his competitive spirit.

Jon smiled at her tactic even as he reached out to take the plant from her. At first, he closed his eyes until he recalled Sofia's advice to keep them open. He opened his eyes and focused his attention on the damage he could see in front of him.

Taking a little of both methods he had witnessed, he gathered elemy and enticed the plant to heal itself while also boosting the cells within to work faster. To his amazement, the leaf healed itself flawlessly, even faster than Behn had achieved. His eyebrows rose in amazement, and a huge grin spread across his face. He held up the plant and declared, "I did it! That was totally cool!"

"I guess it stands to reason, you both were able to watch how it was done first," Valentina said sullenly since her brothers had performed so much better than herself.

All of the boys burst out laughing at Valentina, and the mood finally broke. From that point onward, their conversations were no longer edged in tension. Jon realized Willian might actually be useful, maybe even be a friend over time as long as he kept his hands off of Valentina. So far, they all were behaving.

CHAPTER 17

The bus pulled into the New York City depot just as the sun was setting. Petre stepped off of the platform, followed the flow of passengers out of the terminal, and stared in wonder at the tall buildings all around him. Never in his life, had he felt so out of place and insignificant as he did at that moment.

His original plan of asking someone for directions seemed laughable as he failed to even make eye contact with a single person. The people seemed so preoccupied and unfriendly, and he had no idea what his next step would be now that he was finally at his destination. Several times, he was bumped rudely by passers-by, and he was about to comment on it when he realized everyone else moved. Only his immobility in the center of the sidewalk had caused the problem. He immediately moved over closer to the buildings and out of the main flow so he could assess his situation and maybe discover somewhere to eat or even to sleep for the night.

It was clearly too late to meet with Stephen; he would have to wait until the next day. He looked around and tried to decide which direction in which to walk. The masses seemed to be going left, so he turned and melted into the flow of traffic. Petre was appalled by the levels of noise coming from the cars; he had no idea why everyone put up with the incessant blares of noise which seemed to be continually issuing from them. It was no wonder the people were so unfriendly to have to put up with such racket all of the time.

Petre's nose warned him before his eyes that there was food nearby. His stomach began to growl, and his mouth began to water in anticipation of eating. At first, he was unable to determine where the smell was coming from until he paused a moment to see the group of people standing beside a shiny, silver vehicle with a window cut in the side. Even as he watched, the person inside the box handed a paper tub of food out to the person outside. Petre swiftly walked over to the window to see if they'd hand him some food.

The woman right next to him looked him up and down rudely and yelled, "Hey! You need to wait your turn, mister! Who do you think you are, the President? Get back there and wait with the rest of us!" She pointed behind her with one hand and grabbed his jacket with the other to propel him away from the window.

Petre felt his cheeks turn red even as he heard several people around him begin to chuckle. His rage began to boil just beneath the surface, and he felt himself gathering elemy to do the woman harm. Almost too late, he realized he was in the wrong, but he would not be spoken to in such a manner without repaying the bitch.

He looked into the window and saw the worker had just put together the woman's tray of food. With the elemy already gathered, he turned away from the window and pretended to sulk away; he used his creation power. In an instant, the tray disappeared from the table and reappeared in Petre's hands. He hunched forward and scurried away with a gleeful grin on his face.

Behind him, he heard a cry of alarm from the worker inside the metal box. "Hey! Where did the plate of food go? I just put it down right here!"

Beginning to laugh out loud, Petre had to hasten his steps to get away from the scene before someone figured out he had stolen the woman's order. He melted into the flow of foot traffic and inhaled the mouthwatering scents of the steaming, hot food. Having no idea what any of it was, he used his fingers to pick up several chunks and put it into his mouth. He eagerly scooped several more bites into his mouth and closed his eyes in ecstasy.

Not paying attention to where he was stepping, he accidentally bumped into a group of teenaged boys. "Hey, punk, watch where you're going!" one of the boys yelled as he reached out and flipped the tray of food out of Petre's hands. All of them laughed at Petre's expression of disbelief as he watched food spatter down the front of him and then splat into a pile on the dirty sidewalk.

"Did you see his face?"

"What a moron!" The boys continued to taunt Petre with their rude remarks and laughter.

Without another thought, Petre pulled the elemy from the earth and surrounding himself in a shroud of deception until he disappeared from their view. He chuckled as he saw their expressions change from taunting to fear as he seemed to vanish right before their eyes.

"Where did he go?" One boy asked as his voice cracked in fear.

"Dude, he just disappeared like a ghost!" another one yelled.

As one, they began to back up to get as far away from the spot where they could still see the food on the ground. They knew they had caused it to land on the sidewalk, but now the person was gone. They had no idea what had happened, but they definitely did not want to stick around to see what would happen next. After another few steps, they turned and ran all the while yelling at each other to hurry up and get out of there.

Petre laughed out loud at the revenge he had gotten on the boys, but then frowned when he realized he no longer had anything to eat and he was still hungry. Deciding it would probably be better to remain hidden, he kept the shield around himself as he walked back to the food truck where he had pilfered his meal.

Just as before, he made the tray of food disappear from the table and rematerialize in his cloaked hands. He heard the same commotion from the people inside at the discovery of the missing meal. Remaining where he was, he consumed the food promptly before something else should happen to it.

His first problem was solved with his full stomach, and he was able to begin to consider the solution to the other problem of where he would sleep for the night. He walked with the crowd of people away from the food truck and started looking around him. When he noticed a man standing outside a circulating door, he moved out of the flow to see if the official-looking gentleman might be of assistance. Letting his concealing cloak melt away, he stepped in front of the startled man.

"Excuse me. Would you happen to know of a place where I might be able to spend the night?" Peter asked him.

The doorman regained his composure from the sudden appearance of Petre in front of him. He pointed over his shoulder and said, "There are rooms available here tonight. Let me show you the way." He turned and walked into the opening of the revolving door as if he had practiced it a million times.

Petre was not as skilled, and the doorframe hit his shoulder, causing him to stumble backward and wait until the opening reappeared before he hurriedly stepped inside and rushed to remain in rhythm with the rotation. He almost missed the opening into the lobby as he was watching his feet.

The doorman looked at Petre strangely, thinking it odd that he would have so much trouble with the rotating door. His years of service allowed him to keep a straight face as he said, "Right this way, sir." He led Petre to the front desk and gestured for him to step ahead and talk with the woman smiling at him from the other side of the high furniture.

"Thank you," Petre mumbled to the doorman. He wished he had been able to stand back and watch some other people before he attempted to do this himself. With a sigh of resignation, he cleared his throat and addressed the woman. "I require sleeping accommodations for the night. This gentleman has told me you might have something available."

The receptionist's eyebrows furrowed slightly as she listened to Petre's odd delivery. She smiled and said, "Yes, we can take care of that for you tonight. Is it just for tonight?"

"Yes. Please show me the way. I'm very tired and would like to lie down right away."

"I'm sorry, sir. We will have to take care of the paperwork first. I promise I'll be as fast as I can. Will you tell me your name?"

"Petre MacVeen," he replied in annoyance, thinking this system was highly inefficient. He could not understand how having his name would make his room any better; he merely wanted to have a place to sleep. "Now may I go?"

"I'm sorry, Mr. MacVeen, we still have to take care of the bill. How would you like to pay for the room? Will it be Visa, MasterCard, or American Express?"

"What are you talking about? I would just like a place to sleep."

"Yes, sir, I understand. You will have to pay for the room first."

"What? I've never heard of such a thing. Who's in charge around here?" Petre began speaking louder and looking around for someone else to be more helpful.

"I'm sorry, Mr. MacVeen. I don't know of any place around here where you will be staying for free unless you want to try the Salvation Army downtown."

"I don't need an Army; I need a room." Petre leaned forward menacingly and scowled fiercely at the woman until she backed up a step. Feeling vindicated, Petre turned away from the desk and walked through the lobby. He could hear a commotion behind him as he was not heading toward the door, but rather toward the silver, sliding doors where he noticed other people were heading. They must all be staying in rooms, and he would just pick one for himself.

"Sir! Wait, sir. You can't go in the elevator without a room reservation!" the receptionist yelled out.

Petre stepped around a crowd of people and once again cloaked himself with his shield until he was unseen. He entered the elevator and smiled as he witnessed the commotion left behind in the lobby as a search began for him. The doors closed and the elevator moved up several floors in a matter of seconds. Everyone got out, so he did as well.

He watched secretly as he noticed people using cards swiped across the silver boxes to gain entry to their rooms. With a grin, he walked to the end of the long hall and knocked on a door. No sounds issued from within, so he used his mental power to trigger the lock to open. With no one the wiser, he entered the room and shut the door behind him.

The windows across the way were the only source of illumination as they reflected the city lights into the room. Petre had no idea how to turn on the lights and then shrugged indifference as he could create his own with the elemy. He could see the crisply made bed several feet in front of him. It was terribly inviting, and he was exhausted. He laid down with a gusty sigh and immediately fell asleep.

CHAPTER 18

Shemalla came up from the basement with the box of brochures in her arm. It had taken her much longer than it should have in the disorganized mess and she was more than a little frustrated with whoever had last brought in the shipment. It was not hard to maintain an order if only a little time were invested at the start. She shook her head and marched through the museum to return to the entrance.

Luckily there were only a few patrons as of yet, so she set the box on the floor in the main lobby and kneeled to open it. She used her box knife to carefully unseal the container without damaging any of the brochures; another pet peeve of hers when the other workers carelessly destroyed the top ten brochures by cutting too deep. Her focus was solely on her task and she never even noticed when the people began to walk by her.

What did catch her attention was when she overheard the word "Tuala" spoken nearby. Almost as if it had been said with a loud-speaker, her head shot up, and her eyes turned in the direction from which she believed it had come. She stared as she recognized the three people standing not even ten feet away from her in the lobby.

Slowly she stood up and began walking toward the family she never dreamt of meeting in person. "Amanda?" she asked as she got closer. "Is that really you, Amanda?"

Amanda looked away from her father and saw Shemalla for the first time. Her eyes grew round, and she grabbed for her mother's arm to keep her steady. "You know my name? How?"

"It's a long story, and I'm not going to give you another déjà vu moment which I'm sure you're already experiencing just by seeing me. I'm going to tell my boss I need the rest of today off and I'll meet you in the parking lot in five minutes. Will that work for you?" She waited long enough to see Amanda nod slowly before she turned and rushed away.

Her heart was racing with excitement, yet she had no idea what it could possibly mean that Amanda and her parents had come to Tuala to seek her out. Now she knew why she had felt so out of sorts for the last day or so; it was because of her premonition about this meeting to come. She said a quick prayer for guidance even as she entered her manager's office.

"I need the rest of today off. I'm sorry, an emergency has come up, and I have to leave right now. Please say you understand." Shemalla practically implored him to acquiesce without a fight. Much to her surprise, he nodded.

"Will you be back tomorrow?"

"I'm not sure. Can I call you in the morning to let you know?"

"Sure, sure. I can see you won't be any good to me in your current state. Get out of here and take care of your emergency. Let me know if I can do anything to help, okay?"

"Thank you so much for understanding!" Shemalla gushed as she rushed out of his office and into the employee locker room to get her purse and keys. It would have been faster to have used elemy to bring her things to her, but she had made a promise to refrain from using her powers unless it was absolutely necessary. With her possessions in hand, she bolted toward the back door and burst through it, surprising another co-worker who was on a smoke break. "Sorry," called back over her shoulder as she continued to run out to the parking lot.

She searched ahead of her and almost burst out laughing to see the Covington family standing beside a white 4-Runner, the replica of the one she had seen before. With her target in sight, she slowed down to catch her breath. By the time she came within speaking distance, she had calmed herself enough to make more sense.

Shemalla turned to Amanda and said, "I assume you still remember how to get to my house. Do you want to follow me?"

"Sure," Amanda said even as a small grin appeared on her face. She could hardly wait to find out more about Shemalla and how she came to know all about her without actually ever meeting her. Maybe Shemalla's story was even more fantastic than her own, which gave her quite a thrill since she had felt like a freak on more than one occasion as she told her story to others.

"What kind of car do you drive?" Chris asked, ever the practical guy.

"Amanda knows," Shemalla assured him as she turned to go to her own vehicle.

"She's right, Dad. Let's get into the truck and get ready for our next adventure." Already, Amanda had her hand on the handle of the door and opened it.

Chris reached around Diane and opened her door before he went around the front of the vehicle to get into the driver's seat.

"I don't like this," Diane complained, "It's kind of creepy going to the home of a virtual stranger. What do we even know about this woman?"

"More than you could possibly know, Mom," Amanda said with the utmost confidence. She felt certain this whole trip was for the next few hours they would be spending with Shemalla. Her only wish was that her sister had not had to get into trouble to bring it about. Maybe Shemalla would be instrumental in helping Carrie out of her current predicament.

Suddenly Amanda pointed between her parents out the front window and exclaimed, "There's her car! Follow her Dad!"

"I'm on it!" Chris affirmed. He thought this whole thing was quite exhilarating and reveled in the adventure. He followed closely even though Amanda assured him she could find Shemalla's house should they become separated. Chris did allow a little more space between their vehicles as he realized he was following too close.

Amanda called out which street they would be turning and in which direction even before Shemalla used her blinker. She told them which house and then sat back in satisfaction as they pulled their truck into the driveway behind her car. Shemalla waited for them at the garden gate to walk up to the covered porch with them.

"I never thought this day would happen," Shemalla said to the family as they gathered at the entrance to her yard. She opened the white picket gate and swiftly walked through while holding it open for them to enter. "Of course, I'd always hoped I'd get the chance to meet you, and then you were suddenly there. I'm excited to find out what has brought you all the way here from Florida." She kept up her dialog as she led them through the front door. She gestured to the living room on the left and said, "Make yourselves at home while I go get us some refreshments. I'm sure with all of the talking we're bound to be doing, we'll need it!" She chuckled to herself as she continued down the hall.

Diane watched her retreating figure and scowled at Chris, "Are you sure she's sane?"

"Did she say anything which wasn't true yet?" Chris replied reasonably. "Let's do as she asked and make ourselves comfortable until we can find out her story. We've already read Amanda's account of how this would go, so it shouldn't come as a surprise to you."

"Yeah, but in her account, Amanda was trying to find a way back to Tuala to get her children. She already has her girls and her own telepod. There's something wrong about all of this, and I don't like it."

"Come on, Mom. We've traveled this far, let's just find out why shall we?" She plucked at her mom's sleeve and tipped her head toward the seating area.

With poor grace, she moved into the room and plunked herself down on the couch. She hated feeling insecure, almost as if the situation could turn perilous at any moment. Maybe it was the feeling of vulnerability which caused her so much anxiety. When Chris joined her on the couch, she took some measure of security from his proximity. Surely, he would not put them in a dangerous situation, and he could certainly rescue them if anything went wrong.

Amanda could not even consider sitting at a moment like this. Instead, she prowled the room and noted all of the plants, decorations, and lack of photos. Everything was exactly as she had seen in her dream, including the giant jade plant in the hallway as they entered. She turned as Shemalla entered the room bearing a tray of glasses and a pitcher of liquid and ice.

"Please take a seat, Amanda, so I can tell you everything," Shemalla instructed as she set the tray down on the coffee table in front of Chris and Diane. She looked up at them and held her hand on the first glass as she asked, "Can I pour you some steena tea?"

"Sure, that would be wonderful. Thank you," Chris said for

both of them as Diane remained rudely silent.

Shemalla smiled and poured out four glasses of tea. She handed them out and then settled herself in the chair directly opposite of her guests. "I'm sorry I didn't properly introduce myself back at the museum. My name is Shemalla Paramasivam, and I was born in Pantano, Tuala. I've been working in Roswell for twenty-two years. My current contract still has fifteen years to go until I can go back home."

"That's different," Amanda remarked as she recalled from her dream that she had only been working for fifteen years in her dream. It stood to reason that time would have continued to march on even while Amanda had been in her coma.

"I'm sure you'll discover there are many variances from your prior experience, but nothing of great importance, I assure you."

"You said my prior experience. How could that be since this is my first time to Roswell?" Amanda asked curiously.

Shemalla smiled and nodded her agreement. "You can see now what I'm talking about. We both know one another without ever having met."

"True, do you have an explanation for it?" Chris asked as he leaned forward, eager for the details.

"Yes, but it's a long story," she replied as she took a sip of her tea and sat back to compose her ideas on how to make the accounting as accurate as possible while still making sense. "I guess it all started eight years ago. I received a call from a friend of mine back East who needed help with a few children who had been found. She was someone sympathetic to the people of Tuala and knew I would be interested when she told me about the necklaces they wore."

Amanda's skin began to prickle with goosebumps as she had an inkling of where this story was going to go. She kept her mouth shut so she would not interfere with the telling of the events.

"I flew over to North Carolina and met with the children under the guise of being a social worker who would be taking over their case. You see, I had false documents which would give me proper clearance to get the kids out of the system and into homes where they would have a chance at a normal life.

"When I arrived, I found one of the boys to be very ill, so I used my healing powers to restore his health so we would not have to worry during travel. Through my contacts, I found a family who would take all three children, as unusual as that was. Once the children were all settled in, I planned on going straight home.

"It was when I was making my way back that I ran into some difficulty. I'm still uncertain of all of the details, but the short story was that I was kidnapped and kept drugged at a facility known as Cannon Memorial Asylum."

Amanda gasped involuntarily at her revelation. She began to shake her head as the pieces were all falling together in her mind. This was what she had been missing.

"I see you are putting it together," Shemalla nodded affirmation toward Amanda.

"I am totally lost! What are you saying?" Diane asked in confusion. She turned to her daughter and asked in a frustrated tone, "Do you know what she's talking about?"

Amanda nodded at the same time Chris spoke to Diane, "Let Shemalla finish her story. When she's all done, I'm sure we'll all know what Amanda has already figured out."

"There were two doctors there, each with their own agenda. One of them was truly evil whose name was Dr. ..."

"Gascon," Amanda finished for her.

"That's right. Am I to assume you know the name of the good doctor then?"

"Dr. Medin. How is this possible?"

CHAPTER 19

"I'm getting to that. Okay, where was I? Oh, yes. Dr. Gascon was working on his latest pet project on multi-dimensional disorders, and he had heard me say the word Tuala at some point. Apparently, he has abducted several other people, both from Earth and Tuala who have either been to Tuala or have knowledge of it. He has been drugging them and coercing them to talk about what they know. I'm still uncertain what's in it for him, but he's definitely fishing for something.

"Dr. Medin is a hypnotist who was my advocate. She really is trying to help her patients despite Dr. Gascon's orders against it. It was during my sessions with Dr. Medin that I discovered you, Amanda, and your family. While I was under hypnosis, it felt as though I had been transported to another life...your life, it seems. Everything you experienced, I did as well and shared it with Dr. Medin."

Amanda shifted her gaze to her mother and said, "That's why Dr. Medin asked me if there were more to my story. She had been working with Shemalla and hearing the same things I spoke of when I woke up from my coma." She turned back to Shemalla with a look of utter amazement on her face. "I can't believe how twisted this story is becoming. Why do you think your mind was linked to mine while I was in a coma?"

"You were in a coma? How interesting," Shemalla mused as she thought over the implications of this new disclosure. "I was kept continually drugged to the point where I almost couldn't even remember my own name. When I was being hypnotized, it was as if clarity suddenly returned to my brain except my face and memories were yours instead of mine in the asylum. What happened with your daughters?"

"They've been returned to me. They are now sixteen years old and just beautiful. I couldn't be happier. What I want to know is how you got away from the asylum?" Amanda leaned forward, eager to hear the story.

Shemalla smiled at the memory and chuckled quietly. "I'm not positive, but I'm quite willing to believe Dr. Medin played a hand in it. The asylum was in the middle of moving the facility to New York City, and the staff was all recruited to help with the boxing up of records and equipment. The patients were kept on lockdown with only the medication rounds interrupting their solitude.

"For almost a day and a half, the medication was never delivered to my room. My brain became lucid enough to allow me to call up enough elemy to translate myself out of the hospital. I know it was risky and foolish, but at that point, I probably would have risked even more to get away from Dr. Gascon. I'm sure he never intended on letting me leave. I can only imagine what happened after it was discovered that I was missing with the door still locked." Shemalla gave a good laugh at Dr. Gascon's anger over the disappearance.

Another thought came to mind, and Amanda suddenly asked, "Were you, perhaps, staying in Room 426?"

"Yes! How did you know?" Now it was Shemalla's turn to be surprised by Amanda's question.

"This is going to sound strange, well maybe it won't come to think of it, but I dreamt I was in that room being hypnotized and questioned by both of the doctors. I must have imagined myself living your life as well."

"Amazing! I wonder what it all means," Shemalla exclaimed.

"I have a pretty good idea, but it depends on your answer to my next question."

"What's that?"

"Did you have anything of value in your possession when you were abducted by Dr. Gascon?"

Shemalla was instantly uncomfortable by the question. She had no idea whether or not she should tell the truth. The earnest and eager faces of the group in front of her decided her to say, "Yes."

"So it was you who hid the samara in the wall?" Diane asked suddenly. It had taken her longer than Amanda, but she finally understood what had happened to make Shemalla know them.

Both relief and renewed worry rushed through Shemalla as she asked, "Am I to assume, then, that you found it?"

Amanda nodded thoughtfully and said, "I had an overwhelming urge to go visit the facility and go into the room from my dreams. When my mom and I got there, I was drawn to the comic strip taped to the wall. When I got close enough, I felt the power from the crystal. I was able to hide it in my purse until I got home."

"Oh, thank goodness the treasure is safe. I'd love to get it back to resume my caretaking of it, although I obviously didn't do a very good job the first time!" Shemalla admonished herself.

"There's no need for a caretaker now since its rightful owner has claimed it for himself," Amanda replied.

"Really? Are you serious? The samaras are now being claimed? I had no idea the time was getting so close! It's no wonder you came here to me then."

"What are you saying?" Chris asked in the sudden silence after Shemalla's outburst.

"I'm sorry, I think I've probably said too much as it is about the sacred samaras."

"I'm the one who should be sorry, Shemalla," Amanda replied. "I should tell you that Jehoban has assembled a team of people to seek them all out to fulfill the prophecy which he revealed to me over a year ago now."

"Wow! I wonder if I should schedule a trip back home to get caught up on the news. I feel so out of touch right now. What else am I missing?"

"I'm sorry, Shemalla, I'm not certain how much of the story I'm at liberty to share with you without first consulting Jehoban. I hope you understand."

"Without consulting Jehoban?" Shemalla asked in confusion. "You make it sound as though you've met with him before."

"I have met with him on several occasions," Amanda said with a bit of pride.

"Okay, now I'm definitely going to take a trip home!"

To change the subject to something which was still bothering Amanda, she asked, "Do you remember the names of the children you found homes for before you were abducted?"

"Certainly, they were Behn, Valentina, and Jon. Why? Does that mean something to you?"

Amanda turned and grinned at her parents before she nodded to Shemalla and replied, "They are my daughters' best friends. Juila is actually dating Behn. Small world, huh?"

"This just keeps getting stranger and stranger!" Shemalla exclaimed. She gulped her tea to try to settle the butterflies in her stomach. With everything happening all at once, it was no wonder she had experienced a sense of unrest the day before. Her life was shifting, and it seemed as though the world itself was going to change very soon if what she knew to be true were really coming to pass.

"I'd say it's too much of a coincidence," Diane added as she looked at her husband in alarm. She did not like how intertwined everyone's lives were becoming and how their daughter seemed to be the center of it all. She wished she could have her simple life back, the one where all three of her daughters were little kids, dependent upon her for everything, safe, and healthy.

"It's getting late, and I think we should probably get going," Chris said as he rubbed his palms over his thighs in anticipation of standing.

Shemalla was surprised to see it was actually getting dark outside. She had not realized so much time had passed. "I'm sorry, I should have offered you something to eat. Are you sure you can't stay longer?"

"That's kind of you, Shemalla," Amanda said as she stood. "We do have to go, but if I can get your phone number, I can keep in touch with you."

"Yes, certainly, I'd like that very much. Wait just a sec, and I'll get something to write it down on." She rushed out of the room, eager to get back before they tried to leave without it.

"Does anyone else think this is bizarre?" Diane asked her husband and daughter.

"Absolutely, but it's also rather amazing," Chris said with a grin ensured to annoy Diane because of his optimism.

"Of course, you'd say that!" Diane swatted his knee and chuckled softly.

As he had intended, he was able to break her out of the melancholy mood she had been fostering for the last couple of hours.

Shemalla rushed back into the room with her hand

outstretched with a piece of paper. Amanda reached forward and took it from her.

"Just for grins, can I ask you something personal?" Amanda inquired.

"Sure, what is it?"

"Is your birth crystal filled with white diamonds?"

With raised eyebrows, Shemalla reached up and pulled the pendant out from under her blouse to show the clear crystals on the silver tree of life. "It sure is!"

Amanda leaned forward and nodded. She knew it would be a surprise, so she also pulled her own pendant out from under the collar of her shirt and said, "So is mine, except mine is set in gold. Do you think that means something?"

Shemalla stopped hearing anything Amanda said as soon as she realized the girl from Earth was showing her an unmistakably Tualan birth crystal. "So Alena really did perform the ceremony for you? That's amazing!"

"No, Rasa performed it for me after Jehoban gave this to her to gift to me. Just like you said, there are some things of the story we once knew which would differ slightly with reality."

"Too true! Which reminds me, if you didn't come to Roswell to locate your children, why did you come here?"

"Two reasons, really. First, my sister has gotten caught up with drugs and is now incarcerated in the jail here in Roswell. We need to find out if there's anything we can do for her, but mostly for her children. They've been taken away and put into foster care." Amanda stopped talking as her mother began to sob with the telling of the story.

"You said there were two reasons. What was the second?"

Amanda looked her straight in the eyes and said, "To find you, Shemalla. In fact, given your history with lost children, you might be able to help with getting my nieces released to my parents. What do you think?"

"Definitely! Can we plan to meet for dinner tomorrow night? I can do some asking around and let you know what I've discovered. What are your sister's name and her children's names?"

Chris stepped forward and said, "Carrie Covington is our daughter. Her girls' names are Emily and April. Do you really think you'll be able to get them back for us?"

"I'll do my best," she promised.

Diane rushed forward and hugged Shemalla. She clung to her with the desperation she had been harboring for the hopeless situation. Never had she imagined that this woman might be their savior in this mess.

Amanda ripped the bottom off of the piece of paper Shemalla had handed her. She dug in her purse until she found the pen at the bottom. Rapidly she scribbled down the names as well as her own cell phone number. She held it out to Shemalla and said, "If you need any information, please call me right away. Thank you for everything!"

"I haven't done anything yet," she protested.

"You've restored my hope in this terrible mess," Diane said as she pulled herself away from Shemalla as she wiped the moisture from her eyes. "I can't tell you what a relief it is to know there is someone who will be advocating for us in this." She smiled weakly and took her husband's arm as he offered it to her. They moved past Shemalla on their way to the front door.

Amanda stepped closer to their host and murmured, "I don't expect a miracle. Just knowing you'll try will be good enough for me. Thank you for the offer to help."

"Of course. I'll call you tomorrow to make arrangements for dinner."

"That sounds perfect. Tomorrow we were planning on visiting

Carrie at the jail and then trying to find out the legal process for getting the kids out of the system. Should we leave off on the second part until after we hear from you?"

"No, go ahead. I'll be working a different angle in any event. It won't hurt to have you going through the normal channels."

"Very good. We'll see you tomorrow then," Amanda said and then surprised Shemalla by giving her a quick hug. She moved away from her and hurried over to where her father was holding the door open for her. Amanda raised her hand in farewell and then turned to go to the truck in the driveway.

CHAPTER 20

Amanda could hardly wait to get back to her room to talk to Riccan about what had happened that day. She looked at her clock as they got into the elevator of the hotel. They had stopped to get something to eat before returning so it was already after six-thirty which would make it nine-thirty for Riccan. She knew he would not be asleep so early, so she was able to relax marginally.

When the elevator doors opened, she stepped out ahead of her parents and waited for them to join her in the hallway. "I'll see you both for breakfast," she said as she leaned forward to hug her mother first and then her father. "Sleep well."

"You, too! And don't stay up too late talking with Riccan," Diane admonished.

Amanda blushed at being caught by her mother and once again cursed how transparent her thoughts were on her face for everyone to read. She turned and rushed down the hall, slid her card into the door slot, and entered the room when the latch clicked open. She let her purse and coat slip off of her arm into the chair by the bed as she used her other hand to flip open her phone and hit the speed dial button to call Riccan.

Flopping down on the bed, Amanda held the phone to her ear and waited impatiently as the third ring sounded in her ear. Relief rushed through her as soon as she heard Riccan's voice answer the call. "Hi," she sighed out.

"Hey, babe. It sounds as if you've had a rough day. Do you want to talk about it?"

"Most certainly!" She spent the next half hour going over all of the revelations of the evening without any interruption from Riccan. When she finished, she sighed deeply and waited for his response.

"It sounds as if Shemalla will be coming to the rescue again for your family and I'm really relieved. What was your take on her?"

"I feel like we can trust her, but I want to be certain. Is there any way you can ask your dad if he can do a background search, or whatever it is you call it in Tuala, on her? I don't want to share any vital information about the prophecy with her if she can't be trusted. Do you know what I'm saying? Jehoban has put a big assignment on all of us, and I don't want to be the one to bring it to ruin."

"As if! Amanda, when are you going to figure it out that you are the reason this is even happening at all. You are the center of it all, and we're all supposed to defer to your judgment."

Amanda sat in stunned silence as she absorbed what Riccan was telling her. She had never thought of any of it in the way he proposed it, and it frankly scared her. She did not want to have such a burden of responsibility put upon her. To cover her shock, she asked, "Will you talk with your dad? Please?"

"Of course, but I don't think it's necessary. So are you still hoping to come home on Wednesday?"

"Yes," she sighed in resignation, "unless we can miraculously get everything settled sooner." She could hear a lot of noise coming over the line, and she asked, "What are you doing?"

"I'm in the office, getting the patil out while trying to hold the phone up to my ear. Just a second."

Amanda had to pull the phone away from her ear as a loud noise issued from the speaker as Riccan tossed the phone down on the desk so he could complete his task.

"Sorry about that, the phone slipped out of my hand. Okay, I've got the messaging system up and running. Tell me specifically what you want to ask Dad."

Amanda tapped her fingernail on the back of her phone as she tried to compose her thoughts into something coherent. "Okay, write this: Daven, please petition Jehoban for permission to speak openly with Shemalla Paramasivam. Also, please let me know if you already have any information on her which would preclude me from asking for her help. Thank you."

"What are you really thinking Amanda? And don't tell me you just said it all because I know you better than that!"

"Well, then you must know me better than I know myself because I don't have any answers for you. Maybe I'll figure it out while I sleep tonight, but it just feels important to cover all of my bases as soon as possible."

VINIA HAD NOT HEARD anything back from Elder Daven regarding the discovery of Ozian in their colony. Until she heard otherwise, she could only assume, then, that it was okay for him to stay with them. As it was, Ozian, as he was now being called, was fitting right in and helping out wherever he saw a need. Of course, the women were all intrigued by the handsome stranger in their midst, with the exception of Agetha who continued to spout off negative sentiments to anyone who would listen.

Overall, the community was healing from their ordeal with Viceroy Blair and their unexpected trip to Earth. It had always been the men's dream to return to their homeworld, yet the women had found the new land to their liking and had wanted to remain behind. With the tyrant, Grobin, and his cronies gone, peace had once again descended on the community, and the women were free to talk and laugh with one another again.

No one mentioned what their future would look like with so few men or children to keep the settlement viable. For the time being, it was enough for them to try to maintain a sense of normalcy. Crops had been harvested, what little had remained after being left untended during their absence. The women were no longer fearful for their survival through the winter since Elder Daven had provided them with enough food to keep them through the harsh mesans ahead.

Groups of women moved off into the forest to gather wood for their fires. The birds were singing in the trees making everyone feel at ease since they would not be singing if there were storms brewing or danger around. Vinia sat outside her cabin, watching the industry around her, as she mended the quilt from her bed. She had the ability to fix it with elemy, but she did not openly display her power to the villagers who had shunned the skills since arriving two hundred anons ago, seeing them as abnormal and evil.

Vinia's thoughts turned to her children, wishing they were playing out front as they used to only an anon ago. She sighed as she realized they would never again be young enough, or free enough, to play as they had before. So much had happened in such a short time, and her life was so different now.

Even as she mourned the loss of the childhoods of her three

eldest, Danika began to cry inside her cabin. With a smile at how fortunate she was to still have her youngest, she set her mending to the side and went inside to comfort her baby. "Hi, sweetie. Did you have a good nap?" she asked as she leaned over to tickle the whimpering child's tummy. She could see her clout needed changing, so she used her powers to take care of it before she picked her up.

No matter what injunction the villagers might have against using elemy, Vinia could not see the purpose of dealing with stinky bodily functions manually. It was a relief to have the nasty task handled without any fuss. She picked up her now clean and dry baby and held her to her shoulder as she returned to her chair outside.

Danika was fussy and kept squirming until Vinia opened her blouse and put her to her breast to suckle. Vinia knew she should be trying to wean her, yet she could not get over the idea that this would be the last child who would be needing her in such a way. Nealan had been disgusted by the idea of sharing her breasts with the baby.

Vinia realized suddenly that she had not thought of Nealan in quite some time. Not too long before, she had believed she would marry him, and he was the center of her universe. It was funny how much had changed in such a short amount of time. Responsibility for the village had replaced her dreams for the future, and she found she was quite content with the way things had turned out.

She felt a stab of guilt since the last she had heard was that Nealan had been having a hard time with his recovery. It was too much to believe he would want to return to Tuala after all he had endured at the hands of Elder Vargen. Vinia, herself, could not stomach the idea of living on Earth even though her three other children had found happiness there. She belonged to Tuala as much as Nealan belonged to Earth, this much was unmistakable.

Ozian stood at the edge of the clearing, watching how Vinia and her baby were so content together. It made him wish he could be a part of their world. While he had been attracted to Juila, more than ever, he felt himself being drawn to Vinia even though she was several years older than himself. *Anons*, he corrected himself. He was going to have to remember the proper terms for things if he were going to try to stay and fit in.

With this new idea in his mind, he stepped forward and decided to keep Vinia company. Vinia looked up and smiled at him, which was encouraging. "Hello," he said when he got close enough. Even though he had spoken quietly, the one word startled Danika enough to cause her to lose her hold on her mother's teat.

Ozian saw her exposed breast and felt a thrill of excitement shoot through him. He wished he could trade places with Danika, wished he could hold Vinia close and nuzzle her breasts. The depth of his sudden emotion surprised him, and he blushed slightly and turned his face away until Vinia could resettle her daughter to eating.

"Would you mind if I kept you company?" he asked.

"No, I'd love it, but I don't have another chair out here. Do you want to go inside and get one?"

"Sure." He went inside and returned swiftly with a short bench from the dining table. He positioned it to the side but facing Vinia for easier conversation. "I have a few questions about life here. Would you mind talking about it?"

"Not at all." She gazed lovingly at her daughter as she stared up at her while she suckled. There was nothing else she would be doing until after Danika finished her meal. Talking with Ozian was a welcome change.

"What are your customs for dating? Or do you even date here?"

Vinia smiled suddenly and asked, "Why do you ask? Has some girl caught your fancy?"

Blushing furiously, and cursing his fair complexion for making it so obvious, Ozian looked down at his hands clasped in his lap. "As a matter of fact, someone has."

"I'm sorry for teasing, Ozian, it's just such a novelty to have someone new. Let's see, courtships have been encouraged, but they usually only last a few weeks before the couple would get married. For the past several anons marriages have simply been arranged by the men of the village with little regard to what the women might want. I'm sorry, but I think you might find some resistance to your advances for a while."

"Even from you?" Ozian asked hurriedly before he lost his nerve.

"Me? What are you saying, Ozian? You want to be with me? Nonsense, I'm too old for you." She felt her own cheeks warming at the thought of being with another man so soon after Nealan.

Emboldened, Ozian pushed, "Are you saying you're not interested in me?"

"No, it's not that…" she stammered and finally stopped talking.

"I'd like to court you, Vinia. No, that's not exactly true. I want to marry you and take care of you and Danika."

"I'm flattered, Ozian, but you can't possibly mean that. I mean, what about your people back on your own planet? Don't you think you'll eventually want to go back home? I can't risk another relationship with a man who won't remain content to stay here in Tuala. After all, I have Danika to think about, and she's getting old enough to start forming memories and bonds, and that wouldn't be fair to her."

"I hear what you're saying, Vinia, and I assure you Tuala is where I want to be. My home planet is dying and far too provincial for me in any event. I've seen how you lead the people here and how you care for your daughter, and I admire and respect you for it. I want to help you, but most importantly, I want to be with you…in every way. Please say you will at least consider my offer before you refuse outright."

"I'll agree, but only so it'll give you time to reconsider and possibly choose someone more appropriate for you from the village girls. I don't want you to discover you settled for me because you didn't want to wait to find the right person."

CHAPTER 21

The weekend flew by for the girls. Daven had taken Juila flying in his telepod when he found out about her joy in travel. Nena had shown Jena the family's historical documents which pleased her greatly. All the while they had grown up, they knew they had a family, yet they were kept apart from them until their mother had approached Jehoban.

Now they had both sets of grandparents and a lot of family stories to catch up on. Even though Nena was an only child, Daven had many brothers and sisters whom she already knew from living on Acaim with them. Of course, at the time, she had no idea they were great aunts and uncles to her and her sister.

Their lives still had a feeling of fantasy when she took the time to review it all. She wondered why Jehoban would have kept the truth from them for so long, but instantly dismissed the idea since she knew he always had their best interest in mind. Hopefully, she would discover it all for herself in the future.

"Have you taken any time to work with your samara, Grandma?" Jena asked suddenly, breaking the silence.

"What? Oh, no. I don't think I'm going to," she stammered.

"But you have to!"

The vehemence of Jena's statement surprised Nena into asking, "What makes you so certain?"

"I..." Jena faltered while she tried to come up a reasonable excuse without revealing the truth she knew. "I mean, it was decided at the last meeting that everyone who had a crystal should practice using it. You don't want to be the only one who doesn't understand how it's used, do you?"

"No, but to be honest, the thing scares me more than a little bit. I don't want to risk being caught within it, or maybe it'll force me to do something against my will as it did with Ela Nena. You have no idea who might control my crystal, and I don't want to find out!"

"Oh, Grandma, you don't know, do you?"

"Know what?"

"I've done extensive research on the samaras during my childhood on Acaim. I never knew why I was fascinated by them, but now I'm grateful. The samaras were each created for a specific person. While it is true, they can be used by someone other than their true owner; it is not possible for it to be manipulated by anyone else once the final owner claims it. You are the final owner, Grandma. Once you hold it, claim it as your own, and bond with it, then both you and the samara will be safe from manipulation of a third party. Have you ever held it?"

"No, I can't say that I have."

"Then it's vitally important that we take care of that right away. Your samara is in jeopardy of being stolen as long as it remains unclaimed. Where do you keep it? We need to take care of this immediately!"

Nena was torn with indecision. She could see the wisdom of Jena's words, but her fear kept her rooted to her seat. With a final, desperate thought she asked, "Don't you think we should wait until Daven and your sister return? I think it'd be safer to have more people around to help me should something go awry."

"I know what to do, Grandma, I was there for Juila and you know I wouldn't do anything which would risk her. Let's go get yours, and you can claim yours right away."

Knowing when she was not going to win the argument, she gave in reluctantly. She stood up and led the way to the Ascension Gate room where her samara was being kept hidden. Each step closer brought a fresh wave of nervous energy which she could feel was making her heart race and her breathing come faster. Her sense of dread increased when she held her hand out to the doorknob.

"I can't do it," she suddenly declared, turning to face Jena, ready to bolt around her.

"Yes, you can, and you must. This is possibly the most important thing you will ever do, and it must be done."

"Okay, I'll agree only if you will agree to wait until Daven and Juila get home."

"Deal!" Jena agreed and held out her hand to seal the bargain. She had been surprised when her grandmother had acquiesced too easily and not at all shocked when she changed her mind at the last possible moment. While she knew this next step with her samara was important, she also knew her grandmother's fear would make it harder for her to accept the gift of her crystal.

With a sigh of relief, Nena allowed herself to relax more and more with each step away from the hidden spot where she could feel the samara calling from behind her. The call was easier to ignore when she was nowhere near the room, and she was grateful to get away. Her relief was short-lived when they turned the corner to the main hall and saw Daven and Juila at the other end, clearly back from their day's adventures.

"Great timing," Jena called down the hall.

Nena narrowed her eyes with suspicion at her granddaughter and then had to laugh out loud. Through her link with her sister, she would have known Juila was home and that they would be returning immediately to complete what she had promised to do. "I should have suspected you were up to something," she accused quietly.

Without denying anything, Jena merely smiled and hurried her steps to greet her sister and grandfather. *Did you tell grandpa what I was trying to do?* she asked her sister through their mind link.

Juila nodded ever-so-slightly with a glint of excitement in her eyes. *He was glad to hear you were pushing her to move ahead. He has the same idea as you about getting it claimed to keep it safe.*

Nena was the last to reach the group, and she leaned forward and waited for her husband to bend down to kiss her. She was planning on offering dinner or refreshments as an enticement to keep his mind on anything other than the task Jena had proposed. Before she could even speak, Jena began to talk. She sighed at the lost opportunity and waited to hear what Daven would say, although she already suspected he was in cahoots with the girls.

"Grandma was just commenting on the fact that she wanted to wait until you were both home before she tried using her samara for the first time. I'm glad you showed up when you did so we can go back to the room to complete the task. How about it, Grandpa, are you ready?"

"Sure, that sounds like a great idea," he said with a wink only for her. He put his arm around his wife's shoulders and turned her around to head back in the direction of the Ascension Gate room. "I'm so proud of you for wanting to get this taken care of." He smiled down at her with the most loving expression.

Nena did not have the heart to refuse him when he looked at her in such a way, nor did she dare refute his assumption of her willingness. She was fairly certain he already knew how scared she was to approach the stone, and she wanted to be brave for his sake. If he asked her to take a walk on the moon, she would probably try to make it happen simply because she loved him that much and always wanted to please him.

Soon enough they had reached the dreaded room. Daven led them to the small table in the room before he went to retrieve the wrapped bundle containing the samara from the hidden niche in the wall. Even through the cloth, he could feel the power emanating from it and wondered what it would be like to have his very own. He sincerely hoped this one was actually meant for his wife since there was always the chance it was meant for someone else who also had the same color of birth crystal as Nena.

Seeing the fear on his wife's face as he set the precious item on the table, Daven said, "I think we should say a prayer before we begin." He saw nods of approval and a look of relief from his wife and knew he had said the right thing to help ease her mind. Nena had great faith in Jehoban and His ability to keep her safe from harm.

They reached for one another's hands as they sat in a circle around the table. Daven spoke, "Jehoban, please watch over Nena and keep her from harm as she endeavors to do her part in fulfilling your prophecy. If this is not something which she is meant to do at this time, please give us a sign so we may know to stop. We ask this in Your name. Amen."

They remained with their hands clasped for several more tense seconds while they waited for anything to give them a signal to stop. When nothing happened, Nena sighed in resignation which caused the others to laugh at her display of annoyance. The tension had been broken, and they let go of one another's hands.

Jena uncovered the samara and pulled on the cloth to bring the stone within easy touching distance to Nena. She spoke gently to her grandmother as she instructed her on what she should do. "I want you to relax as well as you're able and then take both of your hands and place them on either side of the stone. There will be an instant of intense contact as the samara makes its initial link with your essence and fusing with your life-line. From personal experience, this is the last time you will feel… What's the word I'm looking for?" She turned to Juila for her answer.

"Incomplete."

"Yes, exactly. This is the last moment in your life where you'll feel incomplete."

"I don't feel that in my life at all," Nena protested as she looked at her husband who had always made her feel whole.

"Trust me, you will feel more. Juila and I have always shared a special bond, but when we each got our own samaras, there was another level of depth to our skills which we never knew we were missing. It's too amazing to properly describe, so you'll have to try to explain it when you're finished. Go ahead and begin." Jena knew her grandmother wished to stall as long as possible which was why she had added a slight compulsion to follow orders with her last few words. She hoped the use of power was subtle enough so as to be undetectable, yet somehow she believed her grandmother knew she had done it since she scowled over at her.

Nena knew her time for stalling had come to an end. With her heart racing and her hands visibly shaking, she stretched out her arms with her elbows resting on the table and let her palms come into contact with the cold, hard surface of the crystal skull. She was thankful for Jena's description of what to expect; otherwise, she might have been tempted to wrench her hands back at the first flash of power she felt course throughout her body.

After the initial fear and shock had worn off, Nena found herself delving into and seeking out the source of the power. At the same time, she could feel the same quest for coming from the samara. Somewhere in the middle, they each found one another and the joining was as indescribable as Jena had spoken. It felt as though every neuron in her brain had been set on high alert and she was able to process every input simultaneously and still have the capacity for even more.

It took a few seconds for her to even register how much information she had been assimilating. The scenes flashed through her head so fast, and yet each detail was memorized and categorized for future use. She could tell the exact second when the samara identified the thing inside her which told it that the samara was hers and hers alone. She was the missing element for the source of power which was hers to behold for the rest of her life. It was unbelievable to think she had been scared of this wonderful object and it made her feel foolish for even doubting.

Input began to slow, and Nena discovered she was able to direct the flow to answer some of her own queries. Time crawled for her as she asked question after question. As if the samara were gratified, she could see even brighter colors emanating from its surface, and she smiled with pleasure.

Suddenly her contact was broken, and she scowled as her eyes refocused on those around her. "What happened? Why was my time cut short? I'd only gotten started, and there's so much more to learn." She stopped talking when she realized those around her were grinning foolishly. "What am I missing?"

"You have been communing with your samara for almost two hours." Juila held up her hand to forestall Nena's protest and added, "I'm sure it only felt like an instant to you, but my bum can attest otherwise." She grimaced as she tried to resettle herself more comfortably on the hard chair.

Nena laughed at Juila's last comment and then realized she was also stiff from remaining motionless for so long. She nodded and said, "You were right; it is indescribable. There's so much more to learn, and I feel so foolish for having waited as long as I have. Thank you for pushing me to begin."

Juila looked over at her sister and said dryly, "I think we won't be seeing much more of Grandma on this visit. You've gotten her hooked on her samara now!"

"Nonsense!" Nena protested even as she was planning her next session with the stone still calling to her from the table. "Daven, dear, will you please put this away so we can go get some dinner before it's ruined beyond redemption."

"Gladly," he agreed as he stood up and began pulling the cloth up over the skull. As if in response to the mention of food, Daven's stomach began rumbling loud enough for all to hear.

Laughter ensued from everyone at the perfect timing. They stood up and stretched their stiff muscles as they waited for Daven to return the samara to its secret niche. As a group, they left the small room and made their way to the dining room.

The ever-diligent staff noted their passing in the hallway and began the seamless process of getting the meal ready to be served. As soon as everyone was seated at the long table, the food was being brought out to them. The aroma of foxl soup and fresh-baked bread was the first course.

Nena ate with more appetite than usual. As she chewed her broth-soaked bread, she reflected on the revelations she had just received and understood there was still a lot more for her to learn. There was also an underlying sense of urgency for her to acquire so many more details for her to do her part for Jehoban. The task seemed daunting if she thought about how many hours there were in a day compared to what was still needed before she was to be called into service.

"Oh!" she suddenly uttered as she realized an important truth: time was relative. She had the ability to travel back in time to add more hours to her day and still accomplish everything she needed.

"What is it?" Daven asked with concern.

"I'm sorry," Nena apologized as she tried to come up with some excuse other than the fact that she had been daydreaming while eating. "I must have bitten my cheek."

Jena and Juila exchanged a significant look. They knew their grandmother's mind was racing and her exclamation had nothing to do with the meal. Events were moving faster, and their original timeline felt as though it were steadily moving up to overtake them.

Jena shivered in fear of her future. She looked down on her birth crystal to make sure it remained the dark amethyst to let them know they were still on the right track. It might have only been wishful thinking, but she could almost swear the purple had lightened slightly, which could only be a good sign.

CHAPTER 22

Sofia looked across the table at McDonald's at Luke, wondering how she was going to bring up the subject of Jena tactfully. Her thoughts must have been apparent when Luke put down his half-eaten hamburger and looked at her pointedly.

"Why don't you just tell me why it was so important that we meet up today? I can see it's eating at you and you're ruining my appetite, which is hard to do." He picked up his soda and took a long pull on the straw as he watched Sofia decide what to say.

"I know you said you were going to back off and let Jena have some space because of Willian. I wondered if you might reconsider," she said hastily.

"It seems like a moot point given the fact that Jena is away at her grandparents for the next couple of weeks."

Recalling the idea that Luke did not know about Jena's true heritage, she had to tread carefully so she would not be the one to reveal the secret regarding all of their friends. "That's true, which is why I wanted to meet with you. I want you to start thinking about being there for Jena when she comes home."

"What are you not saying? Is something going to happen to Jena?" Luke desperately wanted to be with Jena, but he was not going to be the guy who interfered with her love life, he refused to be the third party in the relationship.

"Well…it's possible Willian has found someone else."

"What? That's terrible! What a douche bag! He came all this way to profess his undying love for Jena and get her half-way convinced that he's changed only to turn around and dump her as soon as she's out of town! How did you find out about this?"

"When you put it that way, it does sound pretty bad; and I found out from Jon."

Luke's brow furrowed, and he asked the first thing which came to mind, "Why would Jon know anything about this?"

Sofia's eyes grew wide, and she took a deep breath as she realized belatedly that she would have to explain the circumstances where Jon became involved. She decided to make the account simple and direct. "Jon punched him when he found Willian kissing Val in her bedroom."

Luke's eyebrows rose almost to his hairline as he registered what Sofia told him. He shook his head to clear his thoughts and said, "My head is spinning. I have so many questions. What was Willian doing at the Wilson's house? What was Val doing kissing Willian? When did all of this happen? Why am I just now hearing about this? Does Jena know about it yet?"

Sofia held up his hands to keep him from continuing and said, "Let me try to answer each question as you asked them. Willian ran into Val at school and supposedly said there was an instant connection between them which led him to go over to their house after school on Friday. Apparently, Val felt the same thing, and they ended up kissing. I only heard about it because Jon was so furious afterward that he had to vent to someone. And, no, Jena knows nothing of any of this which is why I'm asking you to be there for her when she gets back."

"I can't believe Jon didn't call me. We're supposed to be best friends and all. Heck, he could've called me over, and I would have helped him beat up that jerk, especially after he took that sucker punch to me at school for kissing Jena." He rubbed his fist into his other hand just thinking about the lost opportunity to exact his revenge.

"Maybe that's the reason he didn't," Sofia said with a wicked grin. "After all, Val kept Jon from getting in a second punch. I haven't had a chance to talk with Val myself to get her take on this since she and her brothers went over to Willian's house today."

"What? Why would they all go over there?"

Again, Sofia could have punched herself for opening her big mouth. How in the world was she going to explain the real reason for them going over there? It was not like she could tell Luke they were learning to use magic from Willian. Instead of answering she temporized, "I'm not exactly sure what their plan was, but they all went over there. Maybe they're trying to get this mess straightened out before Jena gets home."

"Hmm," Luke responded. He picked up his burger and took a vicious bite. He chewed hurriedly and took another bite as he tried to imagine how Jena would need him when all of this played out.

THE COUPLE WAS STILL KISSING and groping one another as they burst through the hotel door. The man pushed the woman backward as he continued to kiss her neck and began unbuttoning her shirt in anticipation of what was soon to come. They fell together on the bed, and the woman turned her head to allow easier access to kisses on her neck. She opened her eyes and immediately began screaming as she discovered another man already in the bed.

"What the hell?" the man exclaimed as he pushed himself off of the bed and prepared a defensive stance against the stranger in the room.

Petre, startled out of his sleep by the woman's screams, sat bolt upright in bed and realized he was in a terrible situation. Even as the man erupted off of the bed on one side, Petre did likewise on the other. Unfortunately, the man was between him and the exit. Thinking as fast as his muddled brain allowed, he gathered elemy around himself and seemed to disappear before the man's eyes.

"Where did he go?" the woman screamed as she sat up on the bed and held her blouse closed with her clutching hand. "Bruce, do something!"

"What do you think I'm doing?" His eyes scanned the room for any sign of movement. He began to edge over to where he had last seen the stranger, thrusting out his fist in the off-chance it might hit something. Hearing a noise behind him, he saw movement and turned just in time to see the door open. He lunged over to the closing door, grabbed it, and hauled it open. He scanned the hallway and thought he saw a glimpse of someone entering the elevator as the doors were closing.

He ran back into the room and grabbed up the phone and hit the zero button. When the operator answered, he yelled, "There was someone sleeping in our room. He ran when I confronted him, and he just got into the elevator! What kind of a hotel are you running? This is unacceptable!"

Petre could hear the man's rantings as the doors shut. He breathed a sigh of relief at the close call and allowed the shielding cloak around him to dissipate as the doors slid shut in front of him. The elevator felt as though it were moving down, which was exactly what he wanted anyway.

It appeared his problems were not over when the doors opened into the lobby, and there were several men wearing uniforms converging on him. In a split-second, he recreated his cloaking shield and slipped between the men. He chuckled at their cries of dismay at his apparent disappearance and kept moving forward until he was through the lobby and back on the sidewalk outside. Keeping the shield in place for the time being, Petre tried to get his bearings from his rude awakening.

It was already light outside, and the streets were busier than they were the evening before. The sounds were deafening, and he felt the tension increasing inside him with each passing step. Thinking he was probably far enough away from the hotel that nobody would recognize him, he let the shield dissipate again, and he stood with his back to a building and watched people pass by without even noticing him.

Now that he was awake, he wondered what he would do to find Stephen. There had to be some way to get to where he was going. For the first time, Petre wished he had taken the time to learn more about Earth before he made the rash journey into this unwelcoming land. There were so many customs and strange happenings that he felt like a lost soul. Suddenly he realized how the people from Earth must feel when they mistakenly found themselves in Tuala, not knowing anything or anybody.

After several hours of watching the people, Petre began to recognize a pattern with their movements. Men and women would step off of the sidewalk, hold out their hands, and a vehicle would stop and pick them up. He had to assume they would then be taken to their destination. With this new idea firmly in his mind, he pushed himself away from the side of the building and did as he had seen.

He stepped off the curb in front of a vehicle. The car screeched to a stop with its horn blazing and the person behind the wheel shaking his fist and yelling at the top of his lungs. "Get out of the street you moron!" He cranked the wheel and pulled around Petre, holding up his middle finger out the passenger side window as he passed.

Petre stepped back up onto the curb and wondered why it had not worked for him as well as it had for everyone else. The woman right in front of him raised her hand, and a yellow car stopped in front of her. She opened the door, sat down, and gave the driver her destination even as she shut the door behind her.

It was only then that Petre realized the car she had flagged down had writing on it and a light on the top. All Petre had to do was wait for another vehicle which looked like that one to come by, and he would try again. Luckily, he only had to wait a few seconds and, just like he had seen the woman do it, it worked for him.

"Where to, mister?" the driver asked as Petre sat down in the back seat.

"Creedmoor Psychiatric Center."

The driver gave him a second look in the rearview mirror to make sure his passenger was not actually planning on being a patient before he pulled away from the curb and merged into the flow of traffic. "Are you visiting a friend there?"

"No, I'm meeting with Stephen Gascon. Do you know him?"

"Can't say that I do."

"How long will it take to get there from here?"

"This time of day, it should take about twenty minutes."

Petre nodded and kept his eyes scanning the crowds and buildings as they passed them. He could not understand why the people would want to live here in such a hustle and bustle. When he got back home, he planned on getting back onto his water craft and disappearing for a good long time to let the peace and quiet of the water ease his nerves.

Eventually, the car pulled up to a tall building and stopped in front of the double-door entrance. The driver turned around and said, "That'll be forty-six, seventy-five."

Petre looked at him with a blank stare.

"It's time to pay up, mister!"

Petre had no idea what he was talking about and said, "Thanks for the ride." He reached for the door handle and was surprised when the driver's hand shot out and grabbed his other arm.

"Not so fast. You have to pay for the drive out here before you get out. Don't make me call the cops!"

"But I don't have anything to pay with," Petre protested and tried to pull his sleeve out of the man's grasp so he could get out of the car. "Let go of me!"

"Not until you pay. You can use a credit card, you know!" He lost his grip on his passenger's sleeve and grabbed his radio. "Dispatch, please call the police and send them to Creedmoor Psychiatric Center. I have a customer who is refusing to pay."

As soon as he was free, Petre shot out the door and rushed to the doors of the building. He wanted to be as far away from the crazy man as he could get. Stepping up to the front desk he waited for the middle-aged woman to get off of the phone before he spoke.

"May I help you?" she asked even as she noticed the commotion going on outside the entrance.

"I'm here to see Stephen Gascon."

"Do you have an appointment?"

"No. I didn't know I needed one."

"Oh, yes. Dr. Gascon is a very busy man. Just one moment and I'll find out when he will have any time to schedule you in. Are you a patient of his?"

"No."

The woman nodded and picked up her phone. She dialed

several digits and then conversed with someone on the other end of the line. "I'll let him know. Thank you." She hung up the phone and looked back at Petre and said, "Dr. Gascon will be out of the office until Wednesday. He won't have any openings until Friday at 2:00 p.m. Will that work for you?"

Not knowing what the days of the week were called, Petre had no idea how long of a wait it was. He shook his head and said, "How many days is that? Where am I supposed to stay until then? This is unacceptable! I need to meet with him and then get back home! I don't want to be hanging around this disgusting city for who knows how long."

"It's only four days away, sir. I'm sorry, it's the best we can do for you without an appointment. I'm actually surprised you were able to get anything this week. Should I put you down for Friday then?"

"It sounds like I don't have much choice, now, doesn't it?" Petre said snidely.

"No, you don't. Can I have your name, sir?" she asked with less enthusiasm because of his rudeness.

"Petre MacVeen." He tapped his fingers on the countertop as he tried to figure out how to get out of this mess. "Do you have any sleeping accommodations here?"

"Only for patients."

"What does it take to become a patient?"

"You have to admit yourself or have a court order admit you. Are you saying you want to admit yourself?"

Looking over his shoulder at the two men talking heatedly and moving closer to the door, Petre nodded and said, "Yes. Is there someplace private where we can make that happen?"

"Certainly," she said as she stood up and grabbed a clipboard off of the countertop. "Right this way, Mr. MacVeen."

"Petre," he corrected as he hurried to catch up with her and put more distance between him and the cab driver's anger.

"Okay, Petre, just step into this room and fill out this paper. I'll have an orderly come in and admit you in a few minutes." She stepped to the side and shut the door behind Petre when he moved into the room.

"Where did that man go?" the driver asked as he burst into the lobby.

"He's being admitted. Is there a problem?" the receptionist asked.

"Yes, he skipped out on paying his fare."

"I can take care of that for you," she replied. She pulled out an envelope which contained donations for indigent patients and asked, "What is owed?"

"Forty-six, seventy-five," he said belligerently.

The receptionist's eyebrows rose at the amount, but she counted out the correct fare and handed it over to the man's outstretched hand. "There you go. Have a nice day."

"Thanks," he said over his shoulder as he had already turned to get back to his cab. He had already lost enough time at this stop, and his dispatcher was certain to yell at him for it. Next time a customer asked to come out here, he would tell them to get a different cab.

Petre heard the whole exchange through the flimsy door of the room. He felt pretty smug about coming up with a great plan to not only get out of that mess but also for finding a place to stay until he could meet with Dr. Gascon. Petre had no idea what a doctor was, but that was the title the receptionist had given to the man.

He looked down on the paper and filled in his name. Nothing else seemed to apply to him, so he left it all blank. Several minutes had passed before a man dressed all in white entered the room.

Petre was forcibly reminded of the Elders by the man's clothing, and he took an instant disliking to him.

"Let me look over your paperwork," the big man said as he held out his hand to take it from Petre. He glanced at it and frowned. He looked back to Petre, offering the paperwork back to him, and said, "You need to finish filling this out before you can be admitted."

"I put in everything I could," he replied with a smile.

"All you entered was your name. What is your address?"

"I don't have one."

"Fine, give me a former address, then."

"I don't have one."

"What are your symptoms? Why are you being admitted?"

"I need a place to stay until Friday."

"This isn't a hotel," he looked down at the name written, "Petre. This is a mental health hospital. You need to have a valid reason for being admitted."

Petre remained silent and simply glared at the man.

"How come you don't have any addresses? Are you homeless?"

"I don't know what that means here."

"What do you mean by 'here'? It means the same everywhere. Where are you from?"

"A different world, one I'm sure you've never heard of," Petre spoke argumentatively.

The orderly's eyebrows rose, and he was beginning to realize this man really did need to be admitted if he thought he was from a different world. He wrote something speedily on the notes section and signed his own name at the bottom of the form. "Fine. Follow me, and I'll get you settled in your room." He turned, opened the door, and waited for Petre to precede him from the room before he stepped beside him and led the way to the elevators.

Once the doors shut and he selected the thirteenth floor, he began his usual speech. "Lunch is served at 11:30, dinner is at 5:00." The elevator stopped, and the doors opened to a wide, white corridor. They exited and turned to the left. They only had to walk a few feet before the orderly stopped, pulled a ring of keys from his pocket, and unlocked the door to Petre's room. "This is your room," he said as he pulled open the door and waited for Petre to enter.

"It's pretty plain in there. Do you have something nicer?" Petre could hardly imagine spending any amount of time in the plain, white room with only a bed and a chair in it. A window would have gone a long way to making it more welcoming.

"This isn't the Ritz; this is a hospital." He was becoming impatient, so he grabbed Petre's arm and propelled him into the room. Without waiting for any other excuses, he used his key to lock the door again.

"Hey!" Petre yelled as he heard the lock being turned. "You can't lock me in here! Let me out right now." He banged on the door a few times before he recalled he had no other place to go. Turning around, he walked over to the bed and sat down on the lumpy mattress. "I should have stayed in another hotel. Oh well, at least I'm already at the place where Dr. Gascon works. As soon as he gets here, I'll be on my way."

CHAPTER 23

The trip to the jail was silent. Nobody knew what they could say that would make the drive any less depressing, so they kept their own counsel. Luckily, Chris had received directions, so they drove straight to the jail and parked right outside the main entrance. Chris got out of the car and went around the front to get Diane's door for her.

Diane took the extra few seconds to check her makeup in the mirror one last time. She had been crying before they left and she wanted to make sure all evidence of it had been erased. The last thing Carrie needed was to see her mother falling apart and not remaining strong. She would be the rock her child needed if it were the last thing she did that day.

Amanda patted her mother's shoulder for support before opening her door and getting out of the vehicle and standing beside her father. "What time are visiting hours?"

"We'll find out when we get in there. Nobody seemed to know for certain." He put his hand out for Diane to hold as they walked to the front doors. Again, Chris held open the door while Amanda and Diane entered ahead of him. They only had a few steps to take before they had to empty their pockets, put their purses on the conveyor belt, and walk through a metal detector.

Amanda had never seen such a thing before, and she was more than a little curious why such a small town would need something so extreme. She turned and saw the same expression on her mother's face as well. She thought better about asking anything about it until after they were well away from the jail. The last thing they needed was to get turned away because of their curiosity.

Once they were through the initial screening, they came to an information window with a bored attendant. "How can I help you," she said drolly.

Chris leaned forward and said, "We'd like to visit with Carrie Covington. We were told she's being held here."

"One moment while I check the intake records." She turned away and tapped out several things on her computer. "I'm sorry, she's not here anymore. After her indictment hearing, she was moved over to county."

"What?" Diane almost screamed.

Chris shushed her and then asked more calmly, even though he was far from feeling calm, "Is she allowed visitors there?"

"Yes, unless she's in solitary. Would you like me to get you the address?"

"Please."

The woman found the proper business card and handed it to Chris.

"Thank you," he said as he turned away. He practically dragged Diane away from the window as she clearly wanted to ask more questions which the woman would not have answers to anyway. It was better to get them all back to the car before Diane really exploded and caused them more trouble.

"Let go of my arm, Chris!" Diane spoke through clenched teeth as she tugged her arm free of her husband's grasp. She was seething with rage and was starting to see white streaks on the sides of her vision. Once she was seated in the passenger seat of the truck, she turned on her husband and accused, "How could you embarrass me like that?"

"I was trying to keep you from getting yourself in trouble." He spoke calmly as he looked down at the business card to read the address of where they needed to go.

"How could they have already sentenced her?" Diane screamed.

"It wasn't a sentencing; it was an indictment hearing. All they did was bring her in front of the judge and read the charges against her and asked her to give her plea. It's just the first step in the process." Chris turned on the ignition and looked behind them, preparing to back out of the parking space.

"What are you now, a lawyer? How do you know any of this?" Diane accused, unreasonable in her anger.

"I did some research on it before we flew out here. I wanted to know what we were up against."

Amanda remained quiet in the back seat; her stomach churned in fear for her sister. This problem was suddenly more real and more serious than she had imagined. She wished she could be anywhere other than where she was at the moment. The buildings whizzed by as her father navigated the streets to the county jail. Only a few minutes had passed before they were once again parking and going into another austere-looking building.

This time, when Chris asked to see his daughter, they were directed to a big, open room and told to sit at one of the round tables. A few minutes later, Carrie, dressed in orange coveralls, was escorted over to them by an armed guard.

Diane rose and put out her arms to hug her daughter.

The guard spoke in a clipped voice, "No physical contact is allowed. Please be seated."

Dejected, Diane seemed to wilt back into her chair, tears forming in her eyes as she stared at her daughter.

Carrie could not bring herself to even look at her mother; she did not want to see the disappointment in her eyes. Instead, she stared at the sister she had believed would never come out of her coma. This was the first time she had seen her in over seven years, and she wondered why she had come. She shifted her gaze to her father and said dully, "Hi, Dad."

"Hi, honey. Are you doing okay?"

"Does it look like it? I guess I really screwed up this time, didn't I?" Carrie sat down hard in the chair between her sister and father.

"My husband offered to help. Can you think of anything he can do to get you out of here?" Amanda offered helpfully.

"I'd heard you'd married some rich dude you hardly knew. How's that going?" Carrie asked rudely.

Amanda blinked at the unexpected attack and remained silent.

Chris cleared his throat and said, "Carrie, be nice. We all want to help. Tell us what we can do?"

"There's nothing you can do for me, but you can do something for April and Emily. They were taken into foster care, and I'm sure they're scared. Find them and take them home with you."

Diane sobbed suddenly and began digging in her pocket for a tissue.

"Jeez, Mom, please stop. I'm not dead; I'm just in jail. Hopefully, I won't be here long, and then I'll come and get the kids."

"Do you really think it'll work out like that? That you can be out of here soon?" Diane sniffled and dabbed her nose with the tissue.

"Sure, piece of cake." Carrie leaned back in her chair and crossed her arms.

"Carrie? Are you okay? Why are you acting like this?" Amanda asked, hardly recognizing her sister through the harsh mannerisms.

Carrie threw her head back and actually laughed. She plucked at the jumpsuit with both her hands and said, "Does this look okay to you? That's about the dumbest thing I've heard today, Amanda. Why don't you go home to your rich husband? You've done your duty and came and saw me. I don't need you rubbing in your perfect life to me anymore." She stood up and turned to the guard, "I'm ready to go back now."

"Carrie, wait!" Chris stood and willed his daughter to turn around.

Carrie's shoulders stiffened, but she did not look back. She walked out of the visiting room without even saying goodbye. It was all she could do to keep from crying until after she could turn the corner to go back to her cell.

Diane whimpered and let the sobs begin in earnest. She felt as though she had lost another daughter; only this time she was not dead. There was nothing she could do or say which would make this any better. The whole trip had been a waste of time.

"Let's go find out what we can do about getting April and Emily," Chris said quietly.

Amanda put her arm around her mother's shoulders to help her up out of her chair. "C'mon, Mom. Let's go."

Daven did as much research as he could on Shemalla and found relatively little of interest. He had been surprised to find she was officially an agent of Elder Vargen. The fact that her assignment was based on Earth was also something which had only been discovered when he peeled back several layers of classified clearances.

He wondered if any of the other Elders knew that the museum in Roswell was being run by Elder Vargen. How many other facilities were being run by the Elder on Earth? This was highly unusual and would need further investigation. Maybe a conversation with Elder Debbon would be in order.

After typing up his reply to Riccan's message, he could not help but think about the prophecy predicting that the Elders would fall. Could Elder Vargen be one who would fall? He never really had liked Vargen's brash style, nor the way he always sided with the most difficult Elders in any discussion regarding policy. Vargen seemed to be the ringleader of the ornery cronies.

Thinking about the other Elders made him realize it had been several weeks since the convocation voting in Rasa as the successor to Elder Wilken. With how terribly the dissenting Elders had behaved, he was surprised no repercussions had been noted. He would have to check in with Rasa soon to see how she was faring in her new post.

In a way, he was thankful to have Rasa blaze the trail for other women to become Elders. After being with his granddaughters for several days, he could easily see either or both of them becoming an Elder one day. Certainly, they were talented enough, and the fact they had both been selected and trained by Jehoban gave them impeccable credentials.

He leaned back in his chair, musing on the possibilities of their futures. Jena and Juila both possessed their own samaras, something which even he could not claim for himself. Daven wondered if Amanda's assumption about all of them from Jehoban's meeting were to get their own samara. So far, each of the known samaras had been claimed by the attendees only.

Thinking about how Captain Ahn had received his, gave him the idea of trying to call his own samara to him. He closed his eyes and tried to visualize the crystal skull resting in his palms. For an instant, he felt as though he could feel a tingling sensation, and he redoubled his efforts. He breathed deeply and focused his thoughts to the exclusion of all else.

Several hours later, a noise startled Daven into opening his eyes and had to laugh at himself because, apparently, he had fallen asleep. Obviously, the idea of calling a samara was more complicated than he had imagined. He stretched the kinks out of his joints and promised himself, one way or another, he would get his own. Right now, however, he had to get ready for lunch, or he was going to be late. His wife hated it when meals were delayed.

Freya asked an innocent question to Agetha, "What do you think Ozian means by visiting with Vinia so much?"

"No doubt, he's after something. She is the only one with a patil in the village. Maybe he's trying to find a way to get back home since he's discovered there's nothing here for him."

"I don't think so," Freya mused quietly to herself. To her mind, it looked like Ozian had found more than enough to keep him around. She had to admit to herself that she was slightly jealous but then chided herself. Vinia had a small child who needed looking after, Ozian would be a good father for her and a helpmate for Vinia.

"What was that?" Agetha asked unkindly.

"Nothing. I was just talking to myself. Do you have enough firewood, or should we go gather more?"

"I'm fine. You should run along home now; it's getting late."

Not really appreciating being told what to do, Freya held her tongue as she turned and began walking toward her home and away from the mean and spiteful Agetha. If Agetha were not her nearest neighbor, she probably would not have become friends with her. Freya shrugged and told herself it was best to get along with everyone since the community was so small. They all needed one another to get through the hard times.

Freya turned and saw Agetha had gone into her own house, so she kept walking until she found herself nearing Vinia's cabin. She really did not have any intention of overhearing Vinia's conversation, but once she was within range, she found she could not turn away either. Freya covered her mouth to keep from making any noise as she listened intently.

"I really am serious about marrying you, Vinia. Please say you'll accept," Ozian pled one more time.

"What would you do if I said yes?" Vinia asked offhandedly, not really believing Ozian would take it as an acceptance.

"Did you just say yes? Oh, I'm the happiest man alive!" He jumped up from the bench and picked up Vinia and turned her in jubilant circles. "We can have the ceremony tonight, or tomorrow, or as soon as it can be arranged. I want you to have everything you've ever wanted. Tell me what you want to do?"

Seeing she had made a serious error in her choice of words, Vinia did not have the heart to deny his words. She realized she would like to be with him; she only wished it would have come later when she had more time to mourn the loss of her previous relationship. Ozian did not have to pay for her past, and she owed her daughter a future with a father in it.

"I will make the arrangements," Vinia spoke with a silly grin on her face.

For the first time, Ozian leaned down and kissed her firmly on the lips. He forgot about everything else, as he lost himself in the feel of her body under his hands. He began pulling on her shirt, and his kisses trailed across her cheek and down her throat.

"No, Ozian, we can't do this yet," Vinia said as she finally came to her senses and pushed him away from her. "I want this done properly or not at all. Do you understand?"

Looking slightly downcast at being denied his prize, he suddenly grinned and said, "I'd do anything for you, Vinia. I'm going to go home now before I forget what you asked. I'll be back tomorrow to help with the planning. I love you, Vinia!" He turned and rushed out of the cabin. He never even saw Freya standing in the shadows near the corner of the house.

She felt tears dropping down her cheeks as she realized Vinia had accepted Ozian's advances. No longer was it just an idea; it was going to be a reality...and soon. Her hopes for a future with the new man in town were dashed, and she felt herself wilting inside with the loss. She picked up her skirts and ran back to her cabin to cry herself to sleep.

The idea of Ozian wanting to marry her kept Vinia's mind from being able to concentrate on anything for more than a few minutes at a time. It was utterly preposterous for him to be serious, yet every time she tried to deny it, Ozian gave her a look otherwise. Vinia blushed like a schoolgirl when she thought about what would happen if she were to give in to his request, which also made her scoff at herself for her foolishness.

In a daze, she stared at the door where Ozian had just left. Had she really just agreed to get married? Surely not! She could not get married until after she talked it over with her other three children. They were old enough to have an opinion on the matter.

She walked over to the patil and turned it on. She tapped the messaging button and composed a quick note to Riccan to pass along to her children. There was no good way of writing what was happening and she struggled to find the right words. "What a mess!" she said out loud to herself. "This can't be happening right now!"

Danika began to cry behind her, and she abandoned her message in favor of soothing her daughter. She settled the baby on her lap and offered her breast to Danika, not sure who would be more comforted by the gesture. Peace descended upon them both as the only noises in the room were the suckling sounds and small grunts of pleasure coming from the little girl. Danika had no idea what was going on in her world, and Vinia envied her for it.

It had only been three weeks since Nealan had been forcibly taken from her life. In such a short amount of time, she had gone from being completely dependent on someone for support, to becoming the leader of a community. No longer did she mourn the loss of her three older children, since they had also been restored to her life, although not in the manner she ever imagined.

Danika had fallen asleep, and her lax mouth had lost its grip on her breast. She pulled her away and covered herself, but remained rocking in her chair for a few more minutes, enjoying the serenity of the warm bundle in her arms. Did she want to give up this private time by marrying Ozian? There really was no rush in moving forward.

Maybe she was even making a mistake with Ozian by letting her old fears control her future decisions. She needed to take some time for herself and her daughter before she made life-changing choices like getting married. With a newfound resolve, Vinia decided she would tell Ozian in the morning that she wanted more time to decide, she owed that much to her children.

With a sigh, Vinia stood up and gently placed Danika back in her cradle by the bed. She tucked the covers carefully around her and stared at her for a few more seconds before she straightened up and walked back over to the patil. She resumed her seat and read what she had already written and decided nothing needed to be said at the moment.

Vinia tapped on the delete key, and the whole message disappeared. For some reason, it felt wrong to dismiss the whole thing so easily, so she immediately opened another message and wrote:

Riccan,
It would be great if the kids could spend some time with me while they are on winter break. Do you think something could be arranged?
Thanks,
Vinia.

She hit send before she changed her mind. Then she hit the compose button again and wrote another note:

Elder Daven,
Ozias has asked me to marry him. Please advise me on this matter.
Your humble subject,
Vinia.

There was nothing more she could do for the night, so she turned off the patil and wandered around her empty house, cleaning dusty corners, and straightening the folded linens. *Some human interaction would be nice in times like these,* she thought to herself. With the fire banked for the night, she stripped off her clothes and got under the covers. Even though it was still rather early in the evening, her mind was tired from all of the turmoil she felt inside. She turned on her side to face the crib, should Danika need anything during the night, and swiftly fell asleep.

RICCAN HAD STAYED LATE at work since there was nobody to come home to anyway. Things had definitely improved on the work front, yet it still was less satisfying than it had been before the blowup with Ela Nena. There had never been an apology from his boss, and he had to come to terms with the idea that there likely never would be.

He sauntered through the kitchen on his way in from the garage. He toyed with the idea of making himself something to eat, yet he was still pretty full from lunch. The place seemed oddly quiet without the girls being home, and he wondered how they were faring at his parents' house. Thinking there might be some response from his father about Amanda's question over Shemalla, Riccan strode to his office and uncovered his patil.

Once it was powered up, he discovered he had two unread messages. The first one was from his father letting him know Shemalla was exactly who she claimed to be. He had also written that if Amanda felt compelled to discuss matters with her, then it was probably the right thing to do. Riccan smiled at his dad's obvious infatuation with his wife, and he was thankful his father thought so highly of his wife's skill at reading people.

The second message caught him by surprise as he discovered it was from Vinia. His father had been handling the situation involving the Roanoke Colony, so he was curious to see what she would need from him. Surely it would have to do with Jena or Juila; otherwise, she would have contacted his father. He clicked the message open and then sat back in his chair, tapping his finger to his pursed lips, trying to decide what he could do with her request.

Without fully thinking the matter through, Riccan pulled his cell phone out of his pocket and looked up the Wilson's phone number. Thankfully, the girls spent enough time over at their house to warrant being put into his phone. A male voice answered his call.

"Behn, is that you?" Riccan asked.

"No, this is Jon."

"Oh, sorry about that Jon. This is Riccan Stel. Do you have a minute?"

"Sure. What's up?"

"Are you somewhere private?"

"I can be, just a second." Jon rapidly moved out of the kitchen where his parents were preparing dinner and through the living room. He gestured at Behn and Valentina to follow him as he moved down the hall and into his bedroom at the other end of the house. He pulled the phone away from his ear and pushed the speaker button so everyone could hear. "Okay, I'm in my room with Behn and Valentina. Is something wrong?"

"I don't think so, but I just got a message from your mom. She is asking for you to come and see her while you're on break. Her request is simple enough, but it feels like there's something she's not saying. The problem is about how you'd get there. I have to be at work and Amanda is still in New Mexico dealing with her sister."

"So you don't think it's anything urgent?" Behn asked for clarification.

"No, it's just a feeling I have. I hate to dump this on you and then leave you with no way to get over there to her."

"There might be a way," Valentina chimed in. "You still have Mrs. Stel's telepod in your garage, right?"

"Yes," Riccan confirmed and then laughed. He had the feeling they were going to say they could fly themselves there. "I know the technology is really advanced, and it almost flies itself, but I can't in good conscience allow you to try to get yourselves there."

"No, no!" Valentina denied immediately. "I wasn't suggesting that at all. What if there were someone who did know how to fly it available. Would you let us borrow it?"

"I'm afraid I'm not following," Riccan replied, more than a little baffled by what she was suggesting.

"Willian could fly us there," she offered.

"Willian? As in Jena's Willian? Why would he do that? How do you even know him or how to get in touch with him?"

Now it was Valentina's turn to be flustered. There was no good way to answer Mr. Stel about what had been happening, so she temporized by saying, "He's been teaching us to use our crystal skills while the girls are away. We've all become friends of sorts."

Jon snorted and had to turn away from the phone at his sister's lame explanation. Behn covered his mouth to keep from making any noise as well. Valentina glared from one brother to the other in her attempt to remain focused on the solution to the problem.

"I guess that would be fine. I'd need to show him how the controls work. Do you think he might be able to come over this evening for a quick tutorial?"

"I'll call him right now and find out," Valentina offered.

"Sounds good. I'll talk to you shortly. Goodbye."

Thrilled with the idea of an off-world adventure with Willian, Valentina grabbed the phone out of Jon's hand and rapidly dialed

Willian's number. When he answered, she told him what was happening and then asked if he could help.

"I'd be more than happy to be of assistance except for the problem that I don't have any transportation out to the Stel residence," Willian answered.

"That's no problem, I can take you over there," Valentina offered.

"I'll take him," Behn interjected hastily. He knew it would be a terrible idea for the two of them to be alone in a dark car together. They would definitely need a chaperone. "What time can he go?"

"Did you hear Behn?" Valentina asked Willian.

"Yeah. We were just sitting down to eat dinner. Do you want to go in about an hour?"

"Sure, we need to eat, too. Okay," Valentina looked at her watch and said, "We'll pick you up in one hour from now."

"Sounds good. Bye."

"Bye." Valentina clicked off the call and handed the phone back to Behn. "Can you call Mr. Stel back and let him know?"

"Sure," he replied as he looked carefully at his sister. "Are you afraid to talk to him?"

"A little, I mean, wouldn't you be if you were in my shoes? I'm planning on stealing his daughter's fiancé from her, and he's being so nice to us."

"It's something you're going to have to live with for the rest of your life if you move ahead with it," Behn admonished.

"Don't remind me!"

Behn raised his eyebrows and then turned his attention to dialing the phone. After a short conversation with Riccan, he hung up the phone and announced, "It's all set. We move out in one hour. Let's go get some dinner!"

CHAPTER 25

Valentina was both thrilled and nervous about the prospect of being near Willian again. The day had been dreadfully long without seeing him, so this unexpected trip over to his house was just what she needed. She felt like a little child, practically jumping up and down in her seat as they pulled into the driveway of his house. Neither of them even had the opportunity to get out of the car before they saw the front door open and Willian come jogging down the walkway to their waiting vehicle.

He opened the back door and sat down. "Thanks for picking me up." Immediately, he could feel the electrical energy from Valentina and wondered if she felt it as strongly as he.

"No problem," Behn replied as he unconsciously rubbed his arm where the hair stood on end. He hoped the couple would be able to tone down their connection when they got around Mr. Stel. It could potentially be an awkward conversation otherwise. He pulled away from the curb and sped down the main road.

Willian remained quiet in the back seat, curious about where

Jena lived since he had yet to ever visit her home. It seemed a moot point since meeting Valentina, but Riccan would not know anything about that yet. He would have to be on his best behavior with Valentina so Riccan would not suspect anything until after he had had a chance to discuss everything with Jena. It was the least he could do with his betrothed since he was planning on breaking it off with her when she got back home.

Soon enough, Behn turned the car off the road and into the Stel driveway. He paused as the gate registered his vehicle and slowly opened. Willian's eyes grew bigger as he realized Jena lived in a place much different than himself or even Valentina. This grand home was more fitting as a Residence back in Tuala. Actually, it was even bigger than most of those, he realized as they pulled up into the circular driveway.

Willian was glad it was dark outside so it would hide his astonished expression until he could control his thoughts. He had had an idea that Riccan was considered wealthy, but this was more than he would have imagined. There was only a slight twinge of anger toward Jena before he realized it no longer mattered because he had found Valentina. She was worth more to him than any amount of monetary gain which could have been realized with his union with Jena.

The three got out of the car, and Behn knocked on the door while Willian and Valentina stood one step behind him. He got the distinct impression they were using him as a shield from Mr. Stel, and it made him grin at how ridiculous it was.

Riccan opened the door and responded to Behn's grin with one to match. "Hey, kids; come on in." He held the door open and then his eyes fell on the last to enter, and he said, "Willian," in a more formal greeting and a grim expression.

He had yet to decide how he felt about Willian's sudden change of heart where Jena was concerned. Riccan wanted to give him the chance to redeem himself for his daughter's sake, but he would pound him into the ground if he so much as spoke wrong to Jena ever again. He watched the young man walk in front of him and thought there was something odd about him which he had not noticed before.

"We can go straight to the garage if you want to lead the way, Behn," Riccan called over to Juila's boyfriend. He wished Jena could be as happy as Juila seemed to be. It was too bad things had ended so badly with Luke, he had really liked that boy as well.

Riccan felt his usual sense of pride when he heard compliments on the styling of his custom telepod which was parked in the closest bay to the kitchen door. He knew there would be a small amount of disappointment for Willian to discover they would be flying Amanda's older model hidden behind his. When they finally moved past his bright red telepod, even he had to admit the silver, nondescript telepod looked very plain in comparison.

"How many flight hours have you logged, Willian?" Riccan decided to get right down to business.

"Around sixty-eight. Will that be okay?" Suddenly Willian felt nervous as he realized all of their lives would be in his hands. He had a terrible premonition that he could be responsible for killing his soul-mate just at the point of getting to know her.

"Good, yes, that's more than enough for what I've got in here." He palmed open the side door and gestured for Willian to precede him inside. "Go ahead and take the pilot's seat. Come inside, you two, it never hurts to have more people understand how the system works."

Behn and Valentina rapidly entered the craft and sat down in the seats directly behind the pilot and copilot's seats. Valentina's apprehension grew as she recalled the ill-fated trip she had experienced in this vehicle with Juila not too long before. She desperately hoped she would not be called into action for flying the craft and she elbowed her brother and whispered, "Pay close attention!"

Again, Riccan felt something strange around him; almost an electrical current. He rubbed his forearm with his other hand and swiftly forgot about everything except the explanation of the components of his favorite topic. It was nice to have an avid listener, and he went through the entire program and then asked if there were any questions.

Willian raised his eyebrows in dismay and said, "I think you've already thought of every contingency when you put this system together. It's very impressive, and you said your other telepod is even better? Amazing. I'm certain I won't have any problem operating this craft tomorrow. Are you still willing to allow me to use it?"

"As long as you're willing, I don't see why not."

"Cool!" Willian said, finally finding an appropriate time to use the new phrase he had learned at school on Earth.

Riccan did a double-take and then burst out laughing. "How long have you been trying to find a time to use that term?"

Willian laughed then, too, and asked, "You could tell?"

"I remember the same thing when I was your age. They say some unusual things here on Earth." He stood up and exited the vehicle. The kids were quick to follow him out, and he palmed the door shut. "I have to leave early for work tomorrow, so I won't be home. I'll leave the garage door unlocked out back here," he gestured to his right so they would know exactly which door he meant. "Here's the door remote," he said as he held out the black box toward Willian. "You might as well keep it with you tonight."

"Thanks. I'm really excited to take that out for a spin. It's much nicer than anything I've ever flown, as I'm sure you already knew. It must be pretty great to be a designer of telepods. You'd always have the latest and greatest devices in your craft." He held the remote in both of his hands, rolling it over and over as his nerves starting getting the best of him, undermining his confidence.

"I've always enjoyed the perks of it, I must admit. Now, I'm sure I don't have to remind you not to time your trip, right? You've never had to fly between dimensions before so you shouldn't try to mix the two steps before you learn them both on their own. Also, even though the 'pod should do the navigation for you, don't depend on it. Make sure you have the coordinates firmly in your mind as well as alternate coordinates. Think of this as a normal flight, and you'll stay safe."

"Got it," Willian said and swallowed hard with his suddenly dry throat. He was beginning to think it would be a simple matter with the advanced technology, but he could see Riccan's wisdom in reminding him that software could always malfunction and he should be prepared for anything to happen. He would not lose his concentration and cause something disastrous to happen.

"I can see that you do, now," Riccan said as he clapped Willian on the shoulder. He could see on Willian's expression that he understood the responsibility he had been given and his training as the heir to an Elder would keep them all safe.

THEIR DINNER WENT BETTER than any of them could have expected. Shemalla had been the first one at the restaurant and eagerly awaited their arrival. She waited until all of them had ordered, and their small-talk had been exhausted before she announced her news.

"I was able to find out where April and Emily are staying. I talked with their foster-mother on the phone, and she said they were doing as well as could be expected given the circumstances. I could hear them playing in the background, and they seemed pretty happy." Shemalla stopped talking and smiled with delight.

Diane picked up her napkin and dabbed at the moisture which sprang immediately to her eyes. After the terrible visit at the jail, and the lack of progress with the social workers, this was music to her ears. At least one thing had gone right that day, and she was able to breathe easier knowing the kids were not scared.

"What's next?" Chris asked Shemalla.

"I'm really good friends with their caseworker, so I should be able to get the kids released to you in a couple of days. Of course, you'll still have to fill out all of the paperwork and pay all of the assessments, but it should be pretty smooth sailing."

Diane's whimpers turned to open sobs as her tightly strung emotions were finally able to find a release with her relief. "Oh, thank you, Shemalla!"

"Yes," Amanda seconded her mother's gratitude, "Thank you!"

Shemalla reached under the table and brought her satchel up onto the bench beside her. "I have the paperwork with me. Would you like me to show it to you?"

"Absolutely!" Chris nodded enthusiastically.

"I know this sounds absurd, but you and Diane will have to petition to become foster parents and be approved before the girls can be released to your custody. There's also the matter of taking them back to Florida, so you'll have to fill out this other form." She held out each group of papers as she told them about the process. "Once all of this is signed by the judge, then you will be free to take the children with you."

"Will we be able to take them to the jail to say goodbye to their mother? I'm not sure they know she's okay, and I don't want them to be afraid for her." Diane's own concern for her daughter was clear to everyone at the table.

"I'm sure that can be arranged," Shemalla agreed. She picked up the thick stack of papers and tapped them back into order on the table before she shoved them into the oversized envelope and folded it closed. She handed it over to Chris and said, "Be sure to call me if you get stuck on any of the questions. Most of it is pretty straightforward, but I understand it can get confusing if you're not used to the ways they ask things."

"Thanks," Chris replied as he took the envelope and put it down on the table between himself and Diane. He patted it, feeling a sense of relief at being able to do something which would bring them closer to getting their grandchildren back.

If it had not been considered rude, he would have left at that moment to get started. One look over at Diane told him she was thinking the same thing. He patted her hand to comfort her as much as himself. Just then, the waitress brought their food, and they ate with lighter hearts and better appetites than they had originally planned.

CHAPTER 26

Daven awoke earlier than normal and lay in bed wondering what had been the cause. He turned his head and saw Nena was still sound asleep on her side, facing him. He smiled and eased himself out of bed, trying to keep from moving the covers too much which would cause an unwelcome cold breeze. It was not very often that he rose before she did, so he was unused to trying to be quiet.

He grabbed his robe off of the chair next to the door and silently let himself out of their room. Daven decided he would use another bathroom to allow Nena to continue to rest. Having the girls visit with them was more tiring than he would have believed, even though they pretty much entertained themselves.

The halls were empty of any people at this hour and quieter than he was used to. There was an eerie sense of something coming which he could not place. He looked around him, not knowing what he expected to see, but had to laugh at himself when there was nothing out of place. He decided to go to his office and drink some hot tea to settle his nerves.

Once he had a few sips inside him, he turned on his patil and decided to try to catch up on his work while there was still some quiet time to concentrate. He scanned the screen for any messages marked urgent and handled the two which were blinking red. Once those were handled, he began going through all of the other messages.

He was surprised when he came across not only one but two, messages from Vinia. One message was marked from several days before, and he had no idea why he had not seen it sooner. When he opened it, he was shocked to read that Ozias had been found. It was nice to have that mystery solved since it was bad for an Elder to lose a foreigner.

The next message left him scratching his head in wonder. He read it again to make sure he had it right and then sat back in his chair and chuckled. He could just imagine Vinia's situation as a new leader for the community and then here comes this handsome stranger. If that were not bad enough, he asks her to marry him? It was almost too much. He sobered slightly as he realized this was actually not a laughing matter, but very serious indeed.

Foreigners were not encouraged to stay in Tuala, but Ozias' situation was unique. He would have to put some real thought into this problem and not be hasty with his answer. Maybe he should plan a trip out to the colony to meet with the couple. It might give him some clarity if he could see the two together.

Noises from the hallway broke into his reverie, and he left his chair to investigate. Once he cracked open his office door, the sounds he had heard became laughter from his granddaughters as they made their way to the great room. "Hey!" he called out causing them both to jump in fright.

Jena's hand had risen to her throat, and they both turned in the same motion to see who had called out from behind them. Relief instantly registered on their expressions, and they both grinned as they began walking back toward his office. "I'm sorry, Grandpa. Did we bother you?"

"No, no, not at all," he said as he hugged them each good morning and stepped back into his office with a gesture for them to follow. "I was just going over some work, and I discovered a couple of interesting things. First, you'll be happy to know Ozias has been found."

Juila blushed slightly at the thought of the older man who had been so infatuated with her when she had discovered him on her telepod after the close call on Viceroy Blair's spaceship. She stammered slightly and said, "I didn't know he was missing. Where has he been?"

Now it was Daven's turn to backtrack as he realized he had never told the girls that Ozias had gone missing during the return of the women to the Roanoke Colony. He wished he had not said anything, but it was too late to take back what he had said. He recovered swiftly and said, "Apparently he was wandering in the wilderness near the Roanoke Colony. He has asked to remain with the women and children there, and I think I might approve the request.

"Would you girls like to take a trip out there with me today? Another matter has come to my attention which I think I should handle personally." He tried to make the visit seem casual, but he had also seen how Ozias had been around Juila and wanted to see if Ozias were beyond feelings for his granddaughter, or if he just loved women in general and would show interest in both at the same time. He felt slightly guilty for using Juila in such a fashion, yet he could not think of another test which would be as insightful before he gave Vinia a final decision.

From the calculating look on Jena's face, Daven could only assume she suspected something was going on, but she was too polite to read his mind to find out. Also, he was too stubborn to say anything, so there was a slight standoff.

Juila, only thinking about being able to fly the telepod, nodded her head enthusiastically and said, "I think it'd be a fun trip. What do you think Jena?"

"Sure. When were you planning on leaving?"

"Oh, probably pretty soon after breakfast. Do you have any other plans for today?"

"I had planned on getting grandma to work with her samara, but it can wait."

Daven approved of Jena's interest in the samaras. All of the prodding and pushing of his own had not resulted in getting Nena to touch her crystal, but Jena seemed to have a way with getting people to do as she wished. He was grateful since a bond had clearly been made between his wife and the object she had previously been afraid to touch, so that had turned out well in his mind.

"I don't think we'll be gone too long. Maybe you could plan a session for her this afternoon or maybe this evening?"

Jena shrugged indifferently. She just wanted to make sure Nena kept a regular schedule with her samara so a proper bond could be maintained. There was something about Nena and her samara which made her think it was more important than it had been with any of the others she had encountered. It was almost as if this new samara had a story to share which would somehow make a difference in their lives. She could not explain the difference, but she meant to find out what it could be before she had to return home.

Daven began making plans for their departure. He turned to his patil and assigned several of his appointments for the morning to his aids. Luckily afternoon was already clear so he would not have any reason to be forced to return early. With a flourish of activity on his keyboard, he turned off his patil and looked over at the girls. "Shall we go to the kitchen to see what Melba has prepared for breakfast?"

"What about Grandma?" Juila asked.

"I think she's going to be sleeping for a while yet." Daven smiled at the thought of how peaceful she had looked when he had left her. The rest would do her good.

THE LAST THING Petre remembered was the burly attendant handing him some pills to take. At first, he had refused, but the attendant had told him that it was standard protocol for someone in his condition. The promise of food immediately after the pills was enough to convince Petre to toss them in his mouth and wash them down with the water from the paper cup, also supplied by the attendant.

By the rumbling in his stomach, Petre was certain he had never gotten the food. He rolled over onto his side and watched in fascination as light streaks of elemy floated through the room. He wondered what kind of power the hospital had to be able to create such a unique display. The light show kept him mesmerized for an unknown amount of time.

Another movement shifted his focus, and he belatedly recognized the man who had brought him to the room in the first place. "Hey, you," he slurred as he attempted to sit up in the bed. "I thought you said I was gonna get sumpin to eat." Petre somehow got his feet up underneath him, and he swayed dangerously as he stood up to confront the man.

"I'll bring your lunch as soon as you take your pills," he answered swiftly.

"I'm not falling for that trick again! No, I want food first." He crossed his arms defiantly and tried to maintain focus on the man who suddenly became two men, then just as swiftly one again. He was starting to get dizzy and shook his head to clear his vision. His balance gave out, and he stumbled to the side, luckily the wall kept him from toppling all of the way.

"Easy now, Petre. Be good and take your pills and I'll go and get your lunch." He held out his hand to offer the medication, believing Petre would cooperate.

"I said no!" Petre pushed himself away from the wall and attempted to punch the attendant's face. His swing was wide of the target, and he found himself face-down on the floor with the man resting his knee in the middle of his back. "Get off of me! I want out of here! I want food! What are you doing?"

"I'm giving you your medication," he grunted as he pulled a syringe and bottle from his jacket pocket and prepared the injection.

Petre continued to struggle ineffectually. He felt the waistband of his pants being pulled down and a sharp stab of pain in his buttock. "Ouch! Stop that! What are you doing? Get off of me!" Petre was surprised when he was suddenly left alone on the floor. He rolled onto his side and rubbed his bottom as he tried to see where the man had gone. From the edge of his vision, he could see the door closing and the bottom of a shoe as it took the last step from his room.

His sight started swimming even more, and he closed his eyes to help reduce the vertigo he was experiencing. Hopefully, the man would be returning soon with something for him to eat. Food was the only thing he could think of which might dull the effects of whatever had been injected into him. He tried to bring up some elemy to assist in clearing his system, but the moment he closed his eyes to focus, he fell fast asleep.

CHAPTER 27

Willian was waiting on the sidewalk when Behn pulled his car to a stop at his house. He hurriedly opened the door and entered the back seat of the vehicle. When he shut the door, he realized Valentina had chosen to sit in the back alongside him, which was much of a relief. The trip was nerve-racking enough without having to worry about sitting next to Jon. Certainly, they were on much better terms, yet Valentina's presence was a welcome surprise.

"So we're going to go see your mom?" Willian asked to end the silence in the car.

"Yes," Valentina answered and nodded. She really wanted to reach over and touch Willian, but she did not dare with both her brothers only a foot away.

"You didn't really go into much detail on the phone yesterday. Is there a problem with your mom that you need to go there today, or is this just a visit?"

"We're not exactly sure," Behn said from the driver's seat.

Valentina nodded agreement to her brother's statement. "Mr.

Stel received a message from her yesterday saying she wanted to see us. He thought it seemed odd, but there was nothing specific indicating there was anything exactly wrong."

"I see." Willian wondered what would cause her to reach out to her kids in such a manner. He was looking forward to meeting her, so he was not going to complain. The moment Willian stopped trying to make conversation, the silence resumed for the remainder of the drive over to the Stel's house.

He patted his pants pocket to make sure once again that the remote for the telepod was still with him. His palms were sweating as he visualized their landing coordinates over and over while his face was turned toward the window, even though he saw nothing outside. Never before had a flight meant so much to him.

While he wanted to impress Valentina with his skill, he also had to keep them all alive. Thinking about their safety made him remember the systems in place already, and he felt encouraged. None of his passengers had much to compare against, so he felt a small measure of confidence on the outset.

Before he knew it, they had arrived at their destination. Willian happened to be looking to the side as they pulled into the driveway and was surprised when the man he had seen hastily ducked out of his line of sight. It seemed rather odd behavior for a neighbor or even for someone passing by. He did not have time to ponder it further as they moved along the driveway and pulled up behind the garage.

Behn parked the car and shut off the engine. He turned around in his seat and asked, "Are you sure you know what you're doing? It's not absolutely necessary for us to go if you are feeling at all uncertain of your ability to get us there and back safely."

"No, I'm good. I've been reviewing the landing coordinates last night and this morning. Even if something were to happen to the main controls, I'd still be able to navigate mentally."

"What do you mean by mentally?" Jon asked as he also turned in his seat to stare at Willian.

"What do I mean? Oh, I keep forgetting, this is all new to you. In Tuala, all flights are managed with mental control rather than having a computerized system like Riccan's. Of course, his method would be the only example you'd ever seen. Riccan's is far from normal in Tualan standards."

Jon's expression had turned from anger at being called out for his lack of knowledge to an understanding of Willian's explanation. He realized Willian had not been criticizing them; rather he had given them vital knowledge of what Tualan people should all know without having to ask. He would have to try to work on his skepticism when it came to Willian.

"Let's get going," Valentina said as she grabbed the door handle and rapidly let herself out. She was the first to the garage door and impatiently waited for the boys to catch up with her. "Hurry up; I want to find out what made Mom reach out to Mr. Stel."

Obviously, she had picked the right thing to say since the boys lengthened their stride and soon they were leading the way to the telepod, and she had to jog to keep up. Behn and Jon had no idea how to get into the craft, so they stood to the side and waited for Willian to take charge. Willian reached up and palmed the panel on the side of the telepod and stepped beside the other boys as the door opened downward until it made a ramp for them to use.

Willian stepped up first and walked through the craft and sat down in the left-hand pilot's seat. He automatically fastened his seat belt and began looking over the control panel, familiarizing himself with the different setup before he needed to activate the system. Not paying attention to anything going on around him, he was surprised into jumping when Valentina spoke to him from the other front seat.

She leaned toward him so only he could hear, "Are you sure you'll be able to fly this safely?"

"Yeah, I was just going over everything again before I start it up." He looked over his shoulder and asked, "Is everyone buckled in?" He both heard and saw their affirmative nods, and he turned back to the front. Without any other excuse to stall, he pressed the button on the panel in front of him to bring the door closed.

He began the startup procedures and was thrilled when the glass panel displayed only green lights indicating all systems were running correctly. After scrolling through several screens, he found the one where their destination was already programmed from a past trip, and he selected it. The telepod was floating several inches above the ground and holding steady when he shifted his hand to the manual control for the transfer.

It was always wise to be ready for anything when they popped back into existence at their destination. With their landing planned for the beach, he was extra nervous about rogue winds or even high surf. He took a deep breath to calm his nerves and then hit the activation button to begin the transfer. Everything went black, silent, and still, as the seconds ticked slowly by. Normally he would have been back in the daylight by now, but this transfer was going to another realm so he knew it would take several seconds longer. Still, it was rather unnerving to remain in limbo for so long.

He let out his breath in a sudden rush when daylight poured through the windows, and he looked out to see the beach directly ahead of them. Immediately, he felt the wind pushing the craft toward the beach, and he steadied the telepod until he felt they were close enough to the ground to begin the landing procedure. There was only a slight thump as the craft touched down and he promptly turned off the processor to complete the flight.

With a huge grin on his face, he turned to Valentina and said, "I did it!"

She raised her eyebrows at his apparent surprise in their success and then had to laugh at his enthusiasm. Hurriedly stripping off her seat harness, she stood up and walked into the main cabin, more than ready to see her mother. From the speed with which her brothers joined her, they were just as anxious to get going. The door began to open as she realized Willian had pressed the release while he remained behind in the cockpit. She let her brothers leave the craft first, and she waited to walk with Willian. This would be the first time she would be able to be alone with Willian, and she found herself unaccountably nervous.

"How many times have you been here?" Willian asked as they walked away from the shielded telepod.

"Only twice this year. I was born and raised here you know." She did not know why she felt the need to remind him of where she had been brought up.

"Yeah." Willian tried to find the right way to ask what he was really thinking. Finally, he just came right out and asked, "Will you tell your mom about me? I mean, about what our plans are?"

"What are our plans, Willian? After all, we're only kids, and I think it's a bit early to be making any other declarations for a future at this time."

"Oh." Feeling stupid for having pushed the point, Willian wished he had remained quiet. He kicked his toe into the sand harder than necessary as they climbed the slight incline to get to the grassy landing before the tree line began. Trying one more time to say what he was thinking he asked, "Are you going to tell her about the feeling we get when we're near each other or touching one another?"

Valentina blushed. She realized the relationship she had with her birth-mother was quite different than what Willian had with his. She hardly knew the woman they were going to meet, and she could scarcely be expected to talk about the bizarre experience with her adoptive mother who would never understand what was happening. "I don't know," she admitted finally.

Having to be content with her non-answer, Willian suddenly took her hand in his. The electrical current from the physical contact caused Valentina to cry out involuntarily. She tried to jerk her hand out of his, but he only tightened his grip. "This isn't some sort of infatuation, Val; you have to admit to that at least." Willian had stopped walking and had forced her to turn to face him.

"I know," she said weakly and then suddenly pulled her hand from his. She turned and almost ran to catch up with her brothers. She hated seeing the pain in Willian's eyes at what she had said to him, but she felt she was too young to make any decisions based on chemistry alone. Valentina wanted to make sure the man she fell in love with was someone she could trust implicitly. She had no idea about Willian's past other than he was not a free man to be talking to her the way he just had.

Willian kept to the path but walked slower. He had no idea what to make of Valentina's sudden mood shifts. One moment he felt as though he were getting somewhere with her and then the next moment he felt more alone than ever. Maybe it was a mistake to break things off with Jena so hastily before he really knew what Valentina would decide. He felt so torn, yet he knew he would never be as happy with Jena and, for that reason, he was going to let her go. It was the right thing to do, of that he was certain.

His steps lightened as he made up his mind on one matter at least. He took the last bend in the trail and found the clearing opening to the village. Behn was knocking on the door to a cabin nearest the trail so he held back to see what would happen next. A woman appeared in the doorway and immediately began hugging the trio and then pulled them inside. The door remained open, so Willian stepped forward to watch the reunion from a distance.

Valentina looked around and discovered Willian was no longer with them. She pulled away from her mother and went back outside. She looked around and spotted him standing off to the side and yelled, "Come inside, Willian. I want to introduce you to my mom."

Feeling relieved that she had extended the invitation, Willian hastened to do her bidding. He stepped up beside her and went into the dimly lit cabin. Having the door open seemed to be a good idea since they would hardly be able to see one another without the light pouring in from the entrance. It was hard to imagine living in such conditions, yet Willian would endure much less if it meant he could be with Valentina. Luckily it would never have to come to such dire conditions given who his father was in Tualan society.

"Oh," Vinia exclaimed as she felt the energy emanating from the pair. She looked swiftly from one face to the other and narrowed her eyes slightly at Willian.

"Mom, this is my friend, Willian. Willian, this is my mom, Vinia."

"It's my pleasure to meet you," Willian spoke formally and gave her a slight bow of respect.

Raising her eyebrows at his polished manners, Vinia simply said, "Likewise." With a little difficulty, she turned her gaze away from Willian to talk to her kids, "I had no idea you'd be able to make it out here so fast. Let's sit down and chat for a bit. Tell me what's been going on."

"Is everything okay, Mom? Mr. Stel seemed to think there might be something wrong with you." Behn addressed their concerns even as they complied with their mother's wishes and sat down on the crude benches around the wooden plank table.

"In good time, Behn. Humor me for a bit, won't you." Vinia

waved her hands distractingly and found herself sitting between Valentina and Jon.

Jon spoke up first, "Willian has been teaching us to use our birth crystals while Juila and Jena are away."

"Oh?" she asked, hoping Jon's voice would not carry beyond the cabin. The people of the town did not use elemy for anything, and she did not want to cause any other contention with her people. "How is school going?"

"We're on a break right now, but otherwise it's pretty good. We have a lot of friends, and our classes are pretty typical," Behn supplied. "Mom, please tell us what's really bothering you?"

Knowing she was not going to be able to stall any longer, she sighed and folded her hands on the table in front of her. "Something has come up, and I wanted to talk to you before I made any decisions." She looked at each of her almost-grown children and wished they were little again. Opening her mouth to continue, she was stopped by Danika waking up from her morning nap. She went to get her but was stopped by Valentina's hand on her arm.

"I'll get her, Mom. You stay put and keep talking." Valentina got up from the table and went over to her baby sister's crib. She held out her hands to the little girl and smiled when Danika did likewise.

The vague memory of her mother being pregnant popped into Valentina's mind and it still surprised her to know so much time had passed for her while so little had passed for their mother and sister, only one year to them. Half of her own life had passed since she had last lived with her mother and she had missed all of Danika's life up to this point. Her heart hurt for the loss, and she snuggled her sister close to her chest. She nuzzled her cheek onto the fuzzy head and breathed in her baby smell as she sat back down at the table.

Danika had been mesmerized by the new person who had

come to her crib. Now she sat at the table and simply stared at all of the new faces in the room. Usually, she wanted to eat as soon as she awoke, but today, she was distracted from her routine and remained quiet.

Without having any other way to say it, Vinia finally stated, "Ozias has asked me to marry him. I don't want to agree to anything without talking to all of you first."

This was the last thing any of them expected to hear on this visit and the silence was deafening. Willian was the first to talk. At hearing the odd name, he knew there was definitely a problem. "Who's Ozias?"

Valentina answered softly, "He's a man who helped us escape from being kidnapped by Viceroy Blair. What's he doing here, Mom?"

"Yeah, I thought he was going to be getting a job with Elder Daven," Behn agreed.

"Isn't he a bit young for you?" Jon asked. He looked down in embarrassment at the scathing looks he received from both of his siblings. Belatedly, he realized it was not a very tactful question, and he mumbled, "Sorry."

Willian remained unclear about who this person was, but decided to keep quiet until he could ask Valentina about it privately.

"I've also asked Elder Daven's advice on the matter. I haven't heard anything back from him yet. You know if all of you, or even one of you, said no to it, then I would just tell Ozias that it's flattering for him to ask, but he'll have to find someone else. There are plenty of other girls here who would gladly take him."

"Mom, it's not about us anymore. We're all almost grown up, and this is your life we're talking about. What do you want to do?" Valentina asked.

Vinia became flustered and tried to cover her embarrassment

by offering to hold Danika. She was denied even that much when her youngest daughter stubbornly clung to Valentina and refused to be moved. Finally dropping her hands back to her lap she said, "I don't know what I want. Only three weeks ago, I thought I was going to marry Nealan, and now everything about my life has changed." She looked up at her kids and smiled weakly as she said, "Even you three. You're all grown up, as you've reminded me, Vala. I wasn't expecting any of this, and it kind of scares me."

"Maybe you should take some time to decide," Valentina suggested even as she looked pointedly over at Willian. "There's no need to rush into anything, is there?"

Willian took her point and desperately needed to get some fresh air. "I think I'm going to take a walk," he said suddenly as he stood up.

Feeling guilty for taking the cheap shot at Willian, Valentina handed her sister to her mother and announced, "I'll go with you." She stepped away from the table and rushed to catch up with Willian as he was already out the door.

"Is anyone going to tell me what's going on with those two? Who is he anyway that you would bring him here?" Vinia played with Danika's hands as she looked at both of her sons to get her answers.

"He is Elder Debbon's son, and he's betrothed to Jena. When he met Valentina at school, he said he found his soul-mate, and he wants to break it off with Jena to be with her."

"Oh," Vinia said almost soundlessly. It seemed her daughter's situation was much more complicated than her own. Now it seemed selfish of her to drag them all the way out here to discuss her problem when her daughter needed someone to confide in herself. She was sure it was a confusing time for both of them. It was almost unheard of for a betrothal to be broken and for it to involve Jena made it even worse.

CHAPTER 28

Valentina caught up with Willian at the far end of the town, still within sight of her mother's cabin. She grabbed his arm and turned him toward her. "I'm sorry, Willian. It wasn't fair of me to say that back there. I know how you feel about me, but you aren't the problem, I am!"

His expression turned from hurt to confusion as he tried to understand what she was saying to him. "Can you explain that to me?"

"Willian, I've been raised on Earth!" She realized her voice had been getting too loud and she modulated her tone as she continued. "I don't know about all of the customs here, or the rules, or anything about Tuala really if you get right down to it. Where I come from, girls our age date guys, they kiss, they might even have sex, and then they break up and move on to the next guy. We don't pick one person to stay with for life at this age. Do you know how crazy your idea sounds to me?" She searched his face to find some understanding, and then her own expression fell. "No, I can see you don't."

"Is that what you've done, Val? Have you dated lots of guys? Have you had sex? Is that what you're really trying to tell me?" Willian was becoming more upset as what she had said started to register in his brain.

"No, yes, no! I don't know what I'm saying right now!" She stomped her foot in her exasperation.

"I just want to know the answer to one question then: have you had sex with anyone?" Willian's tone made it clear he would get his answer.

Valentina simply stared at him, not wanting to answer at all, but more embarrassed than anything that he had even had the audacity to ask in the first place.

"It's a simple question, Val. Yes or no?" Willian pushed for an answer even as he started to dread hearing the truth and wishing once again that he had kept his mouth shut.

Valentina's arms crossed over her chest as she instantly relived the horror she had endured. She turned away and whispered, "Not willingly."

Her reaction was not at all what he expected. She looked so vulnerable, and his immediate instinct was to try to protect her and keep her safe. He hesitantly touched her shoulder and felt her violently flinch at his touch. Instantly he knew something terrible had happened to her, and he had inadvertently opened a wound with his crass demand to get answers.

Desperate to fix the situation, he gently turned her around to face him and folded his arms around her rigid body. He pulled elemy from the earth and wrapped its healing energy around both of them. As soon as he felt her muscles relax, he tipped his head down and kissed her tenderly, pouring every ounce of his love into her so she would no longer feel any pain.

～

Juila sat in the pilot's seat while Daven let her navigate their way to the Roanoke Colony. Each trip made her feel more competent as a pilot, and each new destination enriched her skills for navigation. She landed the telepod perfectly in the sand and powered down the unit.

Her confidence wavered slightly as she stepped out of the craft and recalled the reason for their visit. The last time she had seen Ozias, he had practically hung on her every word, making his interest in her very apparent. It would be interesting to see if any of that would change now that he had professed his love for Vinia. She hoped Ozias was not simply an opportunist, mostly because she really liked Vinia and did not want her to get hurt.

Jena came up beside her sister. She knew what she was thinking and sympathized with her. She leaned her shoulder into her and whispered, "I know it was flattering for Ozias to hang on your every word, are you going to be okay if his feelings for Vinia are real?"

"Absolutely!" Juila's response was slightly too enthusiastic.

"Liar," Jena teased.

"Okay, it was nice to know he liked me, but I'm already involved with Behn. I'd be thankful to know there won't be a problem with him later. You know what I mean."

"I do." She sent warm feelings of love to her sister through their mind link all the while wishing she had such a clear path with Willian. Even though he had professed his desire to work things out with her, she still felt there was a tough road ahead and a lot of concessions to make before they would be in a place they could both live with, let alone love one another.

Juila grunted sarcastically and raised her eyebrows at her sister's thoughts, thinking it would take a lot more than that to satisfy herself where he was concerned.

"Sometimes it's not very fun to share every thought," Jena

mused, even as she knew she would not have it any other way. The sounds of the ocean could no longer be heard behind them as they continued following their grandfather up the path. From their previous trips, they knew there was only one more corner to turn before they would be entering the village.

Daven set a brisk pace as he wanted to talk with Vinia before the rest of the villagers took notice of him arriving. He had told the girls there would only be a few minutes of private time before the others would be looking to him for supplies or advice. By the time they were within view of the cabin, their grandfather was already walking inside the house.

The girls paused to give him a moment of privacy before they went inside. They looked around the area and noticed there were only a few people outside. The last time they had been there, it had been deserted and looking forlorn. It was amazing how much had changed with the reunion of the people to their homes.

Juila pointed to a couple in the distance and said, "It looks like the people here are all starting to move on with mending their relationships."

Jena smiled in agreement. "This place has seen hard enough times. Hopefully, with Vinia leading them, they will be able to find peace and happiness from now on. Do you feel the difference here? It's amazing." Even as she was finishing her thought, the kissing couple moved apart from one another, and the girl turned toward them. The distance was not great enough to disguise the look of shock which registered on Valentina's face.

"Hey, that's Valentina!" Juila exclaimed and wondered who she had been kissing. With the traumatic experience on the spaceship, she never expected her friend to be intimate so soon. A moment later, Juila was the one to be goggling as she saw Willian turn to face them. His suddenly ashen expression told her he knew he was in trouble. "Oh, no!" Juila gasped as she felt the anger rising in her sister.

Anger was not the word Jena would have used for the instant betrayal she felt from the two people she least expected to conspire against her. She could not decide if she should march over there and tear into them for their actions, or if she should turn around and go back to the telepod. Instead, she remained rooted to where she was standing, no longer seeing reality, but rather replaying the scene of the couple kissing.

Willian grabbed Valentina's hand and began pulling her toward the twins. He needed to start talking before Jena could be hurt any further. Already, this situation was less than ideal, and he had no idea how he could fix it. When he came closer, he realized he should not have held onto Valentina's hand since it was another sign of betrayal in Jena's eyes. Now within easy speaking distance, Willian said, "Let me explain, Jena."

"I don't think that's necessary anymore; it's pretty obvious I've been replaced." Jena dismissed Willian easily and turned her attention to her supposed friend, "How could you do this to me, Val? After everything, I never would have expected this from you!"

Valentina could not look at the hurt expression on Jena's face without tears springing to her eyes. She pulled her hand free from Willian and covered her face in shame. She should have controlled her feelings and not allowed Willian to draw her into his delusions.

"Don't do this, Jena. Valentina didn't do anything wrong. If you want to be angry, then blame me." Willian tried to insert himself between Jena and Valentina to draw attention away from her.

"Are you kidding me right now?" Jena screamed, finally at the end of her patience. "Just a few days ago you professed your love for me and told me you'd had a change of heart. You said you wanted to do whatever you could to prove yourself to me and be worthy of me!

"Is this what you had in mind? You go and make out with my best friend! Juila was right about you all along, wasn't she? You never loved me; you were only using me as a means to your end. Guess what, Willian? You've found your end. I'm done with you!" She spun around, ready to flee back onto the path to the beach.

Willian was fast. He grabbed her arm and spun her back around. There was no anger in his expression since he needed Jena to hear what he had to say. "Jena, you have to listen to me. This isn't what you're thinking. Please!"

Jena's eyes grew wide, and her face began to turn a bright shade of red as she looked down on his hand where it held her arm. She could feel the call of elemy coming from inside her without her conscious thought. Not sure what she planned to do with it when it was ready, she felt more powerful than ever before.

Willian also felt the shift in energy and instantly let her go. Never in his life had he witnessed Jena's wrath, and it scared him more than a little. He stepped back and glanced pleadingly over to Juila to intervene. "Please," he whispered to Juila, "keep her from doing something we will all regret."

"I wouldn't regret it," Juila retorted, but immediately began to calm her sister. She sighed with relief when she felt the elemy dissipate.

Nobody had noticed when Valentina had left, but they were all startled when she returned with Elder Daven running beside her. He had felt the surge of power and recognized the trouble just as Valentina arrived at the cabin door. Not knowing what the problem was, he was prepared to do battle, if necessary.

"What happened? What's wrong?" he asked as he looked around for any signs of danger. He looked at his granddaughters and belatedly noticed Willian standing with them. "Willian? What are you doing here?"

The people of the village were gathering around the strange scene. Everyone wanted to know what had happened which would cause the Elder to be running out of Vinia's house. Their whispers were getting louder as speculation rose.

"I think we should take this discussion into Vinia's house." Elder Daven used a compulsion command to get everyone to do his bidding without any hesitation. Something was definitely afoot, but it seemed like it was not meant to be aired in public based on the stony expressions of the people present at the edge of the clearing.

The crowd parted for the quiet group. Valentina was the first to enter the house and immediately began crying uncontrollably. Vinia went to her daughter and tried to soothe her even though she had no idea what the problem could possibly be. Next came Willian, followed by Juila and Jena.

Elder Daven entered last, and he shut the door, effectively blocking the scene inside from prying eyes. Simultaneously, Daven created spheres of light throughout the room as well as made a shield surrounding the house to keep anyone from hearing or seeing the spectacle inside. "Who wants to go first?"

Willian stepped forward and said, "I do. I want to start by saying none of this was planned. Jena, you have to believe me." He looked over and saw her hard expression and then decided it was probably best to keep his gaze fixed on Elder Daven to plead his case. "I literally ran into Valentina at school on Friday, and something happened which I never knew existed. I was going to talk to Jena about it when she got back, but then she came here, and now I've made a mess of everything."

Daven was more confused than he cared to admit. None of what Willian said made any sense, but he could see it had made

Jena more furious, so he began to suspect some indiscretion had been discovered. By looking at how upset Valentina had become, it started to dawn on him that a love triangle was probably to blame. "Start explaining Willian."

"I can probably demonstrate it better than any words," he said as he walked over to Valentina and pulled her away from her mother and brought her in front of Elder Daven. He kept his hand in hers and said, "Touch me and tell me what you feel?"

Daven saw Valentina's shoulders shaking with her sobs and was curious as to what Willian could possibly be trying to prove. Hoping to put a quick end to this drama, he did as Willian asked and placed his hand on the young man's shoulder. The current of electricity raced through him, unlike anything he had ever experienced. His eyes grew wide, and he knew beyond words, Willian had been right to use this method to explain. He withdrew his hand and simply said, "I see." He turned his head to Jena and said, "Come over here, Jena."

She looked defiant, almost as if she meant to refuse his command. Clearly, she was angry, and she had every right to feel that way, but she needed to know what had changed. This was not something which could be ignored or even controlled. This was beyond anyone's power, and it was not to be denied.

Jena stepped to her grandfather's side and looked up at him angrily. She felt betrayed all over again when she felt as though he were siding with Willian in this matter.

"Jena, you have been trained by Jehoban Himself. I want you to use that training to do as I ask and to keep your mind impartial even though every fiber in you tells you not to. Can you trust me in this?"

Surprised by his request, her thoughts shifted as she was sure he had intended. "I'll try. What is your request?"

"Put your hand on Willian's arm and tell me what you experience."

She sighed deeply, wishing he had asked anything other than that, she reluctantly put her hand out and then gasped even before physical contact had been made. Her forward motion brought her fingers to his skin, and she measured the intensity against the emotions which coursed through and around her.

Instantly, she understood Willian's dilemma and wished she had not reacted as she had in the clearing. This had not been planned, nor was it able to be reined in. For the first time in her life, she felt the perfect connection of two souls. With great reluctance, she withdrew her hand and began crying.

Seeing and feeling everything along with Jena, Juila rushed forward and embraced her sister. She was thankful her sister was finally free of Willian, but she also felt her heart breaking for the complete loss of the relationship. There had to be something she could do to help ease the pain, yet she could not think outside of Jena's tumultuous thoughts.

"What's going on?" Vinia asked, unable to bear the strange actions of her guests any longer.

"Something I've never witnessed before," Elder Daven replied. He sat down on the bench as he composed his explanation. "It appears as though Willian and Valentina are soul-mates. When they bumped into one another at school, their life-lines fused together, and now they are bound together for eternity."

Valentina seemed stricken with fear at Elder Daven's proclamation. The way he said it sounded so final, almost like a death sentence. She wanted to have some say in her future, but this changed everything. Her choice was now taken from her all because of a chance meeting in the hall at school.

Using his powers to read her thoughts, Daven reassured her by saying, "It will always feel like a blessing because you will never have to question his devotion to you. Likewise, he will know your heart toward him. Be at ease, Valentina."

She remained mostly unconvinced as she continued to feel sorry for herself. She could not bear to look at Jena or Juila for fear of the rejection she was certain they would have for her friendship. More than anything, she wished she had remained at home and this day had never happened.

Daven was still connected with her thoughts, as it was his duty to arbitrate arguments within his District. He pulled Jena to the side and whispered, "Are you still blaming the two of them even after you have felt the power pulling them together?"

Jena wanted to nurse the anger longer, but she knew it would serve no purpose. She glanced over at her friend, still holding Willian's hand, and then looked her grandfather in the eyes. The lesson he had wanted her to learn was complete; she felt peace in her heart first, and now it was also in her mind. "No."

He nodded his approval and then suggested, "Make your thoughts known to Valentina and restore your friendship. It's the most important thing you could do right now."

She pursed her lips and gave a quick nod of her head in acknowledgment. She moved away from her grandfather and stepped up next to Valentina. "I understand, Val. I promise I'm not angry with either one of you."

With a brief look of hope, Valentina glanced up from staring at the floor. "Are you serious?"

To make her point, she reached out and touched Valentina's arm, resisting the urge to pull away as she felt the electrical current caused by Willian's proximity. "I've never been more serious in my life. We should sit down and discuss everything together." She pulled slightly for emphasis and then took a step toward the table.

Daven liked the way his granddaughter was handling the situation and approved of her idea to sit together to find out all of the details. What he had witnessed between the young couple was rare and needed investigation. If they could find out how it happened, they could possibly replicate it to make better matches for the citizens.

"I still don't understand what is happening," Vinia complained as everyone began sitting down around the table.

Willian looked over at the woman who would eventually be his mother-in-law and said, "Your daughter and I have discovered we are bound together by our life-lines. I wasn't sure what to make of any of this since I went to Earth to work things out with Jena." He looked over at her with an expression which pled with her to understand his original intention.

"I know that now, Willian. Don't worry about what used to be right now; tell us what happened."

He winced slightly at the finality of Jena's tone, but also felt immense relief. Nodding acceptance to her statement, he proceeded to tell everyone present what had been happening up to the moment Jena confronted them. "I'm sorry it worked out this way, Jena. I really did want to talk to you before it went anywhere else."

"I understand, Willian, I really do. I have to admit it hurt deeply until I found out neither of you had a choice in the matter. If either of you had been involved for any of the normal reasons, this would be a very different conversation. As it stands," Jena turned to Daven with a formal tone, "Elder Daven, will you permit the betrothal between myself and Willian to be dissolved without fault or blemish on either part?"

Daven shifted his gaze to Willian and asked, "Is this also your wish, Willian?"

"Yes." The relief was evident on his face as the worry lines vanished from his brow and around his eyes.

"Due to the unusual circumstances, I will grant your request.

You will both relinquish your betrothal rings immediately." He held out his hand, palm up, and waited for them to comply.

It was more difficult than Jena imagined to remove the ring and know it meant she no longer had a planned future with Willian. She was free to make her own choices, and it scared her. She glanced over to her betrothed, realizing she no longer had any claim to that title with him anymore. She twisted and tugged until the ring came free of her finger and dropped it onto Willian's ring with a metallic clang. The noise seemed to resonate in her head like the final note to a sad song. She was free. She was alone.

You're not alone, Jena. You're never alone as long as you have me, Juila's mind link comforted her.

I'm so thankful. This would have been impossible without your support.

I'm just glad it's finally done. Of course, I never would have imagined it would have come about like this, but I'm happy nonetheless.

"What does all of this mean?" Jon asked suddenly.

Daven cleared his throat and said, "It means the betrothal which was blessed by Jehoban between Jena and Willian is as if it had never happened. They will never be able to marry one another, and they are both free to pursue other relationships."

"I'm not ready!" Valentina cried out as all of the eyes turned to her, including Willian's.

"There's no rush," he assured her. "We have the rest of our lives to discover each other."

Valentina was not encouraged by Willian's words and felt even more like crying. Too much had happened in the last couple of weeks and she had never been good with change. All she wanted to do was be by herself and not worry about anyone or anything. Somehow, she believed this was never going to be an option ever again.

CHAPTER 29

Diane hugged her granddaughters close to her chest as she kneeled on the ground. The social worker in charge of their case had made a special dispensation for them to be able to visit with the girls for a few hours since school had let out early and their foster-mother was still at work. This was going to be a bittersweet visit since they had not managed to finalize the paperwork to get the girls turned over to them which meant they would be telling them goodbye at the end of the visit.

"How are you doing?" Diane asked Emily, her voice slightly higher than usual in her eagerness to sound normal.

"Fine, Grandma. Have you seen Mommy?" she asked with a worried expression.

"I have, and she wanted me to give you a big hug and kiss for her. She really wanted to find out if you were both happy and having a good time on your sleep-over."

"It's not a sleep-over, Grandma. We aren't allowed to go home."

The matter-of-fact tone in Emily's voice made Diane look sharply up at the social worker. She stood swiftly and whispered for only the woman to hear, "What have you been telling these girls?"

"I haven't said anything, but I'll make sure their foster family knows the limits of what they can say to the children." She wrote on her tablet and dismissed Diane while she continued to make notations on the case.

Having to be content with the only answer she was going to receive, Diane sat down on the floor of the playroom and picked up a toy. She wiggled it close to April's face and made silly noises to get her to giggle.

Amanda and Chris were mesmerized with Diane's single-mindedness where the children were concerned. They both had reservations about how this visit was going to end, and they had already planned on making some sort of distraction to keep her from being too depressed. The only course of action seemed to be to make another visit over to the jailhouse to tell Carrie about the children's welfare.

After their last visit three days before, they had no idea what type of reception they should expect to receive. None of them had anticipated Carrie's almost hostile behavior, but they put it up to the fact that she had been transferred that same morning to the new facility. Of course, it did not excuse her actions, but it could at least explain it.

Amanda decided to get down on the floor to entertain April while Diane played house with Emily. She thought the two girls were very bright and seemed to be taking the changes in their world very well. She was certain it would have been much more difficult for herself at their ages, and it made her wonder if this were something they had become accustomed to. It made her sad to think these bright little girls were going to be kept away from their family even for a moment longer.

All too soon, the social worker announced the end of their

visit. Diane tried to maintain a stoic expression as she said her farewells to the children and gave them both hugs and promises to see them again very soon. She did not promise to take them home since she had no idea if it were going to work out and she did not want to give them false hope. Even the lack of the promise filled her with grief that the system could be so cruel as to keep the children from their family all in the name of their welfare.

Chris came over to Diane and hugged her as she continued to wave to the children as they skipped and giggled beside the social worker. Their only consolation was that it seemed the woman took her job seriously and loved working with the children. "We should get something to eat and then we can go tell Carrie how the children are doing. I'm sure she's desperate to know about them."

"Right," Diane agreed without enthusiasm. She wished the girls were coming to dinner with them and that they could be heading back home to Florida. She had to believe Shemalla would be able to pull some strings to make the wheels of justice turn a little faster. Every moment which slipped by without the children seemed to last an eternity and felt like a failure to Diane.

Dinner turned out to be a quick and quiet affair where everyone kept their own counsel, and they ate with little appetite. They felt like they were on autopilot as they went back out to the truck and drove to the jail. Several other families were waiting in the visiting room when they came to sit down at the same table they had used before.

Carrie was led out by a different guard. She did not seem any more enthusiastic about seeing her family than she had the first time. Amanda thought she looked tired and downtrodden, which was understandable given the circumstances.

"Why did you come back?" Carrie asked rudely.

Diane looked hurt by her oldest daughter's tone, but she

refused to acknowledge it. "We saw the girls today. They looked really good."

Carrie simply raised her eyebrows at the news.

"We got to spend several hours with them under the supervision of the caseworker. I think she approves of us, but it's hard to tell." Diane hoped something she was saying would help melt the mask of unconcern her daughter wore a bit too well. She knew her daughter loved her children.

"I'm sure Shemalla will be able to move things along faster so we can get the children out of foster care," Amanda added.

"Who's Shemalla?" Carrie asked suddenly.

"She's...an old friend of mine." Amanda did not know how to really explain the circumstances of their acquaintance since it was all virtual experience and none of it from reality.

"Of course," Carrie drawled and rolled her eyes. She wished Amanda had stayed out of all of this. In fact, if it had not been for Amanda's existence, she would have been the favorite daughter, and maybe none of this nightmare would have happened. The way she saw it, Amanda was the cause of all of her problems.

Amanda could see so many emotions flit across her sister's face and she wondered what she could possibly be thinking. They all wanted the same thing, to get the girls back with their family and to get the charges against Carrie dropped or reduced enough to allow her release. "What's wrong with you, Carrie? Why aren't you happy to hear about our plans for your children?"

"What's wrong with me? Really? You have to ask that of me while I'm sitting here in jail. Everything is wrong!" She stood up, her face reddening with unvented rage, started to speak, but then turned and began walking away.

"Carrie!" Amanda called after her sister. She was not going to let her treat them this way again. She jumped up and ran across the room, grabbed her sister's arm to keep her from leaving and said, "You do not get to do this to Mom. Not again!"

"Oh? You mean after the stunt you pulled? After all of the years, you kept mom chained to your bedside while you were in a coma? I don't get to matter for once? Is that what you're saying? You know what I used to think? I thought fate had caught up to you when you were found almost dead. All those years when you should have been dead!"

"Carrie, you say the meanest things sometimes. What are you talking about?" Amanda was genuinely confused about her sister's incoherent rambling.

Carrie threw her head back and laughed until tears rolled down her cheeks. She wiped them away with the backs of her hands and then sobered immediately. She looked straight into Amanda's eyes and said, "You should have died the same day your twin sister did on the day you were born. But you didn't! You escaped death again when you came out of your coma. You are the blessed child of the family, and the rest of us don't matter. Go home, Amanda. Worry about your own life and stay out of mine! I don't need you!"

Seeing her sister's stricken expression, Carrie smiled and walked away. Finally, she had her revenge. Now she knew the truth their parents had always kept from her. She was only half of the person she should have been. They only loved her because she was their last tie to the daughter they had buried and mourned.

Amanda had no words for her sister's revelation. She could not give credence to anything she had said since she was clearly not thinking straight. Maybe she was still able to find a way to take drugs even behind bars. It would go a long way toward excusing her abhorrent manners and her lack of concern for her own children's welfare. She woodenly walked back toward her parents, not wanting even to repeat the lies Carrie had just spewed to her.

"Let's get out of here," she said as she continued to lead the way back to the vehicle.

"What did she say, Amanda?" Chris asked as he caught up to her. He had seen the strange scene but had been unable to hear anything they had spoken to one another.

"Nothing important. I'm going to call Shemalla on the way back to the hotel and see what she's been able to do to move things along. I want to go home to my husband." She wanted nothing more than to have Riccan's arms around her at that moment of uncertainty and torment.

Knowing how her own daughters felt about being twins themselves, she recalled the dozens of times growing up where she had wanted her own twin to share everything with. If what Carrie had said were true, then surely she would have known about it years before. Looking over at her father, she knew it had to be a lie because he would never have kept such a secret from her.

CHAPTER 30

Daven had not wanted to continue the discussion about the proposal of marriage with Vinia and Ozian since tensions were so high. He had made arrangements to return another day so the fallout from the dissolution of the betrothal could dissipate. Several days had gone by, and Juila noticed other duties had kept him close to the Residence.

On more than one occasion, Juila noted him watching Jena and seeing her change before his eyes, and it was apparent he worried for her. Where she had once been so confident and certain of her future, mostly because it had been planned already, now she seemed forlorn, almost lost. Juila was constantly by her side so Jena would not do anything stupid.

"I wish you wouldn't shut me out of your thoughts, Jena. I really want to help," Juila pled yet again. It was hard on her not to have the close connection she had known all of her life. At this point in Jena's life, it was even more important to Juila to feel connected, not kept away.

"There are things I want to think about by myself. I wish you'd understand that and leave me be for a bit. I'm not going to do anything rash or try to hurt myself, Juila. That's just plain ridiculous. You have no idea what it's like to have your life planned only to discover you have no plan at all. It's...I can't even describe it, and it's happening to me!"

"Are you really okay about Willian being with Val?"

"Surprisingly, yes! I know Val was really troubled about my reaction, and I totally get it, but I couldn't deny what I felt when the two of them were touching. It really was extraordinary."

"I felt it even when they weren't in physical contact. I wonder what it feels like to them."

"Probably something we wish we could have." Jena looked down at her clasped hands and realized that was the part which bothered her the most. She wanted Willian to feel for her and look at her the way he did Valentina. It was what she had always dreamt of for the two of them, and now his interest was completely refocused on someone else as if she had never existed. How was she supposed to keep from feeling hurt and rejected with something so absolute?

"I think Jehoban had a plan for you which didn't include Willian."

"Then why would he have blessed the union to begin with? It just doesn't make sense."

Juila thought about it for some time before she snapped her fingers when she came to the obvious conclusion. "Willian never would have come to Earth to meet Val if it hadn't been for you. Don't you think Jehoban would know that?"

"I suppose." She was still not convinced, yet she felt a glimmer of hope at the idea of being useful for Jehoban's purposes. From their special upbringing on Acaim, she always wished there was some way to repay Jehoban for taking them in and teaching them so much.

Taking advantage of Jena's uncertainty, she added more thoughts to her original idea. "Maybe you two being so ill-suited was part of the plan so it would be easier for you to let him go. Or maybe it was to help him learn to be better to Val. If you really wanted to discover the answer, you know you could ask Jehoban directly."

"I know, but that makes it sound as if I doubted His plan and I don't want to go there. Besides, we have no idea if this is even the real reason, we're just guessing."

"It seems like a pretty good guess to me, and we can both agree that my instincts are usually correct."

Jena quirked her eyebrows at her sister's self-confidence. She did not want to admit to anything at the moment; she really wanted to be able to see the scenario from every angle. Just as their grandfather had requested, she wanted to be impartial in her review, especially because she was involved. If she ever wanted to become an Elder, then this could become an important lesson.

Just as swiftly as she had the idea, she slapped her thigh and smiled, startling Juila into looking up at her sister in astonishment. Jena jumped up from where she had been sitting in the window seat and could no longer keep still.

"What happened?" Juila asked, excited to see a change in her sister.

"I just realized something really cool!"

"What?"

"As long as I was going to be married to Willian, I never could have become an Elder because that was his destiny. I no longer have his restriction on my life. I actually could become an Elder if Jehoban wants me for the role. I'm free to allow my dream to possibly become a reality!" This was the best thing to ever happen in her life, and she had no idea what to do with it.

Juila also rose from the cushioned bench and announced, "Let's go share the great news with our grandparents!"

Jena's expression sobered slightly, and she held out her hand to prevent her sister from leaving the room. "I'd like to keep this between us for a little bit if you don't mind. If Grandpa were to tell me I didn't have a chance at becoming an Elder, then I'd be crushed all over again. Promise me you won't talk about it in front of them." She tipped her head toward the bedroom door to emphasize who she was talking about.

"Sure, Jena. I'll promise whatever I have to if it means you'll let me back into our link." In the next instant, Jena's innermost thoughts were in her own head again, and she sighed with relief when she saw the brightness of Jena's soul.

Jena felt the same release as soon as she allowed the twin-link to resume its normal flow. At the time, it had felt important to have her own space, but now she realized their shared space was better for her emotionally. The warmth Juila projected on her was soothing and moving, more so than Willian had ever been for her.

"We need to make plans for our future." Juila was suddenly overcome with the desire to strategize their options since they were both free for it now.

"I'm pretty sure your future includes Behn," Jena replied drolly.

"If that's true, then yours includes Luke," Juila retorted instantly.

Clearly, that had been the last thing Jena planned on connecting with her life. She had been so consumed with the loss of Willian, she had found no other place for another relationship. Squinting her eyes a bit, she considered how her life would work with Luke in it rather than Willian, and she discovered it pleased her. "There's only one problem with Luke, you know."

"What?"

"He's from Earth. At least Behn is from Tuala and knows about our powers and history. Behn is an obvious and easy choice for you to make. Luke…well…not so much."

"Now you're just making excuses. The difference in heritage hasn't stopped anyone in the past. Our own parents aren't from the same world, but they've managed to work it out."

"Wow, that's the biggest stretch yet, Juila. We know how strangely everything came about for them and we also know Jehoban had a big hand in their coming together."

"What, you don't think He'd do the same for you? We lived with Him for most of our lives, Jena!"

"You don't have to tell me that, I was there, remember? Still, it would seem pretty petty for me to go asking the creator of the universe if He'd mind setting me up on a date. It sounds even worse saying it out loud!"

"Now you're just making excuses. What about Barla and Captain Ahn? Or our father's grandparents, Murisa and Edwin? They are family and from different worlds. Both times they managed to find one another without Jehoban's direct intervention…well maybe. They did all have extenuating circumstances for why they were meeting, but that's beside the point. They found one another against all the odds, and they've managed to make happy lives for themselves. You can too if you let yourself be open to it."

Jena held up her hands in surrender. "Can you at least give me a minute to process the end of my relationship with Willian before you set me up with someone new?"

"Luke is hardly someone new! You've dated him several times, and you enjoyed yourself. I think that speaks volumes right there." She could see her sister starting to get defensive, and she relented slightly. "Fine, I'll leave it alone. I love you, Jena, and I just want you to be happy. If you hurt, then I hurt."

"I know, and I love you." She felt a release in her soul, something which made everything possible again. No longer was she feeling sorry for herself; instead, she was ready to look ahead to a future which still had to be written.

PETRE WOKE up in the lumpy bed, feeling weak, cold, and disoriented. Without moving his head, he looked around him with eyes which refused to focus. He saw a strange contraption suspended above him, and he found himself mesmerized by the constant drip, of what looked like water, into the small vial. The vial was attached to a tube which dropped down, looped back up and snaked across the bed. Belatedly, he discovered the tube had been taped to the back of his hand, and his whole hand and arm felt cold.

The idea of the liquid falling from the bag going onto his arm began to concern him to the point of paranoia. The more he looked at it, the more convinced he became that it was slowly poisoning him. He had to get that thing off of him; it could not be allowed to keep dripping. He reached across his body and pulled the tape off and was even more horrified when he discovered the tube was actually inserted into his body with a sharp object. He pulled it out and let it fall to the floor where it began pooling the liquid around it.

Several drops of blood appeared where the needle had been, and he began squeezing his arm to encourage it to continue bleeding. He had to get the poison out of his arm before he was no longer able to control his motions. Already he felt light-headed and believed he was going to die. Spots appeared in his vision, and he closed his eyes, not knowing exactly when he passed out.

The attendant found him bloody and disheveled. He called in several nurses to get him cleaned and reconnected to the IV. He took a vial of sedative and a syringe out of his pocket and extracted a dosage ensured to keep the patient unconscious until they were ready to interview him. They only had a short time before Dr. Gascon would be returning and they had followed protocol precisely to keep the patient calm enough for his initial session.

Petre was certain he had felt people touching him. He wanted to tell them to leave him alone and let him sleep, but he could not get the words to form in his mouth. There was something very wrong with him, and he worried about keeping his promise to Lucinden.

He had to figure out a way to stop these people from whatever they were doing long enough for him to escape. The mantra kept going through his mind as the sedative entered his system and began slowing down his brain even further until nothing made sense anymore except sleep.

CHAPTER 31

Dr. Gascon stood at the foot of the bed and looked down with a critical eye on this man who insisted he came from another world. As soon as his schedule cleared a little more, he was interested in hearing Petre's story. Ever since Shemalla had gone missing, he had been searching for a new subject for his ongoing multi-dimensional disorder study and Petre would fill the slot nicely.

Just thinking of Shemalla again caused his anger to rise. He knew, yet had no way of proving, that Dr. Medin had been responsible for his star patient to go missing. The fact that she had gone completely off of the radar proved she had to have had help. It was impossible to leave without a trace and without assistance.

Dr. Medin was another sore subject, Stephen mused to himself. He should have seen she was getting too emotionally attached to her patients. Her notes had shown a clear pattern of belief which he should have found a way to dissuade. Dr. Medin had been his best hypnotist and had achieved the fastest results with their most delusional patients. The several therapists who had come and gone as her replacement were mostly disappointing who he'd sent packing after only a few sessions each. He would be taking on Petre himself; this was too important to screw up.

He left the room and made his way back to his own office. There was plenty to catch up on since he had been out of the office speaking on major depressive disorders at another psychiatric convention. Crossing in front of the empty desk in the outer room, he recalled how he had fired his last secretary, but a replacement had yet to be chosen. He sighed at the thought of training another woman to his exacting standards even as he sat down at his mahogany desk.

Putting up his feet on the edge of the desk, Dr. Gascon opened the latest stack of paperwork and photos from the private investigator. By the time he read the third line of the report, he had dropped his feet to the ground and began swearing. "Of all of the incompetent, stupid, people! How could he have been so sloppy as to get caught, and by a kid at that!"

He scanned through the rest of the report and slammed it down onto the desktop. He grabbed up the photos and rapidly shuffled through them to find the picture of the boy in question. Turning it over, he found only a first name of Willian as the identifier for the teenaged boy. Since he was in the vehicle with the Wilson triplets, it was being assumed that he was a friend of theirs from school.

What was not apparent was who the kids were visiting since there had been no recent sightings of Jena or Juila and Amanda was currently in Roswell, New Mexico. An idea triggered in Dr. Gascon's mind, and he grabbed the report back up to scan through it. Yes, it did say Roswell. What was in Roswell and why did that seem so familiar to him?

He turned to his computer and searched through his old patient records. It took over an hour, but his diligence paid off as he found the patient notes from someone he had been thinking about earlier that same day. Shemalla's delusions under hypnosis had her working in Roswell. Could it be too coincidental that Amanda would be traveling to the same town?

How come he had never investigated whether or not she had gone back to the town in the report? Most likely because they had been moving their facility and there were so many other problems to resolve, she had simply fallen through the cracks. Besides, she was a charity patient, merely a pet project of his, so finding her did not really warrant any extra expense. Now he was beginning to wonder if he should hire a private investigator in Roswell.

He would have to ponder it a little longer and decide later since his alarm was going off for his meeting with the Board of Directors. With a sigh of resignation for having to deal with the bureaucracy of hospital, he turned off his computer and put his special files away for future review. Luckily he had made several new acquaintances at the conference who had indicated their desire to make donations to further his studies, so the meeting would likely go in his favor.

THEY MIGHT HAVE BEEN GIVEN the all-clear from Jena on pursuing their relationship; however, it did not mean Valentina felt comfortable forging ahead. She had resisted Willian's attempts to come over to her house on two occasions by giving him lame excuses. Of course, this was only a short-term fix allowing her some time to think about the implications of Elder Daven's summary of their situation.

Valentina was terrified of a future predestined with someone not of her own choosing. Of course, whenever she was with Willian, she could not imagine wanting to be with anyone else.

This created the conundrum in her mind of choice versus chemistry; her mind told her one thing while her body told her something quite different.

As she lay on her bed, she vividly recalled Willian lying on top of her, passionately kissing her. Her memory was so clear that she began to smile at how wonderful the whole thing had been. Just a short time before she had met Willian, she had been a ball of misery in her room. She had Willian to thank for almost completely erasing the rape from her mind.

Almost, she told herself, as she could just as swiftly go back to the moment in time on the spaceship where she had not been in control of her body. This uncontrolled feeling for Willian did not make her feel dirty or used; on the contrary, it made her feel desirable and wanted for herself.

Was it herself Willian really wanted, or was it the elemy forcing him to want her? Would this be something which would last, or was it merely temporary? She was not about to throw her heart at something or someone which was only a phase. Willian already had a track record for discarding one person for another. Jena was gracious enough to let him go without too much hassle, could Valentina be so calm about it? She could not see herself behaving as well as Jena had, which made her feel bad all over again.

"Hey, Val, when are we going to Willian's house to train? It's been days," Jon asked from the open bedroom door.

Valentina looked guiltily over at her brother and wondered if he could guess what she had been thinking. She was certain her face was turning red, and she sat up hurriedly to disguise it. "I don't know; I haven't really felt like it, I guess."

"It seems to me that you've been avoiding Willian. Are you having second thoughts about him?"

"Would you be happier about it if I said yes?"

Jon had been teasing, and he instantly became concerned about his sister's serious reply. He stepped into her room and said, "No. Val, I was just kidding. What's wrong? Why are you suddenly changing your mind about him? Did he do something to you?"

Valentina hastily shook her head to keep him from thinking the worst. "No, it's something Elder Daven said which made me question everything."

"What did he say?"

"Something about this being my destiny. What if I don't want a destiny? I've always wanted to have a normal life where we fit in. How come there's always something coming up which makes that dream impossible? We're never going to fit in; are we?"

Jon chuckled at his sister's summary of their lives to date. He shook his head slightly and answered, "No. We'll never be normal as long as we remain on Earth. I think we'd have a better shot at it if we moved to Tuala."

"But don't you get it? We're foreigners there as well since we were raised most of our lives on Earth. We don't fit in anywhere!" She slapped her hands down onto her thighs for emphasis.

"Maybe you should talk to Mr. Stel about it."

"Mr. Stel? Why him? I'd think he'd be about the last person he'd want to talk to given what's happened to Jena."

"I think you'd be surprised. Anyway, I suggested him because he's lived half of his life on Earth like us. He went to high school here and lived with relatives in the U.S. over the years. He might be able to help you figure out a path for yourself where you can fit in."

"How do you know all of this about Mr. Stel?" Valentina leaned forward onto her elbows with her head resting in her hands. She tipped her head toward her brother in her interest in his answer.

"Jena told me about it while we were studying crystal skills together. I don't even remember why it came up, but I think it might be a good solution for you."

"Maybe." Valentina's mind was turning over various possibilities. For some reason, she had believed Riccan had only made a life for himself here on Earth for business. Never had she imagined he had family living nearby. This definitely changed some ideas she had been forming.

"What about our crystal training? Do you want to go with Behn and me?"

"I think I'll skip it this time."

"Okay, but I'm sure Willian will be disappointed that you didn't come with us."

"That's not my problem."

Jon's eyebrows lifted in denial, but he refrained from commenting further. He knew when to leave his sister alone. He walked back to the door and said, "If you change your mind, we're leaving in about ten minutes."

"When did you guys make those plans?"

"Willian called here several times. After you had refused to meet with him, Behn decided to take the call. Willian asked us if we could all come over today and Behn agreed it would be a good idea."

"Hmmph."

Jon chuckled as he left the room and turned down the hall. He knew his sister could take a long time to come to a decision; he just hoped she would get there before she made things more difficult for herself or Willian.

Shemalla's days had not been wasted on museum work alone. She had spent a considerable amount of time on her cell phone, working her contacts, and calling in favors to get April and Emily released from the system and into Chris and Diane's custody.

While the task seemed straightforward enough, there had been more wrinkles in the case than she had previously been made aware.

As it turned out, Carrie was the only person who could identify the leader of the drug cartel in their county. Because of this, extra precautions were being taken to ensure her children's safety. Shemalla believed getting them out of New Mexico would be the easiest way to accomplish the goal and began to exploit the idea.

It seemed she was starting to make in-roads of progress when she finally got the judge to agree to her plan. He said he would sign off on the custodial paperwork in the morning. Hopefully, all would go well, and the Covington family would hear the news from the clerk the next day. She shook her head at how much influence she had had to exert to get everything accomplished, but she knew it was worth it.

With that task accomplished, Shemalla was able to relax and think over everything regarding Amanda. It seemed incredible to actually meet the girl she had only ever known while under hypnosis. She had no idea why she had never thought about going to Florida to look for her.

Amanda had stirred up her life and made her think about things she had not considered in a very long time; one of them being home. Ever since she had joked about going home, she felt the overwhelming desire to actually make it a reality and get the plans made. Whenever she had these types of feelings, she knew they were not to be taken lightly or dismissed. Immediately, she went to her home office and sat down at her desk and uncloaked her patil.

She composed a message to Elder Vargen asking for transfer through his Ascension Gate for the following Minggu, or Sunday as it was known on Earth. She could not imagine the Elder would deny her request as she seldom asked for any time off of her assignment. After hitting the send button, she sat back at her desk and wondered what was driving her to leave Roswell in such a rush. Shaking her head, she realized it was sometimes better not to know.

Just as she was getting up from her chair to get something to eat, her patil beeped at her with an incoming message. She looked in surprise as she saw it was a reply from Elder Vargen already. Thinking it was amazing to hear something so soon, she tapped on the message and sighed in relief as she read the approval for her transfer back to Tuala.

Unfortunately, Elder Vargen moved the beginning date to the following afternoon and only granted four days of leave, which would not be noticed on Earth because he informed her he was going to time her return to Earth to Sunday evening. Shemalla wished it did not have to be so, but it would make it easier with her work schedule. She already had Sunday off, which was already a rare event, but it also meant she would be really tired for her morning shift on Monday.

Instead of heading to the kitchen, Shemalla went to her room and took out her small backpack from under the bed. Just in case she ended up getting out of work late the following day, she wanted to be ready to head out as soon as she got home. She would not need much on her short trip, but there were a few things she wanted to give as gifts to family members.

CHAPTER 32

Daven finally had a few hours available to head over to the Roanoke Colony and, this time, he did not invite Jena or Juila along. Too much drama had been caused by their last visit, and the last thing he wanted to do was to stir up the curiosity of the villagers by bringing them back. He landed his telepod on the beach and cloaked it as he walked away from it to the trail on the bluff.

The winds were fierce as they buffeted him and blew sand up around him as he walked swiftly. The first of the winter storms must be coming in, and he was glad he had decided to visit now rather than after the weather began to get unpredictable. Flying near the water was dangerous enough without any storm surges adding more difficulty.

He just entered the tree-sheltered part of the path when he literally ran into Ozian. "Hey, I didn't expect to see anyone out here. Do you want to walk with me? It'll give us some moments to talk privately."

Ozian looked like he would rather be anywhere other than

alone with Elder Daven, yet he could hardly refuse him. He cleared his throat and looked down at the ground. "I'm sorry I ran off when you were bringing the women home. I don't know what came over me, but I just couldn't leave with you. I felt like I belonged here and now I know why."

"Because of Vinia? Well, I must say you have created quite a stir in our lives, but I'm not upset with you, Ozias. I promise. Can you rest easier now?"

Ozian's expression visibly relaxed, and he nodded as he fell into step beside the Elder. "Are you here at Vinia's request?"

"I am. Why don't you tell me why you're in such a rush to marry Vinia?"

"Oh, well, I wouldn't say I'm in any particular hurry; I just don't see the point in delaying the inevitable."

"By that, you mean being married to Vinia? What if she didn't agree with your timing?"

"I told her I would take as much time as she needed, but I'd be ready the moment she said go!" Ozian laughed out loud as he thought about his future with Vinia. She brought him so much joy, and he merely wanted to get moving forward with his new life on Tuala.

Elder Daven had been reading Ozian's thoughts, even though it was considered rude. Because Ozian was from another world, he had to be extra cautious when it came to his decision with Vinia. He did not want to be responsible for bringing harm to their community or his District by being rash; this was not the time or situation for proper channels. The thoughts he read remained just as he had suspected: genuine and full of love for Vinia, and surprisingly, for Danika as well.

"What about your age difference?"

"Vinia said the same thing! Is there really such a problem with that here on Tuala?"

"No, I just wanted to make sure you had considered it and what it would mean as Vinia got older. If you want to have children of your own, she may not be able to have more, or even want more as she already has four of her own."

Ozian nodded as he considered the Elder's words. He did want to have a family of his own, but if Vinia told him no, then he would have to be content with Danika. She was young enough to know him as her father, and that would probably be good enough if it came right down to it. "I can work with that, whatever Vinia decides."

"You say that now, but are you sure you won't grow to resent Vinia over time? Maybe you'll even call her selfish for denying you children of your own?"

"That's not how things are done on Heliok, Elder Daven. We respect our women and treat them very well. They are responsible for their own bodies, and they decide when children are going to be a part of the family. I will accept whatever Vinia decides."

Daven nodded as he felt the truth behind Ozian's words. He also saw the conversation regarding his name change and asked, "Are you okay with your name being modified to Ozian?"

"I don't want to disgrace Vinia or the village. It seems like a small sacrifice for such a big reward. I will gladly do it if Vinia agrees to have me."

They moved along the overgrown path for several seconds in silence. Daven finally asked the question he most wondered about. "What about your feelings for Juila? You seemed pretty infatuated with her when you first arrived on Earth."

Ozian actually blushed at the memory of how he had behaved. "Well, that's because she's an amazing girl and I was intrigued by her intelligence. I'd never met anyone who was so self-confident in her abilities. The women on Heliok aren't encouraged to go to school or learn any advanced technology."

"What makes you think you'd be content on settling for Vinia then? You don't have much experience with our culture; maybe you won't find it to your liking here."

Ozian shook his head in denial. "I've never agreed with the customs on my home planet. Juila is the perfect example of why; she has ideas and contributions to the world. On Heliok, our planet is dying because the leaders don't allow free thinking and use all available resources.

"Juila was the first girl I had ever really spoken with from outside of my world. Granted, we had the other women and children held captive by Viceroy Blair, but they behaved just as cowed and timid as the women from home. I had no idea there was anything different until Juila began talking with me. I wanted to go to her world to find someone for myself.

"At first I thought it might be her until I met Vinia. When she took over the community, I saw her strength and wisdom and I knew she was the right woman for me. I don't have any other way to put it, but I know Vinia's the one I'm supposed to marry. Age is irrelevant if we both love one another."

"Do you think she feels the same way then?"

"I do, or she wouldn't have asked you to come and talk to her, don't you think?"

Daven smiled at Ozian's reasoning and had to agree he was probably correct. He clapped him on the shoulder and said, "You are wise beyond your years. Can you make sure I have some private time with Vinia so we can talk about you and your prospects on Tuala?"

"Are you saying I'm allowed to stay then? Do I have future prospects here?"

"Yes, I believe you do."

They turned the last corner on the trail and arrived at Vinia's cabin. Ozian nodded his head in respect as he continued walking toward his own home, all the while wishing he could stay and hear their conversation. Daven knocked on the door and went inside after Vinia let him in.

"Thank you for taking the time to see me," Vinia said as she gestured for them to sit at the only table in the room. "Can I get you anything?"

"You're welcome, and no, I just want to talk with you for a while. I hope now is a good time."

"Perfect. After your last visit, there's been quite a bit of talk about the kids. I even heard people talking about me getting married although Ozian insists he hasn't told anyone. I can't imagine how it got out then, but I guess it's inevitable in a town this small."

Daven nodded agreement as he watched Vinia carefully. She seemed nervous, and she was prattling on as if she were avoiding what was really troubling her. "What did you want to ask, Vinia?"

"Are the kids going to be okay? It was pretty tense around here when you left."

"Yes, I think everything has worked out beautifully. I hope you won't mind your daughter marrying the Elder's heir."

Vinia scoffed incredulously at the idea and chuckled nervously. "I never dreamt of such a future for any of my children. I want them to be happy, and if Willian is the one to do that for her, then she has my blessing."

Daven nodded his approval of her assessment of the situation. Although he imagined she probably did not quite understand the scope of the relationship and added, "Valentina didn't really have a choice in the matter. When her life-line joined with Willian's, it took the choice away from both of them."

"That sounds terrible! Will they resent it as time goes on?" Vinia suddenly feared for her daughter's prospects.

"No, as soon as she accepts it, she will only feel perfect contentment, love, and peace."

"And if she doesn't accept it?"

"She'll never find love in that case."

"Oh." Vinia was disheartened by the Elder's proclamation. This was more serious than she had given it credit for when they were all here in her home. At the time, she was more concerned about the problem of dissolving the betrothal and what that would mean for both of them involved. Now it really did impact her daughter and her future happiness.

"They have time to work it out. I came here to talk about your future with Ozian. Will you be happy with him?"

"Of course, but don't you think it's rather sudden? What if he decides he wants to return to his homeworld? I can't go with him, and I can't worry about what it'd do to Danika if he decided to leave."

Thinking about how Vinia viewed Ozian caused Daven to understand more about how her life had played out in her past. She had never had a stable relationship, and it was valid for her to be concerned for her children. Given the fact that Nealan had been taken off-world did not help her to form any other opinion of foreign men, either.

"I've discussed this matter with him at length. He has no desire to return to a world where women are not revered. His planet is dying, and there would be nothing to go home to in any event. He wants his future with you here on Tuala. He has pledged his devotion to you in my presence, and I am convinced of his sincerity. Would you release your fear for that outcome based on my knowledge in this situation?"

Vinia thought about it a moment before she nodded her agreement. "I can do that."

"Do you have any other objections to Ozian's marriage proposal?

"Only concerns for how he'll treat Danika and my other children. I need to keep them safe."

"Absolutely. Ozian will raise Danika as his own if you'd let him. Would you object to that?"

"No! I'd love for her to have a father who can be a good role model for her. This whole village needs good role-models, for that matter. We need another dozen Ozian's for the rest of the broken families!"

Daven laughed out loud and replied, "I'll see what I can do about that!"

Vinia joined him with her own laughter. It felt good to be able to smile and relax for a few minutes. Danika began to fuss in her crib with the added noise. Vinia went over and picked her up. She looked her in the face and quietly asked her, "What do you think about me getting married to Ozian? Would you like to have him here all of the time?"

Danika cooed contentedly at her mother. She could tell her mom was relaxed and it reflected onto herself. She nuzzled close, hoping it was time to eat. When the meal was offered, Danika eagerly latched on and immediately forgot everything else in the room as she closed her eyes with the single-mindedness of hunger.

Vinia draped a cloth over the breastfeeding child and returned to the table to finish her conversation with Elder Daven. This discussion had helped her come to her decision. "I will marry Ozian if you will officiate it, Elder Daven. I want the village to know it has been sanctioned and I want them all to witness it. There has been enough strife in our community, and I don't want this marriage to add anything other than happiness and harmony. This marriage can be a sign of hope for all of our futures here in Roanoke."

"Well said, Vinia. Tell me when you'd like me to do the honors, and I'll be here."

"I'll let you know." Her mind was already racing with plans. She wanted it to be a proper ceremony so nobody could say it was rushed or inappropriately handled.

Petre felt some sense returning and wondered why he was being jostled. What was most confusing was that he was sitting upright yet he was moving down the hallway without any motion on his part. A man dressed in white stepped beside him and reached up to knock on the door they had stopped in front of. He then reached forward and swung the door wide open, moved back behind him, and rolled him into the office where a man sat behind a large, dark desk.

Immediately Petre was reminded of the time he had met with Elder Debbon, and it set his nerves on edge. He did not like the smug expression on the old man's face anymore than he had enjoyed the one on the Elder's. His chair was stopped on the opposite side of the desk, and he heard the attendant leave and shut the door behind him.

"Petre, it's nice to see you awake. I hope you've had a good rest."

"It wasn't very restful. Who are you?"

"I'm sorry, how rude of me. My name is Dr. Stephen Gascon, and I will be personally handling your case. Can you tell me where you're from, Petre?" Dr. Gascon leaned forward and rested his chin on his steepled fingers.

Without any resistance, Petre was horrified to hear himself answer honestly. "I'm from Tuala."

"And you say Tuala is another planet?"

"No, it's the same planet, just a different dimension."

"I see." Dr. Gascon wrote something down on his notepad and then tapped his pen a couple of times on the papers before he asked, "How long have you been here on Earth, Petre?"

"Since Jumat."

"That word doesn't mean anything to me. Do you know the translation for it in English?"

"I don't know your word for it; I only know it as Jumat." Petre's eyes rounded as he snapped his mouth shut. How could this man force him to answer questions when he had no desire to answer him? What kinds of powers did these people from Earth possess? They seemed more powerful even than the Elders themselves. No wonder the Elders were afraid of the *old souls* coming over to Tuala.

"I see." A few more scratches of his pen on the paper as he doodled then he looked up and asked, "How long were you on Earth before you came to this hospital?"

"I came here on my fourth day visiting. I spent the first two nights on a bus and the last night in a room in a tall building."

"Okay, then four days and three nights. I calculate you arrived on a Friday then. So we can say Jumat means Friday. Today is also Friday, Petre. You've been visiting Earth for one week then. Is that what you'd say as well?"

"Yes."

Dr. Gascon wrote: not smart enough to come up with a different term for the word week. "What do you call a month?"

"I don't know." He wondered what this man was getting at with his strange questions. He was swiftly losing interest and patience with him.

"Do you have another term for what comes after a week?"

"Mesan."

"How many weeks are in a mesan?"

"Four."

"Interesting."

"Is there a point to these questions? I'm really hungry, and I have yet to be fed a meal since I've arrived here. How long have I been here?"

"This is your fifth day. I'm sorry to hear you haven't enjoyed your stay so far."

"Enjoyed!" Petre sputtered and laughed out loud. "The burly man who brought me in has given me pills which made me sleep. When I refused to take more, he stabbed me in the butt with something, and it made me sleep. All I've done is sleep since I came here."

"Why did you come here? I see you admitted yourself; you must want help."

The direct question unlocked Petre's foggy mind, and he remembered exactly why he had come. He looked directly at the doctor and said, "I was sent by Lucinden to speak with Stephen Gascon. That's you, right?"

Dr. Gascon looked shaken at hearing the name Lucinden. Only once in his life had he encountered a man by that name and he hoped never again to repeat it. When he was a little boy, he had been kidnapped by a man who called himself Lucinden. While the police had found Stephen later that same day, he had been scared so badly he needed a psychiatrist to help him through the trauma. It had changed him profoundly, and it was also the reason he had entered the field of study in which he found his life's work.

Petre watched in fascination as the self-possessed man across from him turned into a shell of himself. His fear was evident, and it gave Petre great pleasure to have some measure of power back. He took advantage of the momentary silence to press his control. "Lucinden says it's been a long time since he's contacted you."

"Yes, it has been," Stephen whispered.

Even as Stephen's confidence slipped further, Petre found himself gaining strength both physically and mentally as his mission was being accomplished. He recalled Lucinden's exact phrasing as he said, "It's time to give back the gift you were given. If you do not do as you are told, then Lucinden will come to see you again."

An involuntary shudder passed through Stephen. He glanced anxiously over at the wall of shelves and then back to Petre across from him. He did not want to lose the one tie to finding and repaying Lucinden for his childhood terror. He shook his head in denial of Petre's statement. No longer was he a terrified child; he was a grown man with power of his own. All of his years as the Director of Psychiatry had not left him without resources of his own. "I think I'll wait to answer his request. There are still many things I need to learn from you first, Petre."

"Lucinden was pretty vague in his details with me. What happened the first time between you and Lucinden, Stephen?"

"None of your damned business! I'll be asking the questions here, Petre, or you'll pay for your insolence!"

"You're making a mistake if you don't do as Lucinden asks. Don't you know who he is?"

"Yes, he's a sadistic bastard, and we aren't going to be discussing him anymore!"

"He may be that, but he's also powerful enough to snuff out your life where you sit right now. He's given you the opportunity to live, and I suggest you take it."

"Shut up! Shut up! Shut up!" Petre's words were like knives

stabbing into him, causing him more pain than he knew he could still feel. Again he looked over at the object on the shelf and wondered if it were worth keeping. This pain would stop if he would just hand over the thing and get this man out of his hospital. It could all be so simple, yet he would be giving up his power, and that was unacceptable.

Petre caught his repeated glance across the office and turned to see what kept distracting Stephen during their conversation. For several seconds he simply stared in disbelief. Not more than ten feet away from him, there was a samara sitting out in the open for anyone to see or steal. How could this man be so careless with the priceless treasure?

Suddenly it all made sense; Petre had been sent to retrieve the lost samara to replace his own which had been stolen when he had been arrested. He was being tested by Lucinden, and the samara was his payment. It was perfect, and it was his. No longer did he have to muddle through life without the power source backing up his every deal. Wealth would be his again along with a future with Jinya. Once he had this samara in his possession, nothing would stop him from finding his lost love and making her be his bride.

Regaining some composure, Dr. Gascon leaned forward and spoke in a nasty tone to the harbinger of bad news. "I will keep you here, drugged into a stupor, until I find out everything I ever wanted to know about Lucinden and Tuala and there's nothing you can do to stop me!" He sat back with a satisfied, smug grin and felt his power returning to him. He began reviewing all of the things he would do to this patient, ignoring him entirely during his ruminations.

The disclosure of the drug gave Petre exactly what he needed. Straining himself greatly, Petre sluggishly summoned elemy from the earth and sent over a tendril to the samara. If it were a fake, then he would only be tired from his trying. If it were real, then he would use its power to augment his own. At first touch, the power from the crystal skull became evident, and Petre was able to use the strengthened elemy to flush his system of the drugs which were clouding his mind.

In an instant, he had transformed from doped up and sluggish to more powerful than he had ever been. He rose from his chair, much to the chagrin of his interviewer, and he turned to the bookshelf. "I'll be taking this with me," he announced as he walked away from the desk.

Dr. Gascon roared to life as he realized Petre's intention. He raced around the desk and tried to put himself between Petre and the skull of doom, as he had termed it. "That's mine! Sit down, Petre! Guard! Guard! Anyone! I need help in here!"

He suddenly found himself unable to move forward, and his eyes grew wide with fear as he no longer had control over his own body. This felt almost exactly like it had when he was a little child with Lucinden. He felt moisture snaking its way down the inside of his pant leg.

Petre took the crystal skull down from the shelf and caressed it in both of his hands. He missed having this connection of power; it was more soothing than any woman ever could be. Power surged through him, and he could hear a commotion outside of the office as Stephen's cries for help were being answered.

Without another thought, Petre knew he would have enough power to translate himself back home to Tuala. No wonder Lucinden had not made any plans for his return, he had known Petre would do it himself. *This was way too easy*, Petre thought with a grin as he gathered elemy around him. He watched Stephen's eyes register terror as he disappeared from right in front of him.

CHAPTER 34

Amanda's cell phone rang, and she did not recognize the number. With a curious expression, she took the call while she was sitting with her parents at an early dinner. She listened with increased excitement as the woman on the other end explained what was going to be happening.

The call only lasted a couple of minutes, but it felt like a life-time to both Chris and Diane as they could only wonder who their daughter was talking with. Their anxiety was relieved the moment Amanda clicked her phone shut and announced, "This is the call we've been waiting for: the kids are ours! Dad, get the bill so we can get out of here. They're only open for another half hour, so we're going to have to hurry or wait until Monday!"

"On it!" He jumped up and raced across the restaurant to track down their waitress.

"Is this really happening?" Diane asked as she remained rooted to her seat. She had hoped for this outcome, but with how long everything was taking and the lack of communication from any of the county workers, she never believed it could be resolved so swiftly.

"I promise, Mom. Come on; let's get out to the truck so we can be ready to go when Dad gets there." Amanda grabbed up her purse and slung her jacket over her arm. She did not even want to waste time putting on her coat even though it was only in the thirties outside. Her excitement was more than enough to keep her warm until they were safely inside their vehicle.

They had just gotten their seatbelts fastened when Chris jumped into the driver's seat and had the keys in the ignition before his door was shut behind him. As the engine roared to life, he asked, "Where are we going?"

"The county office across from the jail. The woman said they were on the first floor with the red awning."

Chris tried to maintain some semblance of legal while he was pushing the limit of an acceptable speed limit in his haste to get his granddaughters. They had to circle the block once before they found a parking spot. It was pretty far from the building, but they no longer cared. The time was ticking down for the office to close and they ran from the car to the door with the red awning. Ever the gentleman, Chris grabbed the door and held it open for both Diane and Amanda to enter first and was soon following them as they got to the receptionist's desk.

She directed them to a side room where the social worker had all of their paperwork laid out on her desk, ready for signatures. They could hear Emily and April playing in the room next door, but they were not able to see them. It was a comfort knowing they were nearby as they entered the room. Amanda remained standing while her parents took the two seats at the desk.

"I'm sorry for the short notice. Everything just got approved, and I figured you wouldn't mind."

"Not at all," Diane gushed. "What do we still need to do?"

"I've marked all of the locations where you will need to sign with a yellow flag. These documents make you their legal foster parents, and you will have permission to take them back to Florida with you. A social worker will be assigned to you over there, and she will probably visit your house next week to make sure your home is properly safeguarded for children their age. Also, I must caution you that you are not allowed to have any guns in your home as long as you remain foster parents."

"Fine, fine," Diane said absently as she picked up the pen and began meticulously signing her name on the seven different documents. As soon as she finished one, she pushed it over to Chris for his signature.

Chris took another pen from the social worker and added his signature below Diane's. He wished it would be so easy for them to get Carrie out of jail. It seemed there was little hope of her charges being dropped, but they would do their best to care for her children so she would have one less worry during this terrible time in her life.

Once all of the documents were signed, Diane asked, "Can I see the children now?"

"Please wait a couple of minutes. I want to get copies of these documents for you. As soon as you have your copies, then you will be free to take the children out of here without any further delay." She rushed from the room and handed the papers over to the waiting secretary. She came back into the room empty-handed and sat down to wait with them. "You must have some very powerful friends to get this pushed through so fast. I've never heard of this happening before."

Chris raised his eyebrows at her statement. He was unsure of how to respond since he was unaware of any special treatment other than Shemalla saying she would help out as much as she could. It must have been her doing, then, and he was going to have to thank her once they had the children back home.

The secretary came back with a manila envelope in her hand along with the originals in a new case folder. She set them both down on the desk and retreated without a word, yet she did have a slight smile for Diane as she walked by.

"Okay, these are yours. Call me if you have any questions. And here are your kids," she said as the secretary shepherded the two little girls into the room ahead of her.

"Grandma!" "Grandpa!" the girls shouted in unison as they jumped into their laps since they were still seated in the chairs.

"You get to go home with us!" Diane announced happily to Emily as she hugged her tight to her.

"Is Mommy coming with us? Where is she?" Emily asked innocently.

"Mommy has to stay here and take care of a problem. Come on; let's get out of here so these nice people can close up the office and go home to their families." Diane stood up with Emily still in her arms and settled the little girl on her hip. Walking back to the car with both children was definitely the best moment in a really long string of terrible moments.

Amanda brought up the rear, smiling in delight with the outcome of this part of their journey. She still had to work out what they could do to help Carrie which made her think of Carrie's bombshell of a dead twin sister which she had not mentioned to her parents. She also wanted to spend more time with Shemalla to find out what else she might know about the prophecy. But mostly, she wanted to get home to her husband where everything seemed to work out better when he was nearby.

The girls were bubbling with excitement over their new adventure as they were buckled into their seats in the back of the 4-Runner next to Amanda. She had missed these ages with her own daughters and wondered if they were at all similar; somehow she doubted it. They drove back to the hotel, more sedately than they had driven to get the girls, for which Amanda was also grateful.

Once they parked at the hotel and the kids were released from their seatbelts, Diane took one hand from each and led them into the lobby to go back to their room. Chris waited for Amanda and asked, "What's going on with you?"

"Nothing." She wanted to brush it off and worry about it later.

"Start talking, Amanda," Chris said in a tone which told his daughter he meant business.

"Carrie said something in the jail which I'm sure is untrue, and it bothered me. Don't worry about it, Dad." She stepped faster as the wind caught the zippered edge of her jacket and tossed it open. She grabbed the cloth and pulled it closed over her chest.

Chris put his arm around her and tried to shield her from the worst of the wind until they were safely in the lobby. He pulled her in the direction of the seats in front of the fireplace and pointed for her to sit in one of the chairs. He took the one directly across from her and leaned forward, eagerly awaiting her story.

"Carrie told me I should have died with my twin sister. I know it's ridiculous and I shouldn't have even given it the time of day, but..." Amanda looked up from where she had been twisting her fingers together and saw the look on her father's face. "Dad, it's not true, is it? I didn't have a twin, did I?"

Chris closed his eyes and let out a long breath. After a moment, he opened his eyes and looked at his youngest daughter's agonized expression. "I never wanted to keep it from you. That was your mother's doing. She always said it wouldn't do you any good to know about it, but it would hurt you to know. I can see now; it was a mistake to let her convince me to keep this from you. I'm so sorry."

Amanda was stunned by her father's admission. There was no

way Carrie could have been right with this terrible news. How could she have known? Amanda voiced her question to her father and waited to hear his answer.

"I have no idea. She must have found something of your sister's when she was growing up. Your mother kept a few of her things to remember her by. It was really hard on her to lose the baby."

"What happened?"

"We still don't really know; we only know what we were told. Back when you were born, twins were always delivered via Cesarean section. Diane was admitted to the hospital when she was only thirty-four weeks pregnant. Her water had broken, and they took her in right away. Since everything was progressing so fast, they drugged your mom and took her into surgery immediately.

"The doctor came out after only fifteen minutes and told me that the first girl had been stillborn. Her cord was wrapped around her neck, and she was already gone by the time they delivered her. Then they delivered you, and they said you were vigorous and healthy, crying before you were all the way out."

"What happened then?"

"We were crushed, of course. We had the two girls at home, and you were in an incubator, helping to keep you warm since you were a little bit early. There were so many decisions to be made, and we were so sad. We let the hospital make all of the arrangements for her funeral. They called in a clergyman, and we had a memorial service for her at the hospital sanctuary. I'm sure your mother has visited her grave, but I've never been able to bring myself to go. I had you, and you were all I needed."

"Where is she buried? What did you name her?"

"There was a cemetery not far from the hospital where they laid her to rest. Her name was Virginia Ellen Covington. Ellen was for your grandmother. You know that's the first time I've ever spoken her name out loud? I never even got to hold her. They didn't do that back then. They said it was an easier break if you never bonded. I think they were wrong; it would have been a comfort to say goodbye to her." His voice broke, and he felt tears trickling down his cheeks just thinking about the little, lost life who never got to feel her parents' touch or hear their voices tell her how much they loved and wanted her.

"Oh, Dad, I'm so sorry I brought this up. I never even thought about how hard it had to have been for you all of these years. I can be so selfish sometimes." She kneeled on the ground and put her arms around her father's shoulders which shook with the tears of release he had held back for so long. "All I could think about was why I wasn't told, never thinking about how much you lost on the day I was born. I'm sorry, Dad, I'm so sorry." She rubbed his back, wishing she had kept her big mouth shut rather than see how much pain she had caused her beloved father.

Amanda's phone began to ring. She was going to let it go to voicemail rather than take her arms away from her distraught father.

"You should get that," he said as he pulled away and wiped his cheeks with the backs of his hands while he sniffled loudly.

Thinking he probably wanted a little privacy to pull himself together, Amanda nodded and reached into her purse. She opened her phone and hit the button to connect the call. Putting the phone to her ear and looking at the floor, she said, "Hello?"

"Hi, honey. Is everything going okay?" Riccan asked.

Relief rushed through her just at the sound of his voice. She picked herself up off of the floor and settled back into the chair as she said, "Yes, we have the kids. We just got them, in fact. As soon as we can arrange flights, we'll be home. I haven't called the airline yet, sorry."

"Hey, don't be sorry. That's actually good. I'm going to call a plane for you. I'm done with waiting for you to get home, and I certainly don't want you to have to sit around waiting for some stupid commercial flight to finally decide when to bring you home. What good is all of my money if I can't use it to get you home to me?!"

Amanda laughed with relief to hear his plan; it was the best thing she'd heard since the phone call from the social worker. "I'll leave it to you then. Call me when you know what our itinerary is, okay?"

"Will do! I love you!"

"I love you, too." She clicked the phone shut and looked up at her dad. "Riccan's arranging a private jet to get us all home tonight. I hope you don't mind; I kind of just made an executive decision without even consulting you or Mom."

"Don't worry, honey; it was the right decision. Your mom will be much happier at home, and I really can't see how I'd get any sleep in the hotel room with those two rambunctious girls staying in there with us!" His laughter was forced, but he tried to make it sound as normal as possible while he finished composing himself. They were going to have to head upstairs soon, and Diane needed to see him acting like his old self. "Let's not say anything about our conversation just now to your mom, okay?"

"Not today, I won't, but eventually this is going to be discussed."

Chris nodded with understanding. He always knew this conversation was a possibility, but he never believed it would be because of something another of his daughters knew. That was still a mystery to him which he would discover an answer to at a later time.

CHAPTER 35

Shemalla had been right in assuming she would end up getting off work late. Anytime she made plans; it was as if her boss knew she wanted to be somewhere else and made sure to come up with as many trivial tasks for her to accomplish before she was allowed to leave for the weekend. His excuse today was because she was not scheduled to work on Sunday so she would have to make sure her morning duties were completed before she could leave.

She pulled into her driveway and left the car running as she raced into the house and grabbed her backpack from where she had left it on the hall chair. There was no way she could take the time to eat, even though her stomach was rumbling with hunger. Using her forbidden power, she created a sandwich and turned to leave the house. Taking a quick bite, she returned to her car and threw her bag in the passenger's seat.

Carefully looking as she backed up, she noticed a car parked down the street which she had never seen before. She turned around and left the neighborhood the same way she had come in.

The radio was playing her favorite song, so she turned it up and hummed along as she took another bite of her sandwich.

The weather was so cold outside that her windows began to fog up. She had to switch the defroster on in order for the fog to begin to dissipate. She checked her mirrors to make sure the way was still clear as she made the side road turnoff to get to the Gate.

Again, she noticed the same car from her neighborhood. It seemed slightly coincidental for it to be in both places, yet she did not have the time nor the inclination to worry about it much further. Soon enough she would be going through the Gate, and she would be back home in Tuala.

After slowing down for the bumpy, gravel road, she finally reached the end of the 'improved' roads and parked in the visitor's lot of the nature reserve. She grabbed her backpack and slung it around her and pulled it on over her back. Thankful she had eaten on the way, she set a brisk pace up the trailhead to get to the cave where the Gate was located.

Several times she thought she heard noises behind her, but she did not bother turning around to check it out. The only thing which did slow her down was her phone ringing in her backpack. Luckily it was in a side pocket so she could reach around without having to remove it from her back. She saw the call was from Amanda and answered it with concern.

"Hey! Is everything okay?" Her voice was slightly breathless as she continued to climb the hill to get to the cave above. If the call had come only a few minutes later, she would not have had reception.

"Yes, I wanted to call to tell you thank you for whatever you did to help us get the girls back. We are heading home in about an hour. I didn't want to leave without saying goodbye and seeing if there were any way we could keep in touch."

"I'd like that. I'm heading home right now, as well."

"I didn't know you worked this late. I'm sorry to bother you!"

"No, no! I'm heading home to Tuala. Since I talked to you about it earlier, I couldn't get it off of my mind. I'll be back soon so don't worry if you don't hear from me this weekend."

"Cool, I'm glad to hear you're allowed to travel home. Are you on the trail right now? You sound breathless."

"I see you remember that part of the dream too. Yes, I'm on the trail. Another two minutes and you wouldn't have been able to reach me."

"Okay, I won't hold you up then. Call me when you get back, and you're ready to talk. Take care. Bye!"

"Bye for now." Shemalla powered her phone down since it would not be of any use in Tuala anyway. She stowed it back in her pack and entered the overhanging cliff which led to the inner tunnels where the Gate was located. She created a sphere of elemy and walked with confidence. As soon as she reached the last cave, she stepped down in the Gate's depression in the solid granite floor. Only a few seconds went by before she felt the elemy gather around her and take her home.

The many seconds in between the worlds was usually black and silent, a place where she could gather her thoughts and decompress from her work's tensions. The silence was broken with a heartrending, unmistakably female, scream of terror. Shemalla appeared inside Elder Vargen's Residence with her hands covering her ears. "What was that I heard?" she asked out loud. She expected Elder Vargen to be at the controls for the Gate and discovered one of his trusted aides had actually implemented her transfer.

"I don't know what you're talking about. Nobody has used the Gate today except for you." He turned to leave the room and said, "I'll see you on Minggu."

"Thanks," she replied automatically. I guess it was lucky to have Elder Vargen somewhere else, she never really liked or trusted him anyway. Still, it would have been nice to ask him about the odd experience during the transfer. She shook her head without any answer and followed the assistant out of the room and then out to a waiting transport which would take her to her parents' house.

FOLLOWING the woman had seemed like an easy assignment until she decided to leave town. He was certainly not expecting his target to change her schedule, so it had surprised him when she had driven past him in her neighborhood. As if that were not embarrassing enough, now she had led him out to the wilderness.

He shook his head as he continued up the trail, trying to keep as silent as possible on the gravel path while also keeping an eye on where she had gone. It was inconceivable what drove women to do such odd things, including this trip. Still, he was being paid a handsome sum to keep records on everywhere she went, so he doggedly trudged up the path in his penny loafers.

Being so intent on his footing, he almost broke his own cover until he realized she was no longer moving forward. Instead, she had stopped to take a phone call. He moved as close as he could to try to overhear her conversation, but the wind kept shifting directions making it almost impossible. The two words which were very clear were: home and Tuala.

Ducking undercover as she looked around, he almost missed seeing where she turned into the caves. Heedless of noise, he rushed forward and looked into the black abyss. "Damn it, woman!" he whispered to himself. Of course, he had not thought to bring a flashlight on this adventure either, so he was more than a little reluctant to wander inside an unknown cavern.

Wanting to be as thorough in his report as possible, he entered the darkened cave and waited for his eyes to adjust to the dim interior before proceeding further. Keeping the entrance within sight, he went as far as he dared and then had to concede defeat.

Surely, he could wait for her to come back out. How long could she possibly stay inside a cave? Just as he was smiling at his obvious solution, he heard an eerie sound coming from further beyond him. He felt the hair rise on the back of his neck and both of his arms. Then an otherworldly voice which said something like 'ascension.'

This was the last straw; he was certainly not being paid enough for whatever evil was happening in that black hole. His feet could not move fast enough to get him back into the daylight and down the trail to his car. Feeling like a fool, but not wanting to stay a moment longer, the private investigator left the nature reserve and headed back to Roswell to get a drink.

RICCAN WANTED Jena and Juila to be able to meet their cousins as soon as he had discovered they were going to be coming home to Florida. He had sent a message to his father's patil asking if the girls could spend the night at their house when Amanda returned later that evening. Of course, Daven had been more than willing, which led Riccan to wonder what type of drama had been going on for him to be so eager.

The plane was going to be landing in a few minutes, and he scanned the pattern to see if he could see the jet on final approach. Right on time, the aircraft appeared briefly in a clearing and then shot behind another cloud. He could hardly contain his eagerness to see his wife. There was no way he was going to let her be gone for so long again; he would quit his job and go with her before that happened.

Once the jet powered down and the staircase was lowered,

Riccan was out of his car and loping across the tarmac to greet his bride. Chris was holding everyone up as he had stopped to thank the pilot and co-pilot for a smooth flight. He spotted Riccan, clapped the pilot on the shoulder one last time, and then descended the stairs.

Chris gave Riccan a handshake and turned to watch Diane help the kids down the stairs. The girls had insisted on taking the stairs themselves; otherwise, Chris would have taken one himself. He smiled when he saw their smiling faces as they looked around their new surroundings while walking down the stairs, two feet on each step.

Riccan had never even seen pictures of the two little girls. In fact, he hardly even knew about either one of Amanda's sisters or their children or significant others. He kneeled as the girls came closer to their grandpa and asked, "And who do we have here?"

"I'm Emily," the taller of the two girls said confidently.

"It's nice to meet you. I'm Riccan, your Aunt Amanda's husband. I'm glad to meet you. What's your name?" He turned his attention fully to her sister and waited for a reply which was a little longer in coming.

"I'm April." Her whispered reply came just as she ducked behind her grandfather's leg while she continued to peek around him to see the smiling stranger. She stayed hidden while her grandma came down the stairs followed by her aunt. She watched as Aunt Amanda raced over to the man and threw her arms around his neck and kissed him soundly on the lips.

"Let me hold you, April," Diane said as she kneeled and picked her up. April snuggled in close, feeling comforted by her motherly feel. Diane could tell the girl was overly tired but did not want to miss anything on this big adventure. The sooner they got home, the faster they would be able to get them both to bed and begin resuming a new normal life for them.

The pilot had exited the plane and gone to the back to retrieve their luggage. He brought it forward and set it down by where they were standing. "It's good to see you again, Riccan. You should go flying with us soon." He tipped his hat before he turned and went to take the plane back to their home airport.

Riccan picked up two of the bags, and Chris grabbed the third one. The girls did not come with anything other than the clothes on their backs so they would have to do some shopping, which Diane seemed eager enough to do. They turned and led the way back to the car while Amanda took Emily's hand and walked alongside her.

She leaned down and whispered, "You get to sleep in my old bedroom. I'm jealous!"

"I wish I could sleep in my mommy's room," she replied softly.

"Hey, we could probably arrange that if you'd rather." She stood straighter and let her voice carry further as she called out to her mom. "Is Carrie's room available for Emily to sleep in?"

"I'd have to move a few things around, but we could probably get it together. Is that what you want, Emily?" Diane recalled the many boxes which had accumulated over the years in her eldest daughter's room. If it would make her granddaughter feel safer, then it would not matter what she had to do, Emily would sleep in the room tonight.

Knowing what a mess the room had become, Amanda piped in, "We'll all pitch in and get it ready tonight, right Riccan?"

Wishing he could refuse; instead, he nodded and held the back open for Chris to put his suitcase inside. He rushed around and opened the rear passenger door of the SUV for the women as they got near. Amanda sat up front with him as they began the first leg of their trip home.

"I missed you," Riccan murmured so only they could hear up

front. "The girls are coming home for a short visit tonight. Let's try to make this a quick stop, okay?"

"Really? They're coming home? I've really missed them." Amanda was already planning how fast they could rearrange the bedroom so Emily could sleep in there. Suddenly an idea struck her, and she asked, "Could you use some elemy to move the boxes from the bedroom out to the garage. If the girls never saw the mess, they wouldn't know how much effort it would take. They wouldn't have anything remarkable to talk about, and we could be on our way faster."

"You know I try not to do anything outside our own home, but I'll check it out and see if it's possible." He winked to let her know it was definitely happening.

Amanda had her father lean forward so she could whisper the plan to him. She could see from his expression that he liked the plan a lot more than slogging through the house dozens of times carrying heavy boxes of who-knew-what. He nodded and sat back in his seat.

They pulled into the driveway, and Amanda said, "Mom, why don't you show the girls the playset out back while we get the room ready?"

"Okay," she agreed skeptically. She had no idea what they had planned, but she was willing to go with whatever Amanda suggested.

Amanda led the way down the hall and had to push the door to get it to open all of the way. "This," she gestured to the stacked boxes, "all has to go out to the garage."

"Show me where in the garage so I can at least make it as neat as possible."

"What are you planning?" Chris asked.

"I'm going to use one of my skills to get this over with speedily.

No offense, but I want my wife back at home." He grinned to take any sting out of his words.

Chris grinned back, understanding completely. He opened the garage door and stepped aside so Riccan could see the empty third bay. "It can all go over there."

"Why didn't Mom do that in the first place?"

"I don't know. My guess is she planned on doing something with it all until it got out of hand."

Riccan stared at the space for a moment longer before he jogged back to the bedroom. "Wait here. There's no room for all of us anyway," he said as he closed the door behind him after squeezing himself into the path in the room. A couple of minutes later he opened the door fully and pretended to wipe his brow with exhaustion.

Amanda looked past her husband and could hardly recognize the room beyond. Riccan had even used his skill to clean the carpets and make the bed with fresh linens. It smelled clean and ready to use, definitely faster than anything they could have accomplished in an entire evening. "I'm starting to wonder why you hire a housekeeper if you're capable of this," she said in complete amazement.

"We need to get going home." He grabbed Amanda's hand and towed her behind him.

"Wait, I need to say goodbye to Mom and the girls." She tugged her hand back and made him stop. As much as she wanted to be alone with him, she had to do the right thing with her nieces. Besides, she wanted to see her mother's expression to the cleaned room. She opened the back door and called out across the yard. "Mom, the room's ready, and we have to get going."

"Okay, girls, let's go inside and get you settled in your room." Diane rushed the girls along, anxious to see how they might have improved the mess inside the house. She had each of them by the hand and took them over to Carrie's old bedroom and simply stared with her mouth hanging open at the transformation. "Wow," she mouthed over the girls' heads.

Amanda giggled a little and leaned forward to kiss her mother's cheek. "I love you, Mom. I'll call you tomorrow to see how things are going." She kissed her father as she passed him and then let Riccan open the door to the passenger side.

"I wish I had my telepod right now," Riccan said as he started the engine. He knew it was going to be a good twenty minutes before they got home and the girls would already be there by then. He had wanted to talk to his father before he went back home, but now he was certain he would have dropped them off and left.

"Sometimes Earth sucks," Amanda teased, not knowing what was making Riccan so anxious to get home.

"Yeah, you could say that again," Riccan agreed glumly.

Thinking they would have some private time, Amanda told Riccan about her twin sister who had died at birth. Even as she told the story her father had shared, she felt her eyes misting with emotion. She ended with "I'd like to find out where she's buried so I can leave some flowers at her grave."

"Sure, I think that would be appropriate given the circumstances. Why do you think your mom would keep that from you?"

"I don't know, but I promised Dad I wouldn't bring it up with her for now. I did tell him that it would eventually be discussed, but only after we settle Carrie's mess. Speaking of which, what do you think we can do about getting the charges dropped?"

"Unfortunately, nothing. I made some calls and found out she's in pretty hot water. I might be able to get her moved to a safer prison, but she's definitely going to go to trial. I'm sorry."

"It's not your fault; it was her stupid choices which landed her there in the first place. We're doing what we can for her children, and that's all we can do."

Riccan's thoughts returned to Amanda's story about her dead sister. It made more sense for Amanda to have had twins since she was a twin herself. Riccan had always wondered where the gene had come from since twins were not in his family line at all. At least one mystery had been solved, even if he had never shared his concern with Amanda.

CHAPTER 36

Daven was ready to bring the twins home, much to Nena's chagrin. The girls hugged their grandmother goodbye on the patio overlooking the landing field. Inside their hearts, they were touched by Nena's display of emotion as she sobbed again and drew them into tight embraces of farewell.

"We're not leaving forever, Grandma," Juila chided as she pulled back from the hug. She looked her grandmother straight in the eyes, surprised to see she was so small. Her personality was so big that it always caught her by surprise to see her diminutive stature.

"I know, but I can't help wishing you could stay forever!" She wiped the moisture from her eyes and smiled weakly at both of her beautiful granddaughters. She had wished for this relationship for so long, and now that she had it, she could hardly believe how wonderful it felt to finally have them in her life. Her mind wandered back to the idea of them having lived in Tuala all of these anons, and yet, they had been kept from her and Daven. She knew there was a good explanation, but she still could not let go of the idea that they should have been told long before about the relationship so they could have been in the girls' lives as they grew up. *Oh well,* she sighed to herself, *Jehoban knows best. Who am I to question his methods?*

Nena leaned against the railing and waved continually as the girls descended the stairs and marched across the vast lawn toward the telepod.

The girls turned as one to return their grandmother's wave. They smiled at one another at her exuberance, turned, and entered the telepod. Juila made her way up to the co-pilot's seat. Jena took the middle seat in the passenger section of the craft. While both girls were proficient pilots, Juila had a passion for flying which Jena did not share.

Daven blew a kiss toward his wife and then entered the telepod last. He sat down in the left-hand seat and fastened his seatbelt. He looked over to verify both of his passengers were safely secured, and then he initiated the start-up sequence. The telepod rose several inches above the ground and held steady while Daven monitored the control panel to ensure all of the lights remained green and ready for departure.

"Is everyone ready?" Daven asked as his finger hovered over the activation button.

"Yep," the girls replied in unison.

Daven grinned even as he hit the final code to send them on their way. Everything was instantly plunged into darkness as they moved between space and worlds on their way to Earth. The journey which began uneventfully, suddenly took an odd turn as Daven's attention was immediately drawn to something in the vast nothingness between the realms. It was almost as if he were being called into the darkness. Almost as soon as it began, it ended, and they were bombarded with dim light again as they rematerialized in the Stel garage.

Jena knew something was wrong immediately. She had become so close to Daven during their stay at his Residence, and she felt his unease from the back seat. "What is it, Grandpa? Are you okay?"

Daven shook his head slightly as if coming out of a trance. "I'm fine," he assured her as he began performing the shutdown sequence. Initially, he had intended on just dropping the girls off and going back home. Because of the bizarre occurrence, he felt rattled and decided to remain at his son's house for a little while, at least until he could piece together what had just happened.

Jena hurriedly unfastened her seatbelt and moved through the cabin until she could reach her grandfather. She stretched forward and rested her hand on Daven's shoulder. She felt him flinch with the contact which reaffirmed her suspicion about something happening. "Please tell me what's wrong?" she murmured encouragingly.

"I'm sure it was nothing," he replied as he reached up to pat her hand patronizingly. He looked up at her and saw the look in her eyes. Instantly he knew he had misjudged her, and decided to tell her the truth. "I felt something pulling at me while we were transferring here." Daven stopped talking as he heard Juila's quick intake of breath.

"It's too soon!" Juila cried softly.

Daven shifted his gaze swiftly between the two girls, trying to figure out what they were saying to one another. From their expressions, he could tell there was more than what they were saying out loud. "What are you talking about, Juila?" he pressed even as he saw Jena's head shake in negation of her sister's outburst.

Just as Juila opened her mouth to reply, Jena answered, "There was always the possibility this would come sooner. We just hoped it would be in a couple more anons."

Daven was thoroughly confused at the girls' cryptic conversation. "Will somebody please let me in on what's going on? Clearly, you two know something, and it seems to involve me somehow."

Jena sighed and then answered, "When I was a little girl, I began having nightmares about being lost in darkness. The older I got, I started paying more attention to the details and realized it was not some random dream; it was more like a promise of future events. I also began to understand that I was not alone in the darkness; there was someone with me. At the time, I didn't know who the other person was because I hadn't met him yet."

"Do you know now who it is?"

"Yes, it's you."

"Me? Maybe you should tell me everything."

"The details have always been hazy because not all of the pieces had come into place yet. Ever since we've been reunited with our parents, we've started to put together the puzzle. Now that we each have our own samaras, and know that everybody who was in that meeting still needs to get theirs before the prophecy can be fulfilled, it all makes sense."

"I'm glad you think so! I still have no idea what you're talking about."

"The darkness I was always afraid of was the space in between the realms. The pull you felt was of the samara which belongs to you. Somehow your samara has been lost in the darkness between locations."

A terrible sense of dread overcame Daven as Jena's words sank into his understanding. If his samara truly were in the emptiness between, then the prophecy would forever remain unfulfilled. It was common knowledge that anybody or anything which became lost in that realm would remain there for all eternity; there was no coming back from that darkness. "So you're saying the prophecy will remain unfulfilled? My samara is lost to me?"

"Yes!" Juila cried out at the same time her sister shook her head.

"No," Jena said simultaneously. Jena's hand rose, and her fingertips touched her birth crystal. She looked down at the dark amethyst stones and knew she was going to make the journey. "I believe it's my destiny to help you retrieve your samara so the prophecy can be fulfilled."

"But that's impossible, Jena. Nothing has ever been retrieved from between the realms."

"That's exactly what I told her." Juila turned to her sister and practically begged, "Let this go, Jena. You heard Grandpa. This is an impossible task, and I won't risk you! I can't live without you!"

Jena shook her head as her mind raced through the possibilities. Suddenly her mind fixated on one simple solution, and her eyes grew wide with wonder. "It's going to work, Juila, I know it will!"

"What?" Juila cried.

"How?" Daven asked at the same time.

"Through our twin link. When you were lost in space, we were still able to speak to one another through our special link. That is what is going to make the difference! That is what will lead me home!"

"You can't know that the link will work between the realms. I'm not about to let you through yourself between the realms on the idea of something working."

"I have to agree with Juila on this one, Jena. It's too risky."

"No, what's too risky is leaving the prophecy unfulfilled. It would mean we are letting Lucinden win. It says we are unwilling to put our faith in Jehoban and trust that He has given us the proper skills and training to achieve anything with which we set our minds. I, for one, refuse to give in so easily and, frankly, I'm surprised to hear you do likewise, Grandpa." Jena folded her arms defiantly and stared challengingly down at him.

"I don't want to put you in danger, Jena. It's not my place." Daven felt torn between the two options.

"I have an idea to make this safer," Juila suddenly snapped her fingers. As soon as both sets of eyes turned to her, she said, "When I was lost in space, you had Rasa and Sofia here to help strengthen the link. What if I were to have Behn, Jon, Val, and Sofia come over and join with me, don't you think that would be better than just me?"

"If you're going to do that, then you should invite Willian over as well. His link with Val would probably be enough to bring anyone back from between." Jena could hardly keep the tone of bitterness from her voice even as she realized it was probably the best plan of all.

"Are you sure about that? I don't want to do anything which would distract you during this."

"I'm sure. Let's call them and get going. The longer we wait, the more we risk losing everything."

Daven opened the telepod door yet remained behind as the girls rushed into the house.

Jena grabbed the home phone and called Sofia. "Hey, Sofia. This is Jena. Hi! I don't have time to explain, but I need you to come over immediately to my father's house. Please tell me you can leave right now!"

"Sure, I'm already heading out the door as we speak!"

"Great!" Jena hung up and turned to see how Juila was faring.

"Behn, this is Juila. We have a situation with requires your skill as well as your brother's and sister's. Can you come over right now?"

"Are you okay?"

"Yes, but this is to keep Jena alive. Oh, and can you stop by and pick up Willian? I think his bond with Val will be vital to our success."

"This is serious isn't it?"

"Very! Are you on your way yet?"

"Yes! Val! Jon! We need to go right now!" he yelled, barely moving his mouth away from the receiver.

Juila pulled the cell phone away from her ear in pain before cautiously returning to the call. "I'll see you in five minutes! Bye." She had to smile when all she heard was more yelling, and the phone being slammed down onto the receiver. Turning to find her sister right next to her, they both spoke at the same time, "They're on their way."

They broke out in laughter even though the situation warranted a more serious response. If they could not find a way to laugh, then they were apt to begin crying and that would not help the situation and could actually interfere with their success.

Juila was the first to regain her composure as she asked, "Are you sure this is the meaning of your nightmares?"

Jena nodded solemnly. She wished she were wrong, but her senses were all screaming at her to get moving and take action immediately. Even this delay while waiting for their friends was causing her anxiety. She looked at the clock on the microwave in the kitchen where they stood. Only two minutes had passed since they had hung up the phones. "You stay here and wait for every-one. I'm going to get more information from Grandpa on what he felt. If we can pinpoint the place in the journey, we might be able to decrease our time between and increase our chances of success."

"You have to succeed, Jena, I would die without you!"

"I know you think that right now. I'll do my best to stay alive; I want it as much as you!" She leaned forward and grabbed her sister in a tight embrace. "We're going to get through this, and then my nightmares will stop. I can't tell you how happy I'll be to finally sleep peacefully all through the night."

"I'll enjoy that as well so I can sleep in my own bed!" Juila teased as she wiped a tear from her cheek before they broke apart and grinned at each other.

Jena left hurriedly as she felt herself growing emotional again. It was best to leave it on a humorous note if it turned out to be the last thing they ever said.

"I heard that, and you better not mean it!" Juila yelled from the kitchen. "I'm still in your head, remember?" Juila wandered over to the foyer so she could see when the cars pulled into the driveway. Surely, they would be arriving soon. It felt like an eternity had passed, and yet she was certain it had only been another one to two minutes.

CHAPTER 37

Jena climbed into the co-pilot's seat of the telepod and said, "Can you please shut the telepod door. I don't want to have any interruptions before we leave." She knew Juila was listening; in fact, she planned on it. Juila needed to know everything Daven told them, but Daven would be more comfortable only discussing it with Jena. She was sure he had no idea how perfect was the communication link between herself and her sister.

As the door closed, Daven asked, "What do you think are our chances of success?"

"Pretty good if we can get clear on what you felt. Tell me, at what point in our transfer did you feel the strongest pull? How many seconds in were we before it began?"

Daven closed his eyes and began to replay the journey in his mind. He expected Jena to join his thoughts and was pleased to feel her presence in his head. Jena was quite talented at mind-reading, better than himself even.

"Focus, Grandpa!"

Smiling at Jena's chiding, he did as he was bid and replayed every piece of their journey in slow motion so he could take the time to study everything before he moved on. Jena was actually the one to notice the signal even before Daven did. She mentally tapped Daven and pointed out what she discovered. Daven agreed it was the first sign. Jena noted the time, and they finished the review without any further notations.

"That was great, Grandpa. Now, I think we should switch to Dad's telepod since it has a more sophisticated navigation system with plenty of fail-safes built in."

"Good thinking," Daven agreed even as he worried about his ability to use his son's state-of-the-art telepod.

"I'll set it up according to your coordinates, Grandpa. Don't worry; we're going to succeed. I think for safety's sake, we'll end our trip in Tuala since we'll be closer to there than here. We can come back to Earth after we've rested. How does that sound?"

"I'll defer to your wisdom." He pressed the door button and stood up to leave. He waited for Jena to exit first even as he wished they would not have to go at all. It would be so much easier to forget everything he had experienced. If anything happened to Jena, Riccan would never forgive him for his carelessness.

"Don't worry, Grandpa; if anything happens to me, you won't be around to be blamed either. We'll sink or swim in this together."

"Somehow that doesn't instill any confidence in me for this trip." Daven only whispered this to himself since he knew he was not going to change Jena's mind now that it was made up. He spoke louder and asked, "Were your parents home yet?"

"I didn't see anyone inside. I hope they aren't or they would probably try to stop us from going. We both know that can't happen or the prophecy won't be able to be completed." Jena realized she did not have the remote to her father's telepod, so she concentrated on where she knew it was kept and suddenly it appeared in her hand. She dangled it from her finger after she hit the door button, and said, "After you."

"You take the pilot's seat since you're more familiar with this craft than I am."

"Okay, let's see." She mused over the different controls as she activated the telepod and began setting in the coordinates taken from her grandfather's mind. The telepod did not want to accept her directions since they indicated a stop in a location where there was nothing in existence. Jena sighed as she realized she was going to have to manually control the craft while they were between, which was going to be tricky since there were absolutely no perceptions available in that space. She really had planned on using the computer system to stop for her.

Use the manual override to set the coordinates, Juila spoke into her head. *If you have trouble getting it to take, I'll come out there. Sofia just drove up and parked, and I think I can see Behn's car at the end of the driveway. We're almost ready to start.*

Thanks, Jena thought back to her, and she smiled at how wonderful the mind link could be in stressful situations. Her fingers began to shake as her nerves kicked in. She was planning an impossible trip and hoping for a perfect outcome. If her faith in Jehoban had been any less, she would have thrown up her hands and walked out of the telepod in defeat.

Using her sister's instructions, she managed to set the coordinates into the system even though the light remained red. It bothered her slightly to imagine taking off knowing the telepod indicated a problem, but in this instance, it could not be helped. She buckled up her seat harness and listened in as her sister greeted their guests at the front door.

"Hi, Sofia. Please go and sit in the living room. I'll explain in a second." Juila pushed past her friend and waved anxiously for the four newcomers to hurry up and get inside. "We don't have any time to waste, run, run!"

Behn was the first to arrive inside where he barely hugged Juila and said, "Just tell us what to do, and we'll be ready!" He moved through the foyer and nodded toward Sofia. To say he was surprised to see her there would have been an understatement. It was not his place to say anything, so he kept his thoughts to himself. When this was all over, he was certain to get a more thorough explanation.

Willian was the last to enter the house. He nodded acknowledgment to Juila as he walked past her and looked around trying to find Jena. Out of courtesy for the house he was in, he sat across from Valentina rather than next to her, even though his eyes fixated on her and wondered what she thought since she had remained elusive ever since they had been confronted by Jena.

With everyone seated and looking to Juila for what to do, she remained standing. "Willian, I need you to sit next to Val and hold hands with her." Seeing him begin to argue she held up her hands and said, "I don't have time for niceties. Just move. Sofia, can you scoot over, so Willian has room on the couch. I know it's tight with so many of you, but I'm also going to sit there so we can link minds to help guide Jena home."

"Where's Jena that she needs so much guidance?" Willian asked, suddenly scared for his ex-betrothed.

"She's traveling with Elder Daven between the dimensions to search for something."

"For a second there I thought you were saying she's staying between," Willian chuckled nervously.

"That's exactly what I'm saying, which is why you are all needed."

"What!" Willian exploded off of the couch and rounded on Juila, towering over her in his fear. "Staying between the dimensions is tantamount to a death sentence. It's the first thing we all learn when we're taught to fly telepods. How can you be so calm while you're saying she's planning on going where nobody can possibly survive? She's your twin, for Jehoban's sake, you should be talking her out of this insanity!"

Keeping her voice calm even though she was far from feeling it, she held up her hands in surrender and replied, "Don't you think I tried that? Have you ever talked her out of something she's set her mind on doing?" Seeing his look of defeat, she continued. "I haven't either. This has been her destiny. This journey is the reason why her birth crystal has remained so dark. We don't have time to argue the merits of this trip; it's happening. Please sit down and prepare your mind for me to connect with Jena to give her the best chance of survival."

Juila's words haunted him, and Willian's knees seemed to buckle as he wilted back onto the couch and automatically grabbed Valentina's hand for the comfort he was certain to get with their tight bond. Immediately, he could feel his tension begin to dissipate even as his heart raced for Jena's perilous journey.

Juila also sat on the couch next to Behn and took his hand. "Everyone grab one another's hands so we can link our bodies and minds. If you love Jena, let me access everything you have and don't hold back anything. Is everyone ready?"

There was a momentary shuffling as the participants complied with Juila's instructions. Silence descended upon them as Juila called out in her mind, *We're ready to begin, Jena. Are you prepared?*

As ready as I'll ever be, she answered. Turning around to where Daven sat in the back seat, she said out loud, "Here we go."

While her sister had been assembling the team, she had been making her own preparations. Daven was tethered to her with a hundred-foot rope. He was sitting in the back seat, unbuckled, next to the still-open cabin door. When they were between, he was going to move outside of the craft and attempt to grab what he had felt. Since there were no sensory perceptions, he was going to be guided purely by instinct.

She watched for Daven to nod his readiness before she hit the activation button which sent them into the darkness. "Take a deep breath and hold it. We're only going to have less than a minute before everything will go very wrong." Seeing the flashing red warning lights on the glass panel, she pressed the button. Even as she felt herself dissolving, the link with her sister became a massive envelope around her, making her smile at the effectiveness of love being a solid anchor.

Two and a half seconds had passed before something felt different. On the edge of her perceptions, she could feel a desperate call for help. The more she concentrated on it, the clearer it became. She had no way of knowing if Daven were reacting, but she had to assume he would since he was the first to have noticed it.

Daven felt pulled, almost as if he were magnetized, and he concentrated on moving himself toward it, which was trickier than he had anticipated since he could not use any of his senses other than his instinct to guide him. There was an unnerving sensation of floating with no way of verifying the veracity. Although time was irrelevant between the dimensions, Daven was painfully aware of the passing of time as he realized he needed to breathe. Knowing this would be his best indication of time, he focused only on that aspect as he continually searched for the distress signal.

Finally, he came into contact with whatever it was which had spoken to him. Another few seconds passed, and then he felt an explosion of feeling pouring through his body, unlike anything he had ever experienced before. Without knowing if he were succeeding and hoping he had his arms around it, Daven began praying for the best. Just when Daven thought he would pass out from the lack of oxygen, he began to notice his surroundings appearing around him.

CHAPTER 38

Riccan was surprised to see both Sofia's and Behn's cars in the driveway when he pulled up and parked in the garage. He had expected a family reunion with his wife and daughters, possibly with his father still there, but not outside company. This definitely changed his plans for the evening, and he wished he had been consulted before the kids invited their friends over.

He punched the remote to close the garage door behind him as he turned the ignition off and got out of the SUV. He opened the back door and pulled Amanda's luggage out even as he saw Amanda getting out of the passenger side of the vehicle and begin to walk toward the door to the house. "Wait for me," Riccan called. He did not want to miss any part of the reunion, and he rushed to get beside his wife.

"I saw the two cars outside and I'm curious as to why the kids would be here when Juila and Jena are at their grandparents' house. You must be wondering why they're here as well, right?" She turned to Riccan and cocked her head sideways as she saw an odd expression cross her husband's features. "Do you know why they're here already? Are you up to something, Riccan?"

"No! I'm just as surprised as you are." He struggled with the luggage for only another second before he gave up and made the bag disappear up into their room to be handled later. He brushed off his hands and said, "There, that's better. Let's go inside and see what's going on."

Amanda smiled at her husband's unusual display of power. She stepped through the door Riccan held open for her, expecting to hear voices from inside. Everything was curiously silent, causing her steps to slow down and let Riccan take the lead. She did not have a good feeling about the situation as they walked down the long hallway past the library and office toward the living room.

The edge of the couch came into view, and Amanda spotted Juila sitting there with her eyes closed. Amanda smiled and quickened her step as she turned to Riccan and said, "I didn't know the girls would be home!" She stopped moving forward when she discovered all of the kids lined up on the couch, holding hands, with eyes closed, and no expressions whatsoever on their faces. "What's going on? Riccan, what's wrong? Where's Jena?"

"I don't know, Amanda. I don't like this any more than you do." He took in the entire scene and realized something important was happening which probably should not be interrupted. He kneeled next to Juila and gently took the limp hand from her lap into his own.

Immediately, he felt the pull of power against his will, and he did not fight Juila; instead, he tried to make sense of what she was doing. Juila had woven a powerful rope of elemy connecting herself with her sister. It was unclear why this was necessary, yet, knowing how close Juila was with Jena, Riccan allowed his power to be drawn further into the connection.

Juila felt her father's power and was relieved to have another trained mind enter the scene. If anything were to go wrong, surely he could understand the steps to take to fix whatever situation arose. Just when Juila felt her sister's link weakening was exactly when Riccan had entered the grouping, giving Juila just what she needed to keep the connection together.

Amanda watched in horror as her husband seemed to be caught up in whatever spell had overcome all of the others in the room. She had no idea if she should try to intervene or keep her distance to be kept out in case they needed help. The indecision made the waiting seem so much longer.

Her initial joy of seeing her daughter was rapidly replaced with fear for where Jena could be that she was not included in this strange tableau. Her last idea made her think it was probably because Jena was not there that this was happening. Something was wrong with Jena, and they were trying to help her, of this, she was suddenly positive. She kneeled on the floor next to Riccan, ready and willing to help if she should be needed.

Your mother's here, Juila heard her father say in her head. She mentally nodded acknowledgment but declined from bringing her into the connection. Unless something went wrong, they had more than enough to stay linked and she did not want the confusing distraction of their mother's thoughts interfering.

Juila knew exactly when the telepod had ceased moving through space, stopping between the dimensions. The link had a blurry feel to it, like static sounds on a bad phone connection, which made her skin prickle with goosebumps. This was not a place where people were supposed to stay and she would be glad when her sister finally passed through it.

Her instructions were only to provide a link which would guide her sister home in case the telepod malfunctioned. So far, nothing seemed to be going wrong, but she would not relax her diligence until she knew Jena to be safely in one world or the other. The seconds crawled by and she poured loving thoughts toward her sister and was comforted by having them returned.

Juila felt the connection strengthen as the telepod finally moved back into Tuala. She almost cried out in relief when Jena told her they were getting ready to power down the telepod at their grandparents' house. She untangled everyone from the link and gently gave them each back their own power. With a smile of triumph on her face for her sister's safe deliverance, she opened her eyes and said, "She's okay!"

"Thank Jehoban," Willian said in relief. "Why exactly was this necessary?" His tone immediately informed Juila that he was unhappy with being used without proper explanation.

"Yes, I'd like to hear your answer as well," Riccan murmured, still holding Juila's hand. "What were you doing?"

Juila's triumphant expression suddenly turned serious as she realized she was going to have to explain what they had done without her sister by her side. This was not going to be an easy conversation, given the risk they had taken. She only hoped they had succeeded in their mission since Jena still had not reported whether or not they had retrieved anything from between the dimensions.

"Jena's been having dreams about this particular event for most of her life," Juila began.

Willian interrupted rudely by adding, "Those were nightmares. Are you saying she just lived her worst nightmare and you made us all a part of it? How could you, Juila?"

"Just one moment young man, please let Juila talk," Amanda replied, wondering who this boy was who would be included in the group Juila most likely had assembled. She kneeled next to her daughter and waited for her to continue.

Riccan stood up and crossed his arms in concerned concentration as he worried over everything which could have gone wrong. He was not happy with all of this happening without their knowledge or consent. He was definitely going to be having a conversation with his father when this was all settled.

"It's true she'd always thought of it as a nightmare, but mostly because she didn't understand it. Once it all came together, she was most insistent on getting it handled immediately. She didn't leave me any more choice in the matter than she did the rest of us. There was no stopping her from taking this assignment and hopefully succeeding."

"So we don't know if she were successful or not? What was the point then?" Willian asked hotly and then subsided from further comment at Riccan's withering gaze.

"I don't know who you are, but I must insist you remain quiet until I find out if Jena is going to be okay. Juila?" Amanda faced Juila and waited.

"Just a second, let me check." She turned her thoughts to Jena and said, *Mom and Dad are here, and they have lots of questions. What do you want me to tell them?*

We have a situation here. We went into this with just myself and Grandpa, and now there are two other people on board the telepod. I don't have any answers yet, but I'll keep you updated as soon as I know anything. I'm sorry you have to deal with our parents alone.

But what about the power Grandpa felt? Did you locate it?

Yes, and I feel it even stronger now, but I haven't seen anything to indicate anything was recovered except this man and woman.

Okay, I'll report this to everyone. I love you.

I love you, too. Thank you, Juila, this was a lot easier knowing I was never alone. It was much better than in my dreams.

The entire conversation lasted less than a fraction of a second, so Juila immediately was able to report Jena's findings to the group. The looks of relief mixed with curiosity for the two new passengers was almost comical. Then Juila realized her mother had not known who Willian was and thought a belated introduction would probably be appropriate.

"Mom, you should probably know the guy at the end of the couch is Willian." She had spoken softly, only for her mom's ears since she did not want to make a big production out of anything until Jena had a chance to come home and be a part of the conversation.

"Oh," she mouthed back soundlessly and shifted her eyes over to where Willian was still staring in their direction. It made sense now that he had been concerned for Jena's safety, given that they had been betrothed for so many anons. He also noted the fact that Willian was still holding Valentina's hand even though everyone else had let go since their connections were no longer required.

She had so many questions but refrained from asking any of them until the whole family was back together. "Did Jena say when she was returning home?"

"No, but she did say she'd keep me informed as she learned anything new."

"Maybe we should go to them," Riccan suggested.

"They took your telepod. We don't have room for everybody, and I don't think it'd be very nice to leave them here, after all they've done to help."

"No, you're right; that would be rude." He was surprised to hear they'd taken his telepod. "Why were they in my telepod instead of my father's?"

"They wanted to have the best navigation system and Grand-pa's just wasn't as good as yours."

Riccan felt proud that his invention could be so useful in

keeping his family safe. Once again, he was glad he had gone into the technology field of telepods so he could achieve this goal. It made him wonder whether or not he should actually quit working there or if he should continue to safeguard his family and countless others with his innovations.

CHAPTER 39

Strangely, Daven could see outside because the telepod door was still open. He had no idea how it had been accomplished, but he was kneeling on the floor. His attention was drawn back inside as he heard whimpering. Looking down he jumped slightly as he realized there were two other people also inside the telepod who had not been there when they had left the garage.

Daven hurriedly pushed himself forward as he tried to assess the situation. The people turned out to be a woman and a man who were holding one another. The woman appeared unconscious and the man was sobbing uncontrollably. Daven's healing instincts activated immediately as he noted the lack of breathing on the woman's part.

He shoved the man to the side and linked in immediately with her life-line. There was very little left; she was on the verge of being lost forever. He drew strength he did not know he possessed and poured it into the woman's body until he could feel her start to fight for her own survival. Only at that point did he begin to pull away and assess her numerous health issues.

Her lungs appeared to be singed inside and filling with fluid causing her labored breathing. He healed the tissues, and her breathing became a normal pattern of health. She had minor burns on her hands and a gash across her scalp which he healed as well.

When her eyes opened, he withdrew all of his healing power from her and helped her to sit up. "Where am I?" she asked.

"I'm not sure," he replied honestly as he looked over to Jena with a questioning expression.

"We're outside your Residence. In just a moment I'll have the telepod powered down, and I can help you." Jena rushed through the final procedures even as she unbuckled her harness. She turned in her seat and gasped as she saw who else was in the telepod with them. "How did he get here?" She held her hands up to her mouth in astonishment and fear.

Daven heard her tone and looked more closely at the babbling and crying man. He could hardly believe his eyes as he realized who he was. Then the man moved slightly and revealed what he had carried in his hands. Daven immediately reached down and took the object from his grasp and finally understood what had drawn him to that particular spot in between nowhere. This was his samara, and it had called out to him.

"I was chosen, I was chosen, I was chosen," the man kept whispering over and over in a bizarre mantra made almost unintelligible from his panicked sobbing.

Daven tucked the samara into his pocket and reached down to help the man sit up. He had questions, and he was determined to get answers. First, he had to find out why he was so distraught before he was going to get anything coherent out of him. Seeing his eyes remained unfocused, Daven slapped him across the face.

"What's wrong with you? Petre, can you hear me?" Daven

kneeled in front of him, close enough to see sense returning to his expression.

"I was chosen," Petre repeated as he looked Elder Daven in the eyes. "I don't know why, but I was chosen."

"Who chose you?"

"I don't know. They were in my head; they kept me alive until you could find me. They told me I was chosen."

"For what were you chosen?"

"I don't know." Petre shook his head as he tried to make sense of everything, yet nothing seemed to fit anymore. His body began to tremble with shock and he drew his arms around his legs pulled up to his chest and rested his forehead on his knees. He started to rock back and forth, still seeing the men in his head telling him he was chosen. "Where is the woman? I felt her with me. Where is she?" Petre suddenly lifted his head and looked around. Relief spread through him when he saw her lying on the floor nearby. "Is she going to be okay?"

"Yes, I believe so. Do you know who she is?"

"No, I don't know her, but she needed me. She needs me still. I have to make sure she's okay." He scooted across the floor and gently touched her cheek. Feeling her warm and healthy calmed him down and his trembling began to ease. He would make sure she stayed safe, it was his duty, and he would be there for her as long as she needed him.

Elder Daven, going against protocol, was listening in to Petre's thoughts and wondered what had happened between the worlds to make such a drastic change in this man. Petre was known for his selfish, crass ways, especially where women were concerned. What he saw in Petre's mind was so totally changed as to be almost unrecognizable.

Petre looked up at Elder Daven and asked, "Were you able to save the samara as well?"

"I was, but it will be staying with me." Daven had toyed with the idea of letting Petre believe it had been lost, but it went against all of his teachings. Seeing the relief on Petre's face as he heard the news proved he had been correct in owning the truth.

"Good, it belongs to you, you know. I'm glad you saved it." He turned back to face the woman and picked up her hand and held it between his own. "Please wake up. Tell me your name."

Almost as if she had been waiting for the invitation, the woman's eyes opened and she smiled weakly up at Petre. "It was you. You saved me from the darkness. You kept me from being lost and alone forever. Thank you!"

"I'm just glad I was there to help. Can you sit up? What's your name?" He supported her arm as she struggled to move into the telepod seat behind her. He remained in physical contact even as he took the seat beside her, never taking his eyes off of hers.

"Thank you. My name is Tirsha." She looked at Petre first and then turned her gaze to see Elder Daven and finally Jena. "Oh, I'm sorry I didn't notice the two of you. You must think me so rude."

"Not at all," Daven assured her. There were so many questions rolling through his head and he could see Jena was also intrigued. "Jena, I'm assuming you've let them know we're alright?"

"Yes. They are very relieved and asking when we will be returning."

"Very shortly, as soon as we get these two sorted out." He turned back to their unexpected guests and asked, "Would the two of you mind coming inside so we can figure out how you both ended up where you were?"

"Sure, I'd like to figure it out myself." Petre stood up and offered his hand to Tirsha. He was more than pleased when she accepted his invitation. Together they stepped off of the telepod, and the group walked up to the terrace of the Residence. It was such a lovely day; they opted to sit in the sunshine after such a dark and harrowing experience.

Daven's staff were as efficient as ever and had steena tea delivered within seconds of their arrival on the patio. Just as Melba retreated into the house, Nena came outside with a wide grin of welcome for her husband and granddaughter. Her smile lost some of its sparkle when she noticed Petre sitting at the table, but she held her tongue until she could discover the reason for this visit.

"Daven! I didn't know you'd be coming back so soon, and with Jena even!" She kissed her husband on the cheek warmly and smiled fondly at Jena. She turned to the newcomers and said with a clipped tone, "Petre." Her tone changed dramatically when she addressed the woman seated next to Petre, "I don't believe we've ever been introduced. My name is Nena; I'm Elder Daven's wife."

The woman looked startled as she finally took in Daven's clothes and their surroundings. She had been so disoriented that she failed to recognize she was in much-esteemed company. Suddenly shy, she looked down at her lap, seeing her clothes were stained with black streaks and torn, she brushed ineffectually at the dirt in an attempt to be more presentable. "My name's Tirsha. Thank you for your hospitality; it is very...unexpected."

Nena raised her eyebrows in question at Daven and received a puzzled expression in return. This was turning out to be a very odd day. Nena sat down on the other side of the woman and hoped she would hear what was certain to be a very interesting story. She poured tea into the glasses and handed them out to everyone.

Daven cleared his throat as he was the last to sit. "Tirsha, can you tell me how you ended up where we found you?"

"I really have no idea, Elder Daven. I'm sorry to have interrupted you and created such a fuss."

Waving his hand in dismissal of her worry, he continued, "What is the last thing you remember then?"

Tirsha considered his question seriously and then slowly began to recall the events before her rescue. "It was dark, and I got turned around. I was upstairs in my house, and there was smoke filling up every room. I was trying to find my daughter so I could save her…oh no! I need to help my daughter! I have to get back to my house! Please, can you take me there immediately?" Tirsha jumped up from her seat and looked ready to run back to the telepod.

"I understand your fear, Tirsha, please sit back down."

"I can't! Didn't you hear me? I need to save my daughter!" Tirsha took a step away from the table, feeling tears of hopeless despair at her situation.

"There's time, I promise. Once you tell us everything, I will be able to get you back in time to save your daughter. Please sit back down and finish your story."

Seeing she was not going to be taken anywhere until she finished, she felt defeated and wilted back into her chair. She did not understand how Elder Daven could be so unfeeling as to keep her here when her daughter could still have a chance at being rescued.

"Please continue, Tirsha. This is important." Daven felt compelled to hear her story, thinking it might be some sort of clue for using his samara which was resting uncomfortably in his pocket, jabbing itself into his thigh as he sat.

Tirsha felt tears of frustration dripping down her cheeks, making clean streaks appear in the filth covering her face. "My house somehow caught fire. I was trapped upstairs when the fire began billowing up the staircase. I could hear my daughter screaming for me down in the kitchen. I wasn't able to get to her. I tried to fight my way through the flames, but the heat drove me back. In a desperate act, I gathered elemy and translated myself out of the house. I was only trying to get outside, but I somehow messed up and never made it to where I intended. Instead, I ended up finding this man." She looked over at Petre with admiration and wonder. "You saved me."

Petre had never experienced anyone looking at him in such a manner before and he was suddenly shy of the attention. He looked down into his lap and felt like a fool. He had done nothing to help her, but he was thankful he had been of assistance to her, no matter how it had happened.

Daven turned to Petre and asked, "Petre, how did you end up where we found you?"

Knowing better than to lie to an Elder, Petre opted for the truth. "I was sent to Earth by Lucinden to retrieve what you have in your pocket. I mistakenly believed I could properly harness its power to take me back home to Tuala. Somehow, I ended up getting stuck between the two worlds. I don't know how or why, but I'm very grateful that you rescued me...us." He rapidly amended as he glanced hastily at Tirsha.

Nena visibly startled when Petre mentioned Lucinden's name. This was the third occurrence in such a short period of time of Lucinden's meddling in affairs which ended up affecting them personally. This was more than coincidental and it was starting to scare her. She did not like the idea of Lucinden becoming so powerful as to start creating events with which they would have to become involved.

Daven stood hastily and said, "I'll be right back." He did not wait for an answer but walked swiftly into the house. At the mention of Lucinden, Daven felt the need to get his samara into a safe hiding place inside his Residence where it would not be at risk of being taken from him. Thinking about how close he had come to never getting his samara made it even more urgent for him to safeguard it until he could properly claim it as his own.

He reached the Ascension Gate room and created a towel in which he could wrap his samara and keep from touching it again until he was ready. With his hand wrapped, he reached into his pocket and retrieved the small crystal skull. He held it up to inspect it for the first time, wishing he could spend more time exploring its depths. With great reluctance, he pulled the towel over the top of it and set it in the niche next to Nena's. He reset the ward to guard it and swiftly returned to his guests on the terrace.

The table had remained silent while Daven was gone. He cleared his throat and asked, "Tirsha, tell me exactly when you left your house. We need to be careful not to return to your home before you left, but we want to get back as close as we can after your departure."

"I was just getting ready to start dinner, just before my husband got off of work at the docks."

"Where are you from?" Petre asked.

"The Port of Cresdon."

Jena had a funny feeling come over her and decided she would ask the question which popped into her head no matter how odd it seemed. "What is the date, including the year, Tirsha?"

Raising her eyebrows at the strange question, she answered confidently, "It's the sixth of Elul, 3440. Why?"

Everyone's eyes rounded with surprise at Tirsha's statement, yet nobody made any reply as they all considered how long Tirsha had been lost. Daven was the first to recover his voice and said, "That was a good question, Jena. Thank you."

"What? Why was that such a good question? I don't understand." Tirsha was getting even more upset with these people and their obvious unwillingness to help her with her daughter.

"Today's date is actually the twenty-fifth of Adar in the year

3450. Somehow you managed to push yourself ahead in time by over a declan. Since you are from the Port of Cresdon, your house fire would have been recorded in the records. I can see what became of your daughter. What is her name?"

"Corva." Her reply was almost whispered as she tried to understand how she could have lost so much time.

Jena gasped as she heard the name. It was too much of a coincidence to think that the little girl she had been raised with for the first six anons of her life could be the same girl this woman had thought to have lost in her house fire. She leaned toward her grandfather and spoke quietly. "That's Barla's foster-daughter's name. The timing is also right, and so are the circumstances of her coming to live with Barla and Captain Ahn. Do you think it could be true?"

"What could be true?" Tirsha asked excitedly as she strained to overhear the conversation across the table. "Do you know my daughter?"

"I think so. Let's go check the records, Grandpa." Jena jumped up at the same time Daven did, and they raced into the house together to investigate.

CHAPTER 40

"Oh, my!" Juila exclaimed as she discovered the identity of the man rescued from between the dimensions. She looked up in horrified amazement at her parents and said, "Petre MacVeen is the man they rescued."

"What?!" Riccan exploded. He did not want his daughter anywhere near that man. His paternal instincts were kicking in, and he stood up, ready to charge into battle, he would use the other telepod to get to his father's house if he had to.

"It's okay, Dad," Juila continued to hold his hand, restraining him from going very far. "He's mostly incoherent, and Grandpa has the situation completely under control."

"I suppose," Riccan said sullenly, still wishing he were where the action was taking place. Getting his information second-hand was harder than he imagined it would be. The mention of his father reminded him that he was not without his own methods of protection, including mind control over Petre if the situation warranted such drastic measures.

He sat down on the edge of the coffee table and gestured

for Amanda to come closer to him so he could put his arm around her for mutual comfort. This was not the homecoming he had planned for her, and he looked up to see if he could tell what she was thinking. Her face was unusually blank of any expression, which worried him more than anything.

"The woman's name is Tirsha. Grandpa and Jena are going inside to check the records about Tirsha's daughter Corva. Jena thinks this could be the mother of Barla's foster-daughter." Juila looked up at her mother and said, "She's the same girl you saw in your visions, Mom. This would be amazing if Corva could have her mother back. It's been more than ten anons. Can you even imagine?"

"Yes, Juila, I actually can imagine. I got you and your sister back after even longer than that, and it's been the most amazing adventure. I hope Corva and Tirsha will have an easier time of it." Amanda smiled warmly at her daughter, still wondering why Jena was unable to come home. "What was in Jena's dream that made her think she needed to risk herself?"

Juila looked distinctly uncomfortable, yet she knew she would have to tell eventually. "Jena said if she didn't go, then the prophecy would not be able to be fulfilled. She said it was now or never and I've learned to trust her instincts."

"Yes, I imagine you would." Amanda tapped her bottom lip as she tried to put all of the pieces together. If the prophecy were dependent upon them each having their own samara, then it stood to reason a samara had been what had drawn Jena. The fact that Daven had been with her seemed to reinforce the idea since he still had to find his. She looked first at Riccan and then shifted her gaze to her daughter before she asked, "Was Jena on a mission to find Elder Daven's samara?"

"How did you know?" Juila asked in stunned amazement. She

still was uncertain if that were the actual draw, but it stood to reason that would be the answer. *Did Grandpa find a samara, Jena?*

I don't actually know. Let me ask. YES! He got his own, and he's already put it with Grandma's for safe keeping until this whole matter can be resolved with Petre and Tirsha. I still don't quite understand how the two of them came to be where they were. Does Dad or Mom know anything?

Juila's eyes lit up as she delivered the good news. "Grandpa found his own crystal with Jena's help. The mission was successful!"

"Oh, thank goodness," Amanda sighed and felt herself wilt slightly onto Riccan's side with her relief making her knees weak.

PETRE SAT AT THE TABLE, the sunshine warming his shoulders, but his thoughts were still frozen on what had just happened to him. Something amazing had transpired, yet he was unclear how he could even describe it to himself, let alone anyone else. He looked over at Tirsha and all he could see was a woman, not terribly attractive physically, but with a soul so profoundly beautiful. He needed to stay with her, take care of her, until she was able to take care of herself.

Even this was a foreign thought to him since he usually did not take into account anyone else's needs. Wishing Elder Daven would return so he could discuss this matter with him; he looked around anxiously. Hopefully, the Elder would be able to tell him what it meant to be chosen; there had to be some deeper meaning to it which was escaping him.

Seeing Elder Daven and Jena return, he could not help but look at the young girl and wonder who she was; she looked familiar to him. He remained silent while he waited for them to be seated and hear what they had discovered.

"We found the report from your house fire," Daven began, although he was not sure how to continue without upsetting her.

"What did it say?"

"The official report stated that both you and your husband perished in the fire."

"My husband? I don't understand; he wasn't home from work yet. He has to be okay." Tirsha looked from one face to the other around the table trying to find someone to corroborate her story.

"I'm sorry, there was a man's body found downstairs in the house. It was presumed you had died since there was never a body located and nobody came to claim the toddler."

"Corva is alive then?" Her previous anguish was lessened considerably. She leaned forward, anxious to hear how her daughter had managed to survive.

"Yes, she is doing very well and has been in a very loving home."

"I want to see her. I need to see for myself that she's okay. Can you take me to her? She must have been so scared, my poor little baby girl."

"Tirsha, I want you to be very clear about what has happened."

"What do you mean? I want to see my baby. She needs to know I'm okay and that I'm here for her."

"Tirsha, you've been gone for a very long time. Remember when Jena asked you the date? You told her a date from over a declan ago. Corva is no longer a little child; she's a teenager. She has been raised by a family ever since the day her family died."

"Are you saying you won't let me see her? She's my child! I want to see my daughter!"

Petre touched her hand gently and spoke softly, "I think Elder Daven is trying to prepare you for her to be much changed from when you last saw her. It may have only been a few moments for you, but for your daughter, it's been a very long time. She may need time to adjust to the idea of you being alive again. I don't think he's trying to keep you from her, are you Elder Daven?"

"Certainly not. Petre's correct in his summation of the problem. I think we need to proceed slowly with this, so we don't traumatize Corva all over again. I already sent a message to Barla to let her know you've been found. She's going to talk it over with her husband and decide how best to tell Corva. I'm sure we'll hear back from her soon."

"Are you talking about the same Barla who's married to Captain Ahn?"

"I am. They've been raising your daughter as their own."

"You sound as though you know them personally. Do you know my daughter?"

"I do know Ahn and Barla. I've also met your daughter, not very often, mind you, but she's always been a pleasant and respectful child. You'll be very proud of her."

As if this were the last bit of news she could handle, Tirsha covered her face with both of her hands and began to weep with relief, grief, and gratitude all at once. Her shoulders shook with her silent sobs as she realized her whole life had changed in an instant. Nothing would ever be the same again, and she would have to start all over, starting with getting to know her daughter who was now a complete stranger.

Petre floundered for how to react to Tirsha's sudden change of mood. He hesitantly put his hand on her back and began to rub it gently. He hated seeing her in such pain and had no idea of what to do to make any of it better. Again, he was surprised at how he was reacting to this strange situation.

He looked up at Elder Daven and asked, "Do you mind if we take a walk together? I'd like to ask you some questions."

To say he was surprised by the question would be an understatement. Elder Daven merely nodded his head and stood up, all the while wondering what Petre could possibly want to discuss with him. He touched his wife's shoulder as he moved away from the table and joined Petre at the top of the stairs leading down to the landing field.

Petre remained quiet, hands clasped behind his back, eyes focused on his feet stepping, while he composed his mind. Once they were out of sight of the terrace, Petre stopped and turned to face Daven. "I'd like for you to read my mind and tell me what you think happened to me in the darkness. Even from the moment you found me to right now, the memories are fading, and I want another person to know what occurred, I think it's vitally important. I understand if you have reservations, given my reputation. However, will you do this for me?"

Not expecting such a request, Daven blurted out his own truth, "I've already been reading it. I know something profound happened to you out there, and I don't even fully understand it myself. I'll do as you ask and try to see if there's more than what you've already shown me. I agree that something quite amazing has taken place." Daven looked around them and wondered the easiest way for this to be accomplished. "Will you kneel in front of me so I may place my fingers on your head?"

"Absolutely." Petre complied instantly and dropped to his knees in front of the Elder. Typically, he would never put himself in a position of submission for any reason. This new attitude alone told Petre himself that he had changed. There was also the novelty of allowing someone into his mind which could be explored at a later date.

With only a slight hesitation, Daven reached forward and touched Petre's scalp with his fingertips. Having Petre's permission made the meld effortless, and he rapidly went through the scenes searching for some clue. He intended to simply download everything to his own memory so he could study it at his leisure; however, the scenes were so vivid that he also became caught up in the replay.

Darkness surrounded him, and all motion stopped. At first, there was a cold, numbing sensation throughout his entire body which immediately morphed into warmth as another person stood alongside him. There was no physical touch, but the mental assurance was quite apparent. The two were approached by two others, larger and more powerful than anything ever known.

Inside Petre's mind, he was told he was chosen, and he willingly complied without question. He began to see a white, bright, yellow light all around him as a silver multi-dimensional grid appeared in the middle of the light ahead of him quite some distance away. The grid made up a series of lines, and at each place where the lines met up, there were other points of purple brightness.

A man stood beside him on the right who could be none other than Emmanuen, while another man stood behind the grid. The man ahead of him moved from behind the grid over to his left side and made a motion with his hands before moving back to where he started before he simply disappeared. Petre felt an overwhelming sense of the word acceptance. He nodded and the lights turned out and left him back in complete darkness.

Petre wondered if they were going to come back when he started to see a pinpoint of purple light in front of his right eye. As he focused his attention on it, the point expanded until it was covering his whole field of vision before the blackness swept in from the right and pushed it over and away from him to the left. This particular light show repeated itself over and over while Petre remained mesmerized by its display.

Then he felt himself waking up. He was curled on his side,

afraid of what he now knew, but had no way of understanding. He was chosen; for what, he did not know.

Daven took his hands away and drew in a cleansing breath as he assimilated everything Petre had experienced. He was also at a loss for what it could all mean, but he was unwilling to give up just yet. "I will have to study this for a while longer before I can tell you what all it means. Thank you for sharing this with me."

"Thank you, Elder Daven, for trusting me. I'm glad you found us when you did."

Daven laughed out loud, startling Petre, and replied, "I am, too!" He offered his hand to help Petre up from the ground. "Let's go back and see if Barla has answered my message yet. I'd like to give Tirsha some closure with her daughter." They turned around and began retracing their steps back to the Residence.

"I'd like that as well. I feel a connection with her, unlike anything I've ever felt before. It's almost as if I'm meant to look out for her and keep her safe. Does that make sense?"

"Considering what you went through together, I'd say you're probably right. Something drew her to you, maybe the power of the samara, but when you were together between the dimensions, you were bonded in a way we've never experienced before. Take care with her, Petre. You can't treat her as you've treated other women in the past."

"I wouldn't dream of it. I can't even think of what I've done and not feel sick to my stomach. Those days are behind me, and I'm never going back, not now that I've seen a better future for myself."

"Did you?"

Petre looked at him strangely. His steps slowed as he tried to figure out what the Elder was asking.

"See a different future for yourself?"

Realizing what he had said, Petre nodded and replied, "I guess I have. I didn't actually realize it until I said it out loud. I want to see what I can accomplish when I do things the right way, staying in alignment with Jehoban's ways."

"What about your assignment from Lucinden? What are you going to tell him when he discovers your failure to retrieve the samara and deliver it to him?"

Petre shuddered even as he shrugged. "I haven't thought it out that far."

"I don't envy you that conversation. Lucinden is not someone I would want to cross."

"I know I probably don't deserve it, but can you put a ward of protection around me?"

"I will do that for you, Petre, because you have demonstrated that you can do the right thing when it truly matters."

CHAPTER 41

Jena returned home only a few minutes later in Earth time, several hours later in Tualan time. She was greeted by all of her friends and family in the kitchen. Everyone was talking at once, and nobody was able to hear anyone's comments. Feeling the effects of the short time-travel jump, Jena smiled her appreciation of their well-wishes and then held up her hands for silence.

"Let's all go sit down in the living room," she stated calmly when her family was finally quiet enough to hear.

Daven touched her shoulder and said, "I don't think I'm needed here. Are you okay to explain everything on your own; or would you rather I stay?"

Jena hugged her grandfather warmly and whispered in his ear, "You're the best, Grandpa. I'll be okay." She pulled away from him and smiled as she said, "Tell Grandma we'll be back on Senin because we'd like to spend the weekend with our parents."

"That'd be perfect. If you're not ready to come back, we'll understand."

"Thank you! I love you!" She pulled him in for another quick hug and then stepped aside so Juila could do likewise.

The other people in the room left them some privacy for their farewell by heading back to the living room and talking quietly among themselves. They fell silent when the two girls returned. All eyes were focused on them, anxious to hear what had happened.

Jena wanted to set everyone's mind at ease and started with the most important point. "The mission between the dimensions was successful in that Elder Daven and I recovered a samara which we believe belongs to Elder Daven."

Riccan and Amanda were so pleased that they hugged themselves before they rushed over to hug Jena for her bravery. This was the best possible news, yet they knew there was still more to come. They stood back to hear the rest.

Their classmates were less interested in this revelation since they had no idea how important the feat had been. They smiled at the adults' enthusiasm but shrugged their shoulders at one another over the reason behind it.

Sofia was the most confused since she had never even heard of the samaras. "Is this samara so important then?"

The question seemed so ludicrously innocent that Amanda, Riccan, Jena, and Juila burst out laughing. Jena took pity on her hurt look and stopped long enough to say, "It's probably the most important object ever found. One day I'll tell you all about it after we're sure we can make use of it."

"Oh, soon, I hope," Sofia responded, still not convinced of anything, but wishing she had kept her comment to herself.

"Now that we've settled that matter..." Jena began.

"I'm going to need more answers later," Amanda broke into Jena's statement with her arms crossed and her head tilted to indicate she was not satisfied.

"I know, Mom. But, I'm glad you're home so I can tell you my other news," she looked over to Willian and gestured for him to join her. She waited until he was next to her before she continued. "Willian and I have officially ended our betrothal."

Amanda scowled slightly as she looked at the young man standing next to her daughter. Finally, it dawned on her what Jena had said, and she rapidly put the pieces together. She pointed to the boy and stated, "You are that Willian?"

"Yes, I am. I'm sorry this is how we had to meet."

"So…wait…how did this come about already? Why? I thought the two of you were going to try to work things out. What changed?"

"It's slightly complicated, Mom," Jena began. "Willian has discovered he was meant to be with someone else and I agree with his assessment. We asked Elder Daven to dissolve our betrothal, and he has approved our request. It is final, and Willian is free to pursue his true love."

"Just like that? Jena, I don't understand how you can be so nonchalant about this when you've had your heart set on marrying Willian since you were six anons old." Amanda scowled at Willian and wondered what he had done or said to get Jena to agree to this new arrangement.

"It had nothing to do with either of us, Mom. As I said, Willian found the one person he was meant to be with, and I cannot stand in between them. It would be wrong for me to try and I don't want to. Please just be happy for us both."

"I'll be happy for you if that's what you really want, but I must say I'm rather shocked that Willian would throw you over for someone else so easily. Who is this other person and how did you meet her, Willian?"

"That's irrelevant, Mom. I told you it was their destiny."

"I want to know. Willian, I'm waiting." Amanda stepped forward to emphasize her demand.

Willian looked away from Amanda and over to Valentina wondering if he should tell or excuse himself. When he saw Valentina stand up, he became even more confused.

"It's me, Mrs. Stel. Willian and I are destined to be together. Neither of us planned this, but also we don't have any say in it either." Valentina stood by Willian's side and pled with her eyes for Amanda to understand.

"I'd expect this from Willian, based on the things we've been told about him from Juila and Jena, but not from you, Val. You were Jena's best friend! How could you do this to her?"

"Mom, stop!" Jena went to stand next to Valentina and put her arm around her friend. "She's *still* my friend, and I won't have you blaming her or saying things about which you know nothing." She turned to Valentina and said, "Take Willian's hand in yours, please."

When the two complied, Jena turned to her mother and accused, "Can you deny the power you feel from their combined energy? This is something none of us have ever seen and even Elder Daven admitted we should not try to interfere with a connection which is so apparent. I don't want to hear any more blame being thrown around. I want us all to be glad that these two found happiness in all of this chaos." Suddenly feeling drained of the last of her energy, Jena seemed to wilt onto the couch next to her sister.

Juila swiftly put her arm around her and helped her to lie across her lap. She looked down at her twin with love and admiration. She had been so strong throughout this dangerous journey, and now she was home. Jena had more than earned her rest. Juila's eyes saw Jena's pulse in her neck and then her attention was caught by her sister's birth crystal.

"Oh my goodness, Jena! Your birth crystal has changed! It's no longer a dark amethyst; it's now a light lavender!" Juila looked up at her parents and registered their startled, yet pleased, expressions. "Do you know what this means? Jena's perilous journey has been completed, and she survived it. We were worried about this happening in two anons, but now it's done, and we're going to win, and live!"

DAVEN RETURNED HOME and met Nena on the terrace. He held her in his arms for several seconds, comforted by the strength of her arms around him, before he asked, "How are our guests behaving?"

"They're both asleep in the great room."

"Good. I want to claim my samara!" He grabbed her hand and pulled her along with him into the house. As he passed Petre and Tirsha, he added a sleeping ward to them to make sure they remained out of the way. Without missing a step, they continued to the Ascension Gate room.

He had seen how it was done, yet he still wanted to make sure this was actually supposed to be his stone. "Wait here while I go get it," he told Nena as he left her standing at the table in the room. He gestured behind them both and set a ward over the door to keep anyone from entering until they were done. After two recent mentions of Lucinden, he was not going to make the mistake of being careless.

Taking the small bundle out of the niche, Daven held it reverently away from his body as he returned to the table, and set it down carefully. He pulled the cloth away from it to reveal the perfectly clear, crystal skull. "Can you look at its aura and tell me if its color matches my birth crystal?"

Knowing full well that Daven could do that himself, she realized he wanted a second opinion. It also occurred to her that he might actually be scared of having a samara of his own, even though she knew just how amazing an experience it was to possess one. She nodded solemnly and turned her gaze to the newfound object.

It took no time at all for her to see the light sage green, with hints of pearl. The second color confused her for a moment before she realized it must be recognizing the moonstone representing his Elder status. Once she comprehended its relevance, she nodded her head and said, "I'm certain this is meant for you, Daven, but you already knew that, didn't you?" She smiled reassuringly at her husband.

"Yes, but I had to be sure. This is too important to get wrong."

"I know, believe me." She also understood his hesitation to touch the crystal with his bare flesh. Even though he had been told what a wonderful experience it was, the unknown factor made even the most stoic person hesitant to proceed.

His wife would not have known he had already handled it with his bare hands, yet he had shielded himself from its powers. Without waiting for another excuse to come to mind, Daven reached out and put both hands over the dome of the crystal skull. Immediately, a flare of elemy surged through him, claiming all of his cells as its own.

While Daven had thought he understood what would happen during this exchange, nothing could have prepared him for the onslaught of information which flooded his mind. As his training dictated, he categorized everything as it came through to him, making it readily available for recall when time permitted.

Where everyone else's experience had been overwhelming and exhausting, Daven found it intriguing as well as fascinating. He could easily see himself coming back to visit his samara time and again in order to discover answers to the many questions he had accumulated over the anons of service. Daven allowed his mind to expand to encapsulate the instructions he received, showing him a future of fear, pain, and suffering.

He understood his role in the achievement of success, and it saddened him, but he agreed nonetheless. The prophecy took precedence over everything and he would obey. As soon as he accepted, the information stopped coming. Daven opened his eyes as he withdrew his hands from his samara.

"That was amazing! I see why you want to come back to it."

Nena grinned with complete understanding. She also wondered if his visions had been as confusing as her own. He certainly had not spent as much time with his as she had with hers. She also wondered at her husband's ability to pull himself away from the stone with such apparent ease. She had always known he was a powerful man, but this instance seemed to confirm it.

"Let's go back to our guests and see what we can do about getting their matters handled." Nena did not like the idea of Petre being in her house. The sooner she had him gone, the easier she could rest.

Daven nodded his agreement and covered his samara again. As soon as he had it stowed and protected, he canceled the ward over the entrance to the room and they walked back to the great room. Daven noted neither one of the sleepers had moved at all and motioned again for the ward to release them from sleep.

Tirsha was the first to open her eyes. Her head was facing Petre, so she reached out to touch his hand so close to her own. "Petre, wake up. We need to figure out a way to see Corva."

At Tirsha's touch, Petre's eyes popped open, and he turned his hand over to clasp Tirsha's gently. It was nice to be awoken in such a manner; Petre would like to see if he could make it a permanent arrangement. He cleared his throat and sat up a little straighter. He nodded at Tirsha and looked over to Elder Daven and Nena standing nearby. "I'm sorry I fell asleep."

"It's no bother, you both needed it. Now, Tirsha, I have news about your daughter. Are you feeling up to traveling?"

Tirsha nodded enthusiastically, even as she feared the telepod ride to get home. She was willing to risk teleportation if it meant she could have her daughter back. Scooting forward in the chair, Tirsha noted how weak her legs felt even before she tried to stand. She was appreciative of Petre's assistance in helping her stand and felt even more comfortable when Petre put his arm around her middle to steady her as she walked.

It was slow progress back to the telepod on the landing field. Tirsha asked, "What did you hear from Barla?"

"She has spoken with Captain Ahn as well as Corva. They are expecting us at the landing field in the Port of Cresdon."

"Good. I wish I could be more presentable," Tirsha said as she looked down at her soiled dress and dirty hands. She was certain her face looked worse since she had been crying and she could only imagine how her hair must look.

Nena, who had been walking with them, took pity on the woman and used a small amount of elemy to clean the woman's exposed skin as well as the fabric of her clothing. "I took the liberty of fixing you up a bit," she said warmly.

Tirsha's brow furrowed as she tried to understand what Nena was saying.

"Look at your hands and dress and you'll see what I mean," Nena hastily offered.

Doing as she was bid, Tirsha's eyes widened with relief that Nena had been thoughtful enough to make her look tidier. With a heartfelt smile of appreciation, Tirsha gushed, "Thank you so much. You are so kind."

"Think nothing of it. Safe travels." Nena stayed behind as the three others boarded the telepod. She stepped back as the door lifted and closed soundlessly. Thinking it prudent, Nena began walking back to the terrace as she felt the crystal drive activate behind her. She turned and waved just as the telepod blinked away.

Daven expertly landed the craft at the Port of Cresdon and powered down the craft. Immediately upon opening the door, he could see both Barla and Ahn waiting a fair distance away. They had not brought Corva, which was probably a good thing since Daven had not mentioned Petre's involvement.

Captain Ahn's expression darkened as he noticed Petre disembarking from the craft ahead of the other two occupants. He remained where he was only because of Barla's restraining hand on his arm. "I can't believe he has the nerve to show up here," Ahn growled to Barla.

"I'm sure Elder Daven has a good reason. Please hold your tongue until we find out the meaning of all of this," Barla hurriedly replied as she watched the three people walk closer. She smiled at Elder Daven and noticed he had a new spring in his step.

"Thank you for meeting us out here," Daven said to Ahn and Barla when he got close enough for easy conversation. "I'm sure you already know Petre, and this is Tirsha." He waited for Captain Ahn to explode with anger, yet was pleasantly surprised when Ahn appeared to be in control of himself. This was already going better than he expected.

Ahn barely acknowledged Petre with a minuscule nod of his head while he turned his full attention to this woman who claimed to be Corva's mother. It made more sense now that he knew Petre was involved and he wished he had known about him before they had said anything to Corva. Petre had found a way to dispose of the only person who could identify him as the one who had been lurking around their neighborhood, spying on Vinia.

"May I speak with you a moment in private, Daven?" Ahn asked tersely.

"Certainly." Daven expected as much and gestured for them to head away from the group.

Ahn did not want to go too far since he wanted to keep his eye on Petre to make sure he did not try to pull any stunts. "Daven, what's the meaning of this? You can't possibly believe anything Petre has told you. Do you realize he was identified by Corva as the man spying on our house while Vinia was staying with us? He has obviously come up with this scheme to get information out of us on her whereabouts."

Daven nodded his understanding of Ahn's statements. "I can see why you would believe such a thing, however, after you hear what has happened, you might change your mind. Also, to put you at ease, Petre allowed me free access to his mind, and I find he has changed more than any of us could imagine. Please humor me in this matter; I believe both of them."

Ahn shook his head in wonder. If any other man had given him this explanation, he would have told him he was crazy. He knew and respected Elder Daven and recognized him to be a competent and trustworthy person. Finally, he nodded his agreement, and the two of them returned to the group and began the short journey to the Harbor Master's house.

They entered the house and sat down in the formal sitting room near the front door. Corva had yet to make an appearance and Barla asked, "Can I get anyone anything to eat or drink?"

"We're fine, Barla. Please sit down," Daven directed as he remained standing to share the story with them. Using his considerable power, he called Corva to them and waited for her to make an appearance before he began.

Corva came down the stairs, looking slightly confused until she saw all of the people downstairs waiting for her. She held her hands clasped behind her back and looked down at her toes, uncomfortable with the situation. She no longer remembered anything about either of her birth parents, and she loved Captain Ahn and Barla as if they were her parents.

With a quick glance at the newcomers, she recognized Petre

very well. She recalled he was the man who had been watching their house. She hazarded a glance over at Ahn to see how he was reacting to having the man he detested in their home. The expression on his face also left her puzzled because he was only looking mildly irritated and not irate. Corva stepped further into the room, stopping directly behind Barla's place on the loveseat.

Tirsha could not help but stare at the young woman who could only be her daughter. She seemed so tall and poised. It tore at her heart that she had missed out on so much in such a short period of time. More than anything, Tirsha wanted to hear Corva speak to see if she still had the same voice she recalled.

Daven had his group assembled, and he proceeded to share with them all the events of the afternoon. As each detail unfolded, the listeners shifted between interest and uncomfortable. He could see that Corva was concerned for Tirsha's welfare at the discovery of her being found near death.

Petre especially did not like how his role in the matter sounded and wished it could have been told in a more favorable light. However, Elder Daven only spoke the facts of the matter, so he had no way to refute any of his statements. With the mention of the samara, Petre only felt a slight twinge of loss over it. Looking over at Tirsha, he believed he had found a greater prize if he could only overcome his former reputation with women.

When Daven finished speaking, Barla was the first to ask, "So you have your own samara?"

"I do. Petre gave it to me and told me it was mine."

Captain Ahn glanced suspiciously over at Petre to see what kind of angle he was working to give up something so powerful without asking for anything in return. "What's in this for you, Petre?" he asked rudely.

"Nothing," Petre answered swiftly. "I almost died thinking I could control his samara. When he came near and rescued us both from between the dimensions, I knew it belonged to him. I gladly let him have it." He looked over to Tirsha and wondered if he dared to ask for anything from her.

"And how exactly does Tirsha fit into your plans, Petre?" Ahn asked bluntly.

"I hope she'll allow me to watch out for her. We were drawn together from a vast distance of space and time, and I still am unsure why. I would hope we can have the opportunity to find out for ourselves. That is if Tirsha wants it as well."

Tirsha looked as if she were surprised by Petre's statement and floundered a bit before she answered. "Everything has been happening so fast for me. Only a short time ago, I was with Corva, and she was a toddler. My husband was," her voice broke as the realization hit her. "He was alive earlier today, in my mind. I don't know what I want to do now, or even where I will be sleeping tonight, for that matter."

"You can stay here, Tirsha. Absolutely, you must remain here until you can get yourself sorted out," Barla insisted. She reached up and touched Corva's hand to reassure her. "You probably want to get to know Corva as well. I think it would be best and easiest for everyone involved if you spent your time here to do so." Just the idea of Corva calling someone else mother was making her heart ache, yet she was thrilled to think Corva would have another chance to have her mother back.

Corva's other hand reached out and covered Barla's in reassurance. She was intrigued by this woman; however, Barla was the mother she remembered from her entire life. This other lady was a complete stranger who happened to look similar to herself.

Petre stood up and drew all eyes to him immediately. He could tell that as long as he remained, the reunion between mother and daughter would be postponed. He wanted Tirsha to have her daughter back so she would be happy. "Well, as long as I know

Tirsha is going to be taken care of, I guess I'll be heading out. I should probably get back to my water craft and make sure everything is still there. I'd like to be able to check in with you again sometime soon, Tirsha, if you wouldn't mind."

"I'd like that, Petre. Thank you for keeping me safe."

Petre nodded at Tirsha and then turned to Captain Ahn. "I know we've had our problems in the past, but I hope you can put that aside and allow me to see Tirsha from time to time. I promise I won't cause any trouble."

After hearing Elder Daven's account, and watching Petre closely, he was most surprised by Petre's request. He was even more shocked when he heard himself say, "I will allow that as long as Tirsha agrees she wants it as well."

"On that note, then, I believe I'll be leaving as well. I'll walk out with you, Petre," Daven added into the silence. "Thank you for taking in Tirsha." He turned to Corva and said, "I hope you will get to know Tirsha. I know this can't be easy for you. If you want to talk to me, simply send a message to me on the patil." Petre waited for him at the front door, and they walked back up the sidewalk toward the landing field.

"Do you think Captain Ahn meant it when he said I could come to see Tirsha?"

"He's always been plainspoken before, so I don't see why not."

Petre nodded and then asked, "Do you think you could give me a ride to my water craft?"

"Sure, once we get to the telepod you can give me the nearest landing coordinates of where you're docked." Daven was still impressed by Petre's self-control. He wondered what was to come of him in the future.

CHAPTER 42

Vinia had dinner prepared and on the table by the time she heard a knock on the door. If she were truly contemplating a life with Ozian, she knew she ought to at least spend more time with him. Marriage was more than just liking how someone looked or appreciating how he acted toward her; it was about compatibility and common interests.

She smoothed out her tunic and hastily looked around the house to make sure everything was in place before she walked across the room. Danika was playing quietly on the floor, already full from her dinner. The evening should go smoothly since everything had been taken care of beforehand.

She opened the door and smiled warmly at Ozian. He held out a bouquet of flowers for her and waited to be invited inside. "Thank you. These are beautiful," Vinia said as she took the flowers from him. "Come inside. Dinner's on the table. Go ahead and sit down while I get a glass and water for these flowers."

Ozian watched Vinia as she moved confidently through her house. He could hardly wait to be able to spend every moment with her. Danika squealed on the floor, catching Ozian's attention. He revised his previous idea to include spending time with Danika as well. All his life, he had wanted children, but to imagine there being one so soon was both slightly overwhelming and exciting at the same time.

"Have you heard anything from your other kids?" Ozian asked as he sat at the table.

"No, but Vala seemed to be in a better place when they left. I've never seen anything like what's happening between her and Willian. Could you even imagine? And for him to be betrothed to her best friend? It must've been terrible for her."

"As you said, it seems to have all worked itself out. What'll happen to them now? What's the common custom here in Tuala?"

His question caused her to notice once again how much he still did not know about her homeworld. Would it always be like this? Would he want to stay where he was unsure of the customs? "None of what happened between them is common, here or anywhere I know of. It was special…a miracle you might say. The part which made it okay was the fact that both parties of the betrothal were willing to give it up. There won't be any repercussions from the dissolution, so that's good for all involved."

"Does this mean that Valentina and Willian are now betrothed?"

Vinia set the vase on the table and sat down across from Ozian. "No, Vala wants to wait. However, according to Elder Daven, her reticence won't change the outcome. The two of them are destined to be together. I just hope Vala will accept it sooner, so she won't torture herself with indecision."

"Well, I can understand her position. If she were to marry Willian, wouldn't she have to leave Earth to live with him? I mean, he's the Elder's heir so it's not like he can move to Earth and stay there with her, can he?"

"No, I don't suppose he would although Riccan has figured out a way to live in both places. Maybe Willian can work something out similarly."

"I'm sure they'll figure it out. They have time. Dinner looks amazing." He nodded approval at the many dishes prepared in front of him.

"I can say grace, and you can serve," Vinia offered, knowing Ozian still felt self-conscious about what to say for the blessing of the food.

Ozian readily agreed and bowed his head as he listened to Vinia's eloquent, yet simple prayer. When she finished, he dished up both of their plates and began eating. There were several things which were new to him, but he was always willing to try new things. Vinia's cooking was wonderful, and he felt like a lucky man.

"Tell me about Heliok," Vinia suggested during the lull in their conversation. "What was life like there?"

"It's an old planet with even older customs. The people are archaic in their thinking, and the men make all of the decisions. Like I told you before, I never agreed with this way of living because the women are the ones who do most of the work.

"The planet is dying; all of the lands are barren and sterile. The people live in buildings which are climate-controlled and where food is scarce. They also have a government system similar to here, but the ruling men are only in charge of individual buildings which can house several thousand people. Crime is rampant partially because of the scarcity, but mostly from the uncertainty. I can't imagine the planet will be able to sustain itself much longer."

"What about your family? Are there people there who you need to help?" Vinia had no idea things were so bad on his homeworld. Even at the worst time in her life, Vinia knew she could go to the Elders to give her food or shelter.

"I don't have any family anymore. My mother died quite some time ago. My father couldn't handle being around me, so he left me to work in the slave's dome. I basically raised myself which was the reason I ended up volunteering for duty on Viceroy Blair's spacecraft."

"If your people have the technology for space travel, why can't they figure out how to revive your planet?"

"That's the thing; we don't have the technology. Viceroy Blair stole the craft from visitors to our planet. They had come on a peaceful mission to help our people, but they didn't know what they were getting themselves involved with. Viceroy Blair gathered a group of thugs to kill the crew and take the ship off-planet in search of resources elsewhere.

"We were all figuring out how the spacecraft worked as we went along. Anytime something would break, we had no idea how to fix it. When the food beds broke, we quickly ran out of anything to eat, and that's why we ended up landing on Tuala. I was especially impressed with Juila's skill at fixing the equipment on board the ship, mostly because she was so young and had never actually seen the system before. Even then, Juila had everything running in almost no time at all.

"Heliok could possibly survive if they allowed all of the people to use their brains. As it is, they're too proud, or too stupid to allow any change, even if it means the death of everybody."

Vinia had stopped eating while she listened to Ozian's story. She could not believe how bad his planet had gotten. It was no wonder he was so ready to try a life somewhere else, in a place where he could make a difference. She felt honored that he wanted to make that life with her.

～

DR. GASCON finally cleared everyone out of his office by yelling at them and telling them they were incompetent. He ordered them to search the grounds for Petre even though he knew it was a futile effort. At least this way, he could fire someone and blame them for Petre's disappearance rather than have to admit to anyone that his patient had simply disappeared right in the middle of his office.

He stomped across his office and sat down hard on his chair. Only then did he register the unpleasant, cold wetness from inside his pant legs. He jumped up again and hastily ripped his belt off and dropped his trousers on the floor. He stepped out of them disgustedly and kicked them in a heap across the room and sat back down.

Reaching out to pick up the phone on his desk, he noticed his hand trembling and cursed out loud at his own weakness. He grabbed the phone up and began dialing his secretary when he recalled he had fired her the week before. Slamming the receiver down, he vented his anger by throwing whatever was within his reach across his office, pleased when the items broke against the farthest wall.

One of his throws came close to the place where his skull of doom had always rested. The emptiness of the shelf sobered him immediately. His last tie to his abductor was gone, and now he no longer had any proof of his childhood kidnapping. How was he supposed to get revenge on the man if he had no tie to him?

Instantly, he was a small child again, being held against his will in a dark, windowless van. A man was sitting next to him holding a strange ball of light in his hands and telling him tales designed to scare him into peeing himself. The light moved closer to his face, and he could see images of his family being tortured inside the ball and he screamed and closed his eyes.

The man punched him in the gut and told him to open his eyes and watch, or he would do something worse to him. Stephen could hardly see through the tears filling his eyes, and he was grateful for it because he would never get the blurry images out of his head. He had no way of knowing how long he had been kept, but it was long enough for him to foul his pants, mostly from fear.

"My name is Lucinden. Repeat my name, Stephen." He held his face close to Stephen's, staring at him directly in his one eye.

Stephen felt Lucinden's foul breath on his cheek, and he trembled in fear. He could not force any sound to come out of his mouth. The man wrenched his arm cruelly behind his back until Stephen cried out in pain as a bone snapped. "Lucinden!"

"Very good, Stephen. I'm originally from Tuala. When the time is right, you will recall this conversation." The sphere of light disappeared along with Lucinden, and only a shining object remained where the man had been sitting. Stephen stared at the crystal skull leering back at him, and he became enthralled. The longer he stared at the empty eye sockets, the more fascinated he became with the macabre stone. Unable to help himself, Stephen picked up the skull and put it into his pocket. Never would he tell anyone about what he had found. It was his!

Now it was gone! His despair rapidly changed to a plan of action as his memories and fear returned. He did have a tie to Lucinden, and his name was Petre MacVeen! Not only did he have one tie, he actually had four.

Shemalla had spoken of Amanda's journey in Tuala when she was a drugged patient. Nealand had also experienced the same delusions during his questioning before he had been broken out of the facility which brought his thoughts to Amanda. She seemed to be at the heart of this whole chain of events. It was time for her to pay him a visit.

❧

THE FIRE OF WAR
BOOK SEVEN OF THE CHOSEN

While Amanda enjoyed having her daughters back home for the weekend, she could not get her sister's revelation off of her mind. How could she have gone her entire life not knowing that the twin she had been in the womb with had not survived their birth? She felt terrible because her sister's grave had never been visited, and she had never given her flowers. As soon as her daughters went back to Tuala, she planned on going to the cemetery to rectify the situation.

After their bizarre homecoming, it was nice to have a quiet Saturday with the girls. They would be able to talk about everything which had been going on, which seemed to be more chaotic than normal. She was going to have to tell Jena and Juila about their cousins coming to live with their grandparents. This, of course, would lead to having to tell them the reason for the sudden change in guardianship: her sister was in prison on drug charges.

Then there was the change in Jena's situation where she was no longer betrothed to Willian. Amanda had been told the basics of the story, yet there seemed to be quite a bit more to be learned than time had permitted. She still had a hard time understanding how Valentina had been caught up in all of the drama, even though Jena insisted it was okay.

"You might as well get up. I can hear you thinking from over here," Riccan said as he rolled over in the bed to face his wife.

"I'm sorry, Riccan. I was just trying to make sense of everything which has been going on. Why does it seem like things are happening so fast? Should we be scared?" Amanda scooted up to the headboard and rested her back against it as she looked down at her husband.

"Things are going to be changing; that's the nature of life. Besides, everything has worked out so well, and we should be grateful."

"Oh, I'm grateful, all right. I just keep wondering when it's going to start falling apart."

"That doesn't sound like you, Amanda. You're usually so optimistic."

"Don't listen to me; I'm just having an off day. Maybe after breakfast and talking with the girls, I'll be more like my old self."

"That's a great idea. Let me grab a quick shower, and then I'll fix us some breakfast. I'll make your favorite." He winked at her and slipped out of the other side of the bed.

Amanda grinned at his nakedness and wondered if it would ever grow old seeing him prance around in the buff. She doubted it and then sighed as she heard the shower water sputter. She was going to have to face the day and deal with all of its challenges. It would be easier with a full stomach, and she was glad her husband liked to cook as her own culinary skills were sadly lacking.

She had just touched her feet to the floor to get moving when the phone on her nightstand began ringing. Looking at the clock, Amanda wondered if there were some sort of emergency which would cause someone to call so early on the weekend. Grabbing the receiver, she used her thumb to hit the call button even as she slid it up to her ear and spoke, "Hello?"

"I'm sorry to call so early, Amanda. Do you mind if I came over this morning? I've had a breakthrough of sorts, and I'm starting to feel as though I'm going nuts."

"Neal, I'm sorry…," Amanda started to object but stopped when Nealand began to protest.

"Amanda, I wouldn't ask unless it were important. Please!"

She could hear the desperation in his voice even as she glanced back toward where she could hear Riccan splashing around in the shower. Maybe it would be better if she went to his house. She drew in a breath to offer her alternative when Nealand once again started speaking.

"I need to see you, and we can't talk here…I think you know why. My parents are already so concerned about my mental state, and if they heard what I had to say, then I'd probably have to start worrying about being sent back to Creedmoor."

"Jeez, Neal, don't even joke about that! You can't ever see Dr. Gascon again, that man is deranged and dangerous."

"Who's joking? Unless I can talk this over with you, then I think I might have to admit myself!"

"I think you're being a little bit melodramatic. Fine! What time do you want to come over? Do you need me to pick you up?" She was hoping to have enough time to get a shower and eat before he arrived since it seemed as though he had quite a bit to talk about before she could have her house back to herself for the day.

"I can be there in about half an hour. Is that okay? I really want to get out of here before my parents are awake and start asking me more questions I can't answer honestly."

"Is it really that bad?"

"Yes!"

Amanda sighed in resignation and answered, "I'll see you when you get here."

"Thank you! You're a life-saver, Amanda! See you in a little bit. Bye."

"Bye," Amanda replied even though she had already heard him disconnect the call. She stared at the receiver still in her hand as she lowered it slowly from her head. "The chaos continues," she whispered out loud to herself as she stretched forward and put the cordless phone back on the charger.

"Did I hear the phone ring?" Riccan asked as he stood naked in the doorway rubbing the towel over his hair.

"Yeah."

"Who was it? Is everything okay, Amanda? Did you hear something about Carrie?" He became concerned about what could have gone wrong, assuming it had to be about Amanda's sister.

"What? No. That was Neal. Apparently, he's recovered his memory, and he wants to come over here this morning to talk it through. I'm sorry; I should have asked you what you wanted before I agreed to the meeting."

"It's no problem. We knew this was bound to happen sometime. What time is he getting here?"

"Hmph," Amanda snorted and said, "In thirty minutes, probably less. I'm going to take a fast shower." She pushed herself from the bed and stripped her panties off in one fluid motion. "Don't get any ideas, mister," she admonished as she heard him making approving noises from the other side of the room. "We don't have time for any shenanigans." She danced just out of his reach and squealed as he tried to catch her anyway as she moved into the shower and shut the door just in time to keep him from getting her.

"I'll see you downstairs," he spoke loudly over the sound of the running water.

"Thanks, love!" Amanda replied as she tried to hurry through her routine. She realized she had been extremely fortunate because her parents had so readily believed the adventure she had told them about over a year before. It sounded as though Neal were not going to have as easy a time with it as she had. Now she felt bad for trying to put Neal off knowing the ordeal he had endured first in Tuala and then at the hands of Dr. Gascon at Creedmoor Psychiatric Hospital when she returned him to Earth.

CHAPTER 2

Neal buzzed the intercom at the front gate just as Amanda was finishing her breakfast of scrambled eggs and fried foxl. Amanda hastily swallowed the last bite as she scurried off of the barstool to hit the button to allow access to the property. "Come on in, Neal," she said as she leaned toward the microphone and verified it was he on the video screen.

By the time Amanda turned away from the wall, Riccan had already used his special crystal powers to clean up the dishes, so the only remnant of breakfast was the wonderful aroma in the room. Amanda took the three steps separating her from her husband and then put her arms around his middle and pulled herself close to him. "Thank you for breakfast. I love you."

"I love you, too. I'm glad you liked it." He looked over her head toward the foyer and asked, "Do you think the girls will still be asleep when Neal leaves?"

"I sure hope so. I think it would save a lot of explanations."

"I agree. I'll get the door." He moved out of her grasp as he heard the car door slam. He wanted to prevent Neal from having to knock, possibly waking the girls upstairs. Almost jogging, Riccan rushed through the foyer and grabbed open the door just as Neal was lifting his fist to knock.

"Hey! Hi. You startled me," Neal sputtered in surprise.

"Sorry, I didn't want to wake the girls. Come on inside." Riccan moved back and held the door open wide for Neal to step up into the foyer. He followed their guest through the grand entrance and into the living room where Amanda was already seated on the large leather couch.

Amanda watched as Neal took the seat directly across from her. She could tell he was uncomfortable with his memories and she wanted to get this interview over as painlessly as possible. "Have you been writing in your journal, Neal?"

"Some. Not every day. I should have brought it over with me." He clasped his hands between his knees, and he tipped his head forward as he tried to figure out where to start. After several tense, silent seconds which felt more like minutes, he blurted, "What or where is Tuala?"

Amanda looked over to Riccan who had taken a seat on her left and lifted her eyebrow to inquire if he wanted to take the lead on this question.

Riccan cleared his throat and said, "It's an alternate dimension of Earth."

"I was afraid you were going to say something along those lines. In a way, I'm glad, because then it doesn't seem like I'm the only crazy person in the room. How do you know about it?"

"I was born there."

Neal's head snapped up and his eyes locked onto Riccan's as he re-evaluated the man who had married his ex-fiancé. Finally, he nodded as though confirming something else he had tried to come to terms with from his memories. "Are there such things as Elders there? Are they the leaders of the Districts? Are they all bad people?"

"I'll answer in the same order as your questions. Yes, there are Elders in charge of the different Districts. No, only some of them are bad. They're supposed to be representatives of Jehoban, but some of them have forgotten their promises to Him and have allowed the power of the position to alter their purpose to selfish means. My father's an Elder, and he's the best man I know."

With eyes widening at Riccan's revelation, Neal swallowed and asked, "And Jehoban is God, right? Like God, God?" He pointed his finger heavenward as he tried to clarify his point.

Riccan smiled and nodded confirmation. "Yes, He is one and the same."

"I seem to recall working for a man known as Elder Vargen at a place called the Old Soul Engineering Facility. Is that a real person and place?"

"Yes. Elder Vargen set up the facility to reverse-engineer Earth's technology to use for his own purposes. He's been under investigation for some time as to what happens to the individuals who are turned over to him for questioning. You were one of those people who was kept against your will."

"I see. How was he able to keep me? I can't imagine I would willingly stay."

Riccan took a deep breath and sighed as he tried to come up with an easy explanation for the two parts to his question. "First, you were already at a disadvantage when Elder Vargen got you. You see, there is a protection set in Tuala against people from Earth. When you were transferred into Tuala through the electrical storm, your memory was blocked, so you had no idea about your origins. It's this very confusion which marks people as being *old souls* and gets them turned over to the Elders in the first place.

"Second, when Elder Vargen used his powers to read your

mind, he knew you were from Earth, and he had you drugged with *resh*. You see, *resh* is highly addictive and eventually kills the people who are hooked on it."

Neal shook his head in disbelief even as he knew Riccan was telling him the truth. He remembered getting his special teas every morning and feeling rejuvenated after drinking them. Of course, he never put it together about it being drugged, but now it made sense. "So you said Elder Vargen read my mind. Were you being literal when you said it? He really could read the thoughts in my head?"

"Yes. That is only one of the things the people can do in Tuala. Basically, there are no limits to what a person from Tuala can do. We access the elemental energy from the earth and we can accomplish whatever we decide upon. Of course, some people are more skilled at its use than others, with the Elders being the most accomplished."

"Wow! Just…wow!" Neal leaned back in the chair and tipped his head back to rest on the headrest. Hearing Riccan talk about the things he had only imagined validated his dreams and ideas, yet they still sounded crazy. If he had not already lived through it, he never would have accepted it as the truth. Also, he had traveled through the Ascension Gate in New York City which gave him another point to follow up on. "Where does Vinia fit into all of this?"

"She's someone you met while you were working for Elder Vargen. She was your girlfriend." Amanda spoke up for the first time and only stumbled a little at the idea of Neal being with someone else.

"We lived together, didn't we?" Neal asked Amanda pointedly. He could see she still had feelings for him and wondered if it were causing a problem with her new husband. He shifted his gaze to Riccan's face and could see nothing but concern for the situation in his expression.

"Yes. She was instrumental in getting you back to Earth. We'd never have been able to get you home in time had she not helped."

"Where is she now? She told me she still wanted to be with me the last time I saw her. She wanted me to get my memories back, and she said we could talk about it again."

Riccan cleared his throat as he realized neither Amanda nor Neal knew Vinia was no longer going to be interested in pursuing a relationship with Neal. His father had filled him in on Vinia's request to marry Ozias, which was also an unconventional relationship. "Vinia has other obligations right now, Neal. She won't be coming to see you."

"You mean for a little while, right, Riccan?" Amanda asked, slightly confused.

"No, I mean, ever."

Amanda's brows pulled down, and she cocked her head sideways as she tried to figure out what had happened to change Vinia's mind. She knew the woman was being kept busy trying to lead the Roanoke Colony, but surely she could spare some time for the man she had professed to love. Wishing she had learned more about mind-reading herself, she had to be content with waiting to hear the story later when Riccan's silence let her know he was not going to be forthcoming with his answer.

"I guess that's one less complication," Neal mused as he thought about the woman who had been a part of his life in Tuala. "How come Vinia looks so much like you, Amanda? I mean she's quite a bit older than you, but it's kind of strange how alike you two are, don't you think?"

"It's got to be a coincidence," Amanda said even as she started to feel the hairs rise on the back of her neck. She had wondered about their similarities as had the Wilson triplets when they had first come over to the house to meet her. Thinking of the three time-traveled children who were friends of her own daughters made her wonder if it really were a coincidence. Maybe they shared a distant relative, but who it could be, she could not imagine.

Neal rubbed his temples as he felt his head pulsing with the rhythm of his heartbeat. "You had said 'before it was too late,' when you talked about Vinia helping you. What did you mean? Too late for what?"

Amanda and Riccan exchanged a quick look before Riccan turned back to Neal and answered, "*Resh* is both highly addictive as well as deadly. The toxins build up in your system until it eventually kills the user. You would have died within a couple of months had we not brought you back to Earth. Vinia knew this was true, so she agreed to help us."

"Oh," Neal replied stupidly, not knowing how to reply to such a revelation. "Does this mean I'm dying, then?"

"No," Amanda responded hastily. "The *resh* was instantly removed from your system just by the journey through the veil back to Earth. You also didn't have to endure the withdrawals because of the protection of the transfer."

"Whew, that's a relief." He continued rubbing his temples as yet another piece of his puzzle was put into place. He felt vindicated by the confirmations he had received from Riccan and Amanda, yet he still wondered how it was all possible.

There was no way he could explain this to his parents, but at least he no longer felt like he was going crazy. "I think I've learned enough for today. Thank you for taking the time to talk with me." He stood up and extended his hand out to Riccan.

Riccan also rose from the couch and took Neal's hand firmly in his own and pumped it two times. "Any time. I'm glad we could help out. Give it some more time; don't overthink it too much."

"That's good advice considering this is making my head feel

like it's going to pop off of my neck! Hey, that's weird; my headache just vanished." He looked over to Riccan suspiciously and asked, "Did you do that?"

"Yes, it's one of the many talents we Tualans possess, the ability to heal. I hope you don't mind my taking the liberty without asking your permission first. I find it's more effective to demonstrate than to try to explain."

"Very effective! Thanks." He pulled his hand away a little faster than was polite, but he grinned to try to make up for any slight which could be taken.

Amanda stood up next to Riccan and announced, "I'll walk you out, Neal." She moved between the two men and led the way to the door, expecting Neal to follow her. She was pretty certain she had heard the girls starting to move around upstairs, and she would rather have Neal gone before they made their entrance.

Neal nodded once more to Riccan and walked behind Amanda. When they stood in the open doorway, he leaned close to her and asked, "How long did it take you to really believe all of this?" He stepped down onto the stoop and looked up at her while he waited for her reply.

"I think it's different for everyone. There's no set timeline. Keep writing in your journal; I found documenting everything to be the most therapeutic for myself. Besides, I'd like to read it when you're finished. I have no idea what your life was like before I found you and I am curious. Drive careful on your way home, Neal." Amanda reached out and touched his forearm in sympathy before she stepped back and softly closed the door.

No sooner had she returned to the living room to sit with Riccan than the girls came racing down the stairs, full of energy for the new day. She smirked conspiratorially at Riccan for the close-call before she turned to smile at their daughters. "Good morning, you two. How did you both sleep?"

"I slept like the dead!" Jena announced proudly. "No more nightmares!"

"Thank Jehoban!" Juila agreed eagerly. "I finally got to sleep through the night in my own bed!"

Everyone laughed, and Riccan stood up to hug his daughters and asked, "Who's hungry?"

"Me!" the girls cried out in unison.

CHAPTER 3

r. Stephen Gascon held the investigation report in his hands as he tried to regain his composure. After all, the detective was sitting across from him, and it would not do to lose his temper in front of his employee. As soon as his eyes had fallen on the word "Tuala" he knew the rest of the report was also going to be true.

"I think you realize this does not look good on your record," Dr. Gascon spoke in his most officious tone. He slowly set the papers down on his mahogany desk and took his reading glasses off of his face.

"Excuse me? I reported everything as it happened, sir."

It was easy to see how the investigator took offense at his statement, just as he had intended. He wanted the man to be on the defensive, so that this conversation would end, and he could figure out his next move. "Really? The only thing I got out of this is that you probably got drunk or fell asleep because what it sounds like you're suggesting is that a woman went into a cave and disappeared. Does that sound like something a reasonable person would believe? I think not. I don't believe I'll be requiring any further services from you. Good day."

"Are you firing me?"

"Can you blame me?"

"I did everything you asked…"

"You lost the woman you were supposed to be tracking!" Dr. Gascon stood up and towered over the investigator who remained in his seat.

"I didn't lose her! I swear she disappeared in the cave!"

"I think you should probably leave before I have you committed."

"What about my payment?"

"Ha!" Dr. Gascon picked up the papers from his desk and ripped them in half and threw them at the investigator. "I don't pay for fiction! I pay for facts! Now get out of my office before I have you arrested for trespassing." He pointed toward the door to emphasize his point and stared fixedly at the man until he finally relented.

He could hear the man grumbling on his way across the office but did not bother to confront him about it since he really wanted him to leave as soon as possible. There were too many coincidences with Shemalla, Amanda, and Tuala. The plan he was formulating in his mind needed to be rock-solid if he were going to pull it off.

As soon as he heard the second set of doors slam from the reception room, Stephen knew he would be undisturbed. He rushed across the room and promptly shut and locked his office door which had flung back open with the force of the investigator's slam. He then carefully located all of the shreds of paper and began piecing them back together on his desktop. Once finished, he reread the report and whistled at what could possibly be going on.

Obviously, the hair-raising electrical sensation he had felt in Central Park was the same as the investigator had felt at the entrance of the cave. On the verge of sounding crazy himself, he had to conclude that there were portals between Earth and Tuala in at least these two locations, possibly more. He was going to have to do more research in locations where people had often gone missing to see if there were any correlation between what he believed to be true and what was actually happening.

VALENTINA'S THOUGHTS were interrupted when she heard a knock on her bedroom door. "Come in," she called as she rolled over on her bed, fully expecting her mother to enter the room. She tried to hide her surprise when, instead, she saw her brother, Jon, poke his head around the edge of the door.

"I was hoping you were awake."

"Yeah, I've been up for a while. What's going on?"

"I wanted to ask your advice about Sofia."

"What about her? Is she making you feel uncomfortable?"

"Yes, but it's my fault, not hers."

"Okay, sit down and start from the beginning because you're not making much sense." Valentina patted a space next to her as she scooted up against the wall to make room on her twin-sized bed for her brother.

"I don't have any experience with having a girlfriend, and I think I'm messing everything up." He plunked himself down on the bed and folded his arms across his chest dejectedly.

"Well, none of us have any experience, Jon. We've spent all of our lives just trying to fit in and not doing a very good job at it. At least now we know why we never felt quite right." Valentina's hand moved up to touch the tree-of-life pendant hanging just above her breasts from the leather thong around her neck. Most people did not even notice the gemstones set in a silver setting since it had a protective spell surrounding it.

With his attention caught by her movement, Jon stared at her pendant's clear stones with gold flecks. He knew it was right to come to Valentina with this problem. She always instinctively knew the direction of his thoughts. They were different from everyone around them because they were aliens from another dimension. They were from Tuala and not from Earth, but they had been sent to Earth when they were eight years old to save their lives. Their adoptive parents knew nothing about their true heritage, and they were afraid to share their problem with the only family they remembered having up until recently.

"Are you afraid of getting close to Sofia because we know the truth about our mom?"

"Partly." He shrugged non-committedly. "Mostly, I wonder if it's fair for me to get involved with her if we end up leaving here to go back to live in Tuala. I mean, it's not like she would leave everyone she knows here so she can be an *old soul* in Tuala. She would never fit in."

"Oh, I don't know about that. Mr. Stel told us about how his relatives were from Earth, and they had no problem assimilating to life in Tuala. Besides, Mrs. Stel's aunt lives there, and it sounds as though she hasn't had any problems loving her life there. If you want this, Jon, then you can certainly make it work out."

Jon considered Valentina's words and then sighed heavily. "Maybe Sofia's quick acceptance of our bizarre background is what's really bothering me. Don't you think it's a little strange how she has reacted to all of us? I'd be freaked out, and yet she's not for some reason! Heck, I almost lost it when you and Behn first told me about our mom."

"I remember it all too well," Valentina teased. When she saw her brother roll his eyes at her, she knew she had achieved her goal of getting him out of his funk. "So you think Sofia should have gone running away, screaming that we were all aliens. And since she didn't do that, you wonder if she's the right person to get involved with? Jon, you have a lot to learn about girls!"

"I know! Why do you think I wanted to talk to you?"

"Okay, so let's get everything straight. You like Sofia, right?"

"Yes."

"You want to keep seeing her?"

"Yes."

"She wants to keep seeing you?"

"Yes."

"So what exactly is the problem?"

"Nothing, I guess."

"Look, Jon, I think you're not seeing this the right way. If Sofia didn't know about our real lives, then I think you would be right to be cautious about getting to know her. As it is, Sofia knows all about who we really are, and she's still interested. That should tell you something about her, don't you think?"

"I guess."

Valentina could tell he was not yet convinced but decided to leave it alone for the time being. Instead, she changed the subject by asking, "What do you think about me getting together with Willian. Since Jena has given us her blessing, don't you think it's something worth looking into?"

"Well, I must say my first impression of him wasn't very good." Instantly he recalled the boy in question, lying on top of his sister, kissing her passionately. He held up his hands to keep Valentina from interrupting as he continued, "But, he seems to be a pretty decent guy. I'm still going to keep my eyes on him, though, and if he does anything to hurt you, you can be sure I'll lay him out flat again!"

"Jon, no! That was awful! I don't ever want you to hit him again."

"I'm just saying…" Jon left the threat hanging but relented when he saw the look on his sister's face. "I know you like him and I'll try my best to like him too."

"I think you know it goes a bit further than just liking him, Jon. My life-line is literally tied to his, and my future is already set to be married to him whether we like it or not. At first, I resented the idea of having no choice in the matter, but now I realize it's pretty amazing to be so totally bonded to someone. I'm keeping my mind open to it, and I'll just see where it takes me."

"It seems as though you've changed more than any of us, Val. I never thought I'd hear you accept this so easily. What changed your mind?" Jon was glad to talk about his sister's love-life rather than his own; it was a lot easier to be objective with her.

Valentina considered his question seriously before she answered, "I think it was Jena's reaction to seeing our bond when she touched us at our mom's house. She was genuinely happy for what she felt between us. I think she wished it could have been the same for her and Willian."

"Maybe, but Juila sure was happy to see the two of them broken up. She really despised Willian, and I can't forget about that because I think Juila had some pretty valid reasons for feeling as she did about him."

"But Willian has changed, Jon. Be fair."

"Oh, he's changed in the two minutes you've known him, has he? Come on, can a leopard change its spots so easily?"

"Don't start, Jon. Even Juila admitted he'd changed. Our bond changed him for the better."

"As I said, I'm going to be keeping an eye on him to make sure he doesn't slip back into his bad behavior."

"Fine, but you're wasting your time."

"Good! I'd gladly waste my time if it meant it kept you safe."

"I love you," Valentine relented and threw her arms around her brother.

Surprised by her sudden change of mood, Jon delayed marginally in returning her embrace. It was good to have someone so close who he could trust. He hoped to one day have the same kind of relationship with Sofia. He pulled away from his sister and said, "I think I'll give Sofia a call and see what she's up to today. Maybe we could hang out together or something."

"I think that's the best idea you've had yet." She pulled her arms back from her brother and made a shooing motion with her hands. "Go on, get out of here and get on the phone." She smiled as she watched him scoot off the bed and hurry out of her room without even looking back. She also hoped it was wise for him to continue the relationship. She shrugged as she could hear her own words repeated in her head, *Sofia knows what she's getting into.* "I hope so," she whispered out loud to herself.

CHAPTER 4

Tirsha's attention was torn between her fascination with her almost-grown daughter and her rescuer, Petre. The only thing she knew about either of them was what other people told her. Of course, Corva was beautiful, polite, and smart thanks to Barla's care in raising her since she was a small, orphaned child. She still had a hard time wrapping her mind around the fateful events of the day her house caught fire. One moment she had been upstairs while her toddler daughter waited for her meal downstairs in the kitchen, and the next moment she had been surrounded by smoke and flames.

In her desperate attempt to escape, she had accidentally teleported herself through time and found herself trapped in the nothingness between the dimensions. If it had not been for Petre's intervention, she would have been lost forever and believed to have been killed in the house fire. Instead, she had to face the bizarre fact that she had lost a declan of time as well as most of her daughter's childhood. The three-anon-old she remembered was only vaguely visible in the thirteen-anon-old's facial features.

Luckily, there was enough resemblance she could still see the daughter she recalled from moments before in her own recollection.

It was still a hard idea to comprehend where mere minutes in her lifetime could have been so many anons for her daughter. The pain Corva must have felt thinking she had been left without parents made her want to cry in despair. If only she could figure out how the fire had started, maybe then she could find some sort of closure to their strange story.

Seeing Corva practice her crystal skill lessons sent a pang of envy through her unexpectedly. She should have been the one to first introduce Corva to the magical world of the elemental energy. She had been planning on starting her training in a couple of mesans until the fire shattered the notion. Instead, Tirsha imagined Barla had been the one to train Corva. As if her thoughts had manifested the person, Barla sat next to her.

"She's really very talented. You should be very proud of her; she's at the top of her class, you know."

"Really? That's amazing. Although I had nothing to do with it, I should be congratulating you on teaching her the basics of getting started." Tirsha managed to give the compliment without too much of her disappointment showing.

"Me? No! I wasn't the one to teach her. I hired a tutor for her."

"Oh," Tirsha replied lamely. For a moment she wondered why Barla had let someone else tutor Corva, but then she realized Barla had probably been too busy with the other orphaned children in her care to have the spare time to hold individual lessons. "Is it true Rasa has been confirmed as the heir to Elder Wilken? I didn't think women were allowed to hold that station."

Barla pulled her shoulders back slightly with pride as she answered, "Rasa is the first woman to be honored with the position."

"Why? Weren't there any men to take the post?"

Feeling slightly miffed, Barla replied, "It was Jehoban's request. I'm not going to question His plan."

"Really? Jehoban asked Elder Wilken to take Rasa?"

"No, Jehoban asked Rasa to go to Elder Wilken to be his successor."

"How did that happen?"

"Rasa was chosen to be one of Jehoban's students when she was six anons old. She went to live on Acaim and was raised by Jehoban. It's only natural for Him to want to use the skills He taught her in a manner which pleased Him."

"I had no idea, Barla. You must have been so proud when Rasa had been selected. Why didn't you go with her, though? I thought that's what usually happened when a child was chosen."

Still feeling slightly defensive, Barla looked away from Tirsha and focused on watching Corva practice creating objects on the table in front of her. "It was a hard decision, but we had to think about what was best for the whole family. In the end, Rasa decided to go alone. Ahn had just been appointed as the Harbor Master, and Gravin had all his neighborhood and school friends here."

Tirsha reached over and touched Barla's arm in sympathy. "I'm sorry, Barla. I didn't mean to imply you were wrong for the choice you made. In a way, it makes me feel better because you know what it feels like to miss out on your daughter's childhood." She glanced meaningfully over at Corva and back to Barla. "I've missed out on too much, and I don't know how to make up for the lost time."

"You don't have to try to make any of it up, Tirsha. Having you back is enough. Just enjoy the time with your daughter and don't take any of it for granted."

Tirsha felt tears forming in her eyes, and she simply nodded agreement.

Instantly, Barla felt bad for thinking Tirsha was accusing her. Of course, this woman had come through a terrifying ordeal only to find her life had been completely changed in an instant. She was bound to have moments of bitterness and regret because she had no recourse other than to ask questions. Barla was going to have to keep this in mind with every conversation to avoid getting her feelings hurt.

"Tell me about your experience with Petre," Barla asked. She wanted to change the subject to something more neutral.

Tirsha shrugged and tried to find a way to explain the circumstances when even she did not quite understand what had happened. "I don't really know how it transpired, only that Petre was there with me and I knew I was safe somehow. I've never felt anything like it, so there's nothing to really compare it to. Do you understand?"

"Yes, I do. I'm just wondering what it was like in between the dimensions. Were there smells, sights, any sensations at all?"

"Cold! The bone-piercing cold was what I recall most of all. Then it was the loneliness which almost threatened to drive me mad until I could feel Petre's presence."

"Did you physically feel him then?"

"No, it wasn't anything like that. It was more…" Tirsha shrugged again and began to wring her hands together as she tried to decide how to clarify the unexplainable. "I guess it was more like my life-line felt a link with his. I don't know; it sounds so stupid when I say it out loud."

"Not at all. Do you realize you and Petre are the first people in history to ever survive in that environment? I'd say you experienced a miracle. Surely Jehoban has some special plan for you for Him to give you such a blessing."

"Maybe." Tirsha looked meaningfully back to her daughter and said, "I don't feel very lucky, mostly lost and confused. My whole life has been turned inside out. My husband is dead, my daughter is grown, and I'm living among strangers." Both of her hands flew up to her mouth at her last statement, and her eyes grew round with worry over her rude comment. "I'm so sorry, Barla! Please know I appreciate you taking me in; I don't mean to sound ungrateful."

Barla smiled tenderly and replied, "Tirsha, I want you to know you can always tell me exactly what you are feeling. I'd feel the same sense of loss as you have experienced. I must say, you're handling this situation better than I think I could."

Instantly Barla recalled the confusion and loss she had felt, as a teenager, upon first arriving in Tuala. If it had not been for Ahn's kindness, she knew she would have been lost to the questioning minds of Elder Vargen or another like him. She suppressed a shudder of fear and focused her attention back to Tirsha.

"Don't worry, Tirsha. Ahn and I really meant it when we told you that you could live here as long as you wanted. Technically, you could take Corva and start a life of your own, but we love Corva and want her to stay here. I guess it's pretty selfish of us, but…you know…she's like our daughter now too."

Tirsha nodded her agreement and said, "I can see and feel how much the two of you love Corva. I'm sure that's why she has grown to be such a tender and caring young woman. Thank you for everything you have done and continue to do for my family."

"There's no need to thank us; it's been our pleasure. Having you come back into Corva's life will bring more joy to her life, and I couldn't be happier about how everything has turned out. Now, tell me about your plans with Petre." Hoping the abrupt shift in conversation would lead Tirsha to admit to her feelings for Petre, she pulled a minor amount of elemy through her birth crystal to try to compel cooperation without seeming rude.

Tirsha felt the slight pulse of power and wondered what Barla was up to, but kept her thoughts about it to herself. She had no idea how things were run in the Harbor Master's house, and she was a guest, after all. Deciding to be completely honest, Tirsha replied, "Since I know my husband is dead, I guess I can admit I do have honest feelings for Petre."

"Do you think they are feelings of gratitude or something more?"

"Hmm, they might have begun there, but I think it is something more. It's nothing like what I felt for my husband. He was a hard man to like, let alone love. He drank too much and talked harshly against everything when he was drunk. It's probably pretty terrible to admit I don't miss him at all. In fact, it's a relief not to have to worry about protecting Corva from his tirades. Does it make me a bad person?"

"Not at all, it makes you a mother and a good one at that. I'm sorry Corva lost her father, but I'm glad his bad behavior wasn't able to ruin her life. Maybe things have turned out for the best for Corva, even if her life didn't happen as any of us would have planned."

"Maybe." Tirsha considered Barla's comment with a fresh set of eyes and finally came to the same conclusion as her host. She probably never would have left her husband since he was the sole means of support for the family since she had been disabled. "Oh!" Her eyes widened as she realized another miracle: her disability had disappeared. Now there was nothing stopping her from learning a trade and getting a job.

"What is it? What's wrong?"

The fear in Barla's raised voice caused Corva to look up from her studies and worry for her mother. She stood up and crossed the room to kneel in front of her. She took both of her cold hands into her own and looked up into her face with concern. "Mom, what is it? What's the matter?"

Tears formed in Tirsha's eyes as joy bubbled up through her. She curled her fingers around her daughter's and smiled to dispel the concern from her girl's face. "Nothing! Everything is perfect, just perfect. I just realized my disability has been healed. No longer do I have the shooting pains through my back which kept me from ever getting a job. I don't know how or why it occurred, only that it has happened. Jehoban is wonderful; He has healed me when He kept me from dying between the dimensions."

Corva's lips curled up into a smile to match her mother's. She pulled her hands away so she could reach up and put her arms around her mom's neck in a big hug. "That's incredible, Mom!"

"Yes, Tirsha, it is amazing. Didn't you ever have a wise-woman see to your pains before?"

Tirsha nodded and answered, "Yes, several of them actually. None of whom could find the source of the pain. I even went to see Elder Vargen when my husband's business dealings took him into his District. Granted, his examination was very cursory, but he said it was in my head and not in my body. He told me I'd have to live with the pain. But I don't have to anymore because it's well and truly gone. I can't believe it's taken me this long to realize it!"

"Well, you've been through some pretty shocking things lately. This is the first moment you've had to sit down and really process anything," Barla spoke reasonably. She wondered if the pains really had been psychosomatic. She took a deep breath and asked, "What would you like to do now? Did you want to get a job?"

"I don't know what I'd do since I've never been trained in anything. I always thought I was helpless and useless." Tirsha shook her head in wonder at all of the possibilities in her future since she was free from her abusive husband, free from physical pain, now unencumbered and able to work on her own. Her whole life was still ahead of her, a life of adventure and wonder.

"I'm sure you'll figure something out, Mom. This is the best news ever!" Corva hugged her mom tightly before letting her go and sitting down on the floor across from her. She still could hardly imagine how her mother had been brought back to her. The memories of her mother's face had almost completely vanished over the past ten anons, and yet, as she looked intently at this woman, there was no doubt she looked exactly as she had the last time Corva had seen her.

Barla watched the exchange of mother and daughter with pleasure, and a tinge of jealousy, which surprised her greatly. She shook her head slightly to dispel the strange notion. It was not lost on her that Tirsha had not given her any real answer where Petre was concerned. She only hoped Tirsha's choice in men was not consistent in finding someone who would treat her poorly. Barla would make sure Tirsha knew her own worth so she could have her pick of the decent men of the Port of Cresdon. This idea suddenly became an important mission she was intent on making happen.

CHAPTER 5

Even though it had been four weeks since being appointed Elder Wilken's successor, Rasa still found it overwhelming at times. Not only was she learning all of the duties necessary to become an Elder, but she was also dividing her time with her new charge, Gevena. The young girl was mostly self-sufficient, yet Rasa could not help but wonder if her assurances were only a front to what was really going on.

When Gevena had first come with her to Manzanit, she had just been freed from a forced sex-slave relationship with a much older man. Returning her to her father was definitely out of the question, as it was his idea to basically sell her off to satisfy his gambling debt. Gevena had handled herself admirably given she was only fifteen anons old. Rasa wanted to make sure she received as much mental help as she needed to overcome all of the trauma she had endured.

Rasa shook her head in disgust at what the world was coming to these days. Not only were the people losing their faith in Jehoban and becoming increasingly corrupt, but some of the

Elders were also no longer keeping order within their Districts. She had seen first-hand the discord between the Elders at the conclave voting her in as Elder Wilken's successor.

The idea that she might be part of the problem snuck into her mind, and she instantly dismissed the thought since she knew she was doing as Jehoban desired. It was His express desire for her to have come to Manzanit and to be elevated to her new position. Jehoban would not make a mistake.

No, she needed to keep herself focused on what she could do to help Jehoban. Her position allowed her to influence the people in the most prestigious District. She would do everything in her substantial abilities to redirect the people to the old ways of living. It was also necessary for her to do her part in making sure the prophecy Amanda had found would be fulfilled.

This brought up another sore spot in her mind as she realized how many people had already received their samaras. The list kept growing every time she checked in with the group of men and women who had attended Jehoban's meeting on Acaim. It had been such an odd assortment of people from all across Tuala, from housewives to Elders. There had been thirteen people present, with the exclusion of Jehoban Himself, and now ten of those people had claimed their powerful crystal skulls.

It seemed as though Amanda's idea of each person at the meeting getting to receive one of the thirteen samaras was coming true. The only people who did not have their own powerful talisman were herself, Elder Debbon, and Amanda. The legend of the samaras had told of there being twelve identical skulls and one master crystal tying them all together.

So far, the only glitch in the retrieval of the skulls had been when Alena's had arrived at one of the meetings in several pieces. Luckily, Alena was a skilled wise-woman, and she had been able to fuse the shards back together until nobody could even tell it had been broken. Hopefully, the magic imbued in the crystal had not been damaged and would allow it to function as the rest would.

Thinking of the meeting, she opened her desk drawer and dug down to the bottom to pull out a small envelope. She flipped open the flap with her thumb and removed the much read paper. What was written on it was already memorized, but she wanted to see if she had possibly missed anything. Her eyes saw what her memory supplied:

'FROM A FAR-AWAY LAND, *There will come in time, Intuition is in hand, Strange details known, With ties to the people. From one of my own, There will be a sign. Those born to this one, Will transform all. Lucinden will pursue, Elders will fall, Then all made new.'*

'When the descendants of the Watchers bring these all together then the gates between the worlds will be open for all to pass through without a loss.'

THE PHRASE 'BRING THESE ALL TOGETHER' could really mean anything, Rasa mused, but when you put it together with the 'descendants of the Watchers,' then the words took on a whole new meaning. She had read the ancient library texts when she had lived on Acaim. Those old tomes told the history of the Watchers, and she knew they had received the samaras into their safekeeping.

The part about the gates still remained a mystery, but it certainly held more relevance to her personally since she was now a guardian of the Ascension Gate in Manzanit. Well, she reminded herself, she was the successor to the guardian.

A knock on her office door broke into her ruminations. She swiftly refolded the paper and shoved it back into the envelope even as she called out, "Come in!" Dropping the envelope back into the drawer and softly closing it, Rasa looked up and smiled when Gevena came in and shut the door behind her. Normally Rasa had to seek out the girl's company, so it was a pleasant surprise to be visited willingly.

"I hope I'm not bothering you," Gevena spoke quietly while keeping her eyes cast down to the luxurious carpet beneath her feet.

"No, no! Please come in and sit down. My thoughts weren't being very productive, and I'd much rather talk with you. How are you today?"

Gevena flinched slightly at the question. She had learned to hate being asked about her well-being as if she might fall apart or become unhinged. Rasa meant well and, after all, Rasa never looked at her with pity in her eyes. After seating herself directly across from the young woman, she folded her hands in her lap and replied, "I'm fine. Thank you for asking."

"But you wish people would stop asking you that, right?"

Gevena looked up swiftly, wondering if Rasa had been so rude as to read her mind. The only thing she saw in the woman's expression was kindness without any kind of cunning. No, Rasa would not stoop to mind-reading, she was just adept at reading people's moods. "Yeah, I really am doing fine. I was just wondering..."

Rasa waited for her to continue until it appeared she needed prompting. "Yes? What were you wondering?"

"Well," Gevena cleared her throat gently as she tried to decide if she should even ask. She glanced up at Rasa one more time and saw her expectant, friendly expression. "I was wondering if it could be arranged for Valentina to come and visit me."

This was the last thing she expected to hear from Gevena, and she did not even bother to hide her surprise at the request. Suddenly, she knew this was exactly what her young charge needed to help her through the memories of her abuse. "Yes, I'm sure we can have her come over. I'll have to find out when she's available, but I can send a message today. How does that sound?"

Gevena's worried expression turned to one of joy in an instant as she nodded enthusiastically. She had spent enough time in her own head; it was time to start talking to someone her own age. Valentina had offered to visit, so it seemed like the perfect time. "Wonderful! Thank you!" She stood up and started to back away from the desk. "I'll let you get back to your work. I'm going to take a walk in the private garden before dinner is ready. Thank you." Her heel touched the door, and she turned hurriedly and let herself out of the room.

Shaking her head sadly, Rasa wondered how long it would take Gevena to feel comfortable in the Residence. It was a good sign that the girl was utilizing the gardens. At least there Gevena would be kept safe from prying eyes and away from any strangers. The Residence was a veritable fortress of protection.

With a sigh, Rasa shifted her attention away from the haunted girl and back to the piles of paperwork scattered across her desk. She would send Riccan a message on Gevena's behalf and then she would get as much work done as she could before dinner interrupted her progress. She turned to her patil and tapped on the message button.

Her message was short but to the point. Riccan knew she was being kept busy, so she had no worries about him taking her brevity the wrong way. After all, Riccan was also the successor to an Elder, so he was intimately familiar with the ever-present demands on her time. She hit send with a satisfying tap on her keyboard and then she picked up the first paper nearest her hand and got back to work.

CHAPTER 6

Breakfast had been consumed and cleaned up before Amanda was able to get the girls talking about what they had been doing since she had left them at their grandparents' house the previous week. Even as they had been eating and joking with one another during their meal, Amanda had been watching them carefully and noticed Jena seemed more light-hearted than usual. She supposed it had something to do with ending her betrothal with Willian.

They all took their usual places in the living room: Riccan resting alongside the arm of the leather sofa, Amanda leaning against him, and Jena and Juila sat in the love seat directly across from them.

Not one for standing on ceremony, Amanda immediately got straight to the point. "Tell me what happened during this last week. It seems as though a lifetime of happenings have occurred and I've been left out of the loop."

Juila looked over at her identical twin sister and nodded slightly for her to take up the story. They knew this conversation was not going to be avoided, so they had decided the night before to be as direct and matter-of-fact as possible. The less their mother knew of the danger they had been in, the quicker they could move ahead.

Jena took a deep breath and said, "Willian found his soul-mate in Valentina, and I asked Grandpa Daven to break our betrothal. Grandpa could see it was the only course of action which could be taken, given the circumstances, so he granted it immediately. That's really all there is to it."

"Not exactly," Amanda said as she shook her head. "Isn't there a blemish on your good name if you withdraw from a betrothal agreement? You didn't do anything wrong, so why should you bear the shame of his mistake?"

Jena began to voice her negation when Riccan held up one hand to forestall her. He used the other hand, draped across Amanda's shoulders, to squeeze his wife gently. He looked down at her as he answered, "Normally that would be the case. This matter had extenuating circumstances, as my father told me, so nobody will be blamed for the dissolution."

"How will the people of Tuala know the difference? I don't want Jena to have to explain herself to anyone."

"She won't have to, hon, the people who matter will know, and that will be enough," Riccan spoke with a reasonable tone. He could understand Amanda's concern; he had shared the same ideas with his father when he had first heard about the change in his daughter's status.

"At least now I won't have to give up my dream of becoming an Elder since I won't be the wife of one," Jena announced happily.

Amanda blinked several times as she tried to comprehend what her daughter was telling her. "Is it what you really want? To become an Elder? How come you never said anything before?"

Jena shrugged. "What was the point? As an Elder's wife, it

wasn't even a possibility. Besides, no woman had ever become an Elder anyway."

"Until now," Juila pointed out. "Since our cousin, Rasa, was appointed successor to Elder Wilken, it changed the rules. Jena's credentials are just as good, if not better than Rasa's. They were both students of Jehoban and Jena is the direct descendant of an Elder. Now Jena can be Dad's successor, and nobody would even think twice about it. I think it's great! Don't you, Dad?"

Now it was Riccan's turn to be surprised. He had never even thought about elevating his daughter to be his successor. Of course, since Juila had pointed out the obvious, it seemed foolish of him not to have thought of it himself. "Is that what you want, Jena? Do you want to follow in my footsteps as Elder of Pantano?"

"Wait, as the oldest child, wouldn't the position be given to Juila?" Amanda asked suddenly.

"No! I don't want it!" Juila raised her hands in alarm and shook her head vehemently.

"I guess she answered your question, didn't she," Riccan teased Amanda. "What do you say, Jena?"

Tears began to form in Jena's big, blue eyes as she discovered her most cherished dream might actually become a reality. She nodded, not trusting her voice completely. Finally, she swallowed down the lump which had sprung into her throat and whispered, "More than anything, Dad. It would mean the world to me if I could."

"I'll talk it over with my father and see what we need to do to make it happen, then. Come over here and give me a hug!" Riccan pulled his arm out from behind Amanda and stood up from the couch. He grunted with the impact of Jena's body hitting his as she hurled herself from the loveseat and into his embrace. He wrapped his arms around her slight body and felt her sobs as she cried, leaving wet streaks down the front of his shirt. It was the best moment of his life since he had discovered he had the two girls.

Amanda wiped her own tears of joy away from her cheeks. She had never seen Jena so happy, and it made her heart sing to know Jena would be able to pursue her passion. There were still things she wanted to know about what had actually happened with Willian. The last she had heard, the two were trying to make a go of getting back together, and now, suddenly, they were both content with ending things. Amanda cleared her throat and asked, "I can see this is going to work out perfectly, but what changed Willian's mind? Will someone at least tell me that much."

Juila took up the story as she could see Jena was still feeling overwhelmed by their father's offer. "Willian did come here to Earth to try to work things out with Jena. He was actually being pretty nice, nicer than I've ever known him to be. Anyway, when he was at school on the last day before winter break, he literally ran into Valentina in the hallway. Of course, Val had no idea who he was so she didn't think much of it except she had felt an electrical jolt from the contact. What neither of them knew at the time was that their life-lines actually merged at their contact.

"We've never heard of this happening before, but I guess there has to be a first time for everything. From what we could gather, Willian found out where Val lived and went over to her house to see if it had been a one-time occurrence. As soon as he came near her house, he could feel the pull to her stronger than anything he could ever explain. Val tried to keep herself from feeling anything since she discovered Willian was Jena's betrothed.

"It soon became apparent to both of them it was a lost cause. They were going to wait until Jena, and I came home from Tuala to talk it over with us, but things escalated quicker than either of them imagined. When we," she gestured to herself and Jena, "went to the Roanoke Colony with Grandpa, we walked up to the town and found Willian kissing Val. You should have seen it, Dad, Jena's temper was heated enough to shatter a crystal drive! Anyway, Grandpa came over just in time to prevent anything catastrophic.

"We went inside Vinia's cottage and found out the whole truth. As soon as Jena touched Val when Val was holding Willian's hand, she knew they had not planned anything. Their getting together had been pre-ordained, and she was not going to stand in the way of their future. She asked immediately for the end of the betrothal and Grandpa agreed it would be for the best for everyone involved. I'd say everything has worked out perfectly, wouldn't you?" She nodded her head in satisfaction at her summation of events.

Amanda had been watching Jena, who had resumed her seat, during her sister's recitation of the story and had seen her wince at the point of Jena almost unleashing her power. She knew how it felt to lose her cool, but she also knew Jena's new position would require her to be in control at all times. "Are you truly happy, Jena?" Amanda would be content as long as her daughter was as well.

Jena nodded emphatically.

"Okay, then I will be content with the outcome and let this whole thing with Willian go. Are you still going to be friends with Val, or are you guys done?"

"She didn't do anything wrong! Of course, we're going to remain friends. Besides, it would be kind of difficult since Juila is dating her brother." Jena dug her elbow into her sister's side. She knew Juila never called it dating, but the two had been getting increasingly close, so it may as well be called a dating relationship.

Juila blushed at her sudden inclusion in the conversation. This talk was supposed to be about Jena, and somehow it had been turned back on herself. She did not much like it, but she was willing to endure any amount of ribbing from her sister if it meant Jena was happy.

"Ahem," Amanda cleared her throat to keep herself from laughing at her eldest daughter's discomfort. "I guess I have some news to share with the two of you. I'd thought it would be longer before you knew, but since you're home for the day…"

Both girls leaned forward intently interested in what their mother might share. "What is it?" Juila asked, eager to have the conversation changed.

"My sister has gotten herself in some legal trouble and her two daughters, April and Emily, have come to live with Grandma Diane and Grandpa Chris."

"Really?" the girls asked in unison. "When can we meet them?"

The question in stereo was really quite humorous, and everyone burst out laughing. It felt good to finally have something to be joyful about with all of the tenseness which had been surrounding them for so long.

"I think we'll wait until the end of winter break to allow the girls to get used to their surroundings before we bombard them with more people they don't know. I think they've had a pretty rough couple of years, based on what I could find out."

"What did Aunt Carrie do wrong?" Jena asked, suddenly serious.

"She got involved with drugs and got herself incarcerated. Your dad has done everything he can to try to get the charges dropped, but it appears to be a bigger deal than even money and contacts can take care of. Besides, she got herself into this mess, so she needs to get herself out."

Juila continued to stare at her mother even as she directed a thought question to her sister through their shared mind-link, *That doesn't sound like something our mom would say. I wonder what happened to make her so angry?*

I don't know. Why don't you ask her?

I'm not going to ask. You ask!

Fine, since you're too chicken!

"Mom, did something else happen which you're not telling us about?"

"What makes you ask?"

"Your last comment sounded slightly bitter. We've never heard you talk like that." Jena shrugged.

"Hmmph," Amanda snorted at Jena's perceptiveness. She should have known her girls would have guessed there was more. "Well, I went to go see Carrie in jail in Roswell, New Mexico, while you two were away. She seemed very antagonistic toward me, and I finally called her out on her terrible behavior. Well, that just about made her explode, and she told me she wished I had died along with my twin sister."

"What?!?" Juila cried out.

"What was she talking about?" Jena asked at the same time.

"Apparently, I had a twin who was stillborn. I never even knew about it, but my dad finally admitted it was true. He told me where Virginia was buried. I just couldn't believe nobody ever said anything to me about it in all of these years."

"Wow!" Jena exclaimed as she sat back in the loveseat. "I guess it explains how you could have twins yourself. I didn't think it ran in the family, but I guess it does after all."

"I guess I should have thanked Carrie for finally telling me the truth, but the way she told me was just despicable. The way she looked at me when she said it made me think of the phrase 'if looks could kill' then I would have been struck down at that moment. I've never seen her behave so badly. It was sad, really." Amanda shook her head as she recalled the scene in her mind. At one time she and Carrie had been pretty close, she had no idea where they had drifted so far apart.

"On that note, I think I'll go send a message to my dad about Jena," Riccan announced in the sudden silence. He pushed himself off of the couch and smiled down at his daughters as he walked past them to go to his office. There had been so many revelations in their family lately; he wondered what else could be told which would still shock them. Surely, they had heard all of the secrets there were to be discovered.

He sat at his desk and pressed the lever to open the secret compartment where his patil was located. It would not do to have anyone discover his link to another world, so he had taken great pains to make sure only a few people even knew of the existence of the computer. Riccan tapped on the message icon on the screen and was surprised to see a message from Rasa waiting to be read. Thinking it was odd they had just been talking about her, Riccan's curiosity was piqued, and he opened the message.

Once he read it, he wondered how he would make the meeting between Valentina and Gevena happen. He made a quick reply saying he would see what he could do and then he hit the send command. His mind was still occupied with the meeting when he decided it would be better to have a face-to-face conversation with his father about Jena.

He tapped out of the message screen and selected the video button instead. After entering the coded sequence to reach his dad, Riccan waited several seconds for a response. He was almost ready to end the call when his father's face appeared on the screen.

"Hello, Son. This is a pleasant surprise." Daven smiled at Riccan.

"Hey, Dad. I wanted to ask you a serious question."

"Go ahead; I'm ready."

"Are you alone?"

Daven's smile began to falter as he realized the seriousness of the question. "Yes. What's going on? Are the girls okay? Amanda?"

"Yes, they're all fine. I wanted to ask you a succession question. It was just brought to my attention that Jena wants to be my successor. Do you know if there'd be any problem with her request? I mean, Rasa has just set a major precedent, right?"

Daven's expression cleared immediately, and he began to smile broadly again. "This is the best news I've heard in a long time. I'd consider it an honor to have Jena named! After all, she was raised and tutored by Jehoban! The apple doesn't fall far from the tree; does it, Son?"

Riccan's feelings were slightly hurt by his father's obvious delight in Jena's request. He did not ever remember his father being so enthusiastic about his own appointment as successor. It almost felt as though Daven thought Jena would be more qualified than himself.

Seeing Riccan's fallen expression, Daven realized how his words must have sounded to his son. To mend any damage, Daven said, "I'm very blessed to have the two best successors in all of Tuala. When I die, I will know Pantano will be left in the best care with you, Riccan. I'll send an inquiry to Elder Debbon right away to see what we have to do about Jena. Are the girls coming home tonight or tomorrow? Your mother has been pestering me incessantly to get them back here as soon as possible."

Riccan chuckled as he could well imagine his mother's insistence at getting her granddaughters back to her house. He was thankful they were getting to know the two girls. *Especially now,* he thought to himself. *Dad will probably start grilling Jena on her knowledge of an Elder's duties.* He suppressed a shudder at his memories of getting the same treatment as he had been grown up. "Let Mom know they're coming back tonight after dinner."

Daven blew out a long breath and exclaimed, "Thank Jehoban! We'll see you tonight, then. Blessings." Daven nodded with another bright smile and then disconnected the call.

Riccan stared for a moment at the blank screen. His father seldom ended his conversations with that particular phrase. Their conversation must have been quite special to have him use the term. He did feel blessed as he returned the patil to its hidden location and returned to the living room with his news.

CHAPTER 7

It had been four days since Jena had broken the betrothal and Willian had tried to be patient in waiting for Valentina to call him after they got back to Earth. He had spent every waking moment next to the phone only to be disappointed day after day with no contact. Surely Valentina felt the same thrill of exhilaration for pursuing their relationship.

He rolled over on his bed, bumping up against Pesi, the pudgy, black Pomeranian dog who had taken to sleeping nearly in the middle of his mattress. Pesi let out a dissatisfied grunt at being moved, and Willian reached over and stroked the side of her head in consolation. She leaned her head into the caress and stretched out indolently, taking up more room on the bed.

Willian had been surprised to discover how much he enjoyed having the dog's companionship since he'd never had a pet growing up in Tuala. He smiled at her lazy ways and then continued to reach for the phone, careful to avoid injuring the dog. Pesi backed up as she felt her space was being invaded and shook herself from side to side as if trying to remove his taint from her fur.

"Sorry, Pesi," Willian spoke to the dog and rubbed under her chin to apologize further. Pesi closed her eyes and settled back down on the blankets. "I take it I'm forgiven!" Willian chuckled at the dog's obvious behavior. If he did not know better, he would say she really understood what he was saying to her.

Once again, Willian turned to the phone and dialed Valentina's number from memory. He held the receiver to his ear as he dropped back onto his pillow and waited for her to answer. It was slightly early to be calling, but he did not want to take the chance of her leaving the house for the day without talking to him.

"Hello?" Valentina answered.

"Hey, Val. It's me, Willian."

"Hi."

Willian suddenly felt awkward as the silence continued. He had wanted to hear her voice, but he had no plans for a conversation. He had not really thought this call through very well. Feeling stupid, he sputtered, "How are you today."

"Fine."

She was not making this conversation very easy, and he was starting to wonder if he had made a mistake in calling at all. "I was wondering if we could get together today. We really need to get some things worked out, don't you think?"

"I guess."

"Are you okay? You seem sort of preoccupied."

"I'm sorry; I guess I am. I was just talking with Jon about Sofia. Yes, I think we should talk. Do you want to meet at the park? Like in a half hour?"

"Sure!" he agreed readily and swung his legs around to the side of the bed. His rush to get up nearly flung Pesi onto the floor and she let out a loud squawk of displeasure. "Oh, sorry, Pesi. You're okay, girl." He dropped the phone as he grabbed her with both hands from where she was clinging to the side of the mattress trying not to fall onto the ground. He set her safely onto the floor and rubbed her back in apology. Once again, she shook her whole body and went bounding out of the room with the sound of her claws clicking on the hardwood floors as she ran.

Willian immediately grabbed the phone and shoved it back up to his ear. "Sorry about that."

"What's going on over there?" Valentina teased.

"I accidentally bumped Pesi, and she didn't like it much."

"So I heard!" Valentina chuckled as she imagined what must have happened.

"I'm going to jump into the shower and then I'll see you by the tennis court at the park, okay?"

"Sure, sounds good. Bye."

Willian was certain he heard Valentina laughing as she disconnected the call. He smiled himself thinking he would soon be near the only person in the world who made him feel alive just by her proximity. Just thinking about it made his body hum with electricity. He punched the button to end the call and threw the phone onto his mattress in his haste to get going.

The shower water was still cold when he got in, but he hardly noticed as he hurried through his usual routine. His mind was only focused on how fast he could get himself to the park. Hopefully, the meeting in person would be less awkward than their phone call had been. He was going to have to figure out what he wanted to talk to her about before he made a bigger fool of himself.

He chuckled at his thoughts. Just a few days before, if someone would have laughed at him or put him at a loss for words, his reaction would have been anger. Valentina must really be changing him since he did not mind seeming foolish around her. Just her presence was enough to calm his spirit. This change, more than anything, let him know she was the right woman for his future. He needed someone who soothed his soul since he was going to be the Elder of his District when his father was finished with the job.

Thinking about his father made him wonder what his reaction to his new relationship status would be. Surely, Elder Daven had told his father about his situation. He was surprised he had not heard anything from him or his mother. They were not usually so distant when it came to his future. Granted, being on Earth did make it slightly more difficult for them to get in touch with him. Maybe they still did not know. Willian smiled at the notion of surprising them by presenting Valentina on his arm and introducing her as his future bride.

Willian's smile faded slightly as he recalled how resistant Valentina had been to having her future planned for her. He would have to take things slowly if he wanted to keep her from bolting. Maybe it would be a good place to start in their conversation in the park.

Then another thought hit him, Valentina had not mentioned anything about her brothers coming with her. They were going to be alone together in the park. Before they had talked things over with Jena, they had agreed to always have a chaperone since they had a hard time keeping their hands off of one another when they were alone. The bond between them was so strong; it overrode all thoughts of reason. Maybe it was why she had suggested a public place.

Willian was going to have to control his base urges by firmly reminding himself he had to take things slowly with her. He did not want to screw things up with Valentina as he had with Jena; this was too important. Valentina was his missing piece, and he needed to remain whole.

He dressed hurriedly, brushed his teeth and hair, and then almost ran back to his room to get his shoes. If he had been back in

Tuala, he would have used elemy to bring his shoes to him rather than have to physically retrieve them since his parents had advised him not to use his talents unless it was an emergency. While this meeting was extremely important, he could not rationalize it as an emergency.

After jamming his feet into his shoes without bothering to take the time to pull the backs up onto his heels, he grabbed a light jacket and left his room. He hurried down the hall and found Melissa sitting in the front room with Pesi draped across her lap. "I'm going to the park to meet up with Valentina. I'm not sure how long I'll be."

"Okay, but be sure to call and let us know where you are if you're not back by dark." Melissa smiled at seeing Willian so happy. When he had arrived sixteen days earlier, he had been withdrawn and unsure of himself. His confidence had evidently been restored by whatever had brought him to Earth in the first place.

"Sure, sure," Willian called back to her as he continued his way through the front door. He heard it slam behind him as he walked briskly down the sidewalk and then along the neighborhood road. The park was only about ten minutes from the house, and Willian knew he would get there well before Valentina did, so he tried to consciously slow his steps. His feet had other ideas, and he found himself almost jogging again in next to no time. Giving in, he ran the rest of the way and only slowed down when his shoe flew off his foot when he stepped on the grass.

Feeling slightly foolish, Willian turned and retrieved his shoe from where it had flown ten feet away from him. He looked around to see if anyone had witnessed his stunt and was pleased to note the park was absent of any onlookers. Willian kneeled and jammed his foot back into his shoe, this time taking a moment extra to pull the heels up from under his sole.

While he was just starting to stand, Willian's gaze was caught by movement. He turned slightly and saw Valentina walking toward the tennis courts. She had not yet noticed him, and he could see her expression was troubled. This momentary glimpse into her mood gave him pause to take things easy with her. She was almost like a spooked animal, ready to flee in an instant.

Even without his conscious knowledge, Willian could feel the elemy begin to gather around him the closer she came to where he was standing. Just her proximity triggered the phenomenon, and he knew when she felt it as well. She suddenly stopped, her expression puzzled, as she looked around her and finally spotted Willian. Her expression cleared when she realized he was the cause, and he saw her lift her hand in greeting. His own arm copied her motion, and he moved toward her as if in a dream.

Time had seemed to slow as he stared at her while he walked up the slight rise in the grass. She had stopped next to the picnic bench and sat waiting for him. With their eyes locked, he had no idea what happened as he suddenly found himself flat on his face in the grass. The breath whooshed out of his lungs at the impact, and he spit grass and dirt out of his mouth in disgust. This was not how he had planned on starting their conversation.

He heard chuckling next to him and then Valentina's hands were touching his arm. The electricity shot through them both and Willian no longer cared what had happened. He began to laugh along with her, and he rolled over onto his side and looked up into her smiling face. This is how he wanted to always remember her looking: happy and at peace.

"Are you okay?" She had seen what appeared to be a shadow cross behind him right before he fell. Looking around them both, she could now only see the park and nothing unusual at all.

Still chuckling, Willian nodded. "I seem to have two left feet today. Thanks for coming to my rescue!"

Relieved to see he was okay despite the strange incident, Valentina reached forward and plucked a tuft of grass out of his hair. She held it out between them and said, "I think you should leave the grass cutting to the gardeners!"

"I agree! It tastes terrible!"

They continued to laugh at the silliness of the situation as Willian picked himself up from the ground and brushed himself off. They moved over to the bench and sat across from one another. It seemed safer to have the table between them since the pull to be together was stronger than ever. Willian looked over to where he had fallen but could not see any reason for tripping as it was just smooth grass.

He shook his head slightly to dismiss the accident and looked again at Valentina. Her brown eyes were a striking contrast to her blonde hair. She was tall, almost as tall as himself, and he found that aspect of her very appealing as well. They were so well-suited together, and he hoped she felt the same thing toward him. The silence had become awkward, so Willian asked, "What were to talking to Jon about earlier? You mentioned something about Sofia."

CHAPTER 8

Valentina was more than happy to discuss something other than their own relationship. "Yes. Jon was thinking it was unusual for how well Sofia is taking the knowledge of our heritage. What do you think?"

"I don't know. The family I'm staying with doesn't seem to have any problem with my being an alien to Earth. I guess it just depends on the person. Not everybody is going to be freaked out by us. I mean, we are just like the people here, after all."

"Not exactly!" Valentina sputtered. "I don't see anyone here using elemy to do magic!"

"They could, you know. They just have conditioned themselves to deny that part of their brains. There's no physiological difference between people from Earth and people from Tuala."

"I guess. But you have to admit there's a big difference in the way we think about things. Even though I've spent half my life here, I always knew I was different. Only I thought it was because the three of us were adopted. I never imagined it was because I was from Tuala."

"Maybe you felt the pull of the elemy through your birth crystal, and you didn't know you should be using it. Or maybe you were using it unconsciously, and it made you feel different."

"I don't know. Maybe." Valentina raised her hand to cradle the pendant hanging from around her neck on the leather thong. She had always loved the necklace, knowing it had been given to her by her mother.

As a little girl, she had imagined finding her mother because of the beautiful tree of life pendant. She had never seen anyone other than her brothers wearing such a design, so it had to have been a clue left to them from their mother. Of course, her notion had been disabused when she had seen Juila and Jena wearing the same style of necklace; only theirs were suspended from beautiful, ornate chains.

She looked across at Willian and saw the same chain around his neck whereas the pendant remained hidden underneath his shirt. She wished she could see his pendant to know what color the stones were. "I got a call from Mr. Stel right before I left my house this morning."

"Yeah? Why was he calling?"

"Apparently Gevena has asked for me to come visit her."

"Who's Gevena?"

"Well to make a long story short, she's one of the girls rescued from Viceroy Blair's spaceship. When we finally escaped, we brought her home with the rest of the Roanoke Colony survivors. She's gone to live with Rasa in Manzanit."

Willian perked up at the mention of Rasa's name. He really looked up to her and respected her. He was still confused about the situation and asked, "What do you mean by escaped? Who were you with?"

"Juila took Jon and me to where we grew up in Tuala. It's a place called the Roanoke Colony. Have you ever heard of it?"

"Yes. I've always heard they were a private group, not welcoming to any outsiders. How did your visit go? Is it where you ran into trouble."

"Not exactly. The village had been abandoned."

"What? Where did they go? I thought you said you found the people."

"Well, when we left the ocean-side town, Juila's crystal drive failed in the telepod. We ended up floating in space, unable to get home. I was terrified. We were floating out there for what felt like an eternity and then we were being pulled toward another space-craft. As it turned out, Viceroy Blair had stolen the spaceship from someone else and didn't know how to maintain it. Their own crystal drive system had shattered on their way back to their own home planet. They held us hostage, until they found out Juila could repair their power system."

"Okay, then what happened?"

"The three of us were separated. I don't know what happened with either my brother or with Juila, but I soon found out what happened to the missing people from Roanoke. Most of them were being held as prisoners, to be taken to Heliok to be made slaves. The leader of Roanoke, Grobin, had made some sort of agreement with the Viceroy and he was allowed to wander the ship freely." Valentina shuddered as she recalled the first time he had seen her being hauled to her own room. His eyes had wandered across her body and remained focused on her breasts. He had smiled sickly before he turned and walked away. She felt fresh tears of rage forming in her eyes.

"When did this happen? I wonder why we never heard about it in Tuala?"

"The villagers left Roanoke almost two months ago when Viceroy Blair promised them a trip to Earth."

"Why would they want to go to Earth?"

"Apparently Grobin convinced the townspeople they were originally from Earth. They would only feel free from oppression if they were to go back home."

"I see. How long were you being held hostage?"

"Only two days but it felt like an eternity. Juila managed to get the ship repaired and then made a deal with one of the officers on the ship to help her escape with anyone who wanted to go with us. We brought back all of the women and children. Most of the men stayed behind, thinking they would still be going to Earth.

"Why would Gevena go with Rasa when she could have gone home with the rest of the Roanoke Colony?"

"Oh, she wasn't from there. She's from a place called Desio. Her father basically sold her to a man to pay off his gambling debts. He...didn't treat her very well." Valentina finished the sentence rapidly, hoping to avoid having to explain the actual events which had happened to Gevena.

Sensing Valentina's thoughts shift suddenly, Willian realized he needed to tread lightly with his next question. He looked around them to make certain they were alone before he leaned forward and said, "Tell me what happened to her." To be extra careful and without a conscious thought of his own, he pulled elemy from the earth and created a bubble of privacy around them. He did not want their conversation to be interrupted or overheard.

Valentina shifted uncomfortably, and then her eyes widened as she felt the elemy surrounding her. "What did you just do, Willian?"

"I gave us some privacy. We won't be seen or overheard by anyone. Please tell me what happened."

Still looking around nervously, Valentina took some comfort in knowing they could talk freely. "How absolute is this privacy?"

"One hundred percent. I think you're stalling."

"Only a little bit. It's not really my place to talk about Gevena's story. Can we just leave it with the idea she's too young for the things the man had in mind for her?"

"How old is she?"

"Sixteen, like us."

"I think I understand why she wanted to talk to you," Willian nodded gently. "Something like this has happened to you, too, hasn't it?"

Color flooded Valentina's cheeks, and she suddenly could not look anywhere but at her clasped hands in her lap. She did not want to have this conversation with anyone, let alone Willian. What would he think of her? Would he leave and never look back? She had to say something, but the words would not come to her lips. Instead, she simply nodded sharply.

Willian hissed slightly through his teeth with his hastily drawn breath. She had hinted at something about this right before their first kiss, but then they had been interrupted by Jena finding them out. Everything had happened so fast afterward; he had not even had time to process what she had told him before. Valentina looked like she was about ready to bolt as she had started to look around her like she was trying to find an escape route. "Since you don't feel right telling me what happened to Gevena, will you tell me what happened to you then? I promise to remain calm and quiet." He saw a tear fall from her left eye, and he struggled to keep himself to his side of the table. "Whatever you tell me, I promise it won't change how I feel about you."

"Are you sure? You have no idea what happened. How can you promise such a thing?"

"Because I love you."

"What? We've only known each other for a week. How can you think you love me?"

"I think you know how. Please tell me what happened."

Valentina covered her face with her hands. She knew she

would tell him eventually; she only wished it would be years in the future when the pain had subsided. Not even two weeks had passed since the horrible day when Grobin had violated her body. She still felt shame and disgust because she had not managed to keep him away from her.

Willian reached forward to pull her hands away from her face and was surprised by her violent reaction.

"Don't touch me!" she screamed as she pulled herself out of his reach.

"I'm sorry, Val. I didn't mean to upset you. I just want you to talk to me. Tell me what happened to you. It's apparent you're still hurting, and it'll help for you to talk about it. Don't let it fester inside you. Let it go."

"I can't let it go! You have no idea what he did to me! I should have fought harder; I could have stopped him if I hadn't been so stupid and scared. It's my fault, don't you see! I should have stopped him!"

"Tell me what happened. Now!" Willian used more elemy to compel Valentina to begin talking. He hated having to resort to such measures, but he hated seeing the pain she was enduring by keeping this to herself.

"Grobin raped me! He came into the room where I was locked up, and he held me down and...and I let him do whatever he wanted to do! I was powerless to stop him, and he ripped off my clothes, and he raped me over and over!" Valentina could hardly believe the words were falling out of her mouth. Finally, she threw both of her hands over her mouth to keep anything else from escaping. She had never planned on telling anybody what had happened to her and here she was, bearing her soul to Willian.

Willian had linked his mind with hers as she relived the violent scene in her mind. He could see Grobin towering over her, sneering with lust down at her body. The man was easily twice her size, and he effortlessly overpowered her vehement protests. He felt his own anger begin to seethe inside him and he had to consciously control himself since he had promised to remain calm.

Willian stood up and raced to the other side of the table. He sat next to Valentina, pulling her close to him with his arms around her. Immediately, she began to fight him off as she had with Grobin. She had no idea she was hurting Willian, and he did not care what happened to himself as long as he could comfort his soul-mate. He pulled more elemy around them and used it to soothe Valentina's shattered mind.

He rocked back and forth, rubbing her back and whispering over and over, "It's okay now. You're safe. I love you."

Without any idea how much time had passed in this manner, Valentina eventually calmed down, and her breathing changed from ragged breaths to calm, deep shudders as she came back to her senses. Her momentary relief disappeared as she realized she was being held by Willian, surrounded by electricity and sexuality. She tipped up her chin and leaned forward until her lips were touching Willian's.

Surprised by the emotion pouring into the kiss, Willian responded immediately by kissing her back. Where his hands had been rubbing her softly, they began to knead her flesh with his need of her. Her own hands were pulling at the cloth of his shirt, ripping the buttons from the front in her eagerness to get it off of him.

Willian knew he should stop her from going further, but he wanted her just as badly. When her palms touched his bare chest, he groaned in pleasure as the electricity between them flared to new levels of pain and pleasure. He had to stop them from making a mistake. Now was not the time for this act of love, not after what they had just experienced in her memories. He would not taint their relationship by letting this go any further.

CHAPTER 9

He promptly pulled his mouth away from hers, and he took his hands away from her even as he backed out of the reach of her own questing fingers. "You have no idea how much I want to continue this, but I think you can agree this isn't the right time or place. I'm sorry, Val."

"You don't have anything to be sorry for. What was I thinking, attacking you like that? You must think I'm the worst person, especially after what I just told you." She began to stand up from the bench, intent on leaving as fast as possible to avoid any more embarrassment. "I'd better get home!"

"Val, no! Don't leave. It's okay, I understand. What just happened only proves how much we love one another. Here, let me just go back to my side of the table, and we can keep talking. Please, Val, sit down. Don't go yet." Willian pleaded with her as he tried to pull his shirt back together. Most of the buttons were missing, and he finally gave up and let it hang open in the front.

Valentina stared in horror at the mess she had made of his shirt. This scene would forever be branded in her mind as the

most embarrassing moment of her life. She had lost control…
again. Never before had she been so vulnerable and wonton at the
same time and it scared her more than a little bit.

Abruptly she sat back down and wondered why she thought it
would be a good idea to meet with Willian without one of her
brother's present. Her cheeks flushed brighter as she imagined
how this scene would have played out if her brother had heard
about what had happened to her while she had been held captive
in space. She was certain the scene would have been quite different
and even scarier. Both Behn and Jon were quite protective of her,
and they would have vowed revenge on Grobin, which was the last
thing she wanted. Grobin was not worth it!

Well, she thought to herself, *at least I got to see Willian's pendant.*
The crystals were a bright green like leaves on a tree. She
wondered if the stones had ever changed colors as Jena's had.
Jena's used to be black as night before they had changed unexpect-
edly to a dark amethyst. Then after her escapade with Elder
Daven, they had changed again to be a light pink tone.

"Have your stones ever changed color?" she asked suddenly.

"What? On my birth crystal? Is that what you mean?" he asked
in confusion as he saw where she was staring. He'd never heard of
such a thing happening, so it caught him off guard. He saw her nod
in confirmation of his question and blurted out, "No. Why?"

"I was just thinking about Jena's birth crystal. It's changed
colors twice now. Why do you think that is?"

"Really? That's interesting. I've always wondered why hers
would be black, and mine was light green."

"Jena's is now light pink. I think I recall her saying the darkness
of the stones' color was based on the amount of danger the wearer
was in. Jena has been through some pretty serious stuff lately, and
hers is pretty light now."

"If what you're saying is true, then I'm glad to hear her situation is improving. What about Juila's? Hers was always a dark red garnet color."

"I don't know. I never thought to ask."

Willian could tell Valentina had shifted the subject to something less invasive. He was almost sorry he was going to have to move the conversation back to what they were previously discussing. "Val, I don't want there to be any secrets between us." As he had guessed, Valentina began to fidget and avoid eye contact again. "I have a confession to make. It's something I'm not proud of, but I want to be honest with you."

This was not what Valentina had been expecting, and her curiosity was piqued. She looked up questioningly and asked, "What is it?"

"I used elemy to compel you to tell me your story. I'm sorry."

Valentina's eyes widened, first with surprise, and then narrowed just as swiftly in anger. She slammed her fist down on the table and said in a deadly quiet tone, "Don't you ever do that to me again! Do you hear me? Never!"

"I promise I won't if you promise never to keep secrets from me. We need to be able to tell one another everything if we are going to make this work."

"Trust me; there's nothing for us to work on if you're going to use your considerable power against me!"

"It was never against you, Val. You have to believe me. I only wanted to know what you were keeping from me because I could tell it was hurting you to keep it bottled up inside. I love you, and I want to be there for you. Which brings me to my next confession." He paused as he tried to find the right words to keep her from completely losing it on him.

"You better spit it out right now before I explode. What else did you do?" she spat the words between her clenched teeth. Her cheeks had flushed bright pink again, and her eyes were sparkling with her fury.

In the face of her anger, Willian wished he had kept his shut. He mentally shrugged. His decision had been made; he would be honest, or he would walk away. This relationship was going to be perfect, not the farce he'd maintained with Jena. He took a deep breath and hurriedly spoke, "As you were telling me what happened to you on the ship, I was there in your mind watching what you saw and feeling what you felt." He held up his hands, hoping to stop her from completely coming unhinged as it was apparent she was about to do exactly that.

"I'm glad I did, Val. I know you think you didn't try hard enough to stop him, but I saw how you were. You used all of your strength to fight him off. Don't you see, Val? You fought him, but he was twice as big as you. This was not your fault! You were perfect...you are perfect still. He didn't take anything from you unless you allow him to. Take back your justice and pride. Leave the guilt and shame with him where it belongs. You did nothing wrong! Do you hear me?"

After the initial shock of his admission, she began to hear what he was telling her. Had she really done everything? She had felt so helpless like she had shut down. Maybe she could forgive herself. Willian was right about one thing; the guilt and shame belonged to Grobin. Tears began to course down her cheeks as she felt the release of the pain in her mind and heart.

She was still angry with Willian for invading the privacy of her mind, but she was also relieved to know she would never have to discuss the matter with him ever again. He had already seen the worst thing to happen in her life, and he still wanted to be with her. "Fine, I can agree with your terms as long as you tell me the worst thing you ever did!"

Willian winced slightly as he tried to decide which story to tell her. He tried to sidestep the question by saying, "I'm sure you've already heard plenty of bad things about me from Jena."

"Jena has always stood up for you. The only bad things I heard about were from Juila, and I believe she was a bit prejudiced when she talked about you. I want to hear the story from your side."

It struck Willian harder than he imagined to hear how Jena defended him, even though he mostly never deserved her devotion. "I would hazard to say Juila was probably more accurate than you know. I'm not proud to say I was insanely jealous of Jena and the opportunities she was given. I was intimidated by her crystal skills and by her calm, self-assurance. I treated her terribly, and I never deserved even to be called her friend, let alone her betrothed. There, is that honest enough for you?"

Valentina inhaled slowly and nodded slightly before she answered his question. "Why didn't you just call off the betrothal then? If you felt so strongly, you should have ended it."

"I agree with your opinion." Willian turned his head slightly to the side as he tried to find the right words to explain what his life had been like. "You see, my father's the First Elder and his position holds the most power of all the Elders. The only ones more powerful than he is Jehoban and His son, Emmanuen.

"Jena and I were betrothed when we were six, which was actually abnormally late for such a formal agreement. We didn't even have a normal betrothal as Jena continued to live on Acaim instead of coming to live with my family, as is the custom. I got teased a lot in school because Jena only spent short periods of time at our house. The kids used to say even she couldn't stand to be with me, so she lived on Acaim to get away. You know how cruel kids can be, but I agreed with their assessment, and I began to resent Jena for putting me in such an awkward situation socially.

"Then we began attending special sessions for heirs to Elders. Right away everyone began talking about how skilled Jena was in everything related to elemy, and it's when I started getting jealous of her. I was even more arrogant and overbearing than usual, and I'm sure I said many hurtful things. Yet she never seemed to get mad, and I always ended up apologizing later. It's hard to stay angry at someone who won't fight back, you know.

"The reason I ended up coming to Earth was because I was stupid. I sent her several nasty messages and threats, which Jena never received but were intercepted by Riccan. He brought up the matter with my father, who then came down pretty hard on me for my inappropriate actions. I had disappointed my father, and I had to make it right.

"So I guess my decision to come here to make things good with Jena still wasn't for the right reasons. I was never interested in being with Jena, only in making my father proud. I guess it's why I never even considered breaking the betrothal since it was his idea to begin with. You must think I'm pretty horrible after hearing all of this. But since I've found you, I can turn all of this around. There's no jealousy where you're concerned, and we can start brand new because we want to, not because we're forced to by circumstances beyond our control."

Valentina appreciated his honesty but had to wince slightly at his final summation. "So let me get this straight…you don't have to be jealous of my crystal skills because I don't have any?

"No! That's not what I meant! I'm sorry if you…" he stopped talking when she started to laugh. "What? What did I miss?"

"I was only teasing you! It's true, I don't have any crystal skills, but I promise you I'm going to learn them all someday!" She still kept chuckling as she avidly watched his expression. When he began to smile she continued, "But I don't agree with your last statement. I think the merging of our life-lines is pretty much the same as being forced by circumstances beyond our control!"

"True, but at least we can be happy. I never felt at ease with

Jena. I guess my heart just knew she wasn't the right one for me. Don't you feel the same way with me?"

"I guess."

"Wow, don't be too enthusiastic!" His sarcasm was so thick he could hardly contain the mirth lurking beneath the surface.

"Oh, I won't," she teased right back. "I'm glad you got to tell me your side. It let me know what was going on in your head. One day, I'll learn the mind-reading trick, and you'll have to let me experiment on you."

"Deal!" He pushed his hand across the table waiting for her to shake on it. "I'll even teach you myself if you'll let me!"

Valentina promptly grabbed his hand and smiled at the electric current coursing between them at the first contact. "Deal!" She smiled as she started to plan when they could begin their first training session.

CHAPTER 10

The house was once again quiet as the girls had left the previous evening to go back to the Stel Residence in Pantano. Amanda had remained at home while Riccan flew them in his telepod back to his parents' house. For some reason, Amanda had not wanted to go visiting. There had been so much happening lately, Amanda had decided it would be good to have a few hours of peace and quiet to clear her thoughts.

Riccan was currently out in the garage tinkering with the software for the plascreen panel of his telepod. Amanda had gone upstairs and pulled the diary she had written from her nightstand. She returned to the couch and curled her legs underneath her to settle in for reading. For some reason, she felt as though she had missed an important detail, but she could not figure out what it might be. Hopefully, her journal might shed some light on the matter.

She opened to a random page, thinking it was just as likely to be discovered randomly rather than starting from the beginning. Her life so far had consisted of one coincidence after another anyway, so why change things now! Her eyes scanned the hand-written words which seemed like from several lifetimes ago now.

Without even seeing the page anymore, she began to realize how much her life had changed in such a short period of time. She had gone from being comatose for seven years to now being married with twin sixteen-year-old daughters. Her husband was wealthy beyond belief, she lived in a mansion in Florida, and she had her very own telepod to transport herself to anywhere in Tuala she wished to go. It seemed too good to be true and yet, she had already lived another life while she had been in the coma, so this was her reality. Her dreams had literally come true.

Slapping the book shut, Amanda decided she was not going to spend the Sunday afternoon cooped up in the house. She was going to finally visit her sister's grave. Seeing the words written in the headstone, and being in close proximity to her sister's remains would surely stir something inside her. All the time she had been growing up, she had wished for a twin, never even imagining it had already been true but kept secret from her.

Today would be the change. Today, she would be with her sister for the first time in twenty-six years. She rushed upstairs to put her journal away and change into clothes fit for being seen outside the house. On her way back down the stairs, she ran into Riccan who was coming up to take a shower.

"Hey what's the rush?"

"No rush, I've just decided to go visit my sister's grave."

"Do you want company?"

"If you don't mind, I'd like to do this alone."

"I understand." He gave her a quick hug and then continued up to their bathroom.

Amanda grinned after him. She just loved how easy-going he could be with everything. He never hassled her for what she wanted to do, and he supported her during times of trial. He really was the perfect husband. She continued down the stairs until she reached the foyer. Her purse was still in the kitchen causing her to backtrack slightly before she could be on her way.

As she drove away from the house, she imagined what it would be like to be reunited with her sister, even if only in spirit. Her father had told her the name of the cemetery, but beyond the name, she had no idea where her sister's grave was located. In her mind, the plot would be manicured perfectly with fresh flowers in a wire frame at the base of the stone.

Thinking of flowers, she decided to stop at a florist shop to bring her own flowers with her to beautify the gravesite. Feeling anxious for the delay, Amanda picked the first shop she came upon and hurried inside. For some reason, she felt drawn to the sunflowers over any of the other fancy, or heavily scented flowers. Virginia deserved a little sun of her own. The florist wrapped up a dozen of them and handed them to her in a crinkly pink wrapper. Amanda took the flowers in her left hand and paid for them with her credit card.

Once back on the road, Amanda pressed the gas pedal a little further down to make up for the lost time. She had almost reached the edge of town where she would have to turn off the main road when her gas light lit up and began beeping at her. More than a little frustrated, Amanda slammed her palm against the steering wheel and began scanning the road ahead of her for the closest gas station. The last thing she needed was to get stranded on the side of the road.

She experienced a déjà vu moment from when she had been searching for Riccan in the first place. Unfortunately, she actually had run out of gas then and had to push her vehicle to the station. Luckily, she spotted a station several blocks up the road, past her turn off. She pulled up to a pump and shut off her engine.

After getting out and putting the pump nozzle into the tank, she turned and used her credit card to get the gas flowing. The screen blinked several times and then displayed a message telling her to see the attendant inside for assistance. "Seriously!" she almost screamed at the blinking message. This had to be the most ludicrous situation ever! She never had any issues with her credit card, why would it start today of all days?

She stomped her way across the lot and flung the convenience store door open. The door slammed against the glass panel and made a loud banging noise. Instantly, Amanda felt foolish for creating such a fuss over something so stupid. "Sorry," she called out when the attendant glared at her from behind the cash register.

After waiting in line for several people buying lottery tickets and arguing over which ones they should get, Amanda was again frustrated by the delay. Eventually, she was the next customer to be helped, and she opened her mouth to voice her complaint about the faulty control panel outside.

Before she even uttered a single syllable, the attendant received a phone call, and he picked up the receiver and held up his finger indicating Amanda should wait for him to finish. It soon became apparent it was a personal phone call, which further annoyed Amanda. She turned around to roll her eyes in frustration only to come face-to-face with Dr. Gascon. Panic struck her instantly, and she began to look around her for a way to escape.

"Are you okay, miss?" the man asked her.

Amanda glanced back at the older man and realized it was not Dr. Gascon after all, only someone who looked eerily similar to him. The voice was quite different, which is what had tipped her off. "No, I mean, yes, I'm fine. You just startled me. I'm sorry."

She turned around to face the attendant again and could not help but feel exposed by having her back to Dr. Gascon's double. It was starting to feel as though she should have stayed at home or at least allowed Riccan to come with her. Home was not too far from where she was; she could always go back and get him.

"What can I get for you?" the attendant asked in a bored voice.

"Oh, my card wouldn't work in pump six." She held out her card for him to scan manually.

"Yeah, we've been having problems with the pump. Sorry about that. Would you like to get a lottery ticket today?"

"Sure," Amanda replied automatically. She had no idea what prompted her to accept the offer; she never played the lottery. Apparently, she was more flustered than she had previously believed. Really, what she wanted more than anything was to leave the gas station and her haunting memories behind. When the attendant handed her the lottery ticket and credit card, she shoved them both into her purse without a second glance. "Thanks," she said automatically, and she almost ran out of the store without looking back.

The pump was busily dumping gas into her tank when she stopped beside her truck. She tapped her foot and rested her palm against the side of the 4-Runner until the pump clicked off. As fast as she could, she ripped the nozzle from her vehicle and slammed it back in the pump cradle. She twisted the fuel cap back on until it clicked several times and then shut the side panel carefully.

Almost running, she took the couple steps to get to the driver's side door and got in. After throwing her purse into the passenger seat, she almost cried out in relief when the engine started on the first try. So many things had gone wrong already, it was almost feeling like nothing was going to go as planned, but nothing was wrong now. She checked all of the gauges just to be sure as she put on her seat belt and put the truck in gear.

On her way back to her turnoff, she gripped the steering wheel until her knuckles were white. She took a deep breath and consciously began to relax her overanxious body. She shook first one hand out and then the other as she continued to navigate her way to the cemetery. Twenty minutes later, she pulled up to the quiet location and pulled into the visitor's parking lot. She contemplated leaving or taking her purse with her, finally deciding on the latter.

With purse in one hand and flowers in the other, Amanda got out of the truck and through the open gates. There were more headstones than she imagined. This was going to take a while since she had not thought to ask her father about any directions once she got to the place. He probably thought she would not end up going.

"Well, I'm here now," she said quietly even though there was nobody to hear her. Feeling pulled to go to the left, Amanda picked the direction for no other reason. As she slowly walked up and down the rows, she instantly became fascinated by the inscriptions on the stones. Some, unfortunately, were nearly indecipherable due to neglect and age.

There were several family plots containing numerous stones bearing only the name "Baby" on them. For some reason, these unnamed children bothered her the most as she realized the families had lost five or six children at birth. Times were certainly harder in the olden days; she was thankful for the medical knowledge of her own time.

Amanda dug a tissue out of her purse, glad she had brought it after all. She blew her nose and wiped her eyes. If she spent this much time at each family plot, she would never discover where her sister had been interred. She hurried her steps and only paused for a couple of other stones which were so spectacular she felt she could not help but stop to look.

Her spirits were beginning to flag when she had traversed the entire left-hand side of the cemetery without any success. She tried to recall what her father had said about Virginia's burial and remembered he had said it had been near a building. She looked around her and spotted the back of the hospital on the opposite side of where she had started.

"That figures!" she said as she stomped across the gravel access road to get closer to the building before she got sidetracked with reading the stones again. The grass beneath her feet was longer and unkempt in this section of the property. It was nothing like what she had imagined in her mind. None of the stones had any flowers around them like the ones closer to the entrance, and some were even leaning precariously.

"This can't be right," she mumbled even as she kept getting closer to the edge of the property line where a ragged fence did more to hold up weeds than keep people from trespassing. She used her foot to clear the grass away from the closest headstones. The dates were too old to be of interest. She moved along and repeated the same process until she finally found a small, rounded, white stone which bore the inscription: Virginia Ellen Covington, Born September 28, 1972, Died September 28, 1972, Beloved Daughter of Chris and Diane, In Our Hearts Forever.

CHAPTER 11

Amanda kneeled and angrily grabbed hunks of grass and pulled them out by the roots where they covered the inscription. Why did Mom let this happen? Didn't Dad say she came to visit? From the looks of it, she hasn't been here for years! Amanda's hands were filthy by the time she was done grooming the land surrounding the stone. Absently, she wiped her palms on the grass beside her to get the worst of the filth off before she finished wiping them on the thighs of her pants.

She sat back on her heels and pulled the flowers out of her purse which she had dropped behind her. Letting herself fall back onto her rear, she crossed her legs and simply stared at the words on the stone. Now that the moment was here, she had no idea what she wanted to do or say to her sister. 'It's been twenty-six years, and I finally made it to see you' seemed a bit too cheeky for the solemn occasion.

Not sure what she had expected out of the visit, the emptiness she felt inside was certainly not on the list of emotions. She felt guilty because she had imagined there would finally be a sense of sisterhood or at least kinship by her proximity. This emptiness was unexpected, not to mention disheartening.

"I'm sorry, sis," she whispered as she got her feet back under her and stood up. She stooped over and patted the stone while she picked up her purse. For some reason, she did not think she would ever be returning to this gravesite. There was nothing here for her, not even a sense of peace, nothing except feeling anxious and alone.

The trek back across the property seemed shorter since she did not even look down to inspect any other inscriptions. She was ready to leave, and nothing was going to stop her from getting home to her waiting husband. With keys in her hand, she got into her truck and drove away, not quite squealing the tires in her haste to be on her way again. It seemed strange she had been so anxious to get to the cemetery, only to feel the same sense of urgency to get away.

There was a long line of traffic she had to wait for before she could turn onto the busy main road. She tapped her fingers on the steering wheel and noticed the dirt crusted under her nails. "Yuck," she said out loud.

An opening in the traffic appeared, and she gunned the motor. She had just completed the turn when a loud bang sounded, and her steering became erratic. "What in the world?!" she exclaimed as she promptly pulled to the side of the road and hit the brake pedal to stop before she ran into something. She turned on the hazard lights and again waited for traffic to clear so she could open her door without getting hit. This was not a good road to be stranded on during this time of day. It seemed as though every person in Florida had decided to use this road for a Sunday drive at the moment.

Another break in the traffic allowed her to exit the vehicle and go around the front to find the passenger tire had blown out completely. The rim was resting on the gravel and had a flat spot on it where it had rubbed against the pavement when she tried to slow down. This was not good! She opened the passenger door and searched for her cell phone in her purse. Her digging became more frantic as she discovered it was nowhere to be found. She upended the bag's contents onto the seat and stared in disbelief as the phone was not there.

"No! No! No!" she screamed dramatically and then leaned over the seat for support as she started to feel tears of frustration forming in her eyes. This had to be the worst day ever. Of all the times for her to forget her cell phone, this had to take the cake. "What am I going to do?"

The words were barely out of her mouth before she heard tires crunching on loose gravel behind her vehicle. She used the backs of her hands to angrily brush away the tears from her cheeks. She leaned away from the vehicle to see who had stopped to offer assistance. It was never a good idea for a young woman to be stranded on the side of the road, so she hoped whoever it was at least did not look terrifying.

A few seconds later, a woman exited the car and hurried to get to the front of her vehicle and out of the rush of traffic approaching. "I saw your flashing lights and thought you might need help. Are you okay?"

"Yes, but I'm afraid I won't be going anywhere until I can get the tire changed." To show the stranger the damage, she shut the passenger door and pointed toward the front tire.

"Wow, you totally blew the tire out! I'm glad I stopped. Have you called anyone yet?"

Wishing she did not have to admit it, Amanda replied, "Of all days, I forgot my cell phone at home. So, no, I haven't called anyone."

"It's okay; I got my cell phone. Also, my dad owns his own towing company. I could call him if you want."

"I'd really appreciate it. Thanks!"

"Cool. I'll call him right now. Just a sec." She flipped her phone open and hit the speed dial before putting it up to her ear. "Hey, Dad. I just came upon a woman whose tire is blown on the side of the highway. Yeah, it's just down the road from your shop, going Eastbound. Really? Great! I'll stay here with her until you get here. I'll see you in a couple of minutes. Thanks, Dad!"

She flipped the phone shut and announced, "He'll be here before you know it. He just finished dropping a car off in the yard and was just heading out anyway."

"That's amazing timing. My name's Amanda. What's yours?" Amanda held out her hand for the introduction and belatedly realized how dirty it looked.

The girl did not seem to even notice as she took off her oversized sunglasses and smiled warmly at her. She grasped her hand in a firm shake and said, "I'm Angie McFarland. You know, you look awfully familiar. Are you from around here?"

"I grew up about thirty minutes north of here. But I was thinking the same thing about you, too. I think we went to the same high school together."

"Wait! Did you say your name was Amanda?"

"Yes."

"Amanda Covington?"

"Well, it was. I'm married now."

"Oh, my gosh! I'd heard you were injured in a boating accident and in a coma right after we graduated. This is terrible to say, we all just assumed you died!"

Amanda chuckled and replied, "Well you got half of it right. I was in a boating accident of sorts, and I was in a coma for seven years."

"Wow! That's a long time. Wait! Does it mean you woke up last year? Hmmph, woke up doesn't seem quite right; it's not like you just took a nap."

"A very long nap!" Amanda laughed outright to try to ease Angie's discomfort at her choice of words. "I was very fortunate to even wake up, not many people do after so long."

"We were all appalled to hear about Neal's death in the accident. He was a cool guy. And now you're married?"

Not sure where to start, Amanda hesitated. Being reminded of that period of her life, she also recalled her journal entry where she had come home to find Neal had started dating a girl named Angie. Was it a premonition for when Neal did get home? Was this woman in front of her the person who was supposed to get together with her ex-fiancé?

"Yes, I'm married to Riccan Stel. But, you know Neal didn't die in the accident. It's a really long story, but he's home recovering from his long ordeal. I think he could really use a friend right now. You should stop by his parents' house and say hello sometime."

"Seriously? Neal's alive? This has been the most fascinating traffic stop I've ever encountered. Tell me about your husband. You said his name was Riccan? Oh my goodness, did you mean the Riccan Stel? Like the NHRA racer, Riccan?"

"So you've heard of him, huh? Yes, he's my husband. How do you know him?"

"My Dad has got to be his biggest fan. I've watched him on T.V. for years. Although I don't recall seeing him race this last year, come to think of it."

"Which is probably my fault. I've turned his life upside down ever since we met." Amanda smiled at the recollection of her meeting Riccan.

"I'd love to hear the story sometime. Oh, look, there's my dad pulling up right now." She left Amanda's to be the first to tell her dad about who this woman was married to. He was going to freak out! She opened the passenger door of the tow truck and began speaking hurriedly. She saw his expression change as he took in her words.

Amanda watched as a big man lowered himself out of the tow truck with its lights flashing. She could see he was excited about what Angie had told him and, at this point, Amanda was not above using her husband's popularity to get faster service to get home. Angie was positively dwarfed by the size of her dad as she tagged along by his side as they advanced on where Amanda remained beside her vehicle.

"Billy McFarland," he said as he held out his hand for an introduction when he got close enough.

"Amanda Stel." She shook his hand firmly. At once she saw his hands were dirtier than her own, so she did not even feel ashamed.

Billy leaned his body to the side to assess the damage to the vehicle and whistled. "You sure did make a mess of the rim."

"I think there's a spare under the truck in the back," Amanda offered hastily.

"Okay, I'll check it out. Have you changed your spare recently?"

"No. I don't think so, anyway." Amanda wondered why you would have to change a spare. Did they go bad? She did not think they expired.

"Excuse me," he said as he backed up and opened the rear passenger door and leaned into the vehicle.

Amanda was more than a little curious to find out what he was doing. She moved around the door and tried to peer around his massive frame. Finally, she gave it up as a lost cause and set about to wait to see what he was doing. It all became clear when Mr.

McFarland turned around with a couple of parts in his hand which Amanda had no idea were even in the vehicle.

He walked to the back of the truck and kneeled. With his big hand on the rear bumper, he held himself from the ground while he looked under the truck. "Hmph," he grunted as he pushed himself to a standing position. "I won't be needing these tools after all." He returned to the truck and began putting them away again.

"I don't understand. Are those the wrong tools?" Amanda asked in confusion.

"No, they're the right tools. You just don't have a spare tire. I'm going to have to tow your vehicle unless you want to leave it here and run the risk of someone else towing it."

"What? How come the spare tire is missing? It doesn't even make sense." Amanda knew Riccan was meticulous about the upkeep of all of his vehicles. This was just another strange happening in a long list accumulating for the day. "The spare tire must be at home. Can you tow it to my house?"

"I'll tow it anywhere you like, miss."

"Please call me Amanda. And, yes, I think I'd like you to take it to my house. Thank you." At this point, Amanda was doubly cursing her carelessness for leaving her cell phone at her house. She really needed to talk to Riccan badly, if only for some comfort.

"Okay, Amanda. I'll get you hooked up, and we can be on our way in no time. Sound good?"

"Perfect! Thank you!"

Angie plucked at Amanda's sleeve and asked, "Do you want to wait in my car while my dad gets this taken care of? It'll be more comfortable than standing here on the side of the highway, and definitely quieter." Several semis passed just then, and the wind of their passing almost blew them over.

"Sure, that would be great. Thanks, Angie, you really have been a life saver. I don't know what I would have done if you hadn't stopped when you did. The timing couldn't have been more perfect since it had just happened."

"No problem, I was just leaving my office. I normally don't work on Sundays, but I needed to get a few things handled when it was quiet. I'm glad I could be of assistance."

CHAPTER 12

"Where do you work?"

"I own my own insurance agency. If you ever need any type of insurance, I'd appreciate the business." Angie smiled and then gestured for them to start walking to get into her car.

"That's cool! How did you get into that line of work?" Amanda asked over the roof of the car before she sat in the passenger seat of the BMW. It appeared Angie was doing quite well in her career to have such a nice, new car.

With the doors shut, the noise was all but canceled out. Angie turned and rested her back against the door to make it easier to talk. She could hardly believe Amanda was sitting in her vehicle alive and well. "The opportunity basically fell in my lap. I was working for the agent who used to work in the location, and he decided he wanted to retire. He asked me if I wanted to handle all of his clients and take over the agency. Of course, I then had to go to school and get licensed, but it was too good of an opportunity to pass up."

"Of course! That's really cool. Good for you!"

"What have you been doing? Are you working anywhere?"

"No, I was in rehabilitation for most of last year, and then I got married to Riccan."

"What was the rehab for?"

"Well, I was pretty weak from being in a coma for so long. The rehab helped push me to get back into shape."

"How did you meet Riccan?"

Amanda thought it seemed like a loaded question. If she were to tell Angie the whole story, she would never believe her. She opted for the simple version by saying, "We met during a search and rescue mission. I was the spotter while he flew his airplane."

"Really? He's a pilot as well? You're so lucky, Amanda. Is he as nice in person as he is on T.V.?"

Amanda chuckled and answered, "Well as I've never seen him on T.V. I can't really answer to that part, but I think he's the best man ever. I wouldn't have married him otherwise!"

"Duh! That was about the dumbest question I could have asked. I'm sorry!" Angie covered her reddening cheeks with her hands.

"It's okay. Why don't you come over to the house while your dad is towing the truck? Riccan's at home, and I'm sure he'd be glad to meet you both. What do you say?"

"No, I really couldn't intrude."

"It's not intruding when I asked in the first place. Come on!" Amanda saw Mr. McFarland's tow truck pull out from behind Angie's car and move to the front of her own truck.

"So was it love at first sight then?"

Amanda tore her gaze from outside the front windshield and looked over at Angie. "What?"

"With you and Riccan, was it love at first sight?"

With another chuckle, Amanda replied, "It was for me. I don't think Riccan would quite agree. I think I kind of scared him because I already knew so much about him and he didn't even know who I was."

"Well, I'd think he'd be used to it since he's so popular in the public eye. Of course, you knew all about him!"

Amanda nodded agreement, even though her mind had other ideas on the matter. Amanda's knowledge of Riccan included so much more than what was available online. She had known him intimately from her dreams while she was in her coma. There was no rational explanation for all she had learned while sleeping, yet it was all coming together. Thinking along those lines, Amanda looked at Angie with the light of seeing if she would eventually begin dating Neal, as she had in her dream.

"Are you married?"

"No! No, I've been way too busy to get involved with anyone. It's just me and my work."

The wheels were turning in Amanda's mind. How would she introduce Neal to Angie? Surely this roadside meeting was more than just a coincidence. Amanda no longer believed in coincidental encounters anymore, not after everything which had happened to her in the last year. "Do you have a business card? I'd love to stay in touch with you."

"Sure, that'd be great!" Angie dug in her purse and triumphantly pulled out one of her cards which she handed over to Amanda. Before her fingers released the card, she changed her mind and pulled the card back to her lap. She dug in her purse and pulled out a pen and flipped the card over. "Let me put my cell phone number on the back for you."

Amanda waited for her to finish writing and then accepted the paper. This was just the thing she needed to begin her plan. Surely, the dream about Angie had to mean she was meant to end up with Neal in the end. She had to believe it was the reason Angie happened to be traveling on the road today. It also went a long way to explaining all of the delays she had experienced before getting to the cemetery. If everything had gone smoothly, then she would have been at least an hour or two earlier, and she would have missed this 'chance' encounter.

"It looks like my dad has your vehicle all hooked up. He'll want you to ride with him to give him directions."

"You'll follow us in your car, right?"

"Are you sure it won't be an imposition?" It hurt her to even suggest it; she was almost desperate to see Riccan Stel's house. She had heard stories about the mansion, but she had no idea where it was located. This might be her only opportunity to see it in person.

"Not at all. Please say you'll come over." Amanda reached over and touched Angie's hand to emphasize her point.

"Fine. I'll do it. Oh, my dad is trying to get your attention. I'll see you at your house then."

Amanda opened the passenger door and walked over to where Mr. McFarland stood at the side of his tow truck. He opened the door for her, and she hoisted herself up into the tall vehicle. It was sort of exciting to see the road from this height. She turned around and looked through the back window to see her truck raised in the front and attached to the tow truck. Her eyes moved past the 4-Runner, and she waved to Angie and smiled when Angie waved back enthusiastically.

Mr. McFarland shut the passenger door and went around the front of the truck to get into the driver's seat. "I'll just need you to give me directions. Give me enough lead time to let me know when to turn. Okay?"

"Sure, just keep going straight. We'll be taking the next exit and then turning right."

"Great. Are you warm enough?" He reached forward to adjust the temperature and then removed his hand when Amanda nodded confirmation. He started the engine and put on his blinker while he waited for an opening in the traffic to pull onto the highway.

The ride was quiet as Mr. McFarland was not one for small talk. When they pulled up to the gate, Amanda let herself out of the vehicle and manually entered the code on the security panel. The two sections of the gate slowly opened as Amanda returned to the passenger seat. The curving driveway was too long to simply walk up, so it was easier to hoist herself into the truck.

Amanda looked behind them again to make certain Angie's car made it onto the property before the gate shut. She turned back around and wondered if Riccan had seen the line of vehicles converging upon the house. Suddenly she was nervous about offering the impromptu meet and greet without first clearing it with Riccan. She did not think he would mind, but she had never seen him in any public appearances either.

"Just pull up in front of the right-hand side garage," Amanda directed as they neared the circular section of the driveway. It was the half of the garage where they stored their telepods so it would not matter if the truck blocked the entrance. Of course, she did not share this information with Mr. McFarland.

He expertly backed the 4-Runner up in an out of the way position. The back-up beeper echoed across the wide open space. With the motor turned off, he opened his door and hopped down to the ground in a manner which told Amanda he had done it a million times before.

Amanda exited the vehicle more carefully and started to walk over to where Angie had parked ahead of them. She could see the excited expression of her newfound friend. She could hardly blame her for staring as the house was rather impressive with its four columns supporting the porch and the symmetrical appearance of the six garage doors, three on each side of the massive living space.

As if her thoughts had manifested, Riccan opened the front door and stepped outside. He surveyed the scene in front of him and instantly realized something had happened to the truck. His next instinct was to make sure Amanda was okay. He rushed forward, concern apparent in his expression until he could see his wife smiling. Relief almost overwhelmed him as he stopped in front of Amanda and gave her a quick hug. "What happened? Are you okay?"

"Yes, my tire blew out. Did you know there isn't a spare tire on the truck?" Amanda asked in a slightly annoyed tone.

Riccan pursed his lips and looked down suddenly. "Yes, I took it off to try to find out if it was causing the squeaking sound. I hadn't gotten around to putting it back on yet. I'm really sorry. How come you didn't call me?"

"Oh, I forgot the stupid phone here at home. Of all days!"

"Hmph!" Riccan agreed. "I understand the tow truck, but who's in the BMW?"

"Oh, she's an old high school classmate of mine who came to my rescue. Her father's the owner of the tow truck company." She leaned closer so only Riccan could hear and whispered, "They are fans of yours from your racing days. I sort of promised they could meet you. I hope you don't mind."

Riccan chuckled and replied, "I should be mad, but I owe these two a lot more than an appearance for getting you home safely." He had walked off to the side so he could see the blown tire. His eyebrows rose as he assessed the extensive damage of where the rubber tire used to be. "Boy, you don't do things half-way, do you, Amanda? We're going to have to get a new wheel along with the tire. I'm glad you weren't hurt. Where did it happen?"

"On the highway just as I pulled out from the cemetery. It could have been a lot worse. Luckily I had finished my turn and was going straight when it blew. I pulled over immediately. I'm really sorry about the damage, Riccan."

"Are you kidding? This is nothing compared to your safety. There's nothing to apologize for. I'll be right back," Riccan said as he patted her arm and left her side to go talk with Mr. McFarland as he finished unhooking the truck from his rig. He called out, "Thanks for getting my wife home safely."

"No problem. I wouldn't have had to tow the rig except she didn't have a spare tire. You should probably make sure she has one before she drives again."

Riccan felt abashed at having to admit his guilt in the matter, but he definitely did not want this man to think Amanda had been at fault. "Well, she didn't know I'd taken it off. I forgot to tell her, so really, this is all my doing."

Billy looked up at Riccan, respecting him even more for being honest. He tossed the final rigging equipment into the bin on the back of his truck and then rubbed his palms down the front of his jacket. He held out his hand to Riccan and said, "My name's Billy McFarland. It's a real honor to meet you, Mr. Stel. I've been watching you on T.V. for a long time, and you are a real class act."

Riccan responded by grasping his hand firmly and smiling. "Thanks, Mr. McFarland. Please call me Riccan."

"Only if you'll call me Billy. This here, is my daughter, Angie. If you ever need an insurance agent, she's your girl." His pride was evident in the tone of his voice and the look on his face as he talked about his only child.

CHAPTER 13

"Are you busy? Do you have time to come inside and have a cup of coffee?" Riccan asked.

"Oh, I don't want to impose. I'm sure you have other plans for a Sunday afternoon."

"Please, I'd love to get to know you and your daughter. I heard she went to school with my wife and I think they'd like to catch up. I'd appreciate another man around to keep me company." He smiled endearingly and was rewarded by Billy's reply.

"Okay, but I can't stay long. My wife's gonna have dinner ready shortly." He clapped Riccan on the shoulder and fell into step beside him.

The two men converged on where the women were talking. Riccan said, "I've invited Billy, here, to come inside and have coffee with us. Shall we go inside and I can get you paid as well."

"No, no, you don't have to pay Mr. …I mean, Riccan!" Billy announced hastily.

"Nonsense, you don't work for free, Billy. Besides, how would it look if you didn't charge me? People might think it was favoritism. We can't have that, now, can we?" He grinned mischievously as he stepped up to the front door and led the way inside.

"I guess not," Billy replied weakly. His voice died away once he stepped inside and he took in the grandeur of the massive foyer with the curving staircase on the left-hand side. He looked around and barely caught himself before whistling in appreciation.

Angie stepped into the foyer beside Amanda, and she openly gaped in appreciation. "This sure is a big house for just the two of you!"

"We have our two daughters here as well. They're visiting their grandparents right now, or we'd introduce them to you."

"Two daughters? I thought you have only been…you know…for a year now. How did you manage to have two?"

"Twins."

"Identical twins," Riccan said over his shoulder with pride.

"Wow! How cool! It must be fun having the patter of little feet around," Angie added wistfully. She looked around avidly taking in every detail. One thing she did notice was the complete lack of any personal photos anywhere. She thought it slightly odd for a newly married couple to not at least have their wedding photo proudly displayed. "Where are the wedding photos?" she blurted without thinking about how bad it sounded.

Amanda looked pointedly ahead to Riccan as if accusing him of something before she answered. "We eloped in Reno and didn't get any pictures."

"What? No pictures? It's too bad." Her disappointment was very apparent.

The smell of coffee wafted over to where they remained in the foyer. Amanda smiled inwardly knowing Riccan had used his crystal power to create the coffee. She knew for certain he would not have brewed any for just himself. Sometimes it was fun having special abilities hidden from the public as was the case with surprise guests and always being prepared for anything.

"Let's go sit down in the living room," Amanda suggested as she moved across the foyer and past the dining room. The elegant furniture was impressive, and she knew Angie would be investigating everything as they progressed through the house. She turned to Angie and asked, "Do you want tea or coffee? We have both."

"Oh, coffee is fine. I take it black."

Amanda nodded as she pulled a cup out of the cupboard and poured from a coffee pot she had never seen before. She was about to make herself a cup of tea by hand when Riccan surprised her with a cup already prepared. He winked as she took it from her and she knew he had created this out of Billy's sight. She grinned as she accepted the cup and then turned around to take both back to the coffee table in the living room.

Angie was standing at the wall of windows at the back of the house looking out on the yard. She was amazed at the size of the pool; it had to be Olympic-sized. The grounds were immaculately groomed without a leaf out of place. She wondered how many people it took to keep it all so pristine.

"Come sit down so we can chat," Amanda offered from where she sat on the couch. She had cradled her cup of tea between her two hands and inhaled the minty scent of the steam. It reminded her of the steena tea she usually drank when she was in Tuala.

Angie seemed reluctant to leave the view from the windows, but she turned and joined Amanda on the couch. She reached forward and picked up her own cup and took a sip with appreciation of the perfectly roasted flavor. She thought it might be the best coffee she had ever tasted and wondered what brand they used. Thinking it might be rude to ask, she kept the thought to herself.

Thinking she should move to a more polite line of questions, she asked, "Didn't you say something about Neal being back home? Where has he been and when did he get back?"

Amanda glanced swiftly at Riccan to see if he wanted to answer, she was disgusted by his refusal which left her trying to explain the unexplainable truth. "He just came home on December first, actually."

"Really? Where has he been this whole time? It's been what, eight years?"

"Well, this isn't public knowledge, but he was being held against his will in Mexico. Riccan used some of his contacts to find him, and we managed to negotiate a deal to get him home safely. He's had a pretty rough time adjusting to being back. In fact, he came over here yesterday to talk things over. There aren't many people he can talk to who know about what happened to him." Amanda could see Riccan trying not to laugh at her explanation. She pointedly turned her head slightly, so he was not in her direct line of view.

"Oh my goodness! I had no idea! This really has been a fascinating day! So was Neal shocked to hear you had gotten married? I mean, you two were always an item in school." She leaned forward to add the last part privately, knowing it could be an awkward question with her new husband just a few feet away.

"He'd moved on as well. He had a girlfriend in Mexico."

"Oh, so he's involved with someone else?"

"Not anymore. She decided she did not want to move away from her home. Obviously, Neal didn't want to stay in a foreign land. No, Neal isn't in any relationship right now."

"That's too bad," Angie said without much conviction. She had always had a crush on him, but he was only interested in being with Amanda. *Maybe now...*she thought to herself, hardly allowing herself to believe she might have a chance with him.

Amanda could see Angie's thoughts were heading right where she had hoped they would go. She needed to make sure Neal had someone who could take care of him and comfort him. His mother could only help him so far, but Angie could help him heal physically as well as emotionally. It felt a little strange arranging her ex-fiancé's love life, but she knew instinctively it was the right thing to do. Otherwise, she would not have dreamed about it happening already.

There was a lull in the conversation, and Riccan suddenly asked, "Since you love the NHRA, would you like to see my Wallys? I have them in my office if you're interested."

Billy brightened up immediately and said, "I'd love to! I heard they're pretty heavy. I've never seen one in person, only on T.V."

The two men crossed the living room and went down the hall out of Amanda's sight as they turned into the first doorway. Amanda grinned at Billy's enthusiasm and knew Riccan would have a good time showing off his trophies. "That worked out well, now, didn't it?" Amanda asked Angie with a chuckle.

"Just like two little kids!" she joked back.

They both giggled and then leaned on the couch to relax.

After a few minutes of contemplation, Angie finally asked what was on her mind. "Do you think you could ask Neal if he wanted me to come visit? I think it would be strange to just show up on his parents' doorstep."

"Sure, I'd love to. As I said before, I think he needs some friends to lean on right now. I think I should warn you; he doesn't look the same. I mean, he's still really fit and muscular, but he has aged quite a bit from the ordeal. His heart and mind are still young though. I just didn't want you to be shocked when you saw him for the first time."

Angie nodded like she understood what was being said. Inside her mind, she was thinking it could not be as bad as Amanda was making it out to be. After all, he had only been home for a few weeks. Surely, given enough time in a safe environment and good food, he would relax and begin to look better. She took another sip of her coffee and contemplated Neal's prospects for the future since he was home again.

Amanda did not want to push the subject any further and remained quiet as she covertly watched Angie mull through her ideas. This plan had worked out perfectly. Her thoughts were interrupted by the sound of the men coming back from the office. She had thought they would have been much longer ogling over the wall of awards.

"We should let these two get back to their evening, Angie," Billy announced as he entered the living room once again. "Thanks for the coffee. I think it might have been the best I've ever tasted; just don't tell my wife I said so!"

"Hey, I heard that, Dad."

"Don't go telling on me then!"

Everyone laughed together. Amanda set her cup on the coffee table and stood up at the same time as Angie.

"We'll have to make plans to visit again," Amanda offered.

"I'd love it! I'm really glad to find out you're alive. Maybe I can meet your daughters next time."

"I'm sure it'll happen," Amanda replied, even as she wondered how their conversation would go since her daughters were only ten years younger than herself. There was no good way to say she had been transported back in time and had her babies in another dimension of Earth. It was not really something you brought up over casual conversation.

When their guests had driven away, and Riccan and Amanda were finally alone, Riccan folded his arms around his wife and pulled her into a tight embrace. "I'm sorry about the spare tire."

"I'm sorry about the flat."

"I love you."

"I love you, too."

"Why don't we sit down and you can tell me about your visit to see your sister's grave." He grabbed her hand and began pulling her toward the living room. The one thing he wanted to do was sit down and hold his wife in his arms while she talked. It was one of his favorite things in life.

Amanda snorted as she followed him. He was going to get a kick out of all of her troubles in the day. They snuggled together, and Amanda regaled him with all of the details of the day. She ended with, "Is it bad I didn't feel anything at all at Virginia's gravesite?"

"No. From what you've said about the condition of the grounds surrounding it, I don't think even your mom feels a connection with her there. What you feel for her in your heart and mind are what really matters, not any physical location. I wouldn't worry about it if I were you."

"Thanks, I needed to hear that. I also had another weird premonition."

Riccan had to consciously stay relaxed as he processed what she said. Every time she had experienced premonitions, it had put someone in danger. Trying to remain casual, he asked, "What was it?"

"Do you remember reading in my journal what happened when I came home the first time in my dream?"

"Which part?"

"The part where my dad tells me Neal had moved on and had another girlfriend."

"Oh, yes. I do recall something about it. What are you thinking?"

"Don't you think it was odd for me to have so many delays today? Then Angie told me she doesn't normally work on Sundays and she was heading home at the exact time I had the flat. What are the chances her father would own a towing company?"

"And the girl from your dream reality was named Angie, wasn't it?"

"Yes!" Amanda suddenly moved away from where she had been leaning on Riccan's chest so she could turn and face him. "You think it could be her, too, don't you?"

"Maybe," he agreed slowly. He no longer believed in coincidences either. If this were true, then the part of her day which worried him even more than Nealand's relationship status, was the encounter with the Dr. Gascon look-a-like. He did not like to think the deranged doctor was going to make another appearance in their lives. Their lives were crazy enough all on their own!

Willian knew it was a risk, but he decided the outcome was worth it. He picked up the phone and dialed before he changed his mind. There were several outcomes which could occur from this conversation, and he hoped it would go as he wanted. Several rings had sounded, and he almost pulled the receiver away from his ear when he heard a woman's voice on the other end.

Knowing there could only be one woman in the house, he cleared his throat and said, "Hello, Amanda. This is Willian calling."

"Hello, Willian. The girls aren't home right now."

"I know, I wanted to talk about something with you."

"Me? Really? What is it?"

"There's two things really. First, how's Jena doing? I haven't heard from her, and I wanted to make sure she's doing okay since…you know…since we ended our betrothal."

"It's very kind of you to ask. I've never seen her happier, actually. What was your second question?" For some reason it made her feel better to be snarky with Willian. After everything the boy had done to hurt her daughter, she was not feeling very charitable.

Willian winced slightly at Amanda's comment, but he also felt he deserved it and so much more from Jena's parents. He almost felt lucky to get off as easily as he had. He cleared his throat and promptly asked his second question in one breath.

"Valentina told me Gevena has asked for her to come and visit with her in Manzanit. I was wondering if you would allow me to borrow your telepod to take her there. Valentina really thinks it would be good for Gevena to have someone to talk to about the trauma she went through. Also, I'd like to be able to visit with Rasa and find out how she's getting along with her new duties." He drew a deep breath to recover and was glad to have it all out in the open as he waited for Amanda to reply.

At first, Amanda was amused at how much Willian had packed into one breath, but then she mellowed out slightly as his request sunk in. She felt guilty for her previous comment as she realized Willian was trying to do something nice for other people. "Sure," she replied easily.

"Sure, what?" Willian asked, hardly able to believe it had gone so easily. Surely there had to be some sort of catch.

"You can borrow my telepod. When did you want to go? I don't have any plans for travel anytime soon, so it's just sitting in the garage collecting dust. You may as well get some use out of it."

"Well, I'm not exactly sure. I didn't want to say anything to Valentina until I asked you first. Can I get back to you on it? Like later today or maybe tomorrow?" Willian's hands were shaking with adrenaline at how well the conversation had gone. His respect for Amanda had just risen a hundred-fold.

"Sure. Go ahead and plan the day and time and I'll make sure the telepod is available. Okay?"

"Thank you, Amanda! This will mean the world to Val and Gevena."

"Sure thing. Is there anything else?"

"No, well…maybe."

"What is it?"

"Could you possibly contact Rasa and ask her when it would be okay to come? I can't tell you how frustrating it is not to have a patil to do this myself."

"Sure, I can. I'll message her as soon as we're done talking. Can I reach you at this number?" She looked down on her caller ID to make sure a number was displayed.

"Yes. Thank you. I'm going to call Val right now and see what we can arrange."

"Okay. Goodbye."

"Bye!" Willian ripped the phone away from his ear and fumbled to end the call as he let out a huge sigh of relief.

It took him several attempts, but his fumbling fingers eventually dialed Valentina's phone number. She answered almost immediately, much to his relief.

"Hey, Val."

"Hi, Willian. I was just thinking about you."

"Good thoughts, I hope." Willian was pleased to hear she had been thinking about him. He wanted to be the only thing on her mind for the rest of their lives. Well, she could think of other things occasionally, he supposed.

"Of course!" she teased.

"I was really calling to make you an offer. I called Amanda and asked her if I could borrow her telepod to take you to visit Gevena." He stopped when he heard her gasp. "What?"

"You didn't! I mean, not after what happened with Jena! Did she yell at you?"

"No, she was actually really nice." *Mostly,* he thought. He was not about to tell her about the tone of voice in which he had been addressed at the beginning of the conversation.

"Wow! I don't think I could be if I were in her shoes." Valentina shook her head in wonder.

"Hey, whose side are you on here?" Willian was actually a little hurt by Valentina's comment.

"Yours, of course. I'm just saying...oh, never mind. Tell me what she said."

"She's going to find out from Rasa when a good time to visit will be, and Amanda said we could use her telepod whenever we're ready to go. She's going to call me back with the days and times, and we can coordinate it with whatever you have going on. So, what do you think? Is that cool or what?"

Valentina giggled, and she just had to ask, "How long did it take you to find the right time to use the word 'cool'? I understand it's not a word you use in Tuala."

Willian chuckled in return and admitted, "I've been trying ever since I learned about it, actually!" They both burst out laughing.

Getting back to the conversation, Valentina wiped her eyes from laughing so hard, and said, "If we can arrange it for this week, we won't have to worry about school schedules or anything like that. I think that would be easiest, especially because I won't know how long we'll be in Manzanit. Who knows how much Gevena will want to discuss, you know? What are you going to be doing while we have girl talk?"

"I'm hoping to catch up with Rasa and find out how things have been going with her. Don't worry; I'll keep myself busy and out of your way."

"As long as you don't get yourself into trouble," Valentina teased.

"Now you're starting to sound like my mom!" Willian rolled his eyes at having another woman in his life telling him to be good.

"Well, I should probably get off the phone just in case Amanda is trying to call me back."

"Don't they have call-waiting over there?"

"What's that?"

Valentina chuckled and then gave up. "Never mind. Call me when you know something more, okay?"

"Okay. Bye." His thumb pressed the button to end the call, and he dropped the cordless receiver on his mattress next to the dog. She looked up at him expectantly since the phone had startled her awake. "Now we get to wait, Pesi," he said, and he rubbed the side of her head and watched as she tilted her chin to the side so he could scratch a better spot.

CHAPTER 15

manda had kept the phone to her ear a moment longer and heard Willian's long exhalation. She rapidly hung up her end and burst out laughing. Maybe Willian was going to turn out okay after all. Maybe Valentina was going to be the difference in how he behaved with others.

Today's conversation went a long way toward giving her hope. After all, she was probably going to be dealing with him for a long time when he stepped up to be an Elder and Riccan did likewise. They would be considered equals at that point so it would be better to mend their fences before anything happened.

Thinking it was nice to have a distraction since she was alone in the house, Amanda went into the office and uncovered the hidden patil. She powered it up and tried to decide if she should send a message or try to video chat with Rasa. It had been a while since she had touched base with her cousin, so she opted for the more personal approach.

When Rasa's face appeared on the screen, she could see strain showing around her eyes. Amanda wondered what could possibly have been going on to be so evident in her usually gentle expression. There was a fierceness about her which seemed at odds with her personality.

"Hi, Rasa. How are you doing?" Amanda asked cheerfully.

"Busy! I can't believe how petty people can be sometimes! Sorry, you don't want to hear about my problems. What can I do for you?"

"I don't mind listening if you just need a sympathetic ear. After all, I'm going to be the wife of an Elder someday so it might be a good idea to let me know some of the troubles I might encounter."

"Oh, believe me; you'll learn fast. I don't want to jade your opinion before you even begin."

Amanda chuckled at her tone. She decided not to take up too much more of her time and got to the reason for her call. "I understand Gevena has been wanting a visitor. Willian asked if he could bring Valentina over. We were just wondering when it might be good for them to come. What do you think?"

"Anytime would be good. It would be nice to know Gevena was getting the attention she needs. I've hardly been able to spare a minute since returning home, apart from getting her enrolled in school. Yes, the sooner, the better as far as I'm concerned." She looked down at the piles of work strewn on her desk and then looked back up at the patil. "That would take one thing off of my roster of things to get done."

"I'm sorry I'm not able to do more to help you out. I'm just roaming the empty house without anything to do. It just doesn't seem right; does it?"

"Well, there may be something…" Rasa began as her mind went back to the prophecy Amanda had found in the ancient text.

"Yes, what is it? How can I help?" Amanda leaned forward, eager to do something, anything really.

"I was just looking over the new writings you had found in

Riccan's historical book. It occurred to me you have been right about everything when it comes to the samaras. Only three of them have remained unclaimed. And if your theory about the attendants of Jehoban's meeting are each supposed to have one, then…it would mean I should be looking for mine. I just don't have the time, but I don't want to be the reason the prophecy doesn't come to pass. I know it's a lot to ask, but could you possibly look into it for me?"

"Certainly! But I have to warn you; it might be a personal thing. It might only make itself known to you. Remember, I don't even have one myself. I don't know what they feel like other than the descriptions told to me from the others who have claimed theirs. I will do whatever I can, that I can promise."

Rasa sighed in resignation. "Thanks, I'll have to hope it's enough. If you could, please let Valentina know she can come anytime. I'll leave word with the guards and staff for her to have complete access to the Residence when she gets here."

"Can you grant the same access for Willian?"

"Oh, he doesn't need it. As the successor to the First Elder, everyone here already knows who he is."

"Really? I didn't know about that. I still have so much I need to learn about Tualan culture. Sometimes it seems so daunting and like I'll never know enough." Amanda sighed, worried about her future involvement with the people in the Pantano District.

"Don't worry about it. You already know the important things, the rest will either become apparent or won't be important. I really should get back to work now. Did you need anything else?" Rasa hated having to cut the conversation short, but she had several deadlines looming over her, and she was feeling the strain starting to overwhelm her.

"I'm sorry. No, that was everything. I'll let you go now. Take care!" Amanda smiled one last time before she disconnected the video connection. She had seen Rasa's farewell nod before the screen went blank.

She sat back in her chair and sighed deeply. It had been her discovery of the prophetic words which had set in motion the search for the samaras. They still had no idea what was going to happen once they were all located. It seemed rather daunting to search two worlds for a small crystal which could fit in the palm of your hand. Well, they had done pretty well for themselves given the fact ten of them had been uncovered by various means.

She wished they could all have been as simple as when Captain Ahn had thought his into existence. Nobody else had been able to succeed in the same manner, certainly not for lack of trying! Amanda chuckled as she imagined the amount of time had been spent trying to use willpower to get the remaining samaras to appear out of thin air.

Before she became too absorbed in the mystery of the remaining samaras, Amanda picked up the phone and selected the last caller ID number from the history on the phone. It never even had a chance to ring before it was answered, which caused Amanda to smile at Willian's eagerness to hear back from her.

"Willian? Is that you?"

"Yes."

"Hi, this is Amanda. I just talked with Rasa, and she said she would arrange clearance for the both of you for any time you want to come. She did mention it would be better if you could come sooner rather than later. Have you had a chance to speak with Val yet?"

"Yes, right after I spoke with you. She said she would like to go while it's still winter break at school. Do you think it would be too soon to try to go today? It's still pretty early."

"I don't see why it would be a problem. Just promise me you

won't try to time your arrival. It's not worth the risk involved just to gain a few hours."

"I promise I won't, I'm not sure how it works anyway, and I certainly would never risk Val's life on something so stupid."

"Good, I'm glad to hear it. Okay, well, whenever you figure it out, just head on over to our house. Both Val's and Behn's cars are already programmed with our gate so you won't have any trouble getting onto the property. If we aren't here, then feel free to take the telepod on your own. The remote for the shield and door lock is on the desk in the kitchen. You know what it looks like, right?"

"Yeah, they're all pretty standard. Amanda, I appreciate you letting me do this. I wasn't sure how you would react to my asking, but you've been great about everything. I also wanted to apologize for the things which happened between me and your daughter. She is really a wonderful person, and I'm ashamed to admit I was always quite jealous of her abilities. It's my hope she will find someone to be happy with."

"Thank you, Willian. I know it isn't easy to admit when you've made a mistake, but your sincerity goes a long way to making amends. Things have been pretty tense between you and Jena, but as I said before, she is happy. More than that, I think she is happy with what you and Val have found together. You better be good to Val or I might have to change my mind about you!" She was only half-teasing with her mild threat.

"I definitely will. Besides, I think she could make my life pretty miserable if I didn't since our life-lines are actually joined together. If she ever left me, it would feel as though I had been ripped in half and, believe me, I never want to know what it's like."

"That's good to hear. Okay, enough of my lecture. Go call Val and get this all settled."

"Okay! Thank you again. We'll be seeing you soon!"

Amanda instantly pulled the phone away from her ear as the

sound of him slamming the receiver in the cradle to hang it up was loud and unexpected. She had to chuckle at his enthusiasm, though, so she was not angry at his abrupt end to the call. This would seem like a great adventure to a teenager. She could recall how excited she had been when she was the same age and waiting for a date with Nealand.

There he was again, coming to her mind at an unexpected time. While she had never regretted marrying Riccan, it might have happened quicker than it should have. After all, she had just recovered from her coma and had not really had any time to work through her feelings over the loss of her relationship with Neal.

Well, it was not exactly true, since she had experienced years of her life in Tuala while she had been dreaming. The dream state had included getting to know Riccan and falling in love with him. Unfortunately for Riccan, he had not experienced the same thing with her, but everything had turned out perfectly anyway.

With her mind focused on the things which had happened in her dream, an idea sprang into her mind which caused her to jump to her feet. Something Rasa had mentioned offhandedly made her think her answer might lie in the beginning. She ran from the office, down the hallway, and into the library.

Her momentum moved her through the room until she stopped at the wall of books. She ran her hands under one of the shelves until her fingers found the lever which released the latch on the secret door. The room hidden beneath the bookcase held all of the objects Riccan had collected from Tuala which should not be seen on Earth.

Amanda immediately felt a sense of reverence when she stepped into the narrow room which was illuminated by a high window on one side. She quietly walked over to the bookcase across from the entrance to the room and kneeled in front of a cupboard. She opened the left door and pulled out an ancient-looking text. Never before had she actually held the book in her hands, she had always seen Riccan touch it. She stood up, turned, and walked over to a small desk where she gently set it down.

She was almost afraid to open the cover. Who knew what words it might contain which had not been there previously. This book was not only old, but it was also mysterious, said to have been written by Jehoban Himself. Riccan had once told her it was the most important item in the room which should be returned to his father should anything ever happen to him.

Letting her hands caress the soft leather, she read the ornate script on the front: Elder's Instructional Guide. She carefully opened the hardbound cover and let out a soft sigh of relief as nothing went wrong. She had imagined the spine crumbling apart as she lifted the front, but her fears were unfounded. Even as old as it was, it remained perfectly intact.

Her eyes immediately found the addition she had told Riccan about from her dream. She knew the words by heart:

'Take comfort in one another, combined you will see. Believe in what you Understand, Know what you Do, then you can Be.'

"What is this? When did this get here! Oh, my goodness," Amanda looked around her in a panic. She desperately wanted to write down the new words, but she was afraid to leave the book and have the words disappear. Reading the two new sentences over several times and saying them out loud to enhance her ability to recall them, she reluctantly ran from the room. She ransacked the library tables for a pen and paper only to be frustrated by the lack of supplies.

In utter despair, she ran back down the hall to the office and grabbed the first piece of paper and pencil she came across. She raced back out of the room, and her foot slipped on the hall runner causing her to fall sideways and crash her shoulder painfully into the wall. With a grunt, she pushed herself upright and continued her mad dash back to the secret room.

Her breathing was hard, and her hands were shaking as she bumped into the table in the center of the room. "Thank goodness!" she cried out as she saw the words were still showing on the page. Meticulously she copied the words exactly as they appeared, including even the unusual capitalizations. She had no idea what might be significant with what she was starting to feel were instructions for action. As she got to the last letter, the pressure on the pencil became too much, and the lead broke off and shot across the room.

Amanda stared at the pencil dumbly and then burst out laughing. She had been so intent on accuracy; she had not taken care of her tools. If anyone had been around to witness her actions in the last few minutes, they might have worried about her mental stability.

She put the broken pencil down and then carefully closed the cover of the book. With more care than she'd shown herself, she returned it to its resting place on the shelf and shut the cupboard door. The prophecy must be moving forward if Jehoban had decided to give the next set of directions.

A sense of panic rose in Amanda as she realized they still had the final three samaras to find before they would even be able to think about proceeding with His plans. They were going to have to be more diligent than ever to keep up with His timeline. She picked up the pencil and paper and quietly left the narrow room. Her attention was not too distracted to forget to close the secret passage into the room, however, and she made sure it was sealed before she left the library.

"Maybe I should go see Rasa along with the kids," Amanda mused to herself. As soon as she finished the statement, the familiar clicking sensation in her head made it known she had hit upon the correct thing to do. "Alrighty then. I guess I should get myself ready to take a trip!" She went back to the office and found another pencil. She wrote from memory the first part of the prophecy which, she believed, spoke about herself before she folded the paper to keep it in her hand for safekeeping as she walked through the house to get to her bedroom upstairs. She would change into more traditional clothing for Tualan custom and then she would surprise Willian with her change in plans.

CHAPTER 16

Even though Petre wished he could return to his water craft, he needed to stay near Tirsha. His connection with her was stronger than anything he had ever known. It was even more than when he had kept Jinya with him so many anons ago.

He shook his head in wonder at even having Jinya come to mind considering how much had happened since he had last been spying on Captain Ahn's house. No longer was he interested in pursuing the woman whom he had mistakenly thought he was in love with. What he had felt for her paled in comparison to the heart-stopping pain he had for Tirsha.

This was such a new experience for him since he had always considered his own needs first. It was just a fact of life for the line of work he had chosen. Of course, he would have to change that part of himself, as well, if he intended to create a new future. Nobody would ever have believed how much he had changed from his experience between dimensions. Heck, he hardly understood it himself.

He was not even interested in where Ahn had spirited Jinya off to on the last day he had followed them to the telepod landing field. At the time he had been angry, but now he was relieved to not have to deal with an awkward situation between the two women. Although, if he were being honest with himself, he had to admit he did not think Jinya had wanted to get back together with him after all.

Turning around, Petre looked back toward the docks and wondered when he would be able to get back to his own vessel. He would love to be able to give Tirsha a tour of his humble home on the water. It would be a struggle, but if Tirsha wanted him to give up his water craft, he would actually consider it. Petre nodded confirmation to himself since he would gladly give up anything he had if it meant keeping her by his side.

He turned around and walked the next couple of blocks in silent contemplation of his new future. His mind still felt altered by his encounter with Elder Daven's samara. While he had kept a samara before, it was nothing compared to the Elder's stone. He had known it had belonged to the Elder and had gladly relinquished it to him. What was even stranger for him was the idea of not coveting the Elder's possession of it instead of himself.

Petre stepped onto the wide porch of the Harbor Master's house and knocked on the carved front door. He was pleasantly surprised to find Tirsha had been the person to greet him and even happier yet when she eagerly invited him inside to visit. This feeling of being wanted was what he had been missing his whole life, and he wanted to experience it to its fullest.

"How are you doing today, Tirsha? Have you been able to spend a lot of time with your daughter?"

"I'm doing great and, yes, I've visited with Corva several hours each day when she's not in school or studying. I just can't believe how much she has changed. She's so smart, and I'm so proud of her." She led the way into the front sitting room and offered him a seat. "Would you like some steena tea?"

"If it's no bother," he answered, feeling slightly strange with the formalities.

"None whatsoever. I'll be right back."

Petre wondered why Tirsha did not just create the tea for them while remaining in the room. Maybe she was unfamiliar with where things were located in the kitchen or if they even had enough supplies for her to make it. In any event, he remained seated in solitude while he heard noises coming from down the hallway.

Tirsha entered the room holding a tray containing two cups and a steaming teapot. Petre jumped to his feet and relieved her of the burden. He placed it on the table for her. Before he was able to touch the pot, Tirsha picked it up and began to pour the hot liquid into the cups. Petre took the one closest to him and resumed his seat across from her.

In the past, Petre would have already been drinking his tea and not bothering to wait for Tirsha to join him. Now, he wanted to share the first sip together and enjoy her companionship. Instead, he held the cup between his palms, feeling the warmth begin to radiate from the porcelain, and think about what to ask Tirsha about next to keep her talking with him. He loved hearing the sounds of her voice, no matter what she was actually saying.

"I'm sorry to hear about your husband," Petre blurted and then wished he had kept the comment to himself when he saw her hands flinch at his mention.

"If you knew him, you wouldn't have been sorry," she murmured back. "I'm sorry, Petre. That wasn't nice of me. You see, Filbrun was not a kind man. He...he drank a lot and he took out his frustrations in life on me, both verbally and physically. He was a hard man to love. I was always afraid of what would happen to

Corva as she got older and began having opinions of her own. Filbrun didn't like to be contradicted in anything, and he always wanted his orders followed immediately. You know how toddlers can be when they decide to do something; they won't take no for an answer."

"I haven't really spent much time around toddlers," Petre admitted. *Although*, he thought, *there was a short time when I had taken care of Jinya's daughter.* He shuddered as he remembered what a disaster it had been. "My career really hasn't supported a family lifestyle."

Tirsha cocked her head and wondered what type of a future she would be able to make with Petre if he wanted to keep his career. She did not want to live her life on a water craft, nor did she think it would be a good idea for her daughter. "What is it you do, exactly?"

"Nothing to be proud of, that's for sure. I've decided to make some drastic changes in my life because I want you to be proud of me. I want to do everything I can to please you." He had been frustrated by what he had said to get her questioning him, but he was glad they were having this conversation.

"I don't want you to change for me," she held up her hand when she saw Petre start to protest. She continued, "I want you to change for yourself. It has to be for yourself, or it won't last. Don't you think?"

Petre raised his eyebrows as he considered her point. "I do agree. I want us both to be proud of the man I am becoming. I've disappointed myself for far too long. It's time I actually stepped up to go into the career I was supposed to review. I've dodged my lottery assignment for too long as it is."

"Oh, Petre! Yes, you have to follow the lottery rules. How far behind are you?"

Petre looked down at the cup in his hands, ashamed of himself as he calculated the anons. Finally, he bashfully shifted his eyes up to hers as he answered, "This anon makes it fifteen anons."

"That long? Oh, no! What are you going to do to make it up?"

"I don't know. I hope Elder Daven might give me some advice on what to do."

"Good idea. I really liked him; he was so nice to us. Don't you think?"

"Yes. Tirsha, I have to be honest with you. I've had my problems with the Elders, and I've often criticized them and even cheated them in the past. I can only hope Elder Daven can forgive my past indiscretions and know I'm making an effort to change."

"I'm sure he will; he seemed reasonable to me."

"True, I agree." He sipped his cooling tea, yet he had his doubts whether or not it could work out as well as he had described. It would be a blessing, but he had become used to be continually disappointed with what life handed out to him. *No*, he thought, *I'm not going to think negatively anymore. That's what I used to do in the past, and I'm going to change!*

"What line of work were you supposed to go in?"

"You know, I never even found out. I didn't show up for my assignment."

Tirsha gasped lightly at his complete disregard for the social structure. She did not want to make him feel worse than he probably already did, but it was shocking to hear he had not even shown up on assignment day. She would have done anything to even get an assignment, but her disability had prevented the special day from ever happening.

"You must think I'm a horrible person."

"No, I think you've just been misguided. I'm really glad you want to turn yourself around. And I think Elder Daven will be able to help you. When are you going to see him again?"

Petre had not really considered leaving anytime soon. He had been afraid to be too far away from Tirsha in case she needed him. After visiting with her today, it was apparent she was happy where she was living and getting to know her daughter again. There really was no good excuse to delay his future. Besides, the sooner he began working in an honest profession, the sooner he would be able to entertain starting a relationship.

"I wanted to wait until I talked with you before I made any plans. I had to be sure you were okay, you know."

Tirsha blushed and tried to cover her embarrassment by taking a quick sip of tea. The fluid went down the wrong way, and she began to sputter and cough. She spilled the tea on her legs and jumped up to keep it from burning her skin. Her fear of burning swept through her mind causing her to start having a panic attack. She struggled to catch her breath even as she coughed more violently.

Petre slammed his cup down onto the table and jumped up to try to help her. He held onto her arm and thumped her back, but her coughing just seemed to be getting worse. He looked around to see if there were anyone else who could offer assistance. Intense relief washed through him when he saw Barla heading toward them from the kitchen. "Barla, please hurry!"

"What's going on Petre? What's wrong with Tirsha?"

"She swallowed her tea wrong, and then I think she started to panic. I don't know how to help her; please do something!"

"Step aside, please." Without waiting for his compliance, Barla pushed Petre away to be directly in front of Tirsha. She could see the panic in the other woman's eyes, and she had to agree with Petre's assessment. "Easy now, Tirsha. You'll be fine once you calm down. Let me help you." She began to pull elemy from around her and move it into Tirsha's body to help soothe her.

Almost instantly, she could tell it was the right way to handle the situation. Tirsha's odd expression changed back to normal, and her breathing slowed down. She still coughed from the irritation in her throat, but it was a normal cough. "That's better, Tirsha. Do you feel more yourself again?"

Tirsha simply nodded since her coughing prevented anything further.

Barla looked down at Tirsha's wet clothes and again used her newly acquired crystal skills to dry her clothes. She had never known how gratifying it could be to use elemy to fix things rather than having to do them manually. Her gratitude to Jehoban multiplied because He had given her the birth crystal to let her know He approved of her in Tuala. It was her most prized possession, and her hand reached up to touch it reverently.

Barla had left them alone to continue their visit. As soon as Tirsha's coughing subsided, Petre decided he should take her advice and seek out Elder Daven as soon as possible. Petre cleared his throat and said, "I think I'm going to head out now if you don't need me."

"Go, I'm fine. I promise." She smiled up at him as he rose from his chair. She stood when he came up beside her and put her hand in his. Together, they walked to the front door.

Petre turned to face her and took her other hand in his. He looked down at her upturned face and allowed himself to follow his impulse to kiss her. When their lips parted yet they remained close; he whispered, "I don't want to leave you ever."

"Well then hurry and get your life together. We can be together when you're ready."

Wishing he could honestly say he was ready now, he had to content himself by simply nodding his agreement with her statement. "I'll hurry."

"Thanks," she whispered back and smiled up at him.

Petre's heart melted even more at the blind trust she had for him. He could do anything as long as she believed in him. He could see it in her eyes; he would prove himself worthy. It was hard, but he tore himself away from her and rapidly turned to leave. Seconds later, he turned at the gate and saw her waving sweetly at him. Raising his hand to wave back, he smiled with renewed confidence in his future. His next stop would be a visit with Elder Daven.

CHAPTER 17

The car door slamming outside alerted Amanda to company. She was ready to go and rushed to open the front door for the kids. As she had suspected, Willian had arranged with Valentina to go to Manzanit in less than an hour. "Good morning, you two. I hope you won't mind my slight change of plans."

Willian looked slightly alarmed even as he tried to hide it. "Did you need for us to reschedule? We totally understand if something else came up."

"Something has come up, but I was hoping I could go with you to Manzanit. I have something to discuss with Rasa which would be better done in person."

"Oh!" Willian exclaimed, relief evident in the tenseness releasing from his shoulders. "Sure thing, Amanda. Do you want to navigate then?"

"No, I can be co-pilot. You've flown to Manzanit before, and I haven't yet, so you're the more experienced one for this flight."

"Sure thing! Are you ready to go now or do we need to wait?"

"No, I'm ready whenever you are. I'm as eager to get going as you, I'm sure!" Amanda grinned at Willian. "How are you doing, Val? We haven't seen you since the girls went to their grandparents' house."

She promptly looked over to Willian and then back at Amanda before she replied quietly, "I wasn't sure I'd be welcome."

"Oh, Val; of course, you're still welcome here. You're one of Juila's and Jena's first friends. Just because there's been a change in circumstances, it doesn't mean we don't still care about you!" She pulled Valentina off to the side and spoke quietly, "Besides, Jena has told us she's happy for you."

"I'm so glad to hear that. I've been worried because I haven't heard anything from her even though I know she spent Friday night here at home. When Mr. Stel called me, he told me the girls were home for the day. I hoped everything was okay."

"Your concern is appreciated, but everything is just fine. We had to catch up on some family business, is all. Now, what's this I hear about Gevena wanting to visit with you? Did you two get to know one another well when she was here?"

"No, not exactly. I just think we have a lot in common and she wanted someone her age to talk to about it."

Amanda could see Valentina was uncomfortable with the question, so she let it go for now. At some point, she would probably hear more about it from Rasa. If not, it really did not matter to her. "Let's get going, shall we?" she asked brightly to both of her guests. Without waiting for a reply, she turned and led the way to the kitchen to retrieve the telepod remote.

Willian made small talk along the way and said, "I was wondering why you were wearing that outfit. It's not exactly the style for here on Earth, but it'll fit right in where we're headed."

"Do you think so? I'm glad." She opened the garage door and stepped down onto the concrete. When she got closer to the space where the telepod was parked, she touched one of the buttons on the remote to deactivate the security shield allowing it appear out of thin air right in front of their eyes. Amanda never got tired of seeing it. It reminded her of a magic trick she had once seen on T.V with some famous magician making a seven-ton Learjet disappear on stage.

A couple of steps closer and then Amanda touched the button to open the door on the side of the telepod which dropped down to create a ramp into the mid-section of the aircraft. She entered first and sat in the right-hand seat up in the cockpit. Amanda fastened her seat harness while she waited for the other two to enter the craft and get situated in their respective seats.

Willian took his place next to Amanda up front and, once again, marveled at the sleek control panel. He touched the button in front of him to secure the cabin for departure. It took him a moment longer than usual to fasten his own seatbelt as his hands fumbled nervously to get it clasped correctly. "Since you're more familiar with these particular controls, I'd appreciate it if you can verify I do everything correctly."

"Sure thing," Amanda agreed readily. She had planned on it anyway, but it was comforting to know Willian was smart enough to ask. Amanda knew the surest way to get into trouble was to be too cocky of your own abilities.

With another pause while he looked over everything once more, Willian began the startup procedures on the telepod. He felt the entire craft lift off of the ground and remain hovering in place several inches above the concrete floor. The plascreen panel lit up and, one by one, the lights all turned green indicating all systems were working properly.

He tapped on the navigation screen and scrolled through the pre-programmed locations until he got to Manzanit. He selected it and waited a second or two for the coordinates and map of the landing site appeared on the screen. Leaning forward, he inspected the screen and verified the numbers as those he had memorized previously. Likewise, he agreed with the map displayed as being the same location as where he had landed before.

"I think we're ready to go now." He looked over to Amanda for confirmation.

"Don't forget to have your hand on the manual control during flight."

"Right, yes, I was getting to that part next." He immediately wrapped his fingers around the control, making sure his finger did not trigger the activation switch until he was mentally ready for the transfer. "We're set to go now, Val. Remember the transfer between Earth and Tuala takes about six seconds so count it out in your head."

"Thanks, Willian. I'm ready," Valentina replied from the passenger seats in the cargo area.

"Make sure you keep the coordinates in mind just in case something happens with the programming. The human mind is still more reliable than any piece of software." Amanda smiled to take the sting out of her tone. "At least it's what Riccan kept telling me with each flying lesson."

"Thanks for the reminder. I agree with Riccan. Okay, coordinates are visualized, and I'm ready to activate the transfer."

"Okay, carry on," Amanda offered. She made sure she had the coordinates firmly focused in her own mind just in case something went wrong.

Once the activation button was pressed, everything around them disappeared. All sensory perception was instantly lost save the sound of their own heartbeats within them. The seconds rolled by like an eternity until they popped back into the daylight hovering over the landing field at Manzanit.

Willian manually guided the craft to an open spot on the grass and set it down near the ground without contact. He sighed with relief and began the standard shut-down procedures. The last process automatically moved the craft the last several inches to the soft soil. He pressed the button to open the side door with one hand while he unlatched his seat harness with the other.

"Expertly done, Willian. I couldn't have done it better myself," Amanda praised with a smile on her face. She unfastened her own harness and waited for Willian to exit the cockpit before she followed him out into the cool, bright sunlight of Manzanit. She looked around in wonder at the number of telepods parked as far as the eye could see. There must have been hundreds of them of various sizes throughout the grassy field. "Did you happen to see where the entrance was before you landed?"

"Yes, it's not too far over to the right." Willian pointed to a distant area.

"I'll have to trust you on it," she teased. She looked back into the telepod and saw Valentina was still seated. "Are you coming, Val?"

"Yes, I'm just having trouble getting my seatbelt undone."

"Here, let me help you," Amanda hastily offered when she saw how badly the girl's hands were shaking. She must have been terrified during the flight to cause such a violent reaction. "There," she announced cheerfully as she easily released the latch. Amanda held out her hand to the young girl and was shocked at how ice cold her fingertips were as they touched her.

She almost had to haul her up from the seat since her legs were as unsure as her hands had been. "We're okay, Val. Once you get outside and feel the firm ground beneath your feet, you'll know it too. I was pretty scared the first couple of times I flew in a telepod, you know."

"Really? How did you get over your fear?" Valentina looked up at Amanda, thinking it would be wonderful to have as much confidence.

"Mostly by repetition, but also by learning how to fly the telepod myself. Knowing how it works helps to keep my mind occupied on the process rather than the fear."

"Oh, I was hoping it would be something which didn't involve flying. Why does it have to be so empty and black during the transfer? I hate the dark; it feels like drowning."

"Like drowning? Have you almost drowned?"

"Yes, when I was really little. I don't remember much except for the feeling of not being able to breathe and all the darkness around me."

"I'm sorry, Val. I had no idea you'd been through that. Maybe we can talk to Riccan and see if he has any ideas on how to help you. Would you like me to ask him?"

"You'd do that for me? Even after what happened with Jena? Really?"

"Look, Val, I'm going to tell you this one last time; you were never to blame for what happened between Willian and Jena. Things were set in motion long before he even met you."

Willian stepped over to Valentina's other side and said, "It's true. Remember when I told you how bad I'd screwed up with Jena? My terrible actions were the reason I went to find her and make things right again. My dad told me the betrothal was going to be annulled if I didn't get things straightened out."

"So, you see, you had nothing to do with it. You just happened to be walking down the hall at school, and Willian bumped into you. Suddenly your whole life shifted, and you think I'll blame you for it? I don't think so. Please just forget about it and be happy. Jena has accepted it, and the rest of us have as well."

"I guess I can see your point." She smiled at Willian, for the first time really feeling free of any guilt about being with him. "But I can't promise you I'll like flying in the telepod right now!"

"I can live with that!" Willian said with a grin. "Here we are at the entrance. Let me flag down a transport."

"How did we get here so fast?" Valentina asked in amazement. She looked behind her and saw the rows of telepods parked. It was true; they had walked the length of a football field while they had been talking.

The ride lasted only a couple of minutes, and they exited the vehicle in front of the gates to one of the entrances to the Residence. Valentina was awed by the size of the building as it took up at least two city blocks. Her experience of Tuala had only ever consisted of seeing her home village which was a remote town located on the eastern coastline in the Pantano District. They did not have transports or any multi-storied buildings, so this was eye-opening, to say the least.

There was only a slight incident regarding their entrance into the Residence when Amanda had to wait to receive clearance. For some reason, it had not occurred to her that her own identity would be questioned, even after she had heard Valentina would need clearance. It was probably because she had already been inside the Residence which allowed her to believe it to be a non-issue. Of course, the trip had been through the Ascension Gate and had been rather rushed, along with being accompanied by Rasa. As soon as Rasa issued the clearance, the three of them proceeded into the grand reception gallery of the massive estate with Rasa's personal assistant, Ulwin, leading them.

The young man asked, "Since you ladies have not been to the Residence before, I'll give you some history if you'd like."

Amanda replied, "I've been here once with Rasa, but I'd love to hear more about it. Valentina, here, has never been so it'll be nice for her to learn."

"As you surely know already, the fortress represents the seat of power for all of Manzanit and its sheer size alone lets everyone know how esteemed our Elder is for us. This Residence is the first of its kind in Tuala. We take great pride in making certain everything is maintained perfectly. There are over one thousand staff members whose only job is to keep everything pristine and ready for any occasion."

"Wow! I had no idea there were so many people here. I've hardly ever seen anybody around," Amanda exclaimed.

"Then we are doing our jobs properly," he said with a grin of satisfaction.

Amanda could imagine it would take some adjustment on Rasa's part since she had come from the elegant estate setting on Acaim. Her new surroundings were too large to be classified as classic elegance; she would be more apt to call it medieval grandeur with its thick stone walls, tall barrel-vaulted ceilings, interior support columns, and arched stained-glass windows.

The many generations of Elders had put their personal touches in the decorations to keep it from feeling cold and stark. The thick tapestries hung from sturdy rods between the deep window sills. They walked on luxuriously woven rugs of foxl hair, which Amanda felt certain would be as soft as silk if she were to touch it. Dark furniture with elaborately carved scenes adorned the edges of the walkway should a person care to rest while they waited for an interview. No expense had been spared.

CHAPTER 18

Amanda glanced over to Valentina to see her reaction to her surroundings. She was rewarded with the look of awe and admiration. Her thoughts were cut short when Ulwin began speaking again.

"Valentina, Pelka will be taking you to the west wing where Gevena awaits your visit." He stopped his walking and gestured to a girl hardly much older than Valentina who smiled prettily as she was acknowledged by the guide.

Valentina looked both alarmed and surprised because she was going to be separated from the only two people she knew. She still held Willian's hand, and her fingers clenched his in a bone-crunching grip at the idea of leaving. "Please come with me!" she pled in an urgent whisper.

Willian nodded and said to Ulwin, "I'll walk with her until we reach Gevena. She's understandably nervous being in the Residence with strangers."

Their guide pursed his lips and shook his head slightly. "I'm afraid it won't be possible. Elder Wilken heard you were coming

"

and he has requested you to join him for his morning tea. I'm sure you won't want to keep him waiting."

"Oh, Willian, you'll have to go then. I may be scared, but I did ask you to bring me here. It's not your job to babysit me."

Reluctantly Willian nodded in agreement. He was eager to visit again with his mentor. He released Valentina's hand and watched while she stepped closer to Pelka. In his previous visit, he had recalled seeing Pelka around, he had always received smiles of admiration from her so he knew no harm would come to Valentina while she remained in her care.

As if in answer to Amanda's thought, Ulwin said, "Rasa has asked for you to come and visit with her in her private chambers." He turned to Willian and asked, "Do you need a guide to Elder Wilken's tea room?"

"No, I know my way around. Thanks, Ulwin. I'd best not keep him waiting!" He sprinted ahead and turned left at the next corridor.

Amanda wondered how the three of them would know when each was ready to leave. This was not something she had really planned through very well in her eagerness to come and see Rasa with her incredible news. Even as she thought about it, her hand touched the pocket in the side of her tunic. She felt the crinkle of the folded paper and felt relief rush through her at its existence.

"We shouldn't keep Rasa waiting either," Amanda suggested as Ulwin remained standing in the hall in front of her. He had an odd expression on his face as he stared at Amanda.

Ulwin had not really paid much attention to whom he was guiding, nor had he given any of them more than a cursory glance. As Amanda stood with her face bathed in sunlight from the upper window, he had an eerie sensation he had met her somewhere before. Amanda's question startled him out of his reverie, and he became slightly flustered at being caught staring. "What? Oh, yes, we should get going; you're very right!" He turned and set a brisk pace to keep from having to talk while his cheeks remained bright pink.

They walked at the quick pace for another six or seven minutes when Ulwin turned down a short corridor which ended in a set of elaborate double doors with ornate bronze handles. He pulled one open and remained standing where he was as he swept his arm in front of him with a grand gesture. "This is where we part ways. Have a good day, Amanda."

"Thank you for the history lesson and being my guide. I never would've found my way here without you." She swept past him and felt the breeze of the door as it shut silently behind her. Sweeping her eyes around the room, she saw Rasa sitting in one of the intimate groupings of chairs near a floor-to-ceiling window which overlooked the central garden.

"Hello, Amanda. I had no idea you were planning to accompany the kids today. Although, I am pleasantly surprised," Rasa said as she rose from her chair and began walking toward her cousin. It still gave her a thrill to have a cousin near her own age, and they had yet to really spend any quality time getting to know one another.

"It was a last minute decision. I hope you don't mind too much; I know how busy you are."

"No bother at all. You saw me at my most weary when we talked earlier. I've gotten through the most urgent matters, and I decided I've earned a break! Come; let's sit down and have tea together." She led the way back to the chairs and poured the steaming steena tea into another cup.

They sat and held their warm cups in their hands. It was pleasurable silence between them as they relaxed into the chairs. Rasa's curiosity got the best of her, and she broke the silence by asking, "What brought you here today?"

"A couple of things, really." She took a sip of her tea to whet her throat in preparation for a long talk. "First, I'm sure you were aware of Willian's intention of working things out with Jena."

"Yes, I was the one who made arrangements for him to go to Earth and I sent him through the Gate. Are you thinking he might still have a chance with Jena?"

"No. Jena asked Elder Daven to break the betrothal, and he allowed it immediately."

"What? When did this happen? Why would Elder Daven get involved without letting Elder Debbon know about it? This is a very serious matter which involves the First's successor." She pulled at her lower lip as she tried to imagine all of the implications the separation could have on other Districts and Elder Debbon's position as First Elder. "Amanda, this is really not good! This is way bigger than you can imagine, all of it to Elder Debbon's detriment."

"I only heard about it after the fact. I had nothing to do with Jena's decision. Willian didn't leave her with any decision at all."

"Wait, I don't understand what you're saying. If Jena requested it, then, of course, she had a choice."

"No, she didn't. Let me tell you what happened..." Amanda proceeded to share with her all of the details which had been given to her regarding the whole sordid situation. She could see an intensely interested expression come over Rasa's face and wondered what it could possibly mean. She filed her thought away for a time when it would be more convenient to discuss and then she ended with, "So you have to see how Jena's hand was forced."

Rasa laughed outright and then had to explain herself when she saw Amanda's puzzled expression. "It struck me as an odd choice of words when you said Jena's hand had been forced because your hand in marriage is a common term. I'm not sure if it's the same on Earth. It always seemed as though Jena had been forced into the relationship…sorry, it just struck me funny. Never mind." She could see Amanda had been too concerned with her daughter's happiness to see any humor in it at all.

"Well, I agree," she continued in a more serious tone. "Elder Daven was left with no other choice if the bond is as strong as you say. I'd like to witness their bond personally. Maybe I'll have time to visit with them both before they leave. Elder Daven might be on to something in trying to figure out how it happened so we might replicate it to make happier unions. I've felt the change in people's feelings for one another slipping to an all-time low lately."

"It sure would be good if the same formula could be used on Earth. The divorce rate is probably fifty percent or better these days. When my parents were kids, it was shameful to divorce, and now everyone seems to think it's okay. I agree things are changing and I'm not sure it's for the better."

"I don't think we'll be able to solve all of the world's problems over one cup of tea," Rasa grinned over the edge of her cup as she tipped it to take another drink. After she swallowed she set the cup back on the table and crossed her hands in her lap. "What was the other reason you decided to come all this way to speak to me? Surely it wasn't just to update me on Willian's failure in getting back together with Jena."

"No, but it does have to do with Jena since she's single again." Amanda scoffed at herself. "It sounds so strange to talk about my daughter in such a way. You know we don't have arranged marriages on Earth in America anymore."

"They aren't very common here either, you know. It's mostly just with people in positions of power so they won't have to worry about someone getting together with a person for the wrong reasons."

"I would have thought your ability to read minds would put a damper on being able to pull something like that off." Amanda was mostly teasing, but she did think it would be a deterrent.

"We need to review your lessons! The first lesson in mind reading is to get permission first. If you do it at any other time, it's considered very rude, the same as eavesdropping."

"I was just kidding…well mostly, anyway!" She chuckled and then turned serious as she returned to her original point. "I wanted to ask your help, well advice really, about Jena."

"What do you need?"

"Jena told her father she wants to be his successor."

Rasa's eyes grew wide, and her mouth moved into the shape of a big O as she realized how she had paved the way for her young cousin. "And since I've set the precedent, then she felt like it was okay to pursue it, right?"

"Yes! What do you think her chances are? I don't want her to set herself up for failure."

"No worries on that score, Amanda. I've often thought Jena would make a better Elder than Willian. Oh, this is just perfect! I'm thrilled for Jena being able to go after a future which makes her happy. You have no idea how talented she is with her crystal skills. I've never seen anyone so innovative or eager to learn. She was probably Jehoban's favorite student, you know!"

"Really? I was hoping I wasn't just being biased since I'm her mother. So you think she'll have a good shot at this?"

"I don't see why not. In fact, her claim to successorship is much stronger than mine was. I only had the blessing of Jehoban. Jena has the right lineage as well as Jehoban's blessing. The more I think about it; I'm starting to believe Jehoban allowed Jena's betrothal to prepare her to be a compassionate Elder. She had to learn a lot of patience with Willian."

"I never thought about it quite like that. My idea was they were paired together for Willian to come to Earth to find Valentina. I can't imagine how they ever would have found one another otherwise."

"Maybe so. Or maybe we're both right, did you ever think about that?" Rasa sat back with a pleased smile on her face. She was relieved to hear Jena had decided on a new path for her life which would bring her happiness and fulfillment. *Their horrible situation turned out perfectly, probably just as Jehoban had planned,* she thought to herself with an inward giggle at His maneuvering ways.

Rasa reached over to pick up her cup, only to discover it was empty. She had no idea when she had finished it; her companion-ship was so stimulating, she had lost track of time. As Amanda still seemed inclined to talk, she picked up the teapot and poured herself another cup. She raised her eyebrows to inquire if Amanda would like a refill as well and then filled the other cup at her nod of assent.

Rasa took another sip of tea and asked again, "What else is on your mind? I can see the wheels turning in your head!"

Amanda set down her cup and reached into her pocket. She handed the folded slip of paper over to Rasa without saying a word. She sat back in her chair and waited to see the reaction when Rasa got to the new line.

"What's this?" Rasa asked rhetorically. She placed her teacup on the table and used both hands to unfold the paper. Her brows furrowed as she saw the familiar opening line and then she gasped in astonishment as she realized there was more explanation than there had been before. "Where did you get this? What does it mean?" Who else knows about it? When can we get the group together to figure out what we should do with this?" There were so many other questions twirling through her mind, all ideas of getting back to her mundane paperwork flew completely out of her head.

Rasa's reaction was everything and more than Amanda could

have wished for and she laughed out loud. "The only one you missed was 'why' in your flood of questions. To answer you in the same order: I discovered it in the same book as before at our home, I don't know what it means; you're the only person I've shared it with, and I was hoping you'd have a better idea of when we can all gather for another meeting."

"And to think, I was just talking to you about the last three samaras still needing to be found, and then you find this? Amazing!"

"It was actually because of you I even went looking in the book again. I was thinking about how we only had the two samaras before I discovered the prophecy and then they seemed to come flooding to their rightful owners. I know how you feel about not having one of your own, I don't have mine yet, either. My best guess is it's because the timing isn't quite right yet."

"Maybe," she agreed reluctantly. She re-read the paper, using her memorization techniques to keep it with her forever. Her former discouragement turned back into hope as she realized Jehoban was still helping them figure this whole thing out. Deep within every fiber of her being, she knew they would succeed!

CHAPTER 19

illian's meeting with Elder Wilken ended when a courier had come to deliver important documents which needed immediate attention. The timing could not have been better as Willian had just stood up to take his leave anyway. He made a low bow of respect to the oldest Elder in Tuala, and then he left the reception room.

Not sure where to go next, he decided to seek out Rasa's company. He was eager to tell her about his relationship with Valentina. There was only a slight twinge of fear she would tell him he was a fool for giving up on Jena. Of course, Rasa would have no idea about the power of his union with Val.

As Elder Daven had stated, it was a new bond which should be studied and encouraged among the populace. He felt proud to be the first at something finally. He would set the example for any who followed his path.

Elder Wilken had commented on his improved state of mind. When he had heard the reason for it, he had been concerned, and eventually convinced it had been the right course of action. The

Elder said he had even met Jena several times when he had visited Acaim for a consultation with Jehoban. He knew a student of Jehoban's would not end the betrothal lightly, so he had listened intently to Willian's reasons.

Willian felt lighthearted, and his jaunty steps mirrored his mood. He kept his eyes and ears open for any sign of either of the women he had arrived with. Not seeing anyone at all, Willian eventually found himself outside the double doors of Rasa's private chambers which was where Ulwin had said they would be meeting.

Not wanting to disrupt their meeting, he quietly let himself into the room. He pushed the door shut behind him and remained with his back resting on the carved wooden surface. He could see Rasa's attention was riveted on a piece of paper she held. Just as he was about to call out, he was shocked into silence again as he overheard their discussion of a prophecy and the fabled samaras.

His mind reeled with memories of Jena obsessing over old, musty tomes talking about the thirteen samaras being held by the Watchers for who knew how long. He wondered why Rasa was even entertaining the topic until he heard Amanda claim ten of them had been found. Why would Amanda know anything about the Tualan's mysterious history?

A tingling sensation crawled all over the back of his neck as his hairs began to stand on end. Elder Wilken had just been teasing him about being a descendant of the Watchers. At the time he had laughed along with the ancient man. Was he really telling Willian the truth?

Willian's musings made him miss the end of the conversation in front of him. He pushed away from the door and cleared his throat loudly. Rasa's curious actions of folding the paper she held and tucking it under her leg made him wonder if she were up to something she should not be involved in. He was going to get to the bottom of this before he went home. This could not be left alone.

"What are you talking about? I thought I overheard you saying something about a samara?"

"Willian, were you eavesdropping? I was just telling Amanda mind-reading was as ill-mannered as eavesdropping. I can't believe this."

"Never mind, Rasa. Answer my question about the samara. What was on the paper you are trying to hide?" He pointed to the leg she had hidden the note under.

"I think you are forgetting who you are speaking to, Willian. This matter doesn't concern you!"

"Rasa, for the first time, you and I are actually considered equals. Both of us are successors so you can no longer pull rank on me. You are not Jehoban's student anymore, so cut the pompous act and tell me what you're trying to hide!"

"Actually," Amanda swiftly interrupted before this conversation escalated into outright hatred, "Willian is somewhat involved. After all, both of his parents are part of the group. If anything happened to them, then Willian would become the Elder in his father's place." She turned and faced the young man, eager to see if he could shed new light on their confusion. "You've obviously heard about the samaras. Tell us what you've learned and then we'll share with you what we were talking about."

"You first," Willian said stubbornly.

"No, it has to be you or else we can't keep you safe."

Shaking his head in a puzzled expression, he finally relented. His first line of questioning was getting him nowhere. At least if he held up his end of the bargain, they would be obligated to share their secret.

"There is an ancient legend where the descendants of the Watchers hold the samaras in hiding until the day comes where they will be united again to change the world as we know it. Jena used to bore me to death with all of the legends which she said could keep us safe in the future. I don't see how the writings in books which are as old as time itself will ever be of benefit to us now. If they were going to be useful, they would've already. Are you saying you believe the old tales?"

"They aren't children's stories, Willian. In the past several mesans, we've witnessed many unbelievable things. One of those miracles is the samaras are being found again. The phrase you used about the descendants of the Watchers almost sounded like a prophecy in and of itself. Were those the exact words you recall or were you paraphrasing?"

"Really? Yes, those were the exact words. By the time I heard them I had already progressed past the crystal skill lesson on memorization." He moved between the women to sit down heavily in the third chair in the grouping. Ideas were swirling through his mind in a confusing whirlwind. He leaned forward suddenly with his elbow resting on his knees and his hands gesturing his frustration. "This doesn't make sense. Elder Wilken just told me he was a descendant of the Watchers. We both laughed about it! I was sure it was just a joke, but what if he had been serious?"

Rasa and Amanda looked at one another in alarm. Could the answer to their question be as simple as meeting with the man who lived right here in the Residence? They both stood up at the same time. Rasa had grabbed the folded paper on her way out of the chair, and she shoved it back into Amanda's hand. She was not going to sit around wondering. "Let's go ask Elder Wilken what he meant!"

"I like the way you think!" Amanda agreed and hurried to keep up with her cousin.

"Wait for me!" Willian yelled after them as they had made themselves quite the head start.

"Hurry up, Willian! Where do you think Elder Wilken is right now?" Rasa asked over her shoulder. Every nerve in her body was screaming out at her indicating she was doing the right thing. Her life was about to change with one simple conversation. Her breathing began to become ragged with her excitement.

"He was just meeting with a courier with important documents," Willian said through his labored breathing as they had gone from sprinting to a full-out run. "I don't think he's going to get away, Rasa. Can't we slow down?"

Willian's words registered in her mind, and she realized how truly he had spoken. She stopped dead in her tracks and began laughing hysterically between her gulps of air. "He won't get away, he says! Ha! Oh, Willian, you are wise beyond your years! Besides, I don't think Elder Wilken would appreciate us barging into his meeting out of breath and sweaty. Let's walk the rest of the way to give him time to finish his discussion." She looked over to Amanda and said, "It's waited this long, I can't think of any reason why it would change in the course of another five to ten minutes of time."

"Thank goodness you came to your senses, Rasa, I think my heart was about to burst with all of this exercise!" Amanda strode at a more leisurely pace between her cousin and Willian, who had finally caught up to them when they had stopped. "I think Elder Wilken will be a font of knowledge after all the anons he has experienced."

CHAPTER 20

"Gevena is waiting for you out in the garden. I'll make sure the two of you won't be disturbed by any of the staff," Pelka offered as she pointed out to Valentina the direction she should take for the meeting.

"Thank you, Pelka. You've been so patient with me."

"It's been my pleasure." She turned away and was gone from sight almost instantly.

Valentina stared after her in wonder. Ulwin had said the staff tried to be as elusive as possible, but it was crazy how fast her guide had gotten out of sight. Their proficiency at hiding also made her worry whether or not their conversation would actually remain private. There could be twenty people within hearing distance, and they would have no idea.

Gevena was sitting in the middle of one of the ornate gardens on a carved wooden bench. She had carefully chosen the location knowing she would have plenty of advance warning of anyone approaching on any of the four gravel paths leading up to the seating area. Also, the shrubs nearby were low enough not to allow any cover for someone trying to listen in. She had been around enough deception, growing up where she had, to know how to avoid detection when she wanted privacy.

When she spotted Valentina exiting her own private rooms, she stood up and smiled brightly at seeing a familiar face. Her fear of rejection subsided knowing Valentina's offer to talk had not just been for the sake of kindness, but of true friendship. She had shown up, which was more than Gevena had hoped would happen. Not only that, but Valentina had also come to meet with her within a relatively quick period of time given the request had to be routed through third parties.

"Thank you for coming to see me, Valentina," Gevena said warmly as she gave her an awkward hug, unsure of how to greet her first guest in Manzanit.

"I wish I could have come earlier; it's just been a bit crazy at home right now." Valentina patted her back and then moved away to sit down on the bench. "It's very beautiful here. How do you like living here?"

Gevena sat close to her new friend, trying not to crowd her on the narrow seat. She shrugged slightly and said, "It's sure a lot nicer than where I came from. I like the school here. The kids are okay, not overly welcoming, though, when they heard I was living at the Residence."

"Why would it matter?"

"I have no idea."

"Well, at least I know how you feel. When we enrolled in our school on Earth when we were eight, everybody stared at us, and we ate lunch alone for a long time."

"At least you had your brothers with you, so you had people to talk to. It's pretty lonely until I get home in the afternoons."

"I guess being a triplet does make it so I'm never alone."

"How neat. I've never known any other triplets before. I don't think they're very common in Tuala. Are they common on Earth?"

"No."

"Oh." Gevena wished this conversation was not getting so strained. She had hoped they would be able to just talk like girl-friends did. She had always seen the groups of girls talking at school, and they never seemed to have trouble coming up with things to say to one another. Maybe it was because she knew they were avoiding the one thing she had experienced in life which made her different from everyone else.

"Gevena..."

"Valentina..." they both spoke at once and then they began laughing. "You go first, Valentina."

"My friends call me Val," Valentina offered to ease the formality between them and then became confused by Gevena's horrified expression. "What? Did I say something wrong?"

"Why would you take the 'a' off the end of your name?"

"What difference does it make?"

"Do you want people to think you've lost your honor? You mustn't do such a thing here!"

"What does my name have to do with my honor?"

"I thought you said you were from Tuala? How could you not know how important a person's name is?" Gevena was becoming confused and then wondered if this meeting had been a good idea after all.

"I was born here, well, not here in Manzanit. I was born in a place called the Roanoke Colony in the Pantano District. When we were eight, my mother was afraid for our safety and sent us to Earth accidentally. We were adopted by the people who we call our parents, and we have spent the last eight years on Earth."

"What's a year?"

Valentina shook her head in confusion. "What do you mean?

It's a year. You know, 365 days make up a year. Do you call it something else here? Now I'm confused."

Gevena's expression cleared as she heard Valentina's explanation. "Yes, we call it an anon. So you were eight anons old when you went to Earth."

"I guess. Hmph. I never knew there were differences in language. I wonder what else is different."

"Your clothing, for one," Gevena said with a slight smirk as she looked Valentina's outfit up and down. She touched the blue cloth on Valentina's leg and asked, "What's it made out of?"

"Denim…I guess it's probably made out of cotton or something like that. I don't really know. What do you make cloth out of here?"

"Mostly of woven foxl hair. It's really soft and versatile."

"What is a foxl?"

"Seriously? Oh, my! We have a lot to learn from one another! Are you planning on ever coming back to Tuala to live or are you going to stay on Earth?"

"I had hoped to live in both places. After all, I have parents in both so it's what made the most sense. Now, I'm not so sure it'd be a good idea. What if I did or said something which would make people wonder about me? I wouldn't want to jeopardize my mom's standing as the leader of the colony."

"I don't think it would happen there since they all know you live on Earth. It's just the rest of Tuala you'd have to worry about."

"Oh," Valentina chuckled, "Is that all? Just the whole rest of Tuala. No problem!"

They both laughed, relaxing as they did so. Neither knew the beginning of their friendship had formed, but their conversations became less forced.

Valentina was the first to speak. "You were saying something about my name and honor. What was that all about?"

"Okay, this will be your first lesson in Tualan culture. All girls' names end with an 'a' and all boys' names end with an 'n' unless they've lost honor. Then they are forced to drop the honorific letter at the end of their name to let everyone know their shame."

"It sounds pretty harsh. Does it happen often?" Instantly she made a mental note to make sure her brothers did not call her by her shortened name if they ever visited their mother. She did not want to bring any shame to her mother by slipping up in front of the villagers or any other people who might be around while they were in Tuala.

"Not as often as it should!" Gevena spoke bitterly as she recalled other people in her life who had treated her badly but still retained their whole name.

This was the opening Valentina had been hoping for in their conversation. She asked, "Tell me about your life in Desio. What was it like?"

Gevena instantly sobered, her sense of ease vanished as she recalled her tough life with her father. "My father drank a lot, and he liked gambling. He met a man named Politun who was from the Roanoke Colony."

"I remember him; he was always so sneaky and secretive. He was the second in command of the colony and Grobin's best friend. Grobin was our leader and the reason we were sent to Earth," Valentina interjected as her memories of her childhood began to sharpen upon hearing Politun's name. "Where was your mom?"

Gevena agreed with Valentina's assessment of the man even as she answered her question. "My mom left us when I was a toddler. I don't know where she is or if she is even alive anymore."

"I'm sorry. Do you think you might want to try to locate her someday? Maybe she was trying to get away from your father," Valentina offered.

"Leaving me behind to deal with him! I'm sorry; you didn't

deserve that." She paused to collect herself before continuing her story as if she had not been interrupted. "As I said, the colony had recently started camping outside our village, causing all kinds of problems as they stole food and clothing from our people.

"We don't know why they came, but my father was only interested in his gambling and drinking. Nobody in town would play with him anymore because he couldn't pay what he gambled. Politun was an outsider, and he was willing to play cards with him. For a while, my father was winning. He bought more liquor and got sloppy.

"After losing several nights in a row, my father came home and told me to gather my things. I had no idea what he had done, and I did as he asked. He took me away from our home and gave me to Politun. He took my arm and began dragging me away from the village. I kept crying and asking my father to help me. He turned around and walked back to our house.

"Politun told me to shut up. He said he had won me fair and square in their last card game. I could not believe what he said was true. I called him a liar and told him to let me go home. When we got to his tent in the woods, he shoved me on the ground and told me I was home. He ordered me to make him dinner so I did it. I figured I'd be able to sneak away when he was sleeping and go home.

"He must have anticipated my plan because he tied my leg to his tent stake that night. After we were done eating he told me to take my clothes off. I refused, and he ripped them off of me. I screamed and screamed knowing someone would come and help me. Nobody seemed to notice. Politun hit my face until my eye swelled shut and my nose was bleeding.

"He told me I was his property and he could do to me whatever he wanted. I had no idea how far he would take this idea until..."

She stopped talking. She had no idea why she had even told Valentina as much as she had.

"Until what? What happened to you, Gevena," Valentina pushed gently. "I know this is hard, but sometimes it makes it easier to talk about bad things so you can begin to forget them."

"What do you know? Apart from being sent to Earth, how can you possibly know what I've been through?" Gevena accused rudely.

Trying not to be offended and also taking her own advice, Valentina answered softly, "Because the day you were rescued from Viceroy Blair's captivity, was the same day I was raped by Grobin."

Gevena's eyes grew wide in disbelief and shock. "I'm so sorry, Valentina. I had no idea!"

"There was no way you could know." Suddenly Valentina laughed harshly and said, "Do you know what the stupid thing is?"

Confused by the sudden change of mood, Gevena shook her head dumbly.

"The reason our mom sent us away was because Grobin was going to make me his wife when I was eight. My mom knew what he had planned for our 'wedding' night, and she was trying to protect me from his disgusting advances. I guess he got what he wanted after all."

"Oh, Valentina, how awful! But you'll have to admit it would have been even worse for you when you were only a small child."

"True, but then it would have been over a long time ago rather than just two weeks ago. It wouldn't still be fresh in my mind. So since you know I truly do understand, do you want to finish telling me what happened to you?"

Reluctantly, Gevena decided it would be nice to tell someone else her story who knew what it felt like to be helpless. She swallowed and took a deep breath before she continued. "He removed his clothes and pinned me to the ground. I couldn't get away with my leg tied to the tent. I didn't have anywhere to go since my father had betrayed me.

"At first, I struggled and clawed at him, but he only hit me with a sick grin on his face. I immediately figured out he enjoyed it when I fought him so I forced myself to be completely still. When he realized I wasn't going to challenge him anymore, he finished and got off of me.

"I didn't dare move a muscle until I heard him laughing with Grobin over by the fire. It was like my mind was no longer inside my beaten body. I curled up on my side and cried. That was when I knew nobody cared what happened to me. I was alone." Her last words came out in a whisper.

"I know the feeling as well; it was almost the same thing I did when Grobin left me after…you know. Thank you for telling me. Someone very wise once told me as long as I let what was done to me haunt me, then I was giving up myself to the other person. The shame and guilt belong only to Politun; you did nothing wrong. Do you understand?"

"I guess." She sighed deeply and felt as if a weight had been lifted from her soul. Rasa had been very wise when she had suggested she invite Valentina for a visit. Suddenly she wondered if Rasa knew what had happened to Valentina as well. She remembered seeing Rasa with her when they were leaving the telepod at the Stel's house. "Does Rasa know about your story?"

Valentina nodded. "She's the first one who helped me when we got back to Earth. I was pretty much a mess when Juila had her see me."

"So that's why she wanted us to talk?"

"I think Juila had something to do with it as well."

"It makes sense, Juila is the only person I've ever told about what happened to me, until now." Thinking of Juila and her twin sister, Gevena wanted to change the subject and asked, "Do you know what happened between Jena and Willian? The last I heard, Willian had gone to Earth to try to work things out with Jena. She was pretty upset to learn he was staying close to where she lived."

Now it was Valentina's turn to be uncomfortable. "They weren't able to work things out between them. Jena requested for their betrothal to be broken and Elder Daven granted it."

"Oh, no! That's terrible! There has to be a way for them to work it out and get back together. But I guess it's too late if the Elder approved her request. Was it just a verbal break or did they give up their bond symbols?"

"Bond symbols? What are those?"

"They are usually bracelets, rings, or sometimes a necklace. Both of them would have had a matching set of whatever it was."

"Oh, then yes. Elder Daven asked them to relinquish their rings immediately."

"Definitely too late then. Both families must be mortified."

"Why? People get divorced all of the time. What difference does it make?"

"You do have a lot to learn, Valentina. Let me see how I can explain this...people get married here, but betrothals are different, they are more than just a marriage." She pulled at her bottom lip with her thumb and finger as she tried to find the right words to express the magnitude of a betrothal.

"We don't have very many betrothals. They are rare because of what it means to the families involved. Betrothals are arranged between two infants by applying to an Elder to take the matter to Jehoban. Usually, the reason for the arrangement is because the families are in important positions or are influential in the society. Sometimes it's because it's believed the match will enhance the crystal skill lineage in the children they will bear when they're grown.

"The children are raised together by the boy's parents so they will share the same background and beliefs. They grow up knowing they will be married. They also know they will have a blessed marriage because it was sanctioned by Jehoban Himself. Their special relationship will always produce children who have unique talents and their standing in society is held in high esteem."

With a sick feeling in her gut, Valentina forced herself to ask, "So what will happen to them since the betrothal is dissolved?"

"They will both be ridiculed and shamed by their peers. It will always be remembered by the people, and their lives will never be the same. It's too bad it didn't work out. Do you know why?"

Wishing she did not have to admit her part in the situation, Valentina looked down at her hands. She saw her fingers were almost white with the strain of holding them so tightly. Consciously, she relaxed her fingers and thought about what Willian had told her. Finally, she nodded and replied, "It's because Willian and I are bonded."

"Wait, what? You did this to them? How could you ruin Jena's life?"

Valentina shook her head in denial and kept her voice calm. "It wasn't like that. Willian bumped into me at school, and something happened. He says our life-lines merged together or something like that. I tried to keep away from him, but it's like trying to avoid oxygen. I need him to live, and he feels the same about me. When Jena realized we didn't have any say in the matter, she asked for the dissolution of the betrothal. I recall her asking Elder Daven to dissolve it without fault or blemish on either part. Do you know what it could have meant?"

The horrified expression on Gevena's face disappeared when she heard the last part of Valentina's explanation. She sighed in relief as she answered. "Yes, thank Jehoban Jena added the phrase to her request. They both would have been ruined without it."

"Oh, good, but what does it mean?"

"It means Jehoban will remove the betrothal from everyone's minds. They will still recall Willian and Jena were in a relationship, but the stigma of a broken betrothal will not haunt them. The only way people will know about it is if they tell anyone. I suggest you don't talk about it in Tuala so it will stay gone from everyone's memories."

"That's good to know. I had no idea Jehoban would be such an active participant in the whole process."

"So what are your plans with Willian? I guess it really means you're going to be moving to Tuala. It would be hard for him to be an Elder if his wife were on Earth. You do know most people in Tuala don't even believe Earth is real. Most of the Elders have gone to great length to let them think the *old souls* are dangerous individuals who should be turned over to them for the cleansing of our culture."

"Isn't it a contradiction then? How can Earth be a myth and *old souls* be a problem? Where do they think the *old souls* come from then?"

"I never thought about it in such a way! I don't really know the answer! Wow, how funny. I guess I might be able to learn something about Tuala from your perspective being so different."

Valentina grinned at the idea of them being able to compare notes. She was intensely relieved to know she had not ruined Willian's or Jena's lives simply by being in the wrong place at the right time. Things had worked out for all of them in the end.

CHAPTER 21

"Dr. Stephen Gascon is here to see you, Dr. Medin," the receptionist said over the intercom.

Jasmine cringed at the idea of meeting with her least favorite colleague. She had not known he was coming, and if she had, she would have found a way to be out of the office. Since she had worked with him years before, she had first-hand knowledge of his idea of patient treatment which she found completely unethical.

Her last contact with him had been when he had requested a meeting with her long-term coma patient, Amanda Covington. She had been shocked when he had even asked then considering how they had left things off when she quit working for him. It was her phone call to the medical board which had caused him to be placed under investigation.

After sighing in resignation, knowing he would only come back until he got his interview, she pressed the button on the intercom and said flatly, "Send him in."

As if he had already been standing at the door it opened immediately, and the stern-faced man stalked into the room as if he owned it. Her dislike of him intensified as soon as he sat and began talking in his condescending tone.

"I hear you're seeing a former patient of mine, Nealand Taivas." He watched the woman across from him to see if she would give anything away.

"I'm sure you know I would never discuss any case with you, even if he were my patient. What is this visit really about, Dr. Gascon?" She kept her gaze steady and did not allow her fingers to fidget. She knew his methods too well to fall for any of his intimidation tactics.

"Well, if you were hypothetically seeing Nealand, I wanted to share with you my deep concern for his special case of psychosis. His extended captivity created a split personality of sorts, allowing his delusions to seem as though he had lived in an alternate dimension or another world. I believe he called the place "Tuala." I simply wanted to make sure you were taking precautions for your safety when you meet with him. He is a young man with a lot of pent up frustrations. I know your aversion to drug therapy, but he really should be on a regimen of anti-psychosis drugs."

"That sounds very interesting Dr. Gascon. I see you haven't bothered to observe your discretion regarding doctor-patient confidentiality. If there's nothing more, I really do have a lot of work to get done. Please see yourself out." It was important for her to maintain a sense of professionalism when dealing with his kind. He took pleasure in making others uncomfortable, which was why she had chosen the dismissal tactic with him.

She knew a prolonged visit would only lead to him gleaning small pieces of information from her. She wanted him out of her office as fast as possible. As she pretended to be busy reading a chart on her computer screen, she tried to ignore the fact the other doctor had not made any move to leave. Suppressing a sigh of irritation, which would only make Dr. Gascon feel like he was getting to her, she asked in as bored of a tone as she could muster with her heart racing, "Is there something else?"

"There's something about you which has changed. I'm just trying to figure out what it is." Dr. Gascon shrugged like he was trying to be friendly.

Jasmine knew better than to fall for his act. "It's called confidence. I no longer have to follow orders I don't agree with. I treat my patients by dealing with their emotional issues by talking to them and not drugging them. You might give it a try yourself and see if your results improve. There, I've answered your curiosity about my difference. I do not have any additional time for socializing. I don't believe we have any further need for conversation."

She stood up confidently and stepped out from behind her desk and over to the office door. When she opened it, she caught the eye of her receptionist as she raised her voice for her to hear, "Dr. Gascon was just leaving, please be sure to validate his parking."

Seeing he had no other choice than to leave or make a scene, Dr. Gascon reluctantly conceded the win to his former protégé. He slowly rose from the chair, scanning her desk for patient's names on her desk files as he did so before he turned and faced Jasmine. As he came up beside her, he spoke in a tone only she could hear, "I'm certain we'll be seeing one another again soon. I look forward to it. Good day."

Jasmine made no reply other than raising one eyebrow slightly. Once he stepped across the threshold, she calmly shut the door and leaned her body against the inside. Her hands began shaking as the adrenaline finally began to show its symptoms. She had been able to fight her flight instinct and stand her ground.

Returning her attention to work again was going to be impossible, so she did not even attempt it. Pushing herself away from the door, she moved over to the chair Dr. Gascon had occupied. She kneeled in front of it, turning it over to see the underside. Just as she suspected, she discovered a small electronic listening device.

Plucking it off of the underside of the chair, Jasmine examined it carefully. She knew Dr. Gascon had used the visit as a means to both intimidate her as well as to plant this device. Now she had to decide what she was going to do with it. If she destroyed it, then she would have to be on her guard everywhere, not knowing where the next one would be placed. If she let it remain, she would have to guard her every word within the private sanctum of her office.

This newest stunt proved Dr. Gascon was capable of anything. She had to play her cards right, or she would discover how far Dr. Gascon wanted to take this new game. Jasmine decided she would play along for now.

After placing the bug in her desk drawer, grabbing her coat, purse, and Neal's patient file, she left her office. She stopped at the receptionist desk and announced she would be heading home for the evening. Once her too-loud announcement was made, she leaned closer to the receptionist and whispered, "Dr. Gascon bugged my office. Make sure you mind your words until I can figure out what I should do with it. I need to see if I can catch him at his own game. Until then, we need to be on guard."

The receptionist's eyes grew wider with each sentence. She had never been involved in anything as scary or as exciting as this. "Should I be scared?" she asked in a whisper.

"I'll let you know if it gets to that stage." Jasmine patted her shoulder and smiled as reassuringly as she could muster. She was feeling pretty vulnerable, but she could not let her staff know, or they would make mistakes. "I'm going to make some phone calls to see what our options are. I know I don't have to tell you this, but we need to keep this situation between the two of us."

"Absolutely," she whispered slightly louder than before. She was afraid to say much of anything, not knowing how much could be overheard. Looking back to the doctor's office, she shuddered slightly.

Seeing her look, Jasmine said, "I put it in my desk drawer. I think if you keep my office door shut, we'll be okay. As I said before, just be mindful of your volume. Okay? I wouldn't mind if you wanted to leave work early today, say four o'clock?"

"Thank you," she replied in a rush of gratitude.

"Goodnight," Jasmine called over her shoulder as she saw the elevator door opening. She quickened her pace to enter the car which only had a couple of other people inside. As the door closed, she dug in her purse for her cell phone.

She opened the phone and tapped out a memorized sequence of numbers and held it to her ear. With a sigh of exasperation, she heard the answering machine pick up the call. Luckily, the other passengers exited the elevator just as it was time for her to speak. "Hey, this is Jasmine. Dr. Gascon just bugged my office after a surprise visit. Please let me know if you have any contacts to assist or any ideas for moving forward. Thanks. Talk to you soon." She hung up and whispered one more word to herself, "Hopefully."

CHAPTER 22

Jena and Juila thanked their grandfather for bringing them home early. They had planned on staying with their grandparents for the duration of the winter break, but they had gotten homesick and ended up coming home just over halfway through the break. With their bags sitting on the floor of the telepod, they both used the elemy to move them upstairs to their rooms so they would not have to lug them through the house.

They stepped off of the telepod and waved goodbye until the telepod blinked out of existence in the garage. Not even a breeze stirred from its departure, the only evidence of a disturbance was the slight static feeling in the air. The girls turned around and went into the house.

"Mom, we're home!" Juila called out as they entered the kitchen. She looked over to her left and noticed the remote to their mother's telepod was not in its usual hanging spot. "Do you think Mom went to Tuala? Her telepod remote is gone."

"I don't know. She never said she had any plans on going, but you never know what might have come up."

The girls split up to search the house. Jena took the upstairs while Juila remained on the main floor. They kept in constant contact with one another through their mental link. With every room searched, they reunited in the living room. "We should check the patil to see if any messages came in. There might be a clue there," Jena suggested.

"Good idea!"

They trooped into the office and uncovered the patil. Juila sat at the desk chair and turned on the computer. She tapped the message icon and saw the message from Rasa to their father asking for Val to come and visit Gevena. "I guess she could have taken Val to Manzanit," Juila offered, still not convinced. She checked several other places on the patil and did not discover any other clues.

"I guess we'll just have to wait and see. I think I'm going to head upstairs and take a bath," Juila announced as she shut off the patil and stored it back in its hidden compartment in the wall. She pushed away from the desk, and they left the room together.

Jena was slightly disappointed to be alone at home. The reason they had come home early was so they could spend time with the parents they had only known existed for the past five months. Thinking about how short of a time it had been seemed almost unreal since so much had happened since arriving on Earth. They had been enrolled in school, had their sixteenth birthdays, gone to homecoming, been on dates, received samaras of their own, and they each had experienced life-threatening adventures which ended in two other people getting samaras as well.

Thinking about dating made her wonder what Luke had been up to since winter break had begun. They had ended their relationship on a weird note when Willian had unexpectedly shown up at their school. Not only had Luke been hurt to find out Jena was in a committed relationship, but he had also been punched by Willian when he discovered them kissing in the hall. She would totally understand if Luke told her he was never going to be interested in her again. After everything, she certainly would not blame him.

She watched her sister head upstairs, and she shielded her thoughts to keep them private. It was nice having a sister who was close, but sometimes she needed to be alone in her own head. Jena walked over to the phone and picked up the receiver. She contemplated whether or not she should call Luke when she saw the message light blinking on the answering machine.

Without hesitation, she pressed the play button and listened to Jasmine's urgent message for her parents. She was unsure of who the woman might be, but the tone of her voice made it seem as though there might be a problem on the horizon. Jena transcribed the message on the pad of paper on the desk just in case something happened to the original message. When one of her parents got home, she would be sure to let them know about it.

Realizing she had been stalling in making her own phone call, her fingers hesitated as they poised over the number pad. What if Luke told her to drop dead? How would she be able to face him in school the next week? What if he were waiting for her phone call and she never called him? This last question decided her action, and she rapidly dialed his number from memory.

She put the phone up to her ear with her thumb resting on the end button just in case he became angry with her call. Jena listened as the third ring sounded in her ear. Her heart thumped loudly in her chest, and she began pacing across the kitchen.

"Hello?" a male voice answered.

"Luke? This is Jena."

"Oh, hi, Jena. I thought you were going to be at your grandparents' house until school started back. Are you home?"

"Yes, we decided to come home early to surprise our parents. I guess the surprise was really on us since nobody's home."

"I could come over and keep you company if you'd like?"

"I...I'd like it a lot," Jena stammered stupidly. She could feel her face getting warm as she blushed at his offer. This was more than she had hoped for with her phone call.

"Are you okay?"

"I just didn't know if you still wanted to talk to me after...you know."

"It's okay, Jena. Sofia told me everything."

"She what?" Jena's mind raced with ideas of what Sofia would have told him. *She knew everything about their family not being from Earth. Luke was the only person in their group of friends who did not know, until now,* she thought angrily. *Sofia had no right to tell him anything about their family. Sofia should know it would put them all in danger if people found out they were aliens.*

"You sound angry. What's wrong?"

"Nothing," she covered. "When do you think you'll be here?"

"I can be there in ten minutes if you want. Otherwise, let me know what time you want me to be there."

"Ten minutes will be fine."

"Okay. See you in a few!" Luke hung up the phone.

Jena's thumb pressed on the end button and then she immediately dialed Sofia's number. She was going to give the girl a piece of her mind and then she thought she might give her a mind swipe to keep her from blabbing to anybody else about their family secrets. Too angry to hold the phone, she pushed the speaker button and slammed the receiver down on the island. She stood with both hands on the countertop and listened to it ring.

Sofia answered in a cheerful tone.

"How dare you tell Luke about us?!" Jena accused by way of a greeting.

"Jena? Is that you?"

"Were you expecting someone else? Are you going to answer my question?"

"Jena, why are you so angry? What do you think I did?"

"Luke told me you told him everything! How could you tell him? Do you realize we're probably going to have to leave Earth because of what he now knows? You've ruined everything for my whole family because you just had to tell someone our secret!"

"Jena, I think you have the wrong idea. All I told Luke was he was probably going to have a chance at getting back together with you after..." Sofia stopped talking immediately. She had no idea if Jena knew what had happened between Willian and Valentina. It certainly was not her place to be the one to tell her.

"Oh, don't stop there, Sofia! What else do you want to share with me? After all, this is my life you're so blithely discussing with other people."

"I'm sorry, Jena. I think you should probably be talking with Willian instead of me."

"Willian? What does he have to do with this? He and I are through so I don't know why I'd have to talk to him."

"You and Willian broke up? Really? That's great...I mean...are you okay with it Jena?"

"Yes. It was my idea. Besides I can't compete with what he and Val have together. Out with it, Sofia! What else did you tell Luke?"

"You know about Val and Willian kissing? How did you find out?"

"About them kissing?" Jena was getting more confused by the minute. She had no idea how Sofia would have known about the kiss she had witnessed in Roanoke. "I saw them kissing myself which was when I told him we were through."

"Oh, it must have been a different kiss then. The one I was talking about was in Val's bedroom when Jon punched him in the gut for making out with her."

Jena smirked at the idea and knew exactly how Jon must have felt. Her reaction had been a little more volatile, deadly really, but she had been stopped before she had been able to unleash her anger. She felt slightly mollified knowing Jon had avenged her honor with Willian. "I didn't know about that part." She was starting to get the idea there was something else going on, and she relented by asking, "Why don't you tell me what you told Luke? You'll have to hurry because he's going to be here in a couple of minutes."

"Luke's coming over to see you? When did you get home?"

"Start talking Sofia!"

"Okay, fine! I told him about what happened with Val, Willian, and Jon. I also suggested he might want to be there for you when you got home because you were probably going to be single soon. He was really angry at Willian for betraying you. He even offered to help Jon beat him up for cheating on you. It was really romantic!"

"Is that it?"

"Yes. Why? Oh, you thought I'd told him about your family secret? Jena! I would never tell a soul about where you all come from. I promised you and Juila your secret was safe with me, and you doubted me?"

"Well, what was I supposed to think when Luke told me you told him everything? Of course, I'd think you told him everything."

"No, never! I'd never betray your trust!"

"I'm sorry, Sofia. I should have known you wouldn't. It's just my life has turned upside down, and I don't know what to expect with anything anymore."

"I'm sorry, Jena. I wish I could be there with you right now." She paused for only a heartbeat before she asked, "Tell me how you ended it with Willian? You said you saw him kissing Val. Where were they? How did you find out? I want details!"

"Oh, I gotta go, Luke just pulled up to the front. I'll call you later. Bye!" Jena promptly hung up before Sofia could ask any more questions. She put the phone back on the charger as she raced to get to the door before he knocked. At some point, Juila would be done with her bath and come down to discover Luke was here, but she hoped she would have some private time before being interrupted.

Breathless from her sprint, she pulled the door open in a rush just as Luke was raising his hand to knock. She grinned foolishly at him and stepped to the side to give him room to enter. "Thank you for coming over."

"I'm glad to see you're so eager for me to be here," he teased.

"Oh, that...I didn't want Juila to know you were here. She's upstairs." She tipped her head up toward the staircase to indicate her direction. Again, she felt stupid since it was obvious where the upstairs was, and he could figure it out without her gesture. "Let's go out back so we can talk."

"Okay," Luke agreed and barely managed to keep himself from smiling at how silly Jena was acting. He assumed it was her way of dealing with her difficult situation with her former boyfriend. At least he hoped Willian was out of the picture, Jena had not come out and said they were over yet. Now it was his turn to be nervous about what Jena might have to tell him.

The temperature had cooled to the mid-seventies, and there was a light breeze as they sat in the patio chairs next to the pool. Both of them waited for the other to begin talking and the silence drew out until they were uncomfortable.

"I thought you weren't coming home until school started again..."

"I'm glad you wanted to come over..." they both talked at once and then burst out laughing. "You first," Jena offered.

"It was nothing. I just remembered you said you wanted to

surprise your parents by coming home early." He sighed as he tried to figure out how to ask what he really wanted to know about. Deciding to just get it over with he blurted, "I hope you're not angry about Sofia talking with me. But I have to ask, are you going to get back together with Willian?"

"No. We are definitely through."

"What a bastard! Just give me the word, and I'll break his lying, cheating face for you!"

"No, Luke, I don't want that either. I'm glad Willian has found someone who makes him happy. He was never happy when we were together. I guess he was one of the reason's we came here to live with our parents."

"What? I'm confused. Haven't you always lived with your parents?"

Wishing she could take back what she had said, Jena frantically tried to come up with an answer to his question. Going back to the lie they originally used when enrolling in school, she said, "No. We were in boarding school in South Africa. Willian was getting jealous and mean with me all of the time, and I needed to get some distance between us. I never believed he would follow me here." Even as she finished talking, she hated herself for having to lie to Luke. He deserved the truth, but his safety depended on him remaining ignorant of their true heritage.

"You must be furious with Val, too."

"No, I'm not angry with either of them. Luke, I promise you I am genuinely happy for both of them. I want you to promise you won't say or do anything to hurt either of their feelings because of what happened between Willian and me. It won't do any good, and it will cause other problems in our group. I want us all to be friends again. Please promise me, Luke."

"I don't understand how you can be so casual about it, but if you're sure you're okay, then I'll leave it alone. But if you ever change your mind, let me know!" He laughed after he said it, but his eyes held hers in a serious expression so she would know he meant every word he said.

"It won't be necessary, but thank you anyway." She looked away from Luke's intense stare and wondered what she should do since the hard conversation was over.

"So you want me to be friends with Willian?"

"Yes, if you can manage it."

"You're definitely a better person than me, Jena. I will try for your sake though. So...where do we stand? Are we friends or maybe something more?"

"I was hoping you'd still be willing to see me. After everything which happened, I didn't think you'd ever talk to me again, but here you are."

"Here I am, and here I'll always be, Jena. There's something special between us, and I want to see where it'll go. Do you feel the same way about me?"

"I do. Can I tell you something and not have you hate me?"

"You can tell me anything."

"We'll see. Okay, here goes. Willian and I were supposed to get married when we were eighteen. It was an arranged marriage made when we were both six years old. He was more than just a boyfriend, but we were like oil and water. Between you and me, I think he was jealous of me and..." she was about to say it was because of her ability to use her crystal skills but stopped herself just in time, "...and lately he hasn't been very nice about our relationship. When he came here professing he'd changed, I had hoped it was true.

"But then I felt guilty because I'd met you. When you and I were together, I felt guilty because I knew I already had someone else, but I liked you more than I ever liked Willian. Trust me; I tried to like him, but he was always saying hurtful things to me. You never did anything like that to me."

"Thank you for sharing how you felt with me. I had no idea your relationship was arranged. It makes more sense now. I was sort of worried about how casual you were about ending your relationship, but I can tell it was because it wasn't anything you ever wanted for yourself."

"Definitely not!"

"Good, then we don't have to talk about it anymore…unless you want to, of course."

"Thanks. I think I'd rather talk about us." She grinned over at him.

"I like the way you're thinking!" He laughed along with her. His tension had dissolved ever since he realized the true nature of Jena's feelings for Willian. He had hated thinking she could coldly cast aside her old boyfriend; she just did not seem the type to be so cavalier.

CHAPTER 23

Juila tried not to splash the water as she lowered herself through the layer of bubbles and down into the warmth of the tub. Careful to keep her hands dry, she picked up her phone from the edge of the tub. She had shielded her mind from her sister's so she could have a private phone conversation.

She touched the speed dial and held the phone to her ear. When Behn picked up the call, she said, "I thought you might want to know we came home early."

"Really? When can I see you? I wanted to talk to you about something important."

"I guess you could come over. I just got into a hot bath. The only thing covering my naked body is a layer of bubbles." She kept her voice low in her first attempt at being sexy and sultry.

"I like the sound of that. Tell me more."

"My skin feels all slippery and wet."

"Well you are in the water, so I'd expect it," Behn teased.

"Oh, I give up! I just can't do sexy; I feel like an idiot!"

"I'm sorry, Juila. I couldn't resist teasing you."

"What did you want to talk about?"

"I wanted to ask you how Jena was doing. Is she really okay with Val dating Willian? Is it going to make things weird when we get back to school? Are we still okay?"

"Wow, Behn, if I didn't know better, I'd say you were feeling insecure."

"Well, what do you think? My sister is now dating your sister's ex-fiancé."

"Ex-betrothed, actually. Well, I was thrilled with them breaking up. At first, I was angry at Val for her part in this, but now I know she's an innocent victim in the whole mess."

"Oh, good."

"Besides, I've never seen Jena so happy. She even asked our dad if she could be his successor."

"Successor to what?"

"Are you being serious?"

"Yes. I don't know what you're talking about."

"My dad is the next in line to become the Elder of the Pantano District when Grandpa Daven steps down or dies. You knew that, didn't you?"

"I didn't really know it was a lineage thing. I just assumed Elder Daven was elected to the office, like a Mayor or something."

"No, the Elders are trained by Jehoban and their son's inherit the title of successor when they are born. They learn everything the Elders are supposed to do and, when the time comes for them to take the office, they meet with Jehoban and get his blessing and instructions."

"But Jena isn't a boy. You just said it went to their sons."

"That was before Rasa was confirmed as successor to Elder Wilken. It means because Jehoban has given his blessing once he will most likely do it for Jena as well. Jena has a better claim to the title than Rasa did, so I'm sure it'll work out as she hopes."

"Why couldn't she be a successor when she was betrothed to Willian?"

Juila raised her eyebrows in dismay at how little Behn knew about the societal structure of Tuala even though he had been born there. She answered patiently, "Because Willian is Elder Debbon's successor. Jena could hardly become an Elder herself if she were the wife of another Elder. It would have been impossible to do both."

"Oh," Behn said softly, thinking through everything Juila had just told him. He realized there was much he still needed to learn about his mother's world, which was how he thought about it to himself: his mother's world. Even though he had been born in Tuala, he had been raised for half of his life on Earth. He did not remember any of the customs of Tuala; he was a foreigner in his homeworld. "Does this mean your family is royalty?"

"I guess. Of a sort. We don't have kings or queens; we have Jehoban, then the Elders, then the wise-woman, and then finally the town leaders."

"Definitely royalty then," Behn determined based on her description of the chain of command. "You know, in ancient times on Earth, the kings would say they were appointed by God. They believed themselves to be the voice of God on Earth, and it was what made them special and untouchable."

"I guess there is a similarity to royalty then," Juila admitted. Her bath water was beginning to be too cool to be relaxing. She asked, "So are you going to come over, or what?"

"Sure. I can help you dry yourself off," he teased.

"If I waited that long for you to get over here then you'd have to chip me out of the ice. I think I can manage on my own," she retorted.

Behn laughed and said, "Okay, I'll be there in a few minutes. Hey, do you know when Willian will be bringing Val home? Mom was asking, and I had no idea."

"How would I know?"

"Because Willian borrowed your mom's telepod to take her to Manzanit. You didn't know about it?"

"No. Nobody was here when we got home. We just assumed Mom went somewhere in Tuala for a visit."

"Oh, well maybe she went with them. She could have decided to visit with Rasa, don't you think?"

"Sure, it would make sense; they are cousins after all."

"Wait! What? Like real cousins, not the fake royalty kind of cousins?"

Juila laughed and said, "I'm not sure what fake royal cousins are, but no, my mom's aunt is Rasa's mother. She really is our cousin by blood."

"Wow, what a small world."

"The worlds are getting smaller by the minute, it seems. Okay, I'm going to hang up so I can get out of this freezing bath. I'll see you in a couple of minutes."

"Okay, bye."

Juila flipped her phone shut and tossed it onto a towel folded on the floor a little distance from the tub. The last thing she needed was to get her phone drenched with bathwater and render it useless. Since she had an idea of where their mom might have gone, she opened her mind-link to her sister and discovered it remained shut on her sister's end. "That's weird," she muttered to herself as she draped the towel around her body and stepped out of the tub.

She dressed hurriedly and flipped the lever to drain the bath water. Juila grabbed her phone off of the floor and tossed her wet towel over the edge of the almost drained tub. Since she was unable to reach Jena's mind, she would have to physically locate her in the house.

After finding her sister's bedroom empty, she continued down the hallway to peer into her own room. Still no closer to finding Jena, she went down the stairs and called out, "Jena? Where are you?" She became concerned when she did not even get a reply. What was happening in their house today? It seemed as though everyone was going missing.

She reached the living room, which was also empty and looked into the equally vacant kitchen. Just as she turned to head down the hallway to the office and library, she caught a flash of motion outside. Her eyebrows rose in astonishment to see Luke sitting outside with her sister. This was a nice turn of events. She thought for certain she would have to pester Jena into calling Luke, and yet there they were chatting and laughing as though he had been there for a while.

Thinking back, she suddenly realized Jena had been the one to first shut off their mind link. "That little sneak," she murmured as she realized Jena had planned this visit knowing she would have time alone while she bathed upstairs. Then she had to laugh at her sister's ingenuity because it really was the only way she would have had a private moment with Luke otherwise.

Juila opened the patio door and nonchalantly walked over to the couple. She realized they did look as though they were a couple with how close they were sitting to one another and the way they never lost eye contact. In fact, she did not even think either of them knew she had come outside; they were so involved with one another. She cleared her throat and said, "I hope I'm not interrupting."

"You know you are," Jena answered snippily after she had jumped in surprise. "I thought you were taking a bath."

"I was about thirty minutes ago. I had to get out eventually."

"I suppose."

"Wow, don't sound too enthusiastic about it or else I might get a complex." She sat on the chair Jena had originally been sitting on. "What have I missed?"

Jena blushed furiously and glared at her sister's presumptive question. "Don't you have anything else you could be doing right now?"

"No, you have my full attention."

Jena continued to glare as she reopened their mind link. She shared everything about her conversation with Sofia and an abbreviated version of Luke's visit in the amount of time it took for three heartbeats.

In the same manner and speed, Juila returned the favor by telling her about her suspicion of where their mother had gone and how Behn was on his way over. She finally relented and stood up and said, "I guess I need to go inside after all."

Luke watched Jena's identical twin sister go back inside the house. He turned back to Jena and said, "If I didn't know better, I'd say you two had a complete conversation while you stared one another down!" He laughed at Jena's expression and was glad to have her alone with him again.

You have no idea how right you are, she said to herself. Instead of answering him, she decided to shift his mind to less dangerous ideas. She leaned forward and kissed him on the lips. Intending only for it to be a quick peck, she was surprised when Luke's arms wrapped around her and pulled her closer. She felt his tongue on her lips, and she parted them to allow it to go further. Her whole body began to sing with the pleasure she felt at being intimate with Luke. This feeling was nothing like it had been before and she wondered if she had changed so much in so short of a time.

That didn't take long, Juila teased as she watched the two from the comfort of the living room couch.

Not now, Juila, Jena retorted. Luckily, all she heard was her sister's chuckle in reply.

CHAPTER 24

As it turned out, the courier was still having a discussion with Elder Wilken when Rasa, Amanda, and Willian arrived at the conference room. They sat on the bench outside the door while they waited for him to leave. Rasa was fidgeting and anxious to find out what her mentor and friend knew about the descendants of the Watchers.

"Are you sure you heard him say 'descendants of the Watchers' Willian?" Rasa asked in a whisper as she tried to make sense of it all.

He nodded emphatically and replied, "Absolutely. Of course, I thought he was joking. What does it matter? You still haven't told me what this is all about. We have time right now."

"We may have the time, but this is definitely not the right place. What we were talking about requires absolute secrecy," Amanda answered quietly even as she watched another staff member cross the corridor in front of them.

"But you will tell me, right?" Willian hated how petulant the question sounded, but he really was earnest in wanting to know.

"If this yields what we think it will, then yes, we'll have to tell you," Amanda agreed. Again, she had the feeling it was the right thing to do with Willian. Her senses were reeling with the expectation of what was certainly going to happen. She looked over at Rasa and wondered if she were picking up on her cousin's excitement.

It was not the definitive answer he had hoped for, but he was going to have to content himself with it for the time being. Besides, because he knew something was afoot, he would keep his eyes and ears open for any other clues even if they decided not to confide with him their secret. From the looks on their faces as they watched him, he believed they knew it was his intention as well.

The conference room door opened and the three of them on the bench each sat there with guilty expressions on their faces. The courier looked at them and wondered what they could have done to warrant such a reaction to his appearance. As Elder Wilken was stepping up behind him, he had no choice but to continue on his way and deliver the news he had gathered to his client.

"To what do I owe the honor of meeting with you three at once?" Elder Wilken asked with a knowing look of amusement in his eyes.

Rasa stood up, faced her mentor, and said urgently "We'd like to talk with you in private if you have the time, Elder Wilken."

"It sounds important. Come inside then. We can meet right now." He took a step back, so there was room for the trio to enter into the conference room. Willian was the last to enter, and he quirked his eyebrow in question at the boy, seeing if the young man would give him a clue as to the meaning of the meeting.

Willian saw the look and shrugged his shoulders in ignorance of an answer. He was just as anxious to hear what the women wanted to ask the Elder. When he came to the small seating area near the fire, Willian took the seat furthest away, knowing the Elder's preference of being near the heat.

Rasa waited for Elder Wilken to get comfortable before she began speaking. "Willian has told us something rather interesting which we would like to discuss with you."

"Go ahead," Elder Wilken responded, and his eyes shifted to look at Willian. He wondered why the boy had denied knowing the meaning of this meeting if he had been the one to bring it up to the women.

Interpreting the look correctly, Rasa clarified, "Willian came to look for Amanda, and he overheard our private conversation. When he asked us more about it, he explained how he had just come from meeting with you."

"Yes, that much is true." He turned to Willian and admonished, "What have I told you about knocking before you enter a room? This is what comes of listening in on other people's conversations."

"Don't be too hard on him, especially if what he told us is true," Amanda interjected in Willian's defense.

Willian was starting to feel pretty bad about where the conversation had been heading. Having Amanda stand up for him raised his opinion of her immensely.

"Well, what did he tell you then? You have me very curious," Elder Wilken leaned forward with an eager expression.

Rasa continued, "He said you joked about being a descendant of the Watchers. Were you joking or is it true?"

Wilken leaned back slowly and sighed. "So it has come to this, has it? I've lived for one-hundred and thirty-seven anons, and I never expected to have the knowledge come to any use."

"Are you saying it's true then?" Amanda asked earnestly. She could feel her pulse quicken with excitement. Elder Wilken could be the first descendant she had ever met which made her wonder what had happened to the others.

Elder Wilken sighed heavily again and nodded, "Yes. It is true I'm one of the last descendants still living."

"Do you have the samara then?" Rasa asked impatiently. When Elder Wilken's eyes glanced hard at her in surprise, she could have kicked herself for not being more respectful with her question.

"What do you know of the samaras?" he asked in an accusatory manner.

Amanda decided to step in and speak since she had been the one to start the whole matter. She reached into her pocket and pulled out the paper containing the expanded prophecy and handed it across the small table to Elder Wilken. "Read this, and let us know what you think."

More than a little curious, Elder Wilken accepted the paper and unfolded it. He turned its writing toward the fire to help his old eyes read the hand-written words.

FROM A FAR-AWAY LAND, THERE WILL COME IN TIME, INTUITION IS IN HAND, STRANGE DETAILS KNOWN, WITH TIES TO THE PEOPLE. FROM ONE OF MY OWN, THERE WILL BE A SIGN. THOSE BORN TO THIS ONE, WILL TRANSFORM ALL. LUCINDEN WILL PURSUE, ELDERS WILL FALL, THEN ALL MADE NEW.

TAKE COMFORT IN ONE ANOTHER, COMBINED YOU WILL SEE. BELIEVE IN WHAT YOU UNDERSTAND, KNOW WHAT YOU DO, THEN YOU CAN BE.

HIS MIND REELED with the implications of the two paragraphs. "Where did you get this? Do you know what this means?" How they answered would determine what he would share.

"Yes. When we first received this message in the Elders' Instructional Guide, there was a group of us which were brought before Jehoban. He informed us it was our task to fulfill what is written.

"At that time, we had already accidentally discovered three of the samaras. Since then, another seven of the samaras have been found and claimed by their rightful owners. This means there are only three samaras still unaccounted for at this point.

"Today, the second paragraph on the paper appeared in the same book, which was why I came to see Rasa. She was at Jehoban's meeting, and she's still in need of finding her samara. When you put that," Amanda pointed to the paper to emphasize her point before continuing, "to what Jena told us about the samara prophecy of 'When the descendants of the Watchers bring these all together then the Gates between the Worlds will be open for all to pass through without a loss.' Then it all begins to make more sense. Willian also supplied us with another version of the saying. Willian, can you repeat it for Elder Wilken?"

"Do you mean what Jena told me a long time ago?" After receiving a nod from Amanda, he recited from memory, "There is an ancient legend that the descendants of the Watchers hold the samaras in hiding until the day comes where they will be united again to change the world as we know it."

A newfound respect for Amanda and Rasa formed in Elder Wilken's mind as well as an intense sadness. He had known both were special, but he had no idea to what extent until this moment. After all of the anons he had lived, he had never received news which shocked him as much as what was written on the paper he still held between his two hands.

Elder Wilken suddenly spoke into the silence. "It is true I am one of the last remaining descendants. I have enjoyed a long life, as have my ancestors. Rasa, have you never wondered why the oldest Districts have been so successful?"

"I thought it had to do with the confluence of the ley lines. Manzanit has the most intersections of any in the world. Is that not the case?"

"Yes, it's a true assessment. However, there's more to it. Originally there were only thirteen Districts, each having their own Ascension Gate. All thirteen were guarded by one of the Watchers and have remained in their line of descent until some of them died. The same has happened with my own post with Pluska not being willing or able to follow after me."

"There are now fifteen Districts. Which ones were added and why?" Amanda asked excitedly. She was beginning to get the glimmer of an idea of a possible plan. Depending on Elder Wilken's answer, she would know if she had the right notion.

Elder Wilken smiled at Amanda's question. "I like the way you think, Amanda. The two which were added were at Gaud and Noidad, and only because there was a dispute surrounding the Gates which were located in each location. The Guardians were eventually voted into the Elder's group to keep them from causing mischief."

"Which would explain why they were so hard to deal with," Rasa muttered.

Amanda looked at her curiously and asked, "In what way?"

Rasa remained quiet since the proceedings of the Council of Elders were to be kept confidential. She glanced over to Elder Wilken and was surprised to see a smirk forming on his lips. "Can I tell her?"

"Yes, you may. I believe it might be important to what you are trying to achieve with this paper." He shook the paper in his hand for emphasis.

Rasa agreed and answered, "The Elders in those two locations were vehemently opposed to my becoming a successor. In fact, Yingun refused to vote at all in the third and final vote. It makes more sense because they come from a line of people who weren't initially placed by Jehoban, so they don't care so much about Jehoban's plan for the people's governing."

"Well spoken, Rasa," Elder Wilken. "For that very reason, Elder Debbon allowed the successorship to go to you without Yingun's vote. I'm sure Yingun felt even more slighted because his opinion was not necessary. Be sure you watch out for him in the future, Rasa. When I'm gone, he's certain to cause trouble for you at every turn."

"Elder Wilken, please don't talk about leaving! We are all in desperate need of your wise counsel for many anons to come," Rasa pled. She was so moved by his statement she had fallen to her knees in front of him and had put both of her hands on his to reassure herself he was going to comply with her wishes.

"We all have our allotted time, dear Rasa." He patted her hand affectionately and then turned his attention to Amanda. "Please remain here for a bit; there's something to which I must attend. Afterward, I'll return to you all here." He gave the paper into Rasa's hands and then pushed himself up from his chair. With a slow step, he shuffled out of the room, feeling exhausted by the morning's revelations.

The trio watched him leave and remained quiet until the door clicked shut behind him. "I've never seen him so downtrodden!" Rasa exclaimed.

"What do you think has happened? What was he going to do?" Willian asked, even more puzzled than Rasa.

"I think we'll just have to bide our time and wait for his return," Amanda announced.

"Well, if we're going to be stuck here for who-knows-how-long, then it'll give you time to explain to me what all of this is about," Willian spoke adamantly as he gestured back toward the paper Rasa had folded in her lap.

Amanda regarded the young boy, wishing he were more mature so she could be certain of his discretion. As it was, Willian had already gleaned many clues from their conversation with Elder Wilken. She nodded and began from the beginning. "While I was in a coma, I had a dream about the prophecy being written in a book at Riccan's house. When I woke up and found Riccan, I told him about it. That was when we discovered the first paragraph of the words written on that page."

"Can I see it?" Willian asked, not really believing they would share it with him. Much to his surprise, Rasa picked it up from her lap and held it out for him. With raised eyebrows, he accepted it, eagerly opened it up, and began reading. The words did not make much sense to him, and by the time he reached the end, he was thoroughly confused. "I don't get it."

"We didn't either at first," Amanda admitted. "But because of where we had found it, we knew it had to be significant. Eventually, Jehoban called together thirteen people, all of whom I had met in my coma induced dream, and we began to piece it together. We believe the first part of it refers to me, and then to my daughters."

"It also stands to reason the samaras were particularly important in this, especially once we realized each person in the meeting began claiming the samaras."

"What does that even mean, 'claiming the samaras'?"

"The samaras only have one true owner. When the correct person comes into physical contact with it, then a bond is formed between them which is unbreakable and very powerful, or so I'm told. In fact, I believe you might have some understanding of such a bond, as what you and Val share is quite similar to it." Amanda wondered if the same bond would happen for the children of all of the samara holders. If such were the case, then neither Juila nor Jena had met their true partners in life.

"Who were the people in the meeting?" Willian asked, leaning forward as he was getting into this fascinating story. This seemed like an epic adventure, just exactly like what all young boys wanted to be involved with.

"That part I won't share with you because it isn't relevant to the story. Needless to say, you already know Rasa and I were there, and neither of us has received our own samaras. We also don't know the timeline for completing the quest, or if there even is one."

"So if you said Juila and Jena were also named in the original journal entry, then I can assume they were also included in the meeting with Jehoban. And if there is only one samara left after your two, then either one or both of them have already gotten their own samara. Am I right?" Willian was madly trying to piece together all of the bits of information he had gleaned so far.

"As I said, Willian, it isn't relevant to the story. There's nothing more for us to discuss at this point," Amanda shut her mouth and inwardly wondered what other intuitive leaps Willian would make. He certainly was smart enough to figure out much of it. In fact, only a minute or so later, her musings were confirmed with his next statement.

"You also said, in Rasa's conference room, both of my parents were part of the group. Is there any danger in them both being involved? Are the samaras dangerous?" Willian wondered what else his parents had kept from him. He was starting to not like being kept in the dark when important things were happening around him. To be fair, he probably had been too involved in his own affairs to notice much of what his parents were involved with anyway.

Amanda looked over to Rasa in consternation.

"You did say it actually," Rasa commented with a grin on her face.

"So that is Rasa, you, Jena, Juila, Mom, and dad." As Willian said each name, he counted them off on his fingers. "That's six of the thirteen. I bet Riccan was there and probably both of his parents, which is now nine people. Eventually, I'll figure it all out, even if you don't tell me!"

Rasa laughed out loud and said, "He probably will, Amanda!"

"I don't think I have to remind you this conversation cannot be repeated outside of this room. All of our lives could be at stake and possibly the lives of everyone in Tuala. Do I make myself clear, Willian?" Amanda admonished in the most serious tone she could muster.

Instantly, Willian's expression of delight in the mystery dissolved and he nodded soberly. "I understand. Jehoban wouldn't have called you all together unless it was important."

Everyone agreed with Willian's statement, and they fell into silence as they all wondered what the outcome of it all would be. They remained in silence for several minutes.

Rasa broke into their thoughts when she asked, "So Willian, why don't you tell me about you and Valentina? The last I heard, you were convinced on getting back together with Jena."

Embarrassed beyond belief, Willian's cheeks burned red hot, and he looked guiltily over to Amanda. The serene look on her face helped tremendously. She had every right to be upset with him over the whole affair, and yet she had already told him she was fine with the outcome. He swallowed hard to moisten his dry throat and began telling Rasa the story of what had happened.

Almost an hour had passed, and they were running out of

things to talk about. Periodically, one or another of them would glance toward the doorway whenever they thought they heard a noise in the hall. It seemed silly for them to all have to wait until the Elder's return.

"Do you think we should check on him? He seemed pretty tired when he left," Willian reasoned.

"No," Amanda answered. "He was quite specific in having us wait for him until he returned. I'm inclined to follow his order as he's more than five times my senior. I'll have to defer to his wisdom." She looked at her watch and was surprised to see how late it had gotten. She wished she had left a message for Riccan about going to visit with Rasa. Never had she imagined it would take so long. Surely she would be home before he returned from work, at least she hoped it would still be the case.

They all jumped when the door did actually open, and Elder Wilken entered the room carrying a small wooden box in his hands. He used his foot to shut the door behind him, with more grace than they knew he possessed as he balanced on his other foot without even a wobble. As he walked across the room, he looked refreshed and livelier than he had appeared on his departure.

As he came to sit in his chair, the three stood in respect and waited until he was seated before they resumed their own places around him. He rested the box on one of his knees and reverently touched the flowery carvings on the exterior of the wooden panels. Never had he imagined how hard it would be on him for this day to come. Without further ado, Elder Wilken held out the box to Rasa and said, "I believe this is yours."

"Mine?" Rasa asked in confusion. "What is it?"

"Open it and see," Willian said eagerly.

Elder Wilken nodded his approval of Willian's statement as he continued to hold the box in front of him for Rasa to receive.

With more than a little hesitation, Rasa accepted the box and rested it on both of her thighs. Her hands were tingling as if elemy were coursing through them. She tried to lift the top, only to discover it was not how it opened. Leaning forward, she noticed the lid was in a slat on three sides and should be slid out of the groove to reveal the contents.

As soon as there was enough space open for her to peer into the opening, Rasa knew it was meant to be hers, just as Elder Wilken had predicted. She felt the energy pulsing toward her hands, and she longed to touch its glassy, smooth surface. Never before had she felt such a bond with something which made her slightly fearful. Knowing each of the other recipients had been unharmed, gave her some measure of comfort.

"What is it?" Willian asked, repeating the same thing Rasa had asked.

Before she answered, she accessed her memory of crystal skills and looked at the aura of the stone. Just as she had hoped, the color of the aura perfectly matched her birth crystal: bright white with two small flecks of light blue. She sighed with relief and answered, "This is my samara."

CHAPTER 25

Petre arranged for transport to Pantano and arrived at the Residence with a few minutes to spare before his appointment with Elder Daven. He had been pleasantly surprised to get an immediate interview with the Elder. In the past, he had experienced endless delays and excuses from all of the Elders, mostly because they did not have time to deal with his lies and deceit.

He walked across the vast expanse of lawn, which was used as the landing field, and admired the stately appearance of the Residence as it was positioned on the slight rise in the land. The last time he had been here, he barely recalled getting into the building, since he had been near death after being trapped between the realms. This time he was a welcomed guest, which was quite a change in such a short period of time.

By the time he reached the stairway, Elder Daven had come out to greet him. The sun was shining above his head, surrounding the older man with light. Petre wondered if there were any significance to the anomaly as he called out a greeting. "Hi, Elder Daven."

"Hello, Petre."

By the time he got up to the patio, he was slightly winded by the exertion. "Thank you for agreeing to meet with me on such short notice."

"It was no problem. Would you care to have the meeting out here on the patio, or would you rather have the privacy of my office?"

"Out here would be fine. Besides, it reminds me of when Tirsha was here with us." He moved over to the same seat he had used before in memory of the former occasion.

Elder Daven sat across from the much-changed man. He had no idea what could have brought Petre back to him so soon and asked him politely.

"I went to visit with Tirsha, and she brought up something which should probably have been remedied a long time ago in my life." Petre was reluctant to even broach the subject. Past experiences had taught him to avoid occasions where he could be ridiculed.

Patience was needed for Petre to finally decide to share with him the heart of the matter. The Residence was nearly empty of staff, and Nena was busy with some of the village people. He had all the time necessary to sit and enjoy the sunshine while Petre formulated his request.

Petre respected Elder Daven's quiet reception, and he was glad he did not feel pressured to talk. Because of this, his tension over the matter eased significantly. "The problem I have is I never appeared for my lottery assignment. I'm afraid I'm fifteen anons late for my appointment, and I don't know if there's a remedy for it. Have you had any experience in this type of matter? Is it something which could be made up? You see, I want to make Tirsha proud by being an honorable and productive member of society, and I think this should be the first step."

"I can see your heart is in the right place. There have been other instances of this in the past." He paused to assess this particular situation and decided to shift his conversation to another tactic. "Are you familiar with Jehoban's teachings?"

"Yes, a fair amount of them, at least." Petre wondered what Elder Daven could be getting at with his question.

"It seems as though your experiences have all been about actions and consequences. Is that a fair assessment?"

"Absolutely. I was forever trying to scheme ways out of paying for something or hiding from someone whom I'd cheated."

"Is this a life you ever see yourself returning to? If Tirsha decided she didn't want to see you again, would you return to your old ways?"

"That's a fair question, and I can honestly say I would not. I no longer want to live a life on the run and on the fringes of civility. I've grown so accustomed to people hating me, I've begun to hate myself. I don't want that way of life anymore."

"I thought such was the case when you gave me my samara." Again he shifted his conversation and asked, "Jehoban's teachings are to guide all of us to be our best selves. He desires for us to achieve all we can in our lives and for us to be happy. The Elders are all taught how to help the citizens in this endeavor. Do you know how the lottery assignments are chosen?"

"No, I always imagined they were drawn randomly."

"They can be, or they can be at the discretion of the Elder in charge of the District. In whose District do you now reside, Petre?"

"Nobody's, I haven't claimed any District since I graduated from school and sailed away in my water craft."

"Have you ever received any retirement benefits?"

Petre scoffed in amusement at the notion. "No. I knew I was destined to begin working immediately since I didn't have the means to continue with post-study. It was one of the reasons I never went to the lottery assignment."

"There's something I need to check on. Will you wait for me here, Petre? I don't think I'll be too long." Daven stood up as an idea struck him. He needed to access his patil before he mentioned anything to Petre.

"Certainly. I'll just sit here and enjoy the view." He smiled up at Elder Daven, wondering how he could ever have thought him to be a spiteful and pompous man. He was startled when a glass of iced steena tea appeared on the table in front of him.

"I thought you might like a refreshing drink while you waited," Daven said with a grin just before he turned to enter the Residence to get to his office.

"Thanks," Petre said as he picked up the glass and made a mock toast in his direction before sipping the minty beverage.

Daven set a brisk pace for himself as he returned to his office and quietly shut the door behind him. He immediately sat at his desk and accessed Petre's records on the patil. He skimmed through the numerous pages of his indiscretions until he reached the lottery assignment date.

The records made his mouth drop open in amazement, and he wondered if there had been some mistake in the entry. After digging through several other layers of documents, he came to the same answer he had received before: Petre was one of the rare people who had received a lifetime pass on a work assignment. He printed it out and folded it carefully in half.

He stood up, with paper in hand, and left his office. The only problem he could see with this whole thing would be Petre's reaction. Petre had lived a life filled with consequences. How would he deal with the idea he had cheated himself out of a life of leisure in his attempt to avoid the perceived responsibility?

Petre watched Elder Daven return and wondered what his

expression could mean. He took another sip of the tea just before the older man came close to the table. Hurriedly, Petre stood up to offer respect for the Elder and waited to sit down until his host did first. "Is everything okay?"

"What? Oh, yes, thank you for asking." He fiddled with the corners of the paper and smiled slightly at how he would give Petre the news. "What type of assignment did you suppose you would receive? Did you have any specialty in school? Any areas of interest?"

"I had no idea, which scared me the most. My teachers didn't particularly care for me since I was continually using my deception skills to get out of most things. I guess it probably would have been something menial or belittling just to satisfy their desire to get even with me."

"Well, I took the liberty of looking up your lottery assignment. I have it printed out here if you would like to begin your task immediately." He held out the paper until he realized Petre was reluctant to take it from him. He placed it on the table directly ahead of where his hand was already resting. "May I remind you that you came to me about getting this situation resolved? I have your answer literally at hand." He smiled a little at his pun, trying to tease Petre into reading the paper.

Taking the bait, Petre pulled the paper across the table with his index finger and let it rest under his palm as he tried to calm his nerves. After all, he had asked for this. His life would never be satisfying knowing this had been left undone. He flipped open the flap of paper and scanned the page. His eyes narrowed slightly in accusation as he looked back up to Elder Daven as he asked, "Is this some kind of a sick joke?"

"No, I promise this is what I found in your graduation file. Either you must have impressed someone, or you are very blessed. I think it was probably a bit of both." Elder Daven smiled sincerely at Petre trying to encourage him to believe his sincerity.

"Is this paper really telling me I was running from my ultimate freedom? All those anons I was thinking I was rebelling against the system, and I was really just making a fool of myself!"

"I don't think you've fully grasped one other thing about what this assignment means."

"What's that?"

"The retirement money which comes along with it."

"You mean the money I forfeited by not showing up?"

"No, I mean the money you are still entitled to, as well as all of the back pay. This assignment doesn't have any contingency clauses. You should take the paper and go see Elder Rylon to receive your back pay as well as make arrangements for your monthly stipend."

"I'm still waiting for you to tell me this isn't real. I've never been this lucky. Surely there's some mistake." Petre's hands shook as he started to feel strong emotions rippling through him. This paper meant he could begin his future with Tirsha as soon as she was ready. He did not have to try to juggle a job and family life as so many others had. This day was ranking right up there with one of his best ever, and he owed it all to Elder Daven for sharing it with him. Another thought struck him, and he asked, "How many others have accessed this record?"

"None. Not even Elder Rylon has opened it; I was the first to break the assignment seal. There hasn't been any conspiracy in this Petre. It was always up to you to go and get this; it just took you a few more anons than it should have. Besides, I think you are ready for the blessing now more than you would have been back then. Don't you agree?"

"Absolutely!" Petre jumped up from the table, eager to get his future going again on the right track this time. "I'm going to go to

Menad immediately!" His eager expression changed almost instantly to one of confusion.

"What is it, Petre?"

"I don't have any money to get me there. I spent my last shillings on the transport here, and I don't even have my water craft nearby in order to sail there myself." He scoffed at his situation and said, "It just figures. I get the best news ever, and I can't even get myself there! When is this endless cycle going to stop, Elder Daven?"

"I'd say right now," he replied, and he gathered elemy and translated Petre immediately to the Residence in Menad. With a satisfied grin, Daven picked up Petre's glass from the table and whistled a jaunty tune as he walked back into his Residence.

CHAPTER 26

Juila invited Behn into the living room and sat next to him on the couch. She had her back to her sister, who was still out on the patio outside with Luke. Her mind link kept her informed as to what was going on, so she felt no need to watch them as well.

"I see Luke and Jena have managed to patch things up already," he said with a silly grin. He watched the pair outside for little longer before he turned his attention back to Juila. With his hand resting on her leg, he imagined how it would have felt had he been beside her while she was bathing. His imagination began to run away with him, and he had to clear his throat and look away from her in embarrassment.

"What were you thinking just now?"

"What? You mean you weren't reading my mind?"

"No! I would never be so rude!" She scowled at his accusation. "Tell me what you were thinking; you had a strange expression on your face."

Behn scuffed his shoe on the carpet, wishing she had not asked him. Part of what he liked about their relationship was their complete honesty. "I imagined what your leg would have felt like while you were in the bath."

Juila smiled, "Oh yeah? It must have been good." She pulled up her skirt until her flesh was bared. "What about now? How does it feel?"

Her skin was smooth and warm under his fingertips. With a groan of pleasure, he laid his hand flat on her thigh and gently squeezed it. He leaned over and kissed her on the lips as his hand continued to massage her flesh. He had not realized how muscular her legs were which made it even more exciting. Her lips tasted of strawberries, and it made him hungry for more of her.

Before long he had managed to have her lying on the couch underneath him. His hand had wandered higher, and of their own volition, his fingers explored her curves. He could tell she was enjoying herself by her gyrations and moans as she kissed him even more urgently than before. His other hand had found its way up her shirt and was cupping her breast, squeezing gently.

"Jeez, you two, get a room!" Luke admonished as he reached over the back of the couch and pushed Behn's head playfully.

The two burst apart guiltily, and Juila pulled her clothes back down to cover her exposed flesh. They both lookup up at Luke who remained standing behind them smiling from ear to ear.

"I'll remember this the next time I catch you in a compromising situation," Behn accused, knowing his cheeks were burning red with embarrassment.

"What's this about compromising situations?" Jena asked as she walked through the patio doors and looked at each person in the room, deciphering accurately what had just happened. She burst out laughing. "You should see the looks on your faces!"

"I'd rather not," Juila mumbled, causing them all to laugh harder.

"Come on, Luke, we've teased them enough. Let's get something to eat," Jena said as she pulled on his arm to get him turned around and give her sister some privacy.

"Why didn't you warn me about them coming back inside?" Behn whispered hoarsely.

"I was a little preoccupied!" Juila shot back in a softer whisper.

"What about your mind link? I thought you always knew what she was thinking!"

"As I said, I was distracted. I'm pretty sure you had a little something to do about it."

"I'm sorry, Juila. I'm not mad at you, just embarrassed at being caught in such a compromising position. Besides I don't know what came over me, attacking you in such a way." He shook his head in dismay. Never before had he been so brazen with another girl and he wondered if it were because of their common heritage which made them more compatible.

"I wouldn't say you were attacking me. As you could see, I never discouraged any of it. Next time we'll have to plan ahead a little better." She smiled at his incredulous expression. Her statement had managed to surprise him, and she enjoyed keeping him on his toes.

Glad to hear she wanted there to be a next time, with a wicked grin on his face Behn asked, "When?"

Juila playfully slapped his arm and said, "Let's see what Jena is making. I'm ravenously hungry." She stood up and adjusted her skirt even more as she could see it had been twisted sideways.

"Me, too," Behn agreed as he pinched her butt as she passed by him. He chuckled as she tried to keep her squeal of surprise from being too loud.

"Stop it!" She glared down at him and stalked away toward the kitchen.

He watched her go, thinking about what would happen the

'next time' as she had promised. There were places he had heard about where they could park in his car. Maybe they could see what happened when they remained uninterrupted. He had to adjust his pants as he stood up and pretend to be interested in something across the room until he became less aroused before he was willing to join the group in the kitchen.

"Where are your parents?" Luke asked from where he sat on the stool at the kitchen island.

"Dad's at work. We're not sure where Mom went, she was gone already when we got home," Jena answered. She was struggling to cut the block of cheese for their grilled cheese sandwiches. "Why do they make this stuff so hard to cut?" she said as she pushed down on the knife harder. In an instant, the knife slipped off the edge of the block and cut through the skin on two of her fingers. "Ouch!" she cried out and immediately cupped her hand to keep Luke from seeing what she had done.

"Did you cut yourself?" Luke asked in alarm. He began to get off his chair.

"No, I'm fine. Stay where you are, I just knocked my fingers hard onto the countertop," she replied hastily. Even as she spoke, she began pulling elemy up from the earth and used it to begin knitting her flesh back together. Once she finished, she went to the sink and washed the blood which had pooled in her palm down the drain.

Knowing it was all better, she lifted her hand facing it toward Luke and said, "See? No problem." She grabbed the knife from the counter and washed it thoroughly before drying everything off. "I wish they made an easier way to cut this," she complained as she contemplated whether or not she had already cut enough.

"Here, let me show you how I do it," Luke said as he jumped off his stool and took the knife from her unresisting hand when he got beside her. He expertly carved off several more slices before he said, "My family uses a wire slicer, but this works pretty well, too."

"A wire slicer sounds easier," Jena she agreed even as she thought to herself, *safer, too!*

"Sit down, and I'll finish this up. I'm pretty much an expert at this type of sandwich since I make them for myself every day after school." Luke began buttering the bread and positioning the eight slices in the grill top. "I wish my parents had a cooktop like this; it sure is cool."

Jena could only think it would have been so much faster if she had been able to simply use the elemy to create the meal without all of the fuss of preparing it. They could have already eaten and been back outside talking again in the time it had taken her to cut the cheese. She rubbed her thumb over where she had healed the deep cuts. Not even a mark remained, her healing ability had seen to it as well.

Juila leaned into her side, commiserating with her over her injury. She had felt the exact moment when the knife had cut her sister as if it had been her own hand. There really had not been anything to get excited about, knowing her sister was an accomplished healer in her own right. If it had been too much, she would have stepped in to assist.

I wish we could tell Luke the truth about us, Jena spoke in her mind link to Juila.

It is pretty nice not having to hide anything, Juila agreed.

I think you should be hiding a bit more from Behn. What were you thinking? What would have happened if Luke and I hadn't walked in to stop you? It looked like you had lost control. You certainly weren't hearing anything from me, that's for sure.

I don't know what happened. I guess I let it get out of hand. She stifled a giggle and amended, *or a little too much was in Behn's hand.*

How far did you let him go? Jena asked even as she saw the details flash through her sister's thoughts. *Juila! What were you thinking?*

It's pretty evident I stopped thinking the moment we started kissing.

Maybe you should do like Val did and keep a chaperone with you at all times.

I don't think that'll be necessary.

"Lunch is served," Luke announced happily as he flipped the last sandwich onto a plate and began placing them in front of the three others sitting at the island. He walked around to take his place in the chair next to Jena. She had been awfully quiet the past few minutes, and he hoped she was not regretting letting him come over.

Jena and Juila both bowed their heads to pray while the boys did not waste any time getting started on the sandwiches. It was only a few minutes later before all of them were finished with the light meal. Jena gathered the dishes and stuck them in the dishwasher they never had to use. Once Luke went home, Jena would use her crystal skills to take care of them.

"Thanks for making lunch, Luke," Jena said.

"Yes, thank you," Juila added.

"Thanks, Luke," Behn chimed in last.

"I should probably be heading out. My mom wants me to run some errands for her before it gets too late since I took her car to get over here," Luke said as he glanced at his watch.

"I'll walk you out," Jena offered hurriedly. She jumped down from her chair and walked beside Luke. "Thanks for taking my call today. It's been a relief getting things straight between us."

"Yeah, I'm glad Sofia told me what was going on ahead of time. It really gave me some time to think things through. I've discovered a lot about how I feel."

"Really? How do you feel?"

Instead of speaking, Luke curled his fingers around Jena's and gave her hand a slight squeeze while they continued slowly walking through the foyer. He opened the front door for her, and they left the house and the other occupants behind them when he closed the door. He leaned against his mother's car and pulled Jena close until her body was leaning against his own.

"You know, I was pretty jealous of Behn back there when we came in from outside. I imagined how it would be if that were you beneath myself. I want that for us, I want there to be an us," Luke said. His eyes searched Jena's intensely as he spoke.

"I want it, too," she whispered back, not trusting her voice to speak any louder.

Her consent was what he had been waiting for. He tipped his head down and softly kissed her lips. His arms tightened around her waist, pulling her even closer. Mindful of where they were, he ended the kiss with several small nips at her bottom lip. "Call me tonight."

"I will."

He gave her another quick peck on the lips and then pushed himself away from the vehicle. Keeping his arm around her shoulders, he walked around his car with her and opened the driver's side door. "I hate leaving you."

"You gotta keep your mom happy if you plan on borrowing her car again to come over," Jena teased.

"When are you going to get a car?"

"I'd have to get my driver's license first." She chuckled at Luke's dismayed expression. "What? Don't look at me like that! I haven't gotten enough practice to warrant taking the test yet!"

"You're birthday was months ago! What have you been doing all of this time?" He tipped his head as he considered his own question. "I think you're scared!"

"So what if I am? After all, I haven't been in this country for very long, and I'm not used to all the rules of the road. I don't want to take any unnecessary chances."

"Okay, I'll give you a pass on that one. Maybe I could give you some lessons."

"Why? Because you've been driving for so long?" she teased.

"Clearly longer than you, so I guess so. What do you say about it?"

"It would certainly give us an excuse to see one another."

"Oh, so now you need an excuse?"

"Keep it up and I will!"

"Fine, fine. I better leave before this gets any worse for me. I'll talk to you tonight." He gave her one more kiss. He meant for it to be quick, but his mind had other ideas as he pulled her close again and kissed her deeply and thoroughly until they were both breathless.

"Okay, I forgive you," she said as soon as their mouths parted.

"Thank goodness!" He got into his car and shut the door. As soon as he had the engine turned on, he rolled the window down and waved goodbye.

Jena watched him drive away. Her arms were crossed over her front as she tried to keep the feeling of him touching her vivid in her thoughts. She had never even dreamed of feeling this way when she was with Willian. Certainly, this had to mean something special was happening between the two of them.

She went back inside after she could no longer see the car in the driveway or hear its engine. The sound of voices traveled through the foyer from the living room, and she headed in that direction. Her sister was just getting up from the couch when she dropped down in the loveseat across from them. "Where are you going?"

"I thought I'd check to see if Mom left a note by the phone," she replied and took another step away.

"I already looked. The only message was one on the answering machine from someone named Jasmine," Jena answered. Her mind was still going over everything Luke had talked about while they had been outside. She was pretty distracted by the idea of starting a relationship of her own choosing. "Behn, do you think it's okay for me to start seeing Luke?"

"Sure. Why not?"

"Oh, I don't know…possibly because I'm not from here. Do you really think it's fair for me to get anything started with him if I don't ever plan on telling him the truth about our family?"

Juila scowled at her sister and sighed. "We've already talked about this Jena. Why are you bringing this up again?"

"I just feel so guilty. It's almost like I'm leading him on because I know I'm going to go back to Tuala when school's finished, and I won't be coming back. How can I let Luke develop feelings for me when I know he can't go where I'm going? It just isn't right."

"We have plenty of relatives who have proven it's possible. I'm not going to list them all again for you because I doubt you're even listening anyway." Juila's reason for getting up was gone, so she flopped back onto the couch beside Behn. She liked how his hand immediately came to rest on her thigh again.

Jena rolled her eyes at how easily her sister could be distracted. Unless she had a relationship of her own, this could get pretty disgusting rather quickly. Still, her sister's love life was hardly any reason to get Luke involved in their family drama. She decided to talk to their mom about it. *If she ever gets home,* she thought to herself sullenly.

CHAPTER 27

Rasa's eyes remained fastened on the contents of the box. She desperately wanted to reach in and feel its power surge through her body. Even through the box, she felt the power pulsing, which kept the temptation alive in her mind.

Willian jumped up from his chair so he could peer into the box. He had never seen a samara and was desperate to know what they really looked like. His expression was puzzled because somehow he had expected the crystal to be showier or something...more. "It's just a small skull. Are you sure it's what you think it is?"

"Oh, yes!" Rasa exclaimed. She looked up at Willian with a gleam in her eyes.

Willian stepped back, unsure of what to think of the change which had come over his old friend and teacher. "Maybe you should put the cover back on," he suggested warily.

"It actually might be a good idea," Amanda agreed. "We will need some time and privacy for you to claim your samara. I doubt this is a good time for it. I've seen how long it takes for a person to get to know their crystal and you're going to want at least an entire day devoted to it."

Rasa sighed with resignation. It was not the answer she wanted to hear, but she could tell it was probably wise to heed Amanda's wisdom in the matter. After all, her whole family had samaras of their own, so she was clearly the resident expert even though she still remained without one of her own. She picked up the lid and shoved it back into the slot until it clicked shut.

"I'm feeling rather tired after all of the day's discoveries," Elder Wilken announced. He levered himself up from his chair and looked around the room and smiled inwardly over the eagerness of this next generation. "I'm going to head up for a quick nap before supper. Rasa, I'm pleased to know you are the one to receive the samara. I couldn't have picked a better person for it." He nodded in her direction and then shuffled slowly out of the room.

"You'll need to store it in a safe place, Rasa, until you can claim it. Until such time, it's still vulnerable to being stolen," Amanda pointed out.

"What? Who would dare?" Rasa asked indignantly.

"Oh, I can think of one in particular. Promise me you'll find it a secure home." She looked at her watch and gasped in surprise. "I need to be getting back home. Riccan is getting off of work soon, and I wanted to be there before him. Willian, why don't you go and find Val and let her know it's time to go."

Willian nodded his agreement and raced out of the room.

Amanda sighed at his energy and wished she felt as carefree. Belatedly, she realized she should have advised Willian to keep their meeting with Elder Wilken a secret. She promised herself it would happen when she met up with him before they left.

"Who do you think would steal this, Amanda?"

"Lucinden, for one, or any of his minions. There has been an increase in incidents which seem to be pointing back to him." She paused as she considered the bits of information she had gleaned from various people. "We really should get the group back together to see what everyone has been discovering."

"I agree. They all need to know about the additional text you found. What did Riccan say about it?"

"He doesn't even know yet. As I said, I came straight here after I discovered it."

"You should put it on the group message before we meet so they can think about the possibilities it may hold."

"That's a good idea. I'll have Riccan do it tonight. Where do you think you'll be storing your samara?"

"I'm not sure. Do you have any suggestions?"

"Elder Debbon said he keeps his and Chelesa's in the Ascension Gate room. He set wards of protection around the room and then additional ones on the two crystals. Do you have the same ability here as well?"

"Yes, I think I can figure something out here. Thanks, Amanda." She tapped the sides of the box still in her lap and said, "I just want to touch it! Did the others feel the same way when they were near theirs?"

"No, there was a lot of unknown factors for them. You have the advantage of knowing it'll be okay. Did you check the stone's aura? Did it match your own birth crystal?"

"Yes, it's a perfect match. You said the bonding process could take hours. How will I know when it's complete?"

"I think it's been a little different for everyone, but plan on scheduling an entire day for it. I'd also advise you have someone around to help you get out of it if it goes on too long. It wouldn't do for you to starve because you didn't pay attention to your own needs."

"Could it really be so bad?"

Amanda nodded solemnly. Having given her final advice, Amanda stood up and said, "I really need to get going. Can you show me the way out? I'm afraid I'd get terribly lost if I had to find my own way."

Rasa chuckled and said, "It does take some getting used to, doesn't it?"

They walked across the room, and Amanda asked, "How do you like it here? Are you going to be okay with the new job?"

"I love it. The energy here is amazing. Can't you feel it, too?"

"I wonder how much of the energy you felt was actually your samara being nearby," Amanda mused as she pointed at the box resting between Rasa's hand and side.

"Hmm, I wonder if you could be right. I don't really know, but it's been a lot of fun learning how the District is run. I've still got a lot to learn and Elder Wilken has been an amazing instructor. Hopefully, he'll be running the District for many more anons so I can get to know all of the delegates and councilors before it's my turn to be the Elder.

"You know, it still sounds crazy to hear my name along with the title of Elder. It just feels like a dream. I never thought it would be a possibility, but Jehoban's plans have been different from my own. When He had me teaching the Elder's successors' school, I never thought it was because He was preparing me to become one."

"I think you'll do amazing!"

"I hope so!"

WILLIAN'S PACE had slowed to a walk as his mind reeled with the implications of what he had just witnessed. If the legend Jena had told him about were true, how many other legends were also true?

He wished he could access the records back at his home to satisfy his intense curiosity. Speaking of back home, he wondered what other things his parents were keeping from him as well as where they might have hidden their own samaras.

He turned down the corridor to take him to the west wing of the Residence where Ulwin had said Valentina would be meeting with Gevena. His curiosity about the girl paled in comparison with his desire to get answers to the hundreds of questions swirling through his mind. It might be a good time to take Valentina home to meet his parents.

Stopping dead in his tracks, Willian realized everything had been happening so fast; he had yet to tell his parents about his betrothal being dissolved. How would they react? Would they be angry at him for being the cause? Maybe it would be unwise to bring Val home until after he had had a chance to get things smoothed over with his parents.

An employee entered the hallway ahead of him. Willian looked up just in time to make eye contact with the young woman before she curtsied and moved out of his line of sight. The distraction was just enough to get his mind back on the track of locating Valentina so they could head home. He lengthened his steps and began looking out the windows, hoping to catch a glimpse of either Valentina or her companion.

By the time he reached the last section of the wing, his vigilance was rewarded as he spotted Valentina sitting with another young girl on the benches out in one of the gardens. He tapped his index finger knuckle on the glass, hoping to catch their attention. His actions were rewarded when Valentina turned her head and waved at him. He saw her stand up, still talking to the other girl.

The two girls walked parallel to where he was standing and disappeared in a doorway out of his line of sight. He had to assume they were on their way to meeting with him, so he remained still.

The last door in the hallway opened, and Valentina was the first to step out. Immediately, Willian could feel the shift in the elemy around him. He wondered if she felt it as well.

From the pleased grin on her face, he had to assume she could. His own lips curled into a smile, his eyes only seeing her graceful-ness as she moved toward him. When she came close enough for easy conversation, he said, "I hate to bother you both, but Amanda wants to head back home now."

"It's alright; we were just finishing today when you came. How was your talk with Elder Wilken?" Valentina asked.

"Very enlightening!" His tone made both girls regard him with interest, and he wished he had thought over his answer before saying anything. He did not really have a good excuse other than the truth, and somehow he thought it might be better left unsaid.

"Anything you want to share?" Gevena asked. She had never met this handsome young man, and she was intrigued about who he might be to warrant a meeting with the Elder.

"Sorry, it was a private matter," Willian said, regret evident in his tone.

"I'm sorry, Gevena. I should have introduced you. This is my boyfriend, Willian. His father is Elder Debbon. Willian, this is Gevena."

Willian nodded his head at the introduction and said formally, "It's my pleasure to make your acquaintance, Gevena. Both Elder Wilken and Rasa have told me how much they have enjoyed having you come to live here with them."

"Really? Oh, I'm glad. I was afraid I was being a bother to them both." She smiled sweetly. Her expression changed to one of wonder rather than timidity. She turned to Valentina and asked, "When do you think you can come back? I've really enjoyed having someone my age to talk with."

"Me, too, Gevena." She looked over to Willian and answered,

"I'm not sure since it'd be up to Willian or Mrs. Stel to bring me. I don't know how to operate a telepod or even how to get here, for that matter."

Taking the hint, Willian answered, "We'll see what we can do about borrowing the telepod a couple more times this week while we're on break from school. I can arrange for a message to be sent to Rasa to let you know, okay?"

"Thanks, Willian. I'll look forward to it." She clasped her hands in front of her tightly, nervous about being in the company of the boy who would one day be an Elder. "If you don't mind, I'd like to walk back with you."

"Sure," Willian replied happily. He wanted to get to know this girl who had captured Valentina's interest. "How have you been getting along here? Is school going okay?"

She took her place next to Willian, wondering what it would be like to have a boyfriend as tall, handsome, and powerful as he. She stammered slightly in her reply since her imagination had run away with her. "Rasa has been amazing! I don't know why she'd want to bother with me, but I'm glad nonetheless. School is…well, it's…okay."

Her experiences so far had been being mostly ignored since she had been placed with younger kids than herself. Because she was several anons behind, she had a lot of catching up to do before she would be placed in classes with kids her own age, if ever. The lessons the others were learning came so easily to them, and she struggled with even the most basic crystal skills. It was rather frustrating.

Interpreting her summation of school correctly, Valentina came up with an idea. "I've been learning how to use my birth crystal with Willian's guidance. Would you like for us to train with you? I could certainly use more practice!"

"Really?" Gevena's eyes lit up with joy. It would be so much easier to learn alongside someone who knew as little as she did herself. The tutor who Rasa had hired to bring her skills up to speed was continually frustrated with her lack of knowledge, and she dreaded each lesson more than the last.

"Sure, I'd be willing to take you both on," Willian teased.

"Watch out, or we might gang up on you," Valentina quipped in return.

"Give it your best shot!" Willian grabbed Valentina's hand, and they both grinned at the electricity which shot through them.

"What just happened?" Gevena asked as she felt the shift in energy.

"We're not sure, but it's something which happens between us," Valentina answered as she held up their joined hands to indicate their touching.

"That's pretty awesome. I wish I could find someone who made me feel like that."

"You never know, maybe Mr. Right is somewhere here in Manzanit."

"Mr. Right?" Gevena asked inquiringly. She had never heard the peculiar phrase before and had to assume it was a colloquialism from Earth.

"It just means 'the right person for you,'" Valentina explained, thinking she would have to watch the things she said while in Tuala. This was a small matter, but there would certainly be others which could cause a lot of uncomfortable questions. She would have to pay more attention to her thoughts before she allowed them to be spoken.

"I seriously doubt I'd find anybody to be interested in me once they found out about my past. I wouldn't blame them, either."

Willian was quick to head off her self-pity and said, "Our past only prepares us for who we will be in the future; it never defines who we are in the present."

"Says the son of the First Elder," scoffed Gevena.

"Trust me; I've done my fair share of stupid things, just ask my father. Well, maybe you shouldn't! But I have learned from every one of them, and I think they all have made me a better person." Willian could well imagine the stories his father would share about him, and it made him cringe to think of them all.

They had entered the main hall and could see Rasa and Amanda coming toward them. Gevena wished her two new friends could stay longer, maybe even move to the Residence so she could have people who wanted to be around her. The days were torture and the evenings were even worse, except for when she visited with either Elder Wilken or Rasa.

"Ah, here are the kids," Rasa announced with a grin. She turned to Amanda and said, "They look as though they've been enjoying themselves, don't they?"

Amanda had seen the three kids approaching. Willian and Valentina were holding hands while Gevena walked beside Willian. She could see the adoring look Gevena gave to Willian and wondered if trouble could be brewing. Shaking her head at such a strange notion, she agreed with Rasa's opinion. "Yes. I hope Gevena won't be too sad when we leave."

"I was wondering if we might be able to come back again this week, Mrs. Stel," Valentina asked.

"Sure, I don't mind. Rasa?"

"It's fine with me."

"We'd need to borrow your telepod again," Willian piped in.

"Yes, now I suppose you would. We can always coordinate our schedules should something come up. I could also take Riccan to work so I could use his telepod. Don't worry; we'll get it figured out." She could see the look of concern evaporate from Gevena's face as she realized her only friends could return soon.

"We're going to practice our birth crystal lessons together,"

Valentina added. "I all but forgot how to use my own until Jena and Willian began teaching me again. It'll be nice to get more practice in."

"I think you'll find it easier here in Manzanit rather than back at your home," Rasa added.

"Really?" Valentina was even more curious than ever to try it out. "Maybe we can come back tomorrow?"

"We'll see!" Amanda laughed. "Let's get going. I want to be home before Riccan. I didn't bother leaving him a note since I never imagined I would be out so late."

"I'll arrange a transport to the landing field," Rasa offered in apology for keeping them so long.

"Thanks," Amanda said as their large group headed out.

CHAPTER 28

To say Petre was surprised by the instant transfer to Menad would have been a gross understatement. At first, he had been terrified to find himself returned to the nothingness between the locations, until he materialized on the grounds of the Residence in Menad. The place had not changed in the fifteen anons since he had last set foot on the island of his birth.

Several people had noticed his appearance. They skirted away from where he stood, wary of his entrance, and speaking excitedly with one another as they left. Petre wondered how long it would take for one of Elder Rylon's people to come and investigate the aberration.

It was a testament to the security of the Residence when Petre saw two officials converging upon him. He could hardly blame them for being suspicious. How many people translated into the Residence unless they were up to no good? Petre was both proud and dismayed to discover Elder Daven had put him in this strange situation. He had been eager to get to the island, but he wished he would have had more time to formulate a proper speech for his interview with the Elder.

"State your business, Petre!" the guard challenged as soon as he came close enough to identify the intruder.

"I was sent here by Elder Daven to meet with Elder Rylon," Petre stated matter-of-factly.

"So you don't have an appointment?" the second guard sneered, not quite asking.

"No, I can come back when it's more convenient." His statement obviously baffled the two officiants. He was certain they were expecting to goad him into anger by the rudeness of their challenges to his mission. He turned to leave when they remained still, simply staring at him in dismay.

"Wait here! I'll see when the Elder has any openings in his busy schedule," the first guard spoke with authority. "Stay here with him, Tiun."

Petre did a double-take at Tiun and tilted his head as he tried to recall a memory. Suddenly it hit him. "We went to school together, didn't we, Tiun? I knew you looked familiar. If I'm not mistaken, the other guard," Petre gestured after the retreating man, "his name's Kemeron, isn't it?"

"Yes, Petre, I had the unfortunate ability to claim you as my classmate. Kemeron was an anon ahead of us."

Used to being dismissed rudely, Petre tried not to let Tiun's reaction to him cause him any pain. He found it was harder than it used to be, that is, before he was changed. Chosen really, Petre admitted to himself.

"So how long have you been a guard for the Elder? How did it come about?" Petre attempted to make small talk while they had to wait.

"I found out about it on assignment day, you know, the one you skipped out on. I've been working here for six anons."

"If you want to know…," Petre began.

"I don't," Tiun rudely cut him off.

"I came here to discuss my assignment with the Elder. I'm ready to take whatever punishment I've got coming to make it right with Elder Rylon."

"Hmph," Tiun replied. Inwardly, he wondered what had caused Petre's personality change. He could tell there was an inner peace which had been severely lacking in him as a teenager.

Petre gave up on trying to be conversational with his old adversary from school. He stood with his hands clasped behind his back and lowered his head until his chin was resting on his chest. His thoughts were racing about what this meeting would be like and when it might actually happen.

Several minutes passed by until he heard footsteps approaching swiftly. He looked up and saw Kemeron returning with a puzzled expression. Petre made a swift decision and turned to Tiun and looked him in the eyes as he said, "I'm really sorry for all of the things which went wrong between us when we were kids. I've made some really dumb decisions in my life, but I'm working on turning it all around. I hope you can accept my apology."

Clearly not expecting such a speech from Petre, he stammered for a reply. His answer was cut off when Kemeron stepped close to them.

He announced stiffly, "Elder Rylon is expecting you. Follow me."

Petre was just as puzzled with Kemeron's announcement, but he no longer questioned the ways of the Elders. He stepped behind the large man and only looked straight ahead. His eyes did not take in any of the stunning beauty around him; his thoughts were too concerned with the upcoming reception with Elder Rylon and what sanctions might be imposed on him for missing the original appointment. Surely, there would have to be a price paid for not following the directives of society.

The room Petre entered was just as grand as Elder Daven's reception room in Pantano. Petre moved past the two guards, alone to discover his fate. The man who held his future in his hands sat in front of a large stained-glass window, backlighting him so Petre could not read his expression. He wondered if it were a planned position to allow the Elder to read his subject's mood without giving away his own.

"Better late than never, heh, Petre?" Elder Rylon spoke quietly when Petre stopped only a short distance away from him.

"I've come here to be at your mercy, Elder. Thank you for seeing me without an appointment. I know your time is valuable and I'm unworthy of your audience." Petre gave the Elder as formal of a bow as he knew how to make, hoping it would be interpreted as a sign of respect and not as a mockery.

"Please sit down, Petre." He gestured to the seat beside him and waited for compliance before he spoke again.

Petre hurriedly took the seat, anxious to get this interview finished so he could begin his life with Tirsha. Whatever the Elder deemed would be proper punishment, he would willingly endure so long as the outcome would be his life being set back on course.

"Just so you know, I received an urgent message from Elder Daven letting me know of his unorthodox method of transporting you to my Residence. Once again, I've been surprised by something you've done. Tell me, Petre, why have you decided to present yourself to me today? What has changed?" Rylon sat back in his chair and studied the various expressions on Petre's face as he thought about his answer.

"I experienced something so profound it has changed my entire perspective on what I want in life." Petre immediately closed his mouth on the other ideas which wanted to be voiced, but which would probably make the Elder question the validity of his story.

"What experience would that be, Petre?" Rylon was still skeptical of Petre's sincerity, but he could see there was a calmness within the man across from him which he had never seen before. Maybe there was something changed within the man who had continually brought shame to his District. Because Elder Daven had chosen to send him home and arrange a private meeting let Elder Rylon know he should take this seriously and not brush it off as another deception perpetrated upon him and his District.

"I almost died, and then I met the woman I want to spend the rest of my life with. She has made me realize I need to get my affairs in order so I can be who she needs me to be. I am changed because she sees me for the man I can be and not the man I've been. I need to prove I'm worthy of her love.

"For the past fifteen anons, I've been selfish, self-absorbed, and generally destructive. I don't like who I've become, and I want a fresh start. I want to make amends for the mistakes I've made, and it begins with apologizing to everyone whom I have wronged. Whatever penance you want me to pay, I will do so willingly if I can have a second chance with my lottery assignment." Petre looked down at his lap as his speech ended. Either the Elder would believe him or find fault, Petre had no one else to blame except himself if it were the latter.

"A fair speech given the fact I know Elder Daven has shared with you the assignment you were given. Do you also realize I have the authority to issue whatever assignment I deem fitting, regardless of what is written on the paper you've read?"

Petre swallowed hard and nodded sharply. He did not trust his voice to remain neutral, so he opted silence instead.

Thinking it was about time Petre learned consequences to his actions, Rylon raised his voice and declared, "The assignment I give you will be as you have seen." Rylon's hands immediately covered his mouth, and his eyes grew large in fear. "No, that's not what I meant to say. Petre your new assignment will be..." his voice faltered slightly, "...permanent retirement."

Rylon jumped up from the chair, angry beyond belief. "What is this that you've done, Petre? How are you able to make me say things I don't intend? What sort of deception are you practicing over me?"

"Me? I don't understand. I've done nothing except put myself at your mercy. Are you saying you don't wish for my assignment to stand? Believe me; I will do whatever assignment you want me to do. I have earned punishment for my prior actions."

"Good! Your punishment will be ...permanent retirement!" Elder Rylon stamped his foot in frustration. He turned and left the room without another word. The double doors slammed open with the force of Rylon's departure and flew back closed.

Petre stared after him in amazed confusion. He could see how the Elder had tried to say something different, and it was almost as if he were unable to get any other words out other than his original assignment. Unsure of what he should do next, Petre stood up, wiping the sweat from his palms onto his thighs as he did so. He retraced his steps across the room and calmly opened one leaf of the great doors.

The guards looked at him curiously but offered no suggestions.

Petre walked past them both and knew they followed at a distance behind him. He left the hallway and went out onto the patio overlooking the island city. The hustle of the people seemed out of place against the quietness of the Residence. He wondered how often Rylon stood just in this spot pleased to look out over the industrious people in his care.

Unsure of how much time had passed, Petre was surprised when Elder Rylon's voice sounded just behind him. He whirled around, his startled expression giving himself away. "I'm sorry, Elder Rylon. I should have left long ago. I'll be leaving right now."

"Petre, wait. I should be the one apologizing to you. I'm ashamed to admit I was acting out of anger and revenge when I spoke with you privately. You came to me with humility, and I repaid you with spite. Please forgive me."

"I've earned it, Elder Rylon. Please don't apologize; I don't blame you one bit." Petre held out his hands in entreaty.

"Still, Jehoban has entrusted me to help His people, and I almost abused my position to satisfy my human desires rather than seeing the wisdom of Jehoban's plan for you. You have taught me a valuable lesson about overcoming arrogance.

"Please walk the grounds with me, Petre. I'm curious to find out about this woman who has made such a difference in you."

Petre smiled, more than happy to speak of Tirsha. As they wandered about the garden paths, Petre told of how he had tried to translate himself and ended up getting stuck inside the transfer. He also spoke of finding Tirsha in the same predicament and how Elder Daven had rescued them both. He withheld the parts of the story about coming from Earth and having the samara, feeling they held no relevance to the tale. He also felt deep within himself that the samara should not be mentioned.

Elder Rylon did not seem to notice the two missing details. He whistled softly as he realized how close Petre had come to finding his demise. It was entirely possible the extraordinary experience had permanently changed Petre.

When they reached the center of the gardens, Rylon indicated they should stop and rest for a bit and enjoy the serenity of the fountain in the shallow pond. He sighed deeply as he sat on the bench facing the view. After a short internal debate, Rylon reached into the pocket of his long, white tunic and handed Petre a folded paper.

With a surprised expression, Petre automatically took the paper, but he left it closed. Instead of satisfying his curiosity, his hand still outstretched, Petre asked, "What is this?"

"It is your assignment, plus an additional amendment I've included. Please read it and let me know if it is satisfactory for you." Rylon pushed his hand toward him to get him to do as asked.

Thumbing open the flap, Petre's gaze fell onto the words of the page. His eyes filled with tears, spilling tears down onto the writing. "I don't deserve this. It would be easier to accept punishment rather than this."

"What, would you prefer it if I banned you from the island of your birth?"

"Yes! Is this what you wish of me? I'll do it, you know." Hope filled his eyes as he looked earnestly at the Elder.

Rylon shook his head in wonder. He knew Petre still had family living in his District so it actually would be a hardship. As much as it would satisfy him to agree to the amended terms, he shook his head in denial. "No, I won't do such to you, Petre. It would not be the right thing." After a moment's pause, Rylon snapped his fingers, and he declared, "Promise me, no matter what happens with this woman, you will remain changed for the good. Denounce all of your former ties and illegal activities. Treat everyone with respect and make amends with everyone you've wronged. If you will do all of those things, then I will consider this your punishment for delaying your assignment."

"Yes, I'll do it. You're wise to challenge me to this task. I'll make you proud of me yet."

"Good, we have an agreement then?" he asked as he held out his hand for them to shake on it.

"Gladly," Petre replied with a relieved grin on his face. He grasped the Elder's hand firmly and gave it a single pump to seal the deal.

"Since we've gotten that out of the way, I want you to know your money has been held in an account for you, with interest. I'm certain you'll find the sum to be satisfactory. You will also be receiving a mesanly stipend to be withdrawn on the first of each mesan. If anything should happen to you, there are rights of survivorship for your spouse and children, should you decide to make Tirsha your wife." Elder Rylon grinned at Petre's look of wonder as he handed Petre his own chit for accessing the account. Feeling charitable, he added, "As a bonus, I've included a house with the retirement so you can begin enjoying your new life on land."

"No, Elder Rylon, it's too much!" Petre stood up; his mind muddled over being treated so well. The chit felt heavy with responsibility in his hand.

"I insist! Besides, don't you think your new partner would appreciate a place to live?"

Petre's eyes grew round as he took in the suggestion and began imagining how he would be able to get started right away. No longer was the prospect of being married to Tirsha a far-off dream; it was an immediate possibility. "You're right. You are so wise, Elder Rylon. I can't wait to tell Tirsha! Wait! Where is the house located? I'm going to have to live near the Port of Cresdon if this is going to work out."

"Well then, it's truly your lucky day, Petre! The house is not only in the Port of Cresdon, but it's also across the street from Captain Ahn's house. Will it do well enough for you?"

Petre fell into a heap onto the ground, unable to support himself under the weight of the news. Never could he have planned this any better for himself. All of his dreams were being realized even as he was discovering them for the first time right along with Elder Rylon.

"Petre? Are you okay?" Elder Rylon asked in alarm. He kneeled beside Petre and tied himself into the other man's life-line to help determine his health and assist if necessary. As soon as he connected the link, Elder Rylon knew there was no deception in Petre's joy. Noting there was no medical issue, Rylon pulled his power away from Petre.

He had been terribly wrong in treating Petre badly. There was no deception anywhere within him, and he had not tried to guard his thoughts against him at all. A true change had been achieved during his incident in the nothingness between the dimensions. Maybe there was something to his experience to be learned for reforming other miscreants.

Rylon returned to the bench and allowed Petre to pull himself back together. He wished to speak more with him, but he knew the time for talking would be at a later date. The ripples in the pond reminded him of the shifting ideas of man. How far would the effects reach? He hoped he had done enough on his own part, enough to make Jehoban proud of him.

Willian expertly landed the telepod in the Stel's garage. The only unexpected thing to happen was when Riccan's telepod popped into its place next to Amanda's. After finishing the shut-down procedures, Willian turned to smile at Amanda sitting in the co-pilot's seat.

"Well, we beat Riccan home, at least," he said with a huge grin on his face.

Amanda chuckled at his expression and nodded. "Yes, we did." She did not wait for Willian to leave the cockpit first, as she had before, she was too anxious to see Riccan and share all of her news with him. She palmed the side panel open and stepped out just in time to see Riccan walking around his own telepod to greet her.

She rushed forward and threw her arms around his neck, squeezing him close to her. With Riccan's arms surrounding her, she felt her feet being lifted off of the ground. "I've got some major news to share when we're alone," she whispered in his ear just before he set her down.

Riccan's eyebrows rose with interest, but he merely nodded to let her know he would wait as soon as he saw Willian and Valentina exit her telepod. "What's been going on?" he asked Willian, keeping his arm across his wife's shoulders when she turned away from him.

"Valentina received an invitation from Rasa to visit with Gevena, so we just got back from Manzanit. If it's still okay with Amanda, we'll be returning tomorrow to give Gevena some crystal lessons."

"Sure, that'll be just fine," Amanda agreed readily, hoping it would expedite their departure to leave Amanda to speak freely with her husband.

"Great!" He turned to Valentina and helped her down the ramp as she was still unsettled by the trip between. "We should probably be getting you home, Val."

"Yes, you're right. I hadn't expected to be gone so long. Thank you, Mrs. Stel, for the use of your telepod today and in advance for tomorrow. Do you think you'll be accompanying us tomorrow, as well?"

"Oh, I doubt it." She smiled to take away any insult from her quick answer. "Shall we go inside?"

"Sure! I can't wait to tell you about my adventures at work today."

"Ugh, not more about the engineering of another telepod!" Amanda half-heartedly teased her husband. He knew she had almost no interest in the workings of the aircraft, even if she did enjoy his innovations to her telepod.

"It's too bad Juila isn't here to enjoy it and ask intelligent questions," Riccan joked back.

"I wouldn't mind hearing about what's new in the telepod industry," Willian chimed in from behind them.

"Maybe some other time when you're not pressed for time," Riccan agreed. He opened the garage door leading into the kitchen and paused in alarm when he heard voices inside the house. Nobody should be home. "Wait here!" he whispered back to the others standing still behind him.

Riccan cautiously and silently entered the house. He paused just out of view of anyone in the kitchen and realized it was his daughter's voice he had heard. With a joyous shout, he called out, "Jena! When did you get home?" He trotted forward and spotted Behn and Juila also sitting at the island with Jena. "Hey, the whole gang is here! What's going on? Is everything okay?"

Hearing Riccan's statements, the others in the garage knew it was safe to go inside. The three entered the kitchen just as Jena began to reply.

She shut her mouth as soon as she spotted Willian and Valentina walking into the room. Expecting to find unease within herself, she was pleasantly surprised to realize she really was okay with Willian and Valentina being a couple. They looked good together: happy. "You guys were gone a long time. Is everything okay in Manzanit?"

"How did you know where we were?" Amanda asked curiously.

"Behn told us about Willian and Valentina's trip, and we put two and two together," she answered with an offhanded shrug.

"Too smart for your own good!" Riccan stated as he tugged Jena's hair playfully.

"Don't blame me! I got it from you!"

"Ouch! I think I've been offended!" Amanda teased.

"Come on, Val, we should get out before there's bloodshed!" Willian grabbed Valentina's hand to hurry her along.

"I'm going to head home, too," Behn announced as he hopped off of the barstool between the twins.

"I'll walk you out," Juila offered, slipping off her own stool.

The two couples left while the rest remained in the kitchen.

Jena pointed to the answering machine and said, "Someone

named Jasmine left you an urgent message. Something about a Dr. Gascon. I wrote it all down, but the message is still on the machine if you want to hear it."

Amanda was instantly on alert. This could not be good news, so she hurried over to the piece of paper and read the transcript of the call. She thrust the paper at her husband and declared, "Oh, Riccan, this is bad. What are we going to do?"

He scanned the note and pursed his lips in concentration. "We should call her back and get more details. Do you have her cell phone number?"

"Yes, it's on my speed dial." She dug in her purse and pulled out the phone. She held it out to Riccan and said, "Here. Press the three button. I'm too upset to do it myself."

"What is it, Mom? Who's Jasmine?"

"She was the doctor who treated me while I was in my coma. Now she's treating Neal to help him through his ordeal concerning Tuala. She's read my journal of my time there, and she believes us. Neal was being treated by Dr. Gascon before we broke him out of Creedmoor and brought him home."

"I already knew about your involvement," Jena said impatiently. "Jasmine said something about a bug. What's wrong with bugs?"

Amanda had to chuckle at Jena's confusion, even though it was not even remotely funny. "It's a term we use for a listening device. He left an electronic device in her office to hear her conversations with Neal, myself, or anyone else who comes into her office." Her explanation suddenly made her nervous, thinking if he were going to such an extreme, then it was possible he had done the same thing inside their house. After all, they did have staff coming and going intermittently.

Turning to Riccan to discuss her fear, she swallowed her remark when Riccan began talking on the phone.

"Hey, Jasmine. This is Riccan Stel. Is this a good time to talk?"

Amanda could hear a faint voice as the phone was being held to Riccan's ear. She motioned rapidly and was pleased when Riccan understood her sign language. Once Riccan hit the speakerphone button, they were all able to listen to both sides of the conversation.

"...now. I just got home, but I'm still in my car. Do you think it's s..." Jasmine stopped talking.

"Jasmine? Are you afraid your car might be bugged as well as your home?"

"Yes. I just thought of it as I was talking. What should I do?"

"I'm coming over. I should be able to help," Riccan offered. "What's your address?"

She gave him the address which Riccan hurriedly wrote down. After hanging up the phone, Riccan grabbed his car keys and began walking toward the other garage where the cars were parked.

"What do you think you're doing?" Amanda demanded as she grabbed his arm and stopped him.

"You heard me; I'm going to see Jasmine."

Amanda leaned close and whispered in his ear, "What if Dr. Gascon has done the same thing here in our house? I don't feel safe here anymore!"

Thinking back on the break-in they had had recently where nothing of real value was taken, Riccan thought Amanda might be onto something. He motioned for Jena to come over to where they stood. When she got close, he pulled her into a huddle and whispered, "Let's get the samaras and scan the house from top to bottom for any electronic signals which don't belong here. Get your sister back in here. Use your mind link to tell her what we're doing."

The two raced into the library to get into the secret room. Amanda stood transfixed to where she stood in the living room, feeling helpless to assist in the search. She watched Juila run through the open front door, through the foyer, past herself, and then down the hallway. It felt as if a whirlwind of activity had begun around her. She sank wearily onto the couch and waited for her family to discover if their sanctuary had been infiltrated.

WILKEN EXHALED as he finished the last few pressing files on his desk. There never seemed to be enough time to get everything done. He heaved another sigh of relief as he shut off his patil, preparing to retire early after the exertions of the day.

He rang the bell next to his desk and was pleased with the speedy response of the maid. "I'd like to take dinner in my room tonight."

"At the usual time, Elder Wilken?" she asked.

"No, you'd better bring it up in the next twenty minutes or so. I'm going to retire early tonight."

"As you wish." She curtsied expertly and backed out of the room.

Wilken smiled as he imagined the commotion he had just set into motion with his change in plans. After turning off his patil, he pushed away from his desk and turned out the light as he left his office. Most of the newer Residences had automatic lighting, but Wilken had resisted the change, preferring to do it himself.

Thinking of all of the changes happening in the world made Wilken shake his head in wonder. It was a good thing the younger generation was getting ready to take over the responsibilities of governing their world; it was getting more complicated by the minute. He was just getting ready to turn down the hallway to his own wing when he spotted Rasa sitting outside of the conference room where they had met earlier. She still had the wooden box resting on her lap. He turned and went to her.

"Rasa, are you okay?"

"What?" she asked in a daze. Her thoughts were far away from her body, and she had not seen Elder Wilken approach. She jumped to her feet and stammered, "Elder Wilken, I'm sorry. Yes, I'm okay, just slightly overwhelmed I guess."

Wilken smiled down on her as if she were his favorite child, even though there was no blood relation between them. "It's been an eventful day, hasn't it? I just told my maid I'm heading off to bed. What are you going to do with that?" He pointed to the box held reverently between her hands.

"Amanda suggested I store it in a safe place until I can claim it."

"That sounds like sound advice. Do you have someplace in mind?"

"The Ascension Gate room."

Wilken nodded agreement, "I think it's a good spot as well. Would you mind if I walked with you?"

"I'd appreciate it," Rasa said with a sigh of pleasure. She always liked these quiet, intimate moments with her mentor. It was comforting to have his presence, even if they only spoke of ordinary things in life. Right now, she felt dazed by the day's events and did not trust her own judgment.

They entered the guarded room together. Wilken pointed to a likely location, and Rasa put the box in the small niche which seemed made for the container. She stood back, pleased with the locations. "Will you put a ward of protection around it? I don't trust myself enough to do it just now," Rasa asked.

"Certainly. Pay attention, so you know how it's woven," he instructed his student as he pulled elemy from its source and wove it expertly around the opening until the box became invisible to any observer. "That should do it. Did you understand what I just did?"

"Yes, it was very elegantly done. I'm going to use the same technique in healing; I think it will be very beneficial. Why have I never seen it used in such a way before?"

"Oh, it's a little technique I've been working on for the past few declans," Wilken shrugged offhandedly, enjoying the praise from his successor. "I like your idea of using it for healing. I agree it could possibly speed up the healing process. I don't know why I never thought of it myself."

Rasa bit her lower lip in embarrassment of his praise. "Thank you, Elder Wilken. I'm so glad I'm able to learn so much from you."

"You've been a wonder for me, as well. Now, I'm off to bed. We have a lot of petitioners coming in tomorrow morning. I suggest you get plenty of sleep yourself." He gave her a side hug and kissed her temple. "Blessings to you, my child."

"Blessings to you, Elder Wilken." She took his fragile hand in her own, and they silently walked back to his bedroom. The maids were just setting up his meal, so she excused herself hastily.

He stood in his doorway, watching her departure. "Thank you, Jehoban, for sending her to me."

The maids curtsied as they passed by where he stood, quietly leaving so he could eat.

His room was luxurious and well-appointed. The aroma of the food briefly invigorated him. He sat at his small table in front of the fire, said his prayer of thanks over the food, and began sampling the various dishes.

The heat from the fire was making him drowsy. His eyes kept closing even as he was bringing his fork up to his mouth. It seemed pointless to keep trying to fight the fatigue. He set his fork down. Lacing his fingers across his belly, he leaned back in his chair, sighed deeply when he closed his eyes, and fell peacefully asleep, feeling content even as he drew his last breath.

STEPHEN WAS RATHER pleased with his progress in bugging Jasmine's office, car, and home. He felt certain he would gather some rather damaging information in at least one of the locations. When he put it together with the device he had planted in the office of the Stel house, he felt certain he would be able to catch one of them in their illegal activities.

His paranoia about Riccan Stel being involved in some sort of drug ring still had no evidence based on the strange conversations he had previously recorded. Thinking Riccan's home office would be the most likely place for any such transactions had seemed to be a mistake since the room was hardly ever used. He made a mental note to send in another person to plant a few more listening devices in the other rooms.

When his voice-activated recorder switched on, he turned his full attention to Jasmine talking. It appeared she had received a phone call. Unfortunately, he was unable to determine who was on the other end. Another mental note was made to put a tracker on her cell phone.

All he had to do was wait for Jasmine's unknown visitor to come to her house for him to find out who she had been talking with. He was a patient man; he would eventually discover all of her insidious secrets. Then he would be able to repay her for launching the investigation against his medical practices.

A thorough investigation revealed only one bug planted in the office of the Stel house. Riccan had been the one to discover it, and he had wondered whether or not he should say anything to his family about its discovery. He did not want them to feel unsafe in their own home. However, it was important to find out what types of discussions were had in the room.

Instead of removing the device, Riccan wove a silencing ward around it, making it soundproof but still operative. He left the room and met up with the rest of his family in the living room. "Well? Did anyone discover anything?"

"No," the twins said in unison, looking relieved.

"I did," he admitted reluctantly.

"What? Where?" Amanda demanded.

With a sigh of resignation, Riccan replied, "In the office. I neutralized the threat, but I've left it in place. We need to think about what things we've talked about in the room since the house was broken into. I agree with you, Amanda, it must have been the purpose of the intrusion."

"We've only used the room for talking on the patil," Jena admitted and then groaned at what was probably said. "What do you think will be done with the information? Do you think he recorded it?"

"Probably. You know…" Riccan said with an excited look on his face, "…those devices only have a short range of transmission. There must be another device somewhere nearby recording our conversations. We should check the perimeter of the property where someone could go unnoticed to collect the tapes. While you guys work on that, I'm going to go over to Dr. Medin's house to investigate."

"I want to come with you," Juila announced.

"Sure," Riccan replied. As he turned to leave, another thought struck him, and he looked over to where Jena stood next to her mother. "Jena, weave a protection around yourself and your mother before you go outside. We don't know if we are also being watched."

"I could do one better," Jena perked up at the challenge. "I could make us invisible."

"Perfect! Good job. Okay, Juila, let's get going."

The two of them hurried down the hallway to the garage. When the door slammed, Jena looked at her mother and could tell she was scared. "It's okay, Mom. We can do this. Do you want to link with me so you can see how this is done?"

"Yes, I should probably learn how to protect myself, even if it's only becoming invisible. I didn't even know it was something you could do." She continued to be amazed at the abilities of her husband and children. It really was true that whatever the imagination could think of, they could make happen with the elemy.

The energy around them began to shift and rise at Jena's

command. Amanda felt herself being pulled into the maelstrom of elemy and watched in fascination as it wove itself around their bodies, shifting and re-shifting in a constant random pattern. If she focused too long on any one spot, it made her feel slightly ill.

"Did you understand what I did?" Jena asked.

"I think so. It makes me feel sick to look at it too long."

"Good, that's the idea. People tend not to look at something if it makes them not feel okay. Let's get going. The sooner we check the perimeter, the quicker I'll feel better about this whole mess. Who is this Dr. Gascon anyway? Why does he want to hear our conversations?"

Amanda tried to think of a simple explanation, but she only shook her head and said, "Can you read my thoughts on it? It might be faster than any explanation."

"Really? You want me to do that? This must be bad."

"Not only bad but complicated as well. Yes, go ahead."

Jena did as her mother requested. She had never attempted to read her thoughts before, and it felt strange to do so even at her mother's behest. At first, she tried to only look at the surface thoughts, but she soon became engrossed in the tangles of the story. Several minutes passed before she unwillingly pulled herself away from the ongoing saga within her mother's brain. "Wow! Wow! Mom, you have so much of this which you've been keeping from us. I wish you would have said something before!"

"I'm sorry; I just didn't want you girls to be concerned. I thought Dr. Gascon was eccentric but essentially harmless. I guess I was wrong. We'll be more diligent since we now know he's taking this to illegal levels to prove his theory."

Jena nodded. Her mind had already wandered in another direction entirely. *Juila, did you get all of this, too?*

Yes!

This situation is worse than we thought.

We'll add wards around the property just to be certain we can be safe.

I agree; I'll start right now when Mom and I go around the property. You can check my work later when you get home. Why don't you do a little scan on Jasmine while you are there? She might know something which hasn't meant anything to her on its own but will be clear to us.

Good thinking. We just turned down Main Street in town. Be safe.

You, too.

"Were you just talking with your sister?"

"How did you know?" Jena asked guiltily. She wondered if her mother had her own form of mind reading.

"Your expression changes when you two are talking."

"Oh."

"Let's get outside and start searching. I don't want anybody getting access to our private conversations."

"I agree! By the way, Dad and Juila are in town right now."

"Who needs a GPS tracker when I've got you?" Amanda joked even though the situation did not warrant the humor. She needed to find some lightheartedness with their predicament, or she would become despondent with fear.

They toured around the house first and made ever-widening concentric circles of the grounds. It was beginning to look as though Riccan had been mistaken. Amanda was feeling relieved to think the device might have been inoperative with the recorder having been removed long before.

"Let's walk along the fence line outside of the property," Jena suggested.

Amanda nodded and began to have an uneasy feeling. They exited their land by entering a modified code into the main gate to allow one leaf to be opened only a small enough gap to let them walk through single file. As soon as they were through, the gate's magnetic lock clicked shut, letting them know the property was once again secure until their return.

"Do you see that?" Jena asked as she pointed out an anomaly.

Almost a hundred feet from the gate they discovered several footprints in the ditch which looked suspicious. Amanda kneeled and inspected the prints which headed toward their fence. She looked up and around to see if she could spot anyone watching their location. She felt exposed even knowing Jena's ward was still in effect around them.

"Can someone still hear us talking even if they can't see us?" Amanda asked suddenly in a hoarse whisper.

"Yes. Just a minute and I'll take care of that as well." Jena shut her eyes and pulled another layer of elemy around them. "Done."

"What did you do?"

"I effectively surrounded us in a bubble. Nobody can see or hear us until I let it dissolve."

Amanda stood up and followed the direction of the prints. It led her straight to a recorder hidden under a bush next to the fence. She kneeled, unsure of what to do. Should she call the police? Should she see if there were a tape recording inside it?

Jena kneeled beside her and said, "I think we should see if there's a tape. No matter what, we don't want anyone hearing the conversations we've had in the office. After all, it's where we go to use the patil." She kept a lookout behind them as her mother leaned forward.

Amanda nodded. Without trying to disturb the machine more than she had to, she located and pressed the eject button. There was a tape inside which appeared to be half full. Her anger made her hand shake as she extracted the tape and closed the cartridge door again. She held the evidence by one of the reels, not wanting to destroy any fingerprints which might still be on the surface. It seemed sort of pointless to be concerned about prints, but if it could lead them to the person who was assigned to collect the recording, then she would be happy to interrogate him.

Jena surveillance paid off when she realized there was someone in a car parked within the line of sight of where they were. Feeling angry beyond belief, she allowed her mind to travel the space between them to read his thoughts. Even knowing it was against tradition to do so without permission, she no longer cared.

After several seconds of searching, she began to wonder if she had made a grave mistake. She was about to exit his mind when he let out a long sigh. His mind clearly thought: This assignment is boring beyond belief. If Dr. Gascon weren't paying so well, I would've taken the gig the other dude wanted me to take to frame his cheating wife. This music is crap. I should've brought my CD case today; I can't believe I forgot it. The only exciting thing to happen this afternoon was seeing Riccan and his daughter leave the house. They sure didn't seem to be in any hurry. I wonder if Dr. Gascon would pay me a bonus if I followed them instead...

Jena immediately disconnected the connection between them. She gasped at what she had just learned and did not want to hear more about what he was planning. One thing she did know, they were not being followed...yet. "Let's go, Mom. The guy over there was hired to watch our house. He's probably the one to change the cassette tape when it's full."

Amanda looked over to where Jena was staring. She felt a trickle of fear to know there was someone watching them. Careful to watch her footing, Amanda hurried back along the fence until she got to the gate. Once again, she entered the special code and then they were back on the property. Her footsteps lengthened, and Jena kept pace with her as they jogged until they were safely back inside the foyer.

Jena released the elemy from around them, allowing it to sink invisibly back into the ground. "Do you have something to play this on?"

"Yes, but I'd like to wait until your dad gets home just in case there's evidence on the outside. I don't want to mess it up by touching it too much."

"Evidence?" Jena asked in confusion.

"Yeah, you know, like fingerprints or something."

"Oh." Jena had never heard of fingerprints being called evidence. She wondered what it could possibly tell them. They already knew it was a person who put it there, most likely the man who she had spotted.

Amanda regarded the house around her, no longer as her haven, but rather as a tainted reminder of Dr. Gascon's continued search into her history. She felt powerless to stop him from pursuing his agenda with her. More than anything, she wished her family could uproot itself and move to Tuala permanently where nobody would question her story.

PETRE HIRED a transport to return him to the Port of Cresdon. Leaving the landing field behind him, he viewed the homes nearby with a new appreciation. His home was now one of these grand estates. In all of his scheming and cheating, he had never even come close to achieving what was given to him this day.

He had to laugh at how much he had struggled to prove he was worthy of the best, when all along it had been waiting for him. He could have begun his adult life having everything and yet he had moved away from his destiny. The hardships and pain were all self-inflicted, none of which moved him into the man he always dreamed of becoming.

Shaking his head at his own stupidity, he had to admit he had learned valuable lessons about himself these past fifteen anons. He knew what he did not want to be anymore. Maybe the most important thing had been discovering how he could love.

Pausing outside of the gate, Petre pulled out the deed papers and verified the address of the house in front of him. He shook his head in disbelief as he stared in wonder since this house was actually his. Elder Rylon told him there was already a full staff of people to maintain it for him.

"Petre you can't be hanging around here like you were before," Captain Ahn spoke from across the street.

Whirling around, Petre had to contain his usual response to being addressed rudely. It was understandable from the captain's perspective that he was loitering. Petre decided to change tactics and smiled. He crossed the road, approaching his former foe in a friendly manner. "I have the most amazing news."

"I don't have time for you, Petre." Ahn began to open his own gate when he was stopped by Petre's hand on his sleeve.

"Please, Captain."

The tone of the request did more to dispel Ahn's anger, combined with the fact he did not think he had ever heard Petre say the word 'please.' "Fine, tell me your news," he ungraciously spoke.

"This is my new house. I have the deed for it here." He held up the papers so Ahn could read them if he cared to do so.

"Who did you swindle to get it?"

"I know why you'd think such a thing about me, but I promise this was an honest transaction. I'd like to tell Tirsha, Barla, and yourself what has happened to me today. It was absolutely amazing."

Reading Petre's body language told him more about the story than his actual words. Ahn was naturally suspicious given the fact Petre was a master deceptor. Still, Elder Daven had asked him to trust the scoundrel, so he relented and said, "Come inside then." He held the gate for Petre, and they entered the house together.

Ahn pointed to the room on the left and said, "Wait here while I find everyone."

Petre nodded politely and went into the formal sitting room at the front of the house. This was more than he was expecting from the captain, given all of the trouble he had caused him in the past. The only way his new life was going to work out was going to be for him to have to admit to the mistakes of his past. This was one of those times, and he was excited to begin.

True to his word, Ahn gathered the requested audience and sat across from Petre. Tirsha chose a spot next to himself while Barla remained standing behind where Ahn sat. Petre cleared his throat, suddenly nervous about how to begin. To gather his courage, he kept his eyes trained on Tirsha.

"I did as we talked about and arranged to speak with Elder Daven. I told him about how I never went to my assignment day and asked him how I could fix it. I imagined all sorts of punishments for shirking my duties, and I told Elder Daven I was willing to undergo any penalty for my mistake. He told me I would have to discuss the matter with Elder Rylon in order to make it right.

"He translated me to Elder Rylon's Residence immediately. I can tell you I was scared silly during the transfer since he didn't give me any forewarning. Anyway, Elder Rylon was able to see me as soon as I arrived, also courtesy of Elder Daven sending him a message.

"So here I am, meeting with the Elder and I just know this isn't going to go well. You see, Elder Rylon and I didn't get along very well when I was growing up. He always told me I could do better… be better, and I never listened. He took it rather personally because I ignored him whenever I could get away with it.

"I could see he was angry with my arrival, but I remained calm. I explained my case to him and told him I was ready to accept responsibility for my actions. He got this look in his eyes as he read my assignment and said he was going to assign me differently than what was originally posted. Of course, he has the option, and I didn't object. So he begins talking, and no matter how hard he tried, the words coming out of his mouth would only speak what was written on the original assignment. He was furious and stormed out of the room.

"I left and waited on the verandah, not knowing what else to do. A little while later, Elder Rylon found me there, and he actually apologized for his actions. To make up for his indiscretion, he gave me the deed to a house." Petre held up the papers again. "Isn't this amazing?"

"It is amazing! But, Petre, what was your assignment? You never said," Tirsha asked excitedly.

"I didn't? Oh, that was even more amazing! I was granted permanent retirement. I don't know how or why, but it was mine all along. Elder Rylon gave me a chit," Petre felt around frantically in his pocket for the small disk and finally pulled it out to display it as well. "He said there'd been an account set up for me, with interest, for the last fifteen anons of retirement pay."

"This is the most ludicrous story I've ever heard!" Captain Ahn jumped up from his chair and abruptly left the room. He did not even pause when Barla called after him. He was going to get to the bottom of this even if it meant he had to go to the source. If Petre was going to be living across the street from him, he was going to be certain it was done honestly.

"Ahn! What are you doing?" Barla grabbed his arm but did not try to stop him from walking toward the kitchen.

"I'm going to get Elder Daven on the patil and find out what's really going on here. Does Petre honestly expect me to believe the cockamamie story he just told us?"

"Be careful, Ahn."

"What? Are you saying you believe him?"

"No, I'm asking you to calm down before you address an Elder in anger."

Ahn took a deep, calming breath and stopped walking. He pulled Barla into a quick hug and said, "You're always looking after me, aren't you?"

"Yes, and I must say, it's a full-time job!" Barla smiled up at her husband with adoration even as she teased him.

Ahn chuckled and let her go. More calmly than before, he entered the kitchen and sat in front of the patil. He tapped out the code for Elder Daven and was slightly surprised to get an immediate connection.

"Hello, Ahn. To what do I owe the honor of your call?"

"Hello, Elder Daven. I wanted to verify Petre's story with you. He just told us he received permanent retirement, is this true?"

Daven nodded with relief. He had wondered if Elder Rylon would change the assignment, but now he knew the original document had been honored. "Yes, Ahn, it's true."

"Wow! Just wow! How did this happen? And how did he end up owning the house across the street from mine?"

"Now I didn't even know about that! Hmm, I wonder. I don't really know, but I can find out for you if you'd like."

"I'd appreciate it. I have to look out for my neighborhood, you know."

"Ahn, please reconsider your opinion of Petre. I've told you truly that he's changed."

"I'm trying, Elder Daven, but my memory runs deep, and he's screwed up too many times for me to blindly let it go."

"I understand. All I ask is for you to keep trying."

"I will. Thank you for your time. Good evening."

"Good evening, Ahn."

Ahn switched off the patil and turned in the chair. With a look of utter amazement on his face, he asked his wife, "Can you believe this?"

"It's pretty remarkable."

"Crazy is the word I'd be more inclined to use," Ahn spoke in a disgusted tone.

CHAPTER 31

The crashing sound of her chamber door startled Rasa half to death. She whirled around, ready to accuse whomever it was of carelessness, but then her words froze in her throat as she saw the look on Ulwin's face. "What is it? What's wrong?" she asked in a panic as she rushed forward to meet him.

"It's Elder Wilken. Please come quick."

Grabbing Ulwin's arm and hauling him back the way he had come, Rasa demanded, "Where is he? What happened?"

"He's in his chamber. Rasa, I think he's dead."

"NO!" Rasa screamed. She dropped his arm and instantly translated herself into his chamber. Never before had she attempted such a thing, and it even startled herself.

Seeing the scene in front of her, she knew Ulwin had spoken the truth. To the casual observer, the Elder was sleeping in his chair by the fire. Rasa could see no life in him. She rushed over to his side and pulled his hand into her own. For a moment she was confused by his warmth but then realized the fire had kept him from becoming chilled.

Faster than ever in her life, she used her healing powers to attempt to tie into his life-line. She searched valiantly, but no connection could be made. Her mentor and surrogate father was truly gone. Her grief poured out in an agonizing wail of despair, overpowering her senses because she was still tied into the elemy. "NO!" she cried out again. "I'm not ready, Elder Wilken. I'm not ready for this," she said in a whisper only for her mentor to hear.

Other cries in the room brought Rasa back to her senses. She gently placed the old man's hand back against his stomach and lifted herself off of the floor. The maids who had discovered him were looking scared and mournful, much like how she felt herself. "He's gone," she announced. "Please prepare his body. I must make the announcement to the other Elders."

Rasa used the formality of the occasion to hold herself together long enough to escape the stares of the women in the room. As soon as she entered the Ascension Gate room, she let herself fall apart. There was nobody left in the Residence who was able to come into the room because of the wards set in place, so she was free to rant, rage, scream, and cry for her friend. None of the staff would ever bear witness to her fear or her loss.

Unsure of how much time had passed, Rasa finally pulled herself together. She wiped her eyes with the backs of her hands and sniffled loudly to control the flow of snot from her nose. When she had arrived, only a mesan before, she had believed she had anons to learn everything. Now, she was performing her first formal act as Elder Rasa.

She switched on the patil and dialed the emergency number for First Elder Debbon.

The connection was immediate.

"Rasa? What's the matter?"

"First Elder Debbon, I regret to inform you Elder Wilken has passed."

"I'll be right there." He disconnected the call.

Rasa was relieved to know she would not be left alone too much longer. She would let Elder Debbon handle the arrangements. It was impossible to think clearly at a time like this, and she needed someone with more experience to handle the situation in the most honorable manner: Elder Wilken deserved it.

Just as she had done earlier, Elder Debbon translated himself directly into the Ascension Gate room next to Rasa. She stepped back, startled by his close proximity. When Debbon held out his arms, she gratefully accepted the comfort of his embrace. "He was well-loved, Rasa. I'm sorry this came so soon for you."

Rasa cried even harder than she had when she was alone. Knowing Debbon shared the same love for Wilken only intensified her grief. How was she going to get through this?

"You'll be fine, Rasa. Wilken told me on many occasions how brilliant you are. Besides, Jehoban never would have sent you here unless you were ready." He pulled her gently away from himself and put his finger under her chin so she would look him in the eyes. "I know you're sad, but we have a lot of work to get done in a very short period of time."

"What? I don't understand. We can't do anything until Elder Wilken has been taken care of!"

Debbon shook his head sadly. "On the contrary, we must assure the people of the Manzanit District they are still protected by an Elder. We are a long-lived group, luckily, so each generation of citizens generally only experience one transition in their lives. Still, we must get you promoted to your position. To do so, we must convene the other Elders."

"I'll send them messages," Rasa said as she began to turn back to the patil.

"No, Rasa. This is where the work will come in…you have to bring them here using your Gate."

"What? How? This gate is set to go to Central Park in New York City on Earth."

"It's just its default setting. As an Elder, you must know how to program your Gate to send people anywhere in any of the worlds. Your first task will be to bring the Elders here into this room. Then, and only then, will they consent to vote you in as a fellow Elder. If you cannot control your Gate, then you are not an Elder. It is the first rule we must all follow."

"Why is this the first time I'm hearing about it? I could have been practicing with Elder Wilken instructing me. I don't understand!"

"Only the Elders know about this ability of the Gates. You can understand why it must remain a secret. If everyone knew we could send anywhere, there would be pandemonium. I must also warn you if you fail this task, then I will be forced to mind swipe this conversation from you. It must remain a secret."

Rasa's eyes grew wide at his last statement. He had certainly made the gravity of the situation quite clear. She knew how serious a matter this was becoming. She also understood the importance of moving things swiftly for the least amount of disruption for the people of Manzanit. "Tell me what I must do."

Elder Debbon nodded in approval. He motioned for them to sit down while he explained the procedures. For over an hour, Debbon talked about the nuances of her Gate.

His explanation made it sound so simple; she could hardly believe anyone would have a problem with its execution. She sat back and rubbed her temples. Her mind was filled with questions and concerns for herself. Suddenly she recalled her conversation with Willian earlier in the day.

"Elder Debbon, I've been so preoccupied with what's been going on here, I forgot to ask you how you've been. When I heard about Willian's betrothal being broken, I wondered what your reaction to it had been. I never got the chance to ask Willian. When he was staying here under Elder Wilken's guidance, he was so hopeful about his future with Jena. This must feel like a whirlwind for you and Chelesa."

Debbon stared at Rasa in stony silence. He had no words to describe what he was feeling at that moment.

Rasa looked up from her folded hands as Debbon remained quiet. She saw his expression and asked with dread, "You didn't know yet, did you? I'm sorry, Elder Debbon. I thought you knew! Willian never said anything differently when we talked today! I'm so sorry!"

He patted her hands and said, "This isn't your fault. I'll get to the bottom of this mess. Did Willian happen to mention if it were a formal dissolution?"

"Yes, Elder Daven granted the request at Jena's behest while they were at the Roanoke Colony." Rasa felt like she was betraying everyone's confidence by sharing her knowledge.

"What were they doing back in Tuala?" Debbon stood up and began pacing. "I'm going to get to the bottom of this. Right now, however, we need to focus on what you need to do tonight. When Debbon stopped talking, Rasa inhaled a shuddering breath and nodded. "I understand. I'm ready to begin, although I'm really glad to have you here with me to make sure I get it right."

"No, Rasa, I won't be. I will be leaving you here alone. You are to bring here all of the Elders in the order I described. I will be the last one you bring here."

"What? Why?" She instantly felt terrified of her task.

"It is to prove to all of the Elders you did this of your own knowledge and power. If I were here when the first ones came, they could assume I had helped you. No, you must do this without me here. I believe in Wilken's assessment of your skills. I'm not worried." He stood up and said, "Send all of the Elders the message, including myself. Once you receive every confirmation of receipt, begin bringing them here."

Without so much as a goodbye, Debbon translated himself back to his own home to await the sad news.

Rasa stared at the spot he had just vacated. How had it all come to this so fast? Was she really ready or had she been lying to herself and to Elder Debbon? She stood up and walked over to the patil. Her hands were shaking badly as she began to type the message to go out to the entire group of Elders. Her eyes blurred with tears as she read the message several times over before she hit the submit button.

She imagined she could hear cries of mourning breaking out all over the world with her terrible news. Certainly, her own heart was breaking, and she had to pull herself together. Some other time she could fall apart, today she had to be strong for Elder Wilken. She had to prove herself worthy to be his successor by performing at her peak.

There would be several minutes before she heard back from all of the recipients of the list. She hurriedly left the room and rushed down several hallways to get back to her private suite. Even before the door had shut behind her, she was ripping her garments off over her head. This was an official occasion, and she should look the part.

In her wardrobe hung the perfectly white, ornate garments of the Elders. Wilken had insisted hers be made for her the day she arrived. Standing naked but not feeling any cold, she reached up to pull it from the hanger, and her hand caressed the foxl fibers, so smooth, almost slippery in her fingers. She could vividly recall seeing Elder Wilken in a similar garment on her day of appointment. Now was her time to emulate him in everything. Her destiny had arrived.

CHAPTER 32

Riccan and Juila arrived home to report finding four more listening devices; three in Jasmine's home and one in her car. The matter regarding Dr. Gascon was becoming more serious by the minute as far as they were all concerned. Where else might he try to listen in on them? How was he getting access to their private spaces? How many people had he hired?

"What I want to know is how are we going to stop him? It's not as if we can go down to the police station and file a complaint. What if they were to investigate Gascon's claims and find out there was some truth to us? We can't risk being under police scrutiny, Riccan!" Amanda was both frustrated and fearful, and this latest news did not inspire any new confidence in their situation.

"Don't worry, honey; I've faced worse in the past. You don't grow up in two worlds without having resources to fall back on."

"What are you going to do?" Amanda demanded. "How are you going to stop him?"

"I'll give him a mind swipe if I have to," Riccan stated flatly. He held up his hand to quiet his daughters' vocal responses to his drastic solution. "First, I'll go pay the good doctor a visit and request for him to cease and desist from all of his illegal activities. I've found people are usually much more submissive when they know they've been caught."

"You can't go see him alone, Riccan! What if he holds you hostage?" Amanda's fear level just escalated several steps higher with the idea of her husband being alone with the crazed doctor. "Who knows what he'd do to you?"

"I've a few tricks up my sleeve, Amanda. I didn't grow up as the Elder's son and not learn anything about using the elemy to my advantage. Gascon won't be able to keep me, but, just to satisfy you, I'll take extra precautions when I meet with him."

"What? What can you do?"

"First, I'll set up several wards of protection around myself. The girls can test them for any weak spots before I go. Second, I'll keep myself tapped into the elemy so any action I need to take can be instantaneous. Third, the doctor's mind will be linked with my own, so I'll know anything he plans almost before he does. What do you think? Does it sound safe enough?"

"Do I have any choice? I still don't like it one little bit!" She turned away from the watchful eyes of her family so they would not witness her weakness of fear. They all looked so confident with their abilities, and she suddenly felt lacking. Her abilities with the elemy were years behind even her daughters' skills, and she felt it deeply.

Her gaze fell upon the tape they had found. She turned back to Riccan and pointed at it on the table, "Jena and I found this outside the fence a ways down from the main gate. I touched it as little as possible to preserve any fingerprints or other evidence."

Riccan pulled a pen out of his breast pocket and slipped it through the reel of the tape. He held it up and noticed the inside tape was halfway used. "Hmph," he commented as he sat on the couch. "What do you think, girls, can we use the elemy to replicate the exterior of the surface of this?"

Jena's eyes lit up with interest. "I don't see why not!" She sat next to her father.

Juila's brain began working on the logistics of the problem, and she took a seat on the other side of Riccan. "I think we should join forces so we can all experience the process."

"Good idea!" Riccan looked up with an eager expression and asked, "Amanda, do you want to join us? I think it'd be a good learning exercise for you."

"Yeah, Mom! Come sit next to me," Jena exclaimed as she patted the sofa beside her.

Seeing the three expectant expressions of her family, she could hardly refuse. Besides, she was just chiding herself for not practicing enough with the elemy. What better time than to join with the three most talented people she knew? "Fine," she relented and crossed the room to sit beside her youngest daughter.

Almost instantly, the powerful pull of elemy surrounded them. It took Amanda's breath away since she had only experienced small portions of it on her own. She braced herself for the continued onslaught only to realize it had been harnessed and focused on the tape which Riccan still held at eye level in front of them with the pencil.

"Juila, try what you were thinking," Riccan instructed.

Juila nodded, and a replica of the tape appeared suspended in the air beside the original. Her expression showed she was pleased with the result. "Like that?"

"It's a start. Jena, what did you have in mind?" Riccan asked without moving his gaze from the objects in front of them.

"Mom mentioned fingerprints being useful. How about if I did this?" She followed her question with action, and a thin, transparent layer appeared between the two objects. When she leaned closer, she could see small smudges of prints.

"Perfect, Jena, now use the elemy to document the prints into a solid, permanent form."

Jena's lips formed a small line as she concentrated on performing the task her father assigned. In an instant, she had done as requested and nodded her satisfaction at the result. She let the film drop to rest on the table for later inspection. "What now?"

"Just a little something I learned as a boy," Riccan said mysteriously. Even as he spoke, he began pushing elemy through the tape. Almost as if a projector had been turned on in the middle of the room, they could all see the scenery beyond the cassette. A man appeared, holding the tape in his hand and they watched him place it in the recorder and stand up again. He peered through the gate toward their house before he turned and walked out of the field of view. Riccan let the images dissipate, and he grinned at first Juila and then Jena. "What did you think of it?"

Jena was the first to speak, "He was the man I saw in the car across the street! I read his mind, and he was definitely hired by Dr. Gascon. He was bored with his assignment, and he wished he would have followed you and Juila instead of having to stay put in his car!"

"What? There's someone out there now? Why didn't you say so when I first arrived?" Riccan's control of the elemy ruptured, and all of them felt the backlash from it. "Sorry," he said hurriedly as he regathered the elemy and then let it dissipate naturally back into the earth.

The twins grinned at their father's loss of control. They had begun to believe he was infallible and this made them feel better to know they could all make mistakes.

"I'm going to go confront the man!" Riccan announced as he shot up from the couch to take action.

"No, Riccan! Think about it, if you go out there and speak to him, he's going to call Dr. Gascon and let him know he's been made. If you want to catch the doctor by surprise, you can't tip your hand," Amanda reasoned.

"True…fine, I'll take my telepod to Manzanit and use Elder Wilken's gate to go to Central Park, which should give the doctor something to think about. First, his spy sees us driving from and then back to the property and not even an hour later, I'm showing up in his office. The timing is impossible, and I want him to realize he shouldn't mess with us!"

"Please be careful!" Amanda admonished again.

Riccan stood still in concentration, his face empty of any expression.

Amanda looked at him, both puzzled and concerned for his sudden change.

"Girls, check out what I've done. I'll keep this around me until I return."

Both Juila and Jena stood up and circled their father. Their faces were intent on something Amanda could not even see. It suddenly donned on her he had created his fields of protection and wanted the twins to search for any weak spots. At least Amanda hoped this is what was happening. Once again she felt left out because of her limited skill set.

"It's amazing, Dad," Jena praised.

"Yes, it's perfect," Juila agreed.

"Fine, I'm ready to go then." He reached out and gave the girls each a hug and a kiss on the tops of their heads. When they stepped away from him, he held out his hand to Amanda who remained seated on the couch. "I'll be back soon," he said as he folded Amanda into his embrace. He kissed her on the lips and murmured, "I love you."

"I love you, too. Be on your alert with him, Riccan. Don't get cocky just because of this…this shield you have. I wouldn't put anything past him, Riccan."

"I agree. I'll pretend I'm meeting with Lucinden and expect the worst." He grinned at his comparison.

"Sometimes I think Dr. Gascon is Lucinden; he's so wretchedly bad."

Riccan kissed Amanda's forehead before he stepped away and strode into the kitchen. He grabbed his telepod remote by the phone on the desk as he kept walking. Nothing was going to stop him from sorting out this issue. Nobody messed with his family and got away with it.

THE TRIP to Manzanit was uneventful. However, Riccan was grateful for the upgraded system. He doubted his mental state would have allowed for such a smooth transfer. He was able to immediately locate a transport to the Residence and paid the driver once they pulled in front of the main gate.

The guards looked wary, and Riccan was puzzled by his greeting. "Thank you for coming so soon," one of them had said to him.

Riccan stepped inside and found the staff was all running about, almost in a disorganized manner. Never before had he seen so many people in the open spaces. Usually, they prided themselves on remaining unseen, so he was beginning to become alarmed. What had happened for everyone to be acting so strangely?

He grabbed the arm of a passing girl and asked, "Where's Rasa?"

"She's in her chambers, Riccan," she said hurriedly. As soon as her arm was released, she was moving to complete her errand and was out of sight.

Riccan shook his head in wonder, yet his stride lengthened as he started to feel the unrest in himself as well. When he got to Rasa's private chambers, he knocked three times rapidly on the door and waited. There was no answer, so he let himself in.

He had gotten no further than the second room when he stopped short. Rasa was standing naked in front of her closet. She had the white Elder's robes held close to her as she cried uncontrollably. His instinct to help her moved him into action and he ran across the room until he was standing next to her.

"Rasa, what is it? What's made you so upset? How can I help?"

Forgetting her nakedness, Rasa let go of the cloth still hanging in the closet and turned to the comforting arms of her friend. "Oh, Riccan," she cried as she clung to Riccan's solid frame.

Riccan was at a loss, but he put his arms around Rasa. It felt strange to be embracing a naked woman who was not his wife, but he did not have time to worry about such a thing. He needed to discover what had upset Rasa this much. "Tell me what has happened. Let me help you."

"Elder Wilken has died!" She clung to Riccan harder, and wracking sobs shook her body.

Everything came into clear focus for Riccan. It all made sense, from the guards to the staff to Rasa holding her ceremonial robes. He knew time was not on their side and he pulled her body away from his.

Without looking at her body, he reached over her shoulder and grabbed the robe off of the hanger. In a fluid, practiced motion he gathered the fabric up and put it over her head. She was completely unresisting as he pulled it down the length of her body and he helped her to put her arms in the sleeves.

"Pull yourself together, Rasa. Elder Wilken's memory is still with you. You have to call the Elders together so they can formalize your promotion." He began to pull her through the rooms toward the exit.

"I've already sent them messages. I'm waiting for them to reply so we can begin. I came back here to get dressed, but it all hit me, and I seemed to have fallen apart. Thank you for helping me, Riccan. I don't know what I would have done without you."

He could see sense returning to her eyes as she told him what had already been done. It was a relief to hear things had already been set in motion. He personally dreaded the day when her actions would be his own at his father's passing.

"I'll walk with you to the Gate room," Riccan announced. He kept his hand on her elbow to keep her moving.

As they came back into the public spaces, Rasa's senses began to sharpen. She had to maintain a sense of peace during the troubling, sorrowful time. The staff expected her to know what to do and they could not see her seeming uncertain and weak. Her spine straightened, and she walked with confidence again.

"What are you doing here, Riccan?" Rasa suddenly asked.

"I've discovered some troubling news of my own; although, not on the scale of your news. Dr. Gascon is threatening my family, and I came to ask if I could be sent to Central Park to confront him. I can see now is a bad time, though."

"No, no, Riccan. I'd be happy to help you out; you've earned it by helping me through this. I'm still waiting for the replies from the other Elders and, until then, I need something to do. Please, let me send you right now."

"As long as you don't mind, Rasa. I am really sorry for your loss. Elder Wilken was a gentle soul, and he's been an inspiration for me and many others over the anons."

"Thanks, I agree with you. I'd hoped to have many anons more to learn from him. My only solace is it appeared he passed peacefully in his sleep. He didn't appear to have suffered at all."

"That's good, a gentle end for a gentle man." Riccan opened the door to the Gate room and let Rasa enter first. He promptly followed behind and shut the door firmly. Riccan could feel the power emanating from the Ascension Gate and, once again, realized just how powerful a location this place was. He did not envy Rasa the coveted position.

Rasa moved over to the patil and scanned through the messages. There were still two confirmations to be received. She would have time to send Riccan before her skills were called into action. In a way, it was comforting to operate the Gate normally to get her nerves settled before she had to test the newly learned procedures.

She tapped a few buttons on the control panel and looked up at Riccan. "I'm ready for your transfer as soon as you are."

"Are you sure? I don't want to be a bother." He felt guilty at his unfortunately timed arrival.

"No bother at all, just step down into the Gate, and I'll get you on your way."

Rasa's confident manner went a long way toward easing Riccan's reservations about letting her operate the transfer. She appeared to be back in control of herself. He nodded agreement and walked over to the far wall. He stepped down into the depression and turned to face her. He smiled and said, "I'm ready. Thanks, Rasa. The next time I'll see you, I'll have to call you Elder Rasa."

"Thanks for the vote of confidence, Riccan. Be safe with Dr. Gascon," she replied as she hit the activation button. The Gate's energy charged up, and Riccan disappeared before her eyes. She watched the controls and confirmed all was functioning perfectly, and he had arrived in Central Park unharmed.

The patil next to her beeped two times in quick succession. She turned her attention to the screen and saw the remaining confirmations had been received. It was time for her to begin the complex transfers.

CHAPTER 33

With a sigh of relief, Riccan stepped out of the twisted branches which shielded the Gate from casual view. He stepped through the ferns and underbrush until he came to the trail leading out of the wooded area and into the open, grassy fields of Central Park. The chill wind pushed against him as he left the sheltered area of the trees. There was a drastic temperature difference between Florida and New York City this time of year, and he wished he would have brought a jacket with him.

Instead, he pulled more elemy around him to keep the chill away. He walked swiftly away from the tree line and followed the jogging path until he came to the edge of the park. He hailed a cab and instructed the driver to take him to Creedmoor Psychiatric Center, located in Queens. He recalled Amanda saying it was a fifteen to twenty-minute drive, so he sat back and looked out the window at the passing buildings and throngs of people.

The cab drove unerringly to the requested location and parked outside of the front doors. Riccan paid with his credit card and left the warmth of the car. He entered the building and strode confidently up to the receptionist's desk.

"How may I help you," she asked brightly.

"I'd like to see Dr. Stephen Gascon."

"Do you have an appointment?"

"No."

"One moment and I'll see if he has any openings." She turned and tapped several keys on her keyboard while staring at her computer screen. Her lips pursed and she began to shake her head sadly. Not wanting to disappoint the devastatingly handsome stranger, she turned back to Riccan and said, "I'm sorry; Dr. Gascon isn't available right now. If you'd like to schedule an appointment, I can check his availability."

"So he's in the building?" Riccan persisted.

"Yes, he's currently meeting with another patient."

"This is an urgent matter. Please have a message sent to him directly indicating Riccan Stel is here to see him. I'm certain he will make the time. Also, let him know if he doesn't see me in five minutes; I'm leaving."

The woman's eyebrows rose higher with each word Riccan said. She had never encountered anyone who was so confident in their presence. "I'll message him right now," she replied and instantly turned and began typing the note to the doctor. She was just turning to tell Riccan the message was delivered when she received a reply to let him come up to Dr. Gascon's office. Apparently, this mysterious man had been right with his prediction. "Mr. Stel, Dr. Gascon has approved your request. Please take the elevator right there up to the thirteenth floor. His office is the third one on the right."

"Thank you, miss," Riccan replied with a tilt of his head even as he moved away from the desk. He tapped the call button on the elevator and entered the car as soon as the doors opened. Riccan turned to face the doors and took several breaths to steady his anger. He must appear in complete control in front of the psychiatrist. His position of authority must be apparent even for the egocentric doctor.

Riccan followed the receptionist's instructions and came to the doctor's official office. Without knocking or waiting for an invitation, Riccan entered the room as though it were his own personal space. He crossed the secretary's room, which was absent of anybody anyway, and opened the second door into the doctor's personal domain.

Dr. Gascon looked excited as he stood abruptly from his chair and said, "To what do I owe this honor, Mr. Stel. Have you finally decided your wife needs my professional help?"

Riccan took the momentary surprise of his arrival to link his mind with the other man's. Instantly he was bombarded with convoluted scenarios of what the doctor would like to see done to himself. He compartmentalized the doctor's thoughts so he could mentally record everything for later review. He stepped up to the desk and leaned forward until his knuckles rested on the mahogany surface.

"This isn't a social call, Gascon. I'm here to warn you."

Dr. Gascon sneered in derision as he casually sat in his over-sized, leather chair. He knew this man's secrets, and he had the upper hand. Riccan had no idea what he was stepping into by coming here today. "Please sit down. There's no need to be hostile. Tell me what's on your mind."

"I'll remain standing. I know you've hired people to watch my house. I've discovered the bug you planted in my office. I even know the identity of the man who has been collecting the tapes for your review."

The expression on Dr. Gascon's face remained bland and unconcerned. He was not about to let this pompous ass try to intimidate him. Besides, he had another angle covered with Jasmine Medin since his original plan had been exposed. "I'm sure I have no idea what you're talking about. You sound more like a paranoid delusional man with your unwarranted accusations."

Riccan heard his thoughts and continued, "I've also disabled the bugs you have on Dr. Medin."

Stephen's expression altered slightly. How could Riccan have discovered them so fast, it had just been done this afternoon? Surely he was bluffing, and he decided to call him out on it. "Why should I believe this any more than I believe your other accusation?"

"Because Dr. Medin found the bug you put in her office and called me. I located and neutralized the devices in her office, kitchen, living room, and her car. Does it sound like I'm bluffing to you? Listen, Gascon, listen well. I'm only going to give you this one warning. Call off your hounds. Do not have anyone follow us or try to record us or our movements in any way. Leave my family alone, or you'll be sorry you ever messed with me!"

"Oooh, I'm so scared. What are you going to do, kill me? You don't seem the type. You're way too civilized, Riccan. Besides, the information I have on your family is quite damaging. If you touch one hair on my head, I've left instructions for the documents to be released to the authorities. Would you care to find out how thorough I've been?"

"I have no interest in your theories or your illegally gathered so-called evidence. Leave my family alone, or you'll be getting one last visit from me."

"Hmm, I don't think so. I rather think you'll be staying here as my guest." Dr. Gascon pressed a button on the underside of his desk and was pleased with the quick response of his orderlies. They barged into the room and waited for his command. "Please make sure Mr. Stel has a room near my office. I believe he and I are going to have quite a few conversations during his stay here."

Riccan shook his head in disbelief at Dr. Gascon's actions. "Watch and learn, Gascon. We are not to be underestimated… ever!" He turned and walked calmly past the orderlies.

"Don't just stand there like imbeciles! Grab him and take him to a room!" Dr. Gascon jumped up from his chair and pointed at Riccan's retreating back. His face grew purple with anger as the guards regarded him strangely.

"Doctor, are you feeling well? There's nobody in this room but you," one of the burly men replied.

Raging with fury, he said, "Of course, there is; he just walked past you! Oh!!! I'll do it myself!" Dr. Gascon flew out of his office, shoving rudely against the two men until he caught up with Riccan in the outer office. He reached out and grabbed Riccan's arm in a firm grasp and tried to turn him around. "You're not going anywhere! I'm not done with you!"

"If I were you, I'd release my arm," Riccan spoke casually.

Abruptly, Dr. Gascon complied, a startled expression on his face even as he did so against his wishes.

Riccan used his momentary confusion to translate himself out of the office. He was watching Dr. Gascon's face as he disappeared and could see the stark terror in his eyes. Riccan looked down and could swear he saw liquid pooling around the doctor's feet. He smiled at his own theatrics and fervently hoped he had made his point clear to the doctor.

He reappeared back in the woods of Central Park. His plan had not been fully formed and it had been a serious risk to perform the translation. However, he felt the ends had justified the means when he began to go over Dr. Gascon's final thoughts as he left.

Originally, Riccan had planned on going back home through the Gate in Manzanit, but now he wondered if he should leave

Rasa alone. With another sigh of resignation, Riccan once again trekked through the park and hailed a cab. "Take me to JFK," he instructed. His trip home would take hours longer, yet it would also give him time to go over all he had just learned from his visit.

The cab pulled up to the terminal and Riccan got out. He made arrangements for a private charter jet and sat in the secluded waiting room designated for priority guests. Normally, he would have called ahead and had the plane waiting, but he did not mind the twenty-minute delay as the pilot filed the flight plan and prepared the airplane for immediate departure.

CHAPTER 34

Rasa used her memorization skills to good use as she reprogrammed her Gate. She set up a simple code so she could promptly recalibrate the coordinates as soon as each Elder stepped far enough away from the core to safely begin again. With a cautious breath of anticipation, she entered in Gamb's location coordinates and punched the button to activate the transfer. Instantly Quentien appeared on the depressed platform with an impressed look on his face.

"Very nicely done, Rasa," he complimented as he stepped up and out of the way. He was surprised to find he was the first to arrive. As the initial witness of her power, he watched her carefully as she tapped the next coordinates into the control panel.

Uvan of Secar arrived second. He went to stand next to Quentien. The two had never been close, but they were both invested in Rasa's success or failure with the following transfers. Faster than either of them had ever seen, Yingun of Gaud appeared. His scowl of disapproval was ignored by both of them as they gestured for him to join them in watching the performance. He took his time in exiting the platform.

The delay had given Rasa enough time to program the fourth command and she hit enter, possibly sooner than she should have since Yingun had just cleared the danger zone when Xylen of Noidad materialized in the chamber.

"Don't be too cocky, girl," Yingun called out derisively.

She deigned to ignore his snide comment as she entered the next set of coordinates. She did, however, wait until Xylen had joined the group before she activated the transfer.

Vargen of Apio was next followed in rapid succession by Olguin of Genip, Zigern of Neum, Tarshen of Sambur, Senjin of Argot, Rylon of Menad, Daven of Pantano, Jedon of Neve, Emmin of Telae, and finally Debbon of Elder Isle.

Debbon solemnly stepped up from the depression in the earth and turned to bow in congratulations to Rasa for a job well-done. "Thank you, Rasa, for demonstrating your skill in operating this Gate."

He turned to the two groups of men who had formed off to the side of the room. The division was no mystery to the First Elder, the ones on the left were those who disapproved of a woman becoming a formal member of their group, not so coincidentally they were also first to be brought to the assembly. Without telling Rasa, he had organized the transfers so even the dissenters would not have cause to accuse she had obtained any help from another Elder in bringing them all here.

"We have gathered together because of the sorrowful news of the passing of one of our own. Rasa has demonstrated the first task of control by successfully bringing us all together."

"She was much too cocky with her speed. She was reckless!" Yingun objected vehemently.

"Not so, Yingun. Your opinion has been duly noted on many

occasions. We are all safely arrived, which was the task. Speed was never a factor for consideration." He turned back to Rasa and asked, "Will you take us to where Wilken has been laid out?"

"Certainly," she replied humbly, but firmly. She stepped past the men and exited the room knowing they all followed her, yet she did not look back to verify it. Her confidence must not be questioned in this procession.

They marched silently down the hallway until they reached Wilken's private rooms. The staff had lined the walls, heads bowed with sorrow, as the esteemed group passed. Rasa opened the double doors and entered the room. Her eyes located her friend much where she had last seen him. The table and chairs had been removed, and the fire had been quenched. Wilken was lying on a table, dressed in his formal attire, with his hands once again resting across his stomach.

Each Elder vividly recalled his own time when he had performed this same task with their father. Several men unsuccessfully tried to hide their tears or sniffles as they circled Wilken's body. Rasa remained by Wilken's head and she looked down at him through tear-filled eyes. This would be the last time she ever saw her dear friend. Trying not to see the straps crossing over his body, including across his forehead, she soaked in every detail down to the slight smile still on his lips. She imagined he was enjoying the show of making the dissenting Elder's squirm at what would happen soon and hoped she would make him proud.

Without a single word, each Elder reached out of one accord and grabbed the handles of the gurney on which Wilken had been placed. Only Rasa remained unburdened as she turned and led the group back the way they had come to return to the Gate room. She dreaded her final task, yet she knew it was necessary for her to be elevated to Elder status.

The men crossed the room until they were at the Gate itself.

They shifted their burden until the gurney stood upright, resting against the back wall. It appeared as though Wilken were standing inside the Gate even though the straps were the only thing keeping him from slumping down.

Rasa stepped forward then and said, "I commend you back to Jehoban. May your soul be guarded and protected. Your District has been served well with your wisdom, kindness, and knowledge. You will be missed, dear friend." She touched her hand to Wilken's birth-crystal and felt an odd tingling sensation flow through her body. She stepped up and backed away from Wilken's body. She turned and walked to the control panel for one last transfer.

Frustrated by her suddenly blurry vision, she hastily wiped her eyes and began programming the panel for the one-way trip between the dimensions. She glanced up one last time and smiled farewell to Wilken.

"It is time, Rasa," Debbon said quietly beside her.

She nodded and pressed the button to send him on his journey home. The Gate activated, a bright light blinded them all as if Jehoban were welcoming Wilken back to Him. When the brightness dissipated, the platform was empty.

While Debbon was consoling Rasa, the men began to gather into tight groups throughout the room. Their conversations were hushed as they all theorized about the meaning of the odd departure of one of their own.

"I say it was a sign indicating this is not right," Yingun accused as he leaned indolently against the wall. He received nods of approval from Quentien and Xylen.

Quentien leaned forward and said, "Maybe Wilken took the Gate's power with him. Haven't any of you noticed how powerful Manzanit has always been?"

"It's true," Xylen agreed. Not to be outdone, he added, "I've noticed all of the Gates have been losing power. More recently it's become obvious to more than just us Elders. The people using my Gate have been complaining about how long the transfers have been taking. Have either of you noticed the same?"

"No, I haven't," Yingun sneered. "Maybe it's just a product of your ineptitude, Xylen." His accusation was only designed to deflect his own reaction to Xylen's observation. He had been worried it had only been his Gate's power being affected. Never would he admit such a thing to the other Elders, however.

As Xylen stormed off, Yingun looked around the well-appointed room. He did sense more power here than in any other Gate and wondered at it. While this was the second oldest Residence, he had somehow believed the power had come from Wilken's line and not from the location at all. Since Wilken had been disposed of, the power still remained. He glared over at Rasa, knowing she was no relation to the old relic who had finally departed from this world.

Debbon pulled on Daven's sleeve and motioned for them to move to the side of the room, too. As soon as they were out of earshot, Debbon accused, "How dare you dissolve my son's betrothal? Don't you think I should have been consulted first? I had to find out today from Rasa. The poor girl was mortified to learn that I didn't know anything about it. I was equally mortified. I'm the First Elder, don't you think I should have known what was going on in my own household?"

Daven waited for Debbon to run out of breath before he urgently whispered his own reply. "I was left with no choice, Debbon. I'm sorry; I assumed Willian would have told you right away."

"No choice? Really, that's the angle you're sticking with? There's always a choice. Believe me; this is not the last you've heard about this from me. There might even be sanctions in store for you for interfering in another Elder's District."

"Do as you wish, but I'd suggest you talk to Willian about it first."

"I'd thank you not to tell me how to handle my own family."

"Debbon, it's been almost a week. I would have expected Willian to have contacted you by now."

"A week?!" he asked incredulously with his voice rising. "Didn't you think it strange I hadn't contacted you by now? If I had known, I would have been at your Residence asking questions! I can't believe how you would betray my trust like this! I thought we were friends."

"Debbon, please talk to Willian. I don't want you to say anything you might regret."

"I won't regret any of this, Daven. You have betrayed my trust; I know this for certain. I will not forget or forgive your transgression against my family and your insult to my position. I have Rasa's ceremony to complete. I don't have time for you right now."

He turned his back on his friend and cleared his throat to get everyone's attention. "Elders, Rasa has been trained and approved by Wilken. She has also been accepted as Wilken's successor by our majority. There is only one thing left to do which is to welcome her to our ranks as Elder Rasa."

He put his hands on Rasa's shoulders and said, "Please kneel, Rasa. As First Elder, I hereby appoint you the position of Elder to the citizens of Manzanit. May all of your decisions and considerations be done with the will of your people first in your mind. May Jehoban bless you in this endeavor and welcome you to our ranks." He placed his hand on the top of her head and mumbled something under his breath.

Rasa felt the warmth of his hand and the tingling sensation returned. She felt it travel throughout her body until it seemed to coalesce at her birth crystal. When Debbon's hand lifted from her, she looked down on her pendant to discover it now contained the circular disk denoting her status as an Elder. Jehoban was the only one who could place the new crystal, and nobody could deny it was His wish for her to become one of them.

She rose from the floor and smiled up at Debbon. Seeing his glance down at her newly bejeweled birth crystal, she said, "Thank you, First Elder Debbon. I will do my best to be an asset to the people as Jehoban's representative."

"Well spoken, Rasa." He clapped her gently on the shoulder and turned to face the others in the room. "Jehoban has placed the moonstone in her birth crystal. What Jehoban has declared, we will join in the celebration of his decision."

There were cheers of approval from many of the men and Rasa chose to ignore the glares of disapproval from those who remained silent. No longer could an argument be made against her ascension to their ranks. She was now their equal in every way.

"I'm positive there is much for you to do yet today, Rasa. As your final task, please be so kind as to begin sending us all home."

"Certainly." She leaned closer so only Debbon could hear and asked, "Is there a particular order?"

He shook his head and said with a wicked grin on his face, "No, but I can probably guess who's leaving first!"

Her task did not take long, with Debbon being the last to leave. She felt physically drained and imagined the room around her did as well. With her feet dragging, she left the room and retired to her personal suite to change out of her formal attire. Morning would come all too soon; she was going to bed.

CHAPTER 35

The windows of the car were completely fogged up as Willian and Valentina sat in the front seat and talked about their days. Valentina had driven him home over an hour before only they were reluctant to part ways. They were holding hands, but they knew if they did not have the console between them, it might easily turn into something more.

"I was so scared of the ride in the telepod," Valentina said again.

"I know. You know, I could take the fear away for you," Willian offered.

"No, I'll work through it over time. Maybe it's a good thing we'll be traveling again tomorrow."

"Yes, although I don't know how well I'll be able to instruct Gevena. If she's afraid to use her powers, it'll be difficult for her to learn the concepts."

"But you're a great teacher, Willian!"

"For you, yes; you wanted to learn and competing with your brothers fueled your desire to succeed."

"True."

"You know, Val, when I was coming to find you today, I was thinking about what it would be like to take you home to meet my parents. What do you think? Do you want to go?"

"You told them about me already?" Valentina was amazed and wondered when he had been able to do so. "What did they say?"

Willian blushed a little as he realized Valentina had gotten ahead of him in his story. "Actually, I haven't even told them about the betrothal yet."

"Willian! You have to tell them. Your dad set up the betrothal when you were little; he needs to know right away. I can't believe you've let it go this long!" She pulled her hands out of his with her shock and anger at his selfishness regarding his parents.

"It's not my fault, Val. I haven't had access to a patil. How would you suggest I let them know?"

"Oh, I hadn't thought about it. Here on Earth, we'd just pick up the phone and call, but I guess this situation is slightly more challenging for you."

"I'll say! I'm afraid my mom's feelings will be hurt and I'm fairly certain my dad will be disappointed in me."

"It can't be undone, Willian, you told me so yourself. You're going to have to face them some time and it'd be better to hear the news from you than from someone else. Don't you think?"

"I suppose. Maybe when we go to Manzanit tomorrow, I'll use Rasa's patil to talk to Dad."

"Don't you think it'd be better in person?"

"No! I'd much rather do a video call and let him rage without my neck too near to throttle." He chuckled, but he was actually pretty serious about the situation.

"I think they'll be happy for you when you tell them the reason behind it. I'm sure they only want you to be happy."

"Hmmph, I hope so," Willian answered. His thoughts turned to Valentina's family situation. He was certain his father would not be too thrilled with him being with a woman whose family had a questionable background. It was not like he had planned to fall in love or that he even had a say in the matter.

"You don't regret anything, do you, Willian?"

"What? No! I wouldn't change anything. My future is with you no matter what happens. I promise to tell my father tomorrow. Then we'll know where we stand moving forward."

"Good." She looked at her watch and sighed. "I should get going. Mom will have dinner almost ready and she hates it when we're late."

"Okay. I'll call you tomorrow when we have things arranged for the trip." He reached out and pulled her hand, so she was forced to lean forward. His lips met hers and the next few minutes were unaccounted for in both of their minds.

Valentina broke free and breathed deeply. "We have to be careful with that, too." She turned on the engine of the car and turned on the window defroster. The condensation did not change. "This might take a while," she teased. She rolled down her window in an effort to speed things along.

Willian saw the problem and accessed the elemy to clear the glass in an instant. He smiled at his success and asked, "Is that better?"

"Showoff! Someone might have seen, you know!" Valentina accused.

"I don't care. I want you to be safe and for that, you'll have to see out all of the windows." He flashed her another grin at his logic and then pulled on the door handle. Once he was out of the car, he leaned down and said, "I can't wait to see you again tomorrow. Have a great night and say hello to your brothers for me."

"Thanks, I will. See you tomorrow." She drove away as soon as Willian shut the door. She saw him waving in her rearview mirror and smiled in disbelief at her luck in having him find her. The fear she had withheld from Willian surfaced since she had seen the look of doubt on his face when she asked him if his parents would like her.

Jena certainly has a better pedigree than my own. After all, Jena is the grand-daughter of an Elder and had been Jehoban's student since she was six. What do I bring to the table? Valentina asked herself. Heck, I've only recently found out I'm from Tuala and I barely understand how to use the elemy. Maybe I should break things off with him before I cause him more trouble than he already has.

Her lips were still tingling with the intensity of their kiss. Just the idea of never seeing him again almost made her heart stop and breathing became difficult. She felt like she was on the verge of a panic attack and had to abandon her line of thinking before she began to feel better. There's no hope for it; he's stuck with me.

BEHN CAME into Valentina's bedroom after tapping lightly on her open door. "Hey, sis, do you have a minute?" When she nodded, he turned and closed the door for privacy. He could not risk their adoptive parents overhearing their conversations.

"This must be serious to warrant a closed-door meeting," Valentina teased to lighten the mood.

"It's not exactly serious; I just wanted to find out how today went in Manzanit. This is the first time you've been there. How were Rasa and Gevena?"

"And Willian?" she guessed.

"Well, of course!" Behn sat on the bed once she moved off to the side to give him room. "Are you two being careful? You've had a couple of outings now without one of us with you. I know how you are drawn together."

"Behn! It's not like we planned it! Besides, Mrs. Stel went with us to Manzanit today, so we weren't actually alone for very long, just when I drove him home."

"Really? Why did Mrs. Stel go with you? Did she say?"

"No, but she seemed pretty excited about discussing something with Rasa. Our guide separated us almost as soon as we got into the Residence. Behn, the place was ginormous. I've never been in a building which covered two city blocks before."

She spent the next few minutes describing the building and its people. Her brother was a good listener and hardly ever interrupted. She ended with, "Willian and I are going back tomorrow to practice crystal skills with Gevena. She's woefully behind in her studies and I think she's embarrassed to be in the classes with much younger students. I know I would be, too."

"Hmm, do you think I could come with you? I'd like more practice as well."

"I guess...I mean I don't mind, and I don't think Willian will care either. I just worry about making Gevena uncomfortable. She's pretty shy, you know."

"Okay, how about this, ask her about it tomorrow and then I can come the next time you go if she says yes."

"Cool. I like it!"

"So, what was Willian doing the whole time you were visiting with Gevena?"

"He was invited to tea with Elder Wilken. I'm not sure how long he was with him, but he seemed like he was pretty excited about something when he came to get me when it was time to leave."

"You didn't ask him about it? What were you doing the whole time after you returned from the Stel's house?"

"Well, I drove him back to his place and we parked out front. We just...you know...talked."

"Oh? Like with actual words or was it something different?"

Valentina blushed and had to look away from her brother's intense stare. When she heard him laughing, she had to laugh as well. "We did actually talk…a little."

"Hah! I knew it. Please be careful, Val! I'm not ready to be an uncle anytime soon."

Valentina's eyes grew round with disbelief. Just as quickly, her fist shot out and punched him in the arm. "That's not even funny, Behn!"

"Ouch!" he exclaimed while rubbing his arm. "Who said I was joking. I've actually experienced the intensity between you, remember?"

"As if I could forget, you scared me half to death. Anyway, that brings up something I'd like to ask you advice about."

"What's that?"

"Do you think I'm good enough for Willian?"

"Yes! Of course, you are, but sometimes I wonder if he's good enough for you!"

"No, Behn, I'm serious. Think about it for a second from his parents' perspective. Willian will one day become the Elder and his wife will be an important person in their society. Our background is a little…unorthodox, to say the least. Behn, we don't even know who our father is! Compare our life to that of Jena's. She's accomplished in many ways and her grandfather is an Elder himself. How am I supposed to compete with her?"

"You aren't. There's no competition when it comes to matters of the heart."

"Matters of the heart? Really, Behn, since when have you become so poetic?"

"Since I started falling for Juila, I guess."

"Really? Start talking mister!"

"What's there to say? I enjoy spending time with her. I think about her all of the time. I just worry about what's going to happen when they decide to return home to Tuala. Will it be after high school is over or will they leave sooner? I can't imagine leaving Mom and Dad; they deserve better."

"I know, I've thought the same thing. If we continue our relationships, then we'll both be in the same boat. Maybe Jon has it right with Sofia. She knows about us, but she isn't pressuring him one way or another."

"Has Willian been pressuring you?"

"No, no. It's not like that. He did mention today he wants me to meet his parents."

"And then you started doubting whether or not you were worthy of his special status?"

"Something like that."

"Look, Val, it's not like the two of you are going to run off and get married this week. You have a couple of years to discover whether or not you want to stay together. In the meantime, meet his folks, let them get to know you. Your crystal skill lessons will continue and eventually, you'll be right up to speed with anyone else in Tuala…probably better than most. Give it time, okay?"

"I guess. I just don't want to get in too deep if it's the wrong thing to do."

"As if you had a say in the matter!"

"I know, right?"

CHAPTER 36

Riccan hired a driver to take him home from the Miami Executive Airport. The different car gave him a chance to look for anyone suspicious near their home without being spotted. The tinted windows kept his identity secret from any onlookers. It was the perfect cover considering he had left the house via telepod and not in another vehicle.

Just where Jena had said, there was a car parked across the street from their property. He saw the same face as he had seen in the image he had projected from the cassette. Apparently, the spy had not received word yet from Dr. Gascon his assignment had been canceled. Riccan pulled out his phone and dialed 911.

"Yes, I'd like to report a suspicious person parked outside my property," he told the operator. He gave the details and then smiled as he hung up his phone. One more person was not going to be harassing his family.

When the car pulled into the driveway, he used his crystal power to open the gate without the code. They drove onto the property and the driver parked in front of the house. Riccan thanked the driver and let himself out. He watched the Towncar circle the driveway and go back down the long curving road.

Riccan turned around and let himself into the house through the front door. He hardly made it through the foyer before Amanda came running toward him. He was almost knocked over by the force of her body hitting his as her arms encircled his waist.

"Are you okay? Where have you been? What took you so long? How come you came in through the front door?"

"I'm alright, honey." He smiled down at her upturned face to reassure her. "Let's go sit in the living room, and I'll tell you all about my discoveries today." His expression turned serious as he realized he would have to tell her about Elder Wilken's death. Amanda may not have known him well, but she had just seen him earlier in the day. He was afraid it would upset her, so he wanted her to be sitting for the news.

Once his family had convened in the living room, Riccan turned to Amanda and said, "I 'ported to Manzanit to ask for Rasa's help with the Gate. Once I got there, I could tell there was a problem; the staff was running around, the guards outside seemed relieved to see me. I found Rasa crying in her room." He paused as he omitted the part of the story where Rasa had been naked. "When I asked her what was wrong she told me Elder Wilken had died."

"What? No! I was just talking with him! This can't be right, Riccan! He was fine; a little tired maybe, but he was laughing, and…and he was fine!" Amanda jumped up from the couch and stared down at Riccan in disbelief.

"Please sit down, Amanda. Rasa told me he died peacefully in his sleep. She was preparing for the release ceremony when I found her crying."

"What is a release ceremony?" Amanda asked as she returned to her seat.

"It's what we call it when an Elder dies. He is sent into the Ascension Gate without an end destination. His body will forever be between dimensions."

"That's terrible, Riccan!"

"No, think about it for a moment. Wilken spent his entire life guarding the Gate and the dimensions. Now he can continue to do so from within. Do you see now?"

"Not really. So, now Elder Wilkens has been 'released,' what happens now with Rasa?"

"I'm sure she's already been elevated to Elder status."

"This has got to be so hard on her. First, Elder Wilken gave her her own samara and then the same day he dies, and she has to take his place. It's too much, Riccan."

"What about a samara, Amanda? You said Rasa got a samara today?"

Amanda nodded and told the story of the day's events to her avid audience. "I was going to come home and tell you about the new part of the prophecy and have you set up a meeting with the group. But now I think we'll have to postpone it until Rasa gets settled into her new job.

"She was going to wait until tomorrow to claim her samara. I told her to keep it in a secure place until she had enough time to devote to the connection. Who knows how long she'll have to wait now?" Amanda suddenly went silent as her mind made an intuitive leap. "Do you think Elder Wilken died because he no longer had control of the samara? He did say his family was all long-lived and they had held the samara since they were first given. He said he was a descendant of the Watchers."

Riccan considered her questions and then nodded. "It's possible. Amanda, nobody forced Elder Wilken to give up the samara. You said yourself he gave it freely to Rasa and was pleased to find she was the true owner of it. He made the decision himself."

"I suppose, but it's still horrible to think he knew he was going to die by giving it up. I'm certain if Rasa knew the consequences, she never would have agreed to accept it. She loves Elder Wilken; she told me how much she still has to learn from him. Now she can't do it; she's left alone. I'm sure she's got to be scared."

"She has people there to help her. I'm sure Elder Debbon is going to be instructing her as well; he is First, after all, it's his job."

"I guess, I still feel horrible." She shook her head and tried to refocus. "So did you stick around to help her? Is that why you've been gone so long."

"No, Rasa insisted on sending me through to Central Park. She said it would help calm her nerves to have something to do."

"So you let her send you? Didn't you worry she'd lose her concentration and 'release' you, too?" Amanda was beginning to wish she had convinced Riccan to stay home for the evening rather than race off to defend the family. Just the thought of losing Riccan made her feel sick. She looked over at their daughters and wondered how they had remained so calm throughout the story. They did not even look concerned.

"Am I missing something here?" Amanda asked.

"You don't understand the dynamics of the Gates. There was no risk to my journey. Central Park is where it's designed to go, so she just had to make sure there was enough energy. Technically, I could have sent myself, and I was monitoring the power as I went. I'm not stupid, Amanda. I do have some self-preservation."

"Okay, so go on with your story, Riccan."

Riccan went through the events and how he decided to come home by conventional means. "One good thing, I most likely neutralized the stalker on the way in. He must have left his cell phone on silent and didn't receive the message from Gascon yet. Anyway, he's out of the picture."

"So what are you going to do about your telepod? It's still in Manzanit, right?"

"Maybe you could take me there tomorrow in your telepod," Riccan suggested with a quirked eyebrow. "It's either that or I take your telepod to work tomorrow leaving you without one at all. The choice is yours."

"It's not much of a choice," she pouted. "Besides, Willian asked to borrow my telepod to go to Manzanit tomorrow with Valentina. Maybe you could hitch a ride with him; I want to be able to sleep in."

"Oh, really? Foisting me off already, are you? Even after I avenged the family honor?"

"Oh, please, I think you're being a bit melodramatic. I would offer to go if I thought Rasa might need me, but somehow I think she'll be much too busy to entertain a social call."

"You're probably right. Okay, I'll call Willian and see if he can get here early enough for me to be to work on time."

WITH TIRSHA HOLDING onto his arm, Petre walked across the street to his house. It was pretty spectacular to be seeing inside it for the first time with the woman he hoped to spend the rest of his life. How perfect would it be for Corva to live across the street from the family who had raised her and still be with her mother? This was the solution to Tirsha's problem for which he had been searching all along.

"It's beautiful, Petre! I just can't believe how lucky you've been. Aren't you glad you went to see Elder Daven now? I'm sure your conscience feels lighter," Tirsha whispered. They stood in the foyer, and she was nervous about who might hear their conversation.

"So true, Tirsha. You were right to talk me into it. Let's take a tour; shall we?" Petre began to walk down the hallway and had to smile. "Is it just me, or does this floor plan seem like the mirror image of Captain Ahn's house?"

"You know, I think you might be right. There is a slight difference, though. I think these rooms might be slightly smaller. Does all this furniture come with the house, too? Oh, I hope so, it's just perfect. Don't you think?"

Petre had actually been thinking about how formal everything looked, which made him slightly uncomfortable, but if Tirsha liked it, then he could learn to as well. He grinned at Tirsha and said, "Elder Rylon said the house was fully equipped, even with staff. I have to assume the furniture stays."

They walked through room after room, encountering a cook in the kitchen and a maid in the family room. When they went upstairs and discovered the three bedrooms and two bathrooms, each space had its own theme of color and design. Nothing was left to do to make the house more livable.

"I'm so happy for you, Petre. This home is so lovely, and I'm sure you'll be content here."

"It'll only bring me joy if you are here with me, Tirsha."

"What are you saying, Petre? I can't live here with you; we're not married. I'm not even sure what we are to one another."

"Do you really think that? I thought I made my intentions clear where you're concerned. Tirsha, I want to be with you forever. I want to marry you and have you move in here with me." He turned to face her and held both of her hands in his. "Please tell me you want the same thing."

"Oh, Petre, I do! I just…I just need more time. My whole life has changed in a matter of days; please understand." Tirsha's eyes began to fill with tears.

"Hey, hey, don't cry, Tirsha. I understand, and I'll take this as slow as you want. I'll wait forever for you." He pulled her against his chest and rubbed her back slowly as he continued to make shushing noises.

"Thank you, Petre. I'm sorry I'm such a mess of emotions. I didn't used to be like this."

"Hey, no worries. We can take things slowly; you can come over and visit whenever you want. We can eat our meals together, and you can bring Corva over here so she can get used to both of us. This is going to work, Tirsha; trust me."

Tirsha sniffled loudly and pulled away from him as she nodded. "I believe you, Petre, and I agree this is the perfect solution for all of us. I never wanted to take Corva away from Barla and Ahn, she thinks of them as her parents. I've been trying to find a solution short of living with them forever, which just seemed like I was asking a bit too much of their hospitality."

"Good, then we're agreed. You are welcome in this house any time, day or night: no invitation needed, you understand?"

She nodded and smiled up at him with excitement over the new possibilities for their lives together. For the first time, she could see a way to work everything out for everyone to be happy. She had the ability to be with a man who loved and adored her and, she had to admit to herself, it was slightly scary to contemplate.

To keep from thinking too long on her last thought, she shook her head to clear her mind and said, "Let's walk through the house again. I'm sure I missed so much the first time, and I want to know it all!"

Petre smiled and gestured for her to lead the way. He happily followed after her, listening to her running commentary of the beauty of each room, the proportions, and so many other details which interested him not at all. This was probably the happiest day he had ever known.

CHAPTER 37

Riccan had let Willian pilot the telepod to Manzanit just as Amanda had done the day before. He was interested in seeing how other pilots operated the machinery since it gave him insights in innovations for future models. He gladly answered all of Willian's questions about the programming and the placement of different controls. It was fun having an interested listener when he talked about one of his favorite subjects. As an avid pilot, both in Tuala and Earth, Riccan loved all things avionic.

They arrived on the landing field only a few spaces away from where Riccan had parked his telepod. He did not want to have to time his arrival to work, so he hustled out and jogged over to his own 'pod. In less than a minute, he was ready to leave. With a final wave out the window, Riccan and his telepod blinked out of sight.

Willian turned around in the pilot's seat and smiled mischievously at Valentina. "We don't have anywhere to be until lunchtime when Gevena gets out of school. What do you want to do? What do you want to see?"

Valentina, sitting in the back seat in front of the open telepod door, shrugged her shoulders as she peered outside. "I don't even know what to ask to see. I've never been to a city before in Tuala. You've seen where I was born; it's slightly primitive compared to this. I mean, we didn't even have a patil until a couple of weeks ago when Mom asked for one. Why don't you surprise me?"

"Great! I know just the thing! Come on; let's go." Willian jumped out of his seat and held out his hand for Valentina. He noticed her fingers shook slightly when he wrapped his fingers around hers. "Was this trip a little better?"

"Yes. I just kept concentrating on where we were going and not how we were going to get there. It was a little easier."

"And each time will be better than the last," he assured her as he stepped onto the ramp and into the sunshine. "The day sure looks a lot warmer than it feels," he commented as the wind blew his hair over his eyes.

"Oh, brrr! I'm so glad it doesn't get this cold in Florida," she announced as she grabbed the lapels of her light jacket and pulled them close together.

"Hey," Willian leaned close and whispered, "don't mention the names of places on Earth here. Okay? If you want, you can call it Pantano, after all, it is the same geographical place."

"Oops, I'm sorry. I'm going to have to watch what I say so I don't draw attention to us." She looked down at her feet and chided herself again for her carelessness. She knew what the people of Tuala thought about *old souls*, as they termed the people from Earth, they were scared of them. It still did not make much sense to Valentina since the *old souls* were essentially powerless in Tuala. It would be scarier for a Tualan to come to Earth when they knew how to use extraordinary powers through their birth crystals using the elemy.

Willian tugged on Valentina's hand until she moved off of the ramp. He palmed the door to close, and they walked across the landing field to the exit they had used the day before. Once there, Willian flagged a transport vehicle and instructed the pilot to take them to the marketplace. A few minutes later, they got out. Willian let Valentina stare for a bit to get her bearings before he led her down the many aisles of goods, wares, textiles, and trinkets.

"There's so much stuff here, I almost feel drunk with the sights," Valentina whispered. She paused to touch the fabric hanging from the corner post of a stall. "This feels amazing, and I love the bright colors."

"You know, we should buy you a couple of outfits to help you fit in a little better," he suggested.

"Do I stick out too much?"

"Only a little." He turned his head, pretending to look around, as he smiled at her consternation.

"Okay, smarty pants, pick me out some stuff then. Make me look unremarkable."

"Unremarkable? Never! I'll make you look amazing, like a first-daughter!"

"A first-daughter? What's that?" she whispered.

"It's the term used to describe a boy's betrothed. Jena was the first-daughter to my parents. I'm sorry; I probably shouldn't have brought it up." Willian began to fiddle with some garments on the table in front of them.

"Hey, Willian, I don't want you to think you can't talk about your time with Jena. She was a big part of your past, and she's my friend. I know how things were and how they are now. It's really okay, you know?"

"I'm glad you understand. I just haven't said much about that time because I didn't want to make you feel like a replacement."

"Am I? A replacement, I mean?"

"NO! Never," his gaze immediately turned to her face and saw her smiling devilishly. "Hey, that wasn't funny!"

"Come on, quit stalling and pick something out for me."

They continued to wander through the market, gathering supplies, gifts, and clothes. The people seemed rather subdued as they moved through the crowds. Willian wondered what had happened to make the usually cheerful people so quiet and withdrawn.

Willian checked his timepiece and realized they were going to have to hustle to get back to the Residence in time for Gevena's lesson. He was unsure if they were going to be able to eat so he grabbed some hot glawlets from one of the vendors near where they could catch a transport.

He handed one of the rolls to Valentina with a grin and said, "Have you had one of these before?"

"I don't think so. What is it?" She took the warm roll, surprised at how heavy it was, and looked at it carefully.

"A glawlet is filled with a poached egg and sausage gravy. If you have it at home, then the gravy would be on the outside, but here in the marketplace, it would be pretty messy, so they inverted it. Give it a bite and let me know if you want a second one before we go."

Valentina complied and took a large bite. She was pretty fearless when it came to food, and this time was no disappointment. Her mouth was too full to reply, but she hummed her pleasure and nodded her head in agreement.

Willian turned and ordered two more before he flagged a transport. They ate on the way to the Residence with their bags of purchases stacked around their feet. By the time they got to their stop, they were almost finished eating. Willian shoved his last bite into his mouth and began gathering the bags after he paid the pilot.

They got to the main gate and received the same solemn reception as they had found in the market. "Is it just me, or does everyone seem sadder today than they were yesterday?" Willian whispered to Valentina as they entered the main corridor.

"I was just thinking the same thing. I felt it in the market, but I just thought it was normal for there. But, then the guards looked downright beat when we go here. There's definitely something going on. Maybe Gevena will know something. Let's hurry up and go see her. Besides, you still have a promise to keep with me when we get there."

"A promise?"

"You know, calling your dad on the patil?"

"Oh, that promise."

"Yeah. You need to get it handled, Willian, and you know it."

"I know. I know. Fine, I'll do it as soon as I get to a patil. You might have to remind me, however."

"You can count on it."

They finally arrived at the West wing and entered the outer public rooms where Gevena lived. They did not even have to search for her as she was already waiting for them. She seemed down, like everyone else. When they got close enough, Willian asked, "What's with everyone today? It's so quiet around here."

"Haven't you heard?"

"No, heard what?"

"Elder Wilken died yesterday."

"What? No! I just had tea with him. We spent the whole afternoon together. There's got to be some kind of mistake." Willian sank onto the couch and held his head between his palms. It seemed unreal; his friend was gone? He had a hard time making sense of it all. He felt an arm cross over his shoulders and pull him to the side.

"I'm sorry, Willian," Valentina soothed him while she rubbed his arm and held him tightly to her chest. "I know you respected him and thought of him as a friend. We don't have to stay if you want to go home to grieve."

"I just need a minute to process this, besides, leaving won't bring him back. Maybe I should go see Rasa, I mean Elder Rasa, and see if she needs anything." It felt so strange to give her name the title to which she was not entitled to use. To him, she was just a teacher and a friend. He drew in a deep breath and shook his head, lifting it from his hands. The tears flowed freely down his cheeks, and he suddenly stood up. "I'll be right back." He promptly left the room.

RASA WOKE up with the sunlight caressing the side of her face. She stretched and rolled over out of the bright light wishing she could continue the dream which was slipping away even as she tried to recall it. Her thoughts suddenly turned dark as she recalled a nightmare as well. She shook her head and sat up in bed, rubbing the sleep from her eyes as she did so.

She blinked a few times before she could clearly see the white garment draped across the foot of her bed. Shaking her head in confusion, she crawled across the top of the bed and touched the cloth. "No!" she groaned out loud as she realized the nightmare had been real. Elder Wilken was dead, and she was the new Elder for Manzanit. Fresh tears poured from her eyes as she pushed the clothing away from her and sat hard, rocking back and forth to comfort herself from the pain.

The chill of her nakedness made her come back to her senses. She scooted off the side of the bed, picked up the ceremonial robe, and walked over to the wardrobe. The fabric was badly wrinkled, and she hung it up, hoping it would smooth out over time. Her hand caressed it lightly and reverently, recalling the ceremony making her the Elder and changing her life forever.

Her jaw began to shake with the cold which was now seeping up her legs from the cold floor under her bare feet. Slightly embarrassed, she also recalled this was the exact spot she had stood the evening before when Riccan had walked in. She had not even considered her nakedness as she had clung to him for comfort. She wondered what Riccan had thought about the whole thing and if she had made him uncomfortable. Hopefully, their relationship would not be affected by the whole incident.

She grabbed another outfit, also white, which was indicative of her new status. The fabric was perfect; she had never even tried them on before, as there had been no need. She draped the items over her arm and crossed her room to take a warm bath. From the angle of the sun, she determined there was still time for herself before she had to face the day.

After a satisfying soak, thoroughly warming her body to the core, she pulled the plug on the drain and sighed as she pulled herself out of the tub and began drying herself off. She braided her hair and looped it up to keep the long locks out of her way. Knowing she was stalling, she finally picked up her new clothes and put them on. Turning first one way, and then the other in front of the mirror, she was impressed with the perfect fit. Her seamstress was an absolute wonder with her invisible stitches and attention to detail.

With one final look to make sure she looked the part of her new position, she turned and left the room. She only paused slightly as she passed the sitting area where just the day before, she had been visiting with Amanda, enjoying her company, and living carefree. Today was a different matter altogether. Her first task of the day was to go back to the conference room to gather any documents left behind by Elder Wilken so she could review them and begin where he left off.

CHAPTER 38

Willian ran down the halls until he reached Elder Wilken's rooms. The doors were open, and people were coming and going carrying laundry, clothes, and cleaning supplies. Any personal touches of the previous occupant were gone, the room was just that: a spare suite of rooms.

His last hope died thinking it might have been a terrible mistake. He turned and sauntered, his eyes shifted toward the last place he had spent with the old Elder. Motion caught his attention, and he realized the white-robed figure was who he had been searching for. "Rasa?" he called out.

She turned rapidly and looked over to him, clearly not expecting to see him. Willian thought she looked tired and wondered if she had slept at all the night before. He rushed forward to catch up with her and to offer his condolences.

"I just heard about Elder Wilken. Are you okay? Do you need anything?"

"Thank you, Willian. I'm fine for now, but I may take you up on your offer once I start getting into all of the details."

"Anytime. Really."

"What are you doing here so early?"

"Early? It's already noon. Did you just wake up?"

"Noon? Seriously. Yes, I got up a while ago, but I thought it was rather earlier. Why are you here?"

"Oh, I offered to tutor Val and Gevena together to get them both up to speed in their lessons."

"Val…oh, Willian, I think I might have messed up." She guiltily looked away from him as she recalled her conversation with his father.

"What are you talking about?"

"Your father was here last night for the ceremony. I asked him how he was doing since the betrothal was dissolved…"

Willian groaned, feeling physically ill as he realized what she was telling him.

"I'm sorry, Willian; I thought you already told him. I had no idea…I'm so sorry."

"It's not your fault, Rasa, I should have told him already. I actually promised Val I'd call him today, but it's going to be a little more difficult getting a word in edgewise since he's drawn his own conclusion."

"I could talk to him for you if you want. Amanda told me the circumstances…" Rasa stopped talking once Willian began shaking his head.

"No, this is my mess to clean up. Do you think I could use the patil in your office? I should take care of this right away."

"Sure, yes! You remember where it is, right?"

"Yeah, but I wish I could lose myself along the way. I've been dreading this conversation. You know, I'm not sure who'll be more upset, my father or my mother."

"Good luck, Willian. I'm sorry I made it more difficult for you."

"Don't worry about it. I'll let you get back to your work. If you need me later, I'll be with Gevena."

"Okay, thanks. Talk to you later."

Willian watched her walk away; her carefree spirit seemed diminished. He felt the same way himself since he knew his father was upset. He turned around the corner and dragged his feet more as he got closer to the office. *This isn't going to get easier with any more delaying,* he scolded himself.

Once he got to the office, he carefully closed the door behind him. He crossed the room and sat at her desk, shifting the chair until it was the right angle, and pulling the keyboard out to use. Taking several deep breaths, Willian tapped the screen of the patil, selected the video call button, and then typed in his father's personal code, used only for immediate family.

His hopes that his dad would be away from his desk were soon dashed when his face filled the screen. He did not look happy to see his son.

"So you finally got around to calling me, huh?"

"Sorry, Dad, it's not very easy to do on Earth."

"I talked with your mom last night; she's pretty upset. What do you have to say for yourself?"

Willian closed his eyes, wishing all the more he had found an opportunity to present his case to his parents before they learned on their own. *Too late for that,* he thought. "As you know, I went to Earth to work things out with Jena. Well, things were going really well, and I thought I was going to make her want to stay with me. Then I found my soul-mate and everything changed.

"There was no way Jena and I could be together once that happened. It wouldn't be fair to either of us. Jena saw it was true, and asked for the dissolution."

"And Daven just happened to be there and all-too-happy to oblige? I had a few choice words for him last night as well. This matter is not going unpunished for him or for you, Willian. I hope you understand."

"Dad, please listen. Elder Daven had no choice; he's not to blame. Blame me if you have to, but don't do anything to Elder Daven. Please!"

"Don't worry, Willian; you're in plenty of trouble and don't try to tell me how to handle the other Elders. You're not one of us yet, so you don't get a vote."

"Dad! Will you let me explain?"

"Yes, you can do it in person. Your vacation to Earth is hereby canceled. Plan on returning home today by dinner. Your mother has something she'd like to say to you."

"No, Dad, I won't be doing that. I will come home to talk with you, but I won't be coming alone, and I won't be staying."

"Willian, watch your tone with me. If you value your place in our family, you will do as you're told. I see you're in Manzanit; it won't take you long to get yourself here."

"I'm sorry, Dad; but I have other obligations for my time today. I'll let you know when I can arrange a trip home. I'll talk to you soon." He disconnected the call and almost hyperventilated because of his brazen act of defiance.

Still a little shaky in the knees, Willian stood up and had to hold himself up against the edge of the desk as he took several deep breaths. Never before had he openly been defiant with his father and he was certain this was going to have some negative repercussions. He wished he had handled the situation better, if not for himself, then for Val or Elder Daven. They were going to get punished for him being a coward, and it just was not right.

Feeling self-righteous, Willian returned to Gevena's suite of rooms and sat across from the girls. He could see the two had been keeping themselves busy talking. He wished he would have stayed with them rather than going off to find Rasa.

"Are you ready to begin?" he asked.

"Are you?" Valentina asked back, leaning forward and searching his face for any indication of how the conversation had gone.

"Yes. I need a distraction right now. Gevena, why don't you show me what you know already? Once I get a base-line of your skills, I'll know how best to move you further along."

Gevena proceeded to demonstrate her skills in the order they were traditionally taught. She sat back on the couch and closed her eyes to concentrate as she pulled energy out of her birth crystal, moved it over in front of Valentina, and then put the elemy back into her birth crystal. Once completed she sighed with satisfaction and opened her eyes, hoping to get approval before continuing.

"Well done, Gevena. Please keep going," Willian offered, correctly interpreting her look.

She smiled shyly and then closed her eyes again.

Willian felt a breeze blow by him and nodded with satisfaction of the fourth skill properly performed. "Keep going," he encouraged.

She opened her eyes and said, "I need to get a glass of water to continue."

"I'll get it," Willian offered and then pointed down at the table in front of them where the needed glass suddenly appeared. "It's your turn now."

"You made it look so easy! Will I be able to do it someday, too?"

"Absolutely. Are you stalling?"

"Maybe a little." She took a dramatic breath and leaned forward to concentrate on the water in the glass. Nothing seemed to be happening, and she suddenly stopped trying. She turned to Valentina and asked, "Can you do this already?"

"Yes, I just learned. You're doing great. Try again."

"Oh, fine!" She returned her attention to the glass until small bubbles appeared on the bottom of the water. They floated to the surface and more formed until all of the water contained bubbles, and the steam was rising from the hot liquid. "I did it!" She looked up with a satisfied grin over at Willian and then at Valentina.

"Great, Gevena. Now make it freeze," Valentina suggested.

"Oh, I should wait for it to cool down first. It'll make it go faster." She sat back, fully prepared to wait for as long as it took. Her skills were getting sketchier, and she hated showing people how miserable she was at it.

"Actually, hot water turns to ice much easier than cold," Willian contradicted her. "Try imagining the molecules moving and sticking to one another to form a solid block."

"Okay, I think I can do it," she said with less enthusiasm this time. Using his direction, she found it was much easier than ever to get the water to form ice, effectively completing the sixth skill. "Hey, it was pretty easy! I've always thought cold water would be faster, but you're right, having it hot was even better. You know, I've always wondered why we learned these things in this order. Do you know why?"

"Yes, the skills build on one another. Each one teaches you a new aspect of either the elemy or the object you're working with. Once you get to the really advanced levels, you will be using both at the same time as well as your imagination instead of a physical object."

"Oh, my, I don't think I'll be up for anything so innovative. What level have you achieved, Willian?"

"I'm only on the twenty-fourth level, but I know others who are beyond any of the numbered skills, creating their own levels with their imagination. I hope to get there one day myself."

Gevena shook her head in awe, "Only level twenty-four, he says!" She looked over to Valentina and rolled her eyes. "Where are you?"

"I've gotten through the first eleven levels with relative ease.

I'm still working on mastering the creation level. My brothers and I are pretty competitive, so we keep helping one another to move along."

"That would be nice," Gevena said wistfully. "I don't have anyone here to compete with. The little kids in my class only laugh at me when I mess things up. Nobody has offered to help me get better until you two."

"I know it's not easy, but you need to ignore what others think about you and your skills. They each learn in their own way, much as you do. We all have unique talents, and I think you're base skills are done very well. We just need to polish them up a little, and then you'll find them easier and faster to achieve."

"Do you really think I can do this? I've had so many doubts!"

"Belief in yourself is the first step to success," Willian quoted his father's favorite saying.

All of them turned around in surprise when a male voice spoke from the doorway. "It's good to know you've heard something I've told you, Willian."

"Father!" Willian said as he jumped up from the couch and turned to face him.

Gevena also jumped up and dropped her head in submission to the Elder. Even though she had never met him before, his clothing and stance indicated his position.

Valentina remained sitting on the couch, wondering what she should do, concerned for Willian's confrontation with his father. Belatedly, Valentina stood up and awkwardly mirrored Gevena's pose while she tried to keep watching the scene unfolding before her. This powerful-looking man was the one person she needed to impress if she planned on having a future with his son. She was terrified of failing.

CHAPTER 39

"It's good to see your 'prior obligation' is using your talents to help others here in Tuala," Debbon remarked sarcastically. He had been furious when Willian had hung up on him, but he also had a grudging respect for his son's ability to stand up to him in the face of his anger. Willian had come a long way in the past few mesans, and he was proud to see he was using what he had learned to help others rather than just helping himself. This was progress, but he was not going to let his son know.

"Yes, Father. I had promised Gevena I would tutor her until her skills were equal to the other kids our age. She has been treated poorly and has not been allowed to attend school in several anons."

"I see. That explains one of these girls. What about the other one?"

Willian looked back at Valentina and knew this was his opportunity to introduce his future wife to his father. He walked around the table and held out his hand to her. When their hands touched, the electricity between them flared with the emotions they were both feeling.

Gevena gasped beside them and hastily stepped aside.

Debbon's eyebrows rose as he also felt the spike in power. He had never experienced anything like it, and he was instantly curious as to its source. He watched his son's expression change from timid to determined as he brought the girl forward to him.

"Father, it is my pleasure to introduce to you Valentina, my future wife."

Expecting a simple introduction, Debbon was caught off guard at his son's declaration. He immediately inspected the girl to see what made her so special to capture his son's interest so rapidly and fully. The hair on his arms had risen when they approached, and he noticed the hair on the back of his neck was also beginning to move. "What's the meaning of this, Willian? Why do you two practically spark with energy? Who is this girl and where did she come from?"

Valentina took her hand out of Willian's and offered it to Debbon. She saw he was reluctant to touch her, but he mastered himself enough to touch her fingers in greeting. "I was born in the Roanoke Colony to Vinia. I'm pleased to meet you, Elder Debbon. Willian has told me a lot about you."

"It's nice to meet you, as well. Unfortunately, Willian has told us nothing about you." He looked pointedly over at his son and said, "When you are through with your lesson here today, then the two of you will come home to have dinner. It will give us a chance to learn all about you."

Valentina's head swiveled immediately to Willian, and her eyes were wide with fright.

"We won't have time, Father. I promised Valentina's parents she'd be home for dinner."

"We have all the time in the world, Willian, and you know it.

Now, I won't take no for an answer. Your mother wants to see you."

Knowing when to back down, Willian nodded and said, "As you wish, Father."

"Good! Since we've settled the matter, I'd like to see Gevena's crystal skills for myself." He moved past where Willian and Valentina stood over to the frightened girl. She looked like a scared foxl, ready to bolt in an instant.

"I'm sorry, Val. This was bound to happen at some point."

"I'm scared."

"Well, at least you have an outfit to wear for dinner."

She rolled her eyes and quipped, "That's not much comfort!"

"It's all I've got for you. Come on; we need to rescue Gevena from my father."

Both Willian and Valentina were impressed with how Elder Debbon handled Gevena's fear of him. Within a few minutes, the girl was demonstrating the first six skills with the ease of someone who had been doing them for anons. Even Gevena was shocked and pleased to find she was able to do them.

By the time they needed to leave, Gevena was laughing with Elder Debbon as she moved objects from one location to another. With his expert instruction, Gevena had advanced another three levels in one sitting; an almost unheard of feat.

"I think we've done enough for today, Gevena. You are an excellent student and a joy to work with," Debbon said with a genuine smile for the gentle girl. While she had been concentrating on her lessons, he had gently prodded her memories to find out what was blocking her from accessing her full capabilities. It was a simple matter of untangling her fear of failure to allow her to feel success instead.

"Thank you, Elder Debbon. I really enjoyed learning from you. I had no idea it could be so much fun. Why I don't even feel tired, and we got so much accomplished!" Gevena grinned more confidently than any in the room had ever seen her.

"It was my pleasure, Gevena. It's been anons since I've taught these lessons and it was a good refresher for me as well." He slapped his palms on his thighs and rose to his feet. He turned to Willian and asked, "Are you ready?"

"Almost," Willian answered. "Valentina wanted to change for dinner first." He looked through several of the bags before he came to the one he wanted. He handed it to Valentina and winked.

She wanted to say something snide back to him, but she managed to hold her tongue and reached for the bag. "May I use your bedroom for a minute, Gevena?"

"Sure. I'll come with you. I'd like to see what you bought as well." Gevena came up beside Valentina and accompanied her into the room. She sat on the bed and watched while Valentina dug through the bag and pulled out the clothes.

"What are these?" she asked in confusion.

Gevena giggled at her friend's frustration and said, "Here, let me help you." She sorted out an appropriate outfit and helped her get dressed as swiftly as possible. "There! You look amazing."

"I do? I feel foolish. Are you sure this is what it's supposed to look like?"

"Yes, trust me; it's perfect for dinner at the Elder's house. You're so lucky, Valentina. Elder Debbon is such a nice man. At first, I was scared of him, but he is a really great teacher, better than any I've ever had before. I can't wait until I go to school tomorrow and show them how far I've progressed. Maybe now they won't laugh at me so much."

"Yes, Elder Debbon did say you were an excellent student. Maybe you should tell the other kids about how you were tutored by an Elder; it might shut them up."

"He's not just 'an' Elder; he's First Elder. I might just happen to mention it, or maybe not." She shrugged as she thought of all of her different options. It might be more satisfying to have them wonder at her new skills and let them stew over it.

"Okay, I guess I don't have any other reason to stay in here much longer. Will I see you tomorrow? Oh, my brother wanted to know if you'd mind if he tagged along to get extra lessons with us."

"No, I think it'd be fun to have a bigger group. Since I'm not so far behind, it'll be easier for all of us to practice, don't you think?"

"I do!" She reached over and gave Gevena a quick hug before she dumped her Earth clothes into the bag and hauled it all out of the bedroom. "I'm ready," she announced as she entered the sitting room.

"Great, we can take the Gate back to our Residence," Debbon announced. He never even noticed Valentina's alarmed expression since he was so eager to get his son home. Debbon walked out of the room, expecting the others to follow him.

Willian once again reached for Valentina's hand to offer whatever comfort he could. This was not how he had planned for his parents to meet her, but she looked amazing, and he told her so. They were moving ahead with their lives, and it was starting with dinner with his folks.

Debbon had them stand in the depression of the Gate while he fiddled with the controls a few feet away. Valentina's eyes were wide as she took in her first glimpse of the fabled Gates and hoped she would not disgrace herself during the transfer. It was one thing to have a telepod surrounding her between locations; it was quite another to have nothing to keep her safe. She felt dangerously exposed and wished she were anywhere but where she was at the moment.

Satisfied with his changes, Debbon joined the two kids in the center of the Gate's depression in the ground. He concentrated on their destination and used a small amount of elemy to activate the transfer. Within three seconds they were moved over three thousand gania southwest to Debbon's Residence. They marched up the stairs, out the side hallway door, and across the lawn to Debbon's personal telepod. One more short telepod trip and they were parked outside of Debbon's personal estate.

"This is my home," Willian announced the obvious.

"I'm glad you still recognize that, Willian," Debbon said sarcastically as he opened the telepod door and left the aircraft ahead of them.

"I'm sorry my father's being so rude, Val. He's normally really nice."

"I know, I saw how he was with Gevena. Trust me; it's the only thing which has kept me from running scared!" She looked around and admired the grandeur of the home. It was bigger than any other house she had seen in Tuala but smaller than Jena's home back on Earth.

Willian, once again, took Valentina's hand in his own and led her into the house. He knew she was nervous, mostly because he shared the same sentiment. This was probably the most significant meeting to ever take place for him, and it had to go perfectly. They walked through the foyer and to the first set of doors. Willian knew his parents would seat themselves in the meeting room; it's where they held all important discussions.

"Are you ready for this?" he asked, gulping down his own anxiety.

"Just don't let me go," she whispered back with a nod of her head.

"Never." Squeezing her hand, he opened the door to find both of his parents staring at them, their expressions mirrors of disapproval. Willian squared his shoulders, fully prepared to defend his relationship regardless of their opinions in the matter of his personal life.

They entered the room together and remained standing in the awkward silence. Chelesa was the first to make any move as she stood up and moved directly in front of her son. She never even looked over at Valentina; her focus was solely on her son and his best interest.

"Willian, why have you been so hasty? Didn't you consider what this would mean for your father's standing with the other Elders? I've never been so heart-sick as when your father told me about Jena dissolving your betrothal." She had to stop talking as a strange feeling came over her. The hairs raised all over her body, and she absently brushed her hand over her forearm.

"I don't know what happened to you while you were on Earth, but it's obvious something has changed you, Willian, and I'm not sure it's been for the good." She lifted her hand and touched Willian's cheek in concern. "Oh!" she exclaimed as her eyes grew wide and she remained frozen in her place.

"Chelesa! What's wrong? Willian, what are you doing to your mother?" Debbon raced forward to grab his wife away from their son.

At the same time, Willian released Valentina's hand to hold his mother's shoulders to keep her from collapsing. The moment his bond was broken with his soul-mate, his mother's senses returned. "Mom! Are you okay? What happened?" he asked even as he began to realize exactly what she had experienced.

Chelesa's eyes darted over to Valentina, wonder still evident in her expression. Staring at Valentina, Chelesa spoke to her husband behind her, "Debbon, I need to speak with you privately. NOW!"

Debbon was shocked at his wife's tone since she was usually soft-spoken and never raised her voice to him, not even in private. "Of course, Chelesa. We can go to your office."

She nodded curtly, stepped around her son, and left the room without looking back.

CHAPTER 40

Debbon glared once at his son before he also left the room. When he reached the office, he was surprised at his wife's animated expression and her pacing across the room. "What is it? What happened?"

"At first, I was scared, but then I had a flash of memory come to me."

"What are you talking about?"

"That girl, Debbon! Pay attention."

"I would if you were making more sense."

"Fine, remember when we were called to meet with Jehoban?"

"I could hardly forget. What does this girl have to do with the meeting?"

"Nothing directly. Okay, so after the meeting, the same group of people met again, and Amanda gave us the history she remembered and asked us to review it."

"Yes, I still don't understand. Chelesa, please get to the point."

"I'm working on it. Do you remember anons ago when Willian

was little how you had the strange episode like you were glimpsing the future."

"Yes, we've talked about this before when we agreed to betroth Jena to Willian. She was the one I had seen."

"No, I don't think so. Let's go through that time again and compare it to the version of it which Amanda wrote down in her journal."

Debbon did as he was asked, still slightly unnerved by Amanda's ability to know things she had not even been present for in the first place. "So, I had the vision right after I read Petre's mind after I found out he had held Jinya hostage. In Amanda's journal, she had herself in the place of Jinya, so that part was different."

"Keep going."

"So in my vision, I had received a child from Petre who was in danger, which also happened, but it was anons after Willian and Jena were already betrothed."

"We kept the child long enough for her mother to come and get her from us. We knew Petre's story was a lie when he said she was his child," Chelesa reminded him.

Debbon shook his head, still trying to figure out where Chelesa was going with this. "Yes, Jinya came and got her from us before we could adopt her because we wanted to keep the child away from Petre."

"Do you remember feeling that child's energy?"

"Yes, it was hard to forget. Yet, if you recall, I felt the same thing when I was around Jena when she was a child. It's what made me know she was the girl for our son's future."

"Yes, you felt the energy, but Willian never did! Well, I just got the same feeling when I touched Willian's cheek back there," she stated as she pointed behind her to where they had left the kids.

"So...I don't understand how the one relates to the other, Chelesa."

Chelesa's excitement dimmed slightly because she was hoping Debbon would see the correlation which was eluding her as well. There was something special about this girl Willian had brought home, but it still did not make sense. "I think we should hear these two out before we begin making any accusations. Maybe we were wrong about Jena and Willian being a good match, this girl might be better suited, based on what I just felt."

"So you want us to make nice and get answers from them before we tell them it's not going to work out?"

"Something like that. Can you do it, Debbon?"

"I will because you asked, but I still don't see how it'll ever work out for those two. We don't even know anything about her or how they met. Willian's going to be in a position of power one day, and we can't have some interloper coming along and ruining his future."

"I know, Debbon. Let's just see." She led the way back to the meeting room and announced to the kids, "Dinner is served. Shall we go in and eat?"

Willian and Valentina had been sitting on the couch, heads almost touching as they were discussing what could possibly be happening with his parents. They both sprang up instantly and hurried over to where his parents were waiting. As a group, they silently entered the formal dining room, and all congregated around one end of the twenty-person table.

As the dishes were being served, Debbon turned to Valentina and asked, "You said you were from the Roanoke Colony. Is that where you and Willian met?"

"No." She turned and looked urgently at Willian to answer as he saw fit.

There was continued silence as Willian waited until the room had cleared of all of the house staff and they were left in privacy. "We met in the high school on Earth," Willian rushed to answer.

Debbon set down his fork and turned his full attention on his son. "Why don't you tell us the whole story because right now we are confused?"

Valentina looked questioningly at Willian and saw his slight nod to continue. "When I was eight, my mom sent my brothers and me to Earth to keep us safe from the leader of Roanoke. We were adopted by a family and have been living there for another eight years."

"Anons," Willian corrected automatically. "We call 'years' anons here."

"How did your mother manage to do it?" Chelesa asked, suddenly interested in this new twist, and ignoring her son's interruption.

"She had this thing, a crystal skull, which I found out later was a samara, which had been given to her by a wise-woman. She was told to use it in the event of an emergency. I just found out recently my mother sent us away the day before the leader was going to make me his wife."

"But you said you were only eight!" Chelesa exclaimed.

"Where is the samara?" Debbon asked at the same time his wife spoke.

"Mrs. Stel went back to the Colony and recovered the samara already," Valentina answered.

"I didn't know about that, Val. Why didn't you tell me?"

"Maybe because I didn't know it was important to you."

"Why do you call her Val, Willian? Has she lost honor?" Chelesa asked suddenly.

"No, Mom, it's just her nickname on Earth. I'll have to remember to use her full name when we're here."

"Always, unless you want others to question her suitability," Chelesa agreed. "How did Elder Debbon come to be involved in the breaking of your betrothal?"

"He was helping Valentina's mom with the Roanoke Colony, and he brought Jena and Juila with him," Willian replied vaguely.

Chelesa tried to puzzle it all together and finally turned back to Valentina and asked, "How come you spent so much time on Earth if you knew where your mom was?"

"We were so young when we went to Earth, we forgot about everything here. It wasn't until we met Jena and Juila at school a few months ago when we even discovered we were from Tuala. There was always something which made us feel different, but we believed it was because we were triplets or because we were adopted. Never did we imagine it was because we were aliens."

"Mesans," Willian muttered under his breath, referring to Valentina's use of the Earth term month.

"Don't worry about semantics right now, Willian," Chelesa admonished even as she was trying to figure out Valentina's whole story. "So, the girls helped you to realize the three of you were from here. How did they know?"

Valentina pulled the pendant out from under her tunic and said, "Because of these. We each had one, and we saw they had them as well. We'd never seen any others before, so we asked them about where they got theirs. We...well, I was hoping it would give us a clue to finding our birth mother."

"So did the girls take you back to Roanoke to reunite you with your mother?" Chelesa asked.

Debbon's temper flared at his wife's reminder of Daven's involvement in his personal family affair yet he remained silent as he watched the people around him. He was starting to get a bigger picture of the events which had taken place. He wondered where his son had fit into the whole thing.

"No, before that could happen, the girls took us back to their home on Earth to meet their parents. We were shocked when we saw Mrs. Stel because she looked so much like how we'd remembered our own mother looking eight 'anons' before." She paused to give Willian a telling look for remembering to use the correct term. She grinned mischievously, and continued, "We even told her about the resemblance, and she got a strange look on her face. It was a while before we actually came to the conclusion we were from Tuala. Actually, our brother Behn was the first to know about it; then he convinced me when he showed me the crystal skills he'd learned from Juila."

"You don't know how to use your birth crystal?" Chelesa asked incredulously.

"I'm learning now," she looked over to Willian and added, "With Willian's help."

"She's a fast learner; I merely have to remind her of what her mother taught her before she sent them away."

"Back to your story, Valentina…you were saying?" Chelesa prompted.

"Before I was reminded of my heritage, Behn and Mrs. Stel had made a trip to the place of our birth. When they got there, the colony was gone, the place was empty and had been for quite some time. I'm not sure of the circumstances behind it, but Mrs. Stel arranged a group of us to go back to the colony to retrieve my mother's samara. I don't know where she took it, but when she came back, she said she thought she might know where our mother was.

"Only there was a complication. Our mother's children were only nine in her time, and Mrs. Stel knew we were sixteen. Yet she also knew there couldn't possibly be two sets of triplets with the same names to a woman who also resembled Mrs. Stel, so she had to be our mother. It appeared when our mother sent us to Earth, she also sent us back in time, so we ended up reliving the same eight anons. When we were reunited with her, she had to come to terms with the idea we were almost adults rather than small children. It was hard on her, as you can well imagine."

"Yes, I can imagine," she said with a slight choking sound, her mind whirling with the possibilities. "Is…is your mother's name, perhaps, is it Jinya?"

"No, it's Vinia."

Disappointment passed through Chelesa as her hopes had been for naught.

"But, my grandmother's name was Jinya. Did you know her?" Valentina asked innocently.

Optimism returned, and Chelesa turned to Debbon and said, "It's possible, don't you think?"

"What's possible?" Willian asked with total confusion. He looked from his mother to his father without comprehending the silent conversation happening between them.

Debbon leaned forward on the table, ignoring his plate of food as he formulated his question carefully. "Did your mother ever say anything about an incident with you as a toddler?"

Valentina shook her head slightly, not understanding what he was asking. "She's told me a lot of things about my childhood. Is there something specific?"

Thinking there was no better way to ask but plainly, he said, "Were you abducted by Petre MacVeen as a toddler? Did you almost drown and then get bit by a beetlesnatch on the cheek while you were with him?"

Valentina's hand flew up to her cheek where there was a slight divot. Her eyes grew wide as the memories of falling into the dark water and not being able to breath brought back her reoccurring nightmare. Now she knew, the nightmares were based on truth; it made total sense. "I don't know, but it would explain my fear of water. I don't remember, but it certainly could be true."

CHAPTER 41

Debbon pushed himself away from the table. The food remained mostly untouched as nobody seemed to have much of an appetite. "I can do some research. It would be simpler if I could contact your mom, but the Roanoke Colony has always refused outside help, I'll have to…"

"There's a patil in my mother's house in Roanoke. She asked for one as one of the conditions for becoming a leader of the community," Valentina volunteered. She still did not understand what Elder Debbon wanted to confirm, but she was still trying to be helpful nonetheless.

"Really? Your mother is the leader there now? There must have been some serious changes out there…anyway, I'll be right back." Debbon was troubled by the changes in the backward community and because he had not heard anything about it. Even as he walked to his own office, he had to let go of the anger surrounding the community considering it was not in his own District but in Elder Daven's. The Districts were autonomous, so it was unnecessary for Daven to have to report on any changes.

Once seated at his desk, he spent a few minutes searching out the call code of the patil in Roanoke. It was certainly easier to make contact with his intended recipient since it was in her own home. He entered the number on a video call because he wanted to see if Valentina's mother was the same person he thought she might be.

The call was picked up by an unknown man. Debbon was slightly thrown as he had only expected a woman to answer. He hurriedly recovered and said, "This is Elder Debbon. I'm looking for Vinia. Is she available?"

"Certainly, I'll have to run outside to get her. Hold on, please."

Debbon could hear a lot of commotion through the connection and a muffled exclamation of a woman's voice. Several more seconds passed before he saw a woman's chest on the screen as she sat at the table in front of the patil. His eyes grew wide as he looked upon the face of the woman he had known so many anons before as Jinya.

"Jinya? Is that you?" he asked before he could stop himself. He watched intently as her complexion turned a bright red and she could no longer look at the screen.

"Elder Debbon, I'm sorry to have lied to you so long ago. You'll have to know I was trying to protect my identity from Petre at the time. I never expected to see you or hear from you ever again; otherwise, I would have informed you before of my deception."

Even as he continued to stare, he could see the resemblance of this woman to Amanda even though there were many anons difference in their ages. "I'm sorry I keep staring; is your name actually Vinia then?"

"Yes, Elder Debbon."

"Did you know your daughter is here at my estate with my son, Willian?"

"No. What are they doing here in Tuala? She's not in trouble: is she?"

"No, no trouble at all. She's been telling us about her strange upbringing. She is the same child who Petre claimed was his own, yes?"

"Yes, she is the same child, but Petre is nothing to her!" Vinia protested vehemently.

"I'm sorry; I didn't mean to imply...I just wanted to make sure it was the same child. I can't believe she's almost grown and I imagine you can't either!"

"It was quite a shock to which I'm still adjusting. Elder Debbon, I'm sorry about the betrothal. I hope you don't blame my daughter for it; after all, Willian kissed her and not the other way around. Jena saw it happen, but she already knew she wanted to end things. It just worked out Elder Daven was here with me, and she requested the dissolution immediately."

Debbon hid his anger at the knowledge of his son messing up his relationship with Jena and replied, "Don't worry, Jin...I mean, Vinia. Valentina is not in any trouble. Thank you for taking my call and clearing up the mystery for us. I'm going to head back to dinner now. Have a nice evening."

"Good evening, Elder Debbon."

He tapped the screen and ended the call. The conversation left him with several things to think about, some of them not entirely pleasant; others were possibilities to be checked out. Tapping his fingers on his desktop a couple of times, Debbon promptly made up his mind and pushed himself up from his chair. It was time to make some plans.

When he got back into the dining room, he noticed the meal had not progressed in his absence. He leaned over to make it look as though he were going to kiss Chelesa's cheek only to whisper in her ear, "Read Valentina's aura." He did kiss her and then took his place at the head of the table. "Mystery solved, Valentina. You were the child kidnapped by Petre. Your fear of the water is warranted since you almost drowned while he was busy stealing a cargo shipment and not watching you. It's good to have the details cleared up." He picked up his fork casually, stabbed a chunk of foxl steak and brought it up near his mouth. "What's this I hear about Jena catching you kissing Valentina just before she ended the betrothal? Do you think it might have sealed the deal with Jena?"

"What?" Willian sputtered.

Valentina dropped her head low and could not bear to look at either of Willian's parents through her humiliation. How could her mom have told Elder Debbon such a thing? It had to have been her; the timing was too perfect to be anything else.

"No, it wasn't what 'sealed the deal' with Jena. Yes, she was angry about it, but it was only a matter of time before she knew there was no future for us. As soon as she calmed down and she felt the connection which Val...entina and I share, she calmly requested the dissolution without fault or blemish on either part. Jena has declared she is happy for Valentina and me. They are still friends. If you don't believe me, then ask Jena. This was mutual, and it's final.

"Dad, I'm disappointed you haven't followed your own advice you've given me so often about getting all of your facts straight before you open your mouth and say things you'll regret later!" Willian abruptly stood up and reached for Valentina's hand. Giving up on trying to appease his parents, he declared, "C'mon, Val; we're leaving!"

"Willian! You will apologize to your father this instant!" Chelesa said sternly, also standing to address her errant son.

Debbon remained sitting and said, "No, Chelesa, he won't be apologizing because he's right to point out my error. At least I know he's been listening to me all of these anons." He stood slowly, gathering all eyes to him and he turned to Willian and said, "I'm sorry, Willian. I'm sorry, Valentina. I've been the worst possible host as Willian has so eloquently reminded me. I don't have all of the facts, and I've been speaking out of turn because of it."

Valentina was mortified because this was not the first impression she wanted to make on Willian's parents. There was no way to rectify the mess which had been created. More than anything, she wished she had stayed at home on Earth today rather than have everything turn upside down so swiftly and irrevocably. She still held Willian's hand, yet they had not moved away from the table, it was almost as if they were in limbo, not knowing what their next move was going to be.

Debbon spoke again, softly this time, "Can we go back to the meeting room and you can tell me everything. I promise not to interrupt."

"Hmmph!" Chelesa sounded with an amused expression on her face. "That'll be the day!"

Willian chuckled at his mother's amusement, effectively diffusing the tension in the room. The tightness in his hand lessened, and he nodded. "I'd like that very much, Dad. I've had the most amazing past few days, and I've wanted to share them with you, but time and circumstances have prevented me before. We're here now, so let's go talk."

They returned to the meeting room which was no longer filled with tension. As promised, both parents remained silent as they listened with fascination as Willian recounted his whole adventure since arriving on Earth. When he got to the part about the electricity, he touched Valentina's hand and asked, "Don't you feel the difference when we're in physical contact? I mean, it's still there even when we're near one another, yet touching makes it so much stronger."

Breaking the silence, Chelesa admitted, "I did feel it earlier when I touched your cheek. I even mentioned it to your father." She turned and nodded at him to confirm her statement. Satisfied when he dropped his chin slightly in reply, she turned back and said, "I'm sorry. Please keep going."

Willian grinned at their receptiveness, this is what he had wanted all along and never really expecting to receive. Maybe he had learned a few more things on his adventure than he had initially realized. Or maybe it was the death of Elder Wilken which had made him learn to stand up for what he wanted before it was too late.

He told the rest of the story, only omitting the parts where he and Valentina had been intimate, and then he sat back and declared, "And that's all there is to it. We are forever bonded in perfect harmony, and I can't possibly be any happier!" As he said the last part, he had turned to face Valentina with a silly grin on his face. He gave her hand another squeeze for emphasis before he turned back to his dad, awaiting his approval.

"You've given us a lot to think about. It's getting pretty late, we should probably get you back to Manzanit so you can take Valentina home," Debbon declared.

"What? That's all you're going to say about it?"

"You said yourself 'that's all there is to it.' What more can I say at this point?"

"Oh, I don't know…maybe congratulations or I'm happy for you, son."

"I am happy for you."

"Oh, goodness! Don't listen to him, Willian. I'm thrilled you've found happiness! Let me give you both a hug in congratulations!" Chelesa cried out and crossed the space between them to lean over and put her arms around both kids sitting so closely together.

At first contact, she immediately began to see visions of future events and feel energy coursing through her in ways she had never experienced. She jumped back from them and straightened her tunic in confusion. "I'll have to remember not to do that while you're holding hands! Whew!" She stepped back another step and looked away from them uncomfortably.

Now it was Willian's turn to be anxious to leave. He did not enjoy seeing his mother flustered and at a loss for words. He stood up and was pleased when Valentina did as well. "You're right, Dad, we should be going now."

"Go ahead and start without me. I'll be out in a minute," he told his son with a dismissing wave of his hand. He went to his wife and murmured, "Are you okay? Do you need anything? You look flushed; what happened?"

"I don't really know, although I can tell you, it was powerful!"

"Did you read her aura?"

"Yes."

"And?"

"She's only half-Tualan. I could tell by the odd white shimmering around the edges which I usually associate with the *old souls*. Do you think she knows?"

"No, but I mean to get to the bottom of this!" He kissed his wife on the forehead, patted her shoulders hastily, and then left the room to meet the kids outside by the telepod. His mind was reeling with ideas and possibilities, so much so that he suggested Willian take the controls of the telepod to get them back to the Residence.

They had just gotten to the Gate at Elder Island's Residence when Willian asked, "Why didn't we just take your telepod to Manzanit and skip the Gate trip?"

Debbon chuckled and replied, "Because I didn't think of it! It would have made more sense, but you've muddled my brain with all of your revelations this evening. There that does it!" He had finished tapping the final sequence to shift the Gate to take them to Manzanit. He stepped into the large circle, careful to keep himself from touching either of the kids for fear it would make him lose focus on the transfer coordinates in his mind. He activated the Gate, and they were on their way.

They materialized in the secured room in Manzanit and stared in wonder at the mess all around them. Debbon was the first to step up and away from the Gate's energy field. "What's wrong, Rasa? What happened in here?"

"Elder Debbon! I thought I was going crazy, but I'm not, and the worst thing ever has happened!"

"What is it?"

"Someone stole my samara!"

"That's impossible, Rasa. Once you've claimed your samara, nobody else can possibly steal it."

"Ooooh, I know! But I hadn't claimed it yet! So, yes, it was still vulnerable to theft!"

"What? How could you be so careless?" Debbon accused.

"All of the facts, Dad, remember," Willian whispered to him from behind. He moved around his father and asked reasonably, "Where were you keeping it, Rasa?"

She pointed miserably to an open niche in the stone wall. "Elder Wilken put it in there for me and wove a protective ward around it just last night. I was going to claim it this morning when I was rested, but then, Elder Wilken died. We had the ceremony, and I was too tired to do anything other than fall asleep.

"I was so drained I even imagined the Gate itself had been diminished. I just got through all of the matters which required immediate attention, and I came in here to take care of the samara. But it's GONE! It wasn't my imagination after all!" She whirled around, eyes wild with fright and anger and declared, "One of the Elders stole it!"

~

Want more?

When plotting against evil, everyone is at risk.
The odds are stacked against her as she faces her greatest
challenge yet...

THE WAR OF REALMS.

GET MY FREE NOVELLA NOW

To let others know how much you enjoyed this book, please leave a review at your favorite retailer.

To keep updated on new releases, visit www.AmyProebstel.com.

Receive a FREE exclusive novella,

Tuala's Lost Boy: Ceren's Story

at https://geni.us/BMNLSU

by signing up for Amy Proebstel's newsletter.

You can also follow Amy Proebstel on Facebook at www.facebook.com/ATwistOnReality.

ABOUT THE AUTHOR

USA Today bestselling author, Amy Proebstel, writes epic dragon fantasy, magical realism fantasy, clean fated mate shifter romance, clean contemporary romance, and sweet young adult medical romance.

When she's not busy writing about young heroines and dragons saving the world, she spends her time binge-watching YouTube adventures, taking her husband and daughter flying, playing with her Pomeranian and Pomskies, or reading. If you like her books, she recommends you also check out Anne McCaffrey and Ava Richardson. They're the reason she started writing.

Subscribe to Amy's newsletter for a free book to get started on the journey today!

Feel free to email Amy at Amy@LevelsofAscension.com.

Chosen Origins Trilogy, A Portal Fantasy Series
    The Chosen, A Portal Fantasy Series
    Romances Beyond Tuala, A Fated Mate Shifter Series
    Billionaire's Venture Romance Series
    Dragon's Magic: An Epic Dragon Fantasy Series
    Sweet Young Adult Medical Romance Series

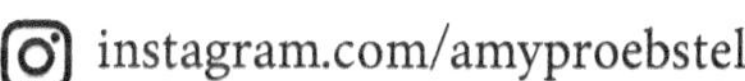 instagram.com/amyproebstel

PEOPLE

Agetha – / **ay** gah thuh / – Resident of the Roanoke Colony. Mother of Romen.

Ahn – / ah n / – Husband of Barla. Father of Gravin and Rasa. Harbor Master at the Port of Cresdon in Thulen. Former shipping captain.

Alena – / ah **leyn** a / – Born Ab 26, 3417. Maiden name: Bellen. Marriage Date: Tishri 16, 3436. Wife of Bryon Kesh. Mother of Justan and Kyclon. Former adoptive mother to Jena and Juila as known in Amanda's coma reality. Trained as a wise-woman.

Amanda – / uh **man** duh / – means 'beloved'. Born September 28, 1972, in Florida. Maiden name: Covington. Daughter of Chris and Diane. Wife of Riccan Stel. Mother of Juila and Jena. Sister to Carrie and Deanna. Cousin to Gravin and Rasa. Aunt to Emily and April. Former fiancé of Nealand.

Andera – / an **dair** uh / – Born Tishri 12, 3439. Daughter of Zeka. Betrothed to Justan. First-daughter of Bryon and Alena.

Andy Brun – / **an** dee **broohn** / – Neighbor friend of Riccan's on Earth. Involved in rock throwing trouble.

Angie – / **an** jee / – Nealand's girlfriend in Amanda's coma reality. Maiden name: McFarland. Daughter of Billy. High school classmate of Amanda's.

April – / **ay** pril / – Daughter (6yrs) of Carrie. Granddaughter of Chris and Diane. Niece of Amanda.

Barla – / **bahr** luh / – Born January 21, 1945, in Wisconsin. Maiden name: Silnack. Birth name: Barbara. Nickname on Earth: Barla. Sister of Diane. Aunt of Amanda. Wife of Ahn. Mother of Gravin and Rasa. Raised Jena and Juila until they were six anons old. Birth crystal color: bright blue.

Behn – / **ben** / – Earth Surname: Wilson. Triplet brother to Valentina and Jon. Sent to Earth by mother, Vinia, from Tuala when he was eight anons old. Tall with brown hair and brown eyes. Crystal color: smoky grey. Boyfriend of Juila.

Billy – / **bil** ee / – Surname: McFarland. Father of Angie. Owns his own towing company in Southern Florida. NHRA enthusiast and fan of Riccan Stel.

Bistea – / bis **tee** uh / – Vendor at the marketplace in Kirma. Patient of Alena's.

Bruce – / **bru** s / – Man in the hotel room in New York City to confront Petre.

Bryon – / **brahy** uh n / – Born Heshvan 2, 3416, in Kirma. Surname: Kesh. Marriage Date: Tishri 16, 3436. Husband of Alena. Father of Justan and Kyelon. Former adoptive father to Jena and Juila as known in Amanda's coma reality. Manager of Kirma Shipping and Receiving.

Carrie – / k **air** ee / – Born April 21, 1970, in Florida. Maiden name: Covington. Daughter of Chris and Diane. Sister to Deanna and Amanda. Divorced, mother of Emily and April. Reclaimed maiden name when ex-husband was convicted of murder. In jail in Roswell, New Mexico, on drug charges.

Celia – / **see** lee uh / – Surname: Scamp. Gypsy family who stayed with Thomas Rockwood in France around 1800. Wife to Sampson. Mother of a sick daughter who received help from Thomas.

Ceren – / **sair** in / – Born approximately 3412. Adopted son of Ahn and Barla. Works at the Port of Cresdon for Captain Ahn.

Chelesa – / **chuh** lay suh / – Married name: Potts. Wife of Elder Debbon. Mother of Willian.

Chris – / **kris** / – Surname: Covington. Husband of Diane. Father of Carrie, Deanna, and Amanda. Grandfather of Juila, Jena, Emily, and April.

Cleon – / **klee** on / – Transport operator at Kirma Shipping and Receiving.

Copa – / **kohp** uh / – Wise-woman for the district of Desio. Person who healed Ninan. She helped Amanda escape from Elder Vargen and found a home for Jena and Juila. Wise-woman who performed Amanda's birth-crystal ceremony.

Corva – / **kor** vuh / – Foster child of Ahn and Barla. Her parents believed to have died in a house fire. Daughter of Tirsha and Filbrun. Reunited with her birth-mother.

Crysta – / **kris** tuh / – Head maid at Elder Debbon's estate.

Danika – / **dah** nee kuh / – Daughter of Vinia. Born in the Roanoke Colony one month early.

Daven – / **dav** uhn / – Surname: Stel. Son of Edwin and Murisa. Husband of Nena. Father of Riccan. Brother of Sanda, Stina, Phen, Zuna, Rucen. Student of Jehoban. Elder whose base of power is on Pantano. Grandfather of Juila and Jena.

Deanna – / dee **an** nuh / – Born April 5, 1971, in Florida. Maiden name: Covington. Daughter of Chris and Diane. Sister to

Carrie and Amanda. Married with two daughters. Suffering from an unknown illness.

Debbon – / **deb** uhn / – Surname: Potts. Elder whose base of power is on Elder Isle. Husband of Chelesa. Father of Willian.

Denana – / **day** naw nuh / – Employee in the Engineering Department at Telepod Engineering Company.

Diane – / dahy **an** / – Born October 1, 1947. Maiden name: Silnack. Sister of Barbara and Saul. Wife of Chris. Mother of Carrie, Deanna, and Amanda. Grandmother of Juila, Jena, Emily, and April.

Dilela – / dih **lay** luh / – Resident of the Roanoke Colony.

Dr. Flores – / **flohr** ez / – The doctor treating Amanda in the hospital in Cancun.

Dr. Huddleston – / **hud** ul stun / – The psychologist treating Neal Taivas, Jr.

Edda – / eh **duh** / – Resident of the Roanoke Colony.

Edwin – / **ed** win / – Surname: Stel. Husband of Murisa. Father of Daven, Sanda, Stina, Phen, Zuna, Rucen. Engineer at the Roswell Museum. Started a Construction Supply Company on Tuala. Started a Consulting Business when they moved to Acaim when Daven was six.

Ela Nena – / **eluh** nay nuh / – Married name: Dunless. Wife of Teden Dunless. Executive VP of Customer Operations at Telepod Engineering Company. Riccan's boss.

Ellen – / **el** uh n / – Maiden name: Hill. Wife of Sydney Silnack. Mother of Barla, Saul, and Diane. Married name: Silnack.

Emily – / **em** ul ee / – Daughter (7yrs) of Carrie. Granddaughter of Chris and Diane. Niece of Amanda.

Emmanuen – / ee **man** you ehn / – Son of Jehoban.

Faegan – / **fay** ghin / – Presenter of the award given to Ela Nena at the Engineering Excellence Awards dinner. Also known as Vanion.

Farmer Joe – Washington asparagus farmer and former owner of the outhouse used by Riccan for senior prank.

Filbrun – / **fil** bruhn / – Former husband of Tirsha. Father of Corva. Died in house fire.

Fordin – / **ford** in / – Former seaman friend of Ninan. Confidant of Ninan's dealings with Petre.

Frasnia – / **fraz** nee uh / – Secretary at Kirma Shipping and Receiving.

Fraya – / **frī** yuh / – Resident of the Roanoke Colony.

Gatson – / **gat** *suh* n / – Personal body guard for Elder Debbon. Main home is on the Elder's Islet at the seat of power.

George – / jorj / – Attendant on duty at Creedmoor Psychiatric Center when Neal went missing.

Gevena – / jeh **vee** nuh / – Sixteen anon old refugee found on Viceroy Blair's space ship. Originally from Desio where she was raised by her drunk father after her mother left when she was a toddler. She stopped going to school at the age of twelve. Moved to Manzanit under the care of Rasa.

Gilora – / **gil** or uh / – Employee at Telepod Engineering Company under Riccan. Interviewer of Amanda.

Gravin – / **gra** vin / – Born Elul 30, 3421, in Port of Cresdon. Son of Ahn and Barla. Brother of Rasa. First cousin of Amanda.

Grobin – / **grow** bin / – Leader of the Roanoke Colony in Tuala.

Gwenda – / **gwen** duh / – Employee at Telepod Engineering Company under Riccan. Interviewer of Amanda.

Hashma – / **hash** muh / – A prostitute at the Lookout Tavern. Filed a sexual assault lawsuit against Petre. Mother of Petre's child.

Issyn – / **ih** sin / – Shipping captain who rescued Amanda from swimming. Friend of Captain Ahn. Main port of call is Port of Cresdon.

Jasmine Medin, MD – / **med** in / – Doctor at Cannon Memorial Asylum under Dr. Stephen Gascon. Amanda's attending doctor in the Florida hospital while she was in her coma. Treated Shemalla while she was being held at Cannon Memorial.

Jehoban – / juh **ho** ban / – Means 'of all the people' who is the creator of everything. Earth equivalent: God.

Jena – / **jen** uh / – Born Iyar 22, 3443, in Kirma. Daughter of Amanda and Riccan. Twin sister of Juila. Former first-daughter of Elder Debbon and Chelesa. Formerly betrothed to Willian. Dating Luke.

Jenny – / **jen** ee / – A dance team member from Amanda's high school.

Jern – / jurn / – A trusted friend of Bryon's.

Jesisca – / jes **is** kuh / – The name given to Amanda from Petre.

Jessa – / **jes** uh / – The name given to Elder Debbon from Petre for Jena's mother.

Jessica Taivas – / **jes** i kuh **tay** v*uhs* / – Wife of Nealand Taivas Sr. Mother of Nealand Taivas Jr.

Jinya – / **gin** ya / – Mother of Vinia.

Jon – / **jawn** / – Earth Surname: Wilson. Triplet brother to Behn and Valentina. Sent to Earth by mother, Vinia, from Tuala when he was eight anons old. Leaner and slightly shorter than Behn. Brown hair and blue eyes. Quiet by nature. Dating Sofia.

Jonan – / **jawn** uhn / – Bullying neighbor of Ahn and Barla.

Jose – / hohz **ey** / – Mexican man who found Amanda on the beach in Cancun.

Juila – / **joo** ee luh / – Born Iyar 22, 3443, in Kirma. Daughter of Amanda and Riccan. Twin sister of Jena. Dating Behn.

Justan – / **juhs** tan / – Born Elul 21, 3439, in Kirma. Surname: Kesh. Son of Bryon and Alena. Betrothed to Andera. Brother of Kyelon.

Kanekoa – / kan eh **koh** uh / – Person who sells her house to Ninan in Kirma.

Kemeron – / kem er uhn / – Head guard at the Menad Residence for Elder Rylon.

Kendon – / **ken** duhn / – Employee at Telepod Engineering Company under Riccan. Interviewer of Amanda.

Kenen – / **ken** un / – Manager of the telepod crystal quarry in Beewa.

Kiya – / **kahy** uh / – A wise-woman in training with Alena.

Kyelon – / **kahyl** on / – Born Tishri 30, 3440, in Kirma. Surname: Kesh. Son of Bryon and Alena. Brother of Justan.

Lana – / **law** nuh / – Maiden name: Gurdin. Receptionist at Telepod Engineering Company in Durseni.

Lillia – / **lil** ee uh / – A Tualan who gave a crystal skull to Maria's family in Campeche, Mexico. Consort of Lucinden. Keeper of the master samara. Also known as Wibawa. Friend of Shemalla.

Lindon – / **lin** duhn / – A friend of Bryon's who took him to Earth as a teenager.

Lucinden – / loo **sin** den / – One of the original angels of Jehoban. He confronted Jehoban for rule of the people and Jehoban banned him and his followers to Tuala. Dating Lillia.

Luke – / **lük** / – Surname: Thompson. Friend of Behn, Jon, and Ryan. Very athletic.

Lukon – / **lük** on / – Community leader of tainted bread town in Tuala. Husband of Scarola.

Marcus – / **mar** kus / – Surname: Parker. Husband of Melissa. Friend of Shemalla. Foster parent for Willian on Earth.

Maria – / mah **ree** ah / – The keeper of the crystal skull in Campeche, Mexico.

Mary – Riccan's housekeeper. Cleans every Friday.

Melba – / **mel** buh / – Head house maid for Elder Daven. Lives in Pantano.

Melissa – / mel **ih** suh / – Married name: Parker. Wife of Marcus. Friend of Shemalla. Foster parent for Willian on Earth.

Mitelda – / mih **tel** duh / – Resident of the Roanoke Colony. Mother of Semsen.

Miorlen – / mee **ohr** len / – Legal advisor for Elder Debbon.

Mosan – / **mow** san / – The second-in-command in the Roanoke Colony in Tuala.

Mr. Smith – The false name for the burglar paid by Dr. Gascon to investigate the Stel house.

Mrs. Shoreham – Sofia's 4th period typing teacher.

Murisa – / m **yur** ih sah / – Born in Tuala. Employee of Elder Vargen sent to work in the Roswell Museum in 1947. Wife of Earthborn Edwin Stel. Mother of Daven, Sanda, Stina, Phen, Zuna, Rucen. Grandmother of Riccan.

Nealand Taivas – / **neel** uh nd **tay** *vuhs* / – Son of Nealand Taivas Sr. and Jessica Taivas. Former fiancé of Amanda. Also known as Neal on Earth and Nealan on Tuala. Former employee at the Old Soul Engineering Facility owned by Elder Vargen. Addicted to the drug *resh* until Amanda rescued him from Tuala and took him through the veil between dimensions. Former boyfriend of Vinia.

Nealand Taivas Sr. – / **neel** uh nd **tay** *vuhs* / – Husband of Jessica. Father of Nealand Jr.

Nedan – / **nay** dan / – Willian's best friend and neighbor.

Nena – / **nay** nuh / – Married name: Stel. Wife of Daven. Mother of Riccan. Occupation: Teacher. Lives in Pantano. Grandmother of Juila and Jena.

Ninan – / **nahyn** un / – Surname: Tigua. Unemployed seaman. Worked undercover for Petre to locate Jesisca. Traveled to Kirma to look for Jesisca. Works for Bryon at Kirma Shipping and Receiving. Address: Thursto Block 43-3, Kirma.

Nurse Bota – / **boht** uh / – The nurse who took care of Amanda in the hospital in Cancun.

Oliver – / awl ih ver / - Surname: Wilson. Husband of Zoey. Adoptive father to Behn, Valentina, and Jon.

Ozias/Ozian – / oh **zi** as / – Crew member of Viceroy Blair's pirate space ship. His mother died when he was little. His father left him soon after to work in the slave's dome. Ozias raised himself before joining Viceroy Blair's crew. Now known as Ozian in the Roanoke Colony.

Pelka – / **pel** kuh / – Employee of Elder Wilken's Residence. Around eighteen anons old.

Pesi – / **peh** see / – Black, female, Pomeranian dog owned by Marcus and Melissa Parker.

Petre – / **pee** ter / – Surname: MacVeen. Birthplace: Menad. Formerly known as Petren, lost social status and forced to lose the honorific 'n' at the end of his name. Wears a black onyx ring showing his status as a Master Deceptor. First person on Tuala to encounter Amanda. Kidnapped Jena and sold her to Elder Debbon under the guise of a betrothal agreement as known from Amanda's coma reality.

Phen – / **fen** / – Surname: Stel. Son of Edwin and Murisa. Brother of Daven, Sanda, Stina, Zuna, Rucen.

Pluska – / **plu** skuh / – Daughter of Elder Wilken.

Politun – / **pol** ih tun / – Resident of the Roanoke Colony. Refugee on Viceroy Blair's space ship.

Rasa – / **rah** sah / – Born Tishri 5, 3423, in Port of Cresdon. Daughter of Ahn and Barla. Sister of Gravin. First cousin of Amanda. Student of Jehoban. First woman to become the successor to an Elder. Elder; base of power is in Manzanit.

Riccan – / **rik** an / – Surname: Stel. Son of Elder Daven and

Nena. Husband of Amanda. Father of Juila and Jena. Great nephew of Roderick. Chief Engineer at the Telepod Engineering Company. Popular racer of telepods.

Roderick – / **rod** eh rick / – Surname: Rockwood. Great uncle to Riccan.

Romen – / **roh** man / – Resident of the Roanoke Colony. Son of Agetha.

Rualin – / roo **ahl** in / – A business associate of Petre.

Rucen – / **roo** ken / – Surname: Stel. Son of Edwin and Murisa. Brother of Daven, Sanda, Stina, Phen, Zuna. Died in a telepod accident at the age of 22.

Ryan – / **rī** ən / – Surname: Perino. Friend of Behn, Jon, and Luke. Very athletic.

Sampson – / **samp** sun / – Surname: Scamp. Gypsy family who stayed with Thomas Rockwood in France around 1800. Husband to Celia. Father of a sick daughter who received help from Thomas. Giver of the crystal skull to Thomas.

Sanda – / **san** duh / – Surname: Stel. Daughter of Edwin and Murisa. Sister of Daven, Stina, Phen, Zuna, Rucen.

Saul – / **sawl** / – Born in Wisconsin. Brother of Barla and Diane.

Scarola – / skar **oh** luh / – From the tainted bread town in Tuala. Wife of Lukon.

Semsen – / **sem** sun / – Resident of the Roanoke Colony. Son of Mitelda.

Shemalla – / shem **al** uh / – Maiden Name: Paramasivam. Born in Pantano. Employee at the UFO Museum and Research Center in Roswell, New Mexico. Apprentice to Elder Vargen. Kidnapped and held captive at Cannon Memorial Asylum where she was a patient of Dr. Medin's.

Sherry – / **sher** ee / – Amanda's best friend from high school.

Sofia – / so **fee** uh / – Surname: Castillo. Her family moves to

Florida from Argentina in 1993. First friend of Jena and Juila on Earth. Girlfriend of Jon.

Stavin – / stav in / – A boyhood friend of Bryon's.

Stephen Gascon, MD – / **gas** kuhn / – Former Director of Cannon Memorial Asylum. Director at Creedmoor Psychiatric Center. Abducted by Lucinden as a child.

Stina – / **stee** nuh / – Surname: Stel. Daughter of Edwin and Murisa. Sister of Daven, Sanda, Phen, Zuna, Rucen.

Sydney – / **sid** nee / – Surname: Silnack. Husband of Ellen Hill. Father of Barla, Saul, and Diane. Died in California at the age of sixty-six.

Tana – / **tan** uh / – Next-door-neighbor of Bryon and Alena in Kirma. Caretaker of Justan, Andera, and Kyelon.

Teden – / **ted** en / – Surname: Dunless. Husband of Ela Nena. Accounting Manager at Telepod Engineering Company.

Thomas – / **tom** uhs / – Surname: Rockwood. Born in France in 1776. Great-grandfather to Roderick. Recipient of the crystal scull in trade in 1800 from a gypsy family.

Tiun – / **tee** uhn / – Guard at the Menad Residence for Elder Rylon.

Tirsha – / **tur** shuh / – Mother of Corva. Presumed dead in a house fire. Rescued by Petre between dimensions.

Ulwin – / **uhl** win / – Rasa's personal assistant at the Manzanit Residence. Around twenty-two anons old.

Valentina – / val ehn **tee** nuh / – Earth Surname: Wilson. Triplet sister to Behn and Jon. Sent to Earth by mother, Vinia, from Tuala when she was eight anons old. Tall with blonde hair and brown eyes. Soul-mate of Willian.

Vanion – / **van** yun / – Minion of Lucinden. Alias: Faegan.

Vargen – / **vahr** guh n / – Elder. Co-founder of the Old Soul Engineering Facility.

Viceroy Blair – / **vīs** roi / – Leader of the pirate space ship.

Vinia – / **vin** ee yuh / – Daughter of Jinya. Mother of Behn, Valentina, Jon, and Danika. Leader of the Roanoke Colony. Former girlfriend of Nealan. Engaged to Ozian.

Virginia – Middle name: Ellen. Surname: Covington. Twin sister of Amanda. Died at birth. Buried at cemetery near birth hospital.

Watcher – / **woch** er / – Spoken of in the history of the crystal skulls.

Wibawa – / wee **bah** wuh / – Undercover name for Lillia.

Wilken – / wil ken / – Former Elder. Base of power is in Manzanit. Father of Pluska. Died at 136 anons.

Willian – / **wil** yan / – Surname: Potts. Son of Elder Debbon and Chelesa. Formerly betrothed to Jena. Soul-mate of Valentina.

Zeka – / **zee** kah / – Daughter of Bryon's father's business partner. Mother of Andera.

Zoey – / awl ih ver / – Surname: Wilson. Wife of Oliver. Adoptive mother to Behn, Valentina, and Jon.

Zuna – / **zoo** nuh / – Surname: Stel. Daughter of Edwin and Murisa. Sister of Daven, Sanda, Stina, Phen, Rucen.

ELDERS

Daven – / **dav** uhn / – Base of power is in Pantano. Earth equivalent: Boca Raton, Florida. 68 anons old.

Debbon – / **deb** uhn / – Base of power is on Elder Isle. Earth equivalent: Isla de la Juventud, south of Cuba. 49 anons old.

Emmin – / **eh** min / – Base of power is in Telae. Earth equivalent: Seattle, Washington. 130 anons old.

Jedon – / **jeh** dun / – Base of power is in Neve. Earth equivalent: Denver, Colorado. 113 anons old.

Olguin – / **ohl** gyu in / – Base of power is in Genip. Earth equivalent: Winnipeg, Manitoba. 93 anons old.

Quentien – / **kwen** tee en / – Base of power is in Gamb. Earth equivalent: Bogota, Columbia. 95 anons old.

Rasa – / **rah** sah / – Base of power is in Manzanit. Earth equivalent: New York City, New York. 27 anons old.

Rylon – / **rī** len / – Base of power is in Menad. Earth equivalent: Camden, Bermuda. 105 anons old.

Senjin – / **sen** jin / – Base of power is in Argot. Earth equivalent: Tortuga, Galapagos Islands. 43 anons old.

Tarshen – / **tar** shen / – Base of power is in Sambur. Earth equivalent: Amesbury, UK. 110 anons old.

Uvan – / **yu** van / – Base of power is in Secar. Earth equivalent: Paris, France. 118 anons old.

Vargen – / **vahr** guh n / – Base of power is in Apio. Earth equivalent: Phoenix, Arizona. 99 anons old.

Xylen – / **z** eye len / – Base of power is in Noidad. Earth equivalent: Delhi, India. 103 anons old.

Yingun – / **yin** gun / – Base of power is in Gaud. Earth equivalent: Guangdong, China. 104 anons old.

Zigern – / **zig** urn / – Base of power is in Neum. Earth equivalent: Melbourne, Australia. 86 anons old.

PLACES

Acaim – / uh kām / – Island where Jehoban lives. Earth equivalent: Jamaica.

Apio – / ah pee oh / – Location of Elder Vargen's seat of power. Earth equivalent: Phoenix, Arizona.

Argot – / ar got / – Location of Elder Senjin's seat of power. Earth equivalent: Tortuga, Galapagos Islands.

Ascension Gate – / ə sen SHən gāt / – A link between the levels of reality, most of the Gates are set between Earth and Tuala. Where the ley lines intersect, the elemental energy is the strongest, creating a vortex of plasma power where a person can control movement between Tuala and Earth.

Beewa – / be wuh / – Location where telepod crystals are mined. Earth equivalent: Merida, Mexico.

Cannon Memorial Asylum – Located in North Carolina. Built in 1962 and shut down in 1999.

Cerid – / sair id / – Location of creditors issuing a death and dismemberment order against Petre. Earth equivalent: Corpus Christi, Texas.

Chapel of the Bells – Located in Reno, Nevada, where Riccan and Amanda were married.

City of Thulen – Major city in the heart of Thulen. A place where Petre has many illegal business transactions. Earth equivalent: Mexico City, Mexico.

Coral Reef Senior High School – Located in the Richmond Heights Suburb of Miami, Florida. Earth school which Juila and Jena attend.

Creedmoor Psychiatric Center – Located in Queens, New York. Built in 1912 reaching its peak occupancy in 1960. Mostly abandoned today, it is still partially in use whereas most of the buildings have been sold off or are in major disrepair.

Desio – / deh zee oh / – Location where Ninan was dumped off by Petre. District where Copa is the wise-woman. Earth equivalent: Alvarado, Mexico.

Durseni – / durs en ee / – Earth equivalent: Cozumel, Mexico.

Elder Isle – Location of Elder Debbon's seat of power. Earth equivalent: Isla de la Juventud, south of Cuba.

Florida Middle Ground – Earth's ocean coordinate off the West coast of Florida.

Gamb – / gam / – Location of Elder Quentien's seat of power. Earth equivalent: Bogota, Columbia.

Gaud – / gah ud / – Location of Elder Yingun's seat of power. Earth equivalent: Guangdong, China.

Genip – / jen ip / – Location of Elder Olguin's seat of power. Earth equivalent: Winnipeg, Manitoba.

Gulf of Thulen – / thoo lun / – Large body of water north and east of Thulen. Earth equivalent: the Gulf of Mexico.

Heliok – / hē lē ŏk / – Home planet of Viceroy Blair and crew.

Ishal – / ish uh l / – Coastal town where Petre conducts illegal trade. Location where Petre dumped the freighter telepod. Earth equivalent: Tampico, Mexico.

Isla Mivua – / iz law mih voo uh / – Location where the storm transported Amanda to Tuala. Earth equivalent: Cook Island inside the Bermuda Triangle.

Kendall – Town located southwest of Miami in Florida.

Kendall District Station – Police station in Kendall, Florida. Location where Amanda is introduced to Riccan.

Kirma – / kurm a / – Hometown of Bryon and Alena Kesh. Location of Kirma Shipping and Receiving. Earth equivalent: Campeche, Mexico.

Lookout Tavern – Located in Ishal. Place where the prostitute, Hashma, works.

Manzanit – / man zan eet / – Location of the Residence of Elder Wilken. Strongest lay lines second only to Acaim. Earth equivalent: New York City, New York.

Matza – / maht za / – Small town where Bryon seeks healer assistance when Amanda breaks her wrist and is bitten by a beetlesnatch. Earth equivalent: La Isla located south of Cancun, Mexico.

Mavuno – / mah vun oh / – Location where telepod crystals are mined. Earth equivalent: Villahermosa, Mexico.

Menad – / mee nad / – Location of Elder Rylon's seat of power. Earth equivalent: Camden, Bermuda.

Miami Executive Airport – Airport located in Miami, Florida, where Riccan keeps his airplane hangared. Tower and Ground call sign is Tamiami.

Neum – / nee uhm / – Location of Elder Zigern's seat of power. Earth equivalent: Melbourne, Australia.

Neve – / neev / – Location of Elder Jedon's seat of power. Earth equivalent: Denver, Colorado.

Noidad – / no ee dad / – Location of Elder Xylen's seat of power. Earth equivalent: Delhi, India.

Old Soul Engineering Facility – A place where they study

objects from Earth and reverse engineer them for their own use in Tuala.

Pantano – / pahn tahn oh / – Home of Elder Daven and Nena. Location where Neal and Amanda started their journey. Earth equivalent: as Boca Raton, Florida.

Pinecrest – Town located southwest of Miami in Florida where Amanda's parents live.

Porino's Café – A popular restaurant located at the southern port of Cresdon.

Port of Cerid – / sair id / – Location of the shipment bound for Beewa, but quarantined for a beetlesnatch infestation. Meeting place for Ninan and Petre.

Port of Cresdon – / krez dun / – Main shipping port in Thulen. Home of Ahn and Barla. Earth equivalent: Cancun, Mexico.

Reesun – / ree suhn / – The large land mass north of the Elder Isle. Earth equivalent: Cuba.

Roanoke Colony – A group of 115 colonists from the year 1587 who went missing from Earth and appeared in Tuala. Earth equivalent: Dare County, North Carolina.

Royal Sonesta – Hotel in New Orleans where Riccan and Amanda stayed in the Presidential Suite.

Sambur – / sam buhr / – Location of Elder Tarshen's seat of power. Earth equivalent: Amesbury, UK.

Secar – / see car / – Location of Elder Uvan's seat of power. Earth equivalent: Paris, France.

Southside Town Deli – Located in the Port of Cerid. Meeting place for Ninan and Petre.

Tamiami – Tower and Ground call sign for Miami Executive Airport.

Telae – / tehl ay / – Location of Elder Emmin's seat of power. Earth equivalent: Seattle, Washington

Telepod Engineering Company – / tel uh pod / – Creator and manufacturing facility for telepods. Located in Durseni.

Thulen – / thoo lun / – Country where Port of Cresdon is located. Earth equivalent: Mexico.

Trilli Deli – A restaurant located at the main Port of Cresdon. A favorite place for Captain Ahn to frequent.

Tuala – / to͞o a-lə / – Planet where Jehoban lives. Alternate realm of Earth.

UFO Museum and Research Center – Located in Roswell, New Mexico.

TIME

Minggu – / **min** gew / – Sunday – First day of the week.

Senin – / **sen** in / – Monday.

Selasa – / **say** law suh / – Tuesday.

Rabu – / **raw** boo / – Wednesday.

Kamis – / **kam** us / – Thursday.

Jumat – / **joo** mawt / – Friday.

Sabtu – / **sab** too / – Saturday.

Nisan – / **nee** sahn / – January.

Iyar – / **ee** yahr / – February.

Sivan – / see **vahn** / – March.

Tammuz – / tah **mooz** / – April.

Ab – / ahb / – May.

Elul – / e **lool** / – June.

Tishri – / **tish** ree / – July.

Heshvan – / **hesh** vahn / – August.

Kislev – / **kis** *luh* v / – September.

Tebet – / te **vet** / – October.

Shebat – / sh*uh* **baht** / – November.

Adar – / *uh* **dahr** / – December.

Mesan – / **may** san / – Month.

Declan – / **dek** lun / – Decade.

Anon – / **ann** un / – Year. There are 365 days and 252 working days in an anon.

Tuala Anon 3402 = Earth Year 1950 A.D.

Aquaponics – / **ah** kw*uh* pon iks / – A process for growing food floating on water where the water contains nutrients supplied by live fish. The plants filter the water for the fish to survive. Since nutrients are readily available, the produce grows faster and in less space than traditional gardening.

Beetlesnatch – / **beet**-l snach / – Black beetle 3-4 inches long, migrates by flying, poisonous bite, lethal to humans and animals.

Betrothal – A formal union giving children even higher status in the community, approved and blessed by the Elders through a betrothal petition stating each family's different abilities and what color of crystal each child bears. Only approved if it is a superior union for the good of the society commemorated with a betrothal ceremony along with a pair of matching bracelets or rings with a precious stone. Once the age of majority is reached by both partic-ipants, they get married.

Birth Crystal – A circular pendant containing gem stones arranged as the leaves of a tree assigned to each citizen of Tuala within 24-hours of birth at a crystal ceremony, worn on an ornate chain around their neck. Once in place, the necklace cannot be removed until they reach the age of eighteen. The color of the stone can change with age, friends, or activities. Parents can both see and hear what their children are doing.

Bruskin – / **broos** kin / – An alcoholic beverage served cold similar to beer.

Cessna 182S Skylane – Make and model of single-engine airplane owned by Riccan Stel on Earth.

Chit – A small electronic disk assigned to respected members of the community. Each is unique to the owner and honored the same as money.

Clotted Cream – Sour cream.

Council of Elders – Elders who convene to arbitrate serious matters.

Crystal Skull – See Samara.

Deckhopper – Earth equivalent: a pirate.

Elder – Individual selected and trained by Jehoban in Acaim. Primary role to help/guide the people. Secondary role to protect the Ascension Gates.

Elder's Instructional Guide – Several thousand anon old text written by Jehoban Himself and now owned by Riccan.

Elder's Instructional Guide's New Prophesy: From a far-away land, There will come in time, Intuition is in hand, Strange details known, With ties to the people. From one of my own, There will be a sign. Those born to this one, Will transform all. Lucinden will pursue, Elders will fall, Then all made new. Take comfort in one another, combined you will see. Believe in what you Understand, Know what you Do, then you can Be.

Elemental Energy – The magnetic energy found in the earth used by the people of Tuala through their birth crystal to create. Slang: Elemy.

Elemy – / **el** eh mee / – Slang term for elemental energy.

Enskil Dumplings – / **ehn** skil / – Main dish made with mashed krumpli mixed with flour and egg and boiled into small dumplings. Served with crumbled foxl crisps and butter.

Epeny – / **ep** eh nee / – Drug causing drowsiness and pain relief, an anti-inflammatory. Addictive when used too long.

Facultas – / fak **uh l** tus / – Meaning 'ability'. A book explaining the Tualan people's abilities used daily such as: teleportation, telekinesis, translation, deception, healing, amplification. Anything the mind can think of, the power can create, without any limitations.

First-daughter – A girl who is betrothed to a son and brought into the son's family and raised as a daughter of the family.

Foxl – / **fox**-l / – Mammal with fur five inches long, straight when dry, curly when wet, head like a sheep, body size and shape like a cow, herbivore.

Gania – / **gah** nee uh / – A measure of distance equivalent to an Earth mile.

Genero – / gen **air** oh / – Meaning 'to create' or 'creation'. A book covering the creation of the worlds, Jehoban and his wayward student named Lucinden, and the beginning of the Elders.

Glawlet – / **glaw** let / – A common breakfast consisting of a fresh warm roll filled with a poached egg covered in a sausage gravy.

Golden Jesisca – 60-foot yacht owned by Nealand.

Inside Ascension – Phrase to use at a gate on Earth to get to Tuala.

Invisibility Shield – A plasma field around an object rendering it undetectable from viewing outside of the field.

Java – / jaw vah / – A stimulating beverage served hot or cold similar to coffee.

Kittilee – / **kit**-l ee / – A miniature feline similar to a common housecat.

Krumpli – / krump lee / – Edible tuber similar to a potato.

Ley Lines – / **lay** / – Concentrated lines of magnetic energy in the land. Ascension gates are located where multiple lines intersect. Healers use the ley lines and crystals to assist with their talents to treat their patients.

Life-line – The non-physical core of every living thing which ties into the elemental energy of the earth. Wise-women access a person's life-line to accelerate healing.

Lottery Pool – The two lottery pools are called the short list and the long list. Draw from short list if the person declines post-study education. Short list retirement times range from nothing to one declan. Long list used for post-study graduates separated into two lists: one for general arts students where retirement times range from ten to fifteen anons; the other for declared major students where retirement times range from fifteen to thirty anons.

Master Deceptor – A person who has mastered the skill of making people believe a lie augmented by the use of elemental energy.

Old Soul – A Tualan name for a person from Earth.

Outside Ascension – Phrase to use at a gate on Tuala to get to Earth.

Patil – / pah **til** / – An electronic device used for storing/accessing information, making video calls, and scanning/printing documents similar to a computer.

Pika Juice – / **pahyk** ah / – A fruity beverage similar to orange juice.

Plascreen – / plah screen / – A large touch-screen plastic surface on a telepod which maintains all of the controls for telepod flight.

Plasfilm – / plas film / – An algae-based plastic used to make household items such as plates and cups, also used for making photographs and important documents such as schematics.

Plasprint – / plas print / – A large design schematic printed on plasfilm. Similar to a blueprint on Earth.

Post-Study – Advanced education similar to college.

Release Ceremony – The ritual used when an Elder dies, sending him through the Ascension Gate without an end destination, leaving his body forever between dimensions.

Resh – Highly addictive drug in Tuala used as a sedative. More addictive to people from Earth than from Tuala.

Residence – Place of business for an Elder.

Retirement – The amount of time immediately following formal education where the people are paid by the Elders to not work until their allotted time.

Samara – / suh **mair** uh / – Name of the crystal skulls. Twelve skulls were distributed to the descendants of the Watchers while the master skull is held by Lillia.

Samara Prophesy – 'When the descendants of the Watchers bring these all together then the gates between the worlds will be open for all to pass through without a loss.'

Shill – Smaller denomination of money, a silver metal coin with ribbons of leaves curling around the edges. Ten shills equal one taj.

Spetch – To jump over a narrow area such as a creek.

Sportsman Class – The middle racing class of telepods, with a mid-sized body and crystal drive, achieving decent speed and noise. Sometimes operated with sponsors.

Steena Tea – / **stee** na / – Sweet flavor with a minty finish, settles the stomach, refreshing.

Stock Class – The beginning level for racing telepods, with the smallest body, generally slower because of smaller crystal drives.

Some of these racers use expensive technology to enhance the power causing contention among other stock racers. Almost exclusively privately funded by the drivers.

Supplemental Teaching Guide – Book of instruction inspired by Jehoban to help the Elders understand the way Jehoban wants the world to be maintained.

Swimmers – Anyone found swimming in need of rescue.

Taj – Highest denomination of money, a gold metal coin with a rose on the front. The average wage per anon is 350 taj.

Telepod – / tel *uh* pod / – A wingless aircraft providing a means of air transportation, powered by a large crystal drive where the color and clarity determined the speed and reliability, operated by mind control, transferred from one location to another telekinetically.

Tocolas – / **tow** koh *luhs* / – A red, corn-based chip colored and flavored by tomato juice, lime juice, and salt.

Top Sportsman Class – The highest racing class of telepods. The largest telepod body and crystal drive, achieving faster speed and noise. Almost always operated with sponsors.

Translate – The ability to move telekinetically from one location to another without the use of a telepod.

Tunic – / **too** nik / – An upper garment, either loose or close-fitting, and extending over the pants or skirt to the hips or below.

Unity Song – 'Crystal around the neck, Follow the next step, Changes today, Changes tomorrow, We all become one.' Taught to all children of Tuala to sing.

Water craft – A smaller boat usually operated by one person.

Wise-Woman – A healer formally trained by an Elder. Giver of birth crystals and officiant of the crystal ceremony.